HALFWAY DOWN
THE
STAIRS

by

Gary A. Braunbeck

JournalStone
San Francisco

JOURNALSTONE
YOUR LINK TO ARTISTIC TALENT

For Tom Piccirilli
1950 – 2015

A choir of ill children will always whisper the last kinds words as every place where you drew breath hums with your absence. Miss you like hell, my friend.

Oh, yeah – *fuck* cancer.

JournalStone books may be ordered through booksellers or by contacting:

JournalStone
www.journalstone.com

ISBN:	978-1-942712-59-6	(sc)
ISBN:	978-1-942712-60-2	(ebook)
ISBN:	978-1-942712-45-9	(hc)

Printed in the United States of America

JournalStone rev. date: December 4, 2015

Cover Art & Designs: Chuck Killorin

Edited by: Aaron J. French

What People are Saying About Gary A. Braunbeck

"Braunbeck's fiction stirs the mind as it chills the marrow"
--*Publishers Weekly*

"Braunbeck is much more than a superbly-skilled storyteller; he's a prose poet in action, a consummate composer whose versatile instrument is the English language in all of its colors, shades, and nuances. He is potently aware of its range and power, orchestrating its effects with the sure hand of a master. Popular fiction doesn't get any better than this." -- William F. Nolan, author of *Night Shapes, The Marble Orchard, Helltracks*, and co-author of *Logan's Run*

"Gary A. Braunbeck is simply one of the finest writers to come along in years. His work is chilling, touching, moving, and above all, compassionate and human. He elevates the genre with everything he writes." -- Ray Garton, author of *Live Girls* and *Sex and Violence in Hollywood*

"Braunbeck's writing has enormous range, feeling, surprise, and insight...He mixes pain with humor, tenderness with violence, rage with compassion. He's going to be one of the big and important ones." -- Ed Gorman, author of *The Poker Club* and the Sam McCain series

"Gary A. Braunbeck is one of the best and most original writers to emerge in the last several years. His work is powerful, thought-provoking, terrifying, and not for the emotionally stunted." -- Elizabeth Massie, author of the Bram Stoker Award-winning *Sineater*

Table of Contents

HALFWAY DOWN

THE

STAIRS

Halfway down the stairs
Is a stair
Where i sit.
There isn't any
Other stair
Quite like
It.
I'm not at the bottom,
I'm not at the top;
So this is the stair
Where I always stop.

Halfway up the stairs
Isn't up
And it isn't down.
It isn't in the nursery,
It isn't in town.
And all sorts of funny thoughts
Run round my head.
It isn't really
Anywhere!
It's somewhere else
Instead!

-- A.A. Milne

Foreword

Gary A. Braunbeck

This collection marks a series of firsts for me: it is the first time that the majority of these stories have ever appeared in a collection of mine (not counting the new stories scattered throughout the first section); it is the first time that stories in one of my collections will have introductions—not by me, but by an array of exquisite writers who were kind enough to offer their thoughts on specifically-selected stories (I will be limiting my introductions to the separate sections only); and it is the first time that I have assembled a collection of stories since turning 55, an age I did not think I'd survive long enough to see, hence the title of this collection and the poem from which that line was taken. I'll leave it to you to work out the implications of the metaphor (it isn't that subtle, trust me).

As I assembled these stories and the generous introductions provided for them, I was suddenly struck with the realization that — and I know how silly this is going to sound so no letters or e-mails, please—that there are people out there who *actually read my work*. I know there's a major "Well, *duh!*" factor involved with that statement, but if someone had told me 38 years ago that one day legends like Ramsey Campbell and Graham Masterton would be saying such glowing things about my work, I would have asked them what they'd been smoking and if they had any extra —and these two gentleman (both life-long writing gods of mine) are only 2 of the many writers from the fields of horror, mystery, fantasy, and science fiction who became an enthusiastic part of this project. But here's the thing: every last one of the writers and artists who offer intros herein have read my work—and here's that realization again—*beyond the single story they introduce*. That may not seem like much to you, but it kind of boggles my you-should-excuse-the-expression mind.

I mean, let's face it, Harlan Ellison had it right, when you get right down to it: writers tell lies for a living, so there are readers out there who gladly sacrifice their beer (or pizza, or burgers, or what-have-you) money in order to allow me to spin the *damnedest* yarns, and I cannot tell you how grateful I am for that. I know that what I do isn't all that important in the grand scheme of things; it doesn't help eradicate world hunger, or child abuse, or cancer, or loneliness, or any of the countless little cruelties that we so offhandedly inflict on one another on what seems a quarter-hour basis, but I like to think that it at least provides a brief respite from the weight the knowledge of such things places on our individual shoulders and consciences; I like to think that it gives people their own private spot halfway down the stairs where there is nothing but them and the music of their minds that is perhaps enriched, however briefly, by the stories they take there with them.

I am thankful for and grateful to each and every last one of you who reads my work. Here's a book of offerings you might consider taking to your special place not at the bottom nor at the top, just the special place where you stop to catch a breath and be somewhere else instead.

Part One:

THROW IT AT THE WALL
AND SEE WHAT STICKS

"Hey, hey, my my ...."
Neil Young

"All this I came to report."
Patti Smith

"I will take this one window
with its sooty maps and scratches
so that my dreams may remember
one another and so that my eyes will not
become blinded by the new world."

James Tate, "Fuck the Astronauts"

I was originally going to call this section *Potpourri* but, when I looked at the overall tone and content of the stories, I decided that it was *way* too cutesy a title. What you're going to find here is a selection of stories that vary from the recent ("Crybaby Bridge #25") to the older ("All The Unlived Moments") to the brand-new (five of these, among which, "Attack of the Giant Deformed Mutant Cannibalistic Gnashing Slobberers from Planet Cygnus X-2.73: A Love Story" is very close to my heart, for reasons that will become obvious). They range from horror to mystery to science fiction to suspense; there are longer pieces and there are short-shorts; there are straightforward narratives and some pieces that are more experimental in nature; in brief, the stories in this section are all over the road. Kind of like my thought processes, but let's not get into my dreadful personality problems this soon ....

Crybaby Bridge #25

"Little child, take no fright,
   In that shadow where you are
      The toothless glowworm grants you light ..."

—James Agee, "Song"

The legend says that there are twenty-four 'Crybaby' bridges in the state, and many are the numbers of people who have gone to investigate the mystery. It's a simple, harmless haunting they find once they arrive. There are five steps to each investigation: 1. Park your car in the center of the bridge at midnight; 2. Turn off the ignition; 3. Roll down your windows and listen; 4. Once you hear the sound of a baby crying—sometimes screaming—from below the bridge, close your eyes and count to sixty; 5. Open your eyes and see the hand- and/or footprints of dozens of babies' ghosts on your hood and your windshield.

Some people find that they can't start their cars right way after this, but wait a few minutes and it will start. Another variation instructs you to bring an extra set of keys that you leave in the car when you climb out and lock it. Walk away from the bridge for a little while; when you return, you will find that your car is running, its doors unlocked, and an infant's "binky" lying on the dashboard.

No one knows for certain why these bridges are haunted by the cries of babies, but theories abound: one bridge is not far from the abandoned building that, back in the day, was a home for "wayward girls" whose families sent their unmarried daughter away to have their bastard baby far from the curious eyes of townsfolk—who knows what the matrons of the home did with those children who were stillborn, or came into this world far too sick, or perhaps even deformed?

The legend claims twenty-four, but there is one crybaby bridge that no one ever knew about, save for the middle-aged man who drives there on a rainy October night. This particular bridge has long been condemned but children still ride their bikes over it and the odd teenager will still drive his jalopy across it on a dare. Condemned, forgotten, but the bridge still stands.

The man drives his car slowly toward the middle of the bridge, listening to every creak, every groan. The rain is pelting down, making visibility nearly impossible, even with the windshield wipers going on full power.

For several minutes the man just sits in his car, engine idling, watching the wipers thunk back and forth across his field of vision, clearing the dancing water for only a moment before another wave from above replaces it. Thunder rolls. Lightning flashes and cracks. Below the bridge, the Licking River is raging, swollen well beyond its banks. In town, there is worry of flooding. The man in the car doesn't care. He is beyond caring.

He turns off the engine and removes the keys from the ignition. He opens the door and steps out into the storm, pushing himself against the wind that has doubled in its intensity. He presses his body against the rickety guardrail and looks down at the angry waters. His face looks as if it's going to collapse back into his skull, pulling all flesh and tissue deep into the shadow of bone. He grips the car keys in his fist, pulls back, and hurls them into the night, not bothering to watch as they are taken and beaten by furious the river below. Gripping the rail, he leans out, listening.

At first there is only the bellowing thunder and snapping lightening, the two seemingly colliding overhead in a Wagnerian explosion of fury. It is underscored by the screaming, rising water below. The man forces himself to tune them out, to ignore them, to expunge them from his awareness. He soon succeeds, and everything within and without him is focused solely on hearing the sound. He doesn't have to wait long.

From below, somewhere between the bottom of the bridge and the surface of the screaming river, he hears it; softly, at first, so softly that it could be mistaken for a siren sounding in the distance, but within a few seconds it becomes the unmistakable sound of a baby crying; perhaps because it's hungry, or cold, or needs its diaper changed, or because it is alone and terrified and confused. The man bends from his center until he is nearly doubled over. Perhaps he cries out in answer to the baby; perhaps he screams from rage or anguish or another form of dark and deep despair; who knows? No one else is there to hear it.

He straightens up, leaning his head back so the rain will wash away something from his face, or maybe even cleanse him of something intangible and unspoken. But he speaks anyway.

"Please," he says, "please forgive me. We were so young, and so scared, and we couldn't tell anyone. Please forgive me—forgive *us*. We were so young and stupid and selfish ... we had no idea what we were doing. No one ever knew. We didn't even give you a name."

He shakes his head with great violence and goes back to the car, climbs in, and closes the door. He waits. Soon he sees the impression of tiny hands, tiny feet, appearing all over the hood, appearing like photographed images revealed for only a second before the film is exposed to the light for too long; there one second, gone the next. But there are so many of them, so many hands and feet, and now, now he can hear that the babies are no longer crying, they are giggling, laughing, squealing with glee. He hears the sounds they make as they crawl all over the car, the hood, the roof, the trunk, bouncing themselves up and down, rocking the car.

The man rolls down the front windows and buckles himself in, then tightens the seatbelt until it hurts, making it difficult to pull in a full breath. He leans back his head and smiles as, outside, the babies jump and roll and giggle and bounce. The car too bounces up and down, rocks from side to side. The sound of the river becomes a near-deafening roar. The man can't help himself, and begins laughing at the growing sound of the babies' happiness and delight. He laughs. Below the car, the bridge groans. The bridge creaks. Wood begins to splinter.

"...He Didn't Even Leave A Note..."

It has been a long day and the hour is late and you are impatient to get home. You stayed at the office a bit later than usual, tidying up some last-minute paperwork before leaving for the weekend, but as a result you missed your bus and so find yourself walking. Which isn't really so bad, after all, is it? No, not in the least. It's been ages since last you walked home from work, and at least the weather is nice.

It has been a long day and the hour is late and you are impatient to get home, despite the lovely weather. You wonder if any of your friends are going to bother calling you to see what plans you have for the weekend. "You work too damned much," they say; "We never see you anymore," they say; "It's not good for you to spend so much time by yourself," they say, all the while knowing that your job takes a lot out of you—how else could you have secured the recent promotion, had not you put your career first? "And what's wrong," you say to them, "with wanting to spend my time away from work watching movies or reading or listening to music?"

"Those are *solitary* activities," they reply, "and too much of that can alienate you from the people in your life." You love them all the more for their concern, but wish they'd get it through their heads that there are some people who don't need the constant companionship of other human beings in order to feel that their life has meaning. It doesn't mean you don't care for them, but for some reason they don't understand that. You are involved with them. You are involved with life.

Still, it has been a long day and the hour is late and you are impatient to get home, but there is a man in the distance running toward you. He is a feeble and ragged creature, a depressing sight. There is another man chasing at his heels, screaming. You step aside to let the first man pass. Perhaps the two are running for their own amusement, a good-natured race; maybe they are both in pursuit of a third man you didn't notice; it could even be that the second man wishes to harm or even murder the first and any involvement on your part would make you an unwitting accessory. Regardless of the circumstances, you remain standing off to the side, impatient for the whole incident to play itself out so you can get on home, pour a glass of whiskey, and relax to some music, forgetting about the pressures of the week.

The second man nears you and you see that he, must, indeed, have murder in his heart because he's holding a long and very sharp knife; the early moonlight glints off the blade with an eerie kind of beauty.

The second man runs smack into you, thrusts the blade deep into your belly, and twists.

The pain begins. You grasp the murderer by his shoulders and whisper: "Why?"

He glances in the direction of the running, ragged man, and smiles sadly. "If you hadn't stayed to tidy up the paperwork, you would not have missed the bus; if you had not missed the bus, you would have been home in time for Beverly's phone call; if you had been in time for Beverly's phone call, you would have known that she still loves you and wants to try again."

The first man stops running, turns, and shouts back: "You probably haven't even thought of her in months, have you?"

Then, with a last twist of the blade, the second man pulls the knife from your belly and runs back the way he came.

You can no longer see the first man but, still, you call out to whomever may hear: "Don't I have the right to be tired?" You crumple to the ground and watch your life ooze from your belly, staining the sidewalk. "I didn't want to get involved. It was none of my affair. I only wanted to get home."

Then you die.

Everyone calls it suicide.

Attack of the Giant Deformed Mutant Cannibalistic Gnashing Slobberers from Planet Cygnus X-2.73: A Love Story

Viewed through the fish-eye lens of the pod's observation iris, Captain Brick Morgenstern thought the landing area of the Non Sequitur *looked like a steel diamond peppered with ancient smokestacks, but what else should he have expected from a damn-near ancient mining vessel such as this? The area surrounding the pits and pads and terminal structures was a crazy quilt of rampaging colors—landing lights—to offset the cold blandness of the main terminus attached to it, slate-gray alloys macroscopically homogenized to resemble the space surrounding the massive vessel.*

The heavily-armed, one-man transport pod glided down, down, down into a designated pit, and the view from the iris vanished. Once the vessel settled into place, Morgenstern waited for some sign of life; a technician, and ensign, a mouse, anything. He'd come too far, shed too much blood, and seen too much blood shed to start getting the willies now. After several moments of still-life silence, he initiated communications.

* * *

" … Captain Brick Morgenstern calling Command, do you read, Command?"

"This is Command. Go ahead, Captain."

Morgenstern made his way around the tight enclosed space, albeit with extreme caution. "I have managed to keep possession of the Nonexistium samples from the mines of the planet, but suffered massive casualties."

"We were afraid of that after the com blackout, Captain. What is the level of casualties?"

"The Away Team is dead, everyone except me. The ship is crippled but there is one functioning Transport Pod the enemy hasn't gotten to yet. I managed to get to it and leave the planet surface. I am now in the landing area of the *Non Sequitur*."

"Can the Transport Pod be counted on to make the scheduled rendezvous with The *Unity Gain*?"

"Still gathering intel on that, Command. Life Support systems took some damage from hostile forces on the surface."

"Do you have functioning weapons?"

"Affirmative. Including the last portable plasma canon. I have three shots left before the canon will need recharging."

"Understood. All right, Captain, your orders are as follows: make your way to Level Five, Sector Nine. That's the ship's library. It is imperative, Captain, that you locate and take possession of the Cygnus Theocracy Log Files that are stored there. There will be twenty-seven non-digital volumes. None are very large, but you'll need something to carry them in."

"I've got my supply backpack."

"That will be fine, Captain."

"Captain?"

"I read you, Command."

"You are authorized to use one Nonexistium sample to re-power your plasma canon, should the need arise."

"Thank you."

"Godspeed, Captain. Contact us again when you're back at the pod."

* * *

There was no sign of life anywhere on the ship. It was as if the entire crew had simply vanished in the middle of day-to-day operations. Morgenstern tried not to let memories from the battle on the planet's surface replay themselves in his mind's eye, but all this death was just too recent, too close. He saw his team members falling underneath the great elephantine mass of the creatures that had overrun Cygnus, saw them not so much open their mouths as dislodge *their jaws — or what he assumed were their jaws — and devour each team nearly whole. The ones who weren't swallowed at once were ripped in half, bloody half-bodies littering the ground at the creatures' enormous feet.*

Stop it, *he commanded himself.* There's not a damn thing you can do about it now, so just stop it.

He readied the plasma cannon as the elevator doors opened, revealing Level Five. Sector Nine would be to his right. Pressing his back against the wall, Morgenstern moved stealthily along the hallway, cannon at the ready. He was far too aware of the sound of his own breathing, the beating of his heart, the screaming pain from his unattended wounds.

He arrived at Sector Nine without incident and made his way into the ship's library. Once there, it was easy to locate the Cygnus Log Files and slip the volumes carefully into his backpack. The things looked, smelled, and felt ancient. Containing all the cultural, scientific, political, and theological information of the now-vanished society of the planet below, these logs were and would always be the only *documentation that their race ever existed, that they dreamed, hoped, strove toward ...* something. Anything. *Before the creatures came and began taking it all away in bloody pieces. But at least these records existed, and the scientists and historians back on Earth would know how to translate them, and what to do with the information. That was something, at least. And in this place, at this moment, it was something that Morgenstern was willing to die for.*

Tightening the straps on his backpack so that nothing would accidentally come loose, Morgenstern started toward the door. He was almost there when he became suddenly, inexorably, frighteningly *aware of another presence in the room. Activating the light at the end of the canon, he swept the surrounding area and for the first time saw the dozens — hundreds —* thousands *of cobwebs that fluttered down from the ceiling and attached themselves to every book, every computer, every* thing *in the room where information and knowledge resided.*

Tracking a few of them with the light beam, Morgenstern turned his attention up toward the ceiling. They weren't cobwebs, but dozens of small shiny filaments, each one reaching upwards and out to hundreds of dangling membranous sacks. The sacks expanded and contracted in precise rhythm. Then he became aware of the pulsing of the floor; steady, strong, equally rhythmic. A heartbeat. The organic structure of this deck was changing; steel to tissue, wires to veins, fuel to flesh.

Looking closer at the organic sacks, Morgenstern realized what they, as a whole, resembled.

A brain.

What the hell are you? he thought. I saw your kind down on the surface, saw the way those creatures worshiped you, how they ... how they passed my crew members into you through your filaments like children blowing bubbles into glasses of milk through straws. Did you learn from them, from their deaths? Do you even care that you devoured more than knowledge, that you took away lives by the dozens with each victim? Do you think yourself so powerful that you're indestructible? Let's test that theory, shall we?

Slamming the Nonexistium into the power chamber of the canon, Morgenstern opened fire shooting at the thing on the ceiling until he felt its blood and fluids spattering against his face.

He liked the feeling. He liked knowing that he could still, however briefly, fight back.

He continued firing until the canon could fire no more.

* * *

"Excellent work, Captain."

"Thank you, Command. I believe now that I have enough power and air to safely reach my rendezvous with the *Gain*."

"Affirmative. You'll find a hero's welcome waiting for you."

"Thank you, Command. This is Morgenstern, over and out."

* * *

The young man stepped out into the hallway, futilely trying to wipe the water from his face and clothes. A moment later a nurses' aide came beside him with a towel in her hand.

"Looks like he got you good, this time."

"I should have known that giving him a water pellet gun was asking for trouble." He finished drying his face and handed back the towel.

"Well," said the young aide, "no real harm in it, I suppose." She began walking with him as he headed toward the doors.

"Can you do me a small favor?" asked the young man.

"If I can."

"The books in his room. Can you make sure they get covered up at night with a towel or something plastic? Just in case he fires at them accidentally."

The young lady smiled. "We can do that."

They paused at the doors as the young man looked back in the direction of the room.

"It's so sad," said the young aide. "I understand he used to be a famous writer."

"No," said the young man. "He was once an almost semi-popular writer. Almost everyone's forgotten about him now. Those twenty-seven books are his, everything he wrote. I had a helluva time finding some of them. His work is no longer in print. So, please, make sure they get covered at night. Or sneak the toy gun out when he's asleep or … or something."

"Of course."

The young man nodded his head in thanks, took one last quick look in the direction of the room, and exited the doors, making damn sure as he did—as he always did—to not look at the words **ALZHEIMER'S UNIT** printed on the glass.

"See you next weekend, Dad," he whispered, and quickened his step.

* * *

Safely aboard the Unity Gain, *in his private quarters, freshly showered, his wounds tended to, and with a full stomach from a hero's meal, Captain Brick Morgenstern stood in his PJs and bathrobe before the carefully-stacked volumes of the Cygnus Theocracy Log Files, weapon in hand, eyes wide, senses alert. This knowledge the enemy would never get. It was all that remained. It needed a guardian. He was proud to be the one chosen for this most important task. He stood at attention. He would not fail.*

For J.N. Williamson

Househunting

The fence is tall.

Good.

The mother is typical white trash, too loud.

But the kids ... they seem frightened and quiet.

Good.

Easier that way.

All The Unlived Moments

"Secret of my universe: imagining God without human immortality."
—Camus, *Notebook IV*, January 1942-September 1945

I found the guy outside one of the downtown VR cult temples just like the thin-voiced tipster said I would. He was around thirty-two, thirty-three years old, dressed in clothes at least two sizes too small for the cold December dusk. There were blisters on his forehead, face, and neck. One look in his eyes told me that his mind—or what might be left of it—was still lost somewhere in cyberspace, floating without direction down corridors formed wherever electricity runs with intelligence; billowing, coursing, glittering, humming, a Borgesian library filled with volumes he'd never understand, lost in a 3D city; intimate, immense, firm, liquid, recognizable and unrecognizable at once. The 21st Century Schizoid Man, in the flesh.

I gently placed one of my hands on his shoulder. My other hand firmly clasped the butt of my tranquilizer pistol, just in case.

"You okay?"

He turned slowly toward me, his eyes glassy, uncomprehending. "Who're you, mister?"

"A friend. I'm here to help you."

"D-d-did...did he ever find that girl?"

"Who?"

"John Wayne?"

He seemed so much like a child, lost, lonely, frightened. A lot of VR cultists end up like this. Sometimes I wondered if the mass-suicides of religious cults in the past were really such a tragedy, after all. At least then the cultists—sad, odd, damaged people who turned to manufactured religions and plasticine gods—were released, were freed forever from the Machiavellian will- and mind-benders who turned them into semi-ignorant, unquestioning, shuffling zomboids. Worse, though, were the families who hired me and my partner to get their kids back and de-program them. They always thought that familial love and compassion would break through the brainwashing—and don't try to lecture my ass, because brainwashing is the only thing to call it—but then they find out all too soon that you don't need surgical equipment to perform some lobotomies. Seven times out of ten the kids wound up in private institutions; at least one of the other three are dumped at state-run facilities where they're snowed on lithium for six months, spoon fed first-year graduate school psychobabble, then put out on the streets to join the other modern ghosts, adorned in rags, living in shadows, extending their hands for some change if you can spare it, and wondering in some part of their mind why the god they had worshiped from the altar of their computer monitor has abandoned them.

"That's my car over there. C'mon, I'll take you someplace safe and warm. You can eat."

"...'kay..." His voice and gestures seemed even more childlike as he started toward my hover-car. "How...how come your car don't got no wheels?" He seemed genuinely mystified, as if he'd never seen a hover-car before. Okay, so they weren't exactly commonplace yet, but there were more than enough in the air at any given time that, unless you'd been on Mars since 2026, you'd have seen at least a couple.

"It flies."

His eyes grew wide, awed. "*Really?*"

I smiled at him. "Sure thing. Why don't you get in...uh...what's your name? Mine's Carl."

"Mine's Jimmy Waggoner."

"Get in, Jimmy Waggoner."

He did. I locked his door from outside (the passenger-side door cannot be opened from within) and then took my place behind the controls; soon we were airborne, gliding smoothly and quickly over the cityscape.

Jimmy looked out the window and down on the world he was no longer a part of. "This is *sooooooooooo* neat!"

"Glad you like it."

"Uh-huh, I really do. This is the best birthday present I ever got, *ever!*"

"It your birthday today, Jimmy? December eighteenth?"

"Uh-huh. Mommy says I was her 'Christmas Baby.' She let me watch *The Searchers* on tape and then she gave me some pizza money."

Something cold and ugly crept up my back. "How, uh...how old are you today, Jimmy?"

"I'm seven," he said proudly, pointing to his chest.

Then he saw his hand—

—the thick hair on his arms—

—felt the beard on his face—

—and before I could I activate the autopilot and stop him from doing so, he grabbed the rear-view mirror and turned it toward himself, getting a good look at his face.

"*That ain't me!*" he cried, his voice breaking. "*Where'd I go, mister? Where'd I go?*"

I had to sedate him a few seconds later. If I hadn't, we would have crashed.

Jimmy was one strong child.

* * *

I put the hover-car down in a clearing right smack in the middle of a patch of woodland that surrounds three-quarters of our safe house. A long time ago Parsons and I agreed that the more remote our workplace, the better. This area was near impossible to get to by standard automobile, and if anyone ever did manage to get this far, there was only one road leading to the house. Even without the hidden security cameras that lined the final stretch of that road, we'd see them coming from three miles away.

I radioed in for a medical team to bring a stretcher. Parsons got on the horn and asked me if I'd managed to get any information from the kid—and *kid* is how I thought of Jimmy, his age be damned.

"Just enough to give me the creeps," I replied.

Jimmy was still out of it from the tranquilizer shot I'd given him earlier, and as I stared at his peaceful, sleeping form, I figured it was probably for the best.

I didn't know which VR cult this kid had belonged to—there were dozens that had temples in this part of the country—but what I did know was that none of them were in the habit of simply dumping their converts in the street and then calling the likes of us to come and clean up the mess.

The VR cult phenomenon didn't really get going until 2020, though it had its genesis back in the mid 2000's. Back in the 90's, personal VR equipment was bulky, clumsy to use, and expensive—forget that virtual reality itself on the net was more of a curiosity than anything else, and most of the VR worlds were fairly crude by today's standards. Then there were the computers and servers themselves; the 90's saw the beginnings of the ISDN proliferation, the introduction of NFSnet—God bless fiber-optic cable—but even those couldn't manage a transfer rate faster than 2Gb/sec. Then, around 2017, slowly but surely, the faceless Powers-That-Be began giving people a taste of the Next Big Thing, and like lemmings to the sea they lined up.

Now—Christ, *now* you were in the dark ages if your system functioned under 1000 MIPS and transferred less than 4 million polygons/sec. The power required for color-and illumination-rendered, real-time, user-controlled animation of (and interaction with) complex, evolving, three-dimensional scenes and beings was widely available. The VR equipment needed to function in these worlds was streamlined into little more than a pair of thin black gloves, a lightweight pair of headphones, and some slightly oversized black glasses with a small pair of sensory clips; one for your nose (to evoke smell) and one that you tucked into the corner of your mouth (to evoke taste). In a world overrun with people, where personal space was moving its way up the endangered species list, VR worlds and servers offered people the chance to "get away from it all" without leaving the confines of their computer terminal.

Problem was, when you give an apple-pie American something with endless possibilities, they find a quick way to either pervert or trivialize it. It wasn't long before "cyber-diets" were all the rage—Lose Weight Fast! Slim Down For Summer! Log in, and we'll give your senses the *illusion* of being fed. 3D interactive kiddie porn. Sites where you could virtually torture your enemies.

Oh, yeah—and the gods of cyberspace. Any nutcase with a religious manifesto could buy space and set up a virtual temple to beckon worshipers. Create-A-Deity, online 24 hours a day for your salvation, can I get a witness. Some of the bigger ersatz-religions—Mansonism, Gargoylists, Apostles of the Central Motion, Vonnegutionism (my personal favorite, they used a cat's cradle as their symbol), the Resurrected Peoples' Temple, and the Church of the One-Hundred-and-Eightieth Second—were granted licenses to set up their own servers—and because of that, Parsons and me would always have jobs. There would always be lost souls like Jimmy. First get them hooked on the net, alienate them from the world they know, then draw them into your virtual fold, blur the lines between the person they are on the net and the person they are off the net until you trap them forever in the spaceless space between, imprison them in the *consensual loci.*

I was snapped from my reverie by the medical team, who gently loaded Jimmy onto the stretcher and into the ambulance. I signaled them I would walk to the house.

I had a feeling that walk was going to be the last quiet time I'd have for a while.

* * *

Jimmy was still asleep in the recovery area when Parsons met me outside the computer room.

"You say he thinks he's seven?"

"Yes. You should have seen him flip out when he finally got a look at himself."

"Did he give you any indication what cult he belonged to?"

"None."

"So where does that leave us?"

"We know his name. Let's run it through and see if any bells go off."

"You just love talking in tough-guy clichés, don't you?"

I grinned. "Watched too many Clint Eastwood movies when I was a kid."

Parsons laughed. "You were never a kid."

"I feel so good about myself now."

I liked Parsons a lot. A former VR cult member himself, there was no scam, no form of reasoning so out there, no logic so convoluted, that he couldn't work his way through it to awaken what lay at a subject's core. In the six years we'd been working together I'd only seen him lose two subjects—one to suicide after her family took her away too soon, the other to law school.

Parsons hates that joke, too.

One of our latest residents, Cindy (she wouldn't yet tell us her last name, even though we already knew what it was), age seventeen, approached Parsons and asked him about Jimmy.

"I saw them bring him in downstairs," she said.

Parsons put a reassuring hand on her arm. "You don't need to worry about him, Cindy; Jimmy'll be fine."

"You don't know him, do you?" I asked.

"I don't think—I mean, I don't know. Something about him seems familiar, I guess." She thought about it for a second, then shrugged and said, "I guess not. Sorry."

Parsons looked at his watch. "Shouldn't you be helping with dinner preparation in the kitchen?"

"Omigosh, I forgot all about it." She hurried away toward the elevator.

"She seems a lot friendlier than she did last week."

"I know," whispered Parsons. "Amazing how fast she's progressed, don't you think?"

We looked at each other.

"Think she'll try it tonight?" I asked.

"Not tonight, but definitely before Christmas."

"I'll double outside security."

"You do that."

Escape attempts are commonplace here during the first three weeks; week one, they fight us tooth-and-nail because they see us as the evil ones who took them away from salvation and home; week two, they loosen up a bit, then decide to play along, hoping to give us a false sense of accomplishment; week three, they try to run for it. Cindy was a 3rd-Weeker. Time to try.

We parted after that, Parsons going off to a scheduled session with some twelve-year-old from Indiana we snatched from the Resurrected Peoples' Temple. I went into the computer room to run down Jimmy's name.

One of the things I've learned over the years is that you must take nothing for granted when tracking down a subject's past. Not that we have to do it all that often; usually the family provides us with more than enough information to go on. There have been, however, a handful of burnout cases that have simply stumbled into our hands. These always take extra effort, but I rarely mind.

At least with Jimmy Waggoner I had a name—and a possible temple affiliation.

Cindy of the No-Last-Name-Given had been snatched from the Church of the One-Hundred-and-Eightieth Second, who believed that they and they alone postponed the end of the world because they and they alone owned the last three minutes of existence. Their literature even claimed that these last three minutes were a physical object, one that their Most Holy Timekeeper, Brother Tick-Tock (I'm not kidding) kept safely hidden away, watched over by the One and True God of All Moments, Lord Relativity.

I doubted that Cindy actually knew Jimmy, but at this stage anything was worth a shot. I fed all the information into the system, sat back, and waited.

It took about thirty minutes. I'd guessed about Jimmy having come from the tristate area; most VR cults are localized religions and recruit their members close to home as a rule.

I'd almost nodded off when the computer cleared its throat (a WAV file I installed as a signal) and the words MATCH FOUND appeared on the screen. I rubbed my eyes and pressed the mouse button —

—and there it was.

All the information on Jimmy Waggoner that there was to be found.

* * *

Parsons looked up at me from behind his desk. "Don't bother to knock."

I shoved the printouts in his face. "James Edgar Waggoner, born December 19, 1986. Disappeared on his birthday, 1993, on his way to a pizza parlor half-a-block from his home. It's all there, his kindergarten and first grade report cards, school pictures, health records, dental charts, all of it."

Parsons scanned the printouts, all the time shaking his head. "Dear God in Heaven."

"Do you have the medical report yet?"

"Um...yeah, yes...it's right here." He handed it to me but I didn't take it.

"Why don't you just give me the Readers' Digest version?" I said.

He put down the printouts and rubbed his eyes. "Those marks on his face and neck? There were identical marks on his chest, forearms, and thighs."

"Burns?"

"No. Medical adhesive irritation."

"In English."

"That guy's been hooked up to both an EKG and EEG for a very long time. Plus, there was an unusually high trace of muscle relaxants in his system."

"*Muscle* relaxants?"

"That, and about a half-dozen different types of hypno-therapeutic medications."

We stared at each other.

"Any traces of hallucinogenic?"

"Good old-fashioned Lucy-in-the-Sky-with-Diamonds."

I felt my gut go numb. "So whoever took him has...has —"

" —has kept him more or less snowed out of his skull for the better part of three decades, especially the last year or so," said Parsons. "Tests indicate definite brain damage but we're not yet sure of the extent."

"...jesus..."

"I'll second that. You got an address on his family?"

I nodded my head. "The father died a couple of years ago. Coronary. His mother still lives in town at the same house."

"You suppose she stayed there because she believed he'd come back some day?"

"Seeing as how it was the father who petitioned for the declaration of death, my guess is probably."

"Need anything to take with you?"

"A photograph of the way he looks now."

"I'll take it myself."

I stood staring out at I-don't-know-what.

"You okay, Carl?"

"Almost thirty years," I whispered. "What the hell were they doing with him for all that time?"

"I've got a better question."

"What's that?"

"One minute the kid's seven years old and off to buy a birthday-in-December slice of pizza, and the next —*wham!*—he finds himself in an almost-middle-aged body and doesn't know how he got there. How do you explain to someone that they've been robbed of over one-third of their life and will never get that time back?"

* * *

Joyce Waggoner was fifty-seven but looked seventy. Still, she carried herself with the kind of hard-won dignity that, with the passage of time and accumulation of burdens, becomes a sad sort of grace.

Her reaction to the news that her son was still alive was curiously subdued. I supposed (and rightly so, as it turned out), that she'd been scammed countless times over the years by dozens of so-called "cult busters" who, for a nominal fee, promise quick results. I assured her that I was not after any money, and even went so far as to give her the name and number of our contact on the police force. She told me to wait while she made the call, but then she did the damnedest thing —she stopped on her way to the phone, looked at me, smiled, and asked if I'd like some fresh coffee. "It's really no trouble," she said in a voice as thin as tissue paper. "I usually have myself some coffee about this time of day."

"That would be very kind of you," I replied, suddenly feeling like a welcomed guest.

She made the coffee and then called Sherwood, our police contact, who assured her that Parsons and I were on the level and could be trusted.

"May I see that photograph again?" she asked when she came in with the coffee. I handed it to her and spent several moments adding cream and sugar to my cup while she examined the picture Parsons had taken not two hours ago.

"I guess it could be him," she whispered, looking up at me. "I'm sorry if I don't seem overjoyed at your news, but I've been duped by a lot of people over the years who claim to've had news of Jimmy's whereabouts."

"I understand."

She looked up at the mantel. There were only three framed photographs there: one showed Jimmy as a newborn, still swaddled in his hospital blanket; the next, in the center, was a picture of herself with her late husband that had apparently been taken shortly before his death; and the last, at the far end of the mantel, was of Jimmy, taken on his fifth birthday. I raged at the emptiness up there, for all the photographs that should have been present but hadn't been and now never would be—Jimmy graduating from grade school, his high school senior picture, college graduation, all the unlived moments in between, silly moments with Mom and Dad, maybe a picture of himself with his prom date, both of them looking embarrassed as Mom stood in tears while Dad recorded the Historic Moment on film...all the empty spaces where precious memories should have been, filled only with a thin layer of dust and a heavy one of regret. Even with the smell of air-freshener and what I suspected was freshly shampooed carpeting in the air, there was smell underneath everything that had to be grief. It had been clogging my nostrils since I'd come into the house.

"He was watching *The Searchers*," she said. "You know, that John Wayne movie?"

"Yes, I've seen it many times."

"It was his father's favorite movie, you know. Anyway, he was watching it while I was making some last-minute arrangements for his surprise party later that afternoon and...you have to understand, Jimmy was always the sort of child who *liked* being kept in suspense. I guess that way he always had something to look forward to. So, about two-thirds of the way through the movie—and boy, was he immersed in the story—he had to use the bathroom, so he put the tape on "pause" and did his business, and about the time he was coming out of the bathroom his father was coming in the back door with Jimmy's birthday present — his own VCR. Well, I didn't want Jimmy to see it, so I gave him a couple of dollars and told him to walk up to Louie's Pizza and get himself a couple of slices. Louie's — it's been gone for a lot of years now — it was right at the end of our block so Jimmy didn't have to cross the street or anything like that, and he *loved* Louie's pizza. So he said, 'Okay. I'll have it when I watch the rest of the movie,' and he took off. That's...that's the last we ever saw of him."

"Mrs. Waggoner, I have to ask this question: in the weeks, days, or hours before Jimmy disappeared, do you remember seeing any —"

"Yes."

The immediacy of her answer surprised me.

She saw my surprise and laughed. "I didn't mean to stun you, but the police and FBI must have asked me that about a thousand times. Yes, there was a man I saw walking through the neighborhood that I didn't recognize and, yes, Jimmy once told me about this man trying to talk to him."

"Did you contact the police?"

"Goddamn right I did. My husband had several friends on the force, and for weeks afterward I noticed more frequent patrols through our area. After Jimmy was taken, my husband started buying all sorts of guns, most of them from his friends on the force — old pieces of evidence, no serial numbers, like that. At one point, he had two guns in every room in our house. After he died I got rid of most of them."

"How much time elapsed between Jimmy telling you about this man and his disappearing?"

"About five months."

"Did this man say anything to Jimmy that might —"

"I'm way ahead of you." She reached into the breast pocket of her blouse and removed a small, age-browned business card. "For years and years I couldn't find this and then, this morning, I was looking through a few of Jimmy's old Dr. Seuss books and this fell out of *And To Think That I Saw It On Mulberry Street*. That man had given this to Jimmy."

She handed me the card. It was sketch of a man meant to resemble Jesus, his face turned heavenward, his arms parted wide, a clock in the center of his chest.

The time on the clock was three minutes until twelve.

The logo for the Church of the One-Hundred-and-Eightieth Second.

She stared at me. "You recognize it, don't you?"

"Yes." And I did something then that I'd never done before.

I told her everything.

This is not SOP with me, understand. Usually Parsons and I try to feed the information to the families in bits and pieces so as to make the sordid whole a bit easier to swallow, but this woman, this good, graceful, lonely woman had moved something in me, and I felt she deserved nothing more than the whole truth.

She listened stone-faced, the only sign of her grief and rage the way her folded hands balled slowly into white-knuckled fists.

I finished telling her everything, then poured myself some more coffee while the news set in. I still couldn't get that underneath-things-smell out of my nose.

"The police checked out that church," she said. "I could at least remember some of the details of the card. The church denied that any of their 'apostles' had ever seen or been in contact with Jimmy."

"Can I keep this?" I asked, holding up the card.

"Don't see why not." She stared off in the distance for a minute, then shook herself from her reverie, looked at me, and smiled. She looked like someone had stuck a gun in her back and told her to act natural.

"I still have that damn VCR we got for him," she said. Her voice was so tight I thought the words might shatter like glass before they exited her throat. "Still wrapped up in birthday paper. They don't even make the damn things anymore. Still got that tape of *The Searchers*, too."

I reached over and took hold of one of her hands. It was like gripping a piece of granite. "At least that'll give him something to look forward to."

She nodded, and for the first time I saw the tears forming in her eyes.

"I don't so much mind what they robbed me of," she said. "Seeing him grow up, mature, riding a bike for the first time...I don't mind that so much. But *for him*...I very much mind what those bastards robbed him of. Childhood ends all too soon anyway, but to be...to be *stripped* of it like that, to have it expunged, to never, ever experience it...that's worse than simply robbing a boy of his childhood. It's a hideous form of rape in a way, isn't it?"

"We'll get them for this, Mrs. Waggoner. I swear it."

She wiped her eyes, looked at me, and tried to smile. "I don't doubt it for a minute."

I readied myself to leave and take her back to the safe house. To my surprise, she didn't want to come along.

"I, uh...I don't exactly look my best right now," she said. "I want to clean up a bit, put on a good dress, you know."

"Of course. I'll have someone come for you later this afternoon."

"Around five would be wonderful." She took my hand and kissed me once on the cheek. "Thank you, Carl. I don't know what kind of a life my son and I will have from here on, but at least we'll have one. Together."

I smiled at her as best I could and nodded, then quickly trotted out to the hover-car and took off.

I didn't want her to see how badly I was shaking.

Something had clicked into place while she was speaking to me.

And when she'd craned to kiss my cheek, that underneath-things-smell was on her.

And I recognized it for what it was.

And the implications scared the hell out of me.

* * *

"Detective Sherwood."

"Ian, it's me."

"Carl. How goes the spirit-saving business?"

Usually I'd have had a snappy reply, but not today. Sherwood sensed something in my silence and asked: "Okay, you're in no mood for jokes. How serious is it?"

"It may just be my imagination running wild with me—"

"You don't *have* an imagination, pal."

"Everyone's complimenting me today, first Parsons, now you, I feel giddy."

"*There* you are."

"Look, Ian, this might be damned serious. I need you to get your hands on some records for me, can you do that?"

"I'll need a couple of good reasons."

I listed three.

Now it was Sherwood's turn to be silent.

"Still there, Ian?"

"Uh...yeah, yes, I'm just...wow."

"Like I said, it might just be my imagination, but if it isn't—"

"—if it isn't, a lot of people are going to be in deep sewage."

"I figured."

"How far back do you want me to check?"

"Start with a week ago, going through today."

"I'll dispatch some plain-clothes in an unmarked car to keep an eye on the place."

"Tell them not to apprehend, just follow."

"So now you're my boss?"

"Please, Ian? This one feels bad."

He sighed in resignation. "That last name was W-A-G-G-O-N-E-R?"

"Must've been your junior-high spelling bee champ."

"National finalist."

"You're kidding?"

"I'm kidding...but then *I'm* the one with the sense of humor."

"I gotta get new friends."

"No one but us'd have you. Call me back in an hour and I'll let you know."

* * *

"Cindy?"

She looked up from the dishes, surprised to see me. "Yes?"

"I want you to tell me about the place where Brother Tick-Tock takes all new apostles."

She stared. "That's private. Sacred."

I came toward her. There must have been something in my eyes, because she turned slightly pale and backed up a few paces.

"You listen to me, Cindy. That boy who came in here today, Jimmy, you *know* him, don't you?"

"I don't know, like I said."

I had her backed to the wall. "Tell me about Lord Relativity, then."

This caught her off-guard, but at the same time seemed to perk her up a bit. "He is the One and True God of All Moments, available to His followers on-line at all times."

"And what does He say to His followers?"

"Nothing. We simply log on and become One with His Presence."

"You...you *feel* him, then?"

"Yes, his thoughts and the beating of his heart. Lord Relativity was inspired by Jesus. It was in His Seventh Year that he became aware of His greatness, and in His thirty-third year, he falls into the ashes of cyberspace and emerges reborn."

"Reborn. At age seven?"

"Yes. Praise His name and the etherealization of the New World He promises all."

I grabbed her by the shoulders. "Where does Brother Tick-Tock initiate the new apostles, Cindy?"

"That's a secret, I told you."

"Then try this: Unless you tell me where this sacred place is, I think someone is going to try and kill Brother Tick-Tock before the day is over."

"No! Without Brother Tick-Tock to guide us, to interpret what Lord Relativity thinks in His Cyber Palace, we will be lost and —"

I slapped her. I couldn't help it.

I didn't know how much time might be left.

"Dammit, girl, tell me!"

"CARL!"

I turned to see Parsons standing in the kitchen doorway. He looked livid. "How dare you strike her like that!"

"I don't have time for your subtleties, my friend. Have you talked with Jimmy yet?"

"A little."

"There's a huge hole in his memory, right?"

"Yes."

"One that you're going to have to use hypnosis to fill in?"

"Probably."

"Let me save you a little guesswork. You've got the latest incarnation of Lord Relativity up there."

Cindy gasped.

Parsons tilted his head, looking confused. "How do you know — what do you mean the *latest* incarnation of —"

"Get on the horn and see if any seven-year-old boys have disappeared in the last three days, then call Detective Sherwood and tell him to get a squad over to the address Cindy is about to tell us." I glared at her. "Well?"

"How can that man be Lord Relativity? He exists only in cyberspace, where all intellect and electricity meet to form a new consciousness and —"

I drew back to hit her again — I'd use my fist this time.

"Because Brother Tick-Tock and the elders of the church have been kidnapping little boys, drugging them, then hooking them up to medical equipment which is tied into the church's mainframe server so that followers like you can get online and commune with Lord Relativity. I have no idea how many times they might have done this, or how often your precious lord rises like a phoenix from the ashes of cyberspace, but I *do know* that Brother Tick-Tock may be dead soon, and if you don't tell me where the sacred initiation site is, it'll be your fault."

Parsons must have heard it in my voice, because he did not contradict what I said. We try never to lie to or use threats with people here, but if what I suspected was true, there was no time.

"Are you telling me the truth?" whispered Cindy, looking so scared and broken I almost took her in my arms.

"Yes, Cindy, I am."

She gave me the address.

* * *

On my way to the address Cindy had given, I put the hover-car on autopilot while I tidied myself up and removed the detective's shield and ID from the glove compartment—a gift from Sherwood at the police department. Sometimes I had to impersonate a detective in order to gain access to certain people. Thus far I'd never been called on it, and Sherwood had always promised to take care of any problems that might arise should I get busted.

I hoped he was a man of his word.

My phone beeped and, the car still on auto, I answered.

It was Sherwood.

"You nailed it, my friend," he said. "One call to the church, two from. All within the last twenty hours."

"Your plain-clothes boys there?"

"They are, but I don't think anyone's there."

"I'm listening."

"Right after you left, she called the local precinct and was connected to the Records Division."

"Unlisted phone numbers, legal name changes, private addresses and the like?"

"Two cigars for you."

"Parsons called you, right?"

"I've got two cars on the way, and as soon as I hang up I'm on the way my own self."

"See you then."

I broke the connection and landed right in front of the upscale condo and went inside to find the security guard at the desk unconscious.

Not bothering to remove my gloves, I checked the computer for Roger Buchanan's (a.k.a. Brother Tick-Tock's) apartment number and then grabbed the first elevator.

The ride to the twentieth-floor penthouse seemed to take forever.

When the door opened, I came out with my gun drawn. Across from me stood the door to Brother Tick-Tock's personal initiation space where, I suspected, he'd seduced both boys and girls into the fold.

The door was open.

I nudged it farther with my foot and slipped in, my gun in front of me.

There was no sound.

I went from room to room, until at last I came to a large set of oak doors that had to lead into an office.

I opened them slowly and quietly.

Brother Tick-Tock sat in a plush chair behind his desk, a small splotch of blood staining the center of his shirt.

I could still smell the shot in the air.

Not unlike the dying aroma of gunpowder that I'd sniffed in Joyce Waggoner's sad and hollow home.

I walked over, very slowly, to the person sitting in the chair on the other side of the desk.

Joyce Waggoner was still holding the gun, an automatic with silencer attachment.

There was no doubt in my mind that it was one of the untraceable weapons her husband had bought.

It took a moment for her to register my presence, and when she did she simply shrugged and smiled. "He didn't deserve to live, not after all he's done."

I stepped behind the desk and felt for a pulse.

Brother Tick-Tock was still very much alive.

I came back around and took the automatic from her hands. "You called in the tip, didn't you?"

"Yes." She lifted up her open handbag. It was stuffed to bursting with platinum credit chips. The smallest one I saw was a thousand.

"Jimmy got away from them somehow," she said. "I was so stunned to see him, to know that he was alive, that I just...I just held him a lot last night. Made cocoa. But then I got mad. I called the church and told them that I knew they'd taken my son from me and I was going to make them pay. They called me back, Brother Tick-Tock himself here. I hung up on him and he called right back. He offered...he offered me a lot of money to keep quiet. I don't have a lot of money to live on anymore, you see, and Jimmy, well, he's going to require a lot of care and...and..."

"So you said yes to a deal?"

"Yes. But then it occurred to me that they might try to...to take Jimmy back when they came with the money."

"So you took him to the VR temple downtown and called us to come get him?"

"I wanted him to be safe, somewhere they wouldn't dare try getting to him."

"How many men from the church showed up at your house with the money?"

"Only two. One of them slapped me, threatened to hurt me if I didn't tell them where Jimmy was."

"So you killed them both? Shot them?"

"How did you know?"

"I caught a whiff of gunpowder on you when you kissed me good-bye."

"I thought you seemed awfully sharp."

"Where are the bodies?"

"In the cellar. I have no idea how I'm going to get rid of them...of course, I guess that's all moot now anyway, isn't it?"

Brother Tick-Tock moaned but did not regain full consciousness.

Then I heard another sound.

A whimper; very small, very thin.

Behind a door to the left of the desk.

Not taking my eyes off Mrs. Waggoner, I backed toward the door and kicked it open with my foot.

On a bed not four feet away lay a small boy, dressed in winter clothes, tied to the bedposts and all-too-obviously drugged.

I looked at the child.

Then Mrs. Waggoner.

Then Brother Tick-Tock.

And I thought then of Jimmy, of the childhood he'd been robbed of, of the dust on Mrs. Waggoner's mantel, of the hysteria that the parents of this new boy must be feeling, and a last thought, unbidden, came to me: How many times had Brother Tick-Tock done this? How many seven-year-old boys had he kidnapped, drugged, and then hooked up to the church's computer so the followers could log on to see the Reborn Lord Relativity?

In this age gods, like their followers, can be easily manufactured.

I stepped into the room and saw all of the children's toys that littered the floor—balls to bounce, fire trucks, tiny robots, puzzles; a kiddie's paradise.

Then I saw the bank of monitors from the corner of my eye.

I turned to face them.

There were eighteen in all, most of them showing very small rooms with very small occupants on medium-sized beds.

None of the children were alone.

I will not describe the depravities these children were being subjected to by their roommates. I had to turn away for a moment before I threw up.

I saw a second door, set between two bookcases on the far side of the room. I walked very slowly over to the door and pushed it open. A winding stone staircase led downward.

On autopilot myself, I picked up one of the small bouncing balls, a blue one, and tossed it down the stairs.

I turned back toward the monitors and stared at the one in the center.

It showed a stone archway where a stone staircase ended.

I waited, forgetting to breathe.

A few seconds later, the blue ball bounced from the stairs onto the monitor screen.

I stared again at the empty, glassy eyes of the children on the other monitors, wondering if they knew their degradations were being recorded.

I had been wrong about what was really going on.

In my worst moments, I'd never imagined that I'd ever encounter anything as unspeakable as this.

I knelt down for a moment and pulled open a set of drawers under the monitors.

Hundreds upon hundreds of digital video discs were stored there, identified only by labels such as: LARRY, age 6, blonde; Little Boy Blue; Jessica, age 4, brunette; Little Miss Muffet.

So all of this, all of it—the church, the temple, the cyber-crusades of Lord Relativity and Brother Tick-Tock—all it was an elaborate front for a child pornography ring.

Then I noticed a label on one of the discs: ONE USE ONLY; red and noisy.

There were at least twenty more with the same label.

ONE USE ONLY: New cyber-speak for snuff movie.

All of this flashed through my mind in a second, and, knowing that Sherwood and his men would be here any minute, I made a decision that I knew would change the man I was for the rest of my life.

I came back into the office. "Mrs. Waggoner? You with me?"

"Of course."

"Don't ask questions, just listen and answer 'yes' or 'no,' all right?"

"Yes."

"Do you have a heart condition of any sort?"

She looked at me, puzzled. "No...?"

"Do you have any sort of condition that might endanger your life should you suffer a form of body trauma?"

"No."

I exhaled, nodded my head, made sure my gloves were still firmly covering my hands, then took her gun from her hands and shot her in the shoulder.

She fell off the chair with a shriek.

I stood over her. "Listen to me, Joyce, listen very carefully. You came here to confront Buchanan about what he had done. You were out of your head with anger—that's why you knocked out the security guard downstairs. You came up here and the two of you argued."

I picked up her handbag and slammed it against the side of Brother Tick-Tock's head. "He came at you and you hit him in the head with your purse." I jumped back over to her and punched her in the nose. "He hit you in the face and you went down right where you are—don't move. Still with me?"

"...yes..." she said through a haze of pain.

"Good." I went behind the desk and began opening the drawers, hoping to find a concealed weapon of some sort. I did, second drawer on the left, in a metal box that was unlocked. I removed the pistol and shoved it through my belt under my coat, then wiped Joyce's gun clean before shoving it into Tick-Tock's hand. "He went for his gun and shot you in the shoulder." I hauled Tick-Tock's limp form from his chair, Joyce's gun still in his hand, and threw him on the floor beside her. "He came around after you went down and you kicked him in the balls."

I kicked Tick-Tock in the balls.

"He went down, and the two of you struggled with the gun." I placed her hands on the pistol as well. "You shot him twice, once in the chest, and then—" I put the gun up to Tick-Tock's face and pulled the trigger. Blood spattered Joyce's face and clothes and my gloves. I dropped their hands and the gun, then quickly removed my gloves and shoved them in my pockets. "You killed him in self-defense, Joyce. I came in here just in time to see the end of it, understand?"

"...yes..."

"Can you remember all that?"

"Yes." She was recovering from the pain somewhat. This was one tough lady.

"I'll get rid of the bodies in your cellar later, don't worry about that. I hate to admit it, but I've got friends who have experience in that area." I scooped up her purse and removed all the credit chips, shoving them into my pockets. There was still enough junk inside—medicine bottles, makeup, checkbook, etcetera—to give it some good weight. "You're going to keep this money, Joyce, because you'll need it."

I heard the elevator bell.

She looked up at me, then at Brother Tick-Tock's body. "Why did you do this?"

"Because you're right, he didn't deserve to live...and every little boy deserves to see whether or not John Wayne rescues Natalie Wood."

She smiled at me, and as Sherwood and his men came running from the elevator, I went into the small room to untie the little boy whose childhood would not be stolen from him for the sake of false gods and their followers.

I held the child in my arms, and in the darkness I wept, thinking, *I can feel you breathe like the ocean, your life burning bright, all the unlived moments before you; may that fire be your friend and the sea rock you gently.*

* * *

I don't do as much fieldwork these days; that I leave to the Sherwood, who retired from the force a few years ago and came to work with us. Mostly I trace cyber-trails, gather info, make calls. Every once in a while I'll go on an assignment with Sherwood, but my conscience always manages to get in the way.

When at last it all becomes personal, you're no good in the field.

And I am a murderer whose greatest guilt is that he feels no remorse for his crime.

Jimmy and his mother are doing fine. I stop by their home frequently, and I'm glad to report it's a happy home.

Happy enough.

Joyce has the mantel filled with photos now of her and Jimmy. It looks like a family has lived their whole life there.

Jimmy loves his VCR. We have now watched *The Searchers* twenty-six times. He never gets tired of it.

Come to think of it, neither do I.

Amen to that, pilgrim.

At the "Pay Here, Please" Table

When he was a child of eight he was taken on a camping trip by three teenaged boys who were friends of the family; all three were either about to ship out to Vietnam or were preparing to go off to boot camp in preparation for Vietnam. He was the youngest and weakest of the five children they'd taken along that weekend, so naturally when the fellows got good and drunk and dared one another to prove that there was nothing they weren't prepared to do, he was the one they grabbed from his sleeping bag and dragged deeper into the woods where the others couldn't hear him scream. Each teenaged boy raped him at both ends, two of them going at him at a time while the third held him still and firmly upright so no one lost their balance; guys readying to ship off to fight the dinks had to learn teamwork, after all. They left him there for the night, naked and bleeding and vomiting on himself. When he was dropped off at his house the next day, it was with a warning that if he told on them, he would be killed. He told no one. In the weeks that followed, each of the three teenaged boys visited him at the house, usually when one or both of his parents were at work. They made him dress up in his mom's clothes and put on make-up and lots of lipstick. Sometimes he had to wear a wig. He did the things they demanded of him because he was too scared and small and weak to think he had a chance to defend himself. Afterward, he'd put his mom's clothes back just as they had been, sometimes ironing them because they'd gotten wrinkled. Sometimes he'd wrap himself in a particular dress so he could smell his mom's perfume in the material and feel protected and loved for a few minutes. The lipstick always tasted terrible; it took him days to get that taste—and other tastes—out of his mouth. He didn't eat much and lost weight but no one asked him why. Eventually the teenaged boys stopped coming around. They went off to Vietnam. One of them was killed there. The other two returned unharmed. The first became a petty criminal who wound up being sent to prison for forty years; the second became a mail carrier whose route, until he shot himself and three co-workers a few years back, included the boy's family home.

Sitting at the Pay Here, Please table outside the garage now, the man who was once a boy of eight looking forward to his first (and only) camping trip watches as various young girls and women impolitely grope every last item remaining from the detritus of his childhood. Twenty-five cents for blouses, fifty cents for shoes and wigs, fifty cents for the dime-store jewelry Mom thought was so exquisite because she never knew better, a dollar for jackets and dresses. An appealing woman of perhaps twenty-seven with luxurious red hair says hello to him as she makes her purchase. He recognizes the dress: it's the one he was most often made to wear and sometimes wrapped himself in afterward. He feels a pang of regret (because it can't be grief, can it?) as the appealing red-head buys it (along with some shoes, some books, a couple of LPs), slips everything into a shopping bag, and leaves for her home.

He wonders what her friends will say when they see her in it. Look, they'll say. Look at _____'s new dress. It's so retro-chic. Have you seen it yet? Have you seen _____'s new dress?

He asks his sister to take over at the table. Rising, he feels sick as he begins following _____. That dress was his favorite. He wonders if she'll look as good in it as he did. The boys always said he looked pretty when he wore it. He'll wait for her to put it on and see if she's prettier. Then he'll have her take it off. They can maybe go camping there in her house.

He hopes she'll understand afterward. She should have just left it on the table.

Consolation

"The consolation of imaginary things is not imaginary consolation."
—Roger Scruton, English author, philosopher, and composer

In the early days of Cedar Hill when the Welsh, Scotch, and Irish immigrants worked alongside the Delaware and Wyandot Indians to establish safe shipping lanes, it was decided that a beacon of some sort needed to be erected. Two miles out from the shores of Buckeye Lake was an isolated island twelve miles in circumference; perfect for a lighthouse. Construction began in April of 1805, time and the elements took their toll as they are wont to do, and eventually the lighthouse fell to disrepair and decay. Two hundred years later the island was purchased by the Licking Valley Boaters' Association, the lighthouse was restored, and attached to it now was the Licking Valley Yacht and Boaters' Clubhouse, whose members kept one tradition from the 1800s; every New Year's Eve, regardless of the weather conditions, the tower light came on and circled for one minute as the foghorn sounded.

A few dozen yards from the fishing dock on the Buckeye Lake side, a single Cedar Hill Sheriff's Department vehicle pulled into the parking lot. First its visibar lights shut off (there was no siren tonight; the driver had used Silent Approach); next, the headlights, their beams filled with the swirling mist of fresh snow and the incoming fog, snapped back into darkness; and finally the driver's side door opened and out stepped Sheriff Ted Jackson, zipping up his winter coat and blinking against the vapor-trails of his breath. He unclipped his flashlight, its beam cutting through the night-haze of winter, and shone it in half-circles until its gossamer beam at last stopped. Jackson exhaled, nodded, and snapped off the beam, shaking his head. Reattaching the flashlight back onto his belt, he reached inside the patrol car and removed a medium-sized brown paper bag, tucked it under his arm, closed the door, and walked down to the fishing dock.

He approached the small figure sitting there, careful not to make any sudden loud noises. The figure was rocking back and forth, knees pulled up against its chest, humming a nonsensical and off-key tune and grinning ear to ear as diaphanous bursts of steam exited its nose with the rhythm of smoke from a sleeping dragon. Between its knees and its chest, it clutched a pair of well-read books, covers tattered but still doing their job, yes, indeed.

"Carson," said Jackson as he squatted down next to the figure. "A lot of people are worried about you."

"I-I'm s-sorry," he said.

"How in the heck did you get out here, anyway?"

"I took the Number Forty-Eight express from downtown. I been s-saving my money. I got enough to get back."

"The Forty-Eight doesn't come through here until six a.m. What were you planning to do until then?"

"I got enough to go to the truck stop and have a nice hamburger and m-malted or something. I was g-gonna catch the bus there in the morning."

Jackson nodded. "Well, something told me you'd probably be here.

"I'm w-waiting for McDunn."

Jackson gave the ghost of a smile. "So you finally gave it a name?"

Carson nodded, still not looking at the sheriff. "Uh-huh. And I figured that m-maybe since it's gonna be—hey, you know what? It's gonna be my birthday in a couple days. I want McDunn to come to my party. It'll be—you know what? It'll be *great*! I'll be the only b-boy in Cedar Hill who's ever had a dinosaur come to his birthday party!"

"You're right, that *would* be great," said Jackson as he slipped the paper bag behind him.

It was said of Ted Jackson that his eyes always looked as if he were staring at something a hundred yards away that perpetually broke his heart. They looked no different tonight, save for the distance between them and that at which they stared.

Looking at his watch, Jackson said, "Well, ten till midnight, so what say I wait here with you and we'll see if McDunn shows up?"

Carson looked at him now, his smile radiant with gratitude. "Oh, that ... th-that'd be real great of you, Sheriff. I ain't never had n-nobody wait with me before. They all think I'm s-s-stupid."

Jackson put his hand on Carson's shoulder. "Well, I didn't have any plans tonight, anyway —and, besides, I can't think of anyone I'd rather ring in the new year with."

Carson's smile faltered a little, maybe from the cold, maybe from something else. "I always liked you, Sheriff. I'm real g-glad you're the one they sent." When he said "they" Carson's arms tightened around the books. This did not go unnoticed by Jackson.

"Did they try to take away your books again?"

Carson nodded violently, despairingly. "Uh-huh, and they ... they *can't take them away, Sheriff!* They're the only ones I ever had. I just ... I j-just l-love them. I d-do." His eyes began to water, maybe from the cold, maybe from something else. "*P-please* don't them take away my books. All my friends are here!"

Jackson looked into Carson's eyes. "I promise you, buddy, that no one is going to take your ... take your friends away from you."

"You mean it?"

Jackson had to take a deep breath to make sure he could get it out in a steady voice. "I mean it, Carson. I wouldn't lie to you. I'm a terrible liar, anyway."

Carson laughed. "Me too."

Jackson's radio squawked, startling both him and Carson. Patting the tiny rounded shoulders, Jackson said, "Be right back, buddy."

"Will you be back before the light comes on and the foghorn sounds?"

"Count on it." Jackson rose quickly and walked a few yards away, his bad leg reminding him that it wasn't a good idea in this weather for a man of fifty-one years to squat.

"What is it, Rosie?"

"Sheriff, they've been calling here every ten minutes for the last half-hour. You find him?"

"I found him."

"Oh, *good*. Now I can look forward to them calling every ten minutes to see if you two are on your way *back*. Happy New Year and God bless us, every one."

"You're a born poetess, Rosie. Tell them I'm going to wait with him until after the foghorn."

"They won't like it."

"After everything that's been done to him, all the lousy places he's been shuffled in and out of, after all he went through at the hands of that sadistic waste of carbon the county called his father —"

"—that was a while ago, you gotta let it go, you're getting yourself all worked up again and we both know your blood pressure ain't been the best it's ever —"

"Well goddammit *someone* ought to get worked up on his behalf, so why not me? It's not like I got anyone else in my life to worry about, so if he wants to spend time waiting for McDunn to appear —"

"—McDunn?"

"The dinosaur, the sea monster."

"From that story in one those books of his? Sheriff, that's such a sad story."

"They're trying to take the books away from him again, Rosie."

"Oh, *dear*. No wonder he ran away."

Jackson looked back at the tiny figure sitting on the dock. "Hell, I would, too. If somebody threatened to take all my friends away."

"Beg pardon?"

Jackson closed his eyes, getting hold of himself. "I'll tell you about it tomorrow. Promise."

Back with Carson, Jackson decided to sit this time and not tempt fate. "I miss anything?"

Carson giggled. "You're f-funny."

"You're the only one who thinks so, but thanks."

Carson reached over and took hold of Jackson's hand. "I'm real sorry about ... about Misses Jackson."

The sheriff shrugged. "Things happen with married people, Carson."

"How come she l-left like that?"

"That was a lifetime ago, buddy. I just wasn't ... very interesting to her anymore."

"Well, I think that was a t-terrible thing to do. You're such a nice man."

Jackson shook his head. "Spread that around, will you? I haven't had a date in ten years."

"That's a l-long time." He squeezed the sheriff's hand. "I'll bet you g-get ... lonely."

Jackson looked into Carson's eyes and saw all the deep, sincere sympathy that a child's eyes always had; he also saw the phantoms of terrible years of a childhood damaged, a childhood taken away, a childhood denied. Yet Carson's eyes still maintained that spark of hope and wonder, of dreaming of rockets flying above and inspired chicken motels and million-year picnics, of golden apples of the sun and giant mushroom and happiness machines that he probably wished for before falling into his lonely sleep. He saw all of this, yet behind that warm and glimmering they were also eyes that were just sick about something.

"So, Carson ... what do you wish for the new year?"

"Oh, I wish for a lot! When I grow up, I wish that I'll go to a Halloween party dressed like Stan Laurel and I'll meet a girl dressed like Oliver Hardy and we'll fall in love, and I wish to ride in a rocket, and I wish to build a fake mummy out of scraps of paper and old posters and sticks and pots and pans and anything else I can find so that I can play a big joke on everyone so we'll all laugh, and the town of Cedar Hill, central Ohio, will tell the story over and over to other children so they'll laugh, and I wish to travel to Mars and meet real Martians, and I wish to meet a fox in the forest who will laugh at me and my girlfriend 'cause we dress like Laurel and Hardy, and I wish to meet a famous artist on the beach who will draw a picture in the sand and it'll be only for me, and it'll be of a world that's *just* the way I hope it will be, where I can travel back in time and maybe meet knights who sit on railroad tracks, and I wish to say farewell to Lafayette and not be sad, and I wish to meet the parrot who knows every word of Papa's last book, and I'll talk to it, and then it will tell them to me 'cause nobody ever told me stories before, and I wish to write poems and put them into blue bottles and cast them out to sea, and I wish to meet a man all covered in tattoos and each one has a story all its own and he'll tell them to me 'cause nobody ever told me stories before, and I wish to find a button from a Civil War soldier's uniform, one lost downwind from Gettysburg, and that button will whisper stories of great battles to me when I polish it and hold it to my ear, and I wish ... I wish to fall asleep to soft rains and wake to a golden sun, and I wish to play a far-away guitar at midnight in the month of June ... and I wish to be the world's greatest writer so that I can tell stories to other children 'cause everyone should have someone to tell them stories on account it's awful lonely sometimes when you don't have nobody to tell you stories ... and I wish ... I wish ..." His lower lip began trembling, and his voice become much thinner and unsteady as he fought back the tears. "... I wish to have a place called home with my own room and people who love me ..." he pulled the books closer to his chest. "... and I wish that I maybe won't wish so much 'cause it's lonely when you wish and don't got nobody to tell about them ... nobody ever told me stories ..." He hugged the books close to his cheek. "... except here, only here, where all my friends are." He looked at Jackson. "We should go back, Sheriff. McDunn isn't g-going to show up."

Jackson blinked, shocked. "But ... but the lighthouse and the foghorn ..."

Carson threw himself against the sheriff and hugged him tightly, the precious books falling onto the dock as the fog crept in on silent cat paws, curling around the books until they could be seen no more. Carson wept, fighting against a great sorrow heavy and vast as he quoted from memory: "'It's gone back to the Deeps. It's learned that you can't love anything too much in this world... Waiting out there and waiting out there, while man comes and goes on this pitiful little planet. Waiting and waiting.'"

No light came from the tower. No foghorn sounded. The only noise was that of Carson's weeping and whispering: "Waiting and waiting and no one ever comes. N-nobody ever tells stories. Nobody ever tells ...."

Ted Jackson held the tiny, fragile, weeping figure close. He leaned over and picked up the books before the fog took them forever, gently placing them back in Carson's arms. "You know," he said, "he wrote other books with lots more stories."

Sniffling, Carson turned his face upward. "Y-yeah? He did?"

"You bet." Jackson pulled the brown paper bag from behind him and removed its contents, momentarily unnoticing of the folded, stapled sheets of paper that tumbled out.

Carson's eyes grew wide, the innocent fire reigniting from within, making his cheeks glow. "A *hundred stories*?" he cried out in joy as he took the big, new, red-covered book from Jackson.

"Oh, yeah. And I have more by him, as well. You have hundreds, thousands of new friends waiting for you, Carson. He's given them to you. They've been waiting. You only have to open the book and turn to the first page."

"Nobody ever gave me a new book."

"Happy birthday, Carson."

"... all these new friends, all these n-new stories, all these new places to go ...." He began reading the first story.

Jackson patted Carson's shoulder and gave him a small kiss on the top of his head, then reached out and grabbed the papers that he noticed had fallen out. The top of the first page read: **Petition for Legal Guardianship**.

"You want to come and stay over at my place tonight, Carson? We got some things to talk about. Maybe we can grab a pizza and—"

"Shhh," said Carson, flipping the page with great intensity. "This's a *good* one."

And so the fog danced around them but did not take them into the winter shadows; a sheriff of fifty-one and an old man of seventy-nine who, because of too many blows to the head with cast-iron skillets, would always be seven years old.

As Jackson led him to the vehicle Carson read on, finding worlds of new hope filled with new friends, new more wondrous things to imagine, to dream about, and to wish for. The pages turned, the words drunk in like Bacchus's headiest brew, and a childhood lost, a childhood ruined, and a childhood denied blinked as it woke in the darkness, turned on the lights, and raised its head in glory.

For Ray Bradbury

Bargain

"Then wilt thou not be loth
To leave this Paradise..."
—John Milton, *Paradise Lost*

The night grew silent, an almost majestic silence, as if every living thing was holding its breath for fear of breaking the purity.

As the silence became deeper, so did the darkness, allowing a massive shadow to detach itself from a corner of the night and move unnoticed over the city, over every building, every house, every church, past the farmers' fields and the woodlands, until it reached the north and south forks of the Licking River near Raccoon Creek. Here, the North Fork marked the community's eastern boundary. In this spot the county began to gradually slope from the Mississippian bedrock it rested on to the much trickier Pennsylvanian bedrock; shale lay under the surface of the topsoil from the west where sandstone began mixing in.

A small tributary of the Licking River formed in this spot, and it was here that the shadow hovered as still as the point of an ancient divining rod. This sixty-acre plat had always been extremely weak; the ground here was known to often simply collapse without warning, half-swallowing barns, outhouses, even the corpses of abandoned cars rusting in the nearby automobile graveyard.

This was not a place many visited anymore.

What better spot, then, for a certain corner of Hell to open one of its back doors?

Beneath the clear, still surface of the tributary whose surface was made almost turquoise by the moonlight, lay a series of small, evenly-spaced hollowed boulders, each with a translucent sheet of isinglass covering its front. Inside each of the hollowed objects — which, upon closer examination, the shadow saw were not boulders at all but leathery eggs — huddled a clay-like lump; some were shapeless blobs, others vaguely humanoid in shape; some were skeletal, others so corpulent their shapes could barely be contained; still others were mere hand-sized, featureless fetuses. The figures lay with knees pulled up against their chests. Their dark, sunken eyes stared up blankly at the draping algae and bodies of insects floating on the surface.

The shadowed slumped closer to the surface, whispering *Awaken* to any of the figures who could hear.

A set of tiny fingers broke through the gelatinous fronting of one of the eggs and began pulling apart the shell, sections snapping off and flaking away until the featureless fetal face poked through, followed by two pink arms, hands moving slowly through the water as the Unfinished Soul pushed free of its prison and swam through to the surface. It pulled itself onto the ground, crawling toward the tip of the shadow.

The shadow reached out and helped the Unfinished Soul to stand.

I need a guide, little one, whispered the shadow. *A debt is being collected tonight.*

Lift me up, said the Unfinished Soul. *It will be my pleasure to show you the way.*

The shadow poured over the figure, ink spreading across a sketch, until it vanished completely.

Do exactly as I say, whispered the Unfinished Soul.

And the shadow began churning in the air; slowly, at first, curling wisps of smoke from a forgotten cigarette, growing thicker, its speed increasing, soon twisting itself into a funnel and dropping low.

The ground rippled, then began sinking inward with heavy, dry sounds as the shadow threaded itself into the center of the chasm like string through a needle's eye. Sections of earth spun outward as the shadow-thread drilled deeper, finally disappearing beneath the surface. The ground shuddered, jumped, then grumbled. The remaining eggs in the tributary swirled like flecks around a drain before vanishing down the chasm.

In the heart of the shadow, the Unfinished Soul glanced upward, just once, out of curiosity, and saw the moon vanish behind a blue-tinged night-cloud, then re-emerge a few moments later to reveal it was no cloud at all, but something much more solid—a balloon.

Beneath its death's-head body and the glowing fire within, his hands gripping the flying wires of the basket, a young man who could no longer remember his name watched as the chasm grew wide, then wider. As he stared into the pit he saw a ring of trees emerge around the perimeter—fingers of the dead pushing upward through forgotten grave-soil—and stood helpless as the balloon moved downward, toward them.

The trees were well over thirty feet tall, each with a thick trunk resembling that of a cactus, only black. The branches of each tree were obscured by heavy onion layers of bleak blue leaves which collectively blossomed outward to form human faces, each turning upward to stare at him through milky, pupilless eyes, each wearing a tight, pinched expression of concentrated grief. As the wind passed through the trees, the faces opened their mouths and moaned; deeply, steadily, mournfully: the sound of cumulative anguish.

The young man felt tears welling in his eyes, and wished he could say something to ease their pain.

After all, he recognized every face.

A strong gust of wind howled, snatching the balloon from within the ring of keening trees and hurtling it into the gale. It bounced across the night sky, turning, dipping, rising, caught in the thermals. It ebbed across roads, spun down streets, and arced over buildings, its cast-off rope whipping back and forth as it was tossed into the pocket of a wind that pulled it down until the tip of its rope touched the sidewalk.

It scooted along until it reached an old but noble-looking house where a single dim light burned in the downstairs window.

The balloon moved with great care, positioning itself so that the young man was given a clear look inside the window.

Murky light from a glowing street lamp snaked across the darkness to press against the glass. The light bled into the room, across a kitchen table, and glinted off the rim of a glass held by a man whose once-powerful body had lost its commanding posture under the weight of compiling years; he was now overweight from too many beers, over-tense from too many worries, and overworked far too long without a reprieve. Whenever this man spoke, his eyes never had you; this much the young man watching from the balloon recalled with morbid clarity. His father's eyes were every lonely journey the young man had ever taken, every unloved place he'd ever visited, every sting of guilt he'd ever felt; he stared into his father's eyes that never had you, only brushed by once, softly, like a cattail or a ghost, then fell shyly toward the ground in some inner contemplation too sad to be touched by a tender thought or the delicate brush of another's care. You'd think God had forgotten his name.

Albert lifted the glass to his mouth. The cool water felt good going down, washing away the remnant of the bad dream. He drained the glass, sighed, then went to the sink and refilled the glass. He was thinking about his days as a child, about the afternoons now forgotten by everyone but him, afternoons when he'd go to the movies for a nickel and popcorn was only a penny. He thought about how he used to take his son to the movies all the time when his son was still a boy, how much fun they always had, and Albert longed for the chance to do something like that again, something that would put a bright smile on his son's face and make himself feel less of a failure. His son was now a great success, and Albert was still what he'd always been, a factory stooge, a worker on the line. He tried to remember how long it had been since he and his son had last spoken. Seemed a damn shame, it did, the way they never talked anymore, and his son living just the other side of town.

Why hadn't the boy called in so long?

Albert stood at the sink listening to the sounds of his wife sleeping. Janice snored loudly, and though it used to get on Albert's nerves, he now found the sound comforting. He didn't know how he'd be able to face the rest of his life if she weren't by his side. She was a marvel to him. After all the mistakes he'd made—and, God, he'd made a lot, no arguing that—her respect and love for him never lessened.

Albert raised the glass to his lips and found that he was smiling.

The balloon rose higher, then, toward a window on the second floor, giving the young man a chance to look in on the sleeping form of his mother, and smile; even from outside, he could hear her snoring. *Sawing logs like a lumberjack,* his father used to say.

The keening trees had perfectly captured the faces of his parents, as well as the others.

The young man reached out his hand but stopped just short of placing it against the glass.

Would it do any good if you knew how sorry I am?

As if in answer, the wind kicked up once again and the balloon was swept away, up and over the house.

It rode the breeze above the roofs of the town until its nearly-imperceptible shadow fell across the head of a couple climbing out of a car and running toward another house, one the young man recognized all too well.

As he did the couple; their faces, too, had been perfectly reproduced by the keening trees.

The balloon hovered, unseen by Patricia and her husband, Richard, as they rushed toward the front porch of the house. Patricia had been trying to get in touch with her brother for the last week and had finally given over to panic when she'd called Mom and Dad to find they hadn't heard from him for a long while, either.

"He's probably out of town or something," Albert had said to her. "He's been real…busy lately, what with the company taking off like it has."

The explanation wasn't enough for Patricia, who insisted that Richard and she make the one-hour drive from Columbus to Cedar Hill.

Patricia pounded on the front door, calling out her brother's name.

No response.

She began flipping through her keys until she found the spare door key her brother had given her last year when he'd bought the house.

"I don't know if just barging in like this is such a good idea," said Richard.

"Don't start with me again," said Patricia, slipping the key into the lock. "I don't care how great things are going for his company, you *know* how bad his depression can get when he doesn't take his meds. He pulled this disappearing act the last time he went off them, and it damn near killed him."

"I still think you're panicking over nothing."

"I hope so, Richard. I truly hope you'll be saying 'I told you so' to me in a few minutes."

She got the door opened but Richard stepped in front of her.

"Let me go in first, Pat, okay? He might...y'know...have company or something."

"*Goddammit*, Richard, I'm not going to worry about —"

"Just humor me, all right?"

Patricia exhaled, then nodded her head. "I'll wait here. But not for long."

Richard went inside, leaving the door half-opened.

The young man in the balloon wanted to close his eyes, wanted to cover his ears with his hands, wanted the balloon to leave here right this second because he didn't want to see or hear what was about to happen when —

"*Jesus!*" shouted Richard from inside. "*Oh, good Christ — PAT!*"

As if propelled by the volume of Richard's shouts, the balloon caught a thermal and glided farther on, reaching the banks of the Licking River. The thermal expanded and the balloon lowered its basket and passenger into the waters, the currents carrying it to the junction of the north and south forks.

It bounced off a section of jutting rocks and spiraled upward, pulled into a pocket of churning wind being sucked into the deep chasm in the center of the field.

The keening trees blinked their pupilless eyes and cried out again; louder, this time, and with a deeper anguish.

The young man felt their cries chew through him as the balloon hung suspended over the chasm of collapsed earth.

The balloon's tie-off rope began to unroll and lower itself. The rumbling from deep inside the chasm became a whistle. Small sections of hillside crumbled away, giving way to increasingly larger sections sliding toward the chasm and pouring over its edge.

The chasm grew wider. More ground collapsed.

The whistling was replaced by the sound of a million rocks cracking apart from the center.

The tie-off line pulled taut, a fisherman's line at last making the catch of the day.

The balloon began rising.

An ornate kiosk that might have been a belfry poked up, followed by curling arches that formed the overhang of stained-glass windows where stone gargoyles sat underneath.

A tug, another gust of wind, and the tie-off line snapped tighter, pulling with all its might.

The bulk of the rising church was pulled free of the membranous sac of soil.

The young man looked down and saw the world he'd known — as well as those he'd never know —unfurl before him like wings of a merciless predator.

He saw mountains crumble, the sky change color, and the seas give up their dead.

He saw himself watching a television screen that showed him watching a television screen of himself watching another screen where film of a funeral was shown to him as he watched.

He watched his soul grow wings and take flight.

He watched himself grow older.

He watched himself become a baby once again.

He watched himself never being born.

He watched himself being born a thousand times in a thousand different places.

He watched his soul's wings catch fire and plummet downward into the Pit.

He watched as everything shifted and changed and faded into shadows, only to be replaced by other, firmer worlds; there were skies filled with fire and songs to be sung; there were ships and seas and fields of green; there were races being born, becoming children at play, growing up, growing old, dying, becoming ashes, blowing away; he saw a ghost of himself walk through these ashes and stand over the bones of a child who had once been him, and he wept at the sight, at the wasted potential; he saw the bones rise up and grow skin, replacing the ghost of himself, growing up to become young and reckless, grow strong and virile, healthy and pink-cheeked, suddenly a child, a baby once more, a seed in the womb of its mother who snored too loudly, spinning back in time before starting over once again, clicking off the television remote of the funeral scene and struggle to his feet, old, ancient, his grey hair thinning, back bent, legs thin and weak and unstable, wishing for one last kiss from the wife he never had, then hobbling off to a lonely deathbed to lay down, close his eyes, and become ashes that blew away to land in a field of ashes where the next ghost of himself stood weeping over the bones of a child....

The church shook off the dirt and began to glow from within as candles were set aflame.

The doors were unlocked with a loud, creaking groan, and thrown open.

The Dust Witch stepped from behind the doors and gestured up toward the balloon, the bones in her arthritic index finger cracking as she curled it forward, then back, forward, then back: *Get yourself down here, now.*

The balloon lowered. The Dust Witch took hold of the tie-off line and wrapped it around one of the gargoyles.

The basket touched ground, and the young man climbed out, slowly, with much hesitation and even more sadness.

Around him, the keening trees turned their faces downward, screaming.

He touched his lips, then pulled away his fingers to look at the blood covering them; then he reached toward the back of his head, surprised at the size of the exit wound.

He smiled, shrugged, and looked at the hag standing before him.

"A belated word of advice," said the Dust Witch, taking his hand and leading him through the doors into Hell. "Whenever you sell your soul, don't sell it so *cheap*."

Shikata Ga Nai: A Bag Lady's Tale

We find her, as expected, in her favorite place: the iron bench on the courthouse lawn, the one with the sculpted-bronze figures of two old women doing cross-stitch sitting on it. It's fortunate that it's a big bench, because the old lady needs a good deal of room, she does, for her bags and blankets and such. Judging by her face, she's not a day over fifty, yet she claims to be in her early eighties. No one knows her name, or where she lives, or if she has a home at all. But we know her, in a way. As a neutrino has no mass or electrical charge and can pass through the planet in a blink, so this bag lady's existence can pass through this world; she, like the neutrino, is a ghost, yet both are real, both exist and have presence, even if that presence is unseen or ignored.

We take a place near the little garden a few yards behind the bench and watch as she begins to unfold the quilt; we listen as she tells the story to her still bronze companions, who never seem to tire of hearing it:

"Gene got himself shot overseas during the war and it did something to the bones in his leg and the doctors, they had to insert all these pins and build him a new kneecap and calfbone—it was awful. Thing is, when this happened, he only had ten months of service left. He was disabled bad enough that he couldn't return to combat but not so bad that they'd give him an early discharge, so they sent him back home and assigned him guard duty at one of them camps they set up here in the states to hold all those Jap-Americans.

"Gene guarded the gate at the south end of the camp, and I guess it was a pretty big camp, kind of triangle-shaped, with watchtowers and searchlights and barbed wire, the whole shebang. There was this old Jap tailor being held there with his family and this guy, he started talking to Gene during his watch every night. This guy was working on a quilt, you see, and since a needle was considered a weapon he could only work on the thing while a guard watched him, and when he was done for the night he'd have to give the needle back. Well, Gene, he was the guy who pulled 'Needle Patrol.'

"The old guy told Gene that this thing he was working on was a 'memory quilt' that he was making from all the pieces of his family's history. I guess he'd been working on the thing section by section for most of his life—'cording to what he told Gene, it'd been started by his great-great-great-great-grandfather. The tailor—this fellah in the camp with Gene, that is—he had part of the blanket his own mother had used to wrap him in when he was born, plus he had his son's first sleeping gown, the tea-dress his daughter had worn when she was four, a piece of a velvet slipper worn by his wife the night she gave birth to their son....

"What he'd do, see, is he'd cut the material into a certain shape and then use stuff like paint or other pieces of cloth stuffed with cotton in order to make pictures or symbols on each of the patches. Gene said this old Jap'd start at one corner of the quilt with the first patch and tell him who it had belonged to, what they'd done for a living, where they'd lived, what they'd looked like, how many kids they'd had, the names of their kids and their kids' kids, describe the house *they* had lived in, the countryside where the house'd been ... I guess it was really something, all right. Gene said it made him feel good, listening to this old guy's stories, 'cause the guy trusted him enough to tell him these things, you see? Even though he was a prisoner of war and Gene was his guard, he told him these things. Gene said it also made him feel kind of sad, 'cause he'd get to thinking about how most people don't even know their great-grandma's maiden name, let alone the story of her whole life. But this old Jap—'scuse me, I guess I really oughtn't use that word, should I? Don't show the proper respect for the man or his culture—but you gotta understand, back then, the Japs was the enemy, what with bombing Pearl Harbor and all....

"Where was I? Oh yeah—this old tailor, he knew the history of every last member of his family. He'd finish talking about the first patch, then he'd keep going, talking on about what all the paintings and symbols and shapes meant, and by the time he came round to the last completed patch in the quilt, I guess he'd covered something like six hundred years of his family's history. 'Every patch has one hundred-hundred stories.' That's what the old guy said.

"The idea was that the quilt represented all the memories of your life—not just your own, but them ones that was passed down to you from your ancestors, too. The deal was, at the end of your life, you were supposed to give the quilt to a younger member of your family and it'd be up to them to keeping adding to it; that way, the spirit never really died because there'd always be someone and something to remember that you'd existed, that your life'd meant something. This old tailor was really concerned about that. He said that a person dies twice when others forget that you had lived.

"Well, Gene, he starts noticing that this tailor, he seemed really ... I don't know ... scared of something all the time. These camps, they weren't nearly as bad as them ones the Nazis built for the Jews, but that ain't saying much. Some of 'em was filthy and cramped stank to high heaven, but this camp Gene was at —I can't remember its name, dammit—it had this sign tacked up over the entrance gate, and this sign was on the inside of the gate so everyone in the camp could read it, and it said, 'Shikata ga nai.' It was this old tailor that had made the sign and hung it up, you see. He told Gee that it meant, 'It cannot be helped.' I guess a lot of them poor folks jammed into them camps felt that way, y'know? Like there wasn't nothing they could do about it and never would be.

"Gene finally got around to asking the tailor what his name was. The guards weren't supposed to get too familiar with the prisoners, I guess, and asking one for their name was against the rules something terrible, but Gene was a decorated war hero and figured, what the hell are they gonna try and do to me, anyway? So when he notices that the tailor has been acting real scared, he tries to talk with him, calm him down, right? The tailor tells Gene he needs to tell him a story first, before he tells his name, and then he says —get this—he says that he's older than any piece of land anywhere on Earth. He's crazy, right?

"And then he tells Gene this story. He says that when a child dies its soul has to cross the Sanzu River, that when a person dies, they can cross the river at three different spots—depending on how they lived their lives. Since children ain't lived long enough to have done something with their lives, they can't cross the thing. At the edge of the river, these children's souls are met by this hag named Datsueba, and she takes their clothes and tells them to build a pile of pebbles so they can climb up it to reach paradise. But before the pile can get high enough for the children to reach paradise, the hag and her gang of demons knock it down. If the soul is an adult's, Datsueba makes them take off their clothes, and the old-man Keneo hangs these clothes on a riverside branch, and that branch, it bends against the weight of that soul's sins. If the sinner didn't have no clothes, Datsuba stripped them of their skin.

"That's the part of the story when the old tailor, he told Gene that his name was Keneo, that he'd escaped the underworld and Datsuba because he couldn't take part in her behavior no more. He couldn't watch them poor kids trying to climb their piles of pebbles or them adults stripped of their skin. He said that when he escaped the underworld, he stole every piece of clothing that had ever been left by the Sanzu River, because if he could find a way to make a quilt with one section of cloth from each piece of clothing, them souls would be released and there wouldn't be nothing Datsuba could do about it. But in order to give the quilt this power, the clothes from them souls in the underworld had to be stitched alongside pieces of clothes from the living, and that's why it was taking the tailor so long to finish it. The guy, it turns out, didn't have any grandfather, or great-grandfather, or great-great-great grandfather. They was *all* him! Gene, he thought the old guy had himself quite the imagination, so he just smiled and handed him a needle and watched him do his work.

"'Bout ten months after Gene started Needle Patrol the old tailor came down with a bad case of hepatitis and had to be isolated from everyone else. While this guy was in the infirmary the camp got orders to transfer a hundred or so prisoners, and the old guy's family was in the transfer group. Gene tried to stop it but nobody'd lift a finger to help—one sergeant even threatened to have Gene brought up on charges if he didn't let it drop. In the meantime, the tailor developed a whole damn slew of secondary infections and kept getting worse, feverish and hallucinating, trying to get out of bed and babbling in his sleep. He lingered for about a week, then he died. My Gene, he almost cried when he heard the news.

"The day after the tailor died Gene was typing up all the guards' weekly reports—you know, them hour-by-hour, night-by-night deals. Turned out that the three watchtower guards—and mind you, these towers was quite a distance from each other—but all three of them reported seeing this old tailor at the same time, at exactly 3:47 in the morning. And all three of them said he was carrying his quilt. Gene said he read that and got cold all over, so he called the infirmary to check on what time the tailor had died. He died at 3:47 in the morning, all right, but he died the night *after* the guards reported seeing him—up till then, he'd been in a coma for most of the week.

"Gene tried to track down the tailor's family but didn't have any luck. It wouldn't have mattered much, anyway, 'cause the quilt come up missing.

"He didn't tell me about any of this till our twenty-fifth wedding anniversary. He took me to New York City so's I could see a real Broadway show. On our last day there we started wandering around Manhattan, stopping at all these little shops. We came across this one antique store that had all this 'Early Pioneer' stuff displayed in its window. I stopped to take a look at this big ol' ottoman and I asked Gene if he thought there were people fool enough to pay six-hundred dollars for a footstool. He didn't answer me right away so I asked him again and when he didn't answer this time I turned around to see him all white in the face. He let go of my hand and goes running into this store, climbs over some tables and such to get in the window, and he rips this dusty old blanket off a rocking chair.

"It was the quilt that Japanese tailor'd been working on in the camp. They only wanted a hundred dollars for it so you bet your butt my Gene slapped down the cash. We took it back to our hotel room and spread it out on the bed—oh, it was such a beautiful thing. All the colors and pictures, the craftsmanship ... I got teary-eyed when Gene told me the story. But the thing that really got to both of us was that down in the right-hand corner of the quilt was this one patch that had these figures stitched into them. Four figures. Three of them was positioned way up high above the fourth one, and they formed a triangle. The fourth figure was down below, walking kind of all stooped over and carrying what you'd think was a bunch of clothes. But Gene, he took one look and knew what it was—it was a picture of that tailor's soul carrying his quilt, walking around the camp for the last time, looking around for someone to pass his memories on to because he couldn't find his family and he couldn't go back to the underworld on account of what Datsuba would do to him. He was lost forever, and there wasn't nothing he could do about it. It couldn't be helped. Shikata ga nai. Isn't that sad?

"See here, this's the quilt. And this here needle? Gene gave it to me. It was the one that old tailor used. I been adding things to it, 'cause it seemed to me that's what my Gene would want me to do if he was here. See this? This is part of the suit Gene wore when we got married. And this here come off the baby gown that my mom made for Cindy when I had her. Them things there?—those're the dog tags that the Army sent to us after Jimmy was killed over in Vietnam. The way I figure it, Gene was like family to the tailor, so it's only right that I do this. It's only right.

"Thing is, I'm not as sprightly as I used to be, and except for Cindy all my family's gone—she don't much want to have anything to do with me. I'm not even sure where it is she and her husband are livin' these days. And if—oh, Lord, look at me, will you? Getting all teary-eyed again.

"I don't know what's gonna happen to this after I'm gone, you see? And I don't know where any of them souls' clothes was stored. I can keep adding things from people living in this world, but I got no way to get them souls' clothes. I don't know how I'll know when this quilt is finished, and if it ain't finished and I die and don't pass it on to someone, then them souls will be trapped in the underworld forever. And that scares me something powerful, it does. Right down to the ground."

Patience

"Men always want to be a woman's first love. That is their clumsy vanity. Women have a more subtle instinct about things: What they like is to be a man's last romance."

—Oscar Wilde, *A Woman of No Importance*

He walked slowly down the hallway, the sound of his footsteps swallowed by the deep golden carpet. He stopped at a door that was an ornate slab of burnished teak set within a bronze frame. He knew who waited on the other side, and what he was going to do once he found them.

He stood in silence, aware of the rhythm of his breathing and the sweat covering his face. He checked to make certain the surgical gloves he wore hadn't been torn when he'd taken out the two bodyguards downstairs. The first one had been easy—the man was half asleep at his post, it was just a matter of coming up behind him and making sure he punctured the lung from behind with the knife. Puncture the lung, it creates a vacuum, making it impossible for the victim to scream.

The first guard hadn't screamed. Had barely made a sound while his throat was slit. Easy.

The second guard gave him some trouble, even managed to get his gun out if its holster, but never managed to get off a shot. He'd buried the fillet knife in the guard's eye. To the hilt. He hated having to leave the knife. It had been an anniversary present.

He almost smiled now, remembering the shocked expression on the second goon's face when he'd seen him. The man's eyes had held a thousand questions: *Who the fuck are you? What do you want? How'd you get past the alarms? Does this job pay enough to make it worth dying for?*

At least that last one was answered now.

He pulled a handkerchief from his pocket and dabbed gently at the perspiration on his face, then stuffed it into one of the nine pockets of his heavy coat.

The fake beard was itching like hell. The spirit gum he'd used to apply it was burning his skin underneath. He could smell the theatrical hair spray he'd used to make himself grey. And the blue-tinted contacts were causing him to blink more than he liked.

Still, they were necessary precautions.

There was almost no light in the hallway, save for that from the moon which bled in from a large window across from him. Outside it was purple-gray, 4:40 a.m.; dawn just creeping in, night not quite finished with the world. A thin layer of snowy mist enshrouded the yard as a dispirited breeze sloughed through the trees. Frost glistened on every surface, shimmering at the tips of leaves.

She had always loved this time of night, this time of morning. Sometimes, she'd wake and get out of bed, then just sit in her favorite chair and watch the night with infinite patience, just to see a moment of perfect peace.

He felt a rush of renewed love for her. So giving, so kind, so patient.

He'd learned patience from her. He was being patient now. His soul radiated patience.

He checked his watch. 4:42 a.m.

It had taken him three years to find this house and this door.

Three years and nearly fifty thousand dollars, the time and money doled out slowly.

Almost finished, my love, he thought.

He kept his face expressionless, willing the same emptiness into his eyes.

Emptiness was easy now. He had the person on the other side of the door to thank for that.

He checked his watch again.

4:45 a.m.

Time to finish it.

He pressed his ear against the door, listening.

From somewhere deep in the room, he heard a groan. Soft. Then louder.

"Faster, baby...oooooh, that's it, faster, harder...harder...*harder!*"

So he wasn't alone.

That was all right. He'd planned for this possibility.

The noise made by the woman covered the sound of his opening the door. The room was divided into two separate areas, like an expensive hotel suite. He found the sofa and coffee table.

Behind the bedroom door, the woman was screaming like a banshee, squealing and howling.

He took off his coat and began emptying the pockets.

Two pairs of handcuffs. A hypodermic needle filled with a precisely-measured dose of succinylcholine. Ten milligrams for each fifty pounds of body weight. It would cause instant paralysis but not numb the pain or induce unconsciousness.

Surgical bandages. A rubber tourniquet. Pressure tape. A mini blowtorch. Catheter tubing. A small roll of barbed wire. And a battery-powered bone saw.

He laid everything out nice and neat. He unfolded the large rubber apron and put it on over his clothes. He removed the two pistols and double checked the silencer attachment on the semi-automatic.

Ready, steady.

He checked the time again. 4:48 a.m.

He ran the calculations in his head once again.

He'd disabled all the alarms and video cameras, but if anyone happened to glance at the equipment, they'd see all lights on and blinking as usual. If there was a secondary alarm, it would be somewhere in the bedroom. It didn't matter. If a secondary alarm was set off, the security company would call first. Not getting an answer, they'd alert the police. This place was set far back from the main road. The drive to the house was tricky, a lot of twists and turns, not to mention the heavy foliage. You couldn't just *zoom* up here. At best, even if the police cruiser were right at the entrance to the house's private road, it would take them at least four minutes to get here. If the cruiser was dispatched from the station — and out here that would most likely be the case — then it would take them at least thirteen minutes to get here...and that was if they drove at a steady 80 m.p.h. the whole way.

And odds were they'd be on Silent Approach.

If there was a secondary alarm, and if the people behind the door had time to set it off before he could stop them, then once he went through the bedroom door he'd have somewhere between four and thirteen minutes.

He'd choreographed it for twelve minutes.

Time enough. He'd performed enough dry-runs on stolen CPR dummies and mannequins. Last time, he had it down to an even eleven-and-a-half minutes.

If there was a secondary alarm. *If* it was tripped. *If* he had to be fast.

He wished he could have hours.

Days, even.

He walked to the bedroom door.

"Give it to me *hard, baby! I like it hard. YES!*"

He took a deep breath and remembered the scent of Katie's perfume. The way she smiled during sleep. How she organized her sale coupons before heading out for the grocery store.

His face became a mask of granite.

He lifted the guns, exhaled, and kicked open the unlocked door.

The woman on the bed was on all fours, gripping the sheets in her fists and teeth. Her ass was high in the air. The man behind her was plunging a ridiculously large dildo into her.

They both jerked up their heads in shock as soon as the door crashed into the wall.

The man on the bed was none other than Dr. Barry Brandt, international best-selling author of *Return to Romance: How To Stoke the Fires of Marital Passion*, host of the popular syndicated radio show *Words of Love*, and recent daytime television talk-show star, thanks to the instant ratings success of his *Homefires* program. Add to that his always sold-out seminars for married couples —at a thousand dollars a pop—and his Romance Retreat Institute, and you had yourself a bona fide celebrity approaching pop-culture icon.

It was doubtful most of his followers knew about his adult-film franchise.

Brandt flung himself back against the wall, leaving the dildo inside his bed-mate.

"Who the hell are you?"

He pointed one gun at Brandt's face, the other at the woman on the bed. "It doesn't really matter now. My name's Morgan. My wife and I were just one of God-only-knows how many couples you lured to your Romance Retreat."

"Just tell me what you want and I'll —"

"Keep your hands where I can see them, both of you."

"Can I take this goddamn thing out of me?" said the woman.

"No." He moved closer to the bed, pressing the business end of the silencer against Brandt's upper lip. "Are there any alarms in here?"

"No," said Brandt.

Morgan jerked his arm to the right, firing the semi-automatic into the mattress, just missing the woman's knee.

She shrieked but, to her credit, didn't move.

"Next one goes through something wet and soft," Morgan said, shoving the silencer back up against Brandt's face. "This is very important, *Doctor. Extremely* important. So I'll ask again — are there any alarms in this room?"

"Yes."

"Good boy. Where?"

Brandt's eyes moved to the right. Morgan followed the path. A small pearl button on the right bed-post.

"That the only one?"

"Yes."

Morgan took a step back, looked once at the woman on the bed, and shot her in the thigh with the tranquilizer pistol. Ten seconds later, she was unconscious.

Morgan leaned down to check her breathing. It was fine. "Turn her over on her side in case she pukes," he said to Brandt. "And prop a couple of pillows behind her so she doesn't fall over onto her back."

"Look, w-we can...we can *talk* about this," said Brandt.

"Turn her onto her side."

Brandt complied.

Afterward, Morgan shoved the silencer under Brandt's chin; with his other hand, he grabbed the good doctor's testicles and pulled him along, guiding him to the other room.

"Th-that *hurts!*" shouted Brandt.

"It's supposed to," replied Morgan, shoving the other man down onto the sofa. He grabbed the first set of handcuffs and slapped them around Brandt's ankles. Then he grabbed Brandt's hair and forced him to bend forward so he could cuff the man's arms behind his back.

Morgan noted with neither joy nor fury that Brandt's being naked gave him 45 additional seconds to do what he came here to do.

Of course, with no secondary alarm having been set off, he had all night.

All the time in the world.

Morgan reached over and turned on a lamp.

Brandt got a good look at everything that was laid out on the table. His face turned white. He tried to speak but couldn't find his voice.

Morgan pulled up a chair and sat in front of Brandt, the gun pointed directly at the good doctor's genitals. "The blowtorch is for cauterizing. You know, so you don't bleed to death."

"I've got money. A lot of it. There's almost a quarter of million in cash right here in the house. And I can get more within an hour. I—"

"The thing is," said Morgan, "we really *believed* in your methods, Katie and me. Fourteen years we'd been married. Not every moment was filled with the crippling romantic ecstasy that you see in movies, but we loved each other. We were happy—happy enough." He cocked his head to one side and stared into Brandt's eyes.

"You have no idea what I mean when I say 'happy enough,' do you? I didn't think so. How could someone like you know what it's like to totally love someone. Not just their body, their smile, the way they smell in the morning, not just a check-list of countless individual things...but to love the imperfect whole, unquestioningly. The warmth of her lips, the smoothness of her skin, the silly way they hiccupped? I'd always felt that way about her, even if in later years I didn't show it as often or as well as I should have. Every time I saw her, every time we kissed, every time I caught a whiff of her perfume that entered a room just before she did, I was amazed at the rush of emotions inside me. I never in my life believed I had it in me to love someone so completely.

"Being with her wasn't like having a fantasy come true before I was ready for it; it was like having a fantasy come true before I'd even had the fantasy."

He reached up and wiped something from his eye.

"I remember, when we first met, how Katie would always ask me to tell her the story of my life. So I'd tell her, and when I finished, she'd ask me to tell it to her again, and I did. Only the second time, it was the story of *our* life. I—" He stopped himself when he saw the disgust lingering underneath the fear in Brandt's eyes.

"But you don't give a shit about that, do you, Doc? Or should I say, Lance Rollins? As in 'A Lance Rollins Production'?"

Brandt's eyes flashed something at hearing that name.

"You know that exit packet you give all the couples who attend your weekend Romance Retreat? There's a suggestion in that list of— what is it, 125 tips? Buried in the middle. *'Do not be afraid to watch erotic films together; there's nothing wrong with looking for new fantasies to share with your spouse.'*

"Well, after our weekend at the Retreat, things were going really good. We made love like we were in our early twenties again. Katie became more ambitious. She even started taking the initiative. It was just...great."

Morgan rubbed his temple, sighed, then looked at Brandt and shot him in the shoulder.

Brandt threw back his head and tried to scream but the pain was too intense. He barely managed a squeak. Morgan grabbed a small rubber ball from the pocket of his apron and shoved it in Brandt's mouth, then used a strip of pressure tape to secure it in place.

He waited until Brandt finished thrashing. The good doctor's head slumped forward. His breath shot hard out of his nose.

Morgan reached out and tipped Brandt's head up with the edge of the silencer.

"Not gonna pass out on me, are you, Doc?"

Brandt stared at him with hate-filled eyes.

"So I take it then that my narrative isn't boring you?"

Brandt didn't even blink.

"I would apologize for shooting you in the shoulder like that, but I suddenly saw Katie's face. I don't see it anymore, Doc, and that makes me sad. She's gone, and it's your doing, and what should now be the best time of our lives—mine and Katie's, that is—is just an endless succession of dismal, empty days, followed by dismal, empty nights. She used a garden hose, in case you're wondering. Ran it from the tailpipe through the trunk and between the fold-down back seats.

She did it around 5:16 in the morning." Morgan checked his watch. "About seven minutes from now. That's when I'm going to start in on you, Doc. At 5:16. I think you should die as slowly and in as much pain as she did.

"Oh, her pain wasn't as *physical* as yours is going to be, but her spirit, her heart, everything that made her so loving and kind and decent—that was in unspeakable agony. Had to be to drive her to suicide.

"Where was I?—oh, yeah, the 125 tips For Sustaining the Romantic Flame. Number 87: *'Do not be afraid to watch erotic films together; there's nothing wrong with looking for new fantasies to share with your spouse.'*

"Well, it was about three, four months after our Retreat weekend. God knows that time at the Retreat had helped us —put the spark back into our sex life, but Katie and I were starting to, well...run out of ideas. So we sit down with the cable guide and check out the Pay-Per-View adult movies. We decided to spend an evening watching and taping 'erotic films.' The first couple were pretty tame but we enjoyed them, but it was the third film—*Loving Couples, A Lance Rollins Production*—that really caught our attention."

Morgan rose to his feet. He placed the gun on the coffee table, then picked up the tourniquet and syringe. "Are you so stupid as to think that none of the couples who attend your seminars or go to your retreat will *ever* watch Pay-Per-View adult films? Or does your research show that they prefer to go out and rent? I checked on that, you know —your productions aren't available for rental, only purchase through the mail. And since you have to have exact titles...well, I guess I can see why you'd think odds were none of the couples you secretly filmed would ever find out."

He leaned down into Brandt's face. "Well, one of them did, Doc. There we are, sitting naked in front of the television, and all of a sudden *there we are on the television.* First we're making love in the bath tub, then there we are on the bed. Then later on—after you used tape of other couples —we top off the movie with our simultaneous orgasm, the first time we'd ever tried it with me entering her from behind.

"Do you know how that *killed* her? She pulled away from me and covered up her body like it was something *filthy,* something diseased. She wouldn't talk to me for days. She was so afraid that someone we knew might see that movie and recognize us."

He grabbed Brandt's throat and squeezed. "Sex between Katie and me was always something special and intimate, something that left us feeling even closer to one another than we had before, and in *one instant* you ruined it for us forever. You twisted it, made it dirty and shameful and broke her spirit. She couldn't live with what you'd done. *I* wanted to go to the police but she said no. It would have been too humiliating for her. You *made it* humiliating. You took a weekend that was so precious to us, that gave so much back to us, and turned it into...into...God! There's not even a word for what you turned it into!

"You took the most beautiful weekend of our lives and mutilated it. That's what Katie said to me. 'It's all been mutilated for me. My body is ugly. What we do in bed is ugly. I want it to stop.'"

Morgan held the syringe up to the light and flicked it with his finger, making sure there were no bubbles; it wouldn't do to accidentally burst Brandt's heart before he even got started. He wrapped the tourniquet around the other man's arm and pulled it tight, until a juicy vein rose up.

"You mutilated her spirit, Doc. You mutilated her soul. Since I don't think you've got a soul, I'll have to return the favor with the next best thing."

Brandt's eyes grew wide with terror and he began to thrash.

Morgan grabbed one of the guns and slammed the butt against the side of Brandt's skull.

The doctor fell to the side, still conscious but not struggling.

Morgan stuck the needle into Brandt's vein and sank the plunger.

"Just so you won't be too distracted during everything, Doc, I'm going to tell you the story of our life—Katie's and mine.

"Maybe if there's time, I'll tell it to you again. You're in the last part.

"For a little while, anyway."

Morgan lit the blowtorch, then fired up the bone saw.

He was empty now.

Katie had taken the best of him with her. He hoped it would still be waiting for him to reclaim it after he was done. She would be there, waiting for him, thanking him for avenging her death. She would give back to him all the good things that had made him human.

He would be with her soon.

He was saving the Teflon-coated hollow-point round to make sure they'd be together.

Body and soul.

Always.

"Body and soul, Doc. One's useless once the other's been ruined. Remember that. Can't be romance without body *and* soul."

He inserted the catheter tube—none too gently—and then slipped the barbed wire into that.

"You know," he said to Brandt. "I *almost* hope you live through this."

Not rushing things.

It would all come out fine in the end.

All it took was patience.

Always Something There to Remind Me

"Footfalls echo in the memory
    Down the passage which we did not take
        Towards the door we never opened..."
                —T.S. Eliot, "East Coker"

"The carpeting's the wrong color."

Cindy Harris looked away from the television and said, "What?"

Her husband, Randy, pointed to the television.

"The carpeting's supposed to be light blue. Look at it. It's *green*, fer chrissakes."

"So what's the big deal?"

Randy looked at her with that impatient, condescending expression that told Cindy he expected her to already know the answer. That expression was one of the few things about her husband that Cindy genuinely disliked. She could feel his defensiveness rising and wondered if he'd been forgetting to take his Zoloft lately.

"The big deal," he said, "is that I remember the way my folks argued about the color. *Dad* wanted green, but Mom insisted on light blue, and like every other time they had an argument, Mom won out."

Cindy watched him fiddle with the controls on the remote, then flip down the little door at the bottom of the set and start messing with the controls there.

Sighing, Cindy said, "Maybe something went wrong with the transfer. C'mon, Randy. Those home movies were pretty old, y'know? Maybe we waited too long to have them put on DVD. That old eight millimeter film stock, maybe it started to go bad and this was the best they could do. Most of them have turned out fine up until now."

Randy stopped fiddling with the controls, looked at the picture once more, and then turned toward her, his face losing color.

"What is it?" asked Cindy.

"I, uh…nothing. Nothing." He rose to his feet, walked across the room, and began heading up stairs. "I gotta make a call. Back in a minute."

"Hold on," said Cindy, grabbing hold of his elbow. "What's *wrong*, honey? This isn't worth getting upset about."

He tried smiling at her but didn't quite pull it off. "I just remembered something—I mean, I *think* I remembered something."

"Plan on letting me in on it?"

His face softened, but remained slightly pale. "Please let me make the call and then I promise I'll tell you all about it." Kissing her cheek, he gently pulled her hand from his elbow and went up to his office, closing the door behind him.

Putting her impatience on hold, Cindy went back to the sofa, sat down, and turned up the volume. Randy never talked much about his childhood—something that annoyed Cindy at times but which she respected, nonetheless—so maybe she could use this as a chance to get a glimpse of him as a child.

She watched for several minutes as Lawrence, Randy's father, finished setting up a plastic racing track in the middle of the room (with a running and very funny commentary), plugged in the power supply, and then put a small HO-scale car on the track and gave it a test run.

"Think he'll like it?" asked Lawrence.

"Oh, he'll just *flip*," said the voice of Virginia, Randy's mother, who was holding the camera. Lawrence grinned, obviously proud of himself for having assembled this without bloodshed, and then came the sound of a door opening. Virginia whipped around with the camera, the image blurring for a moment, and came to a stop on the face of a little boy who looked about nine years old. His face was flushed from the cold outside, and he was having trouble unwrapping the heavy wool scarf from around his neck.

"What's goin' on?" asked the little boy Randy had once been. "How come Daddy's home from work so early?"

He finished with the scarf, hung it on the hall tree by the door, and then pulled down his hood to reveal his face, his bangs a little too long and little too shaggy.

"Daddy's got an early Christmas present for you."

The little boy stared at the camera for a few moments, and then his face came alive with realization and a smile that could have been seen for miles in the dark. "The race car set came?" And with a speed and agility that is the special province of nine-year-old boys, rocketed past the camera and into the living room, where his shouts of delight filled the air.

"Turn it off," said Randy from behind her.

Cindy turned, smiling, and waved him away. "Oh, get over yourself. Why didn't you ever tell me you were into racing when you were a kid? God, Randy, you were *adorable*."

He said nothing as he reached down, pulled the remote from her hand, and turned off the DVD player. The screen turned a bright shade of blue when the picture vanished.

Cindy turned all the way around, kneeling on the sofa so she could better face him. "What did you do *that* for?"

"Something's wrong."

"I knew that already. Did you make your call?"

"Yes."

"Going to let me in on it now?"

Randy nodded, came around, and sat down beside her. Cindy readjusted her position and took hold of his hand.

Randy said, "Just listen to me for a minute, okay? Don't...don't say anything or ask any questions, just listen."

Feeling anxious—God, his face was so *pale*—Cindy nodded her agreement.

Randy hit the remote, returning to the race track scene, then hit the **Pause** button and pointed to the screen.

"I called Mom just to make sure," he said. "The carpeting was light blue, not green like this. But that's not...not why I called her.

"Cindy, look at me. How long have you known me? Ten years, right? We've been married for six years—and by the way, I've loved every minute of it, if I haven't told you lately. The thing is, have I ever struck you as someone who's absent-minded or forgetful?"

"No."

"Have you ever thought of me as being unstable in any way? The anti-depression medication aside, I mean."

"Of course not."

He stared at her with an intensity that made Cindy uncomfortable. *He hasn't been taking his meds,* she thought. *That has to be it.*

He started the DVD once again. "Look at the screen, Cindy. Tell me what you see."

"Randy, you're making me nervous."

"*Please?*"

"Okay, babe, okay." She faced the television. I see you and your dad playing with an electric racing car set on the floor of your folks' old living room."

"Look closer."

It wasn't until the little boy on the screen ran over to hug his mother—forcing her to set down the still-running camera—that Cindy realized what was wrong.

"What the—?"

"See it now, do you?" asked Randy.

She did. In the bottom right-hand corner of the screen: a small readout giving the time and the date.

3:42 p.m. 12/16/68.

"That's from a *video* camera," she said, looking at him. "Did they even have video cameras in 1968?"

"It doesn't matter," said Randy. "We never owned anything like that when I was a kid. In 1968, Dad was in the middle of a seven-month layoff from the plant. We had a very...inexpensive Christmas that year. It was nice, Mom had been saving money so we'd have a good dinner, but as far as presents went...I got a couple of Aurora monster model kits and some new shoes, that's it."

Cindy looked back at the scene on the television, then to her husband once again. "Okay, maybe I'm a little slow here today, baby, but are you telling me—"

"—that we didn't own a home movie camera, video cameras weren't available to the public, and what you're looking at"—he pointed to the happy scene unfolding in all its glory —"*never happened.* Yeah, I *wanted* an HO race set, but that was out of the question." He looked back at the screen, and when he spoke again, his voice quavered. "This never happened, Cindy. That's why I called Mom—I wanted to make sure I wasn't misremembering things. I wasn't. The carpeting was light blue, we never owned a home movie camera, and I never got a racing set."

He rubbed his eyes and shook his head. "The thing is, while I was growing up, I used to *pretend* that I *did* get one, y'know? I mean, you do that when you're a kid, you imagine things that didn't happen actually did."

Cindy nodded. "I did that all the time. I still do."

Randy smiled at her, touching her cheek. "When I used to play that scene out in my head, it looked just like *that.*" He nodded toward the television.

"Except the carpeting was the right color?" asked Cindy.

"Bingo."

For a minute they both sat watching silently as the scene played out, culminating in Randy beating the pants off his father in the Big Championship Race.

The scene quickly blacked out and a notice reading **End Of Tape** appeared in the middle of the screen.

Randy stopped the DVD player once again and began rummaging around on the coffee table.

"What're you looking for?" asked Cindy.

"The invoice, the list that came with the discs."

"I put on my desk. Hang on." She went into her office and retrieved the paperwork, and came back to find Randy on the floor with all of the discs spread out in front of him (still in their protective sleeves, thank God).

Holding up the papers, Cindy asked, "What are we looking for?"

Randy smiled at her. "You know, you probably don't notice how you always do that."

"Do what?"

"That 'we' business. Five minutes ago, this was *my* problem, then I tell you about it and suddenly it's *our* problem. Not 'me' but 'we'."

"Don't be silly, baby—*of course* it's our problem. What bothers you, bothers me."

He blew her a kiss, then pointed with his thumb at the television. "This is Disc #3. What's the list say is on it?"

Cindy found the invoice for #3 and read aloud: "Disc #3. Transfers of home movies, Reels 1—5, labeled 'Prom', 'Cindy's College Graduation', 'First Day on the Job', 'Mom and Dad's 40th Anniversary Party' and 'Our Wedding Rehearsal.'" She lowered the paper and stared at her husband. "They mislabeled, that's all."

"Did they?" Randy picked up the remote, pressed **Previous**, and a moment later the screen showed Cindy, ten years younger and damn near in tears, receive her college diploma. Then he hit the **Next** button not once but twice, and there was Cindy, laughing and waving at the camera as her mother videotaped her walking into the high school on her first day as the newest History teacher. Randy then hit **Previous** once, and there was his father, setting up the HO track in the middle of the living room that had the wrong color —

—both Cindy and Randy started —

—the living room that now had the *correct* light-blue color of carpeting.

Randy's hand began shaking. "Jesus Christ, honey, what the hell is going on?" He looked at her with an expression of confusion and helplessness that damn near broke her in half.

This time it was Cindy who turned off the disc, but she also ejected the damned thing and turned off the player. "I don't know, baby, but don't...don't let it get to you like this, okay? Whatever it is, we'll figure it out." Even to her own ears it sounded like a desperate, empty promise, something to say to Make It All Go Away For Right Now.

But Randy was having none of it. He pointed to the discs spread out in front of him. "There are eight discs here, Cindy, *eight*. We were charged for seven." He picked up the eighth disc; both the protective sleeve and label on the disc were blank.

"Randy, you need to calm down, baby, okay? I'll tell you what — let's get something to eat, let's go out for a bit, and then we'll come back and watch all of these from start to finish, okay? Maybe one of us will see something that'll help us figure out how...how..."

"...how an imagined memory of something that never happened could wind up on these things?"

She couldn't think of anything to say. Just blurting it out like that made it sound absurd.

"Okay," she said. "Screw it, then. C'mon, sit down next to me and let's watch it again. Come on." She sat on the sofa and patted the spot next to her. "Come on. Let's do this. You and me."

He sat beside her and took hold of her hand, and Cindy started the disc once more.

They watched Cindy receive her diploma, and then watched as she walked into her first day as a History teacher.

The race track film was gone.

Silently, anxiously, they started with the first disc and worked their way through all of the first seven. There was nothing on any of the discs that wasn't supposed to be.

Which left only the eighth, unmarked disc.

"Jesus," said Randy, looking at it as Cindy slipped it from its sleeve. "Did we imagine it?"

"Baby, I've *never* believed in 'shared hallucinations' or whatever it is they're called." She examined the last disc under the light as if she expected to find some kind of ancient sigil hidden in the reflection. Looking up at her husband, she tried to smile and almost made it. "I'm game if you are."

Randy silently nodded his head, looking for all the world like a prisoner who'd just been told the hour of his execution was fast approaching.

Cindy slipped the disc into the player and sat very close to her husband as she hit the **Play** button.

The first sequence was the missing race track film, which the two of them watched as if it were the most natural thing in the world, as if it were something from the past that Randy had shared with her many times over. At one point, they both even laughed at something Randy's father said as he was assembling the set.

Then came the film of Randy getting ready for his first Cub Scout meeting.

"I don't remember this," he said to her, gripping her hand tighter.

"But you *were* a Cub Scout, right?"

"...no..."

"Oh, God..."

And they watched. They watched as Randy graduated all the way to Eagle Scout; they watched as Randy was lifted onto the shoulders of his football teammates after he'd tackled the quarterback

Halfway Down The Stairs

of the opposing team, preventing the touchdown that would have lost Randy's team the state championship (he'd never participated in sports, much to his father's disappointment); they watched as Randy readied himself for his high school prom (to which he did not go because his father had died the previous week); they watched as Randy and his parents moved his belongings into his college dorm room (he'd done this alone); and they watched as Randy's parents embraced both he and Cindy at their wedding.

"Looks like it would have been a nice life," he whispered.

Cindy looked at him. "What's wrong with the one you have now?"

He turned toward her. "Nothing, honey, nothing at all. I love you, you know that, right?"

"Of course I do."

He looked back at the screen. "This is the past I *wish* I'd've had. Look at all this. It's all so...*interesting*. So happy and exciting."

"There's nothing wrong with the life you've had. It's been a good life—it's *still* a good life, baby."

He shook his head. "Look at me, Cindy. I'm a dull little man, and I know it, okay? I don't have any great sports stories to share with the guys I work with, I don't have any great adventures to impress people with, and I sure as hell aren't the most exciting man you could've picked for a husband.

"I used to resent the hell out of that, you know? I hated Dad for dying like he did and leaving me to take care of Mom and the house. I started college three years late because I had to get a job at the plant to help pay for everything. *God*, I resented it! I resented not having *that* life, the one on the screen. I used to imagine...when I was really angry, I mean really, *really* angry, I used to imagine that—"

His words cut off when he looked back at the screen.

It was a film of a woman giving birth to a child that was obviously dead. The woman insisted on holding the body, and as the camera came in for a close-up, Cindy saw that it was Randy's mother.

A moment of blackness, and then came the image of a teenaged Randy, looking a decade older than his years, stabbing his parents in their sleep, their blood spattering the walls with every plunge of the knife.

Another moment of blackness, and there was Randy, in his twenties but looking much older, tying a naked and severely-beaten woman to a wooden chair. The woman whimpered and screamed and begged him to stop, but Randy ignored her pleas as he turned away and began selecting tools from a table.

A final moment of blackness, and there was Randy, as he was now, sitting beside Cindy, as she was, the two of them staring at a screen that showed them sitting on a sofa facing a television screen that showed the two of them facing a television screen that showed the two of them facing a television screen...

Randy sat forward and buried his head in his hands. "God, Cindy, the...*thoughts* I had when I was that angry. That's why I started seeing a psychiatrist—remember that I had to cancel our third date because I'd forgotten about the appointment?"

"I thought you were just trying to let me down easy," she said. She only now realized that she'd moved away from him, that the last series of images had turned her stomach. How could *this* Randy, this man she loved, ever harbor thoughts so repulsive and violent?

Good God, did she know him at all?

He looked up and saw the expression on her face, saw that she'd moved away from him, and his face went blank. "Just so you know, the girl in the chair was Tammy Wilson, who was the only girlfriend I had during college. She cheated on me with at least three different guys, all of them jocks." He looked at the screen once more. "I won't lie to you, Cindy. Thinking about doing that to her...it helped. I'm not proud of those thoughts but I can't very well deny having them, especially now, can I?

"And sometimes, honey, when you really disappoint me...I think about doing the same things to you. And it makes me happy. It makes me *feel good*...."

She pulled the remote from his hand and turned off the disc, which she then ejected, pulled from the player, and snapped in two.

"There," she said to the empty sofa, and then felt herself starting to cry. She quickly got hold of herself, sat down, pulled in a deep breath, and fingered the jagged scar that ran from her left temple to the side of her mouth, a souvenir from her own father—one of many that she carried all over her body.

Goddammit! She'd almost made it work this time, almost had the perfect husband, the perfect marriage, but Daddy's influence always had a way of creeping back, one way or another.

She rubbed at the burn scars around her wrists, scars now faded with age but still pink enough to remind her of the ropes, of the chair, of Daddy's tool kit.

She looked at the stack of DVDs with the transferred home movies of families she'd never met and would never know, and decided that she'd start looking for new memories tomorrow. She was always alone in the lab—that was the best place for someone who looked like her, anyway. History teachers with disfigured faces weren't exactly in demand these days, and never had been.

There were always dozens, hundreds of home movies people wanted transferred to DVD. So she'd say goodbye to Randy and hope that, tomorrow, she could find some new memories that she could hold on to, ones that Daddy couldn't sneak in and ruin.

She turned off the television set and for a few moments just knelt there, staring at the slightly distorted reflection of her face.

"I'll miss you, Randy," she whispered. "You were the best one yet."

She placed her hand against the screen, imagining that the reflected hand was not hers, but that of a gentle and compassionate man who was reaching out through the glass to take hold of hers and whisper that she was beautiful, the most beautiful woman in the world, and, oh, how he would love her forever....

Return to Mariabronn

There you are. I see you at night.

* * *

Lorena notices right away that Rudy is out of sorts. He always took a stool right smack in the middle of the counter—"I like being close to the action," he'd say. "And if there's no action, I like looking at you and *imagining* some action." Why she hasn't slapped his face after all this time, she can't say. Maybe it's because he always blushes like a little boy who's just told his first dirty joke whenever he tries one of his bad lines on her. There's something sweet about his attempts at crude trucker humor, and that always makes her smile.

But tonight Rudy sits at the far end of the counter, near the bathrooms, the worst seat in the diner. He's been tight-lipped, shaky, and anxious. This is not the same man she's been serving and flirting with for the past couple of years, and she's not sure if it's a good idea to ask him about anything *too* personal. Still, he looks like he's about to crack apart. Lorena finishes refilling everyone's coffee and drifts down to Rudy.

"I gotta tell you, Rude"—the nickname usually gets a grin out of him, but not tonight—"I didn't expect to see you with the weather and the roads the way they been. You musta drove like a bat out of hell."

Rudy attempts a smile, doesn't quite make it, and silently pushes his coffee cup toward her. Lorena fills it again. When Rudy reaches for it, she puts her free hand on top of his and squeezes. "What's up with you tonight, Rude? Usually by this time you've propositioned me at least three times. You never know—tonight I might say 'Yes.'"

Rudy looks at her, at the other customers in the diner and then speaks; his voice is a fragile, sad, frightened thing: "I think I might've done something terrible tonight, Lorena. I didn't *mean* to, but ..." He looks at her with eyes so full of mute pleading that Lorena feels her throat tighten. She can't remember if she's ever seen a man so lonely.

"What is it, Rudy? You can tell me."

"I don't know," he whispers. "I—I kinda really like you—why do you think this is always the first place I stop when I leave on a run and the last place I stop on the way back?"

Lorena feels herself blush a little. "I figured you was just the shy type."

"Your opinion of me means a lot, and I... I don't want that ruined."

Lorena puts the coffee pot back on the burner and tells the cook and the other waitress that she's taking her fifteen-minute break. She picks up Rudy's coffee cup and half-eaten sandwich and gestures for him to follow her over to one of the far empty booths.

Once they're situated and sitting across from one another, Lorena sits back, folds her arms across her chest, and says, "Okay, Rudy, here it is: I like you, too, and I think a lot of you, think you're an okay guy. I done things that I ain't really proud of, either, so I try not to judge anybody. So, c'mon—out with it."

Rudy doesn't look at her as he begins talking. Even when describing the worst of it, he never makes eye contact. Lorena has to lean forward and turn her good ear in his direction in order to make out the words. It's hard for her to pay attention to his story at one point because she's stunned by the tears that are forming in his eyes. But she listens, and feels sick.

Rudy finishes his story, sips at his now-cold coffee, and finally looks at her. Something in him touches her, and she moves over to sit beside him, using a paper napkin to wipe his face.

"Rudy, you gotta listen to me, hon, okay? If it hadn't been you, it woulda been somebody else. Sounds to me like they was pretty determined."

"But, *Christ*, Lorena, I- I ...." He takes hold of her hand. "Am I a bad man?"

"No, you're not. A bad man wouldn't be feeling the way you are." She then cups his face in both of her hands. "You listen to this, Rudy, and you listen good.

"*Yes* ...."

* * *

"Dude, I'm serious—you *gotta* hear what I got on my digital voice recorder last night."

"Oh, for the love of—look, I'm begging you, find a woman, download porn, start collecting Precious Moments figurines—*something else*, all right? This goddamn ghost-chasing of yours is wearing really thin. You're out there alone in the middle of the night and—hell, I worry about you, okay?"

"Please? Just listen, and I swear if you think it's bullshit, if you still think it's a waste of my time and money, I'll drop it, okay?"

"Fine. Let's hear it."

Click. Hiss. *Where have you been? I've missed you.* Hiss. Hiss. (Very softly, sounds of distant traffic nearly obscuring the words) *Dance with me?* Click.

"Well?"

"...Jesus."

* * *

The O'Henry Ballroom is crowded that night, the orchestra in rare form as they play "You Came Along" and "Love in Bloom" and "(I Can't Imagine) Me Without You" (one of her favorite new songs), but her escort for the evening has had far too much to drink and is getting somewhat fresh. She reaches behind her and grabs his left hand, pulling it up to the small of her back where it's supposed to be, and hopes that he understands. He doesn't, and soon his hands are slipping again, touching her in the most inappropriate of ways, and at last she breaks away and slaps his face.

"*Please* stop doing that!"

He glares at her, rubbing his check. Around them several couples have stopped dancing and are staring at them.

"I'm afraid I don't know what you mean," he says.

She looks around at the staring faces and feels herself turning red. She realizes then that she should have stayed home and listened to *The Shadow* with her parents. That new actor, Orson Welles, oh, his voice! Instead, she was here, being made a spectacle of because her escort was a drunkard and a masher.

"I wish for you to take me home now, if you please."

He steps toward her, gripping her shoulders. When he speaks, his words are thick and slurred. "I am not going to take you anywhere ... 'cept back to our table. Let's have another drink an' settle down."

She tries to free herself of his grip but he's quite strong. Finally, she stomps on his right foot. He cries out, releases her, and stumbles backward.

"You will take me home *now!*"

"I will most certainly not. If you wish to go, then *go!* Have a nice walk." With that, he turns away and stumbles through the dancers until he disappears somewhere in the throng of swaying bodies. Fighting back tears of humiliation and anger, she twirls around and walks off the dance floor toward the doors. Her face is puffy, red, and tear-streaked. Maybe the cold air will help.

She pushes open the doors and glides out into the harsh winter night. Less than a mile. She has strong legs, a dancer's legs, and knows that she can make it. Yes, she'll be freezing by the time she comes through the front door, but her mother and father will be there. Warm cocoa, perhaps some soup. Father's heavy coat and a place by the fire. Soft music on the radio. Is *Gershwin Presents* on tonight? (She hopes so).

Crossing her arms across her midsection, she takes an icy breath and moves out toward the road, her white dress blending into the swirling snow.

* * *

The State Police find the car in the spring, after the first thaw. It's on its roof far off to the side of Archer Avenue, not far from Resurrection Cemetery, at the bottom of the incline where the winter snow always piles high to hide the carcasses of animals that crawl into the foliage to die, the litter tossed by teenagers as they drive too fast around the bend, and even—sometimes—the bodies of vagrants who curl up with newspaper blankets in the shadows thinking they'll be on their way in the morning, after they've rested.

The entire driver's side of the car is smashed in, the door and part of the front missing.

"Looks like the damn thing got hit with a wrecking ball," remarks one of the officers.

His partner shakes his head. "Never had a chance. At least the license plate is still attached."

The officers call in it in. They are instructed to make a search of the immediate area which turns up nothing.

* * *

The old man wakes at four in the morning and lies there staring at the ceiling. He hates the way the patterns in the plaster form an endless overlapping series of swirls. They look too much like snow caught in the merciless winter winds coming at a windshield late at night, an endless assault of white that not even the windshield wipers can fight against. White … so much white.

He sits up, swings his legs over the side of the bed, and presses his feet against the cold floor. Looking over his shoulder, he stares at the half of the bed where his wife used to sleep. Dear Henrietta, now six years in the grave. She would know what to say, how to rub his shoulders *just so*, relaxing him, whispering *It's all right, honey, it's all in the past, you know it was an accident* … But she's gone, and the children are grown with kids of their own. Sure, they call and visit often, he has pinochle with the guys at the Eagles on Thursdays, but he's going to be eighty-nine next birthday—a "spry" eighty-nine, as his children and grandchildren always remind him—but on nights like this, nights that have become more and more frequent the past few months, he wakes at some god-awful hour and is all too aware of his aches, his pains, the little snaps and crackles made by his bones when he moves, the silence of the house and the world outside … and he wishes that silence would extend to his conscience. Shouldn't he have started becoming absent-minded by now? An old fart who can't remember if the underwear goes on before the pants. Too bad an old man can't choose *what* to forget.

He shuffles over to the window, pulling back the curtain. It's beginning to snow; not much at the moment, just a few light flurries, but if the Weather Channel is right, this part of the Midwest is going to be under a good nine inches in the next forty-eight hours. He wonders if the snow will be as heavy and merciless as it was on that night. He looks back to the empty place in the bed. "I can't live with it anymore, my dear girl. I have to go back." For a moment he imagines Henrietta sitting there, the covers pulled up around her shoulders—she always did chill easily in winter—smiling at him, a smile tinged with sadness at the edges, and finally he imagines her wonderful voice as she says: *You do what you need to, honey. You deserve some peace.* "Thank you," he whispers to the emptiness. He looks out the window again. "I left a big part of me on Archer Avenue back in '37. I remember Bing Crosby was singing 'Black Moonlight' when I started to go around that bend. I remember all the snow—God, there was so much snow against the windshield. The wipers couldn't keep up.

"I should've slowed down, or pulled off to the side and waited for it to clear up. Lord, I was driving Mom and Dad's Imperial! Chrysler used to make their cars like tanks back then. I could have waited it out. I was just a kid, you know? I shouldn't've ..." His voice fades away as he hears another voice—not that of his wife—whisper from the memory of a dream: *There you are. I see you at night.*

He wanders over to the bookshelf and takes from it an old edition of Hesse's *Narcissus and Goldmund*, one of his favorite novels. He sits on the edge of the bed on Henrietta's side and leafs through the pages, stopping to read a favorite paragraph here, a memorable dialogue exchange there, all the while shaking his head. He looks at his late wife's pillow. "I don't know why, my dear girl, but I just suddenly thought of the two of them—Narcissus and Goldmund, how they became friends and the different paths their lives took, Narcissus remaining at the monastery of Mariabronn to become its Abbot John, while Goldmund set off to live the life of an adventurer and artist.

"I was always moved by the final chapters—I don't know if I ever told you this, so pardon me if I'm repeating myself—but there you have Goldmund, who's squandered and prostituted his artistic talents, led a life of self-indulgence and debauchery, only to wind up waiting to be hanged as a thief. And like the *deus ex machina* I suspect it was intended to be, along comes Narcissus to help him escape and bring him back to Mariabronn where Goldmund, sick and dying, is forgiven by Narcissus. Knowing his time is short, Goldmund sets about creating his last genuine work of art, a Madonna fashioned after the image of Lydia, his one true love, whose heart and spirit he had broken. He finds forgiveness in his heart for himself, my dear girl, because he uses all of his love and regret and guilt to perfectly fashion the Madonna's image. And when Goldmund at last sees Lydia's face again, he knows that he is forgiven, and so can die at peace with himself." He closes the book with a loud snap. "That's probably about as close to sentimentality as Hesse ever came.

"It seems to me now, my dear girl, that unlike fiction, one has to fashion one's own *deus ex machina* if forgiveness is to be found."

He rises from the bed, his hand pushing against Henrietta's pillow, then replaces the book on the shelf and begins preparations for his trip.

* * *

"I got more than just that on here. I talked to a guy who's seen her."

"Let's hear that, too, then."

Click. Hiss. The sound of muffled voices and the *ting!* of silverware. A louder voice calls "Order up!" A waitress yells, "Hold your horses! I only got two legs, you know!" Hiss. The sound of a man clearing his throat. Then: "Is that thing on?"

"It sure is."

"Huh. Don't look like no tape recorder I ever seen."

"It doesn't use tape—it's a digital recorder."

"You don't say? Well, I'll be. Makes you wonder what they'll come up with next."

"So ... you said that you met her one night?"

"Oh, I sure did! Told the story many times. Was even on TV once."

"Would you mind telling it again now?"

"Not at all. Nice of you to not think I'm some kinda kook."

"I believe the stories. So, please ..."

* * *

As the winch pulls taught and the tow truck begins moving the demolished car up the incline, the State Police detective looks at the man standing next to him and says: "Mind if I ask you another question?"

The other man shakes his head and wipes something from one of his eyes. "I don't know what else I can tell you but, okay."

"Do you have any idea what he was doing all the way out here? I mean, a man his age had to've known that driving from Ohio to here in the middle of winter was risky. I just can't help but think he was really determined to do something or see someone. Do you have *any* ideas?"

The other man shakes his head once again. "I swear to you, I don't have the slightest clue."

Something in the man's voice makes it clear to the detective that he's lying. The detective begins to speak, thinks better of it, and stands in silence. No reason to push the poor guy. The detective thinks, *Does anything good ever last in this pitiful world?* Then decides he'd rather not know the answer.

* * *

She's made it as far as the bend in Archer Avenue when she hears the sound of a car, but the wind makes it impossible to tell from which direction the vehicle is approaching. She decides it doesn't matter. She can barely feel her feet or hands. Even if the car is going in the opposite direction, no one with a soul and an ounce of compassion would leave her out in the cold, not on this night.

She moves toward the middle of the road and begins looking both in front of and behind her, then begins waving her arms. Soon, she sees the glow of headlights coming around the bend straight toward her. Oh, how wonderful! They *are* going in her direction. She opens her mouth to shout at the driver and steps to the side, away from the oncoming vehicle, but a sudden gust of wind causes her to lose her balance and her white shoes slip on a patch of black ice and she gasps, spins, and stumbles into the path of the car.

* * *

"Sis? It's Joseph. Listen, I'm over at Dad's house and—what?"

"I said, do you know what time it is?"

"Yes, and I'm sorry, but I've been trying to call Dad for the last three days and haven't gotten an answer."

"Oh, God. Is he all right?"

"He's not even *here*! The car's gone. He left an envelope for us with a bunch of stuff in it—a copy of his will, his bank book, his stock certificates, the deed to the house—he made it out to you—and ... and there's a letter."

"What's it say?"

"No, not over the phone. Can you come over? I called the police and I have to wait here."

"I'll be there in an hour. Are you okay?"

"*Hell*, no. But thanks for asking."

"Where do you suppose he could've gone?"

"When you get here. I'll tell you everything when you get here."

* * *

The driver of the semi doesn't see the parked car until he's right on top of it, and by then there's no time to hit the brakes or swerve, not on this road and not with all the black ice. The front of his truck slams into the car and pushes it along the road for several yards, sparks flying, shattered glass spitting up against his windshield, before finally smashing into a snowman in the middle of the road, splattering it all over before the car at last dislodges and rolls down the incline by the side of the road.

The driver beats his steering wheel and screams a torrent of profanities, but does not stop. The snow and wind are coming in almost full-force now, and if he's late with this delivery, it's his ass.

Stupid asshole should've known better than to park there in this weather, anyway, he thinks. *What kind of nutcase leaves their car and goes to build a fucking snowman in the middle of the road?*

A few miles later, the driver notices the blood in a few of the larger, icy clumps of snow that have lodged up against the center of the windshield, in that no man's land the wipers can never quite reach.

Oh, God, please ... please, no.

He eases off to the side of the road and parks the semi, then grabs a flashlight from under the seat, opens the door, stands on the running board, and shines the light onto the hood.

Blood and hair. There is blood and hair in the clumps of ice and snow. He shakes his head. No, it was just a snowman, that's all. Snowmen don't bleed. It must've been a bird. Yeah, that's it. He must have hit a bird and not noticed.

Birds don't have hair, whispers something in the back of his conscience, where the light doesn't quite reach.

"No," Rudy says out loud. "No. It was a bird. Snowmen don't bleed." And that helps. Not a lot, but some. So he drives on, his hands shaking, knowing that it couldn't have been a bird but telling himself it was, anyway, over and over, knowing full well that this is going to haunt him for the rest of his life.

* * *

" —well, she was a sweet thing, no denying that. Long blonde hair and the prettiest face. She kind of reminded me of my youngest daughter. Anyway, she was at the Willowbrook—used to the O'Henry years ago, until the new owners bought it and decided things needed to be, you know, updated and such.

"She come over and asked me for a dance and I figured, why not, she was awful courteous—not like the girls these days—and we had ourselves a nice little dance. Oh, you should've seen how she was dressed! Long white dress, real fancy-like, and shoes to match. I know this sounds corny as hell, but she looked like some of them paintings you see of angels.

"Thing was ... she was awful *cold,* even though it was only autumn. The small of her back, her hands, her cheeks. Real cold. My wife, she's kind of cold-blooded—not in *that* way, she's a sweetheart, but brother, sometimes her touch is like ice—she says it's 'cause of her circulation problems ... shit, where was I? Oh, yeah.

"This gal was *real* cold, so I offer her my jacket. She thanks me for being such a gentleman, and I drape my jacket over her shoulders. She asks me if I could give her a ride home and I say sure thing. We're driving along a little ways and she asks me to go down Archer Avenue. I oblige her request and we're driving along and talking about the weather, the way the Willowbrook has changed over the years, stuff like that, and then we come up on Resurrection Cemetery and she asks me to stop. I think it's a bit odd but I stop anyway.

"She gives me back my coat and thanks me for being a gentleman, then she gets out and starts walking toward the cemetery gates. Here it is, ten-thirty at night, and she's headin' into the boneyard. I call to her that the cemetery's closed and that she really ought to get back in the car so I can take her home. That's when she turns and looks at me and smiles and says, 'I am home.' Then she just ... faded away into nothing.

"That's when I knew who she was, and believe you me, I damn near wet myself. I mean, you hear all the stories about her, but you never expect that *you'll* ... you know what I mean. Ain't a day goes by that I don't think of her. Makes a body wanna cry, it does, thinking about the way she died, out there all alone on that road, middle of winter. Son-of-a-bitch what hit her didn't even stop. I hope to hell whoever it was, if they're still alive, I hope to hell they ain't had a moment's peace.

"She was a damned sweet girl, and she deserved better than that, you know?"

* * *

The old man impresses himself; he's only had to stop twice along the ten-plus hour drive to make water. The last time, he went outside, writing his name in the snow like he used to do when he was a child. He even laughed while doing so, the first real laugh he's had in at least twenty years.

But he's made it, despite the damn snow and wind. Three times he's almost been knocked off the road by the wind. The radio said there were "blizzard-like conditions" coming, but that hasn't stopped him.

And now he's finally back here, after all the years, after all the bad dreams, after a lifetime. Archer Avenue. But this time, *this* time he drives slowly. This time he'll see her before it's too late. This time he'll stop. This time he'll make it right and hope that will be enough.

He turns the radio to a local "beautiful music" station. Truth in advertising, for once. It's "Big Band" night tonight. Glenn Miller. Stan Kenton. Spike Jones and His City Slickers. This music suits the old man

just fine and dandy, yessir. Just as long as they don't play any Bing Crosby, especially "Black Moonlight."

He slowly rounds the bend and hits the straight stretch dense with trees on either side, some of them obscuring the steep incline off to the side of the road. He knows that if he's not careful, he will drive off and fall a good seven feet where no other passing cars can see him. He has to be careful now. Like he should have been back in '37.

A flicker in the headlights as several swirls of snow dance up onto the hood and skitter across until they explode against the windshield. But this time he's got the defrost on high; this time he's got the expensive wipers that are going a mile a minute; this time, he's careful. He drives up and down the road for one hour, two hours, and only notices the gas gauge nearing E halfway through the third hour.

"Where are you?" he asks the snow and darkness. He wasn't expecting an answer, but, still, he's heard the stories about this road, about the other people who have seen her, talked with her, given her a ride home.

"Where are you?" he asks again, this time much louder than before. He pulls over to the side of the road, taking care to stay as far away from the incline as possible. Too much of the car is still jutting out into the passing lane, but he doesn't care. He presses his forehead against his hands, takes a deep breath, and then turns off the engine.

For a little while he sits there, staring out into the freezing night as the snow whips about the car. He's so tired, so very tired. He imagines that he sees two medieval men on horseback in the distance, making their way back to the monastery where the creation of a final masterpiece patiently waits for one of them.

He opens the car door, climbs out, and begins walking up the road toward Resurrection Cemetery. His knees ache and his legs are weak, but at least he's wearing his good winter coat, his good winter gloves, and the heavenly wool cap Henrietta had given him on the last Christmas she was alive.

He's only a few hundred yards from the cemetery gates when he can't walk any farther. He stops, kneels down, and makes a snowball. The snow is thick and heavy enough to pack well, and with a laugh he sets about making a snowwoman, forgetting that he's now in the middle of the road. It takes him nearly forty minutes to fashion her, and by the time he's finished his hands are nearly frozen, even with the gloves. There is no time for her face, but that's fine because he remembers that face with startling clarity. He's never forgotten even a single detail.

He steps back and smiles at her, then holds out his arms.

"May I have this dance?" he asks his creation.

And there he stands, arms extended, eyes blinking against the wind and snow, until at last he hears the roar and the collision and the metallic scrape and the shattering of glass. He moves closer to her, touching her cold skin—didn't everyone always say that her touch was cold? Poor girl. Poor little thing.

He stands there, smiling, as the lights and roar and sparks screaming down on them form a marvelous winter aura around her. He closes his eyes. *There you are,* he thinks. He does not tremble. *I see you at night.* He holds his breath. He holds his breath. He holds his breath. He holds

Cyrano

"I am going to seek a great Perhaps"
— Rabelais on his deathbed

...now that virtue has become to me a shadow, and happiness and affection are turned into bitter loathing and despair, in what should I seek sympathy? asked the knife-edge of his conscience as he lay alone fighting wakefulness. Slumber, even brief and uneasy, granted him stay from the innate afflictions of his wretched heart, and for that he was thankful; though toward what or whom this gratitude was or should be directed he dared not imagine.

The sea-roar gave way to the memory of the words he had screamed at R. Walton before springing from the cabin window of the ship and landing upon the ice-raft which was borne away on hyperborean waves. Time thereafter was measured by the anguish which, meeting no resistance, continued to poison the vestiges of the "soul" he was still foolish enough to believe within his attain.

I was, then, a monster, a blot upon the Earth, from which all men fled and whom all men disowned.

His unmerciful nightmare continued with the Siberian village of hovels where, despite the villagers' screams and the stones with which they bruised him, he assembled the materials for the funeral pyre he later constructed on a larger, thicker ice-raft, one that could endure the heat of conflagration without collapsing into the sea.

The flames crackled and hissed, consuming his filthy rags and blackening his charnel-house skin, the stench filling him with the writhing pain of a Death beyond the death he sadly called existence.

Oh, earth, how often did I imprecate curses on the cause of my being! Even Satan had his companions, fellow devils to admire and encourage him, but I am solitary and abhorred.

His flame-charred flesh slithered from bone, drooping like the sleeves of a dark cloak, when suddenly he beheld near him a hunched and shivering figure wearing only a dressing-gown, slippers, and nightcap. He pointed at the figure and perceived with a start that he was, indeed, wearing a great black cloak whose hood concealed his hideous countenance. No cursed flesh covered his skeletal hand.

The cowering figure raised its head and cried, "Ghost of the Future! I fear you more than any specter I have seen. But as I know your purpose..."

He cringed.

The dressing-gowned man uttering those words was Victor Frankenstein.

The creature gave a loud gasp and lurched forward, wrenching himself from sleep, momentarily disoriented until he caught a glimpse of the life preserver marked *SS Catapaxi* hanging on a nearby pillar.

A book tumbled from his lap and onto the ship's deck, falling open to the title page: *The Reclamation of My Honor: a journal by Ebenezer Scrooge.*

"A splendid work," said a voice behind him. "It is one of my wife's favorites."

The creature turned in the deck chair to see the ship's captain standing beside him. "I apologize, sir, but my dream was of a rather unsettling nature and I fear I have awakened less than rested, so forgive me if I seem ill-at-ease with your unexpected presence."

To his great surprise, the captain — a tall, healthy-looking muscular man — did not turn away in revulsion. "I am Roderick Usher, captain of this vessel. It pleases me to tell you that, despite the rough weather encountered two days ago, we will arrive in Italy on schedule." He lowered his voice, as if taking the creature into his confidence. "I must confess this is a great relief to me. Many of our guests are ambassadors and other assorted government officials, and must be in Padua in time for the world conference."

"A world conference? Toward what purpose?"

Captain Usher smiled, displaying a mouthful of dazzlingly bright teeth. "My good sir, have you not heard? The conference is to commemorate the signing of the Russo-Japanese Pact five days hence by Nicholas II and Emperor Meiji. Such a covenant not only ensures peace between their warring nations, but crushes the budding revolution in

Russia as well. I understand the pact has prompted several like agreements among smaller allying countries."

"Ah," said the creature. "I seem to recall an article of news which concerned a similar pact between Reza Shah Pahlavi of Persia and President John Brown of Mexico."

"Indeed," said Usher. "Even now, Brown's esteemed Vice-President, Miguel Hidalgo y Costilla, journeys to Italy on this very ship. But enough talk of politics." Usher's face grew pensive. "Since you were afflicted with fever when brought aboard, I found it necessary to isolate you from the other passengers. The medical officer informs me that your crisis is now past. I wish you to know that, having been made aware of your tragic circumstances, I will do everything in my power to ensure that you arrive safely to your beloved."

"My beloved," whispered the creature, placing one of his gigantic hands against his breast and feeling the bulk of the letters within his pocket, letters he had read countless times before this day and would read countless times again before reaching his destination.

"Have you the time, Captain, to indulge me with some answers?"

"If they are mine to offer."

"There are certain...inconsistencies in my memory of the last several months, caused by the post-surgical fever of which you spoke. The man who purchased my passage, did he offer a name?"

"Yes. And what a splendid, amiable fellow he was, of a decidedly distinguished background. Dr. Jonathan Merrick of the Treeves Institute in Dublin."

"I never knew his name," whispered the creature, "only his charity, and the goodness of his soul."

"He seemed to hold you in great esteem. When I pressed him for details, he informed me that he had been giving a series of lectures at the University of Krasnoyarsk when a commercial fishing vessel beheld a fire on a nearby ice-isle and discovered you among the wreckage. As he is considered a maverick in the field of treatment for burn victims, and was only a few days' journey away, he was sent for at once."

The creature looked at his hands, still overcome by their power and beauty. How truly miraculous were the skills of Merrick!

Why could you have not been my creator? he thought.

A flash of memory, then: Merrick's sad expression as he said, *"The damage was restricted to your torso and legs. As much as I wanted to give you the new face you so desperately wished for, it was unravaged by the flames. I had no choice but to leave it as it was. Please understand that it was only through the grace of Providence that we were able to obtain enough tissue to restore those areas destroyed by fire. To have constructed a new face for you under such circumstances would have been perceived as a vain cosmetic indulgence and thus trivialized everything I as a physician believe in. I hope someday you will find it in your heart to forgive me."*

From the lower deck a sultry female voice chimed into the air, announcing that breakfast was now being served.

"Such a sweet voice," said the creature. "One cannot help but wonder if—"

"The sweetness of her voice withers against the truth of her delicate beauty," said the captain. "That is my wife, Madeline. Both she and my sister Camille work the ship alongside the crew. You must dine with us this evening. I insist."

The creature rose from the deck chair and approached the safety rail, his massive body, well over eight feet in height, dwarfing the formidable figure of Captain Usher. Leaning forward to allow a burst of sea spray to bathe his face, he said, "Thank you for your proposed kindness, but I have never been afforded the luxury of knives, forks, spoons and plates, so my manners would be...questionable at the very least, and undoubtedly offensive to your wife and sister."

Joining him at the rail, Usher placed his hand on the creature's immense forearm and said, "It seems to me that unrefined table manners are not what keeps you a solitary soul. I would not be so insistent, but the well-being and contentment of all my passengers is of the utmost importance to me. I suspect that your hesitancy to imbibe of the joy with marks this voyage is a symptom of deeper distress."

"Though your suspicion is correct—and a testament to your perceptiveness and leadership—I can only respond by again thanking you for the invitation which I cannot accept."

Usher, whose outward composure failed to mask his feelings of insult, said, "You disdain the companionship?"

"On the contrary. Nothing would please me more than to sit at a clean table with fresh linen and partake of an agreeable meal in the company of friends. For so long, I have fantasized of such an occasion — the aroma of the food, the bouquet of the wine, the pleasant murmur of surrounding voices engaged in conversation, the ghostly wisps of pipe and cigar smoke filling the air afterward."

"The pleasantries of such an evening await. Why do you deny them to yourself?"

"Because that is only part of the fantasy I have constructed from the fragments of my hope. Shall I tell you the rest?"

Usher, whose expression compassionated the creature, gave a silent nod of his head.

"Very well. The scene goes like this: I put down my emptied brandy snifter and turn to the woman seated next to me. How to describe her beauty to you? It is not so much a physical loveliness, though she us undeniably pleasing to the eye, as a bloom that bespeaks the humble-mindedness at the core of her nature. She possesses time's gift of perfect humility, and it is that gift which makes her so alluring. I ask her to join me for a dance and she rises gracefully, not at all repulsed by my countenance. I fill myself with the fragrance of her perfume and, as her eyes meet mine, I feel as if I am Da Vinci, staring through the face of one of his exquisite madonnas, staring past the layers of marble and dust into the burning heart of some godly truth I have always been seeking. My senses heighten with the satin touch of her hand in mine. I revel in the sparkle of her laughter as it mingles with my own to become a singing our hearts cannot contain. I pull her closer to me, and she does not resist, for I know this time, this breath, this moment is filled with the heat of a thousand secret flames. Then, at the last, after the euphoria of her gentle velvet lips brushing moistly against my cheek and whispers, in a voice so delicate that crystal cannot compare, 'Now you can come home from your ghost so that I may cherish for the rest of our days.'

"Do I disdain companionship? you ask. No, good captain, not at all. This scene of ridiculous fantasy has been my only sanctuary from the loathsome truth of my being for so long that I cannot afford to have it tainted by the brutal truth of reality. Do you not understand? Look at me, Roderick Usher, and tell me truthfully that you do not believe your Madeline and Camille would be overcome with horror at the sight of me! The grave-pallor of my face, the dull pustule-yellow of my eyes. Could any woman not born of fantasy look upon such an obscenity as me and feel tenderness?" He reached into his breast pocket and snatched out the letters, thrusting them toward the captain's face.

"Upon waking in your infirmary I discovered these in my pocket. Written by the hand of a young woman of such refiner and exquisiteness my heart bursts at the thought of her *beaux yeux*, they tell the tale of her painful solitude which was relieved by the first of many missives delivered to her from the northern extremities of the Earth. This tender courtship through words has continued over these past three years, filling her heart with such hope and love I found myself weeping at the yearning which guided her hand as she scrawled her fragile dreams upon the page. She claims to love with a depth and passion usually attributed to poets and gods — and I know it is me she loves, for her narrative betrays she has been made aware of the circumstances under which my grisly and wretched birth was induced."

"I don't understand," said Usher, his eyes glistening with sympathy. "If she knows of your history and claims to love you in spite of it, why are your feelings in such chaos?"

"Because *I did not write to her!* The missives she speaks of were composed by another."

The captain blinked, then turned away for a moment, his demeanor growing deeply thoughtful. Momentarily, he turned to face the creature. "My dear, dear fellow, I think the answer to this conundrum is within your grasp. Dr. Merrick gave a letter to the ship's chaplain, with instructions it be delivered to you upon your recovery. You will find the chaplain's office on this very deck. I will take you."

The creature affectionately grasped the captain's hand, taking care not to employ too much pressure lest he injure this man who had been so kind. "Good Captain Usher, I thank you for your compassion, but if I am to be given the solution to this enigma, I prefer to be alone. So many of my days have been spent thus."

"I know, and my heart breaks for it. Even my dear Madeline has wept at the thought of the misery which has for so long been your only companion."

"Farewell, then, Roderick Usher. It pleases me to call you my friend."

"And your friend I shall remain. But I will not accept a 'farewell' from you, for you will dine with myself and my family this evening. The rancor and malice you have encountered in the world does not exist in this heart, nor in those of my wife and sister. None shall cringe at the sight of you, nor scream and turn away. On this you have my most solemn word."

"Until this evening, then," said the creature.

"Which cannot arrive soon enough for my satisfaction," replied the captain who, with a respectful, affectionate salute, continued on his rounds.

Making his way toward the chaplain's office, the creature chanced to encounter a little boy who was playing at shuffleboard. It did the creature's heart well to see this child, who though alone except for his imagination, was nonetheless enjoying himself. Perhaps, to some, aloneness was not a curse and the knowledge achieved from imagination hung around their necks like pearls instead of chains. The creature was almost envious.

Without warning, the boy suddenly stopped playing and spun around, glaring.

Never before had the creature experienced such an overwhelming dislike. Had he been pressed to describe the boy, he would have been struck dumb, but there was, nonetheless, something wrong with the child's appearance, something displeasing and downright detestable. He could not say why he so disliked this seemingly innocent child, only that for the first time in years, the urge to kill came over him. But such impulses had been his damnation once before and he would not, could not, succumb to their seductions again.

"Methinks I know you, horrid beast," said the child with a sneer creeping onto his face. "Indeed, there is such a mark on you."

Seeing in the child an all too familiar evil, the creature stumbled backward into the rail.

The boy's voice was the hiss of a serpent. "I should call you father, would that Fate had bequeathed us a different lot."

The creature pressed a fist against his mouth to repress the shriek that lodged in his throat, thinking that this terrible boy must be deformed somehow, for he gave a strong feeling of deformity though it was impossible to specify its origin.

Swallowing back the scream, the creature pulled the fist away and said, "If ever I were a perversion, I would appear almost Divine under your shadow."

The boy smiled. "Is that how a murderous abomination addresses one whose life has been inspired by him?"

Before the creature could respond, an angry female voice shot through a far cabin window. "Edward! Edward Hyde! If you are not in front of my eyes in one half-minute, I shall thrash you within an inch of your life!"

The boy glanced in the direction of the voice, the hurled into the creature, grasping his hand and kissing it. Then he was gone.

Shaking with such a force he feared his body might shatter into fragments, the creature stumbled toward the stern, his through clogged in terror at the knowledge that the violence, so much a part of his accursed nature, was not limited to himself, that it was infecting the world like a malignancy, seeping into the psyches of mere children, turning them into the unholiest of demons. But did such a thing exist before his own birth, or was it through him that the malignancy entered the world?

"May God damn you to an eternity of torment, Victor Frankenstein! Through my anger and violence you have begat the seeds of humanity's self-destruction. All in the name of your filthy science!" He stood at the end of the ship, shaking with hatred and self-loathing, and so screamed at the horizon: "Did I solicit thee from darkness to mold me Man? Or was I, like the doomed Iscariot, simply a vessel used to carry out the will of One more powerful than even your science? Here I stand, an ABOMINATION! SHRIEKING TRAVESTY! WHERE, THEN IS HOPE? WHERE REASON? WHERE TENDERNESS? Or is it all a diseased illusion? If there be Any who hears these words, I say this to You: will my sufferings forever endure, or is there an end to it?"

He dropped his head, weeping, unable to stanch the flood of faces and memories that assailed him; the cries of those he had killed—Clerval, William, the dear Elizabeth—underscored the deaths of Justine Moritz and Alphonse Frankenstein who, were it not for the creature's grief-maddened actions, would breathe still. The anvil of guilt so long a part of his every breath weighed even heavier for the glorious sight of the sea before his gaze: what right did he, unholy brute, have to enjoy anything so wondrous?

He thought of the blind De Lacy and his children, and missed them intensely.

He thought of the image of his doomed mate, torn apart by Victor Frankenstein before she could be instilled with life.

He covered his face with one hand.

He remembered the loneliness of all the days leading up to this one.

Imagined the loneliness of his future.

And, deep within himself, he screamed.

And he screamed.

And he screamed.

Then a tiny hand touched him, and he blinked away tears to see another little boy standing beside him, only where the child Edward carried only the sense of deformity, this poor boy's affliction was apparent to even the weakest eyes. A more dreadfully misshapen being had the creature never seen, and where the previous boy had filled his heart with disgust, this one filled it with empathy.

The creature knelt, pulling the twisted child to him.

"Have you a name, sad little man?"

"Erik," whispered the boy through knots of crusty and discolored flesh. "I have been sent for you."

"And who is it that would send such a ... fine ... lad ... as ..." The creature's heart brimmed and he could speak no more, only embrace this boy whose heart, he was certain, had been broken as often and as mercilessly as his own.

"It's all right, now," whispered the boy. "No one is so wicked or ugly that they do not deserve a chance at redemption."

"Thank you, dear child," choked the creature as a shadow fell across his sight.

A woman of chiseled and ethereal loveliness touched the child upon its head and whispered, "Such a serious little boy you are, Erik. How often have I told you that your face will not shatter were you to allow a smile to cross it every now and then?"

The child turned from the creature and said, "I have found him."

"So you have. Such splendid work cannot go unrewarded."

The child's face tensed in anticipation

The woman touched Erik's cheek with great love and said, "You may go to the music room and play the piano until it is time for lunch."

"Oh, thank you!" he said throwing his arms around her neck and kissing her cheek with hard, little-boy glee, then bestowed the same affection on the creature before taking flight toward the stairs.

The woman, smiling after him, looked at the creature and said, "I hope you know, sire, that even though Erik is only my ward, I could not love him any more if he were my own son."

"That you feel such affection for him, dear lady, is proof enough I need not pity the misfortune of his form."

"His soul is pure and full of music. His skill at playing and composing are nearly godlike. How could one not treasure him?" She extended her hand. "I am Christine Daaé, fiancée of D. Gray, chaplain of this vessel. I know well who you are, sir. Jonathan Merrick spoke glowingly of you when he gave this to my betrothed." She removed an envelope from her pocket and placed it in the creature's hand. "I hope the contents gives your tortured soul some degree of peace. If not, then please, please seek out my loving Dorian. He will do for you all that he can, even if it crumbles against the weight of the pain previously inflicted on you." She touched his hand then, flooding his system with warmth and promise and a hope of deliverance he had dared not imagine.

"The sight of your devotion to the child has already given me some measure of peace."

"I am glad for that. More than you can ever know."

And with that, she left him there, the envelope and the mysterious contents clutched in his hand.

Heart pounding, breath staggered, hands shaking, he broke the seal on the flap and slowly removed the folded pages.

He read:

My Dear Friend, Child-of-None:

How even to begin this? Shall I say that your tragedy has moved me to such a degree that I will measure the remainder of my life as blessed? Or would it be more fitting to say that nothing this far in my thirty-one years has compared with the effect you have had on both my heart and my —if you'll pardon my using the next word —science? Suffice to say this: you have moved me deeply and it will be only upon the moment of my death that you shall be elsewhere than the forefront of my thoughts.

There is much to tell you and my time is short (the ship sails in less than five hours) so I will dispense with any further declarations of respect and affection, save for this last: know that, whatever may befall you come the next dawn, you are, and always shall be, welcome in my home and my hearth should you ever choose to return to Ireland.

You have doubtlessly found the letters which I placed in your jacket while you were suffering from fever. The young lady whose hand composed them was and is the daughter of an esteemed Italian scientist who, though well-respected in the community of his fellow scientists, was recently and posthumously stripped of several honors when it was discovered that his quest for knowledge (much like that which possessed your Dr. Frankenstein) led him to commit an act so cold-blooded in its conception, so heinous in its disregard for individual human life, and so atrocious in its consequences, that many in the medical community have official stated our belief that the discoveries he made and the serums he created, though ultimately beneficial, are almost totally negated by the appalling manner in which they were achieved. I tell you this because the girl consistently failed to make mention of these facts in any of her letters—motivated, no doubt, by the fear that, should you recognize her name, your heart would grow cold. And who can place blame on her for that, knowing, as I do, that she herself was the unknowing (at first), then unwilling subject of her father's experiments, which rendered her life, as yours, a painfully lonely one?

Before continuing with a listing of further facts surrounding the girl and her letters, I think it is necessary to tell you of a very strange occurrence which took place after our arrival back in Dublin.

A private wing of the Institute Infirmary had been isolated solely for the purpose of your care. Know that you were wall-attended by every member of my staff during this period. (I say this because you were unconscious during the journey from Siberia to Ireland, and remained thus for several weeks after our arrival.)

One evening, shortly after the midnight hour, I was awakened in my chambers by an orderly who informed me that you had regained consciousness and were asking for me by name. My curiosity and unease were beyond any measure at that moment, for I had never introduced myself to you and had given specific orders that, upon your revival, no one but myself was to speak to you. I dressed quickly and climbed the tower stairs to the private wing.

Imagine my shock when, upon entering, I saw you standing by your bed, examining the intravenous drip attached to you. When I inquired how you felt, you turned to me, smiled, and said, "I suspect that he is fine, Dr. Merrick, being deep in a coma as he is."

"Is this some jest?" I asked.

"Would that it were," you replied, in a voice very unlike the one I recalled hearing when first I saw you in Siberia.

"Have you a name?"

"In life, I was known as Victor Frankenstein."

"Victor Frankenstein is dead, having succumbed to fever and infection aboard the ship of Robert Walton. His death has been documented in newspapers and medical journals world-wide."

"I know. And for what will he be remembered when all the facts surrounding the circumstances of his life and death are made known?" Your hands balled into fists, striking at your chest. "For having remade Man. The dubious morality of the act itself is not why I am now being punished, Dr. Merrick. I am being punished by my Creator for having given life to this tragic form you see before you and then, in ignorance and selfishness, turning away from it in denial and revulsion. My sins against him are multitudinous, but none so fierce and harmful as that of having disallowed him compassion. Because of that refusal he became the tortured killer who robbed my life of meaning. And why not? I gave no thought to the meaning of his life. But I digress.

"Sit down, Dr. Merrick, take the writing pad and fountain pen from your desk. I am about to pay my penance and, insomuch as it can be done now, right the ghastly wrong which I have committed."

It was through him that I learned of the girl, a childhood friend of Victor's from his early years in Italy. Then he bid me write to Professor Pietro Baglioni at the University of Genoa. I complied, writing words which he dictated, and did soon receive Baglioni's reply. The professor, a very intelligent fellow possessing a singularly dry wit, yet often stale in his manners, was quite happy to provide the facts behind the girl and her father —who, at the time, lay on his deathbed.

Over the ensuing months, Victor Frankenstein returned to you every night. Having obtained all the information about the girl from Baglioni, Victor informed me it was time we wrote the girl herself, now that she was orphaned and completely alone in the world. Night after night did your Dr. Frankenstein dictate the most passionate, poetic letters to me, missives so overpowering in their honesty and desire that I often found myself on the verge of tears, having been reminded of my own youth and first love.

We—or rather, I—sent those letters as quickly as they were written. And her responses! Well, you have the letters, so you know well how deeply she reciprocated the feelings expressed on the page. Then, at last, she inquired as to the source of your sadness. (I say "your" sadness for the letters were conceived and constructed with the purpose of making a romantic arrangement between you the girl and yourself. I'd never been part of a matchmaking before, though my mother used to speak of such things, and I found that I very much enjoyed it.)

Before next contacting her, Victor instructed me to write to Margaret Saville in England, sister of Robert Walton, and request that she send me a copy of the journal R.W. wrote to her during his last sea voyage. Since, as I'm sure you know, that journal contains your story, I was most anxious to see it myself. Mrs. Saville was more than kind and sent a cleanly typeset copy of the journal.

I wept for you, my dear friend. None who reads your sad tale could hold you in contempt, even in light of your many violent actions.

After sending the journal to Italy, I prayed each night that the girl would be as moved by your story as I. And it would appear that, sometimes, God hears such prayers.

Soon, the girl's response arrived, and her love for you, her compassion and tenderness, were tenfold what they had been before.

Allow me to impart this one last fact concerning her: there is no living man on this Earth who could be her love. Only you, being already dead yet alive, can fill the void in her life.

And so I was compelled to act quickly.

I booked passage on the *SS Catapaxi*. Your fever was in its final stages. I would not have sent you on your way so soon were it not for the fact that no other ship will sail again for Italy until early next year, and to deny you the promise of happiness for even one hour longer seemed to me a sin of unforgivable measure.

I know not what fate befell the soul of your creator, for his visits ceased after we received the girl's response to Walton's journal. I can only hope he has found the forgiveness he sought. Too much misery has already resulted.

And so, my friend, here ends my take. I shall miss you, and pray that jubilation awaits you on the Italian shore. I take leave of you with these words from Gibran: "Love gives not by itself and takes not from itself; live possesses not nor would it be possessed, for love is sufficient unto love."

Your Friend,

J. Merrick

The creature carefully folded the letter and put it with the others.

He turned back toward the sea and saw the ghost of errant light dancing across the waves, imagined the reflections in the ripples to be figures of himself and his beloved engaged in a waltz.

The radiant sphere of the moon shone down upon him, and he gave himself all the way over into its light.

And there beheld promise.

And there beheld sublimity.

And there beheld forgiveness, bequeathing it as well and saying, for the first time, the name of his creature with no hatred in his heart.

He looked at the letters in his hand.

He wondered if she would be as delicate and lovely as her script (she was even more so), if she would smile at the sight of him (she did, and resplendently, opening her arms for his embrace), and if she would ever dance with him (there was music in the square when he arrived at her gate, and they danced; oh, how they danced).

He raised his arms above his head, the moonlight passing between his fingers to create silver rays which shrugged away the shadows; the sea-spray bathed his face, becoming the scent of perfume as it beaded against his skin; and he recalled having heard a fairy story about a puppet who longed to become a real boy, who wished upon a star, and whose wish was granted.

Aided by the moonlight, he gazed inward, quietly saying the name of his beloved over and over, as if it were a prayer —"My dearest Beatrice, daughter of Giacomo Rappaccini"—until he found a solitary pinpoint of shimmering icestar in the night sky.

Part Two:

WITH A LITTLE HELP
FROM MY FRIENDS

"I see nobody on the road," said Alice.

"I only wish I had such eyes," the King remarked in a fretful tone. "To see Nobody! And at that distance, too!"

Lewis Carroll

"A dreamer is one who can only find his way by moonlight, and his punishment is that he sees the dawn before the rest of the world."

Patti Smith

"Who's on First?"

"Yes."

Abbott & Costello

I'm not going to say too much here because I have been lucky enough to have numerous other writers offer commentaries on the stories in this section. Every last one of them floored me with their words, and even as I write this I remain unconvinced that much of it is deserved. That isn't false modesty, either; once a piece is finished and in print, regardless of how many revisions it has gone through before being unleashed upon the world, I tend to see only the weak spots, sections that could have been made better, dialogue that wasn't quite what it should have been, scenes where the rhythm is still just a bit *off*... and then I remind myself that most writers tend to be wrong when judging the value and/or success of their own work; we are, all of us, our own harshest critics. Unless you're Nicholas Sparks, who is a literary genius that gets it right the very first time, every time, because he's, well, a literary genius. Seriously. *Sincerely*. Just ask him.

The Great Pity

Introduction by Ramsey Campbell

How can I even begin to sum up "The Great Pity"? It's a triumphant experiment that manages to announce its narrative radicalism while simultaneously seizing the reader and interrogating the reader's experience. It's a meditation not merely on loss and injustice but on the nature of existence, not least our own. Its very form expresses its theme, emerging from abstraction into vividly lived experience like an uncanny birth. It's an exemplary instance of horror fiction that refuses to relent, confronting us with insights that linger and expand long after the tale is done. If you need evidence that our field is as vital and challenging as ever, just look to Gary Braunbeck.

The Great Pity

"...all those bodies which compose the mighty frame of the world have not any subsistence without a mind —that their being is to be perceived or known."
    —George Berkeley (1685—1753)

"The great pity will occur before long,
    Those who gave will be obliged to take:
        Naked, starving, withstanding cold and thirst ..."
        —Michel de Nostredame

Prelude: Chalked Gripped In Each Hand

Later, of course, no one is watching when the little girl stumbles out of the burning house and toward the middle of the street, a piece of chalk gripped in each hand. One piece is white, the other is red. She finds a section of the asphalt that is without potholes or cracks and kneels down, brushing away some of the dirt and pebbles so that the surface is as smooth and clear as it can possibly be. She looks at the house she has just left but if she is thinking anything, remembering anything, hoping for or regretting anything, it cannot be seen on her face. The flames that were only a second ago causing the house to screech like some prehistoric beast being pulled into a pit of tar freeze in place, so very still, looking almost artificial; even what remains of the roof pauses in the midst of buckling, snapping, and collapsing inward. When the flames resume their feast, less than one-tenth of a second will have passed; but, for now, time, place, here-and-now, back-then, all of them are no longer fixed in place; this is how she wants it, this little girl. For now, at least.

Leaning forward, she begins drawing a long, unbroken, often-curving line with the white chalk until the basic shape of the fallen body—a woman, in her late twenties; yes, that's it—is complete. Switching hands, she begins to add the blood; a splash near the stomach, a trickle down one leg, a massive fountain on the left side of the head. Leaning her own head to one side so as to afford a different if not better view, the little girl smiles at the parallax effect achieved by this slight change of vantage point. She scoots to the side, brushes away some more dirt and pebbles, and begins working on the shape of the second body. A young boy, this one, with a clubfoot and a jagged maw where the lower portion of his face used to be. It's a good thing the sticks of chalk are brand-new; she has so many figures to outline, so much red to splash, spatter, and spray about. It's nice that no one is watching the house now, not like before. She doesn't like it when people look, when people watch, when people stare; the lookers, the watchers, the staring ones, they never say anything, but, oh, the things they *think*; the things they do think.

Luckily, for us, she does not choose to look up from her task. Not that she would see us, but, still, it's best we remain as we are.

1. And By Extension

Not just anyone can be one who only looks: if the person being observed looks back, the observer becomes the one who is being looked at, and the guise of safety, of an action unnoticed and therefore secret and therefore somewhat holy, is shattered; the moment is unalterably affected. Still, one cannot help but wonder: if the being at whom one stares is something akin to a ghost, a spirit, or phantom, does the moment—and, by extension, the observer—remain unaffected? It will be important for us to remember this as we turn our attention to the moment at hand, the moment that is being sculpted from nothingness into a life-like shape, the moment that does not know it's being observed from a safe vantage point; in doing so, like the sculptor confronting the virgin marble or clay or a child who will soon be drawing chalk figures on the street, we will use our words and trust they will speak accurately to who- or whatever is watching and listening. Should we fail in this task, we risk conjuring deaf idols if we take too literally our descriptions of the sculpted scenes, for not just anyone can be one who only looks: if the person being observed looks back, the observer becomes the one who is being looked at.

2. Geometric Exactness

It is necessary—insomuch as anything can be said to *be* necessary—that we establish certain precincts, particular margins, commonplace boundaries before going any further; let us begin with the *when* of it: right now, in the graceful flow of the present. Now, the where of it: we are hidden here, in the blank spaces between words, paragraphs, pages; we are only *now*, right now, here in this story, here on this page, here in this sentence. And from this place of safety we watch as a young man (not the little girl with the chalk in her hands, she hasn't shown herself yet, and with good reason)—a young man in his early twenties, walks down a street that looks like a lot of other streets, passing houses that look very much like all the other houses. We don't know this young man's name, no one living on this street knows his name, and so, as we observe from our unnoticed and therefore holy vantage point, his identity is of no consequence. What *is* of consequence, what we absolutely must concern ourselves with, is the bouquet of flowers he carries in his left hand, the hand that is, at the moment, facing the house he is passing.

Watch carefully. The young man's face is tight and red. There are streaks down both of his reddened cheeks, but if there were any tears, they have already dried. Is he angry? Hurt? Broken-hearted, perhaps. It doesn't matter; what matters is that he is coming to a stop in front of one of the houses, his entire body shuddering from the anger or broken-heartedness. He closes his eyes, pulls in a slow, deep breath that steadies him, and—bringing to bear a surprising amount of force—tosses the bouquet of flowers aside. They land, still neatly wrapped in green tissue paper, on the second of the three stone steps that lead up to the front porch. The young man wipes his eyes, pulls in another deep breath, nods to himself (perhaps having made a decision to which we are not privy), and walks away, his part played, his purpose served, and leaves our story while we remain here, in front of the house, looking at the bouquet of flowers.

We sense more than realize there is something odd about this image. We squint, blink, and stare. It takes a few moments but at last it becomes so obvious that we momentarily feel foolish: there is a certain, almost geometric *exactness* to the position in which the bouquet has landed. Moving closer, we decide that, yes, yes, most definitely, they *do* look as if they were placed in that position on the second stone step *on purpose*, don't they? Absolutely. And with this image of the bouquet firmly set in our memory we can move forward a few hours, unnoticed, undifferentiated, shape- and shadowless, here on this page, at this paragraph, in this book.

3. The Company and Friendship of Shadows

The first person to notice the flowers is fifty-eight-year-old Eugene ("Gene to my buddies") Benson, a man who discovered only this morning that the cancer was *not* totally removed along with his prostate, that some of it, like an undetected fragrance, has found a new and metastasized home in his liver, his lungs, and—very soon—his brain. Gene—as we now know him, for what person would refuse the company and friendship of shadows at a time such as this?—has been walking for hours, forcing himself to notice all things he'd taken for granted during his thirty-one years working the graveyard shift at Miller Tool & Die, his attention and skill focused not on the world beyond the factory cell but instead on metal forming rolls, lathe bits, milling cutters, and form tools. He wonders why he never married, never raised a family, never did any of the thousands of things, be they special or everyday, that mark the passing moments of one's life so that some sort of memory will live on.

He stops when he sees the bouquet on the second step of the house he was about to pass, and for a minute he simply stares, wondering who would leave such a thing, and why; then remembers stories he's heard on the radio or read about in the paper or seen on the evening news, stories about people—family, friends, even strangers—who assemble at the site of some domestic tragedy to leave gifts, cards, pictures drawn in crayon by children, toys, flowers, trinkets, handwritten notes, photos that mean nothing to anyone except the one who kneels down, makes the Sign of the Cross, and tearfully places it beside any of the dozens of motif candles arranged in odd, geometrically exact rows (as if the positioning somehow ensures that the iridescent light will continue to burn, as if the act of placing these things at the site of a domestic tragedy somehow lifts the burden of accountability from the shoulders of the neighbors and friends who gather to sing church hymns, weep openly, and crane their necks to offer prayers both silent and shrill to a sky where no one looks down, all the time trying to convince themselves and others that they *didn't know* or *didn't want to interfere with other peoples' business*).

Gene has always been secretly sickened by such stories. What the hell good does any physical item do for the person who's now dead? Why amplify the suffering of that person—unless it's simply a way to draw attention to yourself? It makes no sense to him. But now, for some reason, he finds himself unable to look or walk away from the flowers. He feels something on his face and reaches up to discover that he's begun to weep—but whether it's for the person who's died or for himself, he can't decide.

Then he does something that surprises even him; he reaches into his back pocket and removes his wallet, flipping through the credit cards in their clear plastic compartments (cards he doesn't have to worry about paying off now) until he comes to the single photograph he's carried with him for God-only-knows how many years: the photo that came with the wallet. It's of a little girl, maybe six years old. She smiles at the camera that has captured her image on a perfect autumn day. She is the little girl every married couple wants. (Had the photo been of a little *boy*, he would have been the little boy every married couple wants.)

With his thumb Gene touches the cheek of the little girl, realizing that her face has faded over the years. He can make out her strawberry-blonde hair, her light windbreaker, part of her smile, and her left eye. He tries to remember what she looked like when she was new; he tries to remember why he purchased this particular wallet; and, lastly, he wonders why he did not remove this photo of the little girl who never was. Slipping it from its protective sleeve, he stares at her discolored and washed-out face, feeling a rush of grief he's not experienced since the death of his parents. He pulls in a slow, deep breath that steadies him (not unlike the nameless young man in the moment before he tossed the bouquet), and walks over to the house, kneels before the second step, and gently places the picture of the little girl among the roses and baby's-breath, taking a moment to make certain that she's looking out at those who may pass by once Gene himself has left.

We float, first this way, then that, whispering around him, pondering the anomalous tableau. Why is he doing this, making a gesture that he's always thought to be ineffectual, offensive, and hypocritical? For a moment we consider entering Eugene Benson's mind to find the answer, but then he speaks, something in the back of his voice sounding of corroded nails being wrenched from rotted wood:

"May as well give you a name while I'm at it, huh? I always kinda thought that Leigh was a really pretty name. L-e-i-g-h, not L-e-e. So why don't we call you 'Leigh,' then? I'll bet whatever your real name is, you're probably all grown up now with a family of your own, but maybe you still model for photos that'll go inside of wallets and picture frames and … whatever else it is they put them kinds of pictures in these days.

"Oh, hon, you ought to see some of the things people have come up with. They got these picture frames now, they're electronic, and you can hook 'em up to a computer and load it with hundreds of pictures, then you turn it on and it'll change pictures every five minutes or so. I guess how long it shows any one picture is something that you have to decide for yourself. I wish I'd known how to use a computer, maybe I could've got on the Internet and found more pictures of you and …" The words trail off, lay fallen at his feet. We drift nearer, closer now than the space between his breaths, and murmur: *and what? Create a daughter who never existed, not in the same sense that—*

"—I exist," says Gene. "I mean, I know that *you* exist, you're right here in the picture, but that's where it sort of *ends* between you and me, isn't it? You look like the daughter I wish I'd had but never did, so what's wrong with wanting to watch her grow up, even if it's just in pictures that I'd find out there in other wallets, other frames? Maybe that's how she stays in touch with me, popping up in them places like that so that I can see that she still has that great smile and her hair still has that terrific shine and her skin still has that … that *bloom*, just like her mother's, and …" The words do not fall at his feet this time; instead, his left hand snaps up to cover his mouth and trap the rest of them within as he turns quickly away from the picture and the flowers; whatever he was about to say will remain unspoken: we can see as much in his eyes, eyes no longer narrowed against the sight of the surrounding world, eyes that are now wide and glistening at the corners and staring at something we are forbidden to look at from the place where we hide, something only he can see, perhaps a thing of heartbreak or madness, quiet fury or ravenous regret, born from a loneliness that whispers of a life misspent, that any and all chances to find something of joy or meaning or permanence have long since passed by, unrecognized, untaken, now unattainable; and as we try to imagine what physical shape this thing only Gene can see might assume—that is, if it were sentient enough to give itself form—questions must be posed;

have you ever:

passed by an ill-kept house where those inside are screeching profanities at one another and notice there is no fence to block your view of the backyard; and did you, despite yourself, look to see brown, brittle grass covered in many places by broken toys and empty beer cans; looking a bit longer, did you catch sight of the crumbling doghouse back there, and did you observe the dog itself: a too-thin, shuddering, frightened, whimpering vaudeville of what it should be, rheumy eyes focusing on you, pleading for a few moments of kindness because kindness does not gift with scabs and scars crisscrossing the body; kindness does not leave the unwashed bowls empty for days on end, until you are so hungry and so thirsty it takes all of your strength to simply lift up your head and lap at the tepid, dirty liquid or nibble at the mashed and moldy heap; it does not rip away chunks of fur, leaving these raw, glistening, red patches of slowly-healing flesh; it does not swing the belt that leaves one eye forever blinded; kindness does not kick the frail bones and laugh at the sound of their breaking; does not allow those broken bones to remain un-mended; it does not laugh at you when you try to fetch the toy but cannot—the deformities left by the broken bones have shortened one leg and rendered useless another; kindness does none of these; and kindness, even a moment's kindness, is all it asks of you, but as you begin to step closer you see that the dog is not chained to a pole or the front of the doghouse, there is nothing weighing it down or forcing it to stay put; and at that moment, safe and unobserved by the screeching people in the ill-kept house, did you wonder why the dog, seemingly of its own free will, *remains there,* where all it knows or will ever know is mockery, starvation, abuse, and loneliness;

have you ever:

watched the shabby vagrants who gather outside the bus station on Friday night, the way each one tries to make him- or herself a bit more presentable before approaching the sore and weary travelers; have you watched as they put on their best smile, the only one they possess, the one that is kept in cold storage and taken out only to ask for a bit of kindness, a little spare change, have you noticed how these smiles — some straight and bright, others displaying teeth that are crooked and broken and yellowed, jutting up from blackened gums —always show for an instant, just a flash, blink and you'll miss it, an echo of the person they used to be; and, in taking note of this, have you ever wanted to approach one of them (especially the worn-out women with bruised faces who hold the hands of small, shivering children), have you ever wanted to touch their cheek and whisper something of genuine comfort, words that will still have value long after the pocket change you drop into their grateful hands has been spent on liquor or drugs or food for the little ones, something like *anytime you feel lost, call my name and I will carry you back across to the place where you can remember what it felt like to still have human dignity;*

have you ever:

walked into a roomful of people and immediately sensed that something important, maybe ugly, possibly profound, has just occurred, and have you then forced a smile onto your face as you make the rounds, trying to discern what has happened by the way the others behave, the tones of their voices, the manner in which they carry themselves, avoiding too much eye contact, but there you are, digging for clues like some second-rate detective just so you can discover what occurred while you were out of the room;

have you ever:

found yourself weeping for no reason, be it at the office or at home or when you find yourself stuck in traffic with nothing to do but *sit there* and wait for everything to start moving again, and while you wait your mind —without your knowledge or assistance—scrounges through the place where you've stored memories of pain, regret, sadness, despair, guilt, and digs deep until it finds a particularly terrible memory; but instead of throwing that memory into your mind, it sends only the feelings that you experienced at that moment, the ones you hoped you would never experience again; and have you ever

wondered about the purpose of pain; and have you ever

in dreams never spoken of, drank the sky from a silver chalice, reigning over a kingdom where there is no more sorrow, or hunger, or broken spirits; and have you ever

felt your heart skip a beat at the sound of a child's scream because, for just a moment, you can't tell if it's a scream of joy, meant to travel the world, or if it's the scream of absolute terror because someone is doing something *terrible* the child, only you can't see *where* it came from;

and have you ever

railed against the existence of God;

or why it is that movies with happy endings always leave you cold and resentful and wishing you could reach into the film and strangle all the actors;

have you ever

wondered why it is that those who, for some reason, love you, are always forgiving of your mistakes, no matter how cruel; and, in the end;

have you ever asked anyone, say, a little girl drawing chalk outlines on the street, if anything you do or say or hope for or strive toward or dream or regret ultimately matters, or is it all just some protracted, contemptuous, obscene delusion?

Shhh; there-there; it's not necessary for you to have an answer. But we did have to ask; after all, if there is enough pain, if there is enough grief, if there is sufficient desperation and hopelessness, and if they are focused intensely enough, with an adequate amount of belief, on a single point and at a single subject (much as the unseen observer watches from his/her/their place of safety), how could you not accept the idea that something that was *not*, suddenly *is?*

We leave Eugene Benson for just a few moments, rising on the breeze toward an upstairs window. Looking in, we see that there is no furniture in the room. Dust covers the badly-scuffed hardwood floor. But as we continue watching, the dust is being disturbed by something unseen; it swirls in the air like snowflakes until it all twists and turns toward the same spot in the middle of the empty room; here, it becomes a small funnel-cloud that, from its behavior, is trying to drill through the floor. Instead—and it takes us a few seconds to realize this—it is trying to pull something up through the floorboards, and, soon enough, we see the semi-gelatinous substance that is leaking upward from the cracks between the boards; at first it looks like mud left on the hillside after rain, but as the funnel continues to churn and more of the mud leaks upward, it takes on the color and consistency of raw liver, all of it combining to form something like a cocoon made of spoiled pork. There is a soft snapping noise from inside the cocoon, and it begins to split apart on one side, a mouth disgorging something unpleasant, and with a series of wet, tearing sounds, a small, slick knot pushes outward. After a few more moments the knot begins to split apart, fingers uncoiling, flexing, and then clawing at the side of the cocoon, ripping away chunks of meat that fall to the floor with heavy splattering sounds.

We turn away from the window and drift back down to Gene, who is now looking across the street where a middle-aged woman has been is watching him for who-knows-how-long, her narrowed eyes filled with suspicion.

Gene suddenly feels embarrassed, foolish, insufficient, and inept, so he glances once more at the flowers and the picture of Leigh and whispers a farewell before walking on, eventually going back to his house where he will order a pizza for dinner, watch the DVD of his favorite movie, *The Shootist*, the one where John Wayne plays an ex-gunfighter dying of cancer, and when it's over, Gene will smile at the television, reach over to the small table beside his chair, pick up the gun, shove it in his mouth, and squeeze the trigger. It will be ten days before any of the neighbors notice the stench in the air; twelve days before any of his friends become worried enough to check on him.

Interlude: Still-Life(s) in White and Red

With nearly all of the figures completed (there will be twenty-seven once she has finished with them) and the little girl stops with the red chalk, now worn down nearly to a nub, held tightly in her grip. Her brow furrows, creating wrinkles in her face and on her forehead that look as deep as scars, momentarily ageing her by decades. She stands and turns in the direction of the first figure (now several yards down the street), her glance tracking from left to right, examining all of the chalk outlines until she is looking down at this final form at her feet. She considers something—what, we cannot tell—nods her head, and skips a few feet away from this final figure. Looking down the gallery of her chalk ghosts, the little girl raises one arm, pointing straight out, reshaping her hand into an imaginary gun that consists of thumb and index finger. "Bang. Bang. Bang," she whispers. Her brow relaxes, her flesh becomes smooth once again, no longer marked by ageing scars; she is only a little girl, holding nubs of chalk in each hand. She kneels down and begins drawing a new figure, different from the rest; this one—a man in his late thirties, yes, that's it, that's exactly right—is given much more detail than any of the others; he has a recognizable face, a knowing expression; he has clothes—work boots, khaki pants, a tee-shirt, a denim jacket, a work cap, all of them stained by machine grease from a factory floor. He is standing, full of purpose. He begins to move with confidant steps, not too fast, not too slow, just enough that one can take a look at him and know that he will not be deterred from his destination or his task. The little girl smiles at him. He smiles back at her. "Shouldn't I be carrying something?" he asks. The little girl nods her head. A few moments later, he is holding something sleek.

"Hold on," says the little girl. "I gotta finish something on the last person."

"Man or woman?"

"Huh? Oh, geez, I don't know."

"Make it a mother holding her newborn baby."

The little girl considers this for a moment. "I'll have to draw it over again. You'll have to wait."

"That will not be a problem."

"Good."

"That's an impressive fire, by the way."

"Uh-huh."

"It would certainly make *me* want to come outside to watch."

"Well ... they started it."

"Yes. That they did. Hey, Leigh?"

"What?"

"Who am I?"

"*Huh?*"

"Give me a name. Tell me the story of my life. I don't care how much of it is left or what I never had of it to begin with, just ... tell me. Tell me about me."

"Like *they* told me about me?"

"Something like that, yes. Please?"

"That's fair. Okay ... let me ... let me think ..."

"Will it be a happy story, or a sad one?"

"I don't know yet. Just wait a second."

"I can wait. Take your time. Make it a good story, this story of my life ...."

4. A Terrible Thing

We turn our attention to the middle-aged woman across the street. She wears a shabby housecoat and even shabbier slippers, but this does not stop her from coming down off her front porch and crossing over to see what that strange man was up to.

She sees the carefully-placed flowers; she sees the photo of the little girl whose face is no longer smudged and worn down, but clear and bright. For a moment the middle-aged woman—Virginia Thompson, "Jinny" to her friends, recently laid-off from the hospital where she worked as a cafeteria cook—stares at the flowers and the photo. The little girl looks oddly familiar, yet Virginia can't quite place her. It takes her a moment longer to realize what this means, and when the realization hits, she shakes her head, turns around, and heads back to her house where she immediately calls her best friend, Arlene, and tells her all about it.

—I knew it must have been a terrible thing that made them move out in the middle of the night like they did.

—But that was so long ago, wasn't it? Are you sure it's the same house, Jinny? Why would any of them come back? That don't seem like such a smart thing to me.

—Maybe he was feeling guilty and that's why he left the flowers and the picture. Oh, Arlene, you ought to see what this little girl looked like. Poor little thing.

—Did you call the police? I would call the police, Jinny. If he's still nearby, he might hurt some other little girl. You never know.

—And what am I supposed to tell the police? That I seen some strange man leave flowers and a picture on the steps of a house ain't no one lived in for a good two years?

—Well, you know the *names* of the folks who used to live there, right?

—Hell, no! Nobody knows anybody else around here. Everyone minds their own business.

—Don't sound like it's much of a neighborhood.

—It ain't, but the house was the right price. If Herb gets laid off from the plant, I don't know how we're gonna keep up with the mortgage payments, I really don't.

—Hey, Jinny?

—Yeah?

—I just had an idea about that little girl ....

* * *

By seven-thirty that evening, having phoned most of the people either of them could call a genuine friend, Virginia and Arlene stand on the sidewalk, facing the house where the flowers and photograph have now been joined by dozens of small lighted candles, sympathy cards, children's toys, hand-drawn pictures, figurines of Christ and the Holy Mother, several rosaries, photographs of other dead or missing children brought there by family members. Word has spread quickly about the vigil (we smile to ourselves as we observe this night watch, somewhat dumbfounded that two or three phone calls have set into action this chain of events), and there are easily two dozen people milling around the front of the house, many of whom have never met before. A man we have never seen before (and will never see again) turns to the woman beside him.

—I heard that Channel 10 might be sending a news van here tonight.

—Really? God, if I'd've known that, I would have fixed my hair. I can't have people seeing me on television looking like this.

Arlene has come prepared, and walks around handing everyone a sacramental candle (they had been on sale at the religious bookstore downtown, three dozen for ten dollars, and Arlene was not one to pass up a bargain); after everyone has set flame to the wick of their candle, the crowd becomes more orderly, forming a lengthy half-circle in front of the house.

—What was her name? someone asks.

—Leigh, replies Virginia. I think I heard the man call her Leigh when he left the picture.

—It must have been a terrible thing, to weigh on a man's conscience like that.

—Do you suppose she suffered much? asks someone else.

And like a curved row of falling dominoes or a grade-school game of Telephone, the speculations begin running down the line and then back again:

I hope he didn't beat her to death, that would have been an awful way to die; think I heard something about a shooting here a couple of years ago, but I don't remember the little girl's name; heard she was strangled with one of her own belts; he tied her hands behind her back and hung her up by her neck in the closet and just left her to choke to death no it was the flu bet you anything it was the flu it's just been terrible this year just a terrible thing the mother poisoned her a little bit each day y'know like in that movie with the little boy who says he can see dead people got pushed down the basement stairs and it broke her neck they both held her under the water in the tub until she drowned a divorce thing the mother had custody and the father got drunk as hell and decided that if he can't have his kids no one can have to wonder why didn't she scream or cry out for help bet she was terrified the whole time her last minutes on this earth were horrible being beaten like that poisoned like that hanged like that strangled like that raped and stabbed like that starved like that pushed down the stairs like that burned like that starved like that hacked up into pieces like that tortured like that what makes a person do such horrible things to a child or anyone for that matter kind of sick person has thoughts like that anyway ....

On and on it goes, until, at last, they compare notes and decide they have their answers.

Second Interlude: The Story, in Mosaic, of the Purposeful Man, Who is Standing

His name was Frank Thomas and for as long as he was alive he acted like a man who was always looking back in hopes that something joyful from his past would come running forward, jump up, and piggyback him into the future, happier life. But that's not quite how it went.

It happened like this:

He finished high school, did his stint in the military, and then went home to help run the farm. He found a good Christian woman to marry and started a family. His parents retired to Arizona on Social Security and passed the farm and its debts to Frank. Everything seemed to be working out just that way it was supposed to.

One night shortly after his parents moved away, Frank remembered telling his wife as she sat at her piano, "I feel powerful, Betty. I'm a man, living in the strongest nation in the world, and I got all that goes along with that; a good home, a good wife and family, plenty of good food. If I work for it, I can have just about anything I want."

But that's not quite how it went.

As his children, Nadine and Rachael, grew up, he found them to be a burden. "It's your fault they grow up so lazy and disrespectful," he told Betty. He did his best to swallow his anger, but when it got the best of him, he told them all just exactly what he thought of them. Betty was a "fat cow" who "...didn't have the backbone to stand up to her brood and teach them what was right and proper." Nadine was a "slovenly ne'er-do-well" who, if she didn't get better grades, would "...grow up to be trailer trash on welfare surrounded by ten screaming children." Rachael was "sickly," and Frank let it be known he resented the special care and expense necessary to support her. As far as he was concerned, none of them had any gratitude for the life he provided for them.

As a young teenager, Nadine got into drugs and sex. She beat up her mother a couple of times and became useless around the farm. One day she was gone and didn't return.

"I'm glad she's run off," Frank told Betty. "I couldn't love nobody who'd do the things that young girl did."

"She grew up like that because you are a heartless bastard," Betty told him. It was the only time she'd ever stood up to him.

The next day, as punishment, Frank sold Betty's precious piano. He enjoyed watching her cry as it was hauled away.

She never gave him any lip again. But she did take up with another man. Frank knew that he should have felt hurt, but he didn't. On some level that he was never really willing to admit to himself, he didn't blame her, but he never visited that level too often and so it was easy to ignore.

He took to forcing himself on Betty some nights, just to see if she'd refuse him.

She never did. Never much enjoyed having him on top of her, either, for that matter, but Frank got to shoot his wad and that was all he cared about—that, and teaching her that there was a price for spreading your legs for another man when you were Frank Thomas' wife.

Eventually Betty died in a car accident on her way to one of her disgraceful, adulterous meetings. There was some question as to whether or not it was an accident; it seemed that there were no skid marks on the road near the tree she'd hit. "Have you noticed if your wife had seemed depressed lately?" one of the investigators had asked him.

Frank stuffed his resentment down deep inside.

So he found himself middle-aged, not as strong as he once was, and without help running the farm. Money was tight. Frank couldn't afford to hire help. Although he'd worked hard all his life and chipped away at his father's debts, he'd never made much of a dent. Rachael, with her mysterious seizures and the drugs she took for them, couldn't be expected to help out much.

The debts piled up.

The farm started to show signs of neglect and ruin.

Younger debts came along to keep the older ones company.

He was forced to sell off half his property.

But he kept the anger and frustration buried deep as the bodies in his front yard.

All too soon there wasn't enough farm *left* to farm. He got a job at the recycling plant, sorting plastic bottles. He was mired in rancid soft drink residue eight hours a day five days a week. Hank Fenster, who drove a forklift at the plant, befriended Frank. With two weeks on the job, they were relaxing one evening after work at the Echo Hollow Tavern.

"Nothing but a bunch of kids running that plant," Frank said, draining half his beer. "Every one of them got a college degree, but no common sense. They push us around like we're nothing. It's like they think I got no pride, that I'll just take anything offa them."

"Ain't it the truth, though?" Hank asked through a mouth full of beer nuts. "I mean, you're just like me, ain't you? I know I couldn't afford to lose that job."

Frank thought about quitting, but with Rachael's medicines and doctor's bills, the repairs to the plumbing and the antiquated tube-and-knob wiring in the farm house, not to mention the debt his father had been so generous with, he knew Hank was right: like it or not, he was stuck.

Frank stared into his empty beer glass and whispered: "One day I'm going to take my hunting rifle down to the plant and blow all them snot-nosed kids away." He was kidding when he said it and laughed, but when he stepped out of his car with his hunting rifle a month later to actually do it, Frank was a man possessed by a life-time of anger denied. In the mail that morning he had received a letter from his supervisor at the plant, explaining how his wages and benefits would have to be cut back or they'd have to let him go.

The bastard couldn't even say it to my face, Frank thought.

His actions that morning were mechanical and dream-like at the same time: before leaving for work, he went into Rachael's bedroom, kissed her on the forehead, put a bullet through skull, and then headed for work. Hank, just arriving for his shift, saw him in the parking lot, tried to reason with him, and finally tried to stop him. After shooting Hank, Frank paused only long enough to register the surprise on his friend's face, surprise that he realized he shared.

What the hell have I done? I should go home!

No—the bastards had to die, if only to pay for Hank's life.

Frank burst through the front entrance to the plant, headed for the administrative offices.

Alerted by the shots fired in the parking lot, the security guard stood just inside, his pistol drawn. Frank had forgotten about him.

"Drop it," the guard demanded.

If I stop now, Frank thought, *maybe I won't get into too much trouble.* Then he focused on the pistol in the guard's hand. It was such a pitiful little thing, not nearly as powerful as his deer rifle. He raised the barrel toward the man and put a hole in his stomach.

Frank killed three more people on his way to the administrative offices; once he reached his destination, he shot everyone who stood between him and the supervisor's office.

The supervisor got special treatment; Frank blew apart both the man's knees, and then stood over him and shoved the barrel of the rifle into the man's mouth.

"A man works his whole life away," Frank spat at the supervisor, "he reports to work on time and punches the clock and works without complaint and doesn't never call in sick no matter how bad he feels, and what does it mean? Can you tell me that, boss-man? What does it amount to when little snotty-ass college pricks like you make him feel embarrassed by what he is, ashamed at his lack of education, humiliated because he can only provide his family with the things they need and never things they *want?*"

The supervisor had wet himself, red-faced, and shook his head as his eyes filled with tears.

The terror in the man's eyes made Frank feel good; for once in his life, he wasn't powerless.

"It ain't so bad when you're in here," he went on, ignoring the supervisor's whimpering. "It's when you're outside that it bothers you, you know? Because you're *marked, if you* know what I mean. You might be all dressed up at a nice restaurant or buying groceries or just out getting your mail and folks, they look at you and know right away what you are, what you've always been, and that's a worker, a laborer all your life, and they know this because you're marked. The work marks you, the not-enough money marks you... and little college shits mark you because they look down their noses at you and make you feel like dirt, and soon enough you start acting like dirt and then you wake up one morning and find out that dirt's what you've become...and that's just what you want, ain't it?"

The supervisor shook his head as much as he could; Frank pressed the barrel down harder and heard some of the man's teeth crack.

"... ittle ... rl ..." mumbled the supervisor through what was left of his mouth.

"What?" Frank pulled the barrel from the other man's mouth. "What'd you say?"

"The little girl."

"What little girl?"

"Leigh."

"I don't know no little girl named Leigh."

The supervisor nodded toward a window. "Sure you do. She's right out there in the street."

Frank looked over there, as well. "You mean in front of the house that's burning up?"

"Yes. Do you see her?"

"I see her. She's drawing something with chalk."

"Bang. Bang. Bang," said the little girl.

Frank looked at her, looked at the figures she'd outlined in chalk, looked at the burning house where the flames now stood frozen, and then, finally, looked at his empty hands.

"Shouldn't I be carrying something?" he asked her.

5. So It Was Decided

Her name was definitely Leigh. She was eleven years old when her father raped her, beat her unconscious, and then tied her hands behind her back with duct tape before wrapping an electrical cord around her neck and hanging her in her bedroom closet. He then killed his wife but the police still haven't found the body. He threw a bunch of stuff into the trunk and backseat of his car and hightailed it out of town. It was all such a terrible thing.

It is nearly ten p.m. now and many of those gathered here are getting tired. Each person extinguishing their sacramental candle, the group begins to disperse, all of them still thinking about the last horrifying minutes of Leigh's life, poor little thing, and maybe those who gathered here will arrive home and hug their children a little tighter than usual, wanting to never let go, and maybe these children will hug back and kiss Mommy or Daddy's cheek and say *I love you, too.*

Virginia says goodnight to Arlene and the two women go their separate ways.

No one has thought to extinguish any of the candles on the steps and porch of poor little Leigh's house. Soon enough the scene is deserted, excepting us, and we move away from the candles and toys and cards, rising toward the upstairs window once again. Looking into the empty room, we note that the funnel cloud of dust is gone, as is the meat cocoon. But from somewhere in the shadows we hear a soft but nonetheless distinct sound: that of a child crying.

A gust of wind, and beneath us the tissue paper around the flowers flutters backward, just enough so that a small section of it dips into the burning candle beside it. Moments later, the flowers are aflame, and it takes little time at all before all of the candles and toys and cards of sympathy are all burning bright.

We look back into the empty room and are startled to see Leigh standing a few feet back from the window, staring directly at us. She is trembling, her body covered in a sheen of afterbirth that both catches and reflects the light from a streetlamp, making her appear nearly translucent. Her saturated strawberry-blonde hair hangs off her scalp, straggling down to her bony shoulders, and when she moves closer to the window, we see that her skin is the color of a gravestone. The fury in her eyes is unmistakable. And we know that she can see us. We are no longer those who can only look.

From somewhere down the street, we hear the sound of a loud automobile engine. The car reveals itself a few moments later; it is an older model Mustang, a convertible with its roof down. Two teenaged

boys are sitting on the back of the car, their feet cushioned on the backseat. The driver is alone in the front seat. The car slows, pulling up to park in front of the house. The three teenagers get out but the driver leaves the engine running. He is carrying something is his right hand, something red and square and —judging by the way he keeps adjusting his shoulder —rather heavy.

—So this is it, huh? The house where that little girl was killed.

—She was raped first, is what I heard.

—Me too.

—Well, at least some of this shit's already burning.

A sloshing sound, drunken words, and we watch in fascination as the driver hoists the gas can up onto his shoulder and then throws it forward. It shatters the downstairs window, splashing a trail behind it that the flames are only too happy to follow. One of the girls in the backseat hops out, pulls something from her purse, and scribbles the words **fuck death** on the sidewalk in front of the house; **fuck** is written in white chalk; **death** is written in red. She throws the chalk aside and joins the others as they run back to the car and, with the sound of squealing tires and the stench of burning rubber, flee the scene.

Three minutes later the house is nearly engulfed in flames. Leigh is still standing at the window, staring at us, her eyes beckoning, commanding us to observe what is in her mind and heart.

This isn't fair, she thinks. *It isn't fair that all of you went away. You were the ones who beat me.* You *were the ones who drowned me. You starved me. You choked me. You raped and burned and tortured me. You wrote the stories of my life. You gave me life only to kill me over and over again.*

She is not of the dead, nor is she of the living; she is a thing created wholly out of perception, grief, anger, and belief. She is a small fracture in the structure of the multiverse. She has no identity save for that given to her by the vigil group. Her past —*pasts,* we should say —was also given to her by the vigil group.

You gave me life only to kill me and then give me life and then kill me over and over again. And it isn't fair. I never knew what it was like to be alive, to run and laugh and fly kites and blow out birthday candles and hold my first puppy and blush after my first kiss, you took that from me, and then you went away.

The smoke and flames surround her, and at last we hear the sound of sirens.

Leigh smiles.

I'll show you *what it's like,* she thinks. *You'll know how it feels. I know all of you, I know your children's names. You did this to me. Now it's my turn.*

The flames do not harm her. She seems to draw strength from them. We cannot move away quickly enough. We must now find another place from which to watch and observe what Leigh will do to those who so unfairly did this to her.

Now it's my turn.

Perhaps we can find refuge on another age, in another story, in a different book. Somewhere in the white spaces between words. We can watch safely from there.

You gave me life only to kill me over and over again.

We whisper goodbye to her.

I'll show you what it's like.

And it is here that our part in the story comes (almost) to an end.

Should you believe any part of this to be untrue, then perhaps you are one of the people who, one night not so long ago, stood outside an abandoned house holding a lighted sacrament candle and creating a wretched, ugly, painful, and perpetually unfair past for a little girl who did not exist until you gave her a name, gave her death (which was her life), and then gave her life (which was her death).

We can watch what happens to you. But you will not see us. As for yourself, you can only listen now ....

Requiem: Audio Snuff Files

Before each call is replayed, there are these words from the dispatcher: "Nine-one-one, where is your emergency?"

... house across the street is on fire and someone's screaming — there's a fire and it sounds like somebody's shooting a gun — can see him walking through the smoke, sweeping his arms from side to side — little girl in the street, she's laughing and dancing in circles — the fire's so bad the whole goddamn thing's collapsing — ash and sparks and smoke everywhere — Jesus Christ he just killed two little kids, just walked right up to them and shot 'em in their heads and now he's heading toward the house next door — where are the fire trucks — how long does it take for a fuckin' ambulance to get here — the signing girl, she's ... ohgod ... she's picking up part of a little boy's body and she's ... she's *dancing* with it — still shooting, I think it's some kind of semiautomatic, maybe an AK-47 or something like that — old woman is still alive, she's crawling across the lawn and she looks so bad — some of the fire is spreading to the other houses and everybody's running into the street — running around — so much noise — can't see anything — bangbangbang is all I can hear — ohgod, please don't shoot me, please don't — believe something like this could happen here — get some help here, please — he walked right past the little dancing girl, he didn't shoot her —singing's getting louder and her laughing is even louder than the gunshots —help us help us help us—people are falling dead in the street—goddamn chalk outlines, people's dead bodies are dropping right into these goddamn chalk outlines and they land just like the outlines are shaped—so much noise—so much gunfire—so much blood—so much screaming—can't breathe from all the smoke—so much smoke—so much death—helpushelpushelpus—how—why—can't believe this is happening—just killed my husband right in front of our house—can't believe this—why—we're good people—decent people—we didn't do anything—why—two little kids on fire, they just bolted into the street and the ambulance ran right over them—scattered in pieces—a hand on my lawn and its fingers are moving, burning—where's Mom, where is she—we're good people—we didn't do anything to deserve this —we didn't—we didn't—we didn't do anything—can't imagine what would make someone do this—can't imagine why—can't imagine what would make someone

In Hollow Houses

Introduction by Lisa Morton

I should maybe begin this introduction with a disclaimer: Gary Braunbeck is not only one of my favorite writers, he's also one of my favorite people. Gary the human being (or, for those of us lucky enough to have made Gary a part of our own lives, Gary the friend) is like Gary the writer: Richly empathetic, deeply observant of both life's beauty and ugliness, genuinely horrified by everyday evils like casual violence and abandoned children, more interested in society's damaged castoffs than those at the top. If you've read Gary's extraordinary nonfiction collection *To Each Their Darkness*, you probably know why he'd have a special fondness for these damaged characters —because he's suffered some pretty serious damage himself. Gary, however, is stronger than his characters because he found his own road to recovery, without benefit of an extraordinary guide. His recovery is his art.

"In Hollow Houses" wasn't the first Gary Braunbeck story I read, but it has all the same properties that captured me with my first taste: It's squarely situated within the horror genre, but has the Big Ideas found in the best science fiction (if you're anything like me, one of your responses after reading a Braunbeck work might be, "How does somebody think this stuff up?"); the protagonists are impoverished and handicapped, while the antagonist is someone so caught up in their own need that they lack any capacity for human compassion; and the horror —because that is Gary's first and foremost genre of choice—is visceral, the kind of stuff that pricks your skin until it gets in and burrows.

This story was originally written for an anthology called *Whitley Strieber's Aliens*. "In Hollow Houses" could be taught in a master class for writers on how to take someone else's toys and make them your playthings. The story includes all the tropes of a standard alien story — abductees, men in black, experimentation, invasion —but Gary has turned all those tropes so far around that you almost have to read the story twice to get aliens out of it at all. The aliens at center stage here aren't little green men but little broken people. When I asked Gary to tell me about this story, he said, "At its heart I like to think it's about loneliness and how redemption can be found even in the most squalid of circumstances." The next time I hear some other writer say they can't create within someone else's universe, I want to hand them this story, hold up that sentence, and dare them to tell me that "In Hollow Houses" is not a classic Gary Braunbeck story, an exquisitely rendered work about how all of us aliens get through life, told by somebody who knows.

I am very proud to call Gary Braunbeck both a fellow horror writer and a good friend, and I'm also proud of being given the opportunity to introduce and share "In Hollow Houses" with you. This is fiction that gives us all a chance to look up out of the gutter and into the stars.

In Hollow Houses

"Still there are moments when one feels free from one's own identification with human limitations and inadequacies. At such moments, one imagines that one stands on some small spot on an unknown planet, gazing in amazement at the cold yet profoundly moving beauty of the eternal, the unfathomable: life and death flow into one, and there is neither evolution nor destiny; only being."
—Albert Einstein

"Heaven wheels above you displaying to you her eternal glories and still your eyes are on the ground."
—Dante

I

Down in the Rusty Room where Buddy lived these words had been written on one of the walls:

someone come

i'm tired of naming things
and then forgetting their names
the voice in the sky is
loneliness
and the night is
restlessness
someone come

Even though she was only a little girl of six (well, *almost* six), she knew that Buddy had written the words, and that it was some kind of prayer, and that made her sad because she knew what it was like to feel so scared and tired and alone, like you belonged somewhere else but there wasn't anybody listening to you when you asked to leave.

and where do I live?
under the tracks of the l
in a cardboard box
that's falling apart

within the cell life is hard, life is long
within the cell, life is hard

someone please come

II

Leah watched in silence as her mother handed the baby over to the man in the dark coat and knew she wouldn't be seeing her little sister again. It always happened this way: Mommy would go away with the men in the dark coats to the Shiny Place (that's what Mommy called it) and Leah would be all by herself for weeks at a time in the abandoned warehouse that was her home; it was kind of scary for a little while after Mommy left, but it was easier getting the people at the restaurants to give her food when she was by herself—"Oh, you poor child," they all said, stuffing bread and hamburgers and doughnuts and little cartons of milk into the paper bags, "what kind of a mother would do this to a child?"—so she never had to dig through the garbage dumpsters like she had to with Mommy, and there was Merc and Chief Wetbrain who were always on their corner a few blocks away, they were really nice and had helped her before...but mostly there was Buddy. She thought it was a good thing that she had Buddy around to take care of her when Mommy was gone; he always made things better.

The dark-coat man took the baby, smiled down at it, then snapped his fingers; another man in a dark coat and sunglasses (Leah wondered why none of the dark-coat men ever took their sunglasses off, even at night) got out of the car and handed Mommy a thick envelope. That made Leah feel even worse. She knew there was money in the envelope that the dark-coat man was giving to Mommy for the baby, and Mommy would use it to buy more needle-stuff that would last until the next time the men in the dark coats returned to take her to the Shiny Place, and after a couple of weeks she'd come back all pregnant, then have the baby, then the dark-coat men'd be there with their envelopes full of money.

Leah wanted to cry. She hadn't even got to give her little sister a name—and this had been her *first* sister, too.

She felt a tear forming and closed her eyes, taking a deep breath and Removing herself (that's what Buddy called it) from everything going on around her, watching as silvery shimmer-bursts of light went off behind her closed lids, and she did just as Buddy had taught her, she reached out in her mind like in daydream and snagged a ride on one of the shimmers—

—and saw the Earth and the Moon as they must have looked to astronauts moving through the cold, glittering depths of the cosmos; the dry, pounded surface of the moon, its craters dark and secretive and dead as an old bone; just beyond was a milky-white radiance that cast liquid-grey shadows across the lunarscape while distant stars winked at her, then a burst of heat and pressure and suddenly she was below the moist, gleaming membrane of the bright blue sky, Earth rising exuberantly into her line of sight: She marveled at the majestic, swirling drifts of white clouds covering and uncovering the half-hidden masses of land and watched the continents themselves in motion, drifting apart on their crustal plates, held afloat by the molten fire beneath, and when the plates had settled and the rivers had carved their paths and the trees had spread their wondrous arms, there came next the People and their races and mysteries through the ages, and in her mind she danced through some of those Mysteries, Buddy holding her hand as they stood atop places with wonderful and odd names, places like Cheops' Pyramid and the Tower of Ra, Zoroaster's Temple and the Javanese Borobudur, the Krishna Shrine, the Valhalla Plateau and Woton's Throne, and then they started dancing through King Arthur's Castle and Gawain's Abyss and Lancelot's Point, then they went to Solomon's Temple at Moriah, then the Aztec Amphitheatre, Toltec Point, Cardenas Butte, and Alarcon Terrace before stopping at last in front of the great Wall of Skulls at Chichén Itzá: The skulls were awash by a sea of glowing colors, changing shape in the lights from above, their mouths opening as if to speak to her, flesh

spreading across bone to form faces and her heart—oh, her heart felt almost freed and—

Mommy smacked her on the shoulder. "Stop daydreaming, damn you."

The dark-coat man handed the baby to one of his friends, then walked over to Leah, took off his sunglasses, and smiled down at her. His eyes were cold and black and made Leah feel like he'd swallow her up if she looked into them for too long.

"Please don't," said Mommy. "She's all I've got."

One of the other men grabbed Leah's mother and held her back.

"All you've got like my ass chews gum," said the dark-coat man. "You have about as much love in your heart for this child as I do for you, you worthless piece of shit."

"Don't you call my mommy names!" shouted Leah.

"I apologize," said the dark-coat man, kneeling down in front of Leah. "Tell me, sweetheart, how old are you now?"

"I'll be six pretty soon."

"The thirteenth of next month, as a matter of fact," he said. "And you know what's going to happen then?"

"Huh-uh."

"Why, we're going to come back and take *both* you and your mommy to a birthday party for you."

"Really? In the Shiny Place?"

The dark-coat man shot an angry glance at Leah's mother. "Chatty little thing, aren't you?"

"Go fuck yourself."

"And charming, to boot." He looked back at Leah. "Yes, sweetheart, we're going to have a birthday party for you in the Shiny Place. Then you and your mommy can live there, if you want. It's very nice; it's clean and you can watch television and play games and there'll be food every day and you won't have to worry about ever being left alone again."

"Can I still see my friends?"

Something in the dark-coat man's eyes brightened when she asked this. "What friends do you mean, sweetheart?"

"You know...Merc and Chief Wetbrain, and Randi—she's a singer who comes around to visit Merc sometimes."

"*Of course* you can still see them, Leah. We'll even bring them to the party if you want."

"Could they live with us, maybe?"

"Maybe. Are there any other friends you want to come to the party?"

She almost told him about Buddy but something in the way he'd said *any other friends* didn't sound very nice, so Leah just shook her head.

The dark-coat man stopped smiling. "Well, then...you think about it, sweetheart. If there's anyone else you want to be there, you just tell us where they are and we'll invite them." He reached out and touched her cheek. His hand felt like cold, raw restaurant meat. "Listen, sweetheart, we need to, uh...do something to you right now, if it's okay."

"Don't touch her!" shouted Mommy.

"Shut up," said the dark-coat man. Then, to Leah: "Would you do a big favor for me? Would you get into the back seat of my car and let us take a little blood from your arm?"

"W-why?"

"It's all right, Leah; the man who'll do it is a doctor so you don't have to—"

"I don't like needles," said Leah, as much to her mother as the dark-coat man.

"I know you don't, honey, but we need it...we need it in case your little sister gets sick, see? You both have the same blood-type—do you know what that is?"

"Uh-huh."

"Good. You both have the same blood-type, and it's very rare; you're the only other girl in this part of the country who has it, and if something happens and your little sister needs blood, we wouldn't have any."

Leah thought about it for a moment. "Will it hurt?"

"Only a little sting, I promise."

Leah's lower lip trembled. "I don't want her to be sick."

"Oh, she's not sick, hon, but if she *were* to get sick...."

"Okay."

"I won't let you!" shouted Mommy.

"That's enough from you," said the dark-coat man, rising to his feet. "She loves her little sister, don't you, Leah? She only wants to help, and if she doesn't, that might spoil things. We don't want to spoil things for her, *do we?*"

"Will she be there?" asked Leah, pointing at the baby. "At my party?"

"If you want."

"I do, I really do. I never had a little sister before."

"Does she have a name?"

"Huh-uh."

"Ah, well...that can be one of your presents. You can give your little sister a name. Would you like that?"

"Oh, *yes...!*"

"Consider it done, then."

Leah got into the back seat and let the nice old doctor with the gray hair take some blood from her arm; it took a lot longer than she thought it would because he had to fill a clear plastic bag, and it left her feeling a little dizzy but then he gave her some lemonade and cookies and she felt better.

As she sat there finishing off the cookies and starting in on the King Dons ("Maybe you'd better have something more," the doctor had said), she heard Mommy talking with the dark-coat man.

"What're you going to do with her?" said Mommy.

"None of your business. You've not asked about what happened to any of the others, so why the sudden concern?"

"Because...I dunno...she's not such a bad kid, y'know? I love—"

"Oh, spare me. God, you're disgusting."

"You can't talk to me like that!"

"I can talk to you any way I damned well please. Aside from the fact it took us three fucking years to find you, the only reason we've let you keep her *this* long is because she's formed—for whatever bizarre reasons—an emotional attachment to you. *She loves you.* We didn't expect that. But don't think that means you're safe, dearie. You could be disappeared like *that"* —he snapped his fingers —"and no one would give a damn."

"Maybe," said Mommy. "And maybe not. Maybe I got friends around town, you know? And maybe I gave a couple of them copies of a letter I wrote, and they'll send those letters if I turn up missing."

"Do you really think that just because my division works outside the boundaries of the Federal Government we can't affect something so puny as the U.S. Postal Service? Christ! You don't *deserve* to be her mother. "

"What is she to you, anyway?"

"A pinball," said the dark-coat man, then laughed. "Oh, my, the expression on your face—BoBo the Dog-Faced Boy looked more intelligent. You have no idea what I'm talking about, do you?"

"You never made a whole lot of sense in all the years I've known you."

"And I fear it's prevented us from becoming closer. The heart breaks. Listen: A few weeks ago I was in Jerusalem checking out reports on a little girl who we thought might be like Leah. What happened with her is none of your business and secondary to the point of my story, anyway.

"I was walking through one of the oldest sections of the city and admiring its ancient beauty, when I got to thinking about how Jerusalem was perceived in medieval times: Many religious groups considered it — and still *do* consider it —the center of the universe, the naval of the world where heaven and earth join. It was there at the center of the universe that God spoke to His prophets and the People of the Book; Jews come to worship at the wall of their temple near the Holy of Holies, Christians come to follow the steps of their Lord in His Final Passion, and Muslims worship at the Dome of the Rock where Mohammed received the Koran.

"In ancient times, there was a center to the old city marked by Roman crossroads that divided the city and the earth into four quadrants—the fulcrum of medieval geography. Most of the roads disappeared long ago, but to this day, at each corner of the crossroads, there still stands a Roman pillar. So I found myself wandering into the very center-within-the-center of the universe. Do you know what's there? Of all the shrines and statues, temples and rocks, symbols and what-have-you that *could* be there to mark the exact, precise center of the universe, can you guess what I found?

"A pinball parlor. Rows and rows of pinball machines. Astonishing. I laughed, I couldn't help it. Determinists think of the universe as a clockwork device. I see it as a pinball machine. Playing pinball requires total concentration, the right combination of skill and chance, an understanding and mastery of indeterminacy as the balls fly about, interacting with the bumpers and cushions. It creates an ersatz reality that integrates into the human nervous system in a remarkable way, and I realized that it was no accident that pinball machines stand at the center of the universe, because in order to know the universe we must observe it, and in the act of observation, uncontrolled and random processes are initiated into reality. I can see from that blank look in your eyes that I'm losing you, so I'll make it simple: children like your daughter will someday soon become the pinballs in the machine of the universe, and whoever has them, whoever controls them, is master of the game and need not worry that the device will tilt on them."

Mommy shook her head. "Man, you are *so* full of shit."

"I take back what I said about you before; you don't disgust me. I pity you too much to feel disgust."

"Feeling better now?" asked the doctor, jostling Leah's arm.

"Yes, sir," she said. "Thanks for the King Dons. I don't get to have a lot of snacks."

"Would you like some more to take with you?"

"Yes, please."

As the doctor was putting the extra packs of King Dons into a paper bag for her, he asked, "Tell me, Leah, do you get many headaches?"

"Sometimes."

"Are they bad?"

"Yeah. Sometimes they hurt *real* bad."

"Can you show me where they start, these headaches?"

"Sure." She put a finger on the bridge of her nose. "Right here. I get a runny nose, too. Sometimes my nose bleeds a little."

"I see," said the doctor, then reached into one of his pockets and pulled out a bottle of pills. "What you've got, Leah, is a condition called sinusitis. It's not uncommon for children of...for children like yourself. Don't you worry yourself, hon; it's not too serious, if treated properly. Here, you take these pills—and *don't* let your mommy see them, all right? She'd only take them away from you."

"...'kay...?"

"The red ones are for your headaches, all right? Take one when the pain gets real bad. The blue ones are for infection; you should take one of those three times a day. Can you remember all that, Leah?"

"Yes, sir."

The doctor smiled and touched her face; his hand wasn't at all like the dark-coat man's; his hand was warm and kind, like a Grandpa's hand—or, rather, how Leah *imagined* a Grandpa's hand would feel.

"You're a very pretty little girl, Leah, has anyone told you that?"

"No, sir."

"And with the 'sir'! So polite."

"Thank you."

"I know a lot of this must be confusing for you, dear, but when we come back and take you to your birthday party next month, you'll understand everything."

"My little sister's gonna be there. The other man said so."

"And so she shall be." Then the doctor leaned forward, pulled Leah close, and whispered, "Your brothers might be there, as well."

Leah felt her heart skip a beat. "All of them?"

"Yes. And maybe—and you must not tell this to *anyone*—maybe your daddy will be there, too."

Leah was so excited she could barely contain herself. For all of her life she'd wondered about her daddy, who he was, where he came from, what he did for a living. All she really knew was that the men drove Mommy to see Daddy whenever they took her away. And now she might maybe get to see her daddy for the first time.

In her heart, wizards, angels, and faeries danced.

"Oh, *thank you*," she said, then gave the doctor a great big hug and kissed him on the cheek. He hugged her back, and there was something sad in the way he did it, something that made Leah think of the words on Buddy's wall: *the voice in the night sky is loneliness...*

"You remember about the pills," said the doctor, "and about our little secret about your daddy, okay?"

"Okay," said Leah, stuffing the bottle of pills into one of her pockets and climbing out of the car, the bag of King Dons clutched to her chest like discovered treasure. She wondered if Buddy liked King Dons, if he'd ever had them, and looked forward to sharing them with her best-best friend in the whole world.

Mommy grabbed Leah's arm and they ran out of the alley. The only sound Leah could hear now was the laughter of the dark-coat man; it bounced off the alley walls, ugly and mean, coming after her and Mommy like some crazy junkyard dog; the sound wailed and roared in the slick darkness of the rain-dampened streets, and under the laughter Leah could hear her little sister starting to cry and suddenly she felt awful, like she'd just run over a bird with her bike. She felt like a killer. She didn't want to leave her sister in the alley with the dark-coat man. The alley was cold and wet and dark and smelled like somebody threw up.

"Mommy, please go and get her back."

"Be quiet."

"Please? She's c-c-crying, hear? She misses us and—"

"*I said shut up!*" screamed her mother, slapping Leah hard across the face. "Shut your miserable little mouth, goddammit, or I swear I'll...I'll let Jewel take you up to his room next time!"

Leah went rigid with fear. Jewel was the short little bald-headed man Mommy bought her needle-stuff from. He was old and wrinkly and sweated all the time and was always trying to touch Leah whenever he saw her. "Young and tasty," he said. "I like 'em when they're young and tasty." Leah didn't know what Jewel wanted to do with her, but she knew it probably wasn't very nice because Jewel had a little girl named Denise who was with him all the time, and she always had bruises and cuts on her face and over her body and sometimes burn marks around her wrists and she never said anything whenever Leah talked to her and her eyes were always staring out at something only she seemed able to see, and whatever it was she saw made her empty.

"Oh, no, *please Mommy, d-d-don't do that!*"

"Then be quiet. You've caused me enough trouble as it is."

Leah's face twisted into a tight, hard, painful knot, and she couldn't stop the tears from coming then. She thought that her mommy loved her and would never do something like that. But maybe—

—you have about as much love in your heart for that child as I do for you—

—Mommy only said that because she felt about bad the baby. Leah hoped so but she couldn't ask her mother because Mommy would only get madder, so she decided to wait and tell Buddy about it tonight after Mommy did her needle-thing and rolled her eyes and shook and fell asleep sort-of. Buddy would say the right things to make her understand and make it all better.

Leah was glad that Mommy didn't know about Buddy and his secret Rusty Room underneath the warehouse basement.

Buddy didn't like her mother. Not one little bit.

III

and where do i live?
in the alleys behind the
cans
abandonment my blanket
no way to slough the fever

and where do i live?
in songs unheard
in the flutter of bound wings that
don't know they're bound
where?
somewhere else
not here

within the cell, life is long, life is hard,
within the cell, life is hard

who will take me?

IV

Leah smiled as Chief Wetbrain drew a chalk circle around him, scooted into its center (he had to scoot everywhere because he didn't have any legs), and started playing his saxophone. Leah thought it was too bad that people called him Chief Wetbrain (she did it, too, and always felt bad afterward) because it was such an ugly name and they only used it because he got drunk a lot on account of the pain in his leg stumps. His real name was Jimmy NightEagle, and Leah wished he'd tell more people to call him that; it was the name of a king, and that's what Jimmy was in her eyes.

Mommy was down the street at Jewel's apartment buying her needle-stuff and had said it was okay for Leah to go visit with her friends. Leah liked listening to Jimmy play his saxophone; his music made her feel less scared and sometimes, if she closed her eyes and listened real hard, the way Buddy had taught her, she could hear the unspoken words in Jimmy's songs: *Who will take me? I don't belong here.*

(*...someone come...*)

Listening the way Buddy had taught her, she heard Jimmy's song cry out a tale composed of notes that became Kachinas and Crow Mothers and They Who Breathed The Land Into Being; she heard it turn round in the breeze and catch raindrops that held his memories of nights on the plains, soaring above the heads of the people as they passed, sprinkling them with hints of things he still knew and they had long ago forgotten, secrets of the Earth and Time hidden in the silences between the notes; a breath, a beat, songs of the Elders and their tales of the Fiery-Sky Ones, another breath, another beat, and the notes multiplied like the birds of the sky after solstice, power, strength, and courage in his grip as he pulled the sax closer to his ruined body, breathing his soul into the reeds like a fine medicine man should—and over there, a glint in a passing pair of eyes, yes, as the song banked on the winds and came back to him, more than it was before, making him feel that he was back among his people again, back where he should have been all along, grace covering him like tree-fallen leaves in autumn, so good, yes, I am ready: The time is upon me to fly.

Jimmy stopped playing as a young man in a three-piece suit walked by and threw some change into a tin cup setting between his stumps. Jimmy smiled and lifted his hat to the young man in thanks, then looked into the cup. "*Sokelas!*" he said, taking out the three quarters and jingling them in his hand. "And my folks used to worry about me making a living as a jazz musician." He looked at Leah, then gave her one of the coins. "That's just for being a pretty sight to these tired eyes."

"How come you're tired?"

"*How come I'm—?* I'm sorry, I didn't mean to snap like that."

"...s'okay."

"No, it isn't," said Jimmy, taking hold of her hand. "I'm tired because I've been having too many bad dreams lately. I'm tired because I feel more and more like *eceyanunia*—a fool—every day. I'm tired because no one answers the music." He pulled her a little closer, putting his arm around her waist. Leah liked it when Jimmy hugged her, it wasn't at all like when Jewel touched her—moist and chilly and sick-making; Jimmy's hugs were gentle and kind and made her feel loved.

"There was a time, Leah, before I left to be educated in the White schools, when I would play my music at night under the stars and know that it would be heard by *Matotipila*, would linger in the heart of *Wanagitacanku*, answered by *Tayamni*, but not here, not in the city. There's too much noise, too much anger and violence, and the buildings block out the heavens. Sometimes I find myself wondering if the heavens are still really there." He shook his head. "Does any of this make sense to you?"

"Uh-huh, some."

"I like you very much, Leah. You're a good friend and I will miss you when I'm gone."

"You're not leaving, are you?"

"Oh, not right now, probably not for a while, but I've been thinking about it for a long time. Especially since the dreams started."

"What kind of dreams? What happens in them?"

Jimmy laughed but there was no humor in it. "You see, that's the thing, I can't really say what happens because I don't know, exactly. It's not so much what *happens* in them, anyway, as it is...the *impression* they leave when I wake up. I feel like I don't belong here, but I can't go back home because I don't belong there anymore, either. Not that they'd have me, and if they wouldn't, then...who *will* take me?" He reached out and massaged one of his stumps. "Get drunk and pass out under one trailer, have it back over you and crush your legs—do this once, and people think you're incompetent."

Leah giggled.

"Ah, good girl," said Jimmy. "There was a time when you wouldn't've realized I was making a joke."

"But it was only a half-joke. It was still funny, though."

"I'm glad you liked it. I like hearing you laugh; it's a lovely sound. I wish you made it more often."

"I know. Buddy says that I—" She gasped, then covered her mouth with her hands, eyes wide. Oh, God! She'd never mentioned Buddy to anyone before and now —

"Buddy," whispered Jimmy. "So that's his name? In my dream he was called *Peye'wik*: It-Is-Approaching."

Slowly, Leah pulled her hands away from her mouth. "You know about Buddy?"

Jimmy reached into one of his pockets and took out a folded piece of paper that he handed to Leah. "There was one image from the dreams that I remembered early on, and I drew it on that paper. Take a look and tell me if those're—tell me if it looks familiar to you."

Leah unfolded the piece of paper; most of it was blank, except for two large, dark, slanted, opposing almond-shapes in the middle. "*Buddy's eyes,*" she said.

"'Someone come,'" said Jimmy.

"*W-what?*"

"'Someone come.' Buddy wrote those words on a wall somewhere, didn't he?"

"Uh-huh."

"He's very lonely, isn't he, your Buddy?"

"I guess. But with him it's like...it's like with Denise, that girl who lives with Jewel?"

Jimmy closed his eyes and nodded his head. "*A Hollow House.* More pain than person. *Goddamn* that little pervert."

"With Buddy, it's like he's so lonely he don't even know it."

"Oh, I doubt that," said Jimmy. "I think he knows exactly how lonely he is. He's just like us, Leah; he should be somewhere else."

Just then Merc came around the corner pulling something behind him that made a funny *thunka-thunka-shisk! thunka-thunka-shisk!* noise: An orange crate nailed to a set of planks that were supported by roller-skate wheels.

"Oh, *man,*" said Merc, coming to a stop next to them. "I read this article in the science section of the paper yesterday about that damn Wooly Mammoth they found upstate a couple weeks ago—you know, the one that was almost completely preserved? Anyway, these science dudes, they were makin' all this brouhaha over the buttercups that were in the thing's mouth. Seems these buttercups were as totally preserved as the mammoth, right? But what makes everything so righteously fucked—oops, sorry, Leah, gotta learn to watch my mouth—what makes it all really weird, right, is that buttercups evidently release some kind of chemical into your system when you eat them that acts like a natural anti-freeze, y'dig? The mammoth had itself a bellyful of buttercups, so they're saying that's why it was so well-preserved, but—whoa, almost lost track of where I's going with this—but the thing is, buttercups can only grow in a moist, warm climate, like around seventy-eight degrees or so, and these buttercups in the mammoth's belly, they weren't dehydrated, and neither was the mammoth. You know what that means? That means in order for the mammoth to've been preserved so well and without dehydration, the temperature had to've dropped from around eighty degrees to something like three-hundred *below zero* in a matter of seconds! And these science wizards, they got no idea what happened, let alone how it could've happened, and if they can't speculate on what happened, then they got no way of being able to predict if or when it might happen again. Man, I tell you, that *messed up* my breakfast big time! Knowing that at any given second we could all be slammed into the fuc—uh, *friggin'* deep freeze and there's nothing we can do about it. It could all be over"—he snapped his fingers—"like *that*, and I spent ten minutes trying to decide what to wear today. Not that I got what you'd call an *ex-ten-sive* wardrobe. That game on your head, or what?"

"Do you ever just say 'hello'?" asked Jimmy.

"Uh, yeah, right. Forgettin' my manners left and right today. Hello."

"What'cha got there?" said Leah, pointing at the orange crate.

"Huh? Oh, this?" He stood back and gestured with his arms like a model at an automobile show. "This here's the new Chiefmobile, first one off the line."

Jimmy stared. "You...you *made* this for me?"

"I get kinda tired of watching you do the Stumpy Dance when you walk. Them little short steps give me a pain. Takes forever to get anywhere with you. I figure this way, you hop in the Chiefmobile and we'll be *burnin'* up pavement. Do wonders for clearing up my schedule. So, you like it?"

Jimmy shrugged (but gave Leah a quick wink), and said, "It's all right, if you like that sort of thing."

"*That sort of thing?* I been digging through dumpsters for the last two weeks trying to find four sets of wheels that're all the same size and all you got to say is, 'If you like that sort of thing'? Talk about your ingrates. Here we got you *trans-por-tation*, Chief. You hear what I'm saying? Take your act on the road. Make 'em Big Wampum, go truckin' on down that Happy Trail in style."

"It is perhaps one of the ten most wondrous sights I have ever beheld in all my life. Why, in all the history of history itself, there has never been a more resplendent orange-crate chariot. I think I'm safe in saying that, yes."

Merc cocked his head to one side as if trying to decide if Jimmy was yanking his chain or not, then gave a quick nod. "Well, that's more like it. Man needs to know his labors're appreciated."

"Very much," said Jimmy, reaching out and patting the side of Merc's leg. "Very much. Thank you."

Merc knelt down and clapped Jimmy on the shoulder. "No *hombre* of mine's gonna be stumpin' round and giving himself more pain."

The two of them looked at one another for a moment.

In the silence, Leah heard the song of two hearts: Friendship.

She ran over and gave Merc a big hug and kiss; she couldn't help it.

"What's that for?" asked Merc.

"'Cause you're a sweetie."

"Uh-oh, this's starting to get too warm and fuzzy for me—but thanks for the hug and smoochie, darlin'. Nice to know the Merc's still got it for the ladies—speaking of: You seen Randi around here today, Chief?"

"No, but I heard she's selling—uh, I heard she's *singing* at some club in the East End."

"Singing?" Merc looked from Jimmy to Leah, then back to Jimmy again. "Oh, yeah, right! I forgot about her, uh, *singing* engagement."

"I know what a hooker is," said Leah. "You don't have to talk around me like I'm stupid or something."

Jimmy and Merc burst out laughing.

"Here I thought we were being so *co-vert,*" said Merc.

"It's okay," said Leah. "I tell everybody that Randi's a singer so they won't know."

"Well, that's darned thoughtful of you." Merc touched the side of her face. "Where's your mom today?—no, wait, don't tell me." He looked at Jimmy. "Jewel's place?"

Jimmy nodded.

"Jeez-Louise." He looked back at Leah. "You two still squattin' in that warehouse down on 11th?"

"Uh-huh. It's not too bad there."

"She's got no business keeping you in a place like that and usin' her money to buy—"

"*Merc,*" said Jimmy; a warning.

"I can't help it," shouted Merc, rising to his feet. "Shit, when I was workin' over in Panama a couple years ago, we'd been hired to blow a worthless fuck like Jewel right out of his socks. Him, and about forty of his boys. I enjoyed it a little too much, y'know? Won't do for a merc to start takin' sides. That's how come I got out."

"I know," said Jimmy.

Merc smiled—and it wasn't a nice smile. "Still got me a little firepower." He looked around, nervous, then pulled open one side of his jacket to reveal a large silver 9mm semiautomatic tucked into the waist of his pants.

"Oh, great," said Jimmy, "look at this: *Son of The Equalizer*—close your coat, for chrissakes. People will think you're flashing us."

"Hey, if I decided to whip out the man-meat," said Merc, closing his coat, "you'd *know* you been flashed. Didn't mean to shock you, Leah."

"You didn't."

Jimmy laughed.

Merc pulled himself up straight. "Gettin' off the point here a bit, ain't we? I'd just *love* to dust our little Jewel. 'Bout the only way we'd ever get Denise away from him. And you know, don't you, Chief, that it's gotta be us. Nobody else give's a rat's ass. We're just partial people to all of them, and you don't pay no attention to a partial person."

"My father had a term for us," said Jimmy. "He called people like us 'Hollow Houses'; the Unbelonging: Vessels with homeless spirits."

"We don't belong here," said Merc.

"We should be somewhere else," whispered Jimmy.

And Leah thought: *Someone come.*

"Well, Darlin'," said Merc, laying a hand on top of Leah's head, "I imagine your mom's gonna be havin' herself a private little party tonight. Maybe Jimmy and me—bet'cha didn't think I knew your real name, did'ya, Jimmy?—maybe the two of us'll cruise on by in the Chiefmobile later and see how you're doing. Can't never tell how a person's gonna act after they shoot that shit into their veins." He saw something behind them, then rolled his eyes. "Speaking of shit..."

"Watch it, Merc," said Jimmy. "I'm serious."

"Leah!" shouted Mommy, trying to sound nice and almost making it. "C'mon, hon. Time to get something to eat."

"Bitch's gonna buy her daughter some real *food?*" whispered Merc to Jimmy. "Sorry state, when junkies start thinking of others. Almost enough to make you believe there's a God."

"Put a sock in it, will you?" said Jimmy.

Mommy came up behind Leah and grabbed her arm. "Say good-bye to your friends, hon. You can maybe come back tomorrow."

"How's Jewel doing?" said Merc.

"Fine," snapped Mommy. "He said to send his regards."

"I'll bet," muttered Jimmy.

"You see Denise?" asked Leah.

"Oh, she, uh...she wasn't feeling too well today, hon. Jewel was making her stay in bed."

Jimmy snorted a nasty laugh. "What a tactful way to put it."

Mommy pushed Leah behind her. "All right, assholes, you've had your fun. I don't need this shit from the likes of you. Nice crate, by the way."

"That's the Chiefmobile, Mommy!"

"It's a goddamned orange crate, for hauling garbage." And she turned around and pulled Leah along.

Leah managed to turn around and wave at Jimmy and Merc. They waved back, but didn't look very happy.

As they got to the corner, Leah looked over at Jewel's building and saw Denise standing at her window. She looked pale and empty and sad. The lower half of the window was foggy with steam, and Denise was drawing patterns in the condensation with her finger. When she finished her drawing, she knelt down and looked out through the two opposing almond-shapes.

Below the almonds, she'd written: *Someone come.*

Leah wanted to touch her, to tell Denise that she'd be her friend.

Buddy would like Denise; Merc and Jimmy, too.

Partial people; Hollow Houses.

"Who will take me?" Leah whispered.

"*What?*" snapped Mommy.

"Nothin'."

"Christ Almighty. Fuckin' *starchild*. Airhead's more like it."

"I'm sorry, Mommy."

"Not half as much as I am. C'mon. I suppose we should get you something to eat. Just eat it quick. I need to get back."

"Yes, Mommy."

V

Leah finished untying the funny rubber band from around her mother's arm and threw it on top of the box they kept all their clothes in. Leah didn't understand why her mother always left that thing around her arm; she had lots of time to take it all the way off after the needle-thing but she never did: she just loosened it enough so the vein would go back down after she stuck the needle in. Then she shook a lot and made weird noises, sighing and growling at the same time. A lot of the time Leah even had to take the needle out of her mother's arm after Mommy went to sleep sort-of and that made her nervous because she was afraid she might slip and Mommy would start to bleed too much and maybe die. She didn't like these nights because Mommy wasn't her mother anymore, she was like some zombie from those old black-and-white horror movies Jewel watched on his television. Mommy knew a lot of zombies; they always came around to see her after the dark-coat man gave her money for her babies.

They all had black eyes and runny noses and were shaky and smelled like old hamburger. Their skin was gray and crusty and all of them had the same little hole-bruises on their arms. They would give Mommy a little money or food or something for a "taste" of the needle-stuff and then light the candles. Leah thought that part was kind of pretty; all of them sitting huddled over the candles, heating up the shiny spoons and lighting the sticks that smelled like Christmas trees. They would laugh and tell jokes and the candle flames made them all look like broken dolls, and it was kind of soft and glowing...but then they'd take out the needles and those funny rubber bands that they wrapped around their arms and it wasn't pretty anymore.

That's when Leah would leave to go see Buddy.

Just like tonight. She was glad that Mommy had done the needle-thing by herself because that meant Leah didn't have to worry about someone else trying to stop her, so she wadded up some old clothes and put them under her mother's head for a pillow, covered her with an old rug so she wouldn't get too cold, and silently crept to the bottom of the stairs. This was fun, like she was in one of those old movies where they were escaping from jail. She reached the bottom of the stairs and walked straight ahead into the middle of the basement where a bunch of barrels were stacked up, then pushed one of them aside and crawled through the opening, careful not to jostle anything and make the stack come crashing down. In the middle of the floor was a loose board, and Leah slid it to one side. This part was never hard to do, the warehouse was all stinking and falling apart, anyway, like all the buildings around here. There were probably all kinds of loose boards that she could rip up, but she didn't want to. This was her special board, her special secret; she had first seen Buddy's lights glowing from underneath this loose board, and because she wanted to keep it a secret, she had stacked all the barrels around it like a bunch of pop cans so no one else would be able to find it. She didn't ever want Mommy to find out about Buddy because then she'd probably tell the dark-coat man about it and Leah just *knew* that dark-coat man had been talking about Buddy when asked about her having *any other friends*.

Sometimes she felt like she had to be scared all the time.

She couldn't stop thinking about what Mommy had said to her, about letting Jewel take her up to his room. That hurt Leah because she loved her mother; very, very much.

She squeezed through the opening left by the missing board, turned around once she was inside, and pulled the board back into place. This way, no one would ever be able to find her. The way she felt right now,

Leah wasn't sure she ever wanted to go back to her mother; maybe if she didn't come back, Mommy would know how she felt when she was left alone all the time.

In the darkness Leah could hear the sounds of rats running back and forth. That was good, because it meant the rats were scared and *that* meant that Buddy was waiting for her.

She scooted over onto her butt and slid down the dirt incline. This part was fun, too; it was like going down the slide at one of the playgrounds Mommy let her play on once. Even though she'd only been able to go down the slide one time, Leah never forgot what it felt like because it made her think that she was going home; the speed, the feeling that she could take flight at any moment, the wind pressing against her—wherever she was supposed to be instead of here, she'd found some small part of it that day on the sliding board.

She hit the bottom of the sub-basement with a moist thud and heard the rats screech and run into the deeper darkness. It was hard to see down here, so she got on her hands and knees and moved forward very slowly. This was the hard part, making sure she didn't get all mixed-up in the dark. She slid her hands forward, then dragged her legs; once, twice, three times, and on the third time she felt the cold metal under her fingers.

The door to the Rusty Room.

She took a deep breath and rose up on her knees—she had to be strong for this because the door was heavy—and worked her fingers into a crack right along the top and pulled.

The door came up with a loud *screech!* sound that felt like an icepick stuck in her ears. She fell back, panting, then held her breath and listened; she always expected Mommy to wake up when the door made that noise and come looking for her.

But she never did. It was like all she cared about was her needle-thing and not about where Leah was.

She crawled forward once again and peered down; there was a little light tonight, sort of red-blue, and that was enough for her to see the rounded walls of the metal tunnel, so she scooted around, slid her legs in, and pushed forward, sliding down the metal tunnel and laughing. She couldn't help laughing; this was fun, even more fun than the sliding board.

She landed on the floor and slid forward a few more feet because the floor of the Rusty Room was made out of black glass; at least, that's what it looked like to Leah. In the middle of the room was a tall pillar that narrowed in the center and supported part of the domed ceiling. The walls were made out of some kind of metal that was very old and had started rusting over the years; the room smelled like dust and copper, and sometimes when Leah would touch one of the walls, the rust came off on her hands, revealing layers upon layers of much older rust underneath. In one of the corners of the room—and it puzzled Leah that a room so round would actually have squared corners—was a hole that looked like something had exploded there. One time she stuck her head through the hole and saw the River of Ash-People that went on and on, farther than she could see even with a flashlight. Buddy had told her that the Ash-People weren't all people, some of them were animals and other creatures that *didn't quite work out as planned*. She wasn't sure she knew what Buddy meant by that, but, still, they were all pretty neat, like sand sculptures people made at the beach in summer. From what she understood, the Ash-People had all gotten caught in some kind of fire-flood, like volcano lava, and had been washed down here where they were forever frozen in one position when the lava hardened.

It seemed kind of sad to her that all of the Ash-People looked like they were reaching upward, hoping someone would pull them out and take them home because they didn't really belong *here*. She wondered if that mammoth Merc talked about had been reaching up when the scientists found it.

She decided not to say hello to the Ash-People tonight, and hoped they'd understand. She had important things to talk about with Buddy.

Then she noticed that Buddy had written some more words on the wall above the hole:

someone come
be there in the morning
when I
wake up
with your silver thread
to lead me out
I don't belong here
who will take me?

someone come

A few feet away from the central pillar was a doorway, and above the door there was a sign of some sort, printed in raised letters (she *guessed* they were letters, anyway; she'd never seen anything quite like them) that shone with an almost eerie phosphorescence, just like all those neon signs downtown where Jewel lived. The red-blue light she'd seen from above earlier came from those letters, and gave off enough light that she could make her way around the Rusty Room without banging into anything—not that there was much to bang in to; just a large white table like in a doctor's office, and a bunch of things that looked like leather coffins stacked one on top of the other.

"Buddy?" she called softly.

And waited to be answered by music that was both primitive and majestic; clicks, grunts, wheezing whistles, then a series of trills, arpeggios, and multi-toned flutings: all parts of Buddy's language. A long time ago, when she'd first met him, Buddy had put her on the table and done something to her head with a gizmo that looked like one of those things doctors looked in your ears with, only Buddy's gizmo had a kind of liquidy spring attached that uncoiled like a snake and went into her ears and then deeper. It had tickled a lot, but ever since then Leah had been able to understand what Buddy was saying to her.

"I know I'm late. I'm sorry, but Mommy...Mommy sold the baby tonight and then we had to go and get some of her needle-stuff."

Still, she was answered by silence. That was all right, though; sometimes Buddy didn't feel like talking *or* showing himself. It was enough for Leah to just know he was around. She could feel him near.

"I got a bag of King Dons the doctor gave me!" She pulled the crushed bag from under her shirt. "Uh-oh. They got squished. But that's okay, they still taste real good, they're just kinda messy." She worked the remains of one from its package and held it out. "You want one? I saved a package for you."

Silence.

"Okay, if you're sure. I'll probably eat 'em all. I'm still kinda hungry. Mommy bought me a hamburger but I didn't get to eat it all 'cause she was in a hurry." She shrugged. "It was kinda greasy, anyway."

She devoured the first package of cakes and then opened the next one. "I wish you weren't so quiet tonight, Buddy. I missed you. Mommy, she...I dunno. I think she does that needle-thing because she's sad about something and it won't leave her alone. Sometimes, when she talks about how she first met my daddy, she gets all sad, then mean. I don't really understand a lot about it. I don't get what a metal cave is supposed to be, unless it's something like your place. Buddy. I guess maybe that's it, and maybe that's what makes her sad enough to do the needle-thing. I bet that's why all of them do the needle-thing, to make the sad go away. I just wish..." She wiped her eyes, surprised that she'd started crying again.

I just wish that she didn't have to give the babies to the dark-coat man for money. She gave him my little sister. I never had a little sister before and I didn't even get to name her.

"I wish you'd say something. You're my best-best friend. I love you, Buddy."

She was answered only by silence, but in that silence she felt Buddy's confusion; not at her being sad, or hungry, or about Mommy and the babies and the needle-stuff, but at one word: love. It wasn't that Buddy didn't know what love was, because he did, in his way; what confused him was that Leah felt such deep and strong affection for him.

"Okay, I g-guess you don't feel like company tonight. I'll come back again tomorrow night, okay? I'll save you some of the King Dons, in case you change your mind." She made her way over to the metal tunnel and saw that Buddy had, as usual, turned it into a ladder so she could climb back up.

She started up, and then swung out, one hand still gripping a rung, and waved good-night to the Ash-People.

Above the hole, some new words had been written:

> *and where do I live?*
> *in the empty spaces where*
> *a spirit should be*
> *among the odd, damaged ones*
> *in hollow houses of flesh*
> *and bone*
> *that the Belonging will not*
> *see*

> *someone come*
> *one last time*
> *I will wait for you*
> *you ask who will take me?*

> *someone come*
> *and answer*

> *soon.*

> *tomorrow.*

within the cell, life is long, life is hard.
within the cell, life is hard.

and home is a cruel joke.

someone come.

"Okay," said Leah, smiling. "I'll come back tomorrow."

VI

Mommy was wake when Leah got back, but there was a man with her and they were doing the grabbing thing. Leah hated that because Mommy always screamed a lot when she did the grabbing thing with a man, but she knew that the grabbing thing was how babies were made because Randi had told her about it once, because that's what hookers did, except they didn't want to have babies so they just did it for fun. Like Mommy sometimes did with one of her needle-friends.

Leah sat in a dark corner where they couldn't see her, listening to her mother moan and scream and say fuck-me-yes-yes.

Leah cried, wishing that Buddy had felt like company.

VII

After it was over, Leah watched as her mother and the man lay naked in the candlelight, sweating. She hoped that the grabbing thing was over because she was getting hungry again. Maybe Mommy would be in a good mood now and give her some money so she could buy a hot dog or taco or something.

She walked out of the darkness and the man laying next to her mother sat up and smiled.

"So that's her, huh, babe?"

"Yeah..."

"Wow. I ain't never seen a...a whatchamacallit—space-baby before."

"Not much to look at, is she?"

"Hey, I think she's real pretty. Like her mom."

"Mommy's just a former abductee."

"Yeah, but them saucer-men must've got themselves a real taste for that nice Earth-snatch of yours, what with them always asking those dudes to bring you back so they can have some more."

"Fuck you."

"You just did."

"Oh, yeah, now I remember." They laughed, and Leah laughed, too, then came over and stood next to Mommy and said, "Can I have some money to buy a hot dog?"

"You already ate once today."

"Please?"

Mommy jumped up and slapped her hard across the mouth, knocking Leah back into the boxes.

"*I said no!*"

"...'kay," whimpered Leah, wiping the blood from her chin and trying hard not to cry.

"Her blood's the same color as ours," said the man.

"So what?"

"So, I dunno...it's interesting, that's all."

"Shit! Only reason I keep her is because they give me more money each time to make sure I don't accidentally leave her someplace. But that ends next month. She'll be six then, and I guess there's something that happens to them when they turn six, something important, so they're gonna take her to the Center."

"But you said they was gonna take you, too."

"Do I look stupid? I know damn well that when they show up to get us, there're gonna be *two* cars 'cause they'll want us to ride separate, and *hers'll* be the only car with a passenger when they get there. I mean, it ain't like they couldn't still use me, but Mr. I'm-In-Charge, he don't like me so much."

The man *hmmm*'d, then picked up one of the needles. "And this shit don't have no effect on the babies?"

"Nope. They've all been real healthy."

The man looked at Leah. "You ever do any experimentin' on her?"

"Like what?"

"Ever send her tripping?"

Leah wondered then, for the first time, if the needle-thing was their way of Removing themselves from what was going on around them.

Mommy looked at her and smiled. "It's not like *I have* to take care of her now, is it? They won't be giving me any more money."

"I hear Mexico's real pretty this time of year. You 'n me, we take your money and your stash, we maybe hit Jewel's for some extra, then head on down. We could set ourselves up pretty good."

Mommy threw off the rug she'd been using for a blanket. "She's been nothing but a pain in the ass since she was born. Let's do it."

Mommy's eyes looked just like the dark-coat man's and Leah tried to get to her feet and run away but she was still dizzy from being hit so hard and Mommy and the man were on top of her before she could even stand up straight and one of them hit her real hard in the mouth with a fist and everything went white and then she felt the rubber band being tied around her arm and then a sting and she cried out for Buddy to come and save her but then the world went liquid and runny and numb...

VIII

...she was back at the Wall of Skulls, only now the skulls had grown flesh and become faces again, and all of them were talking but no sound emerged from their mouths; all she could hear were tings! *and buzzes and beeps. Climbing on the faces, she made her way up to the top of the wall where a Wooly Mammoth stood in front of a pinball machine, concentrating for all it was worth. She said hello and it looked over its shoulder at her. It had Buddy's black-almond eyes. "Come on," it said. "I'm getting tired. You take over for me."*

Leah stood in front of the pinball machine and placed her hands on the buttons. Even though she wasn't doing anything, the machine went crazy; lights blinking, silver balls shooting all over the place and bouncing off the bumpers, the score ding-ding-dinging higher and higher, and she began to remove her hands but the Mammoth said, "No, just keep a grip on the machine and it'll continue to work." So she did.

The Mammoth stood next to her and pointed with its trunks to field that lay beyond the wall. "Everything dies," it said, "but we only know about it as a kind of abstraction. If you were to go out into that field and stand in the middle, almost everything you can see is in the process of dying, and most of those things will be dead long before you are. If it weren't for the constant renewal and replacement going on before your eyes —even though you can't see most of it— the whole world would turn to stone and sand underneath your feet. Everything dies. But there are some things that do not seem to die at all; they simply vanish totally into their own progeny." The Mammoth paused for a moment to munch on a few buttercups.

"Single cells do this," it said. "Not eat buttercups, but vanish into their progeny. The cell becomes, two, then four, and so on, until after a while the last trace is gone. But you can't look upon that as death; barring unnatural mutations that should be gotten rid of, the descendants are simply that first cell, living over and over again. And sometimes, if things go as planned, eventually the descendants will grow back into their original form; they will re-become the first cell.

"Do you understand what's happening right now?"

"No," said Leah, watching as the stars above came closer, grew colder.

"Buddy is what you were before you became what you are, and he is also

what you will become again one day, if things go as planned."

"Why didn't I just stay like Buddy?"

It was so cold, suddenly; so very, very cold.

"If I knew the answer to that, none of this would have ever happened. But I think it has something to do with worthiness."

The Mammoth screamed as the ice came crashing down like a curse from Heaven...

IX

...the bitch! I'll kill her, I swear to God!" Merc, screaming.

"Not if I get my hands on her first, you won't." Jimmy, crying.

Leah tried to move, tried to say something, but her body was stiff and cold and rigid; she couldn't even blink her eyes.

Am I dead? she wondered, and then figured she must be or else Merc and Jimmy wouldn't be acting this way.

Merc pulled out the 9mm. "I'll bet you anything that cunt went over to Jewel's to get herself a little more candy before she takes off."

Some things do not seem to die at all.

"Jesus—Merc! Get back here!"

"What is it?"

"She's...God Almighty, *she's still alive!* Here, feel her pulse—no, in her neck!"

"Ohgod..."

"Christ, Merc, I don't know what to do."

"Thought you were a medicine man?"

"*Sachem!* I was a *sachem* in training! A *spiritual* healer."

"Oh."

Jimmy lifted Leah's body into his arms. "C'mon, Merc, pull me out of here. We gotta find a cab and get her to the hospi—"

"*Ohgod!*"

"What? Merc, you're scaring me, what're you looking—"

"*Over there! In the light! Do you see it? Ohmygod!*"

A breeze, old and tired.

A touch, warm and safe.

Fingers, long and willowy.

Light.

So much almond-eyes light...

X

...the stars began to fade like guttering candles, snuffed out one by one. Out in the depths of space the great celestial cities, the galaxies, cluttered with

the memorabilia of ages, were dying. Tens of billions of years passed in the growing darkness. Occasional flickers of light pierced the fall of cosmic night, and only spurts of activity delayed the sentence of a universe condemned from the beginning to become a galactic graveyard. Light flowed inward, and the sky snowed a blizzard of galaxies as the lens of night burned brighter than the sun, than all the stars in supernova, and the human race fell on its knees, blinded forever by the white-hot darkness in its eyes.

The air crackled with rage.

"I will do this for you, if you want me to," said a voice. "They deserve nothing better, yet they deserve so much more."

"Buddy?"

"Shhh. Just tell me what to do."

"Be here in the morning when I wake up."

"If that's what you want."

"Can't you ever go back?"

"This is home. It always has been."

"I'm sorry."

"I know. Thank you."

"For what?"

"For teaching me about worthiness. And love."

"Am I dead, Buddy?"

"No. But the time is upon us to fly."

Leah smiled. "Like Jimmy's song."

"Yes, like Jimmy's song."

And then Leah felt herself freed from her body, everywhere and nowhere at the same time, becoming light in its truest meaning, becoming light in its purest intention, including the darkness, and for a moment she was aware of a coldness that transcended temperature, a chilling sense of timelessness that touched her mind rather than her flesh, and within that coldness she heard an echo —distant but strong —of utter loneliness, and she recognized this sound because she'd been hearing it in the back of her own mind for all her life, only now it was fading away, away, away as the empty space left in its wake was filled with a blossoming awareness of all the knowledge left behind by the descendants who had simply been the first cell living over and over again, and though she didn't yet understand everything revealed to her, she smiled deep within herself, knowing she would understand, in time...

<u>XI</u>

...she awoke on the table in the Rusty Room and rolled over to see Jimmy and Merc standing beside her.

"How're you feeling?" said Jimmy, reaching out to touch her, then pulling his hand back at the last moment.

"I feel okay," said Leah. "You don't gotta worry about touching me."

"I know," said Jimmy, "it's just that...well, the last time I touched you...." He took a step backward, and only then did Leah realize that Jimmy was...standing.

"*Oh, Jimmy...*"

"You did this," he said. "You gave my legs back to me."

She rose up on the table and looked at Merc. "Can I do anything for you, Merc?"

"You two're gonna have to...to give me a little while to get my head around all of this." He leaned over and brushed some of Leah's hair out of her eyes. "You sure you're feeling all right?"

"Uh-huh. Did you guys meet Buddy?"

Merc looked at Jimmy. "Well, I guess you could say that. Dude made himself quite an entrance."

Leah giggled. "I'll bet you were scared, huh?"

"No," said Merc. "I *been* scared. This was *way* past that."

"I damn near fainted," said Jimmy, then, looking around, added: "Where is he now?"

Leah smiled. "He went home. Sort-of." She jumped down from the table and walked over and gave Jimmy a hug. It felt *great* to hug him standing up!

Jimmy kissed the top of her head, then stroked her hair. "What do you want to do now?"

"I want to go get Denise."

Merc smiled. "Do we have to be nice about it to Jewel?"

Leah's smile grew wider. "No. Jewel isn't Worthy."

Jimmy and Merc looked at each other.

"Then we're gonna find Randi," said Leah. "And all the others just like us. And the dark-coat man. I want my brothers and my little sister back."

"You sure you're up to this?" said Jimmy.

"Uh-huh. I will take care of you. I will help us all make a home."

Jimmy tilted her head back with his hands and looked into her eyes. "*Peye'wik?*"

"No," said Leah. "It Is *Here.*"

"Well, what're we waiting for?" said Merc, pulling out the 9mm and jacking back the slide. "Let's get this invasion started."

They made their way over to the ladder. Jimmy went first, then Merc, and Leah went last.

But before she began to climb, she crossed over to the hole to say good-bye to the River of Ash-People, then read the last words Buddy had left for her on the wall:

> *someone come*
> *give this body no limits*
> *slough the fevers*
> *with your cool hand*
>
> *make the flesh home*
>
> *within the skin, life is long, life is hard*
> *within the skin, life is hard*
>
> *but not for much longer.*
>
> *where do I live?*
> *someone come*
>
> *who will take me?*

Leah looked down at the black-glass floor and saw her reflection; for just an instant, long enough for her to know for sure, she saw her face become two, one superimposed on top of the other, and smiled as she looked into the black-almond eyes that watched the world from behind her own.

She pressed her finger into the rust and wrote:

> *I am here*
> *Someone has come*
> *And I will take you.*

"No more living in Hollow Houses," she whispered. "We'll make ourselves Worthy again. I promise."

She thought she heard the Ash-People singing thanks.

Then left to join her waiting friends.

The invasion was about to begin.

And a little child would lead them.

Afterward, There Will Be A Hallway

Introduction by Chet Williamson

Life after death is one of the standard tropes of dark fantasy fiction, and it's been handled in many different ways over the centuries. But I think it's accurate to say that Gary Braunbeck's depiction of it here is unique. This particular afterlife has a number of rules and restrictions that the reader, along with the story's protagonist, has to learn and adapt to, but that's part of the fun — and the pain. This story has both in large measure. It's a tale of loss and sorrow and longing and discovery and joy, and to say more about it would spoil your *own* joy of discovery. You're in good hands here, with a fine writer who has created a story both imaginative and emotionally charged, giving his readers a powerful and loving look into other lives...and *after*lives.

Afterward, There Will Be A Hallway

"About suffering they were never wrong,
The Old Masters: how well they understood
Its human position; how it takes place
While someone else is eating or opening a window or
just walking dully along."
                                        —W.H. Auden
                                            "Musée des Beaux Arts"

(*...fingers barely brushing the surface of her skin but still her eyes fall through their sockets and into the back of her skull with soft, dry sounds...touching her cheeks, wanting to hold her face as a lover should, whispering that everything will be all right, it will, you'll see, she only has to come back, please, please come back, don't leave again, dearGodplease, but her head collapses inward, flesh crumbling apart, flaking away, fragmenting, becoming slivers, becoming specks, becoming dust, her face sinking, splitting in half, disintegrating...staring helpless as the rest of her crumples and decays, revealing nothing within, the parched shards of what were once her lips holding their form only one more second, long enough to say that it's time...*)

"...to get up, sleepy-head! *C'mon*—it's Wednesday and it's gonna start in a couple hours."

"You've only reminded me ten times since last night," I mumbled, head still buried underneath the sheet, a preview of that day when the sheet would not be pulled back and I'd be lying in a cold drawer in a cold room in the cold basement of some hospital like the rest of them. Someday. Just not today. As with most mornings, I was ambivalent about how I felt on the subject of that particular eventuality.

I had not been dreaming—I rarely dream these days; no, I'd been lying there envisioning what *might* happen if I were to chance touching—

—*don't. Just...don't. You know better than to do this to yourself, Neal, my man.*

I sat up, rubbed my eyes, and focused on the little girl standing in the doorway to my bedroom. Seven—no, wait, just turned *eight* years old. She still wore the Scooby-Doo pajamas underneath the white hospital robe, and those SpongeBob SquarePants slippers that looked cute from a distance but were in fact unbelievably creepy when you saw them up close. Her complexion was a sickly shade of yellow-white, with dark brownish-purple arcs under her eyes. Her left hand rose up to scratch at the padded, custom-made bandanna covering her bald head. The chemotherapy must have been hellish. Every time I looked at her, I wondered if I could have held on as long as she did.

She stared at me for a moment, then asked: "Can we open it now?"

"You've only been here two days, you know my rule."

Hands on hips, one foot impatiently tapping, lower lip sticking out in defiance. "But it's a *dumb* rule! *A whole week?* How come I gotta wait a whole week?"

"Because I..." I rubbed my face, feeling the first twinges of pain behind my left eye; a sure sign that a migraine was going to visit me today if I wasn't careful. "Would you please come over here, Melissa?"

"Not until you start calling me 'Missy'. I asked you, like, what? A *hundred times*."

"Oh, don't be so dramatic—this is only the second or third time and you know it."

"Still...you better not think it's dumb. Mom called me Missy because it sounded like 'messy' and she was always saying how my room was such a disaster area. 'Messy Missy.' I liked it. So you call me that, okay?"

I actually managed a small grin. "Your wish is my command, oh Messy Missy." I pointed to the foot of the bed. "Now, would you come over here and sit down, please?"

She hesitated for only a moment before doing as I'd asked. I imagine her mother had warned her about strangers, about never, ever talking to them, let alone sitting on their beds.

I turned on the nightstand light, blinking against the sudden bright burst. "Missy, have you ever gotten mad at one of your friends and said something that you felt bad about later?"

"Well, *duh*. Who hasn't?"

"My one-week rule is sort of my way of...of making sure something like that doesn't happen with you and your stuff, *duh*."

She cocked her head to the side and squinted at me. "You know that doesn't make any sense, right? God, you're weird."

I sighed. "Okay, look at it this way. It's like—and I am *not* weird."

"Yes, you are."

"Am not."

"Are too."

"I am not."

"*Shut! Up!* You are too! I've seen weird people before, and you're a freakazoid, mister. You don't have any friends except for that lady who's asleep in the other room and she's never awake so for all I know, she hates your guts, nobody ever calls, you don't go anywhere except to drive around all day stealing boxes, you almost never smile and when you do, you look like you're trying to poop but can't—you're *weird*."

Yep. Lost that one.

Something in my face must have alarmed her, because after a few moments she leaned forward and said, "I'm sorry. Really. I didn't mean it in a *bad* way, y'know? You're weird, but it's a *good* weird, I think."

"You don't have to apologize, Missy. You're right, I *am* weird and I *don't* have any friends."

"Not even that sleeping lady?"

I knew she'd get around to exploring the guest room sooner or later; I'd been hoping for later. "I don't know. I don't know how she feels about me."

"Who is she, anyway?"

"Her name's Rebecca. She was my wife."

"How long's she been dead?"

"Three years this Friday."

"She doesn't look very good. Her breathing's all wheezy and her skin—"

"—could we get back to the subject, please?" I was more than aware of how Rebecca looked and sounded, unless things had worsened since I'd checked on her last night. Though I knew I should (and maybe even a part of me wanted to), I couldn't go back in there, not this morning. Seeing her last night—her hair still falling out in clumps, cheeks more hollow than the day before, lips cracked and parched, the black blotches on her skin that seemed to expand as I stood there watching—was bad enough. A second visit this soon was more than I could take.

Missy looked out toward the hallway, deep in an eight-year-old's thoughts, and then turned back to me and said, "I could be your friend."

"That's sweet, but you're not going to be around that long."

"Because of the one-week rule thing?"

"Yes. I know this seems unfair, but I'm only doing it for your own good." Dear God, did I actually just *say* that? "It's like when you do something or say something that seems like what you want to do or say *right then*, at that second, understand? So you say or do it, and then later on wish you hadn't because it was mean or inconsiderate or just plain dumb. You wish you could take it back, but you can't. Does *that* make sense?"

A shrug. "I guess."

"Well it's the same thing with your stuff, only it's a lot more important. Once we open that box, you *have* to choose something, and it's got to be the *right* something. If you pick the wrong thing, you'll be...." I let fly with a soft groan of frustration; this was more difficult than I'd thought it would be. Throwing off the covers (I'd slept in my shirt and pants), I stumbled to my feet and crossed to the other side of the bedroom, pulling back the curtain covering the window there. "Come here. I want you to see something."

Her eyes narrowed. "It isn't something gross, is it? One time, this boy in my class, Eric, he said he had something real cool to show me, and it turned out he had this fat old slimy nasty water-bug that he'd squished open with his fingers. It looked like a big glob of snot with legs and pincers. I couldn't eat my pudding at lunch that day, and I *like* pudding. A lot."

"No squished bugs or anything like that, I promise."

She came over to the window and looked down at the street. I live on the twelfth floor of one of Cedar Hill's nicer apartment buildings, and the windows in my bedroom and living room all offer a good view of the downtown area.

I pointed. "See that old brick building down the street? With those stone steps?"

"Gargoyle Castle!" she shouted, giggling.

"Wha-huh?"

"Gargoyle Castle, you freakazoid. It's got those stone gargoyles up near the top, see? So I always called it Gargoyle—"

" —I follow the line of reasoning, thanks so much—and stop calling me 'freakazoid,' it's rude and gets old in a hurry."

She smiled. "Says you."

The truth was, I'd forgotten about the gargoyles that squat over the stone archway of what used to be the Building and Loan, so for a moment, I was seeing it through her eyes, and it was, as she might put it, *way cool*. But the feeling passed. It always did.

"Okay," I said. "Look down at the steps of Gargoyle Castle and tell me what you see."

She leaned closer to the window, concentrating for all she was worth, and then said: "That guy sitting there with that tin cup? Is he what you wanted me to see?"

"Yes. His name was Leonard but he liked being called 'Lenny'. Lenny fought in Vietnam, did two tours of duty. That cup—which is steel, by the way, *not* tin—belonged to him. It was part of his C-rations kit. You know what C-rations are?"

"Yeah. I saw this movie one time, with my mom, on TV, about these soldiers in World War Two. Lee Marvin was in it—Mom always watched Lee Marvin movies. She thought he was a hottie. I always thought he looked like someone who was mean but wished he wasn't. Anyway, they had those C-ration kits in the movie that they ate from." She seemed so very proud that she was able to answer my question, so I made sure to look suitably impressed.

I nodded toward Lenny. "He carried that cup inside a pocket of his vest. You can't see it from here, but there's a pretty big dent in the side. That's because it deflected a bullet that would have blown his hip to pieces and probably crippled him. He never went anywhere without that cup afterward. He called it his bad luck shield."

"His *what?*"

"His good luck charm."

"*Ahhhh....*" She looked down at Lenny once again. "So when you guys opened Lenny's box, he chose his cup, his good luck charm, right?"

"Not exactly. The cup was the first thing Lenny saw, and he was...he was *really* happy to see it again, so he just grabbed it without thinking."

She gave a soft but genuine gasp. "It *wasn't* the thing he was supposed to pick?"

"No, and because he grabbed the wrong thing without thinking, he's stuck here. He hangs out on those steps...always. And he always will. Maybe not those same steps, but he'll always be waiting around...somewhere."

"Because he can't take it back?"

I nodded. "Because he can't take it back."

"That's so sad. Does he have anyone to talk to?"

"I talk to him almost every day. Sometimes other people like him come by."

"Really?"

"You'd be surprised how many people like you and Lenny wander the streets around here, Missy."

"And you see all of them?"

"Oh, no, not even close. When Lenny's got a visitor whose...I mean, I can only see and talk with those whose belongings...wait a second — look." Sure enough, Lenny, ever the social butterfly, was chatting away.

"Hey," said Missy. "Who's that pretty lady he's talking to? Oh, wow...isn't her hair *beautiful?* She looks like she's going to the Oscars or something fancy like that." She looked at me. "Don't you think she's pretty?"

"I have no idea. I can't see her."

"But she's *right there!*"

"I don't doubt it, Missy, honestly, I don't. But the thing is, whoever she is, I wasn't the one who took care of her personal effects."

"Her what?"

"Her things. I wasn't the one who picked up the box of her stuff."

"'Kay...so how come I can see her?"

"Because the dead can all see each other."

"Huh." She stared for a moment longer, and then her face brightened. "So it's kinda like a secret club? That's *so cool*. Hey, can we go around today and see how many I can spot but you can't? It'll be like a game you play in a long car trip, 'Bury the Cow' or 'I Spy.'"

"We can do whatever you want, Missy. Speaking of—" I dropped the curtains back into place. " —are you *sure* you want to go to your own funeral?"

"Yep. I wanna see Mom again...and I wanna see if mean old Eric feels bad now about what he did to me with the water bug. That was *so disgusting*." She gave an overly-theatrical shudder. When that got no reaction from me, she repeated it, only this time throwing one arm up, the back of her hand pressed against her forehead. "Oh, *suh*," she said in a not-bad imitation of a Southern Belle, "I do believe I ham about to fa-haint."

"'Ham' is right," I said, trying to stop my (according to her) constipated smile. "That's some fierce overacting, *mah de-ah*."

She flung herself against my dresser, one hand still plastered to her forehead, the other now pushing forward to fend off the eee-vell Yankee. "You *must* leave me my *honor*, suh! You *must* show some *decency!*"

I applauded, and she took a broad, grandiose bow.

"I was gonna be an actress on the soaps."

"You're certainly pretty enough. I'll bet you would have been great."

"Me too." No sadness, no regret, just a simple statement of fact. Most of the people I deal with usually crack at a moment of epiphany like

(*Me too*)

this, their bitterness, anger, fear, and grief reducing them for a time to a crumpled handful of spoiled human material whose potential they now knew would never be realized. I'd been listening to it for nearly three years now, this cumulative symphony of human misery, hurt, loneliness, terror, rage, despair, all of it in search of an outlet, something to give it purpose, an endless sonata of sorrow and hopelessness composed by those whose existence has ground to a halt in a series of sputtering little agonies, leaving them with nowhere to go, nothing to hold onto, and no one to speak with except some stranger whose job it is to gather the detritus left behind by the odd ones, the damaged and devastated ones, the ruined ones, the old, the alone, and the forgotten.

Yeah, I'm a real party monster, a walking chuckle-fest. Just ask my wife. Maybe she'll answer *you*...if there's anything left of her.

Melissa was the youngest I'd dealt with, and she still had all the pent-up, eager, impatient energy of a child. It was probably that very impatience that caused her to show up so soon after her death; when I retrieved the discarded box of her personal effects from beside the hospice dumpster, her body still lay inside her room waiting to be picked up by the funeral home. I put the box in the trunk of my car, drove home, and found her sitting in the middle of my living room when I walked through the door.

"Hey," she said softly to me now (as she did then). Something in her voice warned me she was about to ask a question I didn't want to answer.

"We need to start getting ready—well, *I* need to, anyway." I started toward the bathroom and was mere inches from a clean getaway when Missy asked:

"How did Rebecca die?"

And there it was.

But I was ready. Snapping my fingers as if I'd just remembered something, I made a sharp right turn into the hallway and called back, "I almost forgot—I have a surprise for you."

"A *surprise?*"

She was in the living room before I was, her sudden presence startling the hell out of me.

"Ah, damn—*Missy!* I asked you to please not do that anymore." Three years, and it still unnerves me, the way they can pop in and out of a room whenever they want.

"I'm sorry," she said. "I just got all excited when you said—"

"It's all right. Now…

"Close your eyes."

Find me the kid who can resist those three words. Missy did as I asked, bouncing up and down on the balls of her feet. If I listened hard enough, I bet I could have heard her ethereal molecules going, *Oh, goody, goody, goody….*

I pulled the wrapped package from its hiding place behind the television and held it out to her. This was as much an experiment as it was an evasive tactic. "Okay…open them!"

She did, her eyes growing almost absurdly wide as she jumped up and down, practically squealing, "Oh, *goody! A present!*"

And took it from my hands.

So I was right: if it's an action they performed without thinking when alive, they could continue to do so after death.

I'd expected her to make quick, ferocious work of the wrapping paper as would any child thrilled over a present, but instead she looked it over, studying it. "This is real *nice* paper. You did a great job wrapping it. The ribbon's beautiful." She studied it a little more, a jeweler determining the carat-value of a diamond, then held it up by her ear and gave it a little shake. "Hmmm...I wonder what it is."

By now *I* was ready to tear the paper off the damned thing, but then just as quickly realized she'd not only reaffirmed one of my theories, but also just shown me what an extraordinary little girl she was. Had been. She knew, at age eight she *knew* that a surprise equaled a mystery, and any good mystery was to be savored as much as solved. I froze at the sight of her smile; I had never seen such a radiant smile before...or if I had, was too full of myself to

(*You don't have any friends except for that lady who's asleep in the other room and she's never awake so for all I know, she hates your guts...*)

notice it. It was the kind of smile that told you she'd just been let in on this Big Secret, something so wonderful and great and full of happy promises that nothing would ever seem bad or sorrowful to her again; and standing there in my living room, nailed to the spot by the sight of her smile, her joy, her ability to savor the wonder and anticipation, my defenses taken by surprise, dumbstruck by the sudden rush of emotions, I fell a little bit in love with her.

Don't misunderstand, there was nothing even remotely sexual about it, nothing physical or lustful or perverted; I fell in love with her the same way some people fall in love with a piece of music, or a certain time of day or season of the year—twilight in autumn—or even an idea. It was the kind of startling, forceful, promise-of-salvation love a person experiences maybe two or three times in their life, should they be graced with a long one. My breath caught in my throat and my arms would not move. I refused to blink. Everything I'd once believed to be good and pure and redeeming of life stood less than two feet away from me, in the form an eight-year-old girl who would never know her first kiss, her first dance, or the first time she held a boy's hand; for her there would be no late-night study sessions cramming for the big exam, no prom, no graduation parties; no first job, first paycheck, first promotion; none of that for Messy Missy. For her there was only this moment, this breath, in this place, with this wonderful mystery wrapped in shabby-looking paper I'd grabbed from a discount bin at the last minute before getting in the checkout line.

"Are you okay?" she said, taking a step toward me.

I blinked, wiped at my eyes, exhaled, and took a step back. "Uh, um...yes, yes. I'm fine. I guess my mind just wandered off for a moment." I flashed my best Constipated Smile. "Well, go ahead—open it."

"Okay." Even then she didn't rip the paper to shreds; she carefully unwrapped it—a corner here, a corner there—until the paper was loose enough for her to reach in and pull out the gift, which she did with her eyes closed.

"Oh, this is gonna be *good*, isn't it?"

"For the love of God—*open your eyes and find out!*"

"Geez, don't bust a vein." She opened her eyes, saw what it was, and then squealed loudly, jumping up and down while simultaneously twirling. "*The SpongeBob SquarePants Movie!*"

"You said you never got to see it, right?"

"No, but I'm gonna watch it while you take your shower!" She stopped her twirling and held the DVD against her chest as if she expected some stinking pirate to come sailing out of nowhere and be a-relievin' her of her treasure a-fore makin' 'er walk the plank, yar. "Oh, no—wait! Wait! Hang *on!* You know what would be great? Oh, this'll be *way cool!* Listen—we could make popcorn tonight and watch it then. Mom and me, we had this special recipe for buttered popcorn, I could make it for us. You'll love my popcorn, you will, you will, I *swear* you will!"

I pointed at the television. "But I thought you wanted to watch it now."

"Well, *duh*, I do, but SpongeBob, he's more fun to watch with someone else, not just all by yourself. We could—oh, *hey!* Hang *on!* We could maybe see if Rebecca feels like watching it with us—we could even invite Lenny and his new girlfriend." She gasped, eyes growing even wider. "We could *have a party!* Oh, *rock* out! Let's do that, okay? Let's have a party tonight. A SpongeBob/Missy's Funeral party!"

"You want to have a party to watch SpongeBob and celebrate your funeral?"

She turned into a human Bobblehead figure. On way too much sugar. "It'll be *so awesome!*"

"And you called *me* 'weird.'"

"Oh, this is, like, one of the awesomest presents *ever!* You rock! *Thank you so much!*"

And before I could move, she ran forward and gave me a great big hug and the next thing I knew I was

(...*crying out but there was no sound no matter how much she tried, and she wondered what had happened to her voice and why wasn't anybody here she had to go to the bathroom and ohGod, it hurt, it hurt, ithurtithurtithurt so much, and she tried to roll over and press the button so the nurses would come but she couldn't move her legs and there was sudden liquid fire spreading down the backs of her thighs and she started crying because she'd just soiled her bed again and ohGod it burned so much when her bowels let go and she closed her eyes and tried to think of something funny, something cool, like winter snow and goofy snowmen, but then there were arms, strong arms, helping her up, but she vomited all over herself and the nurse and Mommy, where are you, I hurt, Mommy, I hurt, and now it was me that hurt, I felt all of it, the sickness and pain, the vomiting and pissing and shitting, then she'd get so cold and couldn't stop shaking and it felt like her teeth were going to smash to smithereens every time they chattered together, but then came the shot and she felt warm, so warm again, with fresh sheets and a new gown and her SpongeBob slippers keeping her feet snug, and she began to fade away for a little while, then awoke to see Mommy sitting beside her bed, holding her hand, telling her that she was being such a strong, brave little girl, that she'd feel better soon and did she want another shot, they could give her another shot now if she wanted, and Missy said yes, please, and could I have some pudding, too, I like pudding a lot, I promise not to spill any....*)

on my hands and knees on the floor, my body still wracked with the physical agony of her last few hours, but it would fade, I knew it would, this is why I always made it a point to never touch any of them, or to let them touch me; there were always remnants, some strong, some weaker, but none of them coming close to what had just chewed through me.

"Omigod!" shouted Missy, dropping to her hands and knees beside me. "Omigod, I'm...I'm *so sorry!* I am. Please don't be mad. Is there anything I can do? Do you need me to get you—?" She reached out.

"*Don't*...don't touch me, please? It'll happen again." I turned my head toward her and tried to smile but it hurt too much. "It's not that I didn't enjoy the hug, okay? It was really sweet. But...you...you can't...*I* can't...." I couldn't finish, and so lay stomach-down on the floor.

Missy leaned down and whispered, "Is it okay if I stay with you?"

"...sure, hon, whatever you want..."

"Then I'll be right here."

"...okay..."

"Hey, Neal?" It was the first time she'd called me by name.

"...what is it...?"

"I'm sorry that Rebecca killed herself."

The other reason I try to avoid touching or being touched by them: they always pick up on some remnant within me.

"...so'm I..." *Christ*, why wasn't the pain fading yet?

"Do you know why she did it?"

I shook my head, which—considering the threat of the migraine on top of the rest of it—was perhaps not the best course of action. "...don't know, Missy...I really don't..." I said, lying.

"Shh, there-there. You rest, okay? I'll be right here when you wake up."

"...don't know why she did it...there's...so much I don't know...."

The pain became a wave of cold nausea, and I passed out beneath its force.

* * *

Here is what I *do* know:

They come to me as they were at the moment of their deaths, that is the only thing on which there has never been any variation; they retain their five senses (if they had all of them while still alive); until Missy, the usual period between death and turning up in my life was between ten days and one month (it was exactly twenty-three days after her suicide that Rebecca showed up in the guest room, where I'd found her body), but there are at least a dozen who have *yet* to show up, even after three years; most of them don't like to talk too much the first few days, Missy and Lenny being the exceptions there; and—again, excluding Missy and Rebecca—all of them died alone and forgotten, some in the hospital, some in the nursing home, some in the hospice, no one coming forward to claim either their bodies or the boxes containing their personal effects.

Here is what I have learned:

Death is not instantaneous. The cells go down one by one, and it takes a while before everything's finished. If a person wanted to, they could snatch a bunch of cells *hours* after somebody's checked out and grow them in cultures. Death is a fundamental function; its mechanisms operate with the same attention to detail, the same conditions for the advantage of organisms, and the same genetic information for guidance through the stages that most people equate with the physical act of living. So I asked myself, if it's such an intricate, integrated physiological process—at least in the primary, local stages—then how do you explain the permanent vanishing of consciousness? What happens to it? Does it just screech to a halt, become lost in humus, what? Nature doesn't work like that. It tends to find perpetual uses for its more elaborate systems, and that gave me an idea: maybe human consciousness is somehow severed at the filaments of its attachments and then absorbed back into the membrane of its origin. I think that's all they are by the time they come to me—the severed consciousness of a single cell that hasn't died but is instead vanishing totally into its own progeny.

"I don't have the slightest goddamn idea what you're talking about," Lenny had said to me on his third night in my company. We were sitting at my kitchen table, putting a pretty good dent in a bottle of Glenlivet I'd bought earlier that day, knowing it was Lenny's poison of choice.

"Not all of your cells have died yet," I said, only slightly slurring my words, "and the ones that're still alive *remember* you. And as long as just *one* cell remembers, you're tied to the corporeal—to the physical body—in some form. But when those final cells finally give it up—" I snapped my fingers as if I had actually made my point.

"I'm guessing you weren't a big church-goer," said Lenny, tamping a smoke out the pack lying on the table and lighting up.

I leaned back in my chair, grinning. "Okay, smartass, let me ask you something, then. How is it you're still able to smoke a cigarette?"

Lenny looked at the smoke he held between his fingers as if it were something he'd never seen before.

"You don't remember doing that, do you?"

He shook his head.

"That's the answer—or at least part of it. There's a thousand things we do every day without thinking—walking, eating, breathing, lighting a cigarette, picking up a pen, taking a piss. All done by rote. We explain it away by saying that we do it 'unconsciously,' but the truth is it's our *cells* that remember this stuff for us, that tell the rest of our body how to lift a phone receiver or add a little more sugar to the iced tea because it's not sweet enough. Don't you get it, Lenny? You're here with me because those cells in you that are still alive haven't figured out yet that you're gone."

"Horseshit. I bought the farm almost a month ago. You're not really going to sit there and try to tell me that buried under the ground in Cedar Hill Cemetery there's some part of my body that's still *alive* on a cellular level, are you? I'm here, that's that, and it don't mean nothin'."

I was on my fourth drink—well past my limit of two—and feeling no pain. "You remember Medgar Evers?"

"The Civil Rights leader from Mississippi? Betcher ass, I do! Helluva guy. Took 'em thirty years, but they finally put that bastard Beckwith away for his assassination."

"Remember when they exhumed Evers' body before Beckwith's third trial in '94? How there was almost no decomposition after *thirty years* in the ground?"

"Yeah...?"

"I saw this cable special one night where one of the medical examiners who studied Evers' body was being interviewed, and he talked about how, on a routine examination of some tissue, he detected the smallest amount of cell activity. An embalmed body, thirty years in the ground, and there was *still* cell activity in the tissue. So don't say 'Horeshit' to me, buddy."

He crushed out his smoke, poured himself another shot, and lit up a fresh cigarette. "It ain't exactly like these can hurt me *now*, is it?"

"Is that your way of saying that maybe, *maybe* I'm right?"

"It's my way of saying that maybe, *maybe* you're not full of shit right up to the eyeballs, but that's as far as I go. You know, you remind me of this chopper pilot I once caught a ride with from Two Corps in Pleiku. Son-of-a-bitch musta *loved* the sound of his own voice too because, *man*, he could go on and on about anything and most of what he talked about, he didn't know *jack*, but did that stop him? *Hell*, no...."

It was because of Lenny that I discovered they don't sleep. I found out later that night when I heard him cry out from the small room that I laughingly call my office. I was still in the process of cataloguing the contents of his personal effects and had left the lid off the box. He wandered in there, saw his C-rations cup, and without thinking, picked it up.

They can touch and hold those inanimate things that had meaning for them while they were alive, even if these objects weren't among their final personal effects—a favorite book or magazine, a record or CD, a toy or knickknack, even, believe it or not, kitchen utensils and equipment. I once had a wonderful older lady —Grace (never was someone named more appropriately)—who all but danced a jig when she saw that I had an old-fashioned stand-mounted mixer, and insisted on baking cookies and a cake. Once she saw the mixer, everything in the kitchen took on meaning for her, and she puttered around in there for days. It was actually comforting, listening to her occupy herself; the clinking of dishes, the rattle of spoons, the sounds of the mixer working overtime...it reminded me of when I was a child, sitting in the living room at Christmastime listening to my mother work her magic over the holidays. Grace even hummed while she baked, an old lullaby that my mother used to sing to me when I was young:

You can take the Toy-Town Trolley and meet the jolly Times Express,

No one there is melancholy, it's an isle of happiness.
Don't you keep your dreamboat waiting, hope you have a pleasant stay
On Hush-a-bye Island on Rock-a-bye Bay....

Yes, it's corny as hell, but I don't care (hey, *Sinatra* recorded it, so don't get *too* high and mighty); it was nice, during Grace's stay, to feel something of my mother close again.

Lastly, here is what I hope: I hope...

...ah, mmm, *well*...

...on second thought, let's skip that last one. I would have been pissing in the wind and praying for rain, anyway.

* * *

A photograph of Melissa, taken at her seventh birthday party, had been enlarged and set on an easel near the head of the closed casket. Even from the back of the crowded room, you could see her sweet, grinning face and know how much had been lost.

There must have been at least seventy-five people there, possibly more. I was dressed in my best suit and trying to look like *I* was wearing *it* instead of the other way around as I walked up to the polished-wood podium holding the guest book and signed Lenny's name.

"That's not very nice," Missy whispered to me. "You really ought to sign your own name."

Looking up to make sure no one was watching me, I whispered as softly as I could, "We *talked* about this, Missy."

A sigh. "I *know*... 'I can't talk to you once we're inside, Missy. People might think I'm *ca-ra-zeeee*.' This sucks." She looked toward the closed casket. "How come the lid's shut like that? And—oh, *God*, I can't believe she used that picture! I look like a pug!" She stared for a moment, touching her hospital robe, and then her trembling hand moved slowly toward her bandanna. "Do I look that *awful*?" The tears were evident in her voice before they appeared in her eyes. "I didn't think I looked *that* ugly, not so ugly that Mommy wouldn't...wouldn't want people to *see* me!"

I reached out to take hold of her hand but pulled back almost at once; I couldn't chance another episode this soon.

It had taken the better part of twenty minutes for the pain to subside as I lay on the floor of my living room, and true to her word, Missy never moved away from me the entire time. When I was at last able to speak in almost complete sentences, I asked her to go into the bathroom, get into the medicine cabinet above the sink, and bring me one of the boxes containing the pre-measured shot of Imitrex I took when a migraine hit—and make no mistake, once Missy's pain had faded away, the full-blown migraine was there in all its shimmering, aura-soaked, drilling, nausea-inducing glory. I listened as Missy ran into the bathroom, threw open the cabinet door, and knocked over most of the contents within as she grabbed the Imitrex. I could hear her tearing open the box as she came back to the living room.

"You sure you can hold this thing?" she asked. "You seem real shaky—here, I'll do it."

"P-please don't—"

"Shut. *Up.* Dummy. I'm not gonna touch you. How do you—this doesn't look like any needle I've seen. How 'm I supposed to...?"

I explained, not once having to repeat myself, and she administered the shot like a pro. It took about thirty seconds before it began its voodoo, and then I realized there was something I'd forgotten to tell her.

"I am *so* ahead of you," she said, setting the emptied waste-paper basket by my side as I struggled into a sitting position.

"You might...might want to look away for this next part," I said.

She shrugged. "Don't bother me to see somebody else puke."

I would have said something witty and Noel Coward-like in response, but by then my head was buried deep in the plastic basket and things were taking their natural course. If I don't take the shot in time, if the migraine's in full-tilt boogie mode by the time the medicine enters my system, I vomit. Unconditionally. Like this time; I wouldn't have been surprised if I had seen my *shoes* land in there.

Afterward, shoving the basket away, I fell back on the floor and lay there shuddering.

"You're all sweaty," said Missy, picking up the basket and marching back into the bathroom. I heard her empty its contents into the toilet and then flush it away; after that, she rinsed it out in the bath tub, then did something else at the sink. A few seconds later she was kneeling beside me again and placing a warm, damp washcloth against my forehead. I began to protest but she cut me off.

"I'm not touching you," she said, applying the slightest pressure. "There's a wet rag between us."

True enough. She kept her hand there, maintaining pressure, until the warmth began to sink into my flesh. She'd gotten the temperature exactly right, and I liked the feeling of her hand against my forehead.

"You're taking good care of me," I said, managing to produce a second complete sentence in less than three minutes. Things were looking up.

"Well, a lot of people took real good care of me, and I always paid real good attention, so I learned how to do it, too. Hey, maybe I could've been a nurse, huh?"

"Florence Nightingale's got nothing on you."

"I'll bet you think I don't get that, don't you? Well, I *do*, I know all about Florence Nightingale from school, so there!"

I laughed and it hurt. She laughed, as well.

"Better yet?" she asked.

"Yes, yes it is."

"If you wanna tell me where your suit is, I can go and lay it out for you. I used to lay out Mommy's work clothes for her at night so they'd be all ready when she got up in the morning."

I opened my eyes, relieved to see that the shimmering aura surrounding her and everything else was nearly gone. "There's a tan garment bag hanging on the left side of the closet in my bedroom."

"Your shoes in there, too?"

"Yes."

"You picked out a tie yet? If you haven't, can I pick it out for you?"

"That would be very nice of you."

She stared at me a few moments longer. "Y'know, if I didn't think it'd give you another bad fit, I'd kiss your cheek. You look like you could use a kiss on the cheek."

"I appreciate the thought, though."

"Yeah, well...." Then she did something marvelous; she removed her hand from the wash cloth, bent down, and pressed her lips against it, kissing my forehead through the still-damp cotton. "That worked okay, I guess."

"I liked it."

She shook her index finger at me. "Mommy warned me that's what all dirty old men say before they start perving on you, so you just watch it, buddy."

"I'm not *that* old."

"No, but you *do* need a shower. *Phew!* Dude, you stink. Go deal with it."

Then she was off to lay out my suit and shoes, choose my tie (a silk number in a soft, muted shade of red), my socks (black), and wait for me to pull myself together and shower.

Now, standing in the main viewing room at Criss Brothers Funeral Home, she was crying and feeling embarrassed and humiliated because she thought she looked so ugly at the end (which meant she thought she looked ugly now), and I'd just chickened out on taking hold of her hand and maybe, *maybe* helping her to feel a little bit better.

I knelt down, acting as if I were re-tying one of my shoes. "Stop it, Missy." My teeth were clenched together and I was trying not to move my lips, so it emerged sounding like *stotitnissy*.

"I didn't wanna be *ugly*. Oh, lookit Mommy! She's *so sad*...." And the crying—which before had been only sniffles and a few cracked words accompanying stray tears—now threatened to erupt into body-wracking sobs. She was so scared and ashamed and confused, and me, I just knelt there, scolding her, useless, awkward, self-conscious, ineffectual, and inept, having just denied her the one gesture that might have told her was still beautiful, that no one was ashamed of her, she wasn't repulsive and never had been—

("...I'm sorry that Rebecca killed herself...")

—*no*, I thought. *It will not be this way, not within reach of my arm.*

Maybe if I'd been able to summon this kind of backbone sooner, Rebecca wouldn't have...*wouldn't have.*

I reached out and took hold of Missy's hand, prepared for the onslaught of sensations and memories I was sure were about to kick my ass into next week. That is when I discovered what happens if I mentally prepare myself for the consequences of touching them before doing so:

I felt only the hand of a frightened little girl. Missy looked at me, tears streaming down her cheeks, and tried to say something, but all that emerged was a pained splutter of nonsensical sounds as she gave my hand a squeeze, let go, and threw her arms around my neck. "I'm n-n-not u-ugly, am I, Neal?"

"No, honey, *of course* you're not. Shhhh, there-there, c'mon, Missy."

An old woman seated in a chair near the back row heard me, and turned around to stare. Seeing that I was talking to myself, her eyes narrowed in disgust.

"I'm sorry," I said to her. "I just...I knew Missy and it's just a terrible thing." The emotion in my voice wasn't as much of an affectation as I thought it would be.

The old woman's eyes softened and the slightest ghost of a smile crossed her face. She gave me a slight nod—*Maybe the poor fellow's really broken-up*—and turned away, leaving this stranger to his grief.

Missy pulled in a thick, snot-filled breath, and then laughed. "Boy, *that* was a close one. Don't say anything, freakazoid, or somebody'll call the nuthouse to come get you." She gave me a quick kiss on the cheek and broke the embrace, wiping her eyes and nose on the sleeve of her gown. "I'm gonna go over and see Mommy, okay?"

I gave a quick nod as I rose to my feet again. Missy didn't cross the room, she simply did her imitation of an electron, bounding from point to point without traversing the space between. Her mother sat in a chair off to the side of the casket and photo display. Missy was now by her side, looking uncertain what to do.

As soon as Missy appeared, the area she occupied, as if by silent understanding, became at once forbidden to anyone around her. Maybe people were just giving Missy's mother a little space—God knew the woman looked exhausted from trying to put on a strong face as she listened to mourners tell her how sorry they were about her loss—but my guess was that Missy was unconsciously emitting some sort of energy that made others nearby sense a sudden *otherness* in the room, and it might be best to just keep their distance for a few minutes.

I moved along the wall, trying to be as invisible as a living person could be, never taking my gaze off Missy and her mother. I caught a millisecond glimpse of the old woman who'd been staring at me: she was leaning over and whispering something to a well-dressed man who had just enough detached concern about him to be easily labeled an employee of the funeral home. I knew without actually looking that both the old woman and the man were talking about me.

—*Do you know him, ma'am?*

—*Never saw him before today. I'm not sure, but I think he maybe ought to be watched. I think he's really broken up, poor fellow—he was talking to himself. Not trying to start any trouble, you understand.*

—*I do, ma'am, and I'll keep an eye on him.*

Great. The last thing I needed was to have any attention drawn to me.

Missy was reaching out to take hold of her mother's hand. The funeral home employee was moving away from the old woman and making a beeline in my direction (I couldn't get mad at the guy, he was just doing his job). I didn't have many choices, and what few I did have were depleting fast.

Moving away from the wall, I made my way through the clusters of people toward the casket. A prayer bench had been placed close to its side, and I knelt down, making the Sign of the Cross as I did so and then folding my hands, lowering my head. Even if the funeral home employee did think I was trouble, he wouldn't dare interrupt me while I was praying—not that I *was* praying, but I knew damn well how this looked, and right now the appearance of prayer was good enough to buy me at least two minutes of safety.

I did not close my eyes; instead, I began turning my head in small, slow degrees to so that I could see Missy and her mother, at least peripherally. At first all I managed to do was get the great-grandmother of all neck cramps, but as soon as I saw what was happening, the muscle strain seemed trivial.

Missy was squeezing her mother's hand. The woman's head snapped up, her eyes widening as she gasped. Several people turned in her direction but no one approached.

"Neal?" said Missy, not bothering to whisper because she knew I was the only one who could hear. "Please come over here. Please come right now."

I crossed myself, rose, and with a left-right-left sidestepped the funeral home employee who'd been lurking in wait nearby.

I approached Missy's mother, who looked directly at me, smiled, and said, "*Lenny!* Oh, I'm so glad you could make it."

Missy gave me a quick glance, indicating that I needed to take hold of her mother's *other* hand, which I did at once. Her skin was simultaneously sweaty yet cracked and calloused.

"Lenny," said her mother, gesturing with her head for me to lean down; instead, I got down on one knee. She moved her lips close—but not *too* close—to my ear. "I know how most people would take this, but I think you'll understand...I...I *feel* her near me, right this second. It's so *wonderful*. She's fine. She feels fine. She isn't suffering anymore."

I smiled and looked into her eyes; where before they had been red-rimmed and glossed with that heart-numbed luster from having shed too many tears, now their shine was one of utter bliss, of an inner-peace that transcended anything I had ever experienced, and if I'd fallen in love with Missy's joy and innocence before, I felt an equal rush of emotion toward her mother. I had no idea what Missy was doing—or even how she was doing it—but it was obvious that this grief-stricken woman would end the day not with the same broken heart and spirit that had been her only interior companions since the death of her daughter, but with a sense of tranquility, even serenity, that would get her through this.

Even now I cannot tell you what Missy's mother (Cynthia) and I talked about; I had become, for lack of a more subtle simile, Missy's ventriloquist's dummy; she was filtering her feelings and memories and thoughts through her mother into me, compelling me to put those feelings and memories into my own words (more or less) so that, for the dozens of people who slowly and cautiously gathered to listen, it sounded as if Cynthia and I were old friends, sharing private moments and recollections about Missy. If there had been any doubt in anyone's mind that I *wasn't* a friend of the family, those doubts were erased over the next twenty minutes.

When at last Cynthia noticed that we'd gathered an audience, she smiled, wiped her eyes, stood, and said: "Everyone, I'm sorry—this is Leonard Kessler. He was Melissa's—*Missy's*—kindergarten teacher."

Everyone—including the old woman who'd been watching me, and the funeral home employee—said hello and shook my hand and told me how wonderful it was that I'd come. I discovered, much to my surprise, that Missy had given me a cache of specific memories to share with each person, *detailed* memories exclusive to the individual with whom I spoke.

Finally someone—possibly the minister—announced that the service would be starting in five minutes, and everyone should take their seats. I gave Cynthia a hug, she kissed my cheek, and I wandered (read: half-staggered) toward the back row where Missy stood waiting.

Looking at her now, I realized that I knew her better than I'd known my own wife—hell, I knew her better than I knew myself; she might have filtered her feelings and memories through her mother in order not to chance another physical incident like the one earlier that morning, but it in no way lessened the way the information and sensations both effected and affected me.

"Don't you say a word," she said to me. "I've decided I don't want to stay for the service. I—oh, wait, hang on." She made her way over to a well-dressed woman who'd just entered holding the hand of a slightly plump boy who was roughly Missy's age. The little boy was practically sobbing. Missy walked up beside him, took hold of his free hand, and whispered something in his ear, then kissed his cheek.

The kid looked as if he'd just shaken Spider-Man's hand. His face *beamed*, and the tears just—*viola!*—stopped. He looked to his right, where Missy stood, and smiled. Missy smiled back, then returned to me.

"That's Eric, the guy who did the gross bug-thing," she said. "I told him I wasn't mad so he didn't have to feel, y'know, all guilty and stuff. Then I told him he looked real handsome and gave him a kiss." She looked up at me. "Some kids say he's fat, but you know what I think? I think he's gonna be a real strong football player someday with lots of fans and millions of dollars, and nobody'll make fun of him anymore." She studied him for a moment. "I'll bet he grows up to look like a cross between Johnny Depp and George Clooney. He'll be yummy."

I almost laughed, but she shot me a look that said, *Don't you dare, not in here, freakazoid*, then said, "I learned that word from Mommy—she thought Lee Marvin was 'yummy,' so don't look at me like that. I'm gonna touch you now, so get ready," and grabbed my hand, dragging me toward the door.

"I figured it out," she said as we made our way out into the parking lot. "If one of us sort of...*prepares*...y'know, if we make ourselves ready for touching the other person, then we don't gotta worry about sending you into fits like before."

"'Fits'?" I said.

"Well, that's what it was, wasn't it? All that shaking around and kicking your legs and gagging on the floor and puking in a wastebasket." A shrug. "Looked like a fit to me."

"Missy, why don't you want to stay for your funeral?"

"I told Mommy everything she needs to know to feel better. The rest of its just going to be a bunch of boring prayers and people crying and it'll be *soooo* depressing." She stopped by the car, looked me straight in the eyes, and said: "And I changed my mind about one other thing. I want you to call me 'Melissa' from now on, okay?"

"Absolutely. I think it's prettier than 'Missy,' anyway. May I ask why?"

Her eyes glistened ever so slightly, but she did not cry. "I never knew that it was my grandma's middle name. Mommy wanted to name me after Grandma—I never met her, she died before I was born—but I...I gave her crap about it being such an old-lady sounding name That's what I said: 'It sounds like an old lady's name.' I shouldn't have done that."

"But your mom, she knows now, right?"

Melissa nodded her head, firmly, once. "You. Bet. And she's gonna feel better now. I mean, she'll miss me—" She then posed like a classic movie star, one arm cocked so that the hand was behind her head, the other hand on her hip, legs crossed at the ankles, Carole Lombard hamming it up for the press before putting her handprints in cement in front of Grauman's Chinese Theatre. "—c'mon, look at me, who *wouldn't* miss all this? But Mommy will be okay." She put down her arms and looked at me. "So what about you?"

"What about me?"

"What's gonna make you okay?"

"This isn't about me, Miss—uh, *Melissa*."

"It is if I say so—you said this day was my day, that we could do whatever I wanted, *your* rules, not mine, smarty-pants—and *I* want to know what I can do to make you feel okay."

I got into the car and clipped the Bluetooth cell phone receiver to my ear; it makes it look less weird when I'm talking to no one...well, no one that anyone else can see. Yes, it's a waste of money, but it keeps me from landing in the bin.

Melissa was already sitting on the passenger side, arms folded across her chest, glaring at me, impatient.

"I *asked* you a question, Mr. Gloomy Gus."

"If I'm going to call you by your name, then you have to call me by mine. It's only fair."

"Like your stupid one-week rule thing is fair? *That* kind of fair?"

I stared at her. She stared at me.

"I'd like to see you have fun," I replied.

"*Huh?*"

"There's a nice little playground not too far from here, Dell Memorial Park, you know it?"

"No. Does it have a teeter-totter?"

"Yes, and a Jungle Gym, and a slide, and a bunch of other stuff."

She waved the rest of it away. "Not interested in those other things. Give me a teeter-totter any day. Seriously, dude—uh, I mean, *Neal.*"

I started the car. "Then to Dell Memorial Park it is. You going to meet me there?"

"Nah," she said, settling back into the seat. "Think I'll just catch a ride this time."

"Seatbelt," I said.

She stared at me. "Dude—I mean, *Neal.* Think about who you're talking to. Seriously."

"Oh, yeah...right. Sorry. Never mind."

"Well, *duh.*"

* * *

There has always been something about playgrounds that strike me as simultaneously joyful yet also sad and eerie, despite however many children are running around, shrieking and squealing and laughing their heads off, having a high old time as loving parents sit on the benches off to the side, watching Jimmy or Suzy or Billy or Amy or (insert child's name here) burn off some of that seemingly everlasting energy that could power a small Third-World nation were one to harness it properly. Despite the joy and enthusiasm and laughter, I always see playgrounds from a palimpsest sort of view; while everyone else looks at the children and the life and the brisk activity, I imagine I can see beneath the surface to where the other playground waits, the deserted one, the one that exists late at night when everyone has gone home; a silent, shadow-shrouded place of swings with no occupants moving almost imperceptibly back and forth with the evening breeze, empty teeter-totters that somehow still manage to squeak at the hinges, and metal slides that quietly rattle as something small but hard falls from a nearby tree and rolls down to the ground.

Told you before, I am a walking circus of mirth.

But *this*, what I was watching now, this would have given even the most steely-nerved person a case of the willies.

Melissa was running all over the playground, hitting the teeter-totter, the Jungle Gym, the slide, the swings, all of it (despite her protestations that she didn't care about the rest of the playground's offerings), laughing her head off, having the grandest of all grand times, playing with at least five other children...none of whom I could see. I wondered how the scene looked to those people who drive by; the teeter-totter going up and down with no one on it, unoccupied swings moving back and forth, some of them snapping up fairly high...they must have thought they were imagining things.

Watching Melissa play with the unseen children, hearing the chime of her laughter, seeing the happiness on her face and how she looked like such a normal, healthy, vibrant, *living* child, I don't think I've ever felt so lonely.

After a few more minutes, Melissa ran over to me, still giggling over something one of her playmates had just told her, stopped, caught her breath, and said: "This isn't working, is it?"

"What do you mean?"

"You still look like a Gloomy Gus. The *Gloomiest* Gus."

"I'm fine."

"I'm gonna hold your hand again, so get ready."

I prepared myself, and she did as she'd threatened.

"You're so *sad*," she said.

"I'm just tired, Melissa. That's all."

"Huh-uh, buddy. Don't lie to me." A tear began forming in one of her eyes.

"Oh, hey, *Melissa*," I said, taking hold of her other hand. "Don't you get upset, hon, okay? I just...get like this sometimes."

"You *are* like this a lot of the time. I can tell."

"It passes. You go back and play with your new friends, all right?"

She shook her head, her eyes unblinking. "No. I wanna go for another ride, see if I can spot people you can't."

"Whatever you want."

"What I *want* is not to be dead. What I *want* is for you to, I dunno, *smile* and mean it. It won't break your face, y'know."

"Well, then, why don't we go home—uh, go to the apartment and watch SpongeBob, then? I was promised miraculous buttered popcorn, as I recall."

"Oh, you'll get the popcorn, and you'll *love* it. Okay. Let me say good-bye and then we'll go back."

"You could stay here and play with them a little longer, you know. I mean, it's not like you *have* to ride back with me."

"You asked me not to do that popping in and out thing. It makes you nervous."

"Only if I'm not expecting it. This would be different."

Her eyes narrowed. "You trying to get rid of me?"

"Not at all. But you're having so much fun and...and I'm not so much fun."

"Says you. Gloomy Gus."

"I think I preferred 'freakazoid.'"

She parted her hands in front of her. "I am fickle. *And* I am dead. So we do things my way. I'm gonna go say good-bye to the other kids, and then I want you to take me someplace before we go back to watch SpongeBob."

"Did anyone ever tell you that you were kind of bossy?"

"Yes, but I never listened. Like now." And with that, she ran off to have one more ride on the teeter-totter with her unseen friends, while I sat there trying to think of *where* she could possibly want me to take her.

* * *

"You're *not* serious?"

"Yep," she said. "I wanna see where you keep the other peoples' boxes."

We were driving around the downtown square where I suspected Melissa would be able to spot others like herself, but if she did, she said nothing.

"Why would you want to see...I mean, there's nothing to—"

"I just think it would be interesting, that's all."

I made sure to watch the tone of my voice. "Look, Melissa, I don't go there unless I *have* to."

"Is that another one of your dumb rules?"

"No. It's just the truth." I stopped for a red light near the Sparta and found myself remembering when Rebecca and I first began dating, how we'd always start our Friday nights out at the Sparta for the world's best cheeseburgers. This was back when I was arrogant—or lazy—enough to believe that I knew her.

"Hey," said Melissa, pointing toward the traffic light. "Is there, like, a certain *shade* of green you're waiting for?"

"A—huh? Oh, right…thanks." I pulled away, automatically heading toward the East Main Street Bridge that led into Coffin County.

"How come you don't go there unless you have to?"

My grip tightened on the steering wheel. "It's not exactly Disney World in there. It's a big, cold, depressing room filled with metal shelves and boxes full of dead peoples' personal effects —their *stuff*."

Melissa glared at me for a moment. "I remember what 'personal effects' are from when you told me before, so don't explain it every time you say it. I'm not stupid."

"I didn't mean to make it sound that way, I'm sorry."

She turned away from me for a few moments, waved at someone I could not see, smiled, then said: "Can you see that lady over there by that wall?"

Without really being aware of it, I'd driven over the bridge and into Coffin County. We were once again stopped at a red light, right at the corner where the Great Fire of 1968 began when a local casket company went up and took every business in a 3-block radius with it. The area never recovered.

There was an old but elegant-looking black woman standing in front of a brick wall. If I remembered correctly, this part of Coffin County —what used to be called 'Old Towne East' —used to boast a lot of nightclubs, small museums, and specialty shops. I wondered which type of business that wall had belonged to, and what memories the old woman associated with it.

"Yes, I see her."

She stood there with her arms spread apart, as if waiting for someone to embrace her. Her dress was a thing of tattered, faded elegance, and the gloves she wore looked…cheerless. That's the only word I could think of.

"What's she doing?" asked Melissa.

"I have no idea, hon. There are a lot of…lost people who live in this area."

As if to illustrate my point, a young but horribly disheveled man walked up to the old woman and began asking her, in a very loud voice, to cut something off of his face for him. After a few moments, the old woman smiled, patted his cheek as if he were nothing more than an upset little boy, and gave him a dollar bill from her purse. She then turned back to the wall, her arms spread open for the embrace, while the young man looked at her, looked at the dollar bill, and shuffled quietly away.

"You see him, too?" asked Melissa.

"Yes."

She leaned toward me. "I don't know why, but I got a feeling he might be the next person to come stay with you for a while."

"He's just one of the...lost people here, Melissa, that's all. Poor guy's probably crazy or something, can't afford his medications."

The light changed and I drove on.

"Do you always do that?"

I looked at her. "Do what?"

She looked at the young man who was now stumbling around the corner, then shook her head. "Nothing. You're just a lot nicer than you want me to think you are."

"No, I'm not. But thank you, anyway."

"Hey, I'm bossy, remember? If I say you're nice, then you're nice."

"But —"

"Shut. *Up*."

We fell into a comfortable silence for the next few minutes, Melissa studying the streets and buildings (and ruins of buildings) with an intensity that you are genetically incapable of after the age of 9, and me simply repeating a route I could drive in my sleep.

Cedar Hill Memorial Hospital, both of the city's nursing homes, and the County Hospice Center form an almost perfect circle from my apartment; what makes the circle complete is stopping by the "Old Towne East Storage" before heading back home. While this fact has always been present in my mind, I don't know that it ever really hit me as hard as it did as Melissa and I drove toward the OTES facility; for three years I had been driving and living in one ongoing circle; a moth around a light bulb, deciding whether or not to give into the temptation; a plane in a holding pattern, waiting for clearance to land; a humorless straight-man stuck in a revolving door in some silent 2-reeler from the 1920s, waiting for the punch line to the gag.

I pulled up to the locked gates and dug my key-card from my wallet. I was just getting ready to swipe it when Melissa said: "You'd really do it, wouldn't you?"

"Do what?"

She nodded at the gates. "Take me in there and show me the boxes."

"You said you wanted to see them."

"And *you* said that the place depressed you."

"No, I said that the room was big, cold, and depressing."

"Same thing."

"Technically, no, because—"

"Shut. *Up.* You'd really take me in there and show it to me, even if it makes you sad?"

I said nothing. There seemed to be no point.

"I'm gonna hold your hand for a minute," said Melissa.

She did, and for a few seconds I was *aware* of her being somewhere within one of my memories of the storage room. This wasn't anything like this morning or with her mother at the funeral home; this time, I felt...comforted. Less alone.

She let go of my hand and gave a mock shiver. "Yeech, you're right. That is one *depressing* place, dude. Seriously."

"Told you."

"Can I ask you a question?"

"You mean besides that one?"

She giggled. "Don't be a smarty-pants. It makes me want to smack you."

"And your question...?"

Her face became very serious, very adult-looking. "Why do you do this? How did you get this job? What do you do for money? I mean, jeez, it's not like somebody pays you for this, do they?"

"That's four questions."

She huffed. "What? You gotta be somewhere in, like, ten minutes or something? Okay, it's four questions, big deal. Will you tell me, please?"

By now I'd backed out and was heading to the apartment. I decided to take a few small detours. If I was going to tell her about this, it was going to be in the car, not the apartment. I had never spoken about this while in the apartment, and I never would. Something about Rebecca's presence made talking about it seem distasteful, as if I would be dishonoring my wife's memory. Or the memory of the wife I thought I'd known.

Melissa cleared her throat—dramatically, of course. "*Well...?*"

"Promise not to interrupt me with a bunch of questions?"

She mimed zipping her mouth closed.

"I'm serious, Melissa. I've never told anyone about this, and I don't want you making jokes."

She raised her hand, unzipped her mouth, and said: "I'd never make fun of you. Not about something like this. I promise."

I flashed my most dazzling Constipated Smile. "Okay. If something isn't clear, *then* you can interrupt me. Deal?" I held out my hand.

"Deal," she replied, and we shook on it.

"Okay, I'm going to answer your questions in reverse order, if that's all right."

"Just so long as you answer them."

"I *don't* get paid for doing this. I live on my savings, the early-retirement benefits package from my job, and Rebecca's insurance money."

Melissa held up her hand. "Okay, I don't, like, mean to bring up something sad, but if Rebecca killed herself, the insurance company wouldn't pay."

I grinned and wagged a finger at her. "Oh, no, no, no—that's a myth that a lot of insurance companies do everything they can to keep alive. The truth is, there are several companies who *will* pay on a life insurance policy when the person commits suicide. They wait a year, and they pay only the face-value of the policy, but they *do* pay. Suicide is considered a result of undiagnosed mental illness. You'd be surprised at how many companies quietly do this."

"How do you know all that?"

"Do you know what I did for twenty-two years before Rebecca died and I took early retirement?"

Melissa shook her head.

"I sold life-insurance."

"Oh. My. *God!* That is *so* funny! That is, like, the goofiest thing I've heard all week! Is it okay that I think that's goofy?"

I nodded. "I've come to see a certain irony in it." I gave her a look.

"I know what 'irony' means," she said. "My teachers told Mommy I was 'gifted.'"

"I don't doubt that."

"Yeah, well...what'cha gonna do? Hey—how old are you, anyway?"

"I'll turn forty-seven next month."

"Oh, *man.* Your *birthday's* coming up? Dude, I could *so* make you the *best* birthday cake."

"I stopped celebrating my birthday a long time ago—oh, no you don't, Melissa. No arguments."

She sighed, pouting. "Okay, you were saying...?"

"Rebecca didn't have her policy through my company. *My* ex-company is one that won't pay out on a suicide."

"Well that sucks."

From the mouths of babes.

"Does that answer your questions about my financial state?"

"So you got enough money to live on for the rest of your life?"

"If I'm careful. The apartment is paid for. Rebecca and I made some good investments. I'm not rich, Melissa, but I'm okay."

"Cool beans." She turned toward me a little more and folded her arms across her chest. "So...how did you get this job, and why you?"

"I don't think of it as a 'job,' Melissa. It's more like..."

"Like what?"

My throat tightened a little. I coughed. "Could we go back to that one later?"

"Okay."

I pulled into the underground parking garage and had to dig out the card-key, then drove over to my assigned parking space near the elevators. I turned off the ignition, removed the keys, and sat looking at them in my hand.

"What is it?" asked Melissa. "C'mon, Neal, you were going real good there."

"Can I ask *you* something?"

"Sure."

"Why wasn't your dad at your funeral? You've never even mentioned him."

"My daddy's dead. He died before I was born. He had a big party with some of his friends right after he and Mommy found out she was pregnant. He was drunk and got in a wreck. He hit a tree. There wasn't anybody else in the car with him, though, so that was lucky." She looked down at her hands. "I only know him from, like, pictures and video tapes and what Mommy said about him. It's not the same, y'know? It sounded like he might've been really cool, kinda like you."

"You think I'm cool?"

A shrug. "Don't let it go to your head, though. You'd have been a pretty cool dad, I think."

For a moment we just looked at one another. Then she scooted closer to me and put my arm around her shoulder. "Is this okay?"

"This is good. I like this."

"Me, too."

No jolts, no visions, no sudden rush of sensations; just me with my arm around her shoulders, and she with her head resting against my chest. It was nice.

"Three weeks after Rebecca's funeral," I said to her, "I came back to the apartment and found her sleeping in the guest room, just like you saw her. That's where I'd...found her body. She'd taken a bunch of prescription tranquilizers, crushed them up and mixed them in with a bowl of oatmeal so she wouldn't vomit. She'd been gathering the pills for months and I had no idea.

"At first I didn't know what to think—I mean, I'd watched the coffin with her body lowered into the ground, yet here she was, back in the guest room. The rotting part—if that's what it is, rotting—that didn't start for almost three months. But that night, when she first re-appeared, I couldn't stop looking at her. She was breathing, I could see her chest rise and fall, I could *hear* the air going in and out of her lungs, it was like she was just taking a nap. I just figured that I'd been holding it all in, you know? The grief. I'd been holding it in and I'd simply...snapped. Gone a little crazy. So I pulled out a bottle of booze and got good and tanked, then went back into the room. She was still there. I decided that I was going to wake her up. So I stomped over to the bed and reached out and gave her arm a good shake. And that's when...you remember what happened with us this morning, right?"

"Uh-huh."

"Something like that happened with Rebecca. It wasn't as strong as what happened this morning, but it was bad enough. I had a single flash of what had been in her mind during her last moments, and it...it was awful, Melissa. She was so *lonely*, and I never knew. She felt like I was a stranger to her, had been for years." Even now, hearing myself say it aloud, I still couldn't quite grasp it.

"I mean, people like to think that when someone they love dies, that that person is thinking about them, about those they're leaving behind, right at the end." I shook my head. "Rebecca wasn't thinking about me at all. I wasn't even a *distant* thought. I had pretty much ceased to exist for her."

Melissa reached over and squeezed my hand. "I'm so sorry."

But I couldn't stop, not now. "But then something fell out of her hand." I lifted up the car keys. "A key wrapped in a piece of paper. It was a note, in her handwriting. It had an address on it, and a number, and the words, 'Look in your other wallet.'

"That's where I found the card-key to the storage facility. The other key was for the padlock on the unit door, Number 23."

"That's where you keep the boxes."

I nodded. "But that night, when I went to the place, there was only one box. It was filled with things of Rebecca's I never knew she had. Children's books, stuffed toy animals, a shadow box of antique sewing thimbles, a watercolor pad filled with these gorgeous paintings she'd done—hell, I never knew she liked to paint. Fifteen years we'd been married, and I had no idea. There were notebooks of poetry she'd written, programs from theatrical productions she'd done in high school and college, it was just...these precious keepsakes from someone I never knew.

"But the worst of it were the letters. She'd been having...I can't call it an 'affair' because the two of them never...uh...they didn't..."

"Have sex. It's okay to say something like that to me."

I couldn't look at her, I was too embarrassed. "They'd been high-school sweethearts and had met again about ten years or so after she and I were married. They talked on the phone a lot, met for lunch, but made sure they were never alone together. He was married, as well, with a bunch of kids, but the *letters*...my God, Melissa, he loved her so much, and she loved him. She told him things she never told me. She had both his letters and hers—he'd sent hers back when he finally broke it off. It had just gotten too...I don't know...too painful for both of them. I sat in that damned room all night reading them, and by the time I finished the last one, I knew that I'd been the runner-up for her all along. I was the consolation prize for not getting the man she was meant to have been with.

"I wanted her back right then. I still do. I could have been a better man, the kind of man who deserved to be her husband. If I hadn't been so busy making sure we had all of our ducks in a row, everything paid for, always keeping track of the money, the investments, all that pointless bullshit...then maybe I would have noticed how lonely she was. I loved her just as much as he did, but I was never good at showing it, expressing it with words like I should have. 'You're a very cautious man, Neal.' That's what she used to say to me. 'Cautious.'" I pulled in a deep breath, squeezed Melissa's shoulder, and pushed out the rest of it.

"After that night, I kept checking on her, and I kept finding new pieces of paper, with names on them and the addresses of the hospital, or nursing homes, or the hospice. It didn't take me very long to figure out what I was supposed to do. The first few were kind of tough. I had to dig through the dumpsters in order to find the boxes. But after I began figuring things out, the boxes...they weren't so hard to find. They would be on top of all the garbage, or sometimes even setting beside the Dumpsters. I even know the schedules now. The hospital disposes of unclaimed personal effects every Tuesday night; the nursing home on 21st Street gets rid of them on Thursday; the retirement center puts their unclaimed boxes out on Friday; and the hospice—"

"Sunday night," said Melissa.

"Sunday night."

"So you've been doing this for three years, huh?"

"Yes."

"Must get lonely."

I thought of her on the playground, laughing with friends I couldn't see. "It does sometimes. Even when I've got visitors like you and Lenny and all the rest. I even tried to stop doing it once, but that's when Rebecca started to...*deteriorate*. There, I said it. I keep hoping that if I get to peoples' effects right away that it will stop the process, that she'll start getting better. But then I remember...she's dead. There's no 'getting better' from that."

"So why do you think you're the one doing this?"

I looked at her this time. "I don't know for sure, but I hope...I hope that if I do enough, then she'll forgive me for not being there for her, for being such a bad person, for being so distant and unthinking and...and..."

"Cautious?"

I nodded. "Cautious."

"Maybe it's kind of like what the priests make you do after confession, Say an 'Our Father' or 'Hail Mary' or an Act of Contrition."

"Penance."

"Sounds like that to me. Mommy always used to say, 'If it walks like a duck, and quacks like a duck, it must be—'"

We were both startled by the sound of someone banging on the driver's-side window. I actually shrieked, which made Melissa giggle afterward.

"You ever going to get out of that damn car?" shouted Lenny. "I got something to show you." I opened the door but Lenny was blocking my escape.

"Got me a new toy today!" He held up what could only have been a digital camera, and a fairly expensive one, at that. "Some smartass yuppie-type left this at the library. I always wanted one of these, so I figured, what the fuck—oops, pardon the language, little lady."

Melissa grinned. "That's okay. I've heard worse."

We climbed out of the car. Lenny removed his hat and offered his hand. "My name's—"

"Your name is Lenny Kessler. Hi. I'm Melissa." She grabbed his hand and gave it a solid shake.

"Well, now, it's real pleasure to meet you, Melissa. I guess old Neal here's mentioned me, am I right? Tell me I'm right."

"You're right. Where's your lady-friend from this morning?"

"My lady —? Oh, you mean Theresa? The woman in the dress?"

"Uh-huh. I saw you two talking. I watched from the window. She's *pretty.*"

"Pretty full of herself, but yeah, she's a looker. I'm afraid she and I didn't exactly hit it off." He looked at me. "Pity. I'd've given a year's pay for her to've unleashed the hounds and give me a look at those bazooba-wobblies under that designer dress."

Melissa giggled. "You're funny."

"Glad someone here thinks so." Lenny winked at her, then faced me. "So you were about to ask me why I was at the library in the first place?"

I sighed. "Lenny, it's already been a long day and it isn't even six yet."

"I see you're still your usual bucket of chuckles. That's all right, I'll tell you on the way up to your place. By the way, I hope you've still some of the good hooch left. I'm a bit parched."

The three of us headed toward the elevators. I pushed the **UP** button and waited.

"I was looking through this book at the library," said Lenny, "all about brain science and what the writers called the 'biology of belief,' right? They said that all our brains contain what they called a 'God area,' a place where the spiritual and the biological come together during moments of euphoria. And that got me to thinking about you and that 'your cells remember you' horseshit, so I—"

I held up a hand, silencing him. "You still have your wallet on you, Lenny?"

"Always." He pulled it from his back pants pocket. "Not much money in there, though."

"Gimme." I took it from his hand, opened it, and thumbed through its contents until I found what I was looking for. I pulled out the card, read it, saw Lenny's signature, and laughed.

"What?" said Lenny. "You find a naked picture of me or something? Sorry if you feel inadequate at the sight of it, but —"

"You were an organ and tissue donor, Lenny."

He pulled the card and wallet from my hands. "Yeah, so wha —? Oh, wait a minute..."

"I don't know what they took and what they didn't, but according to that card, you agreed to donate your corneas. The rest of you could have been a godawful mess, Lenny, but corneas are among the first things they take from a donor."

He stared at the card, then looked at me. "So you were right? I mean, the cells in my corneas—?"

"Are still active somewhere in the sockets of some lucky person."

"Well, hell, don't that beat all?"

The elevator arrived and its doors opened. It was empty.

"I want to ask a favor of you two," I said, stepping in and holding the door open. "Would you two mind just popping on up to the apartment and letting my ride up by myself? It's nothing personal, but I just...need a minute or two by myself."

"You're not gonna sneak out or something like that, are you?" asked Melissa.

"Where would I go?"

She nodded. "Good point." She grabbed Lenny's hand. "Okay, Mr. Gloomy Gus—we'll see you upstairs."

The doors closed. I pushed the button to my floor, waited a few seconds until I felt the elevator start moving, and then my legs gave out and I dropped ass-first onto the floor, burying my face in my hands and crying. *Goddammit!*

Three years. Three years it had taken me to get the walls built, to train myself *not* to feel anything, and in the course of two days Melissa had bulldozed right through them, and everything I'd been trying to avoid thinking about, confronting, admitting to myself, all of it followed right behind her, blasting into me like the heat from a furnace.

There should be a way to scrape the guilt and regret and sadness from the places in you where it builds up like plaque on your connective tissue, making it almost impossible for you to get out of bed and face the day because it hurts too much to even *move*; there should be a tool that you can carry for those times when a little undetected piece of that plaque breaks loose and begins moving toward your core, a tool that can enter the flesh without spilling blood or scarring tissue and simply scour it away, cut it out, and leave you in a safe oblivion where nothing touches you, nothing moves you, nothing matters.

"*Fuck....*" I said aloud to no one and nothing. I pulled up my head, saw that I was almost to my floor, and got to my feet, wiping my eyes as best I could and hoping like hell that the damned elevator didn't stop at another floor for someone else to get on. I did not want anyone to see me this way.

The doors opened to my floor. No one was waiting there. I made a beeline for my door, key in hand, and slipped quickly inside.

In the kitchen, Melissa was gathering together the ingredients for her popcorn while Lenny poured himself a generous drink. I walked by them as fast as I could, claiming a need to use the bathroom, and that's when I heard Melissa sing:

"A gentle breeze from Hush-a-bye Mountain
Softly blows o'er lullaby bay.
It fills the sails of boats that are waiting —
Waiting to sail your worries away…"

And I couldn't move.

"Hey, Neal," called Lenny. "You want a belt of this stuff?"

"That doesn't go with my popcorn," said Melissa. "Only soda pop. Or strawberry smoothies."

I pulled in a thick, snot-filled breath, went to my office, grabbed the box of Melissa's personal effects, and stomped back into the living room, dropping the box on the sofa. "It's time for you to pick something," I said, a little more loudly than I would have preferred.

Melissa stuck her head out from the kitchen. "It's time for me to *what?*"

"You heard me," I said, pulling the lid off the box. "Time to go, Melissa. Get in here and choose something right now."

She looked at the box, then at me. She was trying not to show it, but I could see that inside of her, something had crumpled.

"But that's not fair! You said that I had to wait —"

"My 'dumb' rules, remember? I can change them if I goddamned well want to. Now get your ass in here and pick something!"

"But…b-but —"

"But *nothing!* I don't need this, I don't *want* this. Everything was fine until *you* showed up, with your questions and your 'dude' and 'freakazoid' and touchy-feely and 'You'd have been a pretty cool dad,' and all the rest of it. I—*look at me!* I'm not your dad, Melissa, he's *dead,* just like you, just like Lenny, just like Rebecca, just like I'll be someday — and the sooner the fucking better!" Even I was startled at how loudly I was screaming at her.

Lenny stood behind her, a hand on her shoulder. "Hey, Neal, buddy—what is this shit?"

"This shit is none of your business, Lenny." I threw down the lid and started toward Melissa, who backed up against Lenny, her eyes widening with fear.

I stopped again. Jesus Christ, what was I doing? She was actually *scared* of me. And she'd been having such a good time at the playground, too.

But of course I knew what I was doing. I was just being cautious. Remove the source of what makes me feel anything, and I would cease to feel once again, and all could continue as before.

I covered my mouth with my hand. "Oh, God..."

"Have you been *crying?*" said Melissa.

"I think you need a belt of the good stuff," said Lenny.

I looked back at the box, at the lid on the floor, and realized what a horrible, terrible, vicious thing I had just done. Once the lid has been removed in their presence, they *have* to choose. I don't know why it's that way, it just *is.*

"Oh, God, Melissa," I said, pulling my hand away from my mouth. "I'm so sorry. I was...I was upset because...because..."

"It's okay," she said, her tone neutral, her expression unreadable. She set down the bowl she was going to use for the popcorn, squeezed Lenny's hand, and walked right up to the box, examining its scant contents.

"All right," she said, the slightest quaver in her voice. "I made my decision."

"Can you forgive me?"

"We'll have to see about that." She turned away, picked up the lid, and placed it back on the box. "There's nothing in there I want. Sorry, freakazoid. Looks like you're stuck with me."

"What are you doing?"

"Making my choice." She walked over to me, gave me that I'm-gonna-touch-you-now look, and held my hand. "I choose to stay here with you. And I *know* you're not my dad, but I never knew him." She pulled on my arm, forcing me to bend down slightly. "But I know you. And I really wanna stay." And then she kissed my cheek. "You need somebody to take care of you, 'cause it sure looks like you can't do it yourself. I mean, *dude*, have you *looked* at that bathroom of yours? I mean, *really* looked at it? I've seen science experiments that were less gross."

We stood in silence for a few moments, and then all three of us turned in the direction of the guest room.

"Was that you, Lenny?" I asked.

"Yeah, been working on my ventriloquist act, learning to throw the sound of my coughing—*what the hell do you think, Cell-Boy?*"

I looked at Melissa. "She's never coughed before."

"You sure?"

"Yes."

"Well, then—maybe we ought to go check on her...?"

The three of us moved toward the guest room. I opened the door and saw that the light of early evening, golden yet somehow gray at the same time, was filtering through the blind on the window, casting soft, glowing lines across Rebecca's body.

Melissa moved away from me and opened the blinds a little more — not all the way, just enough that Rebecca looked for a moment like a figure in a painting, the black patches on her skin looking more like deliberate shadows added toward the end by the artist's brush or charcoal pencil.

"There's less of them," I whispered.

"Yeah," said Melissa, walking over to the bed and sitting by Rebecca's side. "She still doesn't look too good, but she looks *better*, don't you think?"

I started to say something, but then Rebecca coughed again, a soft, dry sound, and moved her head ever so slightly to the right, as if getting more comfortable. I heard the bones in her neck softly crack as she did this, and then she released a small sound, a low, gentle, but satisfied sigh, *There, that's better.*

Melissa took hold of Rebecca's hand. "Huh, that's weird."

"What?" It was all I could do to say *that* much.

Melissa looked at me. "She's thinking about cheeseburgers."

"Oh, man," said Lenny from behind me. "Neal, you *have* to let me take a picture of her, of all three of you." Not waiting for a response, he powered up the camera and nodded for me to go over to the bed.

I moved as if drunk or drugged, and sat on the other side of my wife.

"Take her hand," said Melissa.

I hesitated.

"I'll make sure nothing happens," she said. "I promise."

I took Rebecca's hand in both of mine; it felt almost no different from the other times I'd dared to touch her hand; clammy, moist, lifeless…but I could sense, far beneath the facade of her tissue, the façade that was ultimately all flesh, the tiniest wave of warmth struggling to swim to the surface.

"It's gonna be a long time, still," said Melissa. "But at least she'll have company. So will you." She leaned forward. "*Please* don't ever yell at me like that again. You scared me."

"I know."

"You hurt my feelings."

"Never again, hon. Never again."

Lenny aimed the camera, got us in focus. "You know, there are some cultures that believe if you take a person's picture, you steal part of their soul."

"Then take a lot of pictures," said Melissa. "You can keep all of our souls together in there." She smiled at me. "That way, we can be a family. Kinda. Does that make sense?"

"Works for me," I said, my voice suddenly hoarse.

"I'm gonna make chocolate cake for your birthday," said Melissa. "Chocolate's good for birthdays."

I thought of the rest of my life, knowing that there was now more of it behind me than ahead, and of the days I would spend in these rooms, watching over Rebecca with Melissa nearby to take care of me, and wondered if maybe I'd find that it had some meaning, after all. Maybe Rebecca would come all the way back to me, and maybe she wouldn't; but if there was even a chance I could win her heart as I should have, that I could love and treasure her the way I always should have, then I would not push it away. I would continue to collect the boxes of personal effects and help those who came to my door to find their way to…wherever they went once their choice had been made. I would grow old with my wife and this little girl for company, and the day would come when I would find myself in a hospital, nursing home, or hospice bed, and I knew they would be there, as well, watching over me, whispering memories into my ear, singing lost lullabies as I release the final, relieved breaths, feeling the weight of purpose and meaning forever lifted from my eyes; and afterward…

Afterward, there will be a hallway, its polished floor shining under the glow of overhead fluorescent lights, and into this hallway there will be wheeled a gurney with a sheet-covered body, and the wheels will squeak softly as it is rolled toward the far end where only one elevator waits, and this elevator goes in only one direction. As the gurney is wheeled away, another person, dressed in hospital or hospice whites, will shuffle from the room carrying a box with my name written on its side, and they will carry this box to the front desk, knowing that come Tuesday, or Thursday, or Sunday, it will be discarded with the other unclaimed possessions, left to time, the elements, or other mysteries best not dwelt upon for too long. It is, after all, only a box of *stuff*, of left-behind things, items with no meaning to anyone except the person who can no longer touch them, hold them, or tell the stories of how this book meant something, this ring was precious, this cross-stitched picture is beautiful *because*…

But for now, right now, this moment, I hold my wife's hand, and Melissa holds her other hand, and in this way we are one, and it needs to be captured, to be noted, in order to make it true not only in the moment, but in memory, as well. I look at Melissa and smile and hope that all I want her to know can be seen in that smile, and hope—God, how I hope, how strange a feeling it is to hope—that we'll know in a few seconds, after Lenny takes the picture. I look at him and think, Take it. Take it as we are now. We are looking at you. As we are now. Take it. Take it. Take it.

For Want of a Smile

Introduction by Sèphera Girón

Who hasn't felt the hollow ache of loneliness? The gnawing of sexual frustration? The yearn for companionship?

When one is single, it seems as though everyone else has found love and is living a grand romance. Maybe they are, maybe they aren't.

However, the reality remains that most people come into life believing they will one day have a partner.

Even Frankenstein's monster craved a mate and tried to get one.

Some people spend years, even decades, an entire lifetime, looking for love. There is no guarantee that we will all find love and happiness. Media fills our minds with the idea that romance is only a mouseclick away or that marital vows will truly last, but the statistics prove otherwise. There are a lot of single people out there bumbling around, trying to figure out how to connect.

Although it's easy to point a finger at modern society and say we're cold and disconnected with all of our technologies, the lonely have walked the earth since the beginning of man.

Several years ago—wow, I guess it's been fifteen! —Gary wrote *The Indifference of Heaven/In Silent Graves* and used my name. When he showed me his work, I was speechless, stupefied with honor and insanely flattered. It blew my mind that now I too was absorbed into his beautifully crafted renderings for eternity. His inclusion of my name in his creation remains one of my favourite gifts that I've ever received. And truly, despite my bias, *In Silent Graves* is a fantastic book and required reading for all Braunbeck fans.

Most of you know that Gary has won many writing awards, seven Stokers alone, for his fabulous work. He was also the President of the Horror Writers Association for a while and did a fabulous job. I've been a member of the HWA since the early nineties and the Ontario Chapter Head so it was a thrill to work with him in that capacity as well.

In "For Want of a Smile," Braunbeck captures the poignant ache of loneliness, of yearning to love and be loved; all of the human things that are elusive to so many.

Wayne is a middle-aged average man slipping in and out of reality and we are along for the ride.

Braunbeck's work is always well-crafted; lyrical and usually melancholy. His ability to articulate nuances of emotion is the reason he wins awards. In Wayne, we find a regular guy who just can't figure out the code for getting a girl or even getting laid. We are treated to his misadventures through Braunbeck's poetic prose with lines like "the bitter taste of *alone* in his mouth."

So now, dim the lights and sit back. Immerse yourself into the world of Wayne Bricker who is having a worse life than you.

For Want Of A Smile

I long to talk with some old lover's ghost
    Who died before the god of Love was born.
                                —John Donne, "Love's Deitie"

When Quasimodo awoke he found that sometime during the night he'd turned back into Wayne Bricker and the woman who was his Esmeralda had broken into particles of dust that drifted before his eyes like so many unattained goals.

He dragged himself out of bed, stoop-shouldered, and made his way down to the kitchen where, for the umpteenth time, he prepared himself a breakfast of toast, tea, one strip of turkey bacon, and half a grapefruit. He ate in silence, trying to recapture the scent of Esmeralda's skin, the soft fullness of her lips, the sparkle in her eyes that promised passion. No good; gone but not forgotten.

Wayne Bricker finished his breakfast, started the day's first cigarette, and thought about his life, all thirty-six years, four months, two weeks, six days, seven hours, and—he looked at the clock—eighteen minutes of it. It was not an extraordinary life—he was no poet, no visionary, no heroic leader of men—but it was usually a good life, if a bit solitary; but what else could an acne-scarred, overweight, prematurely balding bachelor who was still technically a virgin expect?

He crushed out his cigarette and went into the bathroom where he showered and shaved. As he stood in front of the mirror drying what was left of his hair, he studied his average face and wondered why it was that everyone had to be exceptional these days. It wasn't good enough just to do your best and get by; no, that was a bit unadorned for most people's vision of success. If you had no grand accomplishments behind you at twenty-one, people smiled and said, That's okay, you're Young; if at seventy you could not compete, they smiled and said, That's okay, you're old; but if you were thirty-six and the best you had to offer another human being was a steady job, a nice enough home, and a life unencumbered by crowds of friends, meager though that life might be, well, then, these same people looked at you only briefly and whispered to one another: Failure.

"Always start the day on a cheery note, eh?" he said to his reflection. It was a pleasant if unmemorable face (and if anyone *did* remember his face, they remembered only the terrible acne scars), and he decided—as he always did during this morning ritual—that he was happy with it and the man who accompanied it. If only he could find someone who would feel the same—

—ah, the hell with it. That's why he had Esmeralda at nights, or in the afternoons, sometimes during lunch, but she was always with him, more a part of his memory than those few people who were actually a part of his life.

And so Wayne Bricker, perceived by those around him as an average, lonely, unimaginative but decent man, dressed and left for work, still trying to recapture the scent of his dream lover's skin.

Just another day. No fanfare, please.

He stopped by the post office and mailed the letter he'd been carrying in his pocket for over three weeks. He'd never tried the **Personals** before. At least the rejection he knew waited for him in print had the added appeal of not being face-to-face humiliation. Enough of that was ... well, *enough*.

He slipped the envelope into the slot and immediately wished he hadn't done it. Oh, well—the noose was around his neck now, might as well step off that chair ...

* * *

SWM, 36, steady employment, owns own home, seeks SF for companionship and possible romance. Appearance not at all important. "Who, being loved, is poor?" Do you know who said that? If so, we might be right for each other. Respond to P.O. Box 18012, Cedar Hill, Ohio, 43055.

* * *

Come, and I will you teach you the disillusionment of the body as it perishes in the rain of grief, the death in fading roses never sent to one you admire from afar, the emptiness of lonely orgasms in night-flooded, loveless rooms.

How many nights had those words come to him while he was asleep and just about to hold his dream lover in his arms? How many mornings had begun with the bitter taste of *alone* in his mouth?

Too many; far, far too many.

And so he came to find himself writing, then re-writing the ad. Short but not too short, and there must be no hint in the words of the desperation in his heart.

No more, he thought as he stood before the post office box, the key in his trembling hand. *No more.*

He inserted the key and turned the lock.

Inside was only one envelope. He knew that he should be happy that at least *someone* had responded, but he'd hoped for more than —

—no. He would not do this. Someone out there cared enough to reply.

He removed the envelope and opened it. Inside was a single sheet of stationary.

The script was delicate and exquisitely feminine, the spaces between each word painstakingly exact, the angle of her slant almost Elizabethan in its fluid grace, each letter a blossom, each word a bouquet, the sentence itself a breathtaking garland: *Oscar Wilde*, read the first two words. *One of his plays, I believe.*

No more the death of fading roses, he prayed.

No more.

* * *

The morning had been filled with frantic activity around the office, and Wayne's thoughts of his impending blind date retreated to the back of his mind where they curled up in a corner, covered themselves against the cold, and snapped off the light.

When lunchtime arrived, he pulled his paper bag from a lower desk drawer, took the elevator to the lobby, and went outside to his usual bench.

Someone was sitting there.

No one all that special, really; no one who'd merit a second look, no; no one who'd make your heart triphammer and try to squirt out of your ribcage, don't be silly; no one all that special, so calm down, Wayne old boy, this is no big deal, nothing to get excited about, nothing earth-shattering ... just the most beautiful woman you've ever seen. Be cool, be smooth, be suave, and remember to not chew with your mouth open.

Shaking and perspiring, Wayne picked up the pace of his steps and crossed to the bench. He stood in front of her for a moment, noting that she was alone, wore no rings, and didn't seem to be waiting for anyone.

She looked up. "Hi."

Wayne gave her a smile. "Hello. Do you mind if I sit down? I always like to eat my lunch here and this is...well, you're the first person I've ever seen sitting here."

"Please, join me."

He sat down—not too close—and opened his lunch: a tuna sandwich, a bag of potato chips, an apple, and an eight ounce bottle of cranberry juice. Boring.

He glanced at the divine woman next to him. She probably knew well the taste of caviar, rack of lamb, things exquisite. Chicken of the Sea from a tin can never came near those lips, nosiree. Nothing common for this beauty, and beauty always has her way.

She looked at him. Her eyes were a deep, soft green.

He felt his grip tighten on the sandwich.

"Are you all right?" she asked.

"Uh...yes, fine, thank you. I didn't mean to stare, I'm very sorry, please excuse me."

"That's all right, I'm used to it." She said this with a laugh, but her lips never formed a smile.

I'll bet you are, thought Wayne. Her statement lacked the edge of arrogance he usually associated with women this stunning; it was almost self-deprecating. He found that refreshing.

"Are you sure you're all right?" She seemed genuinely concerned, and Wayne wondered why until he looked down and saw that he'd completely crushed his sandwich. He shrugged, embarrassed, and began rummaging through his bag for a napkin.

He wished she'd smile at him, just a little something to let him know that she didn't mind his being clumsy.

She turned away. Wayne cursed himself.

He began eating what was left of his lunch, chewing slowly (with his mouth closed, which he chalked up to the **win** column), hoping she wouldn't leave, feeling the food land in his stomach with all the tenderness of a baseball bat shattering a kneecap. Maybe it wasn't too late to salvage this; he could strike up a conversation, get her to talking, show her that he wasn't a total loss. It would be nice to know her name, where she worked, if she was seeing anyone seriously or if there might be a chance—

—don't send out the wedding invitations just yet, Don Juan.

He gave her a quick glance. She was staring at something.

"Zombies," she said.

"I beg your pardon?"

She pointed to a group of well-dressed business people who were rushing past, briefcases or files or cell phones in one hand, some kind of sandwich in the other, trying to balance everything with all the dexterity of a circus performer as they raced their way up the ol' corporate ladder. Wayne always got a kick out of watching groups like this, wishing that just once they'd get so caught up in their wheeling and dealing they'd lose track of what was in which hand and take a bite out of their Blackberry. It's the little hopes that keep you going.

"Sad," she whispered.

"What makes you say that?"

She looked at him, expressionless, and shrugged. "I just can't imagine anyone functioning in that type of environment for long without shredding their individuality, their specialness, if you know what I mean."

"But it's possible not to sacrifice that...if you're careful and have your priorities in place." He heard himself and almost gagged; why did everything he said sound as if he wrote it down ahead of time and memorized it? He was trying to think of a way to sound spontaneous when she said:

"And what are your priorities, Wayne?"

He started. "How did you know my name?"

A light in her eyes. "*A Woman of No Importance*," she said.

"Pardon me?"

"The Wilde line. I knew it from one of his plays, I just couldn't recall which one. It was *A Woman of No Importance*."

Wayne felt his stomach turn to marble. "Y-you're—?"

"I know that our 'official' date wasn't supposed to be until tomorrow night, but I couldn't wait. I hope you don't mind."

"I, uh...no, no, of course not," replied Wayne. But inside he was screaming *Oh, shit, shit, shit, Shit, SHIT!*

"Besides," she continued, "you always hated the formality of 'official' first dates — let alone the pressure of a *blind* first date, so I thought we could have our lunch together out here and consider *this* our first date. Is that okay with you?"

Something occurred to him. "How did you know where to find me? I never told you."

"You always eat your lunch out here, weather permitting."

"Yes, but...I never told you that. How did you know?"

"I know a lot about you, Wayne Bricker. I know that you've worked as an accountant with Burton, Kroeger, and Denver for the last eight years; I know that you live alone and have never been married — or had a steady girlfriend, for that matter; I know that you spend your weekends reading and going to the movies or renting a DVD if there's nothing playing that you want to see; and I know that you go to the nursing home three times a month to visit your mother, sometimes even take her out to dinner if she's having a good week and remembers who you are. Of course, if she is in good shape, she usually chews you out for spending all your time with your nose in some kind of book."

The food had set his stomach on fire. He swallowed hard as a cramp passed. *"Who are you?"*

"And if none of *those* activities appeal to you, you just ask for one or two weeks of the thirteen months of vacation time you've piled up over the years, hop in your car, and drive somewhere. You never tell anyone where you went or what you did because you think they aren't really interested." She moved closer to him. The warmth of her minty breath tickled his chin. They were so close it probably looked as if they were two young lovers about to kiss.

"You know me," she said. "It'll take you a second, but you'll remember."

Definite panic now. "I'm sorry, but we've never met." He looked around, half-expecting to see some of the office staff hiding behind a bush somewhere, laughing at their little, well-staged joke.

"Yes, we have," she said, her voice low, sultry, the sexiest he'd ever heard. "You've made love to me thousands of times. Sometimes my hair is a different color, and the last time we were together you gave me green eyes." She moved her face even closer. "How do you like them?"

Wayne couldn't speak. This was outrageous, even cruel. He'd done nothing to deserve this kind of treatment Maybe he wasn't the most debonair of men, but he prided himself on being courteous, so why —

—and then, in the back of his mind, something threw back its covers, rose up, wiped the sleep from its eyes, and turned on a light.

Come, and I will teach you the disillusionment of the body...

"Remember me now?"

"...ohgod..."

"While I was waiting out here, I got to thinking about our first night together. Remember that? Your father had gotten drunk and slammed his car into a parked semi. Your mother zoned out when the police told her about his death, so her sister came over and took her to the hospital, leaving you alone. You were thirteen years old. You were so sweet. Didn't have any close friends—"

"Still don't," he said.

"I know." She took his hand in hers. "You rummaged around in your father's room until you came across his cache of girlie magazines, took them into your bedroom, and cried while you looked at the pictures and tried to..."

...the emptiness of lonely orgasms in night-flooded, loveless rooms...

"You did this," she went on, "because you didn't really love your father, though you wanted to. He was just a very cautious man, but that caution came across as coldness. You couldn't find any women in the magazines who did it for you, so you threw them aside, put a Monkees album on, closed your eyes, and when you heard 'Daydream Believer,' there I was."

"...yes..." he whispered, closing his eyes, bringing back the memory of that night.

"I'm glad you remember," she said, brushing his cheek with her lips.

"I...I took the record off and you asked me to sing to you while you taught me how to dance."

"You wanted to learn so you could ask Marti Wilder to the spring dance."

"I never did, you know? Ask her."

"You wouldn't have liked it. You would have felt awkward and foolish."

"What did I sing to you that night?"

"'There Will Never Be Another You,' the Nat King Cole song."

"That's right! I was pretty bad."

"But your heart was in the right place."

He opened his eyes and looked at her. Her eyes were warm and sparkling but her face was a stone mask.

And her eyes were now blue—

—and her cheekbones were higher—

—and her nose was smaller—

—and—

"Want me, Wayne. Want me now. Think of me the way I was in your dream last night."

He pulled her close, kissing her, a deep wet kiss, full of awkward but honest passion, his mind folding in on itself, turning drawers upside-down, shaking out all the excesses and trivialities of the day until he found himself gliding backward in time to the moment last night when she'd come to him, her body ripe and sweaty, her desire strong, her breath coming in bursts as she held him and moved with him, gasping and crying out, loving him as no other could, then lying in his arms afterward, looking up, her face lacquered in sweat that reflected like diamond dust in the candle's light, and he saw her face clearly.

He pulled back now and opened his eyes.

She was as she should be.

"I need your help."

Images from an average life swirled around him, reminding him that he had never had a grand moment and never expected one and now here it was; signed, sealed, delivered.

"Anything," he said.

She wrapped her arms around him, hands caressing the back of his neck. "Make me yours, all yours."

"But you are," he whispered. "You always have been."

She shook her head. "No, Wayne. You're not the only person who's ever been lonely, who's scrambled to the back of his mind to build a fantasy lover and soulmate. Do you remember that old saying about monkeys and typewriters?"

"Yeah," he cupped her face in his hands, reveling in the glory of her eyes. "If you put enough monkeys in a room with enough typewriters, eventually they'll write Shakespeare."

"Yes...and if you have enough lonely people who search their imaginations for a so-called 'perfect' mate, eventually some of them will invent the same one. Oh, maybe this lover, this soulmate, will differ slightly from person to person: one might give her blue eyes, while another dreams her with green; someone may make her cheekbones higher and her nose smaller, but the thing is, she's never so different that she can't be recognized. Do you understand what I'm saying?"

"How many others are there?"

"Seven, eight, I'm not certain."

"And out of all of them, you...chose me?"

She brought her hands around, touched his face, pulled him close and kissed him. "*Of course* I chose you. You were the one who first gave me life. You made me real. The others, they only added to me. But none are as sweet and kind and loving and gentle and decent as you." Tears crept to the corners of her eyes, glistened in the afternoon sun, and spattered onto her wrist

"I can't stand it anymore, Wayne. I have nothing of myself to hold on to, only what they give me. But you'll give me a real life, a fuller life, you'll let me become something *I* want to be and not just what you dream me."

"Of course, you know that"

"Take me home. I need to be with your now."

They rose, arm in arm, and walked quickly to the parking garage, found Wayne's car, and left. Wayne Bricker didn't care about his job at this point; he didn't care about anything except being with the woman next to him, the woman who was as real as he, who was flesh of his flesh, blood of his blood, desire of his desire.

In the sweet darkness, they made love for hours. Her body held discoveries for Wayne, her touch answers, her sounds the power of clarity and destination. Wayne moved with a grace of which he'd always thought himself incapable, never fumbling or making foolish mistakes he associated with being an average, unimaginative thirty-six year old man.

When, at last, they finished, when there was no strength left in their limbs for anything other than holding on to one another, when their aching had been soothed and solitude had fled forever with its head hung in shame, only then did she ask him.

"Give me a name."

"Esmeralda," he said. "My Esmeralda."

"Such an elegant, exquisite name."

"No other would suffice." He wished she would smile.

She traced over his lips with her finger. "But why do you always imagine yourself to be so...ugly? Esmeralda was loved by Quasimodo. As I recall, that story didn't end well. Why do you ... ?"

"I don't know. I've just never felt much like I'm the type women give second glances to."

"That's you father's caution coming through."

"I know." He lifted her head and kissed her. Her lips were different, not as full. And her hair was shorter —

—and her hands thinner —

—and—

"It's time," she said.

He tried to put her back to the way she was but hadn't the strength.

"Don't waste your time," she said, her voice tight with panic. "You don't have it in you to pull me back every time this happens."

"Then tell me what to do."

She held both his hands tightly. Her eyes filled with pleading. "Do you love me?"

"Yes."

"And I love you."

His soul, until that moment trapped in a rain of his own making, was lifted from a cold damp place with those words.

"Then there's nothing I can't do," he said.

"God, I hope."

* * *

His name was Dan Rosen. He wore thick glasses and had a clubfoot. He was a short order cook at a truck stop in Baltimore. When Wayne first walked in and took a seat at the counter, Dan looked across at him.

In a way, they recognized each other.

Wayne wasn't sure he could go through with this, but then remembered Esmeralda's words — "I love you" — and realized that he would, indeed, spend the rest of his life lonely and miserable and a little bit dead, filled with average and unimaginative activities that would help him pass the time until people would smile at him and his failures and whisper to themselves that, well, he was Old, and you know How They Can Be.

He ordered a hamburger and fries, ate them slowly, checking the clock. Dan's shift ended at three a.m. Then he'd go home to his dim and dirty studio apartment over the bar and grille where he filled his evenings with model ship building and dreams of Esmeralda — called Lori by him, the name of the girl who'd broken up with him in public one night, saying she had no desire to spend the rest of her life tied to a near-sighted, going-nowhere cripple. He'd cried, Dan had, more out of humiliation than a broken heart, because Lori had just left him standing there as she ran to a car driven by Dan's ex-best friend, calling "Why don't you run after me?" He'd gone home that night to a house where his drunken, widowed mother was snoring in front of the television, locked the door to his room, laid on his bed, and tried to guess whether or not the ceiling beams would take his weight. As he lay there cursing himself and his affliction, he imagined Lori apologizing to him, declaring her love. But then he decided to change her just a little bit, the hair at first, then the eyes, then lips and cheeks and body, running through hundreds of combinations until, at last—

—Wayne shook his head. He hadn't really wanted to know all that, but Esmeralda had said it was important he understand. The lonely road toward True Love was littered with casualties.

"I've never cared about the physical," she said. "Danny's very nice, if a bit on the self-pitying side."

"What am I supposed to do once he leaves?"

"You'll know when the time comes."

And that time, Wayne noted with sleepy eyes, was just five minutes away. He pulled out his wallet and took out a five and two ones to cover the bill and a tip, thankful that he'd been so frugal over the years about dipping into his savings; he had more than enough to last him for a while and he'd been building up a lot of vacation time at work, anyway. Following his sudden disappearance after lunch the other day, Wayne's department supervisor had called to see if he was all right. In eight years, Wayne had not had a sick day. A quick lie about problems with his mother cleared that up and enabled him to take three weeks' vacation.

He stopped his tired musing as Dan walked by him and out the door. Wayne followed him from the truck stop to his apartment, waiting until Dan was out of the car and on his way up the stairs.

Wayne walked up behind him and said, "Dan?"

He turned, startled, eyes wide. "What the fuck do you want?"

"I need to talk to you."

Dan reached into his back pocket and pulled out a switchblade, which he quickly and expertly flipped open. "I got nothing to say to anyone at three-thirty in the morning, pal, so get away from me."

A figure appeared on the landing behind him and said, "Danny?"

Both men looked up. It was Esmeralda, *Wayne's* Esmeralda.

"What happened to your hair?" asked Dan with deep sadness. He lowered the knife.

Wayne wasted no time. Throwing one arm around Dan's neck, he used his free hand to wrench the knife from Dan's grip and then hit him hard in the center of his face. Dan stumbled backward, tried to regain his balance but his damned foot got in the way again, and he fell to the ground.

"Jesus, Lori," cried Dan, in more than one kind of pain. "Who is this guy?"

She started down the stairs, her eyes clear and glistening. "You can't have me anymore, Danny. I'm sorry."

"I don't...how can you...what's with...I—"

Her eyes met Wayne's.

You said you loved me.

He froze for a moment. This Dan wasn't a bad guy, his sad little fantasies that were almost all he had, and Wayne felt his heart fill with pity for the man who now stood shaking with a knife pressed against his jugular. He thought of loneliness in all its forms of expression: of snipers in towers whose pleas for attention and acceptance were carried on tips of bullets; of plain teenage girls pouring their souls onto paper in the form of poetry that would embarrass them someday; of shabby men wandering into clean, well-lighted places, buying coffee they didn't like, listening to music that was too loud, watching younger men who were too stupid and shallow, all for the sake of not spending another second alone.

Wayne pulled Dan to his feet, whirled him around, and stared deep into his eyes.

"Don't take her away...please?" pleaded Dan.

Wayne looked at Esmeralda, who handed him Dan's knife, which she had changed; it was now a dagger of crystal and jade.

"I love only you," she said.

Wayne looked at Dan's foot. And knew.

"I'll take it away," he said. "I'll take it all away."

And Wayne set about his task.

* * *

"It's odd," said Wayne to Esmeralda as they drove back to his home.

"What is?"

He pointed outside. It was raining. A blinking traffic light scattered rubies across the windshield. "I always used to find the rain so sad. I don't anymore."

"Rain's very pretty," she said.

Wayne looked at her. "I used to imagine that, when I was finally in love, I'd be able to run between the drops and never get wet."

She almost smiled at that, but only almost.

* * *

The task became easier with each successive person.

The next was a hair-lipped woman of sixty in Gettysburg who spent her days doing volunteer work for the county children's agency. Having never married because of her sexual preference, she had no grandchildren. Wayne caught her one afternoon as she was making a run to McDonald's for the once-a-week hamburgers she brought to the children. She'd gone to the ladies' room and found Esmeralda on the other side, backed away in fright, and turned to find Wayne pushing her back in. He'd felt a little funny about her; she reminded him of his mother.

Then came Joe in Brownsville, Texas, a gas station attendant who'd lost one of his legs to a landmine in Vietnam; next was Jerry, a library bookmobile driver in Binghamton, New York, who was lucky to have the job because of having only one good eye, the other having been burned partially closed in a furnace explosion a few years before; after that came Cindy with the facial cleft and Alan in Topeka who was a midget and then that guy in Los Angeles with the shriveled arm that looked more like the flipper on a fish, all of them so full of pain and regret and pleadings, all of them so happy finally to see Esmeralda in the flesh, all of them so easy —

—well, maybe not *that* easy, but when Wayne looked into the eyes of his true love, he knew there was no hardship he could not overcome.

Still, he wondered why she would not smile for him.

But that was soon forgotten, at least for a while.

Wayne had begun to taste Purpose. Yes, it was terrible that he had to take her away from all of them —there was always that moment where they would plead with him—but Esmeralda had chosen him, the only woman ever in his life to choose him, and so he never hesitated to use her magic dagger.

He was taking away their suffering.

He was making Things Better.

He was destroying their pain.

And there were moments when it didn't really matter that she wouldn't smile for him, because Wayne felt a sense of power that he'd never known before.

To take away pain and suffering, to destroy loneliness.

God must feel a little like this.

They traveled many places on the lonely road toward True Love; saw many sights, made love as often as possible, whispering of their plans.

All things considered, it was as close to heaven as Wayne had ever come.

Or as close as it had come to him.

Now his heaven was on Earth, and he was its ruler, the Remover of Pain, the Destroyer of Loneliness, the Taker-Away of Affliction.

This holy knowledge made the physical aspect of what was happening to him easier to accept.

Her love grew more intense with every minute of every day. She had no regrets, she said. It really didn't matter what Wayne looked like.

It didn't matter.

Appearances weren't important.

The physical was illusion.

Come, and I will you teach you the disillusionment of the body ...

Then came the day, finally, that the last of them was found. Wayne claimed what was rightfully his. At that moment, his true love seemed to shimmer, whole and clean and alive, no longer the particles of a diamond but the jewel itself, one that Wayne felt himself melt into until they were one.

Peace. Clarity. Fulfillment.

Everything had been worth it. He was no longer average, no longer a man who'd been denied his golden moment, his grand accomplishment

Hand in hand, in the rain, they went home. Their home.

Between the drops, all the way.

* * *

He awoke in the middle of the night and found her gone. He sat up and saw her silhouette by the window.

He reached over to turn on the light.

"Don't," she said.

"What's the matter?"

"Please come to me."

He rose to go to her and felt his center of balance shift drastically, throwing him to the floor. He tried to break his fall with both arms but only one of them worked. He struggled to his feet, only to find one of them had—

—he pressed his weight against the side of the bed and reached out for the light.

"No!" she cried.

He knew, of course, what he would see even before light flooded the room.

Still...

He spoke as clearly as he could, the words coming out slowly because of the facial cleft and hair lip. "I knew it would have to be soon."

She stared at him. "I knew it that night you met Danny."

He looked down at his deformed leg and its clubfoot. "Do you suppose he's happier now?"

She looked out the window. "I know he is. You took away the thing that drove him to search for me in the first place. Don't you remember the newspaper clipping I showed you a few days ago? Dan and Lori got married. Because of what you did for him, because you assumed his affliction, he found the strength to pursue happiness. With no afflictions, how could he fail? How could *any* of them?"

He smiled. "But we have each other. And I love you so very, very much."

"And I love you, my dear Wayne."

"Then would you smile for me? That's all I need now, just a smile."

"I can't," she said.

"Why?" She seemed to be thinner to him, but it was probably the bad eye playing tricks. He shuffled slowly to her side and took her hand, looked up into her eyes. "Aren't you happy?"

She bent low and kissed him gently on the lips. "Do you remember when I told you that I didn't care about physical beauty?"

"Yes."

Tears crept to the surface of her eyes. "I lied." She broke away and crossed to the other side of the room, hugging herself and shuddering. "I don't know what happened, Wayne, but knowing that you would become...like you are, the thought began to needle at me, exasperate me, sicken me." She faced her own reflection in the mirror. "When I think of all the pain you took away from the others, all the happiness you gave them a chance to obtain after such lonely lives, I can't help but love you with all my heart and soul. And when I look at myself, and see how alive I am, when I touch my flesh *and feel* it and know that, because of you, I have an existence that I can at last call my own, I feel such tenderness toward you I could just..."

"But I have my own mind now, and something has awakened there, something that sees and acknowledges my own beauty yet at the same time is repulsed by the sight of you. And I hate it, Wayne. I hate it so much because it will only get worse. I can see a morning very soon where I won't even be able to look at you and that's the last thing I want."

"This is all new to you," he said, feeling his heart lodge in his throat. "So many feelings denied you for so long, so many thoughts you've never experienced —"

"No, it's more than that. Don't you see? Is your soul so naive that you can't understand that this woman, this thing that I now am because of you, *me* ... I love you so very much, but I ... I don't *want* you."

He remembered the lyrics to some stupid song from the 1970's, something about how imaginary lovers never turn you down, and laughed at himself and his reflection, imagining how he was going to explain his condition to the people he worked with. He touched the hideous mound of flesh that he called a face and said, "So what do we do now?"

She came toward him. "Dream me away."

"I can't. You're all I've got."

She took a deep breath. "Then I have to leave." She dressed and stared toward the door.

"Don't I at least get a smile?" asked Wayne.

She paused by the door, her shoulders tensing as if she were making an unpleasant decision, then turned to him with contempt in her eyes and said, "I don't waste my smiles on freaks, Wayne, and that's what you are, it's what you've always been and always will be. You were beyond saving the day I came to you at lunch. You were worse than those zombies I pointed out to you; at least they had something to strive for in life."

He knew what she was doing, that she was trying to make him angry enough to *tell* her to leave — the noble lover sparing the other's feelings — but even though he knew it was simply a ploy, it nonetheless struck at something in his core, breaking apart his feelings of godliness and purpose, and despite his best efforts to dismiss her words and actions, his chest tightened in fury. "You were what my life was for, you were always the thing I most wanted to achieve."

"Not only a freak but a fool as well. God, how you disgust me."

"Don't say that, please."

"Freak."

"Don't."

"Monstrosity."

"...*please*..."

"You're nothing more than a hideous malignancy, Wayne, and I curse the day you found me."

He felt his hand wrap tightly around the lamp. "Don't."

"I hope you die of loneliness. I hope they find you in a heap on the floor, wallowing in your own filth and beyond help. Then maybe they'll shoot you and put you out of misery."

He pulled the lamp off the table and rushed at her, swinging it with all his strength and caving in half her skull. She crumpled to the floor, bleeding and whimpering. Wayne dropped the lamp and fell to his knees, cradling her in his arms as best he could.

"I'm so sorry," he pleaded. "I just couldn't live without you."

She reached up and touched him, her eyes fading. "Isn't this how your dreams always end? In longing and grand, romantic tragedy?"

"...yes..."

"Well, then...."

He held her until the life faded from her eyes and her limbs went stiff and cold. He held her until her flesh became dried and rotted and gray and began to flake off. He held her until his own strength began to dissolve, and then he kept her close to him, pressing her against his chest until she was little more than hones and at long last —he had no idea how long they had lain together this way —she became nothing more than particles of a diamond that swirled into the air, becoming dust and then nothing, nothing at all. He lay there in silence and loneliness, the cramps in his stomach worsening, his body dwindling away. The sun seemed to rise and fall within seconds, entire years passing in the space of an hour.

Come, and I will you teach you the disillusionment of the body as it perishes in the rain of grief.

He gathered the dust that once was her close to him.

Come, and I will teach you the death in fading roses never sent to one you admire from afar.

He gathered her dust into his hands and pressed them against his face.

Come, and I will teach you the emptiness of lonely orgasms in night-flooded, loveless rooms.

He lay very, very still, his heart breaking as he willed his body to become dust so they could be as one.

Come...

It was weeks before they found him.

No one ever figured out why he'd been smiling.

Had he been capable of speech, he could have told them, could have shared the knowledge, the magic, the great and terrible secret at the core of it all:

True Love never dies ....

Curtain Call

Introduction by Christopher Golden

Spoiler warning: You might want to read this after *you've read the story.*

* * *

If you want to understand the gifts that Gary A. Braunbeck brings to the table every time he sits down to write, "Curtain Call" is a great place to begin. Like every other tale in this collection, it is —of course— beautifully written, but let's take that as a given for any story bearing his byline. The beauty of "Curtain Call" is the way that it incorporates the real life Charles Fort and Bram Stoker with both Fort's actual endeavors and Stoker's fictional creations. For a lesser writer, the clever ideas and elegant execution herein would be enough—their own reward. But what makes Braunbeck one of the best in the genre is the painful humanity he brings to everything he writes. Many writers are clever, but few have the talent and heart to expose the weary sorrow that we all feel at times, and that we all fear is lying in wait for us around the next corner of our lives. We may never thank him for it, but connecting us with that sorrow is Braunbeck's greatest gift, for in its shadow we are always reminded to reach for the light.

Curtain Call

(From the unpublished papers of Charles Fort)

I have been, for most of my life, a collector of notes on subjects of great diversity—such as deviations from concentricity in the lunar crater Copernicus, to the great creature Melanicus and the super-bat upon whose wings it broods over the affairs of Man, as well as stationary meteor-radiants, the reported growth of hair on the bald head of a mummy, the appearance of purple Englishmen, instances of amphibians and blood raining down from the heavens, apparitions, phantoms, the damned, the excluded, wild talents, new lands, and "Did the girl swallow the octopus?"

But my liveliest interest is not so much in things as in the relations of things. I find now, in the twilight of my life, as I pour over the endless data that I have assembled throughout my days, that I think more and more about the alleged pseudo-relations we call "coincidences." What if these events, rather than being happenstance, are the final result of great, secret, dark machinations of the Universe interacting with the subconscious to produce an event or events which guide humanity down certain roads certain of its members were destined to take?

I am writing now of a brief period I spent in London when I was thirty-six, in the early months of 1912 (nearly ten years before I decided to move there), and of a most singularly peculiar bookshop, its even more peculiar proprietor, and a bit of London Theatre history which none before me has ever recorded.

I was staying at a very comfortable rooming house in Bedford Place, just around the corner from the British Museum in Great Russell Street (since my visit to London was solely to search through the Museum's vast archives of manuscripts, the location of my rooms could not have been more advantageous for my purposes). On this particular day—kept from my research at the Museum by a cryptic note delivered to my room early that morning—I was exploring the narrower, less often traveled streets of the vicinity, in search of an address which seemed more and more to me a flight of fancy in the mind of whomever had composed the note, when the heavens opened wide and within moments the rain was pounding down violently. I was in Little Russell Street, just behind the church that fronts on Bloomsbury Way, and there was no way for me to find immediate shelter from the storm. The address written on the note was obviously someone's idea of a joke, for I had been up and down this street no less than three times.

So why had I not noticed the little bookshop before?

It seemed that as soon as the sun was obscured by the rain clouds, the tiny edifice simply appeared out of the rain, set between a baker's and a haberdashery where before there had been only, I am certain, a cramped alleyway.

I shall state here that, despite the path of research my life has been dedicated to, I am not a man who is given to either hallucination or flights of fancy. I neither believe nor disbelieve anything. I have shut myself away from the rocks and wisdom of ages, as well as the so-called great teachers of all time.

I close the front door to Christ and Einstein and at the back door hold out a welcoming hand to rains of frogs and lands hidden above the clouds and the paths of lost spirits. "Come this way, let's see if you can explain yourselves," I say unto these phenomena, always taking care to look upon them with a cold clinician's eye. I cannot accept that the products of minds are subject-matter for belief systems. I neither saw nor did not see a bookshop hidden away on this street. It simply *was*, at that moment, where the moment before it was not.

I crossed the street and entered the place, nearly soaked through.

The first thing that assaulted my senses was the so-very-right *smell* of the place. Perhaps you have to be a true lover of books to understand what I mean by that, but the comforting, intoxicating, friendly scent of bindings and old paper was nectar to my soul.

I called out, asking if anyone were there. When no response was forthcoming, I removed my coat, draped it on the rack near the door and—after patting down my hair and shaking off the remnants of rain from my shoes and sleeves—proceeded to browse through the offerings.

The walls were lined from floor to ceiling with sagging shelves full of books, and I could see at a glance that, though the stock contained everything from academic texts to the usual classics, its primary focus was on matters philosophical and occult; everywhere I turned there were books such as Agrippa's *De Occulta Philosophia*, the ancient notes of Anaxagoras of Clazomenae detailing his conclusions that the Earth was spherical, *The Gospel of Sri Ramakrishna*, the Hindu *Rig Veda*, the poems of Ovid, the plays of Aeschylus, Lucan's *De Bello Civilia*...my heart beat with tremendous anticipation. What treasures would I find here?

It was only as I was admiring an ancient copy of the *Popol Vuh* which sat under a glass case in the center of a great table that I became aware that I was no longer alone. How I knew this I could not then say, though what was soon to follow would make the reason clear.

I turned and saw the proprietor.

Though he appeared to be only a few inches taller than I, there was, nonetheless, a sense of power and great, massive presence about him. His fierce, dark eyes stared out at me from underneath thick eyebrows that met over his knife of a nose. His heavy white moustache drooped down past the corners of his mouth, drawing my attention at once to his red and seemingly swollen lips, which were flagrant and somehow femininely seductive against the glimmer of his face. Though he was obviously an older gentleman, he carried himself with the grace and power of man fifteen years my junior.

"Mr. Fort," he said, in a heavily-accented, full, rich *basso* voice the New York Opera would have swooned to have sing upon its stage, "I am so very pleased you were able to accept the invitation." He offered his hand. "It is a great honor to meet a gentleman such as yourself, who shares my interest is matters of data that Science has excluded."

I shook his hand. His grip was steel. I winced from the great pressure and the pain it sent shooting up my arm.

"I beg your pardon," he said, releasing my hand. "I sometimes forget that, in my enthusiasm, my handshake can be a bit...."

"Formidable?" I said, massaging my fingers.

His smile was slow in its appearance but total in its chilling effectiveness. "What a kind way to put it." He turned and started toward a door near the back of the shop. "If you'll be kind enough to follow me, sir."

I did, though somewhat reluctantly. After all, what did I know of this fellow or his intent? True, in my studies I had come across many strange tales told by sometimes stranger individuals, but (at this point in my life, at least) I rarely had to meet any of these people face to face. Still, I must admit, my curiosity was stronger than either my anxiety or trepidation.

I need speak in a bit more detail of the cryptic note which was delivered to my room as I was readying myself for the day's research at the Museum. It arrived in a heavy envelope which contained—aside from the letter itself—several newspaper clippings, which I will summarize momentarily. It read as follows: "My Dear Mr. Fort: I know that you will read the enclosed with great interest, but also with your Intellectual's eye. Come to the address written below before the noon hour and I will give you irrefutable proof that these incidents are, indeed, based on fact and not myth. I urge you to keep this appointment."

Below the body of the writing were these words: *Denn die Todten reiten schnell* ("For the dead travel fast," a line from Burger's "Lenore").

The letter was signed only: *A.S.*

Having read with great delight Mr. Jules Verne's famous novel, I found myself smiling at the thought that I might encounter the fictitious Arne Saknussemm at the end of my own "journey."

The clippings came from newspapers such as *Lloyd's Sunday News*, the *Brooklyn Eagle*, *Ottawa Free Press*, and the *Yorkshire Evening Argus*. All of them detailed stories of various bodies which were discovered to have died from massive blood loss—often the bodies were drained totally of their blood supply. All of the deaths had another fact in common: each victim, though at first thought to have been the target of a robbery-related assault, was found to have "...tiny puncture marks" near or on a major artery. Sometimes there were more than one pair of these marks (a body found in Chicago had at least thirty such puncture marks on her legs) but, in each case, saliva was found within these punctures, leading, naturally, to the conclusion that each of these victims had been killed by "...mentally disturbed" individuals who suffered "...the delusion of vampirism."

My hope is by now you will understand why my curiosity overpowered any anxiety I might have been experiencing.

The proprietor opened the door and led me down a long stone stairway which emptied out into a surprisingly cavernous basement. Lighting a kerosene lantern, he proceeded to lead me down a slope in the floor to an area which I can only describe to you as being a sort-of hidden theatre; there were a few rows of seats (which smelled of old fire) and a raised stage, more than a few of whose boards still bore the black marks of a fire.

As I sat where the proprietor directed me, I noticed the insignia of the Lyceum Theatre on the back of the seat in front of me, and realized at once that these seats—as well as portions of the stage before me—had been scavenged from the great fire which destroyed the Lyceum in 1830. (That they might have been scavenged from the wreckage of the 1803 fire did not, at the time, seem a possibility to me.)

The proprietor wandered away into the darkness, the light from the lantern growing smaller and more dim as he made his way through a curtain off to the side. I heard him moving around back-stage, then a few squeaking sounds, a cough, and then the curtain fronting the stage rose slowly to reveal a series of chairs and small podiums, each on different levels, arranged in a manner befitting a "dramatic reading"—what is often called "Reader's Theatre" in America.

There was, however, only one person on the stage as the lights came up, and he was neither standing nor seated behind one of the podiums.

He was in a wheelchair, down-stage center, illuminated by a spotlight from above. His face was half in shadow, even after he raised his head to look out at his "audience."

Newspaper clippings of blood-drained victims.

The Lyceum Theatre.

A.S.

I knew even before he spoke in his watered-down but still musical Irish brogue that I was in the presence of none other than Abraham — better known as "Bram" — Stoker.

"Mr. Fort," he said, barely above a whisper. "Thank you for coming. Have you paper and pen?"

"I do," I called from the darkness of the theatre, then produced said items from my jacket pocket. (Fortunately the light from the stage bled forward enough that I could see to make notes.)

"Excellent," said Mr. Stoker, then wiped at his mouth with a dark-stained handkerchief he clutched in one shaking, palsied hand.

I knew — as did many of his admirers — that Stoker had been in seclusion for the last few years. Ill health was rumored — a rumor which I saw now to be sadly true (though whether or not he was suffering from the final stages of untreated syphilis I had not the medical knowledge to ascertain). I can tell you that the rumored feeble-mindedness was true, for several times during his narrative did Mr. Stoker begin muttering gibberish for minutes on end, until he would fall into something like a brief trance from which we would emerge lucid and articulate.

"I am a great admirer of your writings," he said from his place on the stage. "You must assemble your articles into a book for publication one day."

"That is my intent," I replied, suddenly aware of the single bead of perspiration that was snaking down my spine.

"May I suggest, then," said Stoker, "that you call your work 'The Book of the Damned'?"

"Why?"

He laughed. It was not a pleasant sound. "Because all so-called 'unnatural phenomena' comes from damned places, sir. Speak of damned places and you speak of places where powerful emotional forces have been penned up. Have you ever been within the walls of a prison, Mr. Fort? Where the massed feelings of hatred, deprivation, claustrophobia and brutalization have seeped into the very stones? One can *feel* it. The emotions resonate. They seethe, trapped, waiting for release, waiting to be given *form*, Mr. Fort. What you might call an 'unconscious confluence' were you to label it in one of your articles.

"You now sit in the remnants of one such 'damned place,' sir: the charred remains of the Lyceum Theatre. These stage boards, the curtain above me, the very seats which surround you and the one in which you now sit, were discovered by myself in a basement storage area of the Lyceum during my time there as manager —along, of course, with Sir Henry Irving, my own personal vampire."

He spoke Irving's name with a level of disgust that was absolutely chilling to hear. Even though Stoker attempted to hide his true feelings about Irving in his biography of the famous actor, it was now well known that, during the twenty-seven years he worked as stage manager at the Lyceum, Irving treated Stoker little better than a slave, paying him so very little that, upon Irving's death, Stoker was forced to borrow money from friends and relatives in order to survive; when he was no longer able to borrow money, he was forced to write such drivel as his latest (and, I suspected, what would be his *last)* novel, *The Lair of the White Worm.*

I could not help but share the sorrow of this broken man on the stage before me; there had been a potential for true literary greatness there, once, but no more...and the late Sir henry Irving was as much to blame for that as were Stoker's so-called "personal indulgences."

"Remember as you listen, Mr. Fort: emotions resonate. They seethe, trapped, waiting for release, waiting to be given form."

I wrote down his words, though they seemed more the ramblings of mind surrendering to the body's sicknesses.

Stoker coughed into his handkerchief once again. Even from my place in the "audience," I could see that he was coughing up blood. His handkerchief was useless to him now. I took my own, unused handkerchief from my pocket and rose to approach the stage and give it to him, but was stopped by the appearance of a great, dark wolf by Stoker's side.

It wandered on from stage left and seated itself next to his wheelchair. Even sitting on its haunches, it was nearly as tall as he. I had never seen such a magnificent and terrifying creature in all my life. It looked upon me with pitiless eyes that, in the light of the stage, glowed a deep, frightening crimson.

I returned the handkerchief to my pocket and took my seat once again.

"You'll come to no harm, Mr. Fort," said Stoker, reaching out to rub the fur at the nape of the great wolf's neck. The beast growled contentedly. I thought of a line from Stoker's most famous novel, about the Children of the Night, and what sweet music they made.

What follows is my transcription of Stoker's narrative. I have taken the liberty of removing the sometimes-prolonged pauses he took between words, as well as excising those instances where his crumbling mind led him down rambling paths of incomprehensibility.

I ask only that you remember this was a man who could have achieved true literary greatness, but who is now only remembered as the author of "...that dreadful vampire book."

Even now, I still sorrow at the thought of What Might Have Been, had Fate been kinder to him.

* * *

The Narrative of Abraham (Bram) Stoker, as told to Charles Fort.
Little Russell Street, London, 1912.

I was born in Dublin in 1847, one of seven children. Though I was a very sickly child, I was nonetheless my mother's favorite. During those years I spent in my sickbed, my mother tended to me with great and loving care. Having fostered a lifelong fascination with stories of the macabre, she entertained me with countless Irish ghost stories —the worst kind there is, I should add. As a child I was lulled to sleep each night with tales of banshees, demons, ghouls, and horrific accounts of the cholera outbreak of 1832.

My mother was a remarkable woman—strong-minded, ambitious, proud, a writer—she hoped that I, too, might one day become a person of letters—a visitor to workhouses for wayward and indigent girls, and above, she was a proponent of women's rights—much like her close friend, the mother of Oscar Wilde. I sincerely believe that, were it not for her kind ministrations on my behalf, I might have surrendered to the illnesses that plagued my early years. But she gave me strength and a sense of self-worth, and for that alone I shall always cherish her memory.

When I became of college age and was accepted at Trinity on an athletic scholarship—you would not know it to look at this pathetic body now, but there was a time when I was a champion. I was a record breaker, in my day...and, I must admit, I gained a reputation among the members of my class for a somewhat exaggerated masculinity —some would even call it polemical. But I assure you that I was never less than chivalric toward the ladies with whom I kept company. I often wonder now if my way with the ladies back then is not the reason I am being punished in my final days with a wife so distant and frigid I might as well be wed to a corpse.

In 1871 I graduated with honours in science—Pure Mathematics, which enabled me to accept a civil service position at Dublin Castle. That same year I began to review theatrical positions in Dublin, and in 1876 I was privileged to review Sir Henry Irving's magnificent performance in "Hamlet." Shortly thereafter, we became great friends—or so I thought.

The great actor is a strange beast, indeed, Mr. Fort, for his ego is such that it requires—nay, *demands*—constant feeding. Sir Henry was much like a child in that way. He took more of my friendship than he ever did return, but I was simply too awestruck by the man's genius to take notice of this.

I became his stage manager when he took over management of the Lyceum Theatre. That same year, I began to publish my writings—*The Duties of Clerks of Petty Sessions in Ireland*. It was released to unanimous indifference from critics and the public alike. Sir Henry urged me to explore more 'universal' themes in my work, much as Shakespeare and Milton and Marlowe did in theirs. The man was simply hoping that his lap-dog assistant would, perhaps, compose a play in which he might once again take center stage and be the focus of attention...but I digress.

I served Sir Henry well and loyally over the years. His opinion of my writing remained, as always, dismissive...until I wrote *Dracula*. On this, he at last expressed an opinion. 'It is absolute, pandering rubbish,' he said. Still, in 'reward' for my many years of service and friendship to him, he agreed to allow me to stage a dramatic reading of the novel before its release from the publisher.

The novel was, as I'm sure you know, quite dense, and so several long, sleepless editing sessions were required in order to make the work an acceptable length for theatrical presentation. During this period in the latter part of 1896, I insisted on being able to rehearse with a cast so as to determine the success of my editing process. Sir Henry would not allow his personal company of actors to be 'inconvenienced'—his word—with a 'work in progress,' and so left it up to me to assemble a cast of unknowns with whom to rehearse the piece. It took me several weeks, but at last I had my cast—with the exception of an acceptable actor to portray Abraham van Helsing. But I shall come to that.

You need to understand that, during this period of intense concentration, the character of Count Dracula became even more alive to me than he was during the years of research it took to create him and write the novel. He was so alive to me, in fact, that I often found myself talking with him as I would stagger home nights after hours of emotionally draining rehearsal. 'My dear Count,' I would say, 'have I lost all perspective where you are concerned?' I did this to relieve my anxiety: if the novel were not reduced to an acceptable three-hour theatrical entertainment, Sir Henry made it quite clear to me that he would not permit me to present the work to the public...not in his precious theatre. And so the Count became my constant companion, sir, my father-confessor, my only true friend.

I began to realize that the only way for the work to be made right, it was necessary for me to make the cast believe in the Count as fiercely as did I. I spoke to them one night of my imaginary conversations with the Count, and though they were at first amused, they came to understand that my dedication to the project was unflappable. I have to say, they were far more accommodating to me than Sir Henry's personal players would ever be with him; being unknowns, there were no egos to soothe or feed. Until the last rehearsal, it was the purest, most enjoyable theatrical experience of my life.

Soon, all of the cast were holding conversations with the Count. I recall encountering the actress who portrayed Mina Murray one night during a break in the rehearsal: I found off-stage left, sitting with her book, eyes closed, whispering, 'Why does someone as remarkable as you, dear Count, have to be so very, very wicked?' It *moved* me, sir, to hear that—and not only from her, but from all of the cast members.

Oh, the stories I could tell you of their recountings of their conversations with the Count. They came to believe in his existence as much as I.

Remember: emotions resonate. They seethe, trapped, waiting for release, waiting to be given form.

The deadline for my final draft of the performance text was rapidly approaching, and still I had not found an actor who I felt would adequately convey the essence of Van Helsing. It may seem a somewhat selfish point, but the other actors had so refined their vocal interpretations of my characters, had given them such life, that to bring in an actor who would less than their equal would have been an insult to them.

Then one evening, after having ended rehearsal early, I found myself in this area of Little Russell Street, and came upon this very bookshop. As I wandered among its many volumes, the proprietor took my aside and asked, 'Are you Mr. Bram Stoker, author of *After Sunset?*' 'I am,' I replied, seeing with some delight that he held a well-read copy of that very short story collection in his hands. 'I am a great admirer of your stories,' he said, offering the book to me, 'and I would be honored if you would inscribe my copy.'

I took the book from him with thanks, and proceeded to uncap the pen he offered, but somehow I managed to cut the tip of my thumb in the process. I bled a little upon the first page—not enough to ruin it, but enough that it could not be easily or neatly wiped away. 'Please do not worry yourself,' said the proprietor to me as I signed my name to the title. 'It can be taken care of.'

After I returned the volume to him, he took it behind the counter and knelt down behind the shelf of books. A few moments later he merged and showed me—much to my surprise—that the blood had been successfully removed from the title paper. I noticed—but did not think much of—his licking his lips several times after emerging from behind the counter. 'I must say, Mr. Stoker, that I am greatly anticipating the release of your new novel.' 'You may be one of the few persons in England who is,' I replied, and we shared a jovial laugh at my remark.

Something about him seemed terribly familiar to me, and as I listened to his voice with its weary, sand-like quality, I came to realize that I was looking at my Van Helsing. I proceeded to tell the proprietor of my problem, and asked him if he would be willing to read the part of Van Helsing for my presentation to Sir Henry at the end of the week. He was deeply flattered, and of course accepted my offer.

When the time came for the rehearsal, I found him outside the theatre, nervously pacing by the performers' entrance. 'My dear fellow, we are all waiting,' I said. When he said nothing in reply, I opened the door wider and said, 'Please, come in and join us.' He did so, and the rehearsal began.

It was the most magnificent reading of the novel I have ever witnessed. He captured not only Van Helsing's weariness, but his near-mad drive to destroy Dracula, as well. His performance was a prism of compassion, fury, wariness, dedication, sadness, and strength. When it came time for his 'This so sad hour' speech, he had all of us transfixed. He *was* Van Helsing.

Then, at the conclusion of the scene, he began to laugh.

It was the sound of an ancient crypt door being wrenched open.

The spell was immediately broken. 'My dear fellow,' I said to him. 'May I inquire what you find so humorous about this very tragic scene?'

'That you see it as tragic at all is what amuses me,' he replied, only this time his voice was not that of either Van Helsing or the sandy-voiced proprietor I had met at the bookshop the previous day: it was the voice of Count Dracula—not only as I had heard it in my imaginary conversations with him, but as the others in the cast had heard it, as well.

I looked upon all their faces and knew that *this* was the voice of the Count as we had come to believe it would sound.

Speak of damned places, Mr. Fort, and you speak, on some level, of belief. Emotions resonate. Electrons dance. Equations collapse and are replaced by newer, equally possible equations. Call it the collective unconscious or the hive mind of the masses, but the emotional charge had built and surged down the cumulative lines of our psyche and found not only focus but *form*.

He changed before our shocked eyes; from man to bat to wolf to rodent to owl to insect, then back again, then a hybrid of all creatures plus man—a sight so unspeakable I have never been able to bring myself to put its description onto paper for fear of being labeled mad.

Count Dracula rose up before us in all his dark, majestic, terrifying glory. 'My thanks to all of you for our little talks at night,' he said, smiling a lizard-grin and exposing his awful teeth. 'I have searched for centuries for a proper form in which I could enter your world, and you have so thoughtfully provided one for me.'

We began to run for the doors, but he became shadow and beast and speed itself: none of the cast made it any farther than the stage-left dressing room entrance before he fell upon them and opened their veins with his teeth. His strength was super-human, his speed that of the wrath of God Himself—if indeed such a Being exists at all.

I huddled behind a stack of risers, listening to the terrified and soon-silenced screams of my cast as the Count fed on each and every one of them. After what seemed an eternity, he found my hiding place and lifted me up as easily as one would a newborn child.

Holding me by the throat, he glared at me with his glowing red eyes and said, 'I wish to thank you personally, Mr. Stoker, for giving me life. But you have also made it necessary for the others who populated your novel to enter this world behind me, and so I must take my leave of you for now. Since I now know the ending of your story, I feel it is my duty to change it on this side...but you needn't worry about further revising your manuscript. I think it will be satisfactory to have the world believe that I am a fictitious creation who was summarily dispensed with at the conclusion of your little melodrama.'

And with that, he released me, and disappeared into the night.

Shortly thereafter, the members of my cast rose to their feet, undead all, and made their way down into the basement of the theatre and, from there, into the sewers of the city. They are still there to this day.

And I sorrow for what I unleashed upon them and the world. Dear God, how I sorrow.

* * *

I sat in the darkness of the theatre in stunned silence for several minutes after Mr. Stoker finished telling his incredible tale. The man was obviously mad...but there still lingered in my mind a whispering doubt. And there was, after all, that unearthly wolf on the stage with him.

"How can I help your unbelief?" came a voice.

I had been staring at Mr. Stoker. His lips had not moved. I looked, then, at the wolf by his side.

It spoke again: "Your unbelief, Mr. Fort. How can I help it?"

The wolf moved forward, hunkered down as if to pounce, and at once became an army of rats that swarmed across the stage and into the orchestra pit and emerged in the aisle as the proprietor who had led me down here. "Does this help?" he asked of me.

I rose to my feet and began to frantically make my way over the seats toward what I believed to be the staircase I had descended earlier. My heart was pounding against my chest with such force I feared it would smash through my ribs and tissue.

The proprietor became several bats who quickly swooped down and around me, assaulting me with their wings. I fell to the floor and the bats collided in a flash of darkest shadow and became the proprietor again, only now he was much younger in appearance, taller, stronger.

Eternal.

"Look upon me and fear, Mr. Fort. For I am as real as you dread I am."

He reached down and grabbed onto my jacket with one hand, lifting me off the floor with unnerving ease so that my feet dangled above the aisle like some marionette left hanging on a peg.

I could not take my eyes from his blood-red gaze.

"My biographer, my creator, wishes for his cast to be given their proper curtain call, the one denied them so many years ago." He slammed me down into the nearest seat and held me there with one mighty hand on my shoulder.

"Nothing less than your most enthusiastic applause will ensure your safe exit from this place," snarled Count Dracula in my ear.

An iron grate in the floor near the foot of the stage shifted with a nerve-wracking shriek and was cast aside by a hand that was more bone than flesh.

And the parade of the dead began.

How to describe what I saw? How to convey the pathetic, terrifying, sad, depraved sight which my eyes beheld?

Their flesh—what remained of it—had the color and texture of spoiled meat. Worms and other such creatures of filth oozed in and out of the holes in their faces where once their eyes had resided. The stench of death was sickly-sweet in the air. Some shambled, a few crawled, and one—a woman—had to be carried by another cast member because much of her lower torso was gone, leaving only dangling, tattered loops of decayed intestine which hung beneath her like a jellyfish's stingers.

I wept at the sight of them, but I applauded them; oh, how I applauded!

And I was not alone in my efforts.

Surrounding me, each of them as decayed and pathetic as the sad creatures who were assembling on the stage before us, were all the characters from Stoker's novel, all of them flesh and blood, all of them — thanks to the Count's actions—now equally un-dead: here was Mina Murray and Jonathan Harker; there was Dr. Seward and Lucy, Lord Godalming and Quincey and every last character from the novel who had participated in Dracula's destruction, only now they were the destroyed ones...even the great Abraham Van Helsing. All un-dead and applauding those whose portrayals and belief had brought them into this world and given them life—albeit briefly.

I became aware of several women clothed in white encircling me as I continued to applaud and the cast to take their individual bows.

The brides of Dracula surrounded me, caressed me, touched me with their lips and hands. My temperature rose in depraved want for them, and I applauded all the harder for it.

"My cast," intoned Stoker from the stage, gesturing to each member of his troupe. "My fine cast, my dear friends."

Dracula smiled and wiped something from one of his eyes. Looking at me, he smiled his awful, bloody grin and said, "I am moved, are you not the same?"

"I am," I said, quite dizzy.

The applause from the audience grew deafening. Dracula parted his arms and became a giant man-bat thing with slick flesh. He flew above stage and proceeded to land gracefully in the center of the players.

"Let my brides pleasure you, Mr. Fort," he bellowed above the noise in a voice part human and part beast, "and worry not, for they will not feed on you. You are our messenger now. Leave here, and tell the world, if you have the courage, that I am real, and that as long as men read my story, I shall never die. With the coming years and centuries, my story will be read by thousands, millions more, and each time the book is opened, each time a page is turned, I grow stronger and more eternal! Tell this to the world, sir, if you dare! For in the centuries to come my followers will grow, they will read of me, go forth, and multiply, and there will come a night when the entire earth will awaken and pull in the sweet damned breath of the un-dead, and then I will be as I should have been from the very beginning: The true Prince of Night, the king of my kind! Go, then, and tell them, if you dare."

One of his brides fell on her knees before me whilst another began to tear at my shirt.

The applause swelled as Dracula himself took a bow, and then I fell down into a dizzying pit of desire and darkness.

* * *

When I regained consciousness, I found myself outside the Lyceum Theatre, some good distance from where I was staying.

I cannot say for certain how I came to arrive safely back at my rooms at Bedford Place, only that I did find my way back there and was at once taken by the arm and led to an office where I was given a stiff drink of whiskey while a constable was called to take my statement.

"Robbery and Assault" was the official explanation for my condition. I saw no reason to argue their conclusion.

The next day, no fewer than three bodies were discovered around London, the blood drained from their veins.

The next day, I discovered reports of several other deaths in Canada, The United States, and Germany.

I returned home soon after, and for the rest of my life continued to gather such stories of bloodless bodies.

I am now an old man and my time is short. It has taken me a lifetime to muster the courage to set this tale to paper. Whether or not you choose to believe this is a matter between you and your conscience. I can no longer say I neither believe nor disbelieve nothing. Belief or unbelief, the dark forces of the Universe will have their way, regardless.

At my window last night I beheld the countenance of Mr. Bram Stoker, himself among the un-dead now; beside him was his creation, the Count, and in his eyes was a promise: *Soon.*

I fear I may not be alive come morning.

Not that I would have had lived that much longer, anyway.

So I take my leave of you. Do with this recounting what you will. The night is nearly upon us.

An article in yesterday's *New Yorker* listed *Dracula* as one of the best-selling books of all time. To this date, it is estimated that somewhere around five million copies in twenty different languages have been sold.

So many readers. So many pages turned.

And he grows stronger with each word read.

There will come a night, he said.

I fear it may be sooner than we think.

I shall lay down my head for the last time now.

God go with you in all the damned places that you walk.

Soon, such places shall be all there are.

—*Charles Fort, the Bronx, May 3, 1942.*

Ungrateful Places

Introduction by Linda Robertson

I have known Gary Braunbeck for several years. Both of us being native Ohioans and writers, of course we have attended many of the same writing conventions, participated in multi-author book signings around the state, and even been to a few of the same BBQs. Always, he has been pleasant, professional, well-spoken and several other flattering and boring adjectives I could use here. But Gary is far from boring. Though his vast writing credits and many noteworthy awards showcase his penchant for horror, I assure you he can also tell personal and self-effacing tales that evoke much laughter.

I say that to say this: Gary is not merely an author. He is a storyteller. The difference? A storyteller crafts more than words on a page, he hones performance into every syllable—and Gary is unparalleled in dramatic readings. If ever you are presented with the opportunity to hear him, it is my earnest recommendation that you do not miss it.

As for *Ungrateful Places*...

We're told that what's on the inside matters most about people, yet that maternal, reassuring whisper seems like a lie as the vain parade of endless selfies scroll by on social media. We know personality isn't bound in the superficial slopes and planes of a face, yet we make myriad assumptions every day based on others' expressions. We convey our emotions through the subtle extension or contraction of our facial muscles. We distinguish whom we know by who we recognize. We even mark achievements with photos —of our faces. The importance of our personal identity is nowhere more evident than in phrases like *losing face* and *saving face*.

Losing face means 'to suffer the loss of respect, to be humiliated.' It implies *guilt* and *failure*.

We all want to be admired, valued and appreciated for whom we are by our family, friends, peers and neighbors. There is value and a sense of worthiness in the respect of others. It is the reward for hard work and maintaining good character. Which is why saving face, meaning 'to preserve one's reputation,' is essential when transgressions have occurred. The implication here is *in spite of guilt or failure.* The threat of shame and disgrace is a tactic used to make people behave; the threat of exposure of shame and disgrace is enough to cause some to lie, fight, and kill.

With that being said, is there a great cause for which you would be willing to lose face?

Taking a bold stance for something you believe in is unarguably honorable, but in these modern times proclaiming your beliefs to the world is as simple as typing it and hitting "ENTER." Opinions are everywhere while actions grow uncommon. Sacrifice—the willful destruction or surrender of something precious—is rare.

Ponder my question again: is there any one thing for which you would cooperatively accept personal indignity? Perhaps you would shoulder such a burden for your children, or spouse, or family, but on what terms would you consent to rigorous personal shame for strangers?

Take it one step further…is there any purpose for which you would, literally, sacrifice your face?

That chill you just felt in the pit of your stomach confirms the horror of this concept.

Before you read *Ungrateful Places*, ask yourself: Who would I be without my face?

Ungrateful Places

"Once a fool was soundly thrashed during the night and the next day everyone made fun of him. 'You should thank God,' he said, 'that the

night was clear; otherwise I would have played such a trick on you!'
'What trick? Tell us!' 'I would have hidden myself.'"

—17th Century Russian Fable

His name was Edward Something-or-Other and though everyone in
the village recognized him on sight no one really knew much about
him, except that he was a large and strong young man who was
always willing to do odd jobs for reasonable pay, that he never spoke
an ill word against anyone, and that he went off to war one cold and
foggy September morning where he eventually saved many of his
fellow soldiers from certain death, was given many medals, hailed a
hero and great warrior, and came home with no face. But by then he
had been gone for so long that no one in the village could remember
what he'd looked like before war had broken out.

To say he had no face is a bit of an exaggeration; he had eyes for
he could see, and he had eardrums because he could hear but no ears
to speak of, just bits of dangling, discolored flesh on the sides of his
head. The skin which formed his cheeks had been grafted on from
flesh the doctors removed from his thighs, and though he was told
that everything would heal over and appear normal Some Day Soon,
it still hurt him to walk or smile; walking was something he could not
avoid, but not so smiling. His nose was gone, as well; his nostrils
were two small skeletal caves that were often blocked and forced him
to breathe through his mouth, which in turn dried up his throat and
made it difficult—sometimes even impossible—for him to swallow;
as a result, he was often hoarse and coughed frequently. Gone also
were his teeth but his jaw remained intact and his gums were firm,
making it possible for him to wear dentures. Sometimes, though,
when he talked—which he rarely did, due to his hoarseness, and also
because his difficulty in swallowing caused him to drool—the
dentures would slip a little and click and whomever he was talking
with would make sorry work of hiding their amusement.

And so Edward Something-or-Other, heroic warrior and village
handyman, began to speak less and less, until, at last, he spoke not at
all...except to the priest.

Everyone in the village took to calling him only "Soldier Boy,"
and found much humor in it. Edward Something-or-Other merely
nodded his head and went about his business. He took to wearing a
bandage on the space where his nose used to be. The bandage

reached the back of his head and was kept in place with a safety pin. He covered the lower half of his face with a long grey scarf, which he liked to imagine flowed in the wind behind him as he walked, like in the old photos and drawings he'd seen of the aviators in their planes as they flew over the battlefields of Europe. Perhaps, he fantasized, people would see him walking with his flowing scarf and think to themselves, "This is an heroic-looking fellow, and I know he was in the war and was given many medals, perhaps he deserves more respect than we have given to him."

But this never happened.

People left him alone, save for those times when a merchant in the village needed something repaired, or hauled away, or a local farmer needed someone to help spread fertilizer. Edward Something-or-Other was the boy for the job; quiet, a bit disturbing in appearance but seemingly pleasant in nature, no job too hard or too dirty or too undignified.

The odd jobs became sparse, so Edward Something-or-Other, under the name "Soldier Boy," became a fighter with a local carnival. He wore a mask and boxing trunks and was said to be able to knock out any and all challengers before the end of Round One. This he did three times a day, six days a week, throughout the spring and summer. He was always careful never to hit any of his opponents in the face for fear he might leave permanent damage; a good, solid blow to the center of the chest usually did it. "Soldier Boy" was never once knocked down, never lost a fight, and made a great deal of money as a result, though he continued to live as he always had; frugally, in a small and sparse room, continuing to do odd jobs in the village whenever they were offered.

Still, there were times, late at night as he lie in his bed trying to remember what his old face had looked like, when he longed to hear the cheering of the crowds as he fought. There, in the ring—even if it was with the carnival—he was, for a little while, admired and cheered as a hero, and no one cared what he looked like.

But like the scarf and his hopes it gave him the air of a hero, it was only something to cheer him a little before he fell into sleep, a little something to help keep the bad dreams away.

The village grew as more children were born and they, in turn, grew to have families of their own. Every summer people came to cheer "Soldier Boy" as he fought his opponents in the ring at the carnival. He was so tall and strong that tiny children would ask to climb on him as if he were a mountain. Edward enjoyed the children, their laughter, the touch of their warm and affectionate hands on his arms, the way they would hug him.

Those who had been alive when he returned from the war grew old and died; only a few remained, and their memories grew dim and fragmented.

"Who is the big fellow who wears the scarf?" younger villagers would ask.

"I don't quite remember," the older ones would reply. "I think he was a hero in the war or something."

"Why does he hide his face?"

Then they would remember: "Because he doesn't have one. That's 'Soldier Boy.'"

Children stopped wanting to play with him after that.

One morning, after cleaning up a local merchant's basement after heavy rains had caused the sewers to back up, Edward Something-or-Other was drinking a glass of water (being careful to hold the rim of the glass under his scarf) when the merchant asked of him: "Did you see many men die during the war?"

Edward Something-or-Other looked at a space in the air as if it contained a window only he could see through, and beyond this window he seemed to see something that haunted him and made him sadder than he was, and instead of answering the merchant with words, he gave a slow nod of his head, but his eyes betrayed that there was much more to his silence and melancholy than this gestures revealed.

What he did not speak of to the merchant that day, what he dared not tell anyone except the priest, was this: he suspected that he was not supposed to have lived, that he somehow had been accidentally passed over by Death that day on the battlefield when the shells were screaming and the mortars exploding and the mines reducing men to chunks of searing meat.

And he suspected this because of the ghosts.

Now, whether they were actual ghosts, he was not at first certain. He only knew that one night, while he sat in his room reading and listening to his tiny radio, a dog began to howl outside his window. The dog sounded frightened, and so Edward Something-or-Other went outside (taking care to first don the scarf so his face would not alarm anyone who might happen by) and lifted the dog in his strong arms. The animal continued to stare down the darkened street and whine, then snarl, and, at last, bury its head in the crook of Edward's arm.

A procession of figures came out of the darkness, walking without sound, all of them carrying burning candles. As they passed by the opened door of Edward's room, he saw that they were all figures of dead soldiers, many of which he had stepped or fallen over on the battlefield. Some were missing arms, others legs, and many, like Edward himself, were missing parts of their faces. It was these figures—those missing facial features—who slowed their step as they passed by his doorway and nodded to him like old friends. They spoke to him, whispering secrets, imparting promises.

At last one of them—an older man, missing forehead and one eye—broke away from the procession and came toward Edward and gave him a lighted candle.

"Keep this nearby," he said to Edward, "and the next time we pass through this ungrateful place, give it back to me."

And with that, he fell back into the procession of dead soldiers and followed them through the streets of the village and into the darkness of the night into eternity.

Edward took both the candle and the dog inside. He allowed the dog to sleep at the foot of his bed. The candle he placed on his nightstand and let it burn through the night as he slept.

He kept hearing the old man's voice calling the village an "ungrateful place," kept seeing the hatred that was in his eyes as he said it, listening as the night carried echoes of the disgust in his voice.

Or perhaps that was all part of his dreams.

* * *

When he woke the next morning, he saw that sometime during the night the candle had changed into the faceplate of a skull.

The dog at the foot of the bed would not look upon the face. It growled when Edward tried to touch it, then bolted out the door and down the road in the same direction taken by the ghosts.

And it was then Edward Something-or-Other realized that he had been destined to die in battle and not come home with this grotesque remnant of a face.

He went to confession and spoke to the priest. Edward spoke slowly, for his dentures and hoarseness made speech difficult, as did the drooling because he could not swallow at all today. He also spoke in this manner because the priest was now so very old and had trouble hearing.

"Father, they told me that if I were to solve the riddle of the Old Man's Candle, then they would give me back my face."

"Your actual face?" asked the priest.

Edward hesitated a moment before answering. "No, Father, not exactly. One said he would give to me his ears for the sides of my head; another promised me his nose so that I would no longer have to wear this bandage; and yet another said that he would give me his teeth so I wouldn't have to wear these dentures and pretend to not notice when the people laughed at me because sometimes they become loose and click."

"Do you believe them to be ghosts?"

"Yes, Father. I recognized some of them from their bodies on the battlefield."

"This riddle you speak of—"

"The Riddle of the Old Man's Candle."

"—yes. Do you know its solution?"

"No. The candle, Father, it...it changed during the night."

"How did it change?"

"It became...well...." Edward reached into his sack and removed the faceplate and showed it to the priest.

"Lord save us," the priest whispered.

"I know what it is, Father," said Edward. "It is the bone of my face as it will appear when it has been healed and made whole again."

The priest gave the faceplate back to Edward, who, feeling embarrassed and humiliated, slipped it quickly back into his bag.

"Do you read your Bible, Edward?"

"Yes, Father."

"Do you remember what Jesus said to the leper who asked that He heal the sores which covered his body?"

"No, Father, I don't."

"Jesus said: 'Heed not the clay countenance that is the flesh, for bright be the face of the soul.'"

Edward said nothing for several moments.

"Edward?"

"Yes, Father?"

"Do you believe that, if these spirits indeed are real, that they will keep their word?"

"I'm not sure, but I suspect not."

"Ah—you still believe that you were meant to die in that battle?"

"Yes."

The priest was silent, deep in thought and seemingly troubled by what he was about to say. At last, he leaned forward and whispered: "This is what you must do, Edward; take a candle from the altar and I shall bless it for you. Take that candle home and light it and then set it upon the face of the skull you have shown to me. Allow the wax to melt so that it covers the entire face, let it dry and harden, and then set three more candles on it—two on the sides, to represent where your ears should be, and one in the center, to show where your nose once was. Do this, and then wait for the spirits to return to you. Only then should you light the three candles and return it to the old man."

Edward did as the priest instructed.

Autumn passed into Winter, and then came Spring and still the sprits had not returned.

Edward Something-or-Other came to believe deep in his heart that he was not meant to be here, and wondered how many more there might be who were like him, if they too ached for company as they lived out their days in ungrateful places.

Summer arrived, and with it the carnival and the rides and the ring and the return of "Soldier Boy"—only now there not so many to cheer his battles. He fought well but without the energy of years past. He was knocked down once by a young man from another village, but managed to rise and defeat his opponent.

He looked once into the crowd and saw, sitting among the spectators, those spirits whose faces were incomplete as his own.

He knew they would be coming for him soon.

Summer passed into Autumn and with its passing came the dry, whispering leaves which skittered along the streets during the day and gathered in dark corners at night.

It was on just such a chill and whispering Autumn night that the dog returned to Edward's window, howling.

"How are you, old friend?" asked Edward as he came outside and lifted the dog into his arms. He wore neither the scarf tonight nor the bandage; his face was, for the first time in many decades, exposed fully to the world...but no one was there to see it.

The dog buried its face in the crook of Edward's arm as the procession of the dead came out of the darkness, their candles burning bright.

This time, however, they did not pass Edward's door but began to gather around. The old man who had given Edward the candle stepped forward and smiled, then asked of him: "Do you have the candle which I gave to you?"

"Yes," replied Edward, and produced from behind his back the wax-covered faceplate, now decorated with three burning candles.

The old man smiled and took the burning face from Edward, holding it high for the others to see.

"'Bright be the face of the soul,'" said the old man; then, turning to Edward, said: "You have solved my riddle, Edward Howe. You have offered your soul to save your village as you once risked your life to save your fellow soldiers." He handed the burning face back to Edward.

It had been so long since Edward had heard his true last name spoken by anyone that he did not at first recognize it; nor did the words "...save your village" at first register.

"You shall be rewarded," continued the old man, "in two ways: First, we shall not, as we were supposed to do, take you with us."

"So it's true, then," whispered Edward. "I *was* supposed to die that day?"

"Yes, but no matter now, you shall grow to be a very, very old man, and let us hope that it will be a happy life from this night on. Touch your face, Edward."

He did, and discovered that it was now whole and healed; ears, cheeks, teeth, nose, skin—it was a normal face, one that he would never again have to hide behind masks or scarves.

"I am whole again," he said, startled by the sound of his voice, its fullness, its richness and timbre. For the first time in decades he pulled in a deep breath through his nose; there was no pain.

"Secondly," said the old man, "you shall now be the only true face in your village."

"What do you—?" But before he could complete the question, there came from a nearby window a scream of singular horror, and soon a woman ran into the street clutching her face. She spun around, eyes wide with terror, and pulled away her hands to reveal that she had no nose, only a smooth, flat area of flesh.

Soon other villagers spilled into the street, all of them missing facial features, some who had no faces at all, merely blank ovals of flesh where their features should have been.

"No!" cried Edward.

"Why?" asked the old man. "Look at us, Edward Howe. Fallen warriors, all of us. Some of us died in battle, but many of us, like yourself, returned home scarred and disfigured, only to find ourselves mocked outcasts. 'Abomination!' they called us. Well, now, let *them* know how it feels to be the one who is mocked, who is scorned and turned away from, who never again knows the warm touch of a friend, the kiss of a woman's lips upon their own, the feel of a child's loving arms around their necks. We have traveled from village to village to find others just like you, Edward, and they have all accepted our bargain. So many years since the war, and how easily those who never knew battle forget the sacrifices we made for them. Let them know now."

Edward saw the people of his village running, screaming, crying, clutching at their ruined or missing faces, and for a moment, just one moment, a moment he would never forgive himself for, Edward Howe, formerly Edward Something-or-Other and Soldier Boy, felt a brief, bright satisfaction in their pain; but a moment later he realized just how wrong this was and thrust out the burning face. "No. If this is the price of having a normal face restored to me, I do not want it; and if it means that you take my soul and I come with you now, then so be it. Return everything as it was and you can take my soul. I will not fight you. The wars are over. I have no desire to fight again."

The old man took the burning face and an instant later, the villagers found their faces restored to them. None looked in Edward's direction; even if they had, none would have seen the spirits surrounding him.

"So I come with you?"

The old man shook his head. "Not now, but soon enough. A season or three. Listen to the wind, and you'll hear our approach in the whisper of leaves across the cobblestones. Good-bye, Edward Howe. Enjoy your isolation and grotesquerie."

They left him there, alone save for the dog, and he watched them vanish up the road toward eternity.

His throat was dry and his nostril cavities were blocked. It was time to take some medicine and try to sleep.

The dog followed Edward into his room and slept at the foot of his new master's bed, where he would sleep for the rest of his days. Years later, upon Edward's death, the dog would be found sleeping at the foot of his master's grave and would refuse to move. It would lay there until it, too, passed away, and would be buried alongside its master.

But that was many years away.

The next morning, everyone in the village was talking about the horror of the previous night, wondering what they could have done to offend God so badly that He would punish them in such a way.

"But He did not make the punishment permanent," said one merchant.

"True," replied a cook. "It was as if he were...warning us."

"Or reminding us," said the priest.

"Reminding us of what?"

The priest said nothing, only glanced for a moment toward the doorway where Edward stood, scarf and bandage in their place, his dog at his feet.

Later that day, someone left a fresh-baked apple pie on the sill of Edward's open window.

The next morning, he found a tray with a delicious breakfast waiting outside his door. The odd jobs began to become plentiful again. Sometimes children would stop and ask him about his scarf and bandage.

In their sleep, the villagers would often dream of Edward sacrificing his soul for them so they would never know the loneliness of having a face like his.

They began speaking to him, and, eventually, he began to speak in return. He was invited to attend church socials, to join in a game of cards or come to a village picnic.

Toward the end of his life, he stopped wearing the scarf and bandage. The villagers took to carrying extra handkerchiefs with them so that they might have one should Edward need it on a day when swallowing was difficult for him.

He took his medals out of their box and put them in a case and that case was put on display in the village hall.

He had many friends in the village that grew to love and respect him.

When Edward passed away quietly in his sleep, the village closed all of its schools and shops for the day so that everyone could attend his funeral. The day was pleasant but slightly overcast and warm.

Near his grave, there was found an oddly-shaped candleholder with three candles in it. Attached to it was a note that read: *Some Burn Too Brightly For Us To Take.*

As it was placed on the lid of Edward's coffin, the sun emerged from behind the clouds and the day became as bright as anyone in the village had ever seen.

There were tears, and later there was the business with Edward's poor dog, but, for generations to come, there was also a tale to pass along to the children; some of it based on fact, some on supposition, some of it on dreams, but it, like its subject, would be remembered, if not forever, then for long enough.

It began: *His name was Edward Something-or-Other and though everyone in the village recognized him on sight no one really knew much about him, except that he was a large and strong young man who was always willing to do odd jobs for reasonable pay, that he never spoke an ill word against anyone....*

A Little Off The Top

Introduction by Deena Warner

By now, you've read a few stories about Gary and feel like you know him. He makes a mean omelet. He's a crazy cat person who chips a tooth every time he leaves the house. He's a generous teacher and dedicated friend. You're so wowed by his talent, you've saved up a thousand dollars to fly across the country to meet him. Only you can't wait those five months until convention season rolls around. What will it be like to finally hear him speak and shake his hand?

You sit in a hotel conference room as he enters through beige double doors. He's followed by a small group of fans and is naming great books and short stories that have influenced him. You nod in agreement as he moves up the aisle. You're a life-long reader and know a thing or two about the genre... except as soon as he passes, you scribble down the names of each book because you haven't heard of *any* of them. No way you could. Because you're not as well-read as Gary.

You watch him read his latest story before a silent crowd. Kudos if you've survived as more than a sobbing wreck in the corner. Don't tell me you still have dry eyes. His story either ripped out your heart and stomped on it a few times or it opened your soul to beauty you've never experienced before. Maybe it wracked you with guilt over horrible things you haven't even done. Maybe it taught you to connect with the simplest creature, a baby or a butterfly.

You take a deep breath. You sidle up and tell Gary how much you love his work. You ask him to sign your Leisure paperbacks and back issues of Cemetery Dance. You thank him for the thoughtful posts he's put online and congratulate him on his latest award. He nods graciously, but none of this makes him comfortable. He steers the conversation elsewhere. He wants to know about . . . you.

Me?

Yes, you. No matter who you are, Gary honestly wants to get to know you. Many writers spend their time looking up, paying attention to their own heroes or the people above them on the totem pole. Gary looks everywhere. If you have passion as a fan or a craftsperson, he will respect you. He'll lift you up and open doors. Before you know it, he'll introduce you to his peers and make you believe in yourself.

That story he read probably shared a lot of qualities with this one: mystical goings-on near the town of Cedar Hill, mutated beings, everyman characters with sadness and flaws. Whether you experience Gary in person or on paper, you're left with hope. Touched by his empathy and enthusiasm, we all live richer lives.

A Little Off the Top

When my grave is broke up again
Some second guest to entertain ...
And he that digs it spies
A bracelet of bright hair about the bone
Will he not at last let me alone?
—Milton

Concerns.

We concern ourselves with a barber and his wife, as well as the barber's customer and *his* wife. Do they have names, these four? Yes, they do, but since we will never meet them again after this tale is told there is no reason for us to know what those names are; odds are we'd forget them soon enough, anyway.

We must also concern ourselves with a very old tree with gnarled roots that grows from soil very few have ever tilled or tread upon. Its branches, bent, twisted, sometimes growing out and around until they become brittle spirals, are draped in places by a fine scintilla that could easily be mistaken for spiders' webs, only if we moved closer we would note that this grayish matter seems to be breathing. We could dismiss the movement as being caused by the wind, but there is never any wind in this place, so it may be best we just not think about it for the moment.

This tree stands—or, rather, *stoops*, not unlike some mythical hunchback finding sanctuary among the bells—in a field several miles from the outskirts of Cedar Hill. There is, around this hunched and stooped tree, a man-made trench several feet deep from which a fetid, rank odor rises; this, too, is of concern to us, as is the creature that calls this trench home.

There is also a three-quarters moon, and that is of concern not only to us, but to the nameless four introduced above.

And so, as the grass of the lawns in town—the grass that is Whitman's beautiful, uncut hair of graves—ripples with the breeze that drifts through, we watch as the moonlight reveals to us in clearer light those people, places, and things with which we are concerned.

The Shop.

There is a barber's shop on this street, just a few yards down from the church, and like the buildings that set on either side of or across the street from it, there is nothing unique to be noted, save for the traditional red-and-white barber's pole outside the entrance door—in fact, if it were not for that pole, one could and would easily miss this shop if one had never been here before and were looking for it: this is, more or less, the intention of the owner, who we will formerly meet momentarily.

The Regulars.

The regulars of this shop are as nondescript and interchangeable as the buildings along the street; most are blue-collar workers, under- to un-educated, or retirees looking to pass some time in pleasant conversation with men of their own era or mindset who, like themselves, have no need for those fancy so-called "salons" where characterless pop music endlessly drones through hidden overhead speakers, the décor leans toward black and chrome, all the male barbers call themselves "stylists," and everything smells like the reception area of a high-priced whorehouse—not for these fellows, no thank you. Give them a row of comfortable chairs, a television tuned to a sports event or news channel, the local paper or a national magazine, free coffee and a soda machine that never seems to run out Dr. Pepper, and they're a content bunch. Ask, and we would find that all of them had, at one time or another, gone looking for this shop and missed it the first couple of times. If it weren't for that pole out front and off to the side, they'd never have known the place was here. Yes, they're a content bunch, sometimes even jovial, and when they laugh or smile their ruddy faces let us know that these fellows plan on being around here for a good long while.

The Barber and His Wife.

As we first see the Barber, he is napping in the small bedroom he shares with his wife in the 6-room apartment they live in above the shop. It's a Sunday evening, getting close to eleven p.m., and the Barber is sweating ever so slightly as he shudders and occasionally jerks in his sleep. After a few moments, his wife enters the room carrying a glass filled with some frosty beverage. She sets the drink on the nightstand next to the bed, places two pills next to the glass, sits down next to her husband, and gently reaches out to brush away some of the hair that seems lacquered to his forehead. Her touch stirs him, and the Barber slowly opens his eyes and smiles at her.

"It's time for your medicine. I brought you some lemonade," she says, her hand resting against her husband's cheek.

"Oh, good," says the Barber, turning his face into her hand and kissing the palm as he begins to sit up. "I could use something cold." He pops the pills into his mouth and reaches for the glass, drinking nearly half the lemonade before setting it down again. "Did you make this just now?"

She grins. "Fresh batch."

"Thank you." He closes his eyes for a few moments; then his face— a face that was red and anxious —begins to regain its natural color as the tension fades away under the drugs' quick-release action.

"Better?" asks his wife.

He opens his eyes. "Much."

He rises from the bed and slips on his shoes. There is no need for him to dress because he purposely fell asleep in his clothes. He goes into the bathroom and washes his hands, then his face. He combs his hair, rinses his mouth with Listerine, and turns to remove his barber's smock from the hook on the bathroom door. He buttons the smock, checks to make sure his cigarettes are in the pocket, and goes back into the bedroom to see his wife looking at the framed lithograph hanging next to the doorway; nearly sepia-toned, it shows a stern-looking group of people surrounding a man with a harsh expression; he is dressed in a cassock and wearing tri-cornered hat as he holds up a Bible. Next to the man stands a woman in plain long dress whose torso is obviously being crushed by the corset underneath; her hair, mostly covered by the white bonnet she wears, is pulled so tightly back that her face seems on the verge of splitting down the middle. It is a scene so ominous that it's almost comical. Almost. Until we look over their shoulders and study what's in the background, a few dozen feet behind the crowd: three gallows poles, each with a dead figure hanging by the neck. All three, we notice upon closer inspection, seem to have been beaten severely and their hair ripped out; except for a few tattered strands caught in the wind, they are bald.

The barber stands next to his wife and places a hand on her shoulder.

"Tell me," she asks him, "why do you insist on not only keeping this thing, but keeping it in our bedroom?"

The barber smiles and emits a small laugh but there is no joy in either. "Call me sentimental."

His wife leans in to him. "Are you ever going to forgive yourself?"

"Have you followed your own advice?"

"We're not talking about my guilt, we're talking about yours."

"Then my answer is, it doesn't matter. Forgiveness is … a cruel joke. And even if I did, it wouldn't change anything. It's not our forgiveness we need."

She turns her head and kisses his cheek. "I do love you so much."

"And I, you." He turns toward her and they share a warm, brief kiss.

Beams from a car's headlights cut through the window blinds then are quickly extinguished.

"Your new customer is here, I think."

They walk over to the window. The barber opens the blinds just a slit, just enough so he and his wife can see down onto the street. There is a small nondescript blue car parked across from the shop. The glow from the streetlight a few yards away reveals two figures in the vehicle, a man and a woman—but beyond that, the barber and his wife cannot make out anything. But we needn't stay up in that bedroom with them, we can pass through the blinds and the glass and drift down to the car, through the nearest of its windows, and take an unseen place in the back seat; and that is exactly what we do, leaving the barber and his wife standing in bedroom shadows.

The New Customer and His Wife.

The woman is quite pretty, though her features are, at the moment, fixed into a mask of quiet, tightly-coiled fear. She turns off the car and looks at her husband. He is far too thin and is shaking and sweating. His face has a gray pallor and there are dark circles under his eyes, making them look as if they might collapse back inside his skull should he be jostled even the slightest. He wears a wool cap over his head, but we can see a few strands of brownish hair —that are more like cobwebs—

protruding from the left side and back. He crosses his arms over his stomach and leans forward, dry heaving.

"Christ," he manages to say. "What the hell was that thing I had to eat?"

His wife reaches over and takes hold of one of his near-skeletal hands. "Some kind of root."

"Did she tell you *why* I had to eat the fucking thing? I can still taste it. Awful. God, it's awful."

"No, she didn't tell me. Maybe her husband can answer that."

The man turns his head and looks at the shop. "Are we crazy, hon?"

"Probably, but you said at this point you'd try anything. And if there's a chance that it'll work, then I ...." Her voice cracks on the last few words but if she is about to cry, she holds back.

Her husband squeezes her hand and kisses her on the cheek. "Can't be any worse than some of those quacks we've already seen. And at least I'll be well-groomed. More or less."

"Are you sure you don't want me to go in with you?"

"Didn't that woman tell you that I have to be alone?"

"Yes."

"Then just leave. Go home. I'll call you when it's ... it's finished."

"Do you know how much I love you?"

"I do. And I love you, too. So very much."

They embrace for a few moments.

"You're hurting me," says the man.

His wife releases him. "Sorry. I just ... I just can't stand the idea of you ... I mean—"

"You think I'm all goo-goo-gah-gah over the idea? I'm not ready yet to pay the fine and go home, but we're kind of getting down to the wire here."

"Don't remind me."

The man kisses her once more and then opens the car door. "God, I hope he doesn't, like, break out any leeches or something like that." He fumbles the metal arm crutches from the back, slips his hands into the wrist cuffs, and clasps the grips; slowly, painfully, he pulls himself up to stand. He makes his way around the back of the car, not looking at his wife as she reaches across to the close the passenger door. He does not see her watch him stumble his way up the shop's front stairs, does not see how her face fills with concern and a combination of deep love and respect that more resembles awe. After a moment she turns away, starts the engine, and drives away.

The man stands at the shop's front door and presses the buzzer. After a moment, the lights come on inside and someone unseen works the locks. The door opens and the man looks into the face of the barber. The barber asks the man for his name, the man gives it, and the barber steps aside to allow him entrance. We slip in behind him just as the barber closes and locks the door.

"Please, have a seat," says the barber, pointing to the only chair in the shop. "Just let me finish getting everything ready."

The man almost makes it to the chair before another wave of intestinal pain causes his legs to nearly buckle. He lets go of one of the crutches and manages to grab hold of the back of the chair; releasing the other crutch, he does not so much sit in the chair as he does crawl up the cushions, twist, and collapse.

From his place by the sink and mirror, the barber watches this, but neither says a word nor offers the man any assistance. The barber opens an old wooden case made of highly-polished wood and begins removing his tools from their resting place within the dark satin pillows within: a straight razor, a silver comb, and, of course, his scissors. All three gleam in the light; looking over at the man in the chair, the barber picks up only the scissors. Placing them on the tray stand next to the chair, the barber then unfurls the grey apron that he ties around the man's neck—though not tightly, not tightly at all—and adjusts so that his new customer's clothes will be protected.

"Would you mind removing your cap?" asks the barber.

The man does so, revealing a scalp almost totally devoid of hair, excepting the few long, sad strands we saw earlier. Though his scalp—it has the same grey pallor as his face—looks moist, it is, we see as we look closer under the lights, only moist in a few places; the other areas are not only severely dry but have patches of red blisters, some of them so wide they could be mistaken for birthmarks.

"The, uh … the chemo has been kind of hard on me."

The barber nods as he pours some gold-colored liquid from a bottle onto his hands. "I can see that." He places his fingers on the man's head and begins massaging the scalp.

"Is this part of the process?" asks the man.

The barber pauses. "Remember—you get three questions tonight, and three questions only. Do you really want *that* to be one of them?"

The man shrugs. "I guess not."

The barber resumes the scalp massage. The man in the chair begins to relax.

"Man, that feels nice."

"I'm glad," says the barber. He finishes the massage, washes his hands once again, and picks up the scissors. "Shall we, then?"

The man in the chair takes a deep breath, holds it for a moment, and releases it slowly. "Yeah, please." Then, as the barber gently takes a strand of his hair into his hand: "Do you mind if I say I'm scared shitless right now? Or would that count as one of my three questions?"

"Actually, that's *two* questions—and no, those I will not count. It's only specific questions about the process that are limited."

"Okay."

"Oh," says the barber, turning around and theatrically patting his pockets. "I seem to have forgotten the leeches."

The man in the chair turns quickly around—well, as quickly as he can, anyway—and blanches. "*What?*"

"Leeches. It's an old barber joke. I thought it might get a laugh from you."

"Oh," replies the man. "Okay … yeah, I guess that is kind of funny. I made the same joke with my wife when she dropped me off."

"The classics never die." And with that, the barber takes a strand of the man's remaining hair between two fingers, and smoothes it down from scalp to tip.

"So," says the barber. "A little off the top, then?"

And both men laugh. It is a strangely musical sound, but it's not the only music in the air this night. We can hear the other music, the singing that the barber and customer cannot, and it's a mesmerizing sound, ethereal, and our curiosity piqued, we slip out through a nearby vent and follow it to its source.

The Tree, Its Singers, and a Visitor.

We can see there is something different about the tree. Oh, at first glance it's still the tallest, ugliest, thickest, most unnaturally twisted-looking tree we've ever seen, its dense, broad roots disappear into the soil as smoothly as a finger into water; there are no cracks, no gaps, no damaged bark; roots and soil are now perfectly sculpted together. We move closer, tentatively, for we are still not sure what's wrong here, moving slowly closer, focusing on one of the lower branches where something thick, wet, and dark is dripping from a deep gash that has to have been made by an ax. The closer we got to the tree, the more we can see that it bares the marks of several ax strikes, and not particularly skilled strikes, either; the wounds—and *wounds* they are, because every jagged score is bleeding—have begun to scab over in a few places, but not enough to prevent us from seeing that, beneath the bark, instead of wood, the tree is made of soggy red tissue and tightly-wound sinew. And it now it *sounds* like the thing is breathing.

Like most places and things in Cedar Hill, there are legends about this tree; so many, in fact, that the people here have long given up trying to separate fact from fancy. The name it was given in legend is The Choking Tree, because those who have witnessed its so-called breathing claim that it seems to be fighting for breath, as if it's being strangled by some unseen hand or force.

We listen. The sound of someone—or *something*—else breathing is louder now, but also strained, wheezing, filled with phlegm. The smooth bark of the tree begins to crack, thin rivulets of blood trickling down toward the gnarled roots, and the shape of the tree begins altering: the branches twine together to form arms, knots in the center protrude and shift, becoming faces, and the scattered clumps of white scintilla we observed earlier move toward these faces to light upon their shorn scalps and become hair. Then, as the three voices merge into one, they begin singing—and what a sound it is; rain spattering against cold glass on a dim autumn day, the taste of the color of sadness, the cry of a distant, low train whistle in the night, reminding you that you are now and always will be alone … and the taste of anger, the touch of betrayal, the groan of something lost in a cavernous, murky, dank place where no light ever reaches to show the way out; all of this is captured in the sweetly bitter song of these voices and they sing, again and again and again, "*Remember … remember … remember* …."

And in the trench—that we now see is more of circular pit—we catch glimpses of the thing that calls this pit home; rippling scales, appendages that may or may not be tentacles, clusters of eyes where none should be, and, briefly—thank the Fates, so briefly—the shape of a mouth big enough to swallow an infant whole, a mouth filled with circular rows of sharp, yellowed, jagged teeth. It moves with the song as if drawing energy from it, becoming stronger, more frenzied in its ecstasy, until it suddenly stops as the song continues.

We turn to see a reed-thin brown cat, perhaps a tabby, shamble out of some nearby foliage. Its eyes are yellowed, its movement slow and painful. So sick is this tabby that it cannot control its bowels, and so both urinates and defecates with every step; the feline leukemia that has been chewing through its system is in its final stages and this tabby, that has known little to no kindness in its few too years on this earth, manages to make it nearly to the edge of the pit before it crumples to the ground, fighting for its last breaths as the pain becomes all it knows or recognizes. Except for the singing. Somehow, the singing manages to find gaps in the pain and enter the tabby, relaxing it, comforting it.

Slowly, quietly, as the tabby struggles for another breath, one of the tentacle-like appendages slips over the edge of the pit and slides toward the cat, gently wrapping the tabby in its embrace, and pulls it back, over the side, and down into the shadows.

We wait, but hear no sound coming up from the abyss — for an abyss this must surely be, and even the sound of the women's singing cannot keep us here now; no, we must leave at once, seeking sanctuary and comfort in the homey warm light of the barber's shop.

Shop Talk of a Sort.

The barber turns the chair around so both he and the man face the mirror. The man starts at the sight of his reflection, as if he's been avoiding looking at himself in bright light. The barber pats the man's shoulder.

"Don't worry, friend," he says in a soothing voice. "I assure you that I'm not some snake-oil salesman."

The man in the chair says nothing, only gives a slow, sad nod.

The barber continues to smooth out the tufts and strands of the man's hair with his fingers; he has yet to make a single cut.

"Did you know," says the barber, who is not really asking a question, "that the human head has been associated with hundreds of rites and taboos over the centuries? Much of them come from the belief that the head — the scalp, specifically — is the abode of forces of great power, and because of its connection with the human head, hair was assumed to possess magical properties of its own and, naturally, became the focus of many other superstitions and magical rites, devised from protecting the head from — get this — psychic injury. It was also supposed to protect those who had the task of dressing or cutting the hair from the anger of the hair's indwelling spirits."

"Isn't there something like that mentioned in the Bible?" asks the man in the chair. "Or does that count as one of my three questions?"

"Yes, there is mention of it in the Bible and, no, it doesn't count. You're thinking of Samson and Delilah. Judges, chapter sixteen — and here's an interesting bit of trivia if you ever want to win a bar bet: Delilah *did not* cut Samson's hair; she had one of her handmaidens do it … or maybe it was one of her nurses, I don't remember. Regardless, she never touched it. Stories like that caused people to believe human strength resided in the hair, and that cutting it reduced physical vitality. Removal of hair was always regarded as a terrible form of punishment, and many groups fully exploited that belief—for instance, the penal authorities of the Dutch East Indies frequently threatened their prisoners with shaving their heads, and the threat alone was enough to secure confessions without resorting to torture.

"Hair is believed to respond to the emotional state of the person it's attached to. Because of *that* belief, it became accepted that a severe shock or fright could turn a head of hair white or grey in a single night. There are a number of interesting historical accounts to back up that belief, such as Marie Antoinette and the less-than-lucky Damiens, who was tortured in public before having his white hair shorn, and then was ripped apart by being tied between four horses. Seems Louis XV took assassination attempts very seriously."

"Why are you telling me all of this?" says the man in the chair. "I mean, it's interesting, don't get me wrong, but ... why?"

"*That* will count as your first question."

"I know."

"I am telling you all of this because it will help make things easier in a little while. It will help you to understand the process."

"Okay. Thank you."

"You're welcome." The barber finds two strands of hair that command his attention. He smoothes them out, separating them from the others in the clump, snips them off, and carefully places them into a small plastic bag that he immediately seals. Returning to the man, he continues to examine what hair remains.

"Many people believed—and still believe—that even after hair is cut away, it is still linked by an invisible bond to the great forces and spirits in the head. Because of this, there is a practice in many cultures around the world of taking the shorn hair and disposing of it secretly to prevent it from falling into hostile hands. Sometimes it is cast into a stream so it will be borne away from any danger. In ancient Rome the discarded locks of the *flamen Dialis*, the Priest of Jupiter, were buried beneath a magic tree. Some cultures would stuff the hair into a hole in the tree, or tie it around some frog or bird, even worms and snakes that lived in or near the tree. What happened to these creatures afterward is anybody's guess, but if there was any truth in the supernatural power of hair, some believe that it may have produced deformities, caused unholy mutations, created monsters of a sort. It is believed that such trees still exist all around the world, some in the most unlikely of places, and that these trees are guarded by the mutated creatures that were tied to the shorn hair, especially the hair of executed witches.

"You see, it was one of the strongest beliefs in witch-hunting times that dark magical potency of the witch or sorcerer resided in the hair, which is why so many accused witches were shorn of all bodily hair before they were tortured, tried, and executed. In Europe the witches were either drowned or burned at the stake, sometimes both, their hair burned along with them. It was believed that burning a witch's hair once it was removed from her body guaranteed the death not only of the witch and her power, but her very spirit. My God, the people were fanatical back then, arguably crazy—and the sad part is, the people who were accused and convicted of witchcraft were what we now call herbalists, midwives, and homeopathic healers who were merely trying to help their townsfolk. So many innocent lives were lost, but the people and their religious leaders *believed* they were doing God's work. Have you ever heard of the Caporael and Matossian studies?"

"No."

"Stay with me on this, it is important. Let's pick a single location, say, for instance, Salem. The Salem Witch Trials in 1692 resulted in the deaths by execution of twenty people, and the torture and imprisonment of one hundred and fifty others, all of them accused or convicted of witchcraft. The thing is, as the Caporael and Matossian studies concluded, the so-called 'victims' of the accused witches very well might have suffering from nothing more than food poisoning."

"That's *nuts*."

"But the studies make a strong argument. It was a specific type of food poisoning known as convulsive ergotism. People contracted it after eating rye that was contaminated with the fungus ergot. Rye was a staple of the New England diet in the late Sixteen Hundreds. It grew exceptionally well in Salem because there was an abundance of swampland, the type of land that is susceptible to infection by ergot and very likely *was* infected. Ergot flourishes best after a severe winter followed by a cold, most spring. New England endured an extremely harsh winter in 1691-1692, and the spring that followed was abnormally cold and damp.

"The 'victims' of the witches suffered giddiness, tremors, and violent spasms. They had the most fantastic visions, and all claimed to feel the legs of invisible ants or other insects crawling around inside their skin. *All* of these are classic signs of convulsive ergotism. And in addition to the nausea and vomiting and hallucinations, they became afflicted with something called formication—the belief that ants or insects are crawling underneath your skin. As for the hallucination and visions, ergot happens to be a rich source of lysergic acid diethylamide—LSD.

"Those women executed as witches *did not* cause these so-called possessions—they were trying to treat and cure it. But willful ignorance coupled with the arrogance of mob mentality has a way of shredding all reason beyond hope of repair." He discovers a third hair, separates it, and places it in the plastic bag with the others. "Nearly finished now." He pulls the apron off the man in the chair. "Tell me, are you feeling nauseated right now?"

The man rubs his stomach. "Hell, yes. I don't know what that root was or why you insisted that I eat the damn thing, but I've been feeling horrible for the last few hours."

"You didn't take any medicine, did you?"

"Nothing."

"No antibiotics, beta-blockers, nothing for the pain?"

"*Nothing.*"

"Good." The barber takes a chair across from the man and lights a cigarette. "We all have our personal rituals, my friend. Having a smoke after a cut is one of mine."

"Man, that smells good," says the man, coughing.

"So," says the barber. "You have two questions left. Want to ask them now?"

"I'll ask one; why did you only cut certain hairs to put in the bag?"

"Because not only does mystical power reside in the hair, but the infection of all diseases, as well. In your case, since there is so little hair to work with—and so much of it has been ruined by the chemo—I had to find the ones that have managed to stay alive, to hold on to some of their power while also sharing the disease. There were three, but that's all we'll need."

"I didn't think it would be over this quickly."

The barber smiles as smoke curls out of his mouth and nose. "It isn't finished. Oh, we're done *here*, in the shop, but we're not finished yet. We still have to make a little drive. Unless I miss my guess, we've got about twenty, twenty-five minutes before that root you consumed causes you to vomit, and you need to do that at a specific place. Please don't ask where because we'll be there soon enough, and the 'why;' of it will be obvious once this is all over. You now have one question left. I strongly urge you to save it."

The man in the chair nods his head. The barber finishes his smoke, rises from the chair, and offers the man in the chair the crutches he dropped earlier. "Shall we, then?"

The Drive.

The drive is mostly non-eventful. Neither man speaks; instead, they listen to the radio. It's only when the Oldies station begins playing Norman Greenbaum's "Spirit in the Sky" that either man breaks the silence: the begin singing along with it. The man beside the barber sings along as if he's just recalled an until-now forgotten memory, one of cruising around on the weekends when still in high school, a pretty girl sitting beside you, honking your horn and laughing for no reasons at all; he sings along with the remembered joy of youth and budding dreams.

The barber sings the song as if it's a prayer.

Just as the song is ending, the barber pulls his car off to the side of the dirt road they have been travelling. "We have to go the rest of the way on foot. Are you up for it?"

"Not that it matters, but I'll try."

The barber places a hand on the man's shoulder. "Not much longer now."

The man grins. "Doctors already told me that." He looks at the barber. "That was cancer joke."

The barber blinks. "Inside, deep inside, I'm doubled over with laughter."

"You hide it well."

"Yes. I get a lot of complaints about that."

They get out of the car. The barber guides the man over to a narrow path leading into something that looks like a miniature version of the forest primeval.

"Stay behind me—I'll walk slowly. Please don't wander off the path. It would not be a good thing."

The man nods once again, and the two men set off on the last part of their journey.

The Path and Its Inhabitants.

All around them are exotic smells that are both intoxicating and threatening; animal urine, manure, sweet flowers, moist greenery; it would be a somewhat pleasant walk were it not for the animals the men see tracking them at a distance on either side of the trees: a coyote with two-thirds of another growing from its side, the extra head bouncing against the ground, white eyes never blinking; toads far too large for this area of the state, some with eyes that bulge even larger than their expanded vocal sacs, others with extra legs or —in one instance—none at all, moving itself forward by wriggling on its semi-gelatinous belly;

geese with so many wings they cannot fly; opossums the size of bull mastiffs; groundhogs walking upright because they have only two legs; and other animals that resemble nothing the man has ever seen before, or wants to see again.

"Wh-what *is* this place?" he asks.

"As far as you're concerned," replies the barber, "it's where affliction and despair come to die. And that was your third question."

"I was afraid of that."

They continue on wordlessly, slowing their pace as they reach a slight rise in the ground; during the small climb, the barber puts his arm around the man's waist, helping him along. The ground flattens out, the overhead foliage ends, and they stand at the edge of a field. The moonlight seems focused solely on the tree. The terrible figures of the three women jutting from the bark reach out with their brittle-branch arms, hand cupped, beckoning the two men to *come closer … come closer … come closer …*.

"I feel sick," says the man, nearly falling.

"Good," says the barber, grabbing the man under one arm. He nearly drags the man to the tree. They stop at the edge of the trench and the barber takes away the man's crutches. The man drops to hands and knees, his head hanging just over the edge.

"Close your eyes," says the barber. "You don't want to see the thing that lives down there."

But the man says nothing, only begins to cough, to choke, to dry heave, but he cannot vomit. The barber removes the plastic bag from his pocket and takes out the three hairs, holding them out, as far away from his body as he can. The woman nearest to him reaches out, over the trench, her limbs crackling, extending, until her hand grasps that of the barber. She squeezes his hand, then with her jagged index finger, scratches deep, drawing some of the barber's blood. The barber makes no sound as she takes the three hairs from his hand and dips them into his blood like a painter preparing a brush for the canvas. Withdrawing her arm, she stuffs the bloodied hair into the knothole in the center of her torso. The barber kneels next to the man. As soon as the hair is ingested, the man begins vomiting, a torrent of white, red, and black tumors shaped like chunks of cauliflower, mixed in with some blood and bile. His entire body shudders and jerks with each burst of pain-wracked sickness; his face is bright red, veins bulging in his neck, his temples, and his scalp. There is a few moments' reprieve from the violent seizures, and as the man groans and struggles to pull in breath the barber grabs one of the man's arms and with his free hand rubs the center of the man's back, whispering words of comfort, words of promise, over soon, it will be over soon, so soon, I promise, I promise you, my friend, over so soon, and another wave a nausea overtakes the man, this last one the worst of them all, the man grabbing the edge of the trench, his body hitting the ground full force as more small tumors are expelled down into the wide, open, waiting mouth of the creature below.

When at last the seizures and sickness have passed, the man rolls over onto his back. The barber moves him away from the trench, into the cool grass of the field. For several minutes the man simply lies there, pulling in ragged, phlegm-filled breaths, his chest rising and falling rapidly at first, and then slowing, slowing, until he is once again breathing freely and easily. He opens his eyes and stares at the barber.

"You opened your eyes, didn't you?" asks the barber.

"Christ Almighty ... what *is* that thing?"

"I'm not completely sure," replies the barber. "It might have been a worm, or a toad, a snake, it might even have been a duckling or a piglet or a club-footed calf for all I know. Whatever it was, it's now something beyond this world but trapped *in* it. It lives on disease, it craves disease, it *gorges* itself on disease. Parts of it are capable of moving out the pit, but not very far. It's become so distended and bloated by all it's consumed over the centuries that its legs are useless. And I am charged with keeping it alive by feeding it death."

The man does not react; instead, he reaches out and the barber helps him to sit up. The man simply stares at the barber, waiting.

"My name was Jacob Sprenger. I was a witch-finder—I was, in fact, a Witchfinder General. I was known as 'Jacob the Shorner.' When interrogating accused witches, I tried not to resort to the more brutal forms of torture—at least, for a while. I was content to obtain confessions by simply shaving all the hair from an accused witch's body. After a while, I became aroused by their terror, and then intoxicated by their cries for mercy and, toward the end, addicted to the pain in their faces as I ordered them to the rack, or burned them with a blacksmith's searing iron, or ...." He shakes his head. "It doesn't matter. There are some sins too horrible, too monstrous, for remorse.

"I married a woman as pious as I, and together we traveled the land, trying the accused who were already condemned before their trials began." He looks at the tree that has now returned to its previous state— just an old, twisted tree in the middle of a field. "One day, there was a trial of three sisters in a village filled with heat of rampant fanaticism. I know now that those three women were innocent; they were simply healers whose methods were so foreign to the villagers that it seemed like dark magic. Rye was consumed frequently in this village, rye infected with ergot. The villagers were not content with simple torture; they demanded execution.

"Just before they were killed by the hangman's noose, the eldest of the three—a girl no more than sixteen—looked at my wife and myself with deep, deep pity. 'You may never gain our forgiveness, but perhaps you will learn and accept the price of your mistakes. For all of eternity, you both shall always remember … remember … remember ….'

"I was foolish enough to think that my wife and I could escape their power, but I was wrong. And so this is, for lack of a better word, my penance. All the pain and horror I inflicted on so many innocent people … I have to make amends. This is how I try, and how I will continue to try until the day they might choose to forgive me and allow my wife and I to pass from this earthly realm into whatever Paradise or damnation awaits us.

"My wife and I are nearly four hundred years old. Immortality is, eventually, a form of damnation. But I have my wife, I have her undying love, and I have my shop, my regulars who are all my friends. I have their company, and their laughter, and the stories they tell. How do you feel?"

The man seems surprised by the question. At first he only opens his mouth to find no words will emerge; then he takes a deep breath—perhaps the deepest breath he's taken in months, even years—and stands up without the barber's assistance. He touches his head to find the scabs have disappeared. His touches his throat, his chest, his groin. "I … I feel … okay, maybe not *great*, but … better. A *hell* of a lot better."

The barber rises to his feet. "And you'll continue to feel better. Go see your oncologist this week and watch as his or her jaw hits the floor after running what I'm sure will be a battery of tests. It is gone. You are clean. The rest of your life awaits you. By the way," says the barber, lighting a fresh cigarette, "you're now a regular. Once your hair grows back in a few weeks, come and see me for a trim."

"A little off the top?"

"A little off the top."

The man points toward the barber's cigarette. "Those damn things'll kill you, you know."

"Can't blame a guy for trying."

And both men laugh; perhaps there is more genuine mirth in one's laugh than the other but it's of no consequence now; they are enjoying each other's company, and that is, for the moment, enough.

Final Concerns.

There is not much more to our story, a story the barber has lived many times before and will continue to live many times more. The man returned home alive and better. His wife wept and kissed him and held him and thanked Who- or Whatever there was out there in the universe for making this possible; she gave thanks for the night, and for the day and days that followed. And there were so many, many days that followed.

The barber welcomed a new regular several weeks later, and like the other men who patronize the shop, he found himself welcome. He brought his laughter, and his friendship, and his stories.

But we mustn't leave just yet. We find ourselves drawn back to the tree in its field, and the trench surrounding it. We wait, we watch, and we listen. Something is scratching at the wall of the trench, something small but determined. For a moment, the sound stops, then whatever is trying to climb out resumes its efforts with more determination.

A few moments later, a brown tabby cat claws its way over the edge and back onto solid ground. It sits, grooms itself for a bit, and then, on strong legs that carry a now-slightly rotund body, strolls off into the night, perhaps, we hope, to find someone who will show it kindness, give it a little food, maybe a new home.

And we smile, turning away from the tree, as the first dim rays of sunlight begin to bleed across the horizon. The night is finished, as is our story.

Tales the Ashes Tell

Introduction by Graham Masterton

Lyrical, intense and moving, Gary Braunbeck's "Tales the Ashes Tell" is told from a highly unusual point of view. He shows that the value of human life is its variety, and that the real horror is its brevity, and is sadness. A deeply affecting story that breaks all the so-called "rules of writing" – but that's what makes the difference between a good writer and an inspired writer. Gary Braunbeck is an inspired writer.

Tales the Ashes Tell

I was in the darkness;
    I could not see my words
        Nor the wishes of my heart.
            Then suddenly there was a great light —
                "Let me into the darkness again."
                    —Stephen Crane

Some nights, when the visitors have left and everything within me falls into dismal silence, when even the Librarian grows weary of drifting through these halls, maintaining these chambers, and looking at these glass doors behind which rest the golden books, when the rain spatters against the roof and the flashes of lightning create glinting reflections swimming against my marble floors, when I am at last certain there will be no one and nothing to disturb me, I allow myself, for a little while, to flip through these books as one still among the living would flip through the pages of an old family photo album; only where the living warm themselves in the nostalgic glow of reminiscences, I sustain myself on the memories of those housed within the books arranged on my shelves, behind my glass doors with their golden hinges, here in my corridors with marble floors. I have no memories, being born of wood, iron, and stone as I was. But those who slumber here, within these golden books, their memories remain with them, and many are so lonely that they gladly share them with me on nights such as this. I house them from the elements; they sustain me with their stories. I prefer it this way, on nights such as this, when it is just the ashes, the rain, and I ... and the tales the ashes tell.

Tonight it's old Mrs. Winters who's the first to start in with her story of her grandson's death in Vietnam and how it broke her own son's heart and led to the ruination of his marriage and career, ending when her son took his own life in a squalid motel room somewhere in Indiana. Every time she tells this story, her neighbors listen quietly, politely, patiently, for they—like I—have heard this a thousand times before, but she always changes some small detail so it's never *quite* the same; tonight, the scene of his death is not some sleazy roadside hovel but an expensive, five-star hotel in the middle of downtown Manhattan, and this time her son does not decorate the blinds with his brains but instead stands on the roof of the palace, arms spread wide, a joyous smile on his face as he falls forward off the edge and for a moment almost flies until he ... doesn't.

Like her neighbors I am pleased by this new trick of the tale. Each time she changes a bit of the minutiae the story resembles itself less and less, and one night it will be a completely new story that she will begin revising almost immediately. We like this about her. She was never married, our Mrs. Winters. She had no children. She died alone, on a bus-stop bench, a forgotten bag lady whose mortal remains were cremated and placed here by a sympathetic police officer who still comes by once a month to bring flowers and pay his respects; it seems Mrs. Winters reminded him of his own grandmother; beyond that, no one here has any further idea of his reasons, and if Mrs. Winters knows of them, her memory is too fragmented to know for certain if those reasons are true or not. We do not press the matter. Even here, certain privacies are respected.

I find it curious, how many of her neighbors were interred here by strangers, or family members they were never particularly close to. Many of them come here from cities and towns that are hundreds — sometimes *thousands* —of miles away. I know that I am a glorious edifice, and am honored that so many of the living wish to bring their loved ones here to rest. I am a tranquil place, a quiet place, a place of serenity and sanctuary. I know all of the stories of nearly everyone who slumbers here, but not all.

Tonight, we have new neighbors on my shelves, behind my glass doors. I heard only a part of the explanation given by the slightly hunched, spirit-broken man who brought them here. Something about his brother and his niece and a boy his niece once knew. I wonder whom it is he has left with us. I exchange pleasantries with all my friends between the golden covers of their books, and as I do each of them asks, *What do you know about the new arrival?* I have no answer for them, not yet, but being the curious sorts they are—and always so lonely, even when all of them are chattering away—they want me to find out but are too polite to ask. They know they don't need to; I will discover it in time.

I see that the glass doors have been freshly washed and dried so that our new arrival is welcomed into a clean space. She is whispering to herself, our new neighbor, and I become very still, empyrean, allowing the rain and lighting and the slow turning of the Earth to cast shapes of angels in the Primum Mobile of night.

She speaks not of herself, but of *we*, of the uncle who brought *us* here.

Could it be? There are so few books here that contain more than a single person's remains; the last was five years ago, when an elderly husband and wife who died within hours of each other left specific instructions that they were to be burned and interred together, their ashes, like their souls (or so they believed), intermingled for eternity. I find that sort of sentimentality pitiful, but I never speak my judgment to those who need to believe in such antiquated notions. Do not misunderstand—the souls of that elderly couple are intermingled here, but not in the way they were raised to believe; there are no fields of green they run through, hand in hand, laughing as the afternoon sun sets their faces aglow and the scent of autumn leaves fills the air. They are simply *here*, and so shall remain. But it is enough for them, this fate, and that pleases me.

The girl still speaks of *we* and *us*, very seldom does the word *I* make an appearance. At least not at first.

I'm here, I tell her or them. *As are we all, and we are all listening.*

She continues to whisper, but whether she is telling the story to me or to those who live inside my walls, I do not yet know. But she tells her story as if she has told it a thousand times before and expects to tell it a thousand times again; and, perhaps, like old Mrs. Winters, she will begin altering details as the years and decades and centuries go by, until it is a new story, one she finds can spend eternity with and not be crippled with regret.

Mute, voiceless, abandoned and all but forgotten, she begins, *my father's house does not so much sit on this street as it does crouch*; an abused, frightened animal fearing the strike of its keeper's belt, the sting of a slapping hand, the rough kick of a steel-toed boot. No lights shine in any of the windows, which are broken or have been covered with boards or black paint or large sections of cardboard that now stink of dampness and rot. The paint on the front door long ago gave up fighting the good fight and now falls away, peeled by unseen hands, becoming scabs dropping from the body of a leper in the moments before death, but with no Blessed Damien of Molokai to offer up a final prayer for a serene passage from this cheerless existence into the welcoming forgiveness and saving grace of Heaven. This was once a house like any other house, on this street like any other street, in this town that most people would immediately recognize and then just as quickly forget as they drive through it on their way to someplace more vibrant, more exciting, or even just a little more *interesting*.

But we can't blame them, you and I; we can't impugn these people who pass through without giving this place so much as a second glance. If things had worked out differently, we would have burned rubber on our way out, making damn sure the tires threw up enough smoke to hide any sight of the place should one of us cave and glance in the rear-view for a final look, a last nostalgic image of this insufficient and unremarkable white-bread Midwestern town, but that's not the way it works around here; never was, never will be. You're born here, you'll die here; you're a lifer, dig it or not.

We sometimes wonder if people still use that phrase, *dig it*, or if it's also passed into the ether of the emptiness people still insist on calling history, memory, eternity, whatever, passed into that void along with *groovy, outta sight*, "*That's not my bag*," "*Stifle it, Edith*," Watergate, Space-Food Sticks, platform shoes, Harry Chapin flying in his taxi, and the guy who played Re-Run on *What's Happening?*

Wouldn't it be nice if that drunken Welshman's poems had been true, that death has no dominion, or that we could rage against the dying of the light? Odd. It occurs to me that if we were still alive, we'd be looking right into face of our fifties about now, feeling its breath on our cheeks, its features in detail so sharp it would be depressing.

But this never does us any good, does it, thinking about such things? Especially tonight of all nights. Don't tell me you've forgotten? Yes, that's right. This night marks the anniversary of the night my father buried us under the floorboards in my bedroom after he came home early from work and caught us in my bed. It was my first time, and when he saw you there, with his little girl, it was too much for him to take; not this, not this dirty, filthy thing going on under his roof, it was too much; his wife was gone, three years in her grave after twice as long fighting the cancer that should have taken her after nine months; his job was gone, the factory doors closed forever, and he was reduced to working as a janitor at the high school just to keep our heads above water because the severance pay from the plant was running out.

"At least the house is paid for," he'd say on those nights when there was enough money to buy a twelve-pack of Blatz, sit at the kitchen table, and hope with every tip of every can that some of his shame and grief and unhappiness would be pulled out in the backwash.

You never saw it, you never had the chance, you didn't know him as I did. I couldn't look at his eyes and all the broken things behind them any longer; I couldn't listen to his once booming voice that was now a disgraced whisper, the death-rattle of a life that was a life no longer, merely an existence with no purpose at its center…except for his little girl, except for me and all the unrealized dreams he hoped I'd bring to fruition because he no longer had the faith or the strength to fight for anything. A hollow, used-up, brittle-spirited echo of the man he'd hoped to be. Even then, even before that night, he'd ceased to be my father; he became instead what was left of him. I tried to fill in the gaps with my memories of what was, what had been, but I was a teen-aged girl, one who hadn't paid any attention to him during the six years my mother was dying, and so I made up things to fill in those holes. I pretended that he was a Great War Hero who was too modest to boast about his accomplishments on the battlefield; I dreamt that he was a spy, like Napoleon Solo on *The Man from U.N.C.L.E.*, hiding undercover, using his factory job to establish his secret identity, his mission one so secret that he couldn't even reveal the truth to his family; I imagined that he was writing the Great American Novel in hidden notebooks late at night, while I slept in my room with the Bobby Sherman and David Cassidy posters on the walls, their too-bright smiles hinting that some day soon my father's novel would make him so rich and famous that the two of them would be arguing over who would take me to Homecoming, and who would take me to the prom.

But he was no war hero, no spy, no secret great notebook novelist; only a factory worker with no factory who'd exchanged a lathe machine for a mop and a bucket and pitying looks from faculty members. To the students, he was either invisible or an object to mock.

No, I don't remember your name. I don't remember *my* name, but what does it matter now? Our names, like our flesh, were only a façade, an illusion to be embraced, a falsehood to be cherished and mistaken for purpose, for meaning. We have—*had*—what remained of our bodies to remind us of that, beneath the floor, flesh long decayed and eaten away, two sets of bones with skulls frozen forever into a rictus grin as if laughing at the absurdity of the world we're no longer part of.

Let's not stay here for now, let's move outside, round and round this house, watching as the living ghosts of everyone who once passed through the door come and go in reverse; watch as the seasons go backwards, sunshine and autumn leaves and snow-clogged streets and sidewalks coming and going in a blink and…and let's stop here. I want to stop here, in the backyard, just for a few moments, just to see his face as it was on that night.

Watch; see how pretty it all is. Murky light from a glowing street lamp snakes across the darkness to press against the glass. The light bleeds in, across a kitchen table, and glints off the beer can held by a man whose once-powerful body has lost its commanding posture under the weight of compiling years; he's overweight from too many beers, over-tense from too many worries, and overworked far too long without a reprieve. Whenever this man speaks, especially when he's at work, especially when he's holding the mop and bucket, his eyes never have you, and even if they do you cannot return his gaze; his eyes are every lonely journey you have ever taken, every unloved place you've ever visited, every sting of guilt you've ever felt. This man's eyes never have you, they only brush by once, softly, like a cattail or a ghost, then fall shyly toward the ground in some inner contemplation too sad to be touched by a tender thought or the delicate brush of another's care. To look at him closely, it's easy to think that God has forgotten his name.

He lifts the can of beer to his mouth. It feels good going down, washing away the bad taste in his mouth that always follows him home from work. He drains the can, sighs, goes to the sink and pours himself a glass of water. He is thinking about his days as a child, about the afternoons now forgotten by everyone but him, afternoons when he'd go to the movies for a nickel and popcorn was only a penny. He thinks about how he used to take his daughter to the movies all the time when she was still a little girl and her mother, his wife, was still alive. He remembers how much fun they used to have, and he longs for the chance to do something like that again, something that will put a bright smile on his daughter's face and make himself feel less of a failure.

He stands at the sink listening to the sounds of the house, its soft creaks and groans, still settling after all these years. He thinks about his dead wife and doesn't know how he'll be able to face the rest of his life without her by his side. She was a marvel to him. After all the mistakes he's made—and, God, he's made a lot, no arguing that—her respect and love for him never lessened.

He tries to not think about the things his daughter has done for him the past few months, things he didn't ask her to do, but things she's done nonetheless. Just to help him relax, to help him sleep.

And then he hears a sound from his daughter's room. A squeak of bedsprings. A soft sigh. The muffled laughter of a boy.

His face becomes a slab of granite and the broken things behind his eyes shatter into even more fragments. Unaware that he's doing it, he reaches over and picks up the hammer he left lying on the kitchen counter last night while he tried repairing the loose cupboard door above the sink. He turns and marches toward his daughter's bedroom, knowing what he's going to find when he opens the door and—

—what? All right, just this once, we won't watch the rest. He wasn't really *there*. Anyway. I'm glad we know that now. He just wanted to scare us but his frustration, his anger, his heartbrokenness took control.

Let's pretend that we still have hands, and let's pretend to hold them as we play "Ring Around the Rosie" once more, going back just a little more, a year, maybe less, because I've been saving this for you, for this anniversary, this most special anniversary. Why is it special? That's a secret I need to keep just a little while longer. Take my hand and let's go, round and round and round and—

—stop right here. Yes, this is the place, the time, exactly right.

There's a young girl of seventeen sleeping in her bed who, for a moment, wakes in the night to hear the sound of weeping from the room across the hall. She rises and walks as softly as she can to her door, opens it, and steps into the hall.

"....no, no, *no*..." chokes the voice in the other room.

"Daddy?" she says.

"....no, no, *no, oh, God, honey, please...*"

She knows he can't hear her, that he's dreaming again of the night his wife, her mother, closed her eyes for the last time, of the way he took her emaciated body in his arms and kissed her lips and stroked her hair and begged her to wake up, wake up, please, honey, what am I supposed to do without you, wake up, *please....*

She takes a deep breath, this seventeen-year-old motherless girl, and slowly opens the door to this room stinking of loneliness and grief. She takes a few hesitant steps, the moonlight from the window in the hallway casting bars of suffused light across the figure of her father as if imprisoning him in the dream. She stares at him, not knowing what to do.

Then his eyes open for a moment and he sees her standing in the doorway.

"Arlene," he says, his voice still thick with tears. "Arlene, is that you?"

"Shhh," says the young girl, suddenly so very cold at hearing him speak her mother's name in the night. "It's just a bad dream, go back to sleep."

"...I can't sleep so hot, not without you..."

She can hear that he's starting to drift away again, but she does not move back into the hallway; instead, she takes a few steps toward the bed where her father sleeps, tried to sleep, fails to sleep, sleeps in sadness, sleeps in nightmare, wakes in dark loneliness, drifts off in shame and regret.

For the first time, she realizes the pain he's in, the pain he's always been in, one way or another, this man who was no war hero, no spy, no secret notebook novelist, just a sad and decent and so very lonely man, and she feels useless, insufficient, foolish, and inept; but most of all, she feels selfish and sorry.

Her eyes focus on one bar of suffused moonlight that points like a ghostly finger from her father's sleeping form to the closet door a few feet away, and she follows the beam, opening the door that makes no sound, and she sees it hanging from the hook on the inside of the door: her mother's nightgown, the one she'd been wearing on the night she died.

"Oh, *Daddy...*" she says, her voice weak and thin.

Still, her hand reaches out to lift the gown from the hook and bring it close to her face. Her mother loved this nightgown, its softness, its warmth, the way it smelled when it came out of the dryer after a fresh washing, and this girl holds the garment up to her face and pulls in a deep breath, smelling the scent of her mother's body and the stink of the cancer still lingering at the edges.

From the bed her father whimpers, "....no, no, *no, oh, God, honey, please...*"

And she knows now what she can do for him, what she has to do for him, and so she removes her nightshirt and slips on her mother's death-gown, crosses to the bed, and slips beneath the sweat-drenched covers.

"...Arlene...?' says her father, not opening his eyes.

"Shhh, honey, it's me. Go back to sleep. Just a bad dream, that's all."

His hand, so calloused and cracked, reaches out to touch her face. She lies down on her mother's pillow and is shocked to find that it still carries the ghost-scent of her perfume. She remembers that her parents liked to spoon, so she rolls over and soon feels her father's body pressing against her, his legs shifting, his arm draping over her waist as he unconsciously fits himself against her. After a moment, she feels his face press against the back of her —her mother's—gown, and he pulls in a deep breath that he seems to hold forever before releasing it.

She does not sleep much that night, but her father sleeps better than he has in years.

We can watch now, you and I, and see his face, see my father's face when he wakes the next morning and sees her next to him. Shadows of gratitude, of shame, of self-disgust, of admiration and love flicker across his face as he stares down at her now-sleeping form. He feels her stir beneath his arm and realizes with a start that his hand is cupping one of her breasts, the way he used to cup his wife's breast before the cancer came and sheeted everything in sweat and rot and pain.

Still, his hand lingers for a few moments as he realizes how very much like her mother's body does his daughter's feel. Then he feels her stir, waking, and closes his eyes, pulling his hand away at the last moment.

His daughter rolls over and sees how deeply asleep he is, and realizes that she's now given herself a duty that can never spoken aloud, only repeatedly fulfilled. Only in this way can she comfort him, help him, thank him.

She slowly rises from the bed, crossing to the closet where he replaces her mother's gown on its hook, then slips back into her own nightshirt and leaves, closing the door behind her.

As soon as the door closes, her father opens his eyes and stares at the empty space in the bed next to him that now hums with her absence. So much like her mother. So much like her mother. So much like her mother.

This goes on for nearly a year, her assuming the role of her dead mother in the night so her father can sleep. In a way, both know what's going on, what they have become, the roles they are playing, but neither ever speaks of it aloud. And even though nothing physical ever occurs between them in the night as they keep the grief at bay, a part of each of them falls a little bit in love with the other. In this way they become closer than they had ever been, and though the house is never again a happy place, the shadows begin to retreat a little…until the night when her father hears the muffled laughter of a boy coming from his daughter's bedroom and storms in with a hammer that he does not intend to use but does, nonetheless, then collapsing to the floor afterward, vomiting and shaking with the realization of what he's done, what he's become, and it takes only a few frenzied hours for him to mop up the blood and tissue and then tear up the floorboards and move the piles of human meat underneath, burying his daughter in her mother's nightgown. He takes great care replacing the boards, hammering them into place, then covering them with an area rug taken from the living room before gathering a few things —some clothes, what little cash is in the house, some food —and stumbling out into the night.

Shhh, listen —do you hear it? That sound like old nails being wrenched from wood? The front door is opening, someone is coming in, someone who walks in a heavy heel-to-toe fashion as if afraid the earth might open up between each step and swallow him whole.

We watch as the old, hunched, broken thing that was once my father makes his way toward my bedroom. He carries a battery-operated lantern with him, a small backpack, and so much regret that its stench reaches us even in this non-place we wander.

He sets down the lantern, then his backpack, removing a hammer from inside. The same hammer.

In the light we see how he's changed. Well over seventy-five, and the years have not been kind. He looks so much like Mother did toward the end, a living skeleton covered in gray skin, slick with sickness. He moves aside what little remains of the rug and sets to work on the floorboards, which offer little resistance, and within a few minutes, he is staring down at us.

"I'm home," he whispers.

Hello, Daddy. I've missed you.

He sits down, his legs dropping down beneath the hole in the floor, his feet resting between us.

"I thought about the two of you every day," he says. "I've dreamed about the two of you every night...those nights that I can sleep. Ain't too many of those, especially lately."

It's all right, Daddy. I understand. We understand.

He reaches into his backpack and removes something we can't quite make out, because he's deliberately keeping it hidden from our gazes. We're back in what remains of our bodies now, staring up at this lost, broken, sick old man whose face is drenched in sweat, in pain, in the end of things.

"I had no right," he says. "I had no right to love you like that, in that way. I had no right to be jealous, Melissa."

Melissa. So that was my name. How pretty.

"I didn't mean it, I didn't mean to do it." And he brings the object into the light so we can see it. But we already knew, didn't we, you and I? His old gun from the war where he never was a hero, just a simple foot soldier who helped fight the enemy and serve his country before coming home to marry a good woman and build a life for his family.

He begins to speak again: "Oh, *honey*, I..." But the rest of it dies in his throat, clogged by phlegm and failure and guilt.

It's all right, Daddy. We understand. We're not mad anymore.

But he doesn't hear us. He clicks off the safety, jacks a round into the chamber, and pushes the business end so deep into his mouth that for a moment we expect him to swallow the entire weapon.

He hesitates for only a moment, but that gives us enough time to move, to rise up as we are now and open our arms as he squeezes the trigger, and we are with him, and he is with us, and as the human meat explodes from the back of his head we lean forward and take him into our embrace, cold flesh and tissue meeting bone and rot, and he embraces us both, does my father, and we hold him close as his blood soaks into the tattered, rotted remains of my mother's nightgown, and we can smell her, she is within us, around us, part of us, and in the last few moments before we pull my father down into hole with us, I find some remnant of my voice in the release of his death, and have just long enough to say, "I forgive you, daddy, And I love you."

Then he is in the hole with us and in this way are our sins of omission at last atoned.

We remember the way we mingled as we decayed, how we were then found and identified; we remember the way Uncle Sonny claimed our bodies—even yours, my teenaged lover whose name I still can't remember—and had us taken to the place of cardboard coffins with plywood bottoms where we were fed one at a time into the furnace, our tissues charred and bones reduced to powder. We remember the way the workmen swept us into the containers and then into the machine that shook back and forth, filtering out gold fillings and pins once inserted to hold hips together.

And now we are here, all three of us. Our new home; our hushed home; our forever home.

And you are welcomed here, I tell them.

Mrs. Winters thinks Melissa sounds like a nice girl, the type of girl her grandson might have married if he hadn't died in Vietnam, and oh, by the way, don't let me forget, young lady, to tell you all about my son who was a pilot, who flew so high above the clouds you would have thought he was some kind of angel.

I'd like that, Melissa replies. I smile, insomuch as I am capable of performing such a thing, and I continue through my corridors with their marble floors, looking through my glass doors at those who reside behind, and I know that I will never know the loneliness and hurt of those who reside here, for I will always have these hushed and hallowed nights, I will always have those who rest here within me, and—most of all—I will until eternity is no more have the tales the ashes tell.

Just Out of Reach

Introduction by Chesya Burke

One of the most exciting things about the future is that it is a distant, unreachable period of time for which none of us can ever fully know and, more importantly, can never understand. The future is always just out of reach, whether it is ten years from now or just a few moments away. We all race toward the future, often ignoring or putting off the present, but knowing full well that it is a race that we, as individuals, can never win. Our children and grandchildren will one day reach the future but we simply cannot.

Unless, of course, we find ourselves in the pages of a Gary Braunbeck story. Then the future can appear instantly, so that if we tilt our heads just right, we can glimpse a shimmer of it within the image of an old Polaroid photo. And we know – we know for a if only for a split second, that there are more possibilities within that future than we want to admit. That things can go so terribly wrong that in order to protect ourselves, we simply choose to forget.

In that way, Braunbeck does not offer a safe, Utopic future for his characters, but instead an unnerving one from which there is no escape other than their own limited memories. So sit back, ready the covers, and await the future. I have been where you are now, in my past.

Just Out Of Reach

Before my face the picture hangs,
    That daily should put me in mind,
        Of those cold qualms, and bitter pangs,
           That shortly I am like to find...
              —Robert Southwell, 1561—1595

For Richard Matheson

It began on the morning a girl with no hands asked if she could take pictures of the house.

Eric was in the kitchen, lecturing the appliances until the refrigerator got bored, so he then turned his wrath on the pots and pans but they were having none of it; since he'd now lost two-thirds of his captive audience, he resorted to scolding the dishes but their conspiracy of silence continued.

"Ingrates!" he shouted at the lot of them.

No reactions.

Talking to kitchens was not uncommon behavior for Eric; as co-owner and manager of one of Cedar Hill's few genuine upscale restaurants/bistros, he'd found it helped channel his daily frustrations (and God knew, he had *so many* daily frustrations) if he yelled at inanimate objects rather than other people, so it wasn't unusual to find him in the restaurant's kitchen after closing time, screaming at the stove or dishwashing machine. He often joked that as long as he directed his anger at things that could not respond, then everyone around him remained safe.

There is nothing more irritating than recalcitrant cutlery, which he discovered after jerking open the drawer in which the little bastards lay all smug and safe in their proper compartments; arrogant, shiny, disinterested.

"I could switch to an all-sushi diet," he said to them. "Chopsticks are very cooperative fellows. *Then* where would you be?"

He sensed they knew it was an empty threat.

This behavior was the result of a breakfast accident; Eric had been too buzzed on his first few drinks of the day (he was more than a little drunk, so it was a good thing Val was out running errands) to pay much attention to what he was doing, and in the process of using one of the large chopping knives to dice tomatoes for the omelet that was to never be accidentally made a nice slice up the side of one of his fingers.

He jerked back his hand and watched as two large drops of his blood dripped onto the table, his face reflected in both of them.

In one, he looked just like himself; but the drop that spattered against the side of the saucer reflected a man who might have looked something like him, but—

—he grabbed some paper towels and started to clean up the mess, decided it could wait, then went into the downstairs bathroom and fixed up his hand: peroxide, two gauze pads, some medical tape, and half a Vicodin tablet from the prescription leftover from his root canal surgery a few weeks back.

Good thing he had two whole days before having to be back at the restaurant; the Health Department would never allow someone with a bandaged hand to get anywhere near the kitchen, and Eric liked to make sure that his kitchen ran smoothly. Also, it was necessary from time to time to check and make sure his chef hadn't killed anyone. The staff tended to give better service when they weren't dead.

The front doorbell chimed.

Eric's initial reaction was not to answer it and hope whoever it was would just go away, but the pragmatic part of him whispered: *It might be important.*

Thankful that he'd decided to get dressed before coming downstairs (he usually spent his days off in his bathrobe), Eric tucked in his shirt, patted down his hair, and answered the door.

The woman who stood before him looked to be in her early twenties. She carried a medium-sized leather shoulder bag. She was dressed in a very business-like blouse and blazer, with a matching skirt and sensible shoes. She wore a plastic name tag on her left breast pocket, but Eric couldn't read her name because her long, dark hair was swept over her left shoulder.

She was so beautiful that, for a moment, he couldn't find his voice.

She was *that* stunning...and yet somehow familiar. Eric felt as if he'd seen her somewhere before. Maybe at the restaurant? Was she one of the semi-regulars whose name he hadn't bothered learning yet? But if that were the case, what was she doing here? How had she gotten his address?

And that's when he noticed that she had no hands; instead there were two curved, shiny steel prostheses which Eric immediately thought of as "hooks".

"Yes?" he managed to say at last.

"Eric Barker?" She said in a bright, chiming voice.

"Yes?" The blood was rushing through his temples with such force that he didn't hear her name when she said it.

She offered him a business card. Eric glanced at it, saw the words **Modoc Realtors, A Subsidiary of Bright Hand, Inc.** and realized that Valerie must have made this appointment without discussing it with him first. They'd been talking for a while about getting a bigger house, had even looked at a couple of places —even finding one that they both fell instantly in love with —but until this moment Eric had no idea that his wife had gone and signed with realtor to sell this place.

And it pissed him off. Sure, the restaurant kept him busy, but not *so* busy that he couldn't be included in making decisions —like, for instance, when to put the house on the market, and with whom.

He was so surprised that he didn't realize he'd invited the girl inside until he found himself closing the door and turning toward her.

"I'm sorry to be early," she said, "but I've got a last-minute showing in about an hour. I hope you don't mind?"

"Uh...uh, no, no, of course not." He slipped her business card into his pocket without bothering to read her name, then asked, "Did my wife make this appointment?"

"Yes, about a week ago. Now, we realize that you're not firm in your decision to sell yet, but the agency wanted me to do a quick walk-through and take some pictures so we can give you a good appraisal on probable market value." She leaned toward him and lowered her voice to a whisper as if he were her co-conspirator. "You'd be surprised how many couples decide to sell after our agency gives them a potential sales figure."

"I'll bet."

She turned away from him and walked through the downstairs rooms, finishing up in the kitchen. "Oh, Mr. Barker, this is a *wonderful* house! There's so much open space —and in all the right places." She set her bag on the kitchen table and opened it, removing an old Polaroid Instamatic camera. "Is it all right if I take some quick pictures of the house? If you later decide you *are* going to sell, then I'll come back with a much better camera and take some professional-quality photos for our brochure and website."

"Have we met?"

"I beg your pardon?"

Eric rubbed his eyes and smiled. "I'm sorry, I don't mean for that to sound like some kind of middle-aged lecher come-on, but ever since I answered the door I can't shake the feeling that I know you from somewhere. Have you ever been to my restaurant?"

"I'm afraid not. I'm a little...*new* to this area."

He continued to stare at her for several moments as she readied the camera.

I know I recognize you, he thought.

And then something occurred to him.

Over the course of his marriage to Valerie, Eric had encountered many beautiful women and had been attracted to many of them —a few had even hinted that, even though he was married, they wouldn't mind a few quickies in hotel rooms —but he'd never once cheated on Valerie. Not that he didn't indulge in the occasional fantasy about sex with another women, but that was always as far as it went.

Looking at this stunning young woman who stood here in his kitchen, Eric realized that she was prime fantasy material for him, yet —

—and damn if this wasn't one for the books —

—he wasn't attracted to her, not in the way he usually found himself attracted to beautiful women, anyway. No; what he felt toward this woman—who should have had him so hard he could barely stand— was much more tender, beyond sexual attraction. He felt somehow... *protective* of her, in the way that an older brother was protective of a younger sister who'd grown up into a true beauty.

Think about something else, he commanded himself.

It was rapidly becoming his new mantra: *Think about something else.*

So he looked at her hooks.

Okay, they weren't *exactly* hooks, he could see that now; they didn't curve but rather stuck straight out, and when she worked them, each prosthesis opened into three separate...*rods*, he guessed you'd call them, two of them the same length, the middle rod a bit longer.

Just like the three fingers in the middle of your hand, Eric thought.

He'd seen people with hook prostheses before, but never anything like these; these were like something from a science fiction movie.

The girl looked up, saw him staring, so Eric cleared his throat and said, "I used to have a camera almost exactly like that."

"Oh?" she replied, doing her best to sound as if she believed he'd been staring at the camera.

"Yes," he continued. "I lost it about a year ago, but until then I'd had it for the better part of twenty years. Worked as well on the day I lost it as it did the day I bought it. It was the same color as yours, as well. Those scratches on the side? I had the same kind of scratches in almost the same place on mine."

"The old carrying cases weren't as well-constructed as today," she replied, inserting, with amazing dexterity, the eight-track tape-sized film cartridge into the bottom of the camera. "I've lost count of how many times I've scraped this thing on the side of that old carrying case."

Eric grinned. "I remember that I had one of those old label-makers, the kind where you had to punch the words in one letter at a time on those plastic strips? I put my name on the label—I misspelled it, by the way—and stuck it to the bottom of the camera. Don't know why."

"Huh," said the young woman. Snapping closed the bottom film compartment, she pulled out the piece of blank film that slid out with a loud *whirrr* after the new cartridge had been loaded, then held up the camera and said, "All set. Any particular place you'd like me to start?"

"Doesn't matter to me." Why didn't he just tell her it wasn't a good time, that he and Valerie needed to discuss it further, thank you for coming, Miss Modoc or whatever in the hell your name is, but things at the restaurant haven't been great lately, and neither has my marriage, and I'm pissed off and angry most of the time and have no idea why (which may be one of the reasons my wife and have been acting more like housemates than a married couple), and because of all this I've got a busy day of moping planned and you're bringing too much activity into my life.

He couldn't bring himself to ask her to leave...but why?

"I'll start right here in the kitchen, then take a couple of pictures of the living room, the master bedroom and master bath, then the guest room and office area upstairs."

"Ah, so my wife gave you an idea of the layout, then?"

The young woman stared at him for a moment, then shrugged. "I think so. To tell you the truth, I talk to so many people about so many houses, some days it all gets a little blurry. *Is* there an office upstairs?"

"Yes."

"Huh." She seemed both surprised and puzzled. "Lucky guess."

Eric sighed. Maybe he was just being paranoid, but there seemed to be something just the least bit *forced* about her reaction.

She took four pictures of the kitchen from different vantage points, then placed the photos on the counter so they could develop.

The young woman excused herself and went into the living room. Eric poured himself another cup of coffee and sat on a stool at the counter, watching as the Polaroids slowly developed.

He'd always been fascinated by the way these old instant cameras worked; snap a picture and out slides this smelly blank square of white, but as you watched it, like magic this image slowly began to appear. A ghost emerging from the mist.

He took a sip of his coffee.

The girl appeared in the kitchen doorway. "Is it all right if I go upstairs and take some pictures?"

"Knock yourself out."

"Would you care to accompany me, Mr. Barker? I know it must seem strange, letting a stranger walk through your house and —"

He waved his hand. "No, you seem trustworthy."

She gave him a radiant smile. "Why, thank you." And with that, she bounced up the stairs.

Eric examined the developing photos. He couldn't be sure, but it seemed like they weren't going to turn out properly.

The phone rang. He continued looking at the photos for a moment, then turned away and answered the wall-mounted kitchen phone.

"Hey, partner," said Carl. "Enjoying your day off?"

"That depends on why you're calling."

"A man of lesser ego would take that as a personal insult."

"I apologize if I've dampened your splendid mood, Carl." He looked back at the photographs. "What's going on?"

"I got a call from Marciano's a few minutes ago about that special order you placed for the imported Merlot."

"Uh-huh?"

"Seems old man Marciano wants you to sign for it personally. From the sounds of it, he flew over to Italy, picked the grapes, made the wine himself, then had to bribe about a thousand Customs officials to get it into the country."

Eric grinned. "He tends to embellish things. I hope you were gracious and thanked him about a dozen times."

"Of course. He's the best wine merchant in the state. Wouldn't do to piss him off."

"The Merlot's for that wedding rehearsal dinner next Tuesday. Can't think of the family's name right now —"

"Parr."

"Right. The stuff was hard to locate and expensive as hell. I promised Marciano that I'd sign for it myself. Is the check ready?"

"Just needs your John Hancock."

Eric looked at the wall clock. "When's the delivery?"

"It should be here in about an hour-and-a-half."

"I'll be there. Just make sure—" The rest of the words died in his throat when he looked back down at the now-fully developed photographs.

"Eric, you still there?"

"Uh...yeah, sorry. I was distracted by...by...okay, I'll see you around noon, Carl. I gotta go."

"Is everything okay there? You sound a little weird."

"Everything's fine. I'll see you in a little while."

"Word of warning: Chef's in one of his *moods* again. No bloodshed, but he might take hostages."

"Oh, joy." Eric hung up without saying good-bye.

He picked up one of the photographs, then another one, examining each of them until he'd gone through all four of them at least three times.

He looked up at the kitchen, the back at the photos to make sure this wasn't some trick of the light.

It wasn't.

The kitchen shown in these photographs was not the same kitchen in which he was currently sitting. *This* kitchen, *his* kitchen, was neat and clean and uncluttered, your typical, nice suburban kitchen.

But the kitchen in the photographs was *magnificent*.

It was the same kitchen, as far as the structure of the room itself went; all of the windows and counters were in the same place, as were the appliances, every wall was where it was supposed to be and all the angles were in their proper place, but that's where the similarities ended.

The magnificent kitchen in the photographs could have been in the pages of *Better Homes and Gardens*. Impressive copper pots hung on the walls. The kitchen table had been replaced by a marvelous marble island, above which hung a metal, scaffold-like series of shelves that were attached to the ceiling by bright silver chains. The shelves held all manner of baking utensils and pieces of small equipment—electric dicing machines, an expensive food processor, a vegetable steamer, and several other contraptions that Eric had seen only in a professional kitchen. In the center of the marble island was a large square of polished wood that served as a knife holder.

He couldn't take his eyes from the photographs.

The shelves were painted a different color. A wall rack held chubby yellow and orange soup mugs. The kitchen table was set over by the window (it was the *same* kitchen table that was now in the kitchen, he noticed), but instead of the two old wooden chairs, there were three exquisite, hand-polished teak chairs placed around it.

He put the photos back down on the counter.

Good Lord.

Valerie had always wanted a kitchen like that shown in the photos. They had even begun pricing some of the items and once had an architect look the place over to see if some of the additions — like the scaffold-like structure of shelves hanging from the ceiling — would be possible.

There was no doubt about it; the kitchen in the photographs was the one he and Valerie had always *planned* on having, some day.

Some day.

He picked up one of the photographs and squinted his eyes, trying to get a clear look at the calendar that, in the picture, hung not by the pantry door but where the telephone now resided.

Climbing off the stool, photograph still in hand, Eric went into the living room to retrieve his reading glasses from the table next to his recliner. Grabbing up the glasses, he noticed that the young woman had left four photos of the living room on the large coffee table in front of the sofa.

He put on his glasses and held the kitchen photo close to his face, but at a slight angle so that the light coming in through the bay window didn't cause too much glare.

He couldn't be one hundred percent certain — okay, close enough to one hundred to call it, but still not all the way — but he could swear that the calendar, though it displayed the correct month, claimed that the year was 2025.

"This has got to be some kind of joke," he whispered under his breath.

The young woman had used some kind of trick photography. It was a gag camera or something like that.

"Miss?" he called out.

When there was no answer, he yanked the glasses from his face and called her again, only this time about five times as loud.

He wanted answers.

He grabbed up a couple of the living room photographs.

Same architecture, but that was it. The furniture was different, ultra-modern but tasteful, and in different places. Pictures lined the mantel over the fireplace, and as Eric looked closer he saw himself and Valerie in these pictures, but they both looked different somehow.

They were older.

And in these photographs, they weren't alone.

They were a family of four; a girl of perhaps eight or nine, a baby boy no older than 10 months.

And in that moment it all came back to him, the so-called tender talks that escalated into arguments and ended in silent resentment: *We're not financially stable enough yet for kids — Don't pull out that old chestnut, Eric, not with me, not again, things are as good as they're going to get — We're not ready — Bullshit, what you mean to say is* you're *not ready for the responsibility — What's wrong with that? Tell me, Val, what's wrong with not being ready to surrender the rest of your life to kids? — It's* selfish, *that's what's wrong with it, and you know how much I want them....*

He tossed the photos down onto the table, yelled for the young woman from the real estate office once again, and then ran up the stairs.

She was nowhere in the house, but she'd taken care to leave behind photographs she'd taken of every upstairs room, and in each photo the rooms were different, brighter, happier.

The master bedroom much more luxurious than it was now; the office had new computers and sleek, matching white works-stations, not the make-shift collection of disparate office furniture which now occupied its space; and then there was the guest room.

As it was now, the guest room, though comfortable and inviting enough, was nothing spectacular. But in the photographs taken by the young woman from the realtor's office, it wasn't a guest room at all.

It was the room of a teenaged girl fifteen years from now; cluttered, filled with clothes, a stereo and curved-screen HD television, posters of rock stars on the walls, books lying helter-skelter wherever there was an overlooked empty space...and it was all so *bright.*

And then it occurred to Eric.

These pictures showed the kind of happy home that he and Valerie had always dreamed of having when they'd be a family. It was a house full of life and activity, where each realized dream was quickly and joyfully replaced by another dream, a new goal, something the family could work toward *together.*

"This is one hell of a trick, young lady," he whispered through clenched teeth.

He went through the entire house twice more, but he couldn't find her.

How had she been able to leave without his hearing her?

* * *

He arrived at the restaurant in time to take care of business with the delivery man from Marciano's. Carl then handed the case to the wine steward and said, "Anything happens to this, we kill your family, slowly, while you watch. But don't feel pressured, okay?"

After the young man had left for the wine cellar—looking equal parts confused and terrified—Carl pulled Eric aside and said: "Don't take this the wrong way—got nothing but love for you in my heart, partner—but from your appearance I'm guessing you feel like shit. No, wait, scratch that. You look as if you *aspire* to feel like shit."

"You're a real charmer."

"Famous for it. Seriously, though—what's wrong? Things still kind of cool between Val and you?"

Eric rubbed his eyes. "Let's go to the formal bar and get some coffee, okay? I need more coffee."

The formal bar wouldn't be officially open for another three hours, so it was a good place to conduct meetings. Jenise, the bar manager, was already there, setting up for later. She poured Eric and Carl two cups of coffee (offering to add a shot of Irish whiskey, which Eric declined), then went about her duties.

For a moment both Eric and Carl watched her as she walked back into the small office beyond the swinging doors.

"That is one *gorgeous* woman," Carl said.

"No arguments here," replied Eric.

Jenise had been working here for the last two years, having decided to take a couple of years off between college and grad school. She was smart, funny, as pleasant an employee as you could hope for, and easily the sexiest woman Eric had met in ages.

He often felt guilty for thinking about Jenise in that way, but some women simply exude sexuality, and with her long, thick red hair, wonderful large breasts, and several sets of curves that no one could improve on, few men could watch her and not wonder what it would be like to ride those hips or slide their hand down the small of her back until you could grab—

—Eric took a sip of his coffee. It was delicious, and far too hot.

Kind of like Jenise herself.

"...I that riveting?"

Eric blinked, realized that he hadn't been listening to Carl, and said, "What?"

"Man, you *are* out of it, aren't you?"

"It's been a rough...things have been...ah, hell!" He covered his face with his hands for a moment, exhaled loudly, then placed his hands flat on the bar as if to make sure it was real.

"I had a young woman stop by the house this morning," he said to Carl.

"Hooker or nun? Oooh, wait—I'll bet it was a hooker *dressed* as nun, trying to help you over that dormant catholic guilt thing, am I right?"

"*What?*"

"Just trying to get a rise out of you, partner. Who was she?"

"I'm not sure. Have you ever met someone who you know —and I mean right down to the marrow of your bones *know*—you recognize from somewhere, but you can't place them?"

"Well, yeah, sure. I mean, we all run into people we've met before at some point in our lives."

"I'm not talking a passing acquaintance here, Carl. It was a lot stronger than that." There was something else about her that he thought he should mention, but for the life of him he couldn't remember what it was.

Carl cleared his throat, peered over the bar to make sure Jenise wasn't going to come back in, and said, "Maybe it's just the old sex drive coming back. You mentioned a couple of times that you and Van have been having trouble for a while, ever since she started pressuring you about the old biological clock. Maybe this woman just sparked something in you that —"

Eric shook his head. "No, it was nothing like that at all. It wasn't anything sexual. I was just stunned by this feeling that I *knew* this woman. Not just as someone I'd met in passing, a customer here or anything like that, but someone who'd I'd been very close to."

"Did she recognize you?"

"No." *What* was it about her that he couldn't remember?

"You sure?"

"I think I'm bright enough to pick up on signals like that, Carl."

"Maybe you knew her in a previous life," said Jenise from the doorway.

Carl mouthed, "Oh, shit," before turning to face Jenise, smiling. "How long you been standing there?"

"Just long enough to hear Eric say he was sure he'd known this woman. Sounds like a karmic thing to me."

It was at moments like this that Eric was glad he hadn't succumbed to temptation when Jenise had first started working at the restaurant. She had dropped hints that she found Eric attractive, had even once asked him out after work, but he had not let it go anywhere. Not that he wouldn't have loved getting into bed with her, but the employee/employer minefield aside, he was a married man who loved his wife.

It was only after he'd gently rebuked her advances that Jenise had started letting her guard down enough, revealing herself to be a crystal-gazing, herb-taking, Gaia-worshipping, New-Age flake.

Still, she was a sweet young woman and a good employee, and Eric thought it might be rude to send her away at this point.

"Another life?" he asked.

"Oh, yes," replied Jenise, her mood brightening. "It happens all the time. You spend each life trying to make up for all the mistakes you made in the last one, and in each life you will encounter people that you knew in your previous existence. One of them will be the person you were destined to be with for all eternity."

"And when do you meet this person?" asked Carl.

"When you have at last atoned for the mistakes of all your previous lives. That's when your True Love will be made known to you. Your soul will be cleansed, then, and together the two of you can move onto the next plane of existence."

"Uh-huh."

Eric found himself staring at Jenise's blouse. Instead of having only the top two buttons undone, she had the top three, giving him a good look at her perfect cleavage and incredible breasts.

"Eric?" she said.

"Your soul will be cleansed, I know, I was listening."

Jenise smiled. "It would explain why you felt so drawn to her, why you believe so strongly that you've known her."

But it wouldn't explain what I can't remember about the way she looked, or why.

"This is bullshit," said Carl, but there was no anger or irritation in his tone. He was simply trying to get a rise out of Jenise.

"Maybe not," whispered Eric.

"You mean you think she might be right?"

Eric reached into his jacket pocket and pulled out the photographs. Tossing them onto the bar, he pointed at them and said, "You've seen the inside of my house, Carl. Take a look at those, will you? That woman from the realtor's office took them this morning."

"Polaroid Instants? Man, I didn't even know they still *made* these kinds of cameras. I—" He stopped speaking as soon as he saw the first few photographs. He remained silent until he finished looking through all of them, then said: "You didn't tell me you and Valerie had remodeled the place."

"We didn't."

"But it's your house, Eric. I've been in there enough to know the layout of the place—the downstairs, anyway."

Eric pushed the stack of photographs over to Jenise. "Look at those, will you? The ones of the kitchen, in particular. Do you see that calendar on the wall?"

Jenise nodded. "Yeah...?"

"Can you see the date?"

Jenise looked at him, then Carl, then held the photograph under one of the bright lights behind the bar. "Omigod...."

"2025," said Carl. Then, to Eric: "Yeah, I saw it, too."

"This is *amazing*," said Jenise.

"Then maybe one of you can explain it to me," snapped Eric, signaling Jenise to add that Irish whiskey to his coffee, after all.

"Is that a good idea?" asked Carl. "You look terrible—*and* you're driving."

"Tell you what—answer that question to my satisfaction and I won't drink this."

Carl said nothing.

"I was afraid of that," replied Eric, taking a deep swallow of the drink.

"Maybe it's the house itself," said Jenise.

Eric stared at her. "Go on."

"Maybe the woman somehow took these pictures at a time when the fabric of reality was rippling, know what I mean?"

"Not in the least."

Jenise sighed. "Okay, it's like, if you write something down on the top sheet of a notebook and then tear out that page, the page underneath still holds the impression of what you wrote on the *other* page. If you, like, took a pencil or crayon and colored all over the second sheet, the message you had written on the first sheet would come through. I mean, it wouldn't look exactly the same, but it'd still be basically the same message. Know what I mean?"

"Yes...?"

Jenise held up one of the pictures. "Well, maybe this woman took these pictures at a moment when one 'sheet' of reality was being torn away. The house you know now, the one you live in, the one that looks nothing like what's in these pictures...maybe it's the first sheet, and what these pictures are showing you is what's on the second sheet."

Eric took another drink, then shook his head. "You just lost me."

"The past and the future, Eric, they're always around us, we just can't touch them. But that doesn't mean they can't touch us."

Eric slid his coffee cup forward. "I'm going to need another before hearing any more of this."

Jenise fixed him another Irish coffee. Carl looked on, not bothering to hide his disapproval.

"What I'm saying," Jenise continued, "is that everyone knows how…tense things have been between you and Valerie for the last year or so. A house can sense these things, too. So maybe, when that woman took these pictures, the house didn't so much tear away one sheet as *lift* it for a few moments, and allowed her to take pictures of how things *are going to be*.

"Maybe the house was sending you a message that everything is going to get better."

"Here's what I think," said Carl, gathering up the photographs, taking care to make sure all of them were face-down. "I think that you're tired, and you're upset; I think that you maybe need more rest than you've been getting, and your eyes are playing tricks on you."

"That still doesn't explain the pictures."

"What pictures?" said Carl, dumping the photos into a trash can behind the bar.

Eric stared at the trash can for a moment. "If only it were that easy."

"It is—it *can be*, anyway, if you just put it out of your mind and think about something else."

"Think about something else," repeated Eric. "Christ, if I had a dollar for every time I've said that to myself or had someone else say it to me these past six months, I could retire to the South of fucking France. *Damn*, Carl…don't you ever just wish that you could…I don't know…put it all on hold for a few weeks? I mean, just freeze everything in your life, all the family and friends and business responsibilities, just push the 'Pause' button and hold it all in place while you took off somewhere to re-group for a while? Go somewhere and act like you could when you were twenty-two and didn't have all this shit to contend with every minute of every day?"

"Who doesn't, partner? Sounds to me like maybe you're just getting bogged down in the have-to, know what I mean?"

"Some days it feels like me whole life is 'have to', you know?"

"You just need to relax for the next day and forget about all of this; trust me. I've turned it into an art. It's the only way you can get through life, sometimes."

"This is *so* wrong," said Jenise. "You're telling him to just...*ignore* a message the universe is trying to send to him. You can't do that. You don't mess around with the Infinite."

"No, but *you're* going to mess around with your Infinity."

"Huh?"

"Your *car*, Jenise. You're going to get in your car and follow me. I'm driving Eric and his car back to his house, and then you're going to bring me back here and we're going to get back to work and forget all about this."

"But it's *wrong!*"

"*Jenise....*" There was a tone in Carl's voice that made it clear he would tolerate no argument on this. Jenise threw her hands up in surrender and went to get her purse and car keys.

"Come on, partner," said Carl, helping Eric to his feet. "I'm driving you home."

"I'm not drunk."

"Maybe not—but then again, maybe the whiskey will hit you five minutes after you leave here and you'll plow into the back of tractor-trailer. I'm not taking any chances."

"But—"

"No 'buts,' partner. Come on, let's get you home so you can rest."

* * *

Eric said good-bye to Carl and Jenise, let himself back into the house, and was starting upstairs to take a nap when he saw another photograph lying face-down near the entrance to the living room.

Must have dropped this on the way out, he thought, reaching down for it.

That's when he noticed the other photographs, all of them face-down, that were scattered along various points up the stairs.

Okay, I wasn't that out of it; I would have noticed if I'd dropped that many.

Not looking at them, he followed the trail up the stairs and through the hallway, retrieving each one along the way.

He was picking up the last of them when he heard a woman gasp from behind the door to his and Val's bedroom. It wasn't a gasp of surprise or shock, but one of pleasure that soon became a deep moan that broke into a series of ecstatic squeals, growing louder and more intense.

The first thought to cross his mind was: *She's been fucking someone else behind my back. She doesn't care who gives her a baby, just that she gets one.*

He grabbed the doorknob and was about to throw it open — the wronged husband making the dramatic discovery — when a second thought came to him: *Why would she bring him back here, to our bed, on a day when she knows I'm home?*

Answer: It wasn't Val.

Then who...?

He opened the door and stepped inside.

The girl from this morning was sitting at the foot of his and Val's bed, staring at the TV/VCR unit in the corner that was turned on. She was watching a pornographic tape of a couple fucking with such ferocity you'd think their very lives depended on how much sweat they produced and how much noise they made — and they were both loud, moaning and squealing and screaming like animals.

Eric was so stunned by all of this — the girl's presence, the porno tape (neither he nor Val owned any), and his reaction to the tape (the couple's sexual acrobatics were arousing him) — that it took a moment for him to realize that he recognized the woman on the tape: it was Jenise, her thick red hair plastered across her back, her marvelous breasts lacquered in sweat, and she was grinding down, thrashing, tossing her head back to reveal her lover's face —

— as Eric's own.

The girl from the realtor's office pressed a button on the remote, freezing the tape.

Eric stared at the image, and realized that the man on the tape, the man who was fucking Jenise like he was twenty-five again, was at least ten years older than Eric was right now; the gray hair — in several places other than his head — was proof of that.

"Couldn't even take her to a motel, no. He had to fuck his whore here in the same bed where he slept beside Mom."

Eric blinked, shook himself, and faced the girl. "What are you — ? How did — ?"

She opened her prostheses, picked up the Polaroid camera, and snapped his picture, the sudden bright flash of the bulb momentarily blinding him. Instinctively, Eric's hands came up to shield his eyes two seconds too late and he dropped the photos, which scattered at his feet.

It took a second for him to realize that he couldn't move; not a finger, not a foot; he couldn't even move his eyes from where they were looking once the bright flash from the camera began to fade from his sight.

At the pictures around his feet.

One displayed the hallway wall next to the bathroom, covered in blood; another showed the wall beside the stairway, where a bloodied handprint started near the top and began a ragged smear as it traveled downward, as is whomever had made it was trying to remain standing as they stumbled downstairs; yet another showed the chalk outline of a very small body, only where its head should have been was a deep dark stain in the living room carpet; here was the outline of a woman's body, wide splashes of gore all but obscuring the chalk—or was it tape?—that showed the position in which she'd been discovered; here was the banister at the top of the stairs, dripping with viscera and speckled with things that looked like pieces of bone; and here was a picture of the living room—not the living room that was down there now, no, but the living room, nonetheless—where the outline of a man's body was drawn partly on the floor and partly on the wall next to the fireplace, a massive splatter of blood and brains covering the wall, the outline of a shotgun lying less than a foot away from that of his hand.

"He used a meat clever on me," said the girl from the realtor's office. "I was studying piano, had been accepted at Julliard, so my hands were the first things to go, but I got out before he could do any more damage. Mom and Billy were already dead by then. I remember screaming when he bashed Billy's head against the banister. I froze, I was so scared. And all because he had to fuck his whore, and she got off on taping it, and Mom found it. He should have never stuck around if he didn't want kids, a family, responsibility. But that's always the way, isn't it? You do things because you feel obligated, then wake up one day to find that all of these things—your life, your family, your responsibilities—hang around your neck like chains instead of pearls. He always had a problem with his temper, but never did anything to help it."

Eric tried to speak, tried to force some kind of sound from his throat, but he couldn't even pull in a breath.

He saw her shadow approach him, felt her slip the new photograph into his shirt pocket.

"The funny thing is," she said, "that I still love him. I don't want to—he butchered my mother and my little brother, then blew his own head off—but I still find that, when I think about him, I still feel some love. Pathetic, isn't it?"

She dropped the camera at his feet.

Eriq Bakker, read the misspelled name punched onto the plastic blue strip attached to its underside.

"I have to go back now —or go forward, depending on how you look at it. I don't know what of this will remain back here, but if I did this correctly, *something* should stay behind. At least, I hope so."

Eric felt her lean forward and kiss his cheek. "Time will tell, I guess."

He listened as she left the room, went down the stairs, and out the front door.

After a few moments, he could breathe again, and felt his frozen limbs begin tingling back to life.

Slowly, with only a little stiffness, he bent down and picked up the blank photographs, wondering where they'd come from, then saw his old camera by his feet.

Funny —he could remember losing this thing but not finding it.

Looking at the photographs, he realized it was a moot point because the damn thing obviously no longer worked.

He tossed everything into the waste basket beside the bed, noticed he'd left the television on—some old re-run of *The Dick van Dyke Show* he'd recorded a few nights ago—turned it off, and went back downstairs.

He was gathering up the detritus of this morning's breakfast fiasco—he still needed to wash away the blood—when he heard the front door open and Val come inside.

"Eric," she said, sounding unusually chipper. "Hey, baby, you down here?"

He picked up the chopping knife and saw the deep splashes of red that still clung to the blade, but whether it was still his blood or from the tomato he couldn't tell and didn't really care. All he wanted was to spend his two off from the restaurant in peace and not have to deal with anything.

"I'm in here," he called to her, scratching at a spot on his chest. Feeling something in his shirt pocket (when had he gotten dressed?), he reached in and pulled out the photograph.

Funny, he didn't remember taking this one, either.

Not that it mattered, because it was already fading.

Was it just him, or for a moment there, before the image finally gave up trying to develop itself and faded to that dull off-white that was always the bane of the Instamatic owner's life...was it his imagination, or had he seen a flash of family, of two parents and two children, smiling for the birdie?

He blinked, and the image faded, its memory and any meaning it might hold for him becoming mist, a ghost, just out of reach, as so many things seemed to be these days.

Jesus, he needed rest. He needed peace and quiet, a break from the daily pressures.

"Eric," said Val and she started toward the kitchen, "I saw my doctor today, and I've got...God, I still can't believe it...I've got some *wonderful* news!"

He lay the empty photograph on the cutting board amidst the guts of the tomato and impaled in place with the chopping knife, held his breath, and then turned to face his wife whose radiant expression bespoke the joy she was about to bring into their lives.

El Poso Del Mundo

Introduction by Tim Waggoner

One of the many things I admire about Gary's fiction is the unblinking — and all-too-often heartbreaking—honesty that lies at its core, and "El Poso Del Mundo" is no exception. Its primary theme deals with violence—not the stylized hyper-exaggerated ballet of brutality that we see in far too many of our entertainments, but the real deal. Violence which has *consequences*, affecting people not only physically, but emotionally. Gary's story asks a profound and much-needed question: "Who's the true victim of violence?" His answer: "Everyone."

It's because of this question—and even more so, its answer—that I assigned this story as a reading in a Horror Literature class I taught at my college one year. I wanted the students, many of whom had only taken the class because of their love for blood-splattered gorefests like the *Friday the 13th* film series, that true horror—horror that *matters*—isn't about machete-wielding maniacs, but rather the pain that eats like cold acid at the center of the human heart.

El Poso Del Mundo

"The souls of the Mexican people are heavy for the wings of love, they have swallowed the stone of despair."

—D.H. Lawrence, *The Plumed Serpent*

An old piece of *ranchera* music blared from the rusted radio at the edge of the bar:

> *I dreamed of money in the bank*
> *And of driving a Cadillac*
> *I married a blond, hoping to become*
> *A respected U.S. citizen*
> *But she turned out to be a wetback too*
> *Now I'm back home, driving my burro*

Humberto Farais shook his head and quietly laughed at the song, hoping that the ghosts of his family would not think he was showing disrespect. Good Christ! How many times had he heard his own father sing that very tune as he sat with other workers around trash-barrel fires in the migrant camps? Sad, silly, drunken men, all of them, with thick calluses on their hands that smelled of tobacco and dirt and cheap tequila and lemons, clutching at their shabby clothes and even shabbier hopes, crooning into the uncaring night toward some God they believed in but had never seen any proof of, praying he would hear their pleas and grant them safe passage to the plentiful streets of *el norte*.

Well, father, he thought as his eyes searched the doorway for some sign of his target, *it was that desire to reach* el norte *that killed you. More's the pity, for I wish you were alive to see me now, and how I am making them all pay for your death.*

He was sitting in the bar of a transient hotel in downtown Monterrey, waiting to run down one of his most profitable con numbers, one that he fondly called *La Caza De Grillos* — The Fool's Errand. All part of putting *la mordida* — the bite — on the wealthy Americans.

He didn't have to wait long.

A man dressed in a three-piece white suit already caked with dust and grime walked in, quickly spotted Humberto, and came over to his table. Sweating, red-faced, and wide-eyed, he might as well have had a sign hanging around his neck with the words **I AM HERE TO LAUNDER SOME DIRTY MONEY** written on it in capital letters. The man shimmered with panic, and with panic came impatience and carelessness, the two most useful tools.

You're about as inconspicuous as an Israeli at a PLO picnic, thought Humberto, slamming back a shot of tequila to keep himself from chuckling.

The man took a seat at the table. Humberto turned on his Lizard Grin and said, "Hey, m'man, loo-keeng good today." The accent was nice and thick and just slightly overdone, something that Humberto had worked years to finesse; he'd found the more he acted the role of Sleazy Mexican Crook, the more his targets took him at face value. He even went so far as to wear the kind of stereotypical uniform that the *americanos* expected of their Mexican hooligans: a polyester leisure suit circa 1977, with an open collar, a few gold chains, rings aplenty, slicked-back hair and a three-day growth of beard. He could've been an extra in *Bring Me the Head of Alfredo Garcia.*

"C-could we just get on with this?" said the target. "I have to catch a plane at eight." Humberto draped one of his arms around the man's shoulders. "Hey, *no problemo*, man. This don't take long. You have, I think, something to show me, yes?"

"Maybe. If you have something to show me."

Humberto reached inside his jacket and produced a thick envelope that he dropped in the target's lap. The man jerked his head to the side to see if anyone had noticed, then opened the envelope and flipped through the bills.

"Authentic *Banco de Mexico* notes," whispered Humberto. "No bills larger than a fifty, just as you said. Serial numbers out of sequence." He smiled. "Some of those notes are older than we are, señor. A nice touch, no?"

"Where were they printed?"

"Some here, some in the States. All very clean."

The target lifted one of the bills up to the light and examined it carefully. "You got a name?"

"Jarraro. And you, señor?"

"The people I represent call me 'Petey.'" He put the bill back in the envelope. "How much?"

"How much you got, m'man?"

"Seventy-five thousand."

Humberto whistled, long and low. "Very impressive amount. But that would be the *hospital's* money, no? Do not look at me that way, I only repeat what your ... associates tell me over the phone last week. How much of your own money did you bring?"

"Another fifty thousand."

Humberto let fly with his corniest sleazebag laugh and clapped the target on the back as if he were an old friend. "This is very good. Here is what I will do for you, señor; I will give you an exchange rate of sixty-seven cents on the dollar."

"Bullshit. The agreement was eighty."

"That was before your chubby president passed his wonderful trade act so your American companies could use my country for an industrial toilet. I'll give you sixty-nine cents and we'll call it a compromise in the name of international harmony."

The target chewed on his lower lip. "You people are all the same, lazy, shiftless .... Seventy-five cents."

"Seventy."

"Fuck you," said the target, holding up the envelope. "Seventy-three."

Humberto reached over and turned the target's head toward the window. Outside in the street, a short red-haired man with a 35mm camera snapped a quick series of pictures.

"W-who's that?"

"One of my *amigos*. He can have that film developed in thirty minutes and the pictures in the hands of your American authorities before you even get to the airport. I am very popular with your American authorities, señor. They find me curious. They would want to ask you many questions about me, and about the envelope you are holding in the picture. They maybe would want to check on your background. That is, I think, something that would not please you."

"I've got a gun."

Humberto knew he was lying. "I do not think so." He flipped open a switchblade and pressed the business end against the man's crotch under the table. "But if I am wrong you may shoot me now and I will die a fool."

The target swallowed and shook his head. Humberto pulled the knife away and gestured for the man with camera to leave.

"Seventy-two?" whispered the target.

"Senor, we have a deal."

Surprise registered on the man's face, and he shook Humberto's hand. Back in the States tomorrow this man would gloat to his partners how he stood his ground and made the oily little wetback squirm for every penny. Another great triumph for American capitalism.

"You will please give me ten thousand dollars in cash right now," said Humberto.

The man took an envelope from inside his jacket and exchanged it for the one Humberto had given to him, which contained the exact same amount.

"Go back to your hotel room and wait," whispered Humberto. "In one hour an *amigo* of mine will visit you. He will have something in a box. You will understand. If you are still agreeable to the terms, tell him and he will bring the message to me. I will meet you back here at five and we will conclude our business."

"I understand." The target stared, his suspicion obvious.

Time to lay it on thick and play the part to the hilt.

"Hey, señor, how rude of me! You maybe want somebody to pass the time with? They call me *proveedor*, you know? You want eet, I get eet for you. You want maybe some coke for the nose, some lovely wee-men for your bed, no? Get you first-rate poo-see, real clean, yes?"

"I don't think you have anything that would interest me," said the man, rising. "My room, one hour."

"Do not worry yourself, señor. I am Miguel Jarraro and I always come through."

The target left. Humberto slammed back another shot of tequila and winced as it hit his stomach.

This guy was a wimp. In a hurry and harmless as a fly.

And then Humberto Farais—alias Miguel Jarraro, José Baranda, Gonzales Vargas, and a dozen other names—remembered something that made his smile weaken, his eyes grow weary, and his chest so very heavy; something that always took him down a few notches when he was feeling cocky and too goddamned for a mere mortal; he remembered the face of his father and the way it had looked the last time Humberto had seen him alive.

And for a moment he didn't feel quite so self-satisfied and indestructible. His face lost its confident expression and became that of a man whose life had become little more than a low-budget two-reeler serial shown in place of the cartoon at a Saturday movie matinee; it was the face of a man who'd cheapened himself and knew it, a man whose skill and intelligence were rapidly deteriorating under the compiling weight of shame, anger, and loneliness; the face of a man whose only untainted pleasure was studying the stars at night while the ghost of his father looked over his shoulder, whispering, *Behold the light from God's eyes, my son. See how brightly it shines. Always the stars will be watching over you, even when I am with you no longer.*

It was a face filled, for the moment, with a bitter self-disgust that defied boundaries.

But a second later it was gone, replaced by thoughts of *la mordida*.

There was business to attend to.

Always there was business.

* * *

"You're telling me there was no film in the camera?"

"You *said* it was just to scare him. I figured the whole thing was just for show. Besides, I'm getting low and film's expensive down here."

"My God," said Humberto. "We've turned into a Donald Westlake novel." He smiled at the red-haired man. "You know, Patch, for someone who did two tours in Vietnam and managed to come out with only a few scratches, you sometimes make me wonder how."

"Part of my well-honed mystique. Just sit back and be awed, I can take it."

There were three of them in the van: Humberto, Michael Joseph "Patch" McCarthy, and a little boy know to them only as Ruben. Humberto had found the boy in a labor camp outside of Mexico City a few months before. Humberto had given the boy some money, bought him something to eat, and discovered that he had no family at the camp. Before he knew what had hit him, the boy had simply and quietly insinuated himself into Humberto's life with all the subtlety of a stray dog that followed whoever happened to throw it some scraps. At first Humberto chose to keep the kid around because he was useful in running down con numbers; he had that innocent, Bambi-eyed look no one could distrust. The fact that he could not —or would not—speak made Ruben all the more disarming. Today would be the first time the boy had ever been used in something this major.

Yes, Ruben was quite useful.

But now there was much more to it than that. The boy had insinuated himself not only into Humberto's life but deep into the core of his heart, as well. Humberto could not have cared more for him had Ruben been his own son.

"What happens next?" asked Patch.

"We wait forty-five minutes and then send Ruben up with a box of the pencils."

Patch lit a cigarette and opened a window so the smoke didn't kill them. "You wanna explain this little ditty to me once more?"

"I've explained it twice already."

"This is my first time with this number and I'm a little anxious. Besides, I'm driving and if you don't tell me I'll make you walk back."

"No, you won't."

"No, I won't—but it sure sounded full of conviction, didn't it?"

"Not even a little." Humberto smiled. He liked Patch a lot. A full-blooded Irishman with the prerequisite red hair, green eyes, and mean temper, Michael Joseph McCarthy stood a little under five-five, every ounce of it tight muscle. Patch had worked as a radio technician for a few years before getting his broadcaster's license. He soon found the strict regulations of the FCC a little too rigid for his tastes so he quit radio, invested his money in state-of-the-art mobile broadcasting equipment, and set up a pirate radio station in the back of a bread van he'd bought for five hundred dollars and change. He traveled for a while from state to state, spewing out rock'n'roll and energetic, ultra-lunatic fringe politics to anyone who picked up his signal. When the FCC began to clamp down on his one-man operation he emptied his banks accounts, declared himself an expatriate, and made it down Mexico way. He took gleeful pride in being able to cruise the border and broadcast to the lower states—not to mention fuck up the Border Patrol's broadcasts to aid Humberto and his cohorts in slipping illegals over the border, or snap a few juicy pictures to blackmail American businessmen who patronized the local whorehouses. Minor stuff, really.

But if they pulled off the Fool's Errand today, they would no longer be *fayuqueros*—little smugglers; they would move up into the ranks of *pezgordo*, the fat fish whose reputation commanded respect amongst the *bandoleros* and other *contrabandista*.

They would be Big Time after today.

"It'll happen like this," said Humberto. "Ruben takes him a box of pencils and hands him a note from me telling him to break open as many of the pencils at random as he wants. Inside each pencil is a *Banco de Mexico* note—a ten, twenty, or a fifty. He relaxes a little because my note tells him this is how the full amount will be delivered to him so he can get the money through customs. He'll be instructed to give Ruben half of the agreed upon amount. When he meets me in the bar, I give him a salesman's sample case filled with boxes of pencils. The top row of boxes are filled with just pencils—in case customs gets nosey. So he takes a couple of boxes from the second row and breaks open another five or ten pencils. Again, he finds *Banco de Mexico* notes inside. This will satisfy him, he'll give me the rest of the cash, and I'll give him a card with the name and private phone number of his contact at a bank in New York."

"What if he wants to call the number to make sure it's legit?"

"He sure as hell won't do it on this side of the border. His plane ticket was purchased in New York. His plane landed in and leaves from El Paso, so as far as anyone knows that's where he was today. If he makes the call he'll do it from the airport, and by then it'll be too late. We're talking about a guy who took a goddamn tour bus from the airport to here instead of renting a car! This is a man who does not want to leave any traces."

"I take it the bank number's a phoney?"

"Well, *duh*. Two points for the Mick."

"And the pencils ...?"

"There's about nine thousand dollars' worth of notes in the top row. The rest are just pencils."

"Helluva way to find out there's a lot of lead in Mexico."

They both laughed.

Then Ruben came over and climbed into Humberto's lap. Humberto put his arm around the boy, who rested his head against Humberto's shoulder.

"Seems like an awfully nice kid," said Patch. "Does this make you a daddy?"

"There're worse fates I can think of."

Humberto reached under his seat and pulled out his flute. Ruben was nervous—he could sense that from the boy—and Humberto's playing always made him feel better.

The music he played was sad, like Ruben himself, yet comforting; proud, yet humble; glorious, yet pathetically aged. It was the soul of Mexico, the sound of a hundred acoustic guitars whispering soft tales of ill-fated lovers, a hundred children raising up their thin voices to the holy *Virgen* at mass, and countless brass horns in smoky bars calling, *Come, sit down with us and drink some, tell us the story of your life, make yourself at home and do not worry, for you are welcome here.*

Humberto finished playing. Ruben was fast asleep. Stroking the boy's hair, Humberto whispered a prayer that his father used to say every night: "Sleep, oh my soul, sleep. Rest in the age-old cradle of hope and do not be afraid. You can trust in sleep as you would your home. You can lay your sorrow at its feet and rest your head on its bosom. Sleep, and do not grieve. For there will come a morning of great joy and it will find you sleeping the sleep of the Just, the sleep without sorrow, in a cradle guided by the hand of God."

"Do you know any happy songs?" whispered Patch.

"I do a mean rendition of 'My Generation' but I didn't feel it was appropriate."

"Watch it; that was almost a joke."

Humberto reached up and removed one of the gold chains from around his neck. Attached to it was a tarnished medal Humberto's father had once given him: St. Christopher, made in a time before the Catholic Church raised its pulpit of sanctimony a few feet higher and made him *Mr.* Christopher.

He gently hung the necklace and medal around Ruben's neck, then jostled him awake. "It's time." He then gave Ruben everything he would need and told him, "Fifteen minutes, then I want to see you back here, right?"

Ruben nodded his head and gave a smile that Humberto believed was put there by angels, then pushed open the rear doors of the van, jumped out, and made his way down the street toward the hotel, one hand clasping the medal all the way.

Humberto considered, as he'd done at least a hundred times since waking up, calling Ruben back and going in his place, but the whole idea was to assault the target with as many different faces as possible; that way he'd never know who was going to turn up next, or who might be watching, or who might be just outside the door or around the corner. It kept them nervous—and this guy had already seen Humberto and Patch; a third face was necessary if the target was to be kept in a state of constant anxiety.

"Don't worry," said Patch, putting a hand on Humberto's shoulder. "We got it covered. You want me to follow him?"

"We can't chance the guy spotting either of us a second time, not this soon."

"Well, then, stop worrying. You said the stars were favorable last night."

"Who's worried?" said Humberto, then whispered to Ruben's retreating back, "may God go with you and keep you from harm."

* * *

At sixteen minutes and counting Humberto grabbed his shoulder bag from under the seat, unzipped it, reached in, and pulled out a Colt Commander 9mm Parabellum with a nine-round magazine and modified silencer attachment. He shoved it in the back of his pants and covered it with the tail of his jacket, then checked to make sure the switchblade and its sheath were still strapped firmly to his ankle.

"Do you think that's necessary?" said Patch. "He's only a minute-and-a-half late."

Humberto said nothing. Years of experience had taught him to assume the worst when someone was late. He couldn't allow himself to get emotional right now. He took a deep breath and waited another sixty seconds, just in case Patch was right and he was overreacting, waited until Ruben was nearly four minutes late.

They weren't all that far from the hotel.

Four minutes meant something was wrong.

Four minutes meant it was time to move.

He reached into his right jacket pocket and touched the coil of piano wire nestled there. In his left jacket pocket was a set of brass knuckles. If it turned out he needed any more protection than what he was carrying—

—no time. "Five minutes, Patch. I'm not back, go to the hotel, room 407. Bring a weapon." He kicked open the doors, jumped out of the van, and hit the pavement running. They were four blocks away from the target's hotel; he should get there in sixty seconds, ninety at most. He didn't worry about the odd glances people gave him as he hammered past them; the police rarely cruised this area during the daytime, choosing to concentrate more on the center of town where the *bailadoras* and drug dealers transacted their business.

Always there was business.

He broke through a crowd of tourists, took a shortcut through an alley, and was rounding the corner of the hotel's street when a *patrullas*—a police patrol unit—whipped in front of him and came to a stop. Before the dust had settled both doors were open and two Mexican officers were on either side of him, grabbing his arms, shoving him into the back seat, and slamming the doors.

He looked and saw there were no inside door handles back here— but there was also no partition between the back and front seats; in Mexico, few police cars had them.

In the time it took for the two cops to get back in and shut their doors, Humberto measured his options—and none of them were very pleasant. He just hoped these two were only trying to put a little *mordida* on him before sending him on his way. Graft was second nature here.

The cop who wasn't driving—a trim, well-groomed man of forty with a perfect golden complexion—spoke without turning to face him. "Miguel Jarraro, we have received a complaint about you from a Mr. Petey. He claims you have some money which belongs to him."

"No."

Without saying a word the cop whirled around and smashed Humberto in the face with a club designed for just that purpose. Humberto felt his nose pulp as the blood burst forth and splattered on his shirt, sending him face-down to the floor.

The cop reached back and grabbed him by the hair, pulling him to his knees. "Do not lie to me, Mr. Jarraro. Your Mr. Petey provided us with *mucho* information about you." He turned toward his partner. "I think we maybe need to take him for a little interrogation. Give him a taste of *la chicharra.*"

Humberto felt himself go rigid. Mexican police were infamous for using electric cattle prods to torture their prisoners when the mood struck them—and when it involved *mordida,* the mood was always upon them.

"You guys always this melodramatic? I'm surprised your partner isn't twirling the end of his mustache."

Both officers laughed.

"I don't suppose you'd believe me if I said I don't know any Mr. Petey?"

"No."

The other cop put the car in gear and drove the *patrullas* through the streets, past the hotel, and into an alleyway a few blocks down.

"Understand our position," said the well-groomed cop. "Tourists are very important to us and we can't afford to have them leave with a bad impression. It's important that we keep good relations with our friends across the border, especially now that their young president has sent so much business our way. When people encounter a ladròn such as you, it doesn't bode well for the rest of us."

The unit came to a full stop. Humberto swallowed, tasting the coppery blood as it trickled down his throat.

This was more than just putting the bite on him; these guys seemed serious. That made them dangerous. If this were the case, Humberto was in deep. And there wasn't time for that.

Only one way to find out.

"Look, I apologize if I gave this Mr. Petey such a bad impression. Isn't there some way we can get around all this? A ... fine of some sort?"

The cop's face was a slab of granite. "How much of a fine are we talking about?"

"Say a thousand dollars American."

"Each or to divide between us?"

"Each." He hoped this would settle the matter. For a moment back at the van he'd considered leaving the envelope containing the ten thousand dollars "Mr. Petey" had given to him; now he was grateful he hadn't.

The cop climbed out of the unit, opened Humberto's door, and helped him out. For a frenzied second Humberto feared the cop might search him—or worse, handcuff him—but he didn't.

He simply slammed the business end of the club into Humberto's stomach, dropping him to the ground.

"Fucking pig! How dare you attempt to bribe me!"

Humberto winced from the pain. This was no show, the guy was for real. Amazing as it seemed, there were some people this close to the border who could not be bought. For one second while the pain rushed through him Humberto actually respected the cop who stood over him; the man had principles in a place where principles were worthless. He probably even slept well at night. Good for him.

The cop swung down and cracked the club between Humberto's shoulders, knocking him face down in the dirt. As soon as he hit the ground, Humberto heard the cop unbuckle his holster.

He allowed the pain to whip-curl in his guts like a snake attacking a field mouse.

He blinked against the dust and the mud and thought of Ruben's smile, then took a deep and painful breath, knowing what had to be done.

"I'm so sorry," he whispered as the cop unholstered his gun.

Everything happened very fast this close to the border, especially violence. If you understood violence, if you lived with it, breathed it, slept with the threat of it always crouching at your bedside, then you knew it wasn't something poetic or glorious, that the flow of blood was ugly and painful and swift and degrading. One-on-one violence was the swiftest of all, for when it happened there was always one person who would be unprepared in the first few crucial seconds while something reptilian seized the brain of their opponent and sucked all of their survival instincts forward, transforming an otherwise rational human being into a whirling dervish of brutality.

In three rapid, smooth, sharp movements Humberto pulled out the Colt, flipped over onto his back, and with one shot—*snip!*—blew off half the cop's gun hand and sent him down screaming. The driver came around the side of the unit carrying a sawed-off shotgun and was just in time to see his partner's hand turned into tomato paste. Humberto was up on his knees by now and threw himself forward, knocking the driver off-balance and yanking the shotgun from his grip with one hand while plowing off another round—*snip!*—into the guy's knee with the other. The driver crumpled into a heap, clutching at his shattered kneecap, his face contorted and red with agony. Shoving the Colt into his side jacket pocket, Humberto whipped the sawed-off around and came down hard, slamming the butt into the driver's balls with all the force he could muster. The driver bellowed inhumanely and Humberto cracked the butt of the shotgun against the man's mouth, shattering his teeth and turning his lips into two wormy strands of putty, then spun around and threw the shotgun deep into the alley and caught sight of the other cop scuttling around, his ruined hand a smoldering mass of muscle and cartilage and jagged bone. The guy was reaching with his remaining hand for his pistol that lay only a few feet to the side. Humberto staggered forward and swung out a leg and kicked the guy in the ribs once, twice, three times, until he heard something crack down there, and as he was getting ready to kick the guy a fourth time the cop came up on his knees and grabbed Humberto by the balls, sending barbed-wire tendrils of pain spiderwebbing through his groin; as Humberto began to crumple down the cop started pulling himself up and just when it looked like the balance of power was going to seriously shift Humberto brought his knee up into the cop's chin, knocking his head backward and forcing him to let go. The cop spun around and Humberto grabbed the piano wire from his pocket and in a blink had it around the guy's throat, pulling it tight, spattering the alley floor with ribbons of arterial spray as the cop's arms flailed wildly, his one hand balling into a fist and pounding against Humberto's arm, which only made the wire dig in deeper but then the cop's legs started kicking back against Humberto's ankles, finally tripping him but that was bad for the cop because when Humberto went back he yanked hard on the wire and felt it slice all the way back until it caught on the cop's spinal cord and that was that. The blood fountained out of the wound as the cop thrashed and kicked and flailed in one last repulsive seizure before he finally died. Humberto kicked back and pushed himself away from the body, then flipped around to his knees and got on his feet just as the other cop, thick strings of blood slopping from his former mouth, managed to squirm onto his side and unholster his pistol and aim it right at Humberto's chest, so Humberto pulled out the Colt once and did the only thing his now-reptilian brain would allow him to do, and that was shoot straight out — *snip!* — at the driver's face. The first bullet blew in his cheekbone. The second one sheared part of his jaw away. The third one blew his head apart like an M-80 inside a pumpkin, scattering wet red pieces of meat and skull over the trashcans behind him.

Humberto staggered around like a drunkard for a moment, the Colt hanging from his grip, the pain from his nose and shoulders and stomach and balls meeting in the center of his chest, and he knew that he couldn't drop, if he dropped he wouldn't be able to get up too soon and Ruben needed him, four minutes meant something was wrong but they were looking at a good nine minutes now, which meant twenty-four minutes altogether, and his vision was blurry and that wouldn't do, he had to make it right, so he shoved the Colt in his pocket and grabbed onto his nose with his fingers, kneading through the pulp until he felt the bone, latched onto it with his thumb and index finger, snapped it to the left and felt the bone skid, then grind back into place. A small shriek escaped him as the serpent let go of his brain and scurried back into the darkness, allowing the pain to overtake him—but Humberto Farais would not allow it, nor would he allow himself time to regret what he'd had to do to the police officers. Regret would come later.

He stumbled out of the alley, got his bearings, then bolted in the direction of the hotel. He had never run so fast in his life, legs pounding with race-horse fury as he rounded corners, jumped over curbs, vaulted garbage, and shoved past the throngs of people who took little notice of the bloodied, broken man who was providing another common piece of street theatre for their squalid surroundings.

The pain fueled his resolve; gasoline to a fire.

He arrived at the hotel, his heart triphammering in his chest, the image of Ruben's smile still driving him on. He shot through the lobby and took the stairs three at a time until he reached the fourth floor and saw a figure step out from one of the doorways. Hoping that it was his "Mr. Petey" he ran forward—

—and Patch pushed out his arms to stop him. "The guy's gone," he said. He was shaking and pale, his red eyes puffy and moist.

Something clogged Humberto's throat.

"Where's—"

"We have to leave," said Patch. "We have to leave *now.*"

Humberto slapped Patch's hands away and stepped into room 407. Ruben was still there.

What was left of him.

Humberto went numb. There was no anger, no overpowering flood of grief, no shudders or curses, only questions as he shambled toward the small, naked, broken figure handcuffed to the bedpost, its face buried under a blood-soaked pillow; questions like: Was he dead before the man finished torturing him? Did he struggle or remain still, hoping that you would come for him after fifteen minutes and put a stop to it? Did he cry out?

Then the questions ceased as Humberto saw two things: the broken liquor bottle lying on the floor, its neck missing, blood streaking the broken edges of the glass—

—and the St. Christopher medal clutched in Ruben's dead hands.

His legs turned to rubber and began to buckle under him but then Patch was there, arms supporting him, moving him toward the door, talking to him in a smooth, soft, steady voice that held no trace of the tears he'd shed earlier.

"We gotta go, Humberto, gotta go now, it's over, he's dead and the guy's gone—"

"—shouldn't have sent him, I knew it d-didn't feel right—"

"—don't start that now, pal, it ain't gonna do you any good, c'mon, we have to go, we can't be here when they find—"

"—goddamned cops stopped me ... I should've left sooner, I shouldn't've waited so long ohgod—"

"—have to stop this right now, get hold of yourself, get moving or we're gonna be—"

Patch's words were cut off when one of the hotel maids screamed from the doorway behind them.

In the moment of silence that followed the maid's scream Humberto found his legs, found his grief, found his pain, found his anger —

—found his plan.

He and Patch leapt past the shuddering woman and ran for the stairs. They passed no one on their way down and were followed only by the echoing screams of the wretched woman they'd left alone in the room, her horrified eyes locked on the site of Ruben's mangled body.

The lobby and streets were a blur to Humberto: one moment he was standing in the doorway to room 407, then—*blink*—he was climbing into the back of the van.

Patch slammed the doors, jumped into the driver's seat, and wrenched the van into drive, tires squealing as he sped out into traffic.

"Turn left up ahead," said Humberto, his voice cold and hollow.

"Where are we going?"

"The bus station. That's where he'll be."

Patch angrily pounded his fist against the steering wheel. "Fuck that, man! How do you know he didn't just take a cab to the airport?"

"Because only the tour buses are allowed to cross over the border."

"Fine! What're you gonna do once you find him?"

Humberto told Patch exactly, *precisely* what he was going to do.

Patch's face went pale and his throat went dry.

Humberto went to the back of the van, sat down, and wept with more pain and sorrow than he'd known since the night his father had died.

In his mind his father's face kept dissolving into Ruben's, then back to his father's, then Ruben's again.

Then something reptilian slithered forward and took control.

And Humberto smiled.

It felt good to smile, this close to the border.

His father and Ruben smiled back at him from within the reptile's jaws.

* * *

A lizard crept along the grimy tile floor of the bus station until it reached the crushed remains of a spider that it inspected with the tip of its tongue. Then it began to eat.

From his spot near one of the exits, an old man named Valdez watched the lizard with his one good eye. This was the most interesting thing that had happened all day.

His name wasn't really Valdez, people had just started calling him that a few years ago. He didn't know why and didn't much care. Drinking had long ago wiped away most of his memory but some mornings he could still remember a car crash, and a fire, and the strangled screams of a woman and child, the stench of searing flesh, and pain—lots of pain—then a few long swallows of liquor made those memories go away.

If only the drink would give him back his legs.

He reached out and rubbed the two dirty-bandaged stumps that now took the place of his knees and lower legs. They felt like hard knots on a tree. Between them sat a tin cup with a few coins inside; not a good day. There would be no food or drink tonight if this was all he had.

He considered the lizard, and wondered how it might taste.

Then someone stepped over him.

Valdez looked up at the sweaty man in the dirty white suit. "Could you spare a little something, señor?"

The man in the dirty white suite spit in the cup and walked away.

"They are all the same, these *americanos*," said Valdez to the lizard. It lifted its head and looked at him with its cold, bulbous eyes. Valdez sighed and reached behind him, rummaging through the debris on his four-wheeled cart until he found the liquor bottle. It was nearly empty.

As he poured the last of the booze down his throat another man stepped over him. This one was dressed in dark-stained clothes. His hair was slicked back and his nose was broken and seeping.

Valdez froze.

This man reeked of violence and death.

The lizard blinked as if it too had sensed something.

As the dark man walked away Valdez whispered, "I think he is maybe after the other man, no?"

The lizard blinked, then turned to look.

The dark man came up behind White Suit and shoved something into his back, then the two of them quickly turned and came back toward Valdez, nearly stepping on the lizard.

"I need a room," said the dark man, tossing a fifty dollar bill into Valdez's cup.

Not taking his gaze from White Suit's terrified face, Valdez replied, "Behind me there is a cleaning closet."

"Good," said the dark man, shoving White Suit forward.

When they had disappeared behind the door Valdez leaned close to the lizard and whispered, "It is a matter of *venganza*, I think. I saw it in their faces." He dragged himself over by the door, happy that no one had noticed the two men.

Valdez leaned close, and listened.

There was a wet, tearing noise, followed by the sound of a small splash. Then a cough. Then gurgling.

The dark man's voice in an icy whisper: "Did that hurt?"

A whimper, thick with agony.

"Good. Let's see how this feels."

Four quick sounds—*snick-snick-snick-snick*—and then something kicked against the door. Things rattled around with the closet, metallic sounds, as if someone were sifting through tools.

More whimpering.

Valdez looked down and saw a thin line of blood trickle out, then begin pooling under the door.

Another wet, tearing sound, followed by the *crack!* of a bone breaking, then the dark man's voice again:

"Do I have your attention now? Good. Because I'm going to tell you a little story before I finish things. My father always used to say that the greatest gift one man could give another was to tell them a good story at the end of their day, so here's mine."

Snick!

"My father was always working, working, working, taking whatever pissy-assed job he could get just to bring home a few scraps of meat and some milk and maybe a little extra *dinero* to save. He'd go away for weeks at a time when I was a kid and when he came back he'd have milk and candy and more money. He'd go on about how *El Aleman* had taken him and other over the border into glorious, generous America where the people were so kind because they gave him so much. 'Look, my son,' he would say to me. 'Look at how much they pay me.'"

Thwap!

"Don't pass out on me now, I'm getting to the good part. I said don't" —*smack!*—"pass out"—*smack!*—"on me!

"Good boy.

"You see, the thing is, I *loved* that poor, ignorant man. Holding out his chump change like it was some kind of king's treasure, a big, stupid smile on his face. My mother died when I was four and we lived in this festering shit-hole of a camp. The children sometimes killed dogs that wandered into the camp just so we could have something to eat. It was a fuckin' block party when *two* mutts wandered in, let me tell you!" His voice cracked on the last few words and for the next several seconds there was only the sound of heavy breathing.

"My father kept promising me that someday he'd have enough money so that I could go to wonderful, generous *Los Estados Unidos* and live the life of a respected man. He hoped that if he could do that for me, I'd forgive him for being a failure. He never believed me when I told him that he was never a failure in my eyes. 'I can give you something better than this,' he'd say. 'It does not matter if I am with you or not. I'll know that I was able to get you away from *el poso del mundo.*' That's what he called the camps along the border —the lowest hole in the world; the toilet where America so generously shit its turds so we wetbacks could smell it and tell them it didn't stink.

"He was killed one night while trying to cross over into your wondrous Promised Land. He and ten others were shot to death and then stripped of everything they had, even their underwear. When the motherfucking Border Patrol found the bodies, they loaded them all into the back of a pickup truck and dumped them in the middle of our camp so people could identify their loved ones. I had to dig through seven different bodies before I found my father's.

"You know what I figure? I figure that, in a way, you're one of the guys who killed him. Guys like you, you keep coming back regardless of what we do to keep you out. Sometimes you kill young boys' fathers. Sometimes you kill the young boys."

Something snapped loudly.

Then a thump. Then another.

A muffled shriek.

"Did he beg you to stop? *Did he?* "

The sound of something moist being wrenched apart.

Another snap.

Liquid spilling onto the floor.

"I'll bet my father begged, too."

Spitting. Retching. Gagging.

A dry, crinkling sound.

"Would you like to live?"

Whimpering.

Snick!

A high-pitched screech.

"Too bad, you child-murdering cocksucker!"

A metallic *click!,* then several short whistle-spit sounds— *snip-snip-snip-snip-snip!*—followed by the acrid and smoky stench of gunpowder, then the *whump!* of weight hitting the floor.

A puncturing noise.

A deflating hiss.

The sharp scrape of metal against tile.

The widening pool of blood spread outward. Valdez scooted onto his cart and rolled away from it, the lizard in his lap.

A choking noise and several spluttering grunts from inside the closet made him stop and wait, curious. Whatever was going on behind that door was inhuman but necessary and deserved respect.

Valdez sat in silence and looked at the lizard.

The lizard sat in silence and looked at Valdez.

No one passing by looked at either of them, nor did they notice the blood, nor see when the closet door opened and the dark man came out, wiping something red from his face.

He walked up to Valdez and shoved a thick envelope into his cup. "You didn't see me, old man."

"No, señor. My one good eye is very bad."

The dark man smiled and turned away, pulling several items from his pockets and shoving them into a nearby trash receptacle; bloodied pliers, two screwdrivers, a coil of wire, a can of Industrial Strength Drano, a fistful of teeth, and a chunk of slick meat: a human tongue.

He looked over his shoulder and saw Valdez staring at him. "Use the money well, old man." Then he knelt down and picked up the lizard.

It seemed to Valdez that something passed between the dark man and the reptile but it was quickly gone. The man tossed the lizard back into Valdez's lap and walked away.

As he counted the money in the envelope Valdez looked at the lizard and smiled. "Tonight, we sleep in a bed, my friend. I'll buy you lots of bugs to fill your stomach with. Maybe we buy ourselves a whore. *Two* whores, no?" He laughed. "Two whores, *yes!*"

The lizard blinked and turned to watch the dark man leave the station.

* * *

Patch said nothing to Humberto, only put the van in drive and drove back toward the road that would take them to Humberto's house in Matamoros.

Humberto wiped something from his eye, inhaled deeply, and waited for the pain in his core to lessen.

He knew he'd be waiting for the rest of his life.

After a while he picked up his flute, lifted it to his lips, then pulled it away and tossed it out the window.

"What do we do now?" asked Patch, whose face wore the expression of someone who thought he'd seen all the abyss had to threaten him with, only to see another face whose expression proved him wrong.

"I hear there's a bunch of frat boys coming down to Tijuana to bang some whores this weekend," whispered Humberto. "I ... I bet we could roll them for some—oh *Christ!*" He buried his face in his hands for a moment, took several deep breaths, then looked up at Patch.

"Frat boys ought to have a tidy wad of cash. If we get some film for your goddamned camera, we could probably catch a few in ... compromising positions."

"I never cared for frat boys," said Patch.

"I'll make some other calls, see if there's anyone in need of coyotes for border runs."

"Yeah, sounds good to me."

"Yes," whispered Humberto, looking out the window at the dust and death of home. "We've got plenty of business to attend to."

Yes. Business.

Always there was business.

Don't Sit Under
The Apple Tree

Introduction by Elizabeth Massie

Life alienates us from each other by virtue of our individual bodies and the various chemistries of our minds. We're set adrift to navigate, to do what we can, to fix what we can with whatever tools we have. Joseph picks the handiest tool for the job and is determined to get to the root of his problem and fix it. Who can argue with that? (And thanks for the gut-wrenching chills, Gary! Nobody can do it like you do.)

Don't Sit Under The Apple Tree

"There is no such thing as personal responsibility."
—Timothy Leary

Joseph Sandeman discovered the source of all his life's frustration the night after his forty-sixth birthday. He was lying in bed next to his wife who was snoring (again), wide awake because they'd been fighting (again) over the various paths taken by their three children. He drummed his fingers over the flab of his ever-extending waistline as he stared at the ceiling. Finally, unable to endure another ten seconds of his wife's moose calls, he rose, put on his robe, and walked down to the kitchen where he made himself a cold bologna sandwich and stood over the sink, staring out the window into the backyard. Which is when and how he made his discovery.

The revelation was so sudden and stunning to him that he froze with his teeth halfway through the sandwich, unaware of the ketchup that dripped out and spattered down the front of his chest as if he'd just cut his own throat.

He dropped the rest of his sandwich into the garbage disposal and smiled wide as he stood there gawking at his discovery. Then he went down to his workroom in the basement and pulled his new chainsaw down from the wall. He checked the tightness of the chain, oiled it, and thought of his family.

He was so happy he didn't even notice that he cut a small chunk out of his left thumb.

Of course his life hadn't always been one of endless frustration that would one day lead to self-loathing; on the contrary, his younger days with the advertising firm had held a lot of promise for a bright future. He'd finished college on the G.I. bill after WWII eventually dropped his ass right into the middle of Anzio where he earned no less than four different medals for valor and heroism. He was given a hero's welcome by his friends and family upon returning home.

He'd been able to choose the university he would attend, since virtually dozens of offers had come in on the heels of his much-lauded return. (These were still in the days when a local hero was just that: a hero.) He'd breezed through the various and required industrial arts courses that set him on the path to More Serious Study. Once out of college he quickly found employment as a member of the "think tank" for the state's most successful and prestigious advertising firm, married his high school sweetheart, and found himself firmly set in the niche reserved for those few well-adjusted War Heroes who Easily Fulfilled Their Vast Potential.

After fifteen years of cruising along without so much as a ripple, the waves came crashing down.

His wife, Alice, started getting lazy and growing fat after the birth of the twins, Karen and Laura. The firm fell on some hard times which, though they didn't last long, caused him to lose some of the social standing he'd worked so hard for within the community — which was to say he'd had to resign from the country club because its fees were just a little out of his reach. He never rejoined. Both of the girls married badly and often ran up the long distance bill when they called, always in tears, to bemoan the fact to their parents. Somewhere along the line he and Alice had gotten careless, resulting in the birth of Andrew, a Down syndrome child who—though neither he nor Alice would admit it —was a supreme embarrassment to them. Andrew had been injured when he was ten years old and would wear a leg brace until the day he died.

Oh, yes; Joseph Sandeman, now president of the firm, started drinking. He also took a mistress—three times a week, to be exact. Alice was hardly home, what with all her clubs and bingo games, and when she was home they never talked, never smiled, never made love. Alice ate and watched television. Andrew sat in his room and did God-only-knew what. And Joseph...Joseph drank. And brooded. And dreamed of the sweaty, grunting afternoons with his mistress. At least he hadn't lost his knack for advertising. The firm was now listed as fifth in the nation in terms of clear year-end profit. Money was no problem. Everything else was.

As he carried the chainsaw upstairs and placed it on the back porch, Joseph Sandeman knew that all those problems which had been forced upon him would soon be taken care of. None of it was his fault. Never had been. But he would, as it seemed he always did, Take Care Of Things.

Just like a Well-Adjusted War Hero was supposed to do.

* * *

Alice looked up from her morning paper at him. "It's whose fault?"

"That damned apple tree in the back yard. I was sitting underneath it when I decided to join the Army. My father suffered the heart attack that killed him trying to pick apples off the goddamn thing. My mother died of grief because of that tree. Andrew fell from that tree and destroyed his leg. My grandmother choked to death on a pie made with the apples from that tree. I proposed to you under that tree."

She smiled, her nose in the paper, only half-listening. "I remember you'd only been home a few weeks and were getting ready to leave for college. We sang that dumb old song...what was it called?"

"'Don't Sit Under The Apple Tree.'"

"Yes, I remember."

"Laura's wedding ceremony took place in our backyard. She and Walter exchanged their vows under that tree. She's been miserable ever since. Karen was washing apples picked from that tree when John came over and apologized for hitting her and she forgave him and now they're married and he still hits her. Everything that's gone wrong in my life is because of that fucking tree. It's attached itself to my family and it won't let go. And now that it's old and dying it's trying to take my family with it. I won't allow it to happen, Alice, do you understand?"

"Did you read where they voted to raise property taxes? I think that's outrageous."

She wasn't listening. He didn't care. He was speaking for and to himself now.

"I always wanted us to be happy, Alice, but it hasn't worked out. I always wanted for us to be in love, I always wanted for us to be young and thin and attractive. But that tree has taken it all away. It's not my fault. But I'm going to fix things, you'll see. And maybe it will restore some decency to my life."

She looked up from her paper and blinked as she gulped down her coffee. "I'm sorry dear, you were saying about the tree?"

"I'm going to cut it down," he whispered, not looking at her.

"Well, you have a good time, but be careful." She rose and began packing herself into the outfit for that day. "I've got a few meetings this morning for the new cooking class and then Hazel and I are meeting some of the girls for lunch and shopping before class tonight. Andrew is staying over at the group home tonight to see if he likes it. I'll be back around ten. You've got the whole day to yourself." Then, with a dry peck on his cheek that he assumed was her version of a kiss, she was gone.

Forty minutes later his mistress was groaning underneath him in her apartment. When he was finished he gave her a savings account book with a balance of twenty-five thousand dollars and broke it off. She didn't seem hurt. He wasn't even out the door before she was on the phone with someone named Nick and talking about Las Vegas.

Then it was home. Changed into work clothes. Chainsaw in hand. Facing the tree.

Twelve feet high, all its branches barren. Only five thick limbs remained. He chose not to think about all the happy childhood memories he had associated with the beast. The chainsaw was hungry, its teeth oiled and shiny.

He let it roar and began the destruction.

Nine hours later he had the pieces stacked neatly on the front porch. All that remained of his life's frustrations was an ugly stump in the back of the yard. He'd hire someone to uproot it.

He felt good. Tired from solid hard work. Drained. Happy. Cleansed. Renewed.

He fell asleep in his favorite chair with a smile on his face. He was a better Joseph Sandeman.

* * *

Alice woke him a little after ten. "Decided against it, did you?"

"W-what? What time is it?"

"Decided not to cut the tree down after all?"

He jumped from the chair and ran to the back porch.

There it stood, no different than it looked last night.

"So it's to be this way, is it?" he whispered through clenched teeth. "Fine. You got yourself a fight."

The tree offered no response.

It only took him seven hours the next day. He ignored the howling pain of his muscles.

He'd just collapsed into his chair when the doorbell rang. Alice answered; probably the people bringing Andrew back from the group home. Joseph closed his eyes. Then Alice shrieked. Five minutes later he was holding her in his arms and listening to a detective explain how Andrew had turned up missing early this morning from the group home. His room had been destroyed and bloody. The FBI was being called in. Could they set up recording and tracing equipment in case a ransom call came in.

Two hours later, with his wife heavily sedated and several detectives and FBI men squatting in the living room, Joseph went out back and found the tree waiting for him.

After six days and no call the squatters pulled up stakes and left Joseph and his wife to their worry. Joseph had agreed to allow a tap on the phone that would be monitored around the clock for the next seven days. What would happen after that, no one would say.

He cut the tree down again that night. Then he lay in bed listening to Alice snore. It sounded weaker. He could detect the slightest dripping sound and realized that the pipes were going to hell again. If it were anything like the last time, the basement and attic would be flooded by the end of the week. But at least the tree was gone.

* * *

The next morning the FBI was back with news.

Not about Andrew. About Laura.

Her husband had turned up in a drunk tank in New Jersey covered with blood and babbling. When local police searched the house they'd found it a shambles, the walls splattered with blood. The FBI asked Joseph if he had any enemies who would want to hurt him like this. He could only think of one true enemy, and he didn't dare tell them about it.

Alice went into the hospital that night. Catatonia, they said. Shock coupled with extreme emotional trauma.

Joseph stayed up all night and annoyed the neighbors with his work. Then he drove out, rented a pickup truck, and loaded the pieces of the tree into the back. He drove out to an old abandoned strip mining sight and dumped the pieces into a pit, poured gasoline over them, and set them on fire. He stood there until the fire was gone and all that remained of the tree was ashes. Then he drove home. Parked in the driveway. Went to the sink and got himself a drink of water. Passed out when he looked up and saw what was standing in the back yard.

* * *

That night the dripping was back, tap-tapping everywhere. He couldn't find the source. He knew it was the pipes because the whole house was starting to stink.

He sat down and got good and drunk, then realized that, during all of this, Karen hadn't called once. Surely the authorities would have contacted her first, since she lived so close to Laura.

He called his only remaining child.

There was no answer.

The next morning he cut down the tree and let the pieces remain in a pile in the yard. It seemed easier that way. Then he got good and drunk again. He was still drunk when the police came and told him about Karen.

And Alice.

Both missing. Rooms trashed. Lots of blood.

"It's not my fault," he whispered.

The police asked him to please repeat that.

He looked down at his shaking hands. He thought he was holding a bottle of scotch. He wasn't. He was holding the chainsaw. It was rusty, but that couldn't be because it was new. Dark, dripping rust.

He heard the pipes leaking again. Smelled the stench of the backed-up sewage. So did the police, he could see it on their faces.

He walked slowly toward the kitchen. The police followed him. He looked out the window. The tree stood strong and healthy, defiant, black-shiny with blood and shreds of tissue in the moonlight.

He knew he heard a lot of footsteps, people running, voices calling, and commotion. None of it really registered. He dropped the chainsaw and sat quietly at the kitchen table. He made himself a cold bologna sandwich, heavy on the ketchup. The two policemen with him had their guns out. He wondered why. They should be pointing them at the thing in the backyard. After all, everything was its fault, not his. It had manipulated him for as long as he could remember. But no more, never again.

And it all had started so innocently, when young war heroes were full of hope. He smiled as ketchup dribbled down his chest and began singing softly to himself: "Don't sit...under the...apple tree with...anyone else...but me..."

Not his fault.

"...anyone else but me..."

None of it.

"...anyone else but me..."

Large plastic bags, full of lumpy, warm, wet things were carried past him. Some of the pieces looked like things you might pick for use in a pie.

"...oh, no-no-no...don't sit under the apple tree..."

He was pulled to his feet and handcuffed. He stopped singing. He couldn't remember the rest of the words. But that was all right.

The tree had haunted his family long enough. Ruined everything. But that was all over now.

Except when he was leaving the kitchen he heard one of the officers say to another: "It's not even an apple tree. Any moron knows a pear tree when they see one."

Not my fault. I'm not the one responsible, he thought. *I did my part, I fixed it, I left it better than I found it.*

Humming an old tune to himself as he walked proudly out the door....

Redaction

Introduction by Usman Tanveer Malik

Gary Braunbeck's stories aren't written but sculpted. He chisels them out of darkness and shapes them with a hammer or perfect melancholy. He blows his spirit into them until they gleam with his immortal soul. "Redaction," a story as startling as it is inevitable, is no different.

Redaction

"We can't hate ourselves into a version of ourselves we can love."

— Lori Deschene

In college he wrote a paper for a Philosophy 101 class entitled "The Lie of the 'I,' the Deception of All Nouns." It was intended as a joke, a swipe at how utterly pretentious he found the professor, his classmates, and the course as a whole to be. "'I,'" he'd written, "is at once a lie, because once you've spoken that word, you are no longer the 'I' of whom you speak but rather a *representation* of that 'I,' the 'you' you wish others to think of when you say 'I.' By speaking of yourself in the first person, you at once separate yourself from the person you are claiming to be, so what is intended as proof of authenticity is actually the most deceptive pronoun of all; nothing but a 'he' in disguise, wearing a phony moustache and fright wig, a 'her' with hair shorn short and a false beard and breasts held flat by sports bandages beneath the shirt of the tuxedo. It is no better when considering the deception of nouns, for they do nothing more than delineate a class—*my* chair, *my car*, *my* life—it's a blur, a flippant label, a lazy summary, and if the 'my' coupled with the noun—that is, the 'my' that is the 'I' that is 'you'—is also a misrepresentation, then the two taken together create a terminal oversimplification of how we gather knowledge, experience, and memory, the three things that are—or so we are taught—*de rigueur* to forming and maintaining individuality. If the 'I' is a lie, then so is the conceit of individuality, all of it tantamount to the total annihilation of the Self. In short, we're all hosed."

He'd expected to get drummed out of the class after handing it in a day late (on purpose); instead, he received glowing comments from the professor and several members of the Philosophy department, one of whom insisted on entering his paper in a national competition. He declined, feigning humility, but the truth was he'd plagiarized several key passages from papers written by his very professor several decades before. If the guy didn't recognize his own words, it was probably because he was too damned old—but that didn't mean that someone else wouldn't find themselves wondering why things rang a bell. So, as it turned out, the joke he wanted to play on the professor, his classmates, and the Philosophy department, he wound up playing on himself. There was a lesson in there someplace but he was damned if he was going to go digging for it.

He hadn't thought of that paper in years but for some reason, waking from a night's very bad sleep, aching and taut and sluggish and grunting, dry-coughing so hard he could have sworn he saw dust fly out of his mouth, not so much rolling out of bed as crawling toward something like an upright position, he for some reason recalled that opening passage and wished, momentarily, that he could find it in him to swallow a little bit of that happy horseshit, because if the "I" was a lie, then it wasn't "him" who was feeling so lousy.

He made his way into the kitchen, started the coffee maker. Turning on the under-cabinet mounted television, he saw the hot young comedian of the moment adapting his shtick in order to make it sound like conversation with the host of the show. The host, good morning drone that she was, knew precisely the questions to feed the comedian so that he could dazzle the audience with excerpts from his stand-up act.

"You've got a massive web presence," said the host. "Doesn't the threat of having your information hacked worry you—especially considering how highly visible you are, being a celebrity? Is something like identity theft a concern?"

The comedian's eyes brightened considerably—you could tell he'd been waiting for the host to feed him this exact question. He cleared his throat and sat back, trying to look nonchalant. "I don't have to worry about identity theft any longer. Mine got up and left on its own."

It didn't get quite the laugh the comedian had hoped for—that was obvious—but there was a smattering of applause.

The coffee maker finished brewing the morning's fuel, and he allowed himself one large, relaxing cup before readying himself for the day, which turned out to be nothing special until his lunch break; the morning commute, fighting in the garage for a parking space wasn't on the fucking roof, slogging through the crowds to get to his office building, and then up to the Cubicle Farm to spend the next four hours entering data and information and making sure the company's massive website was slick and functional and so easy to navigate that a legally retarded chimpanzee with Parkinson's Disease could find its way through the links while half asleep. *Binary code,* he thought. The "I" might be a lie, and all nouns might be lies, but binary code existed on another plane, where lies did not and arguably *could not* exist. Something coded in binary might be *wrong,* but it could never be a lie; its very existence was all the proof it needed of its own authenticity. A nothing-special thought to end the nothing-special morning of a nothing-special day, until it came time to pay for his lunch.

Like everything else, his lunch was nothing special; a sandwich, potato chips, a soda, and a cup of yogurt at the faux-hip café that catered to the faux-hipsters who only ate at cafés and not "restaurants." He was standing in line waiting for his turn to pay.

When he came up to the young woman at the register he smiled, handed her his check, and began to pull his credit card from his wallet, but as soon as he had the thing in his hand he noticed that his name was missing. Jesus, had he used it so much that he'd worn down the slightly raised letters of his name? He turned toward a window where there was a bright slash of afternoon sunlight glaring off the chrome of the café décor and angled the card slightly. No, it wasn't that he'd worn down the raised letters because there were none there. Shouldn't there have been at least a dim ghost of the letters, a curved bump here, something that might be a middle initial here? But … nothing. It was as if the card had been printed with no name on it. He turned it over to check the strip where his signature should have been and it too was blank. Shit—he was holding up the line. He shoved the wallet and blank credit card into his coat pocket and paid in cash.

More annoyed than confused, he walked outside and took a seat on a nearby bench, examining the card again. No name on either side. What the hell? He'd call the credit card company and request a new one, tell them he'd lost this one. Simple. He'd dispose of the card properly when he got back to the office; use the über shredder that could turn a sheet of Plexiglas into powder if the need were there. He rose, slipping the card back into his wallet, and accidentally knocked loose his driver's license that tumbled out and hit the ground before he could grab it. Picking it up, he wiped if off on the side of his coat and turned it forward. There was his face. There was the state seal. There was the license number; there was his height, his weight, and his date of birth, everything that needed to be there. Except his name.

He felt sore and unsteady and uncomfortably rigid, just as he had upon waking this morning, but now there was the added bonus of a slight ache in the center of his chest. He was too young to be having a heart attack, he didn't smoke, didn't drink (much, anyway), he exercised and watched what he ate, so there was no point in indulging that particular anxiety but, just to be safe, he sat down again and placed a hand against his chest and concentrated on his breathing until it felt normal. It then occurred to him that the pressure seemed to be more in his torso than his chest, and almost laughed at his foolishness; he'd mistaken a case of rapid-onset heartburn for a coronary. It was to laugh, sincerely; it was to laugh. He did then what he always did whenever he had a bit of gas like this; he pressed the side of his fist into the center of his torso and applied a slight bit of pressure. It helped a little but not like it usually did, so he did the same again, only this time putting a little more force behind it, but it still didn't improve things. Feeling both irrational and inept, he sat up straight and hammered the side of his fist into his chest with as much force as he could without drawing attention to himself and this time felt something dislodge up into his throat. God, please don't let him vomit in public. He opened his hand and placed it against his chest, applying pressure, and began to cough—dry, scratchy, harsh coughs that left his throat feeling raw, and with each successive attack he saw the mist splutter out of him—no, not mist, not saliva, not phlegm, it was more like ... dust, and the more he coughed, feeling as if his body might collapse in on itself with each wracking assault, the more dust came out of him, encircling him in a small cloud as if he were some cowboy cliché dusting himself off with his hat after weeks out on the lonesome trail, or that *Peanuts* character who was always surrounded by a churning haze of dirt. He continued coughing up dust for what felt like an hour but was actually less than a minute; if any passersby took notice of this odd little noisy vaudeville, none gave any indication. That was fine by him; he didn't like being noticed under the best of circumstances, let alone for something this embarrassing. The next wave of coughing was the worst yet, each explosion causing his body to double over and lock up, blood pounding through his temples with such force his sight blurred even though there were no tears in his eyes, and for a moment, one moment in which he feared he was about to pass out from lack of oxygen, it seemed to him that the cloud swirling before and around him wasn't composed of dust particles at all but recurring, overlapping series of tiny ones and zeroes scrolling upward with near-blurring speed.

When at last the worst of it passed he rose somewhat unsteadily to his feet, brushed himself off, and began walking back toward his office building. Christ, this day was one for the books; first the business with the credit card, then his driver's license, and then the goddamn coughing fit. Oh, brother—if this wasn't one fucked up day then his name wasn't ... wasn't ....

He stopped, nearly causing the women walking behind to plow into his back and drop everything she was carrying. She cursed at him under her breath and gave him the stink-eye on her way past. He didn't care. He couldn't remember his name.

Okay, hold on, hold on, just take it easy, don't flip out. It had been a bad morning; okay, yes, no argument there. *Bad* morning, after a worse night's non-sleep. The stuff with the cards, it had just thrown him, just caught him off-guard, that was all. Hell, there were probably times in everyone's lives when they momentarily forgot their name; it was no big deal. *I mean, c'mon, how often do you think of yourself* by name, *anyway?* The name is something for *others* to identify you with, so if every once in a while you skip a groove and can't remember it, it doesn't mean you've actually *forgotten* it.

Right?

He closed his eyes and placed his hands in front of him, palms out, as if preparing to stop something about to plow into him. He took a series of deep breaths, clearing his mind of as many cobwebs as possible, and then opened his eyes, looked at his hands, and said, "No biggie. No need to push the panic button. See there, my friend? You're good. You're *good.* You're Good Ol' ..."

Good Ol' Name's-Not-There-Anymore, that's who.

He decided that something must be seriously wrong. Maybe he was coming down with something, a virus, the flu, *something* that would explain all of this. He hadn't been sleeping well lately, he'd been less than his usual sharp self—more than one of his coworkers had told him that—and everyone knew that lack of sleep could really mess with you in more ways than one, because if you don't sleep enough to dream, it was possible that your mind would start to dream while you were awake, or even cause hallucinations like not being to see your name on a card, or remember what it is, or —

He started coughing again, much more violently than a few minutes ago, and this time it was clear that he was coughing up dust and reflected against the curtain of that dust, as if being shone on it through a powerful projector, the ones and zeroes of the rushing binary code scrolled through the dust, cutting off wherever the cloud curved or dissipated.

Go home, he told himself. *Go check in with the supervisor, finish the last little bit of coding, and go home.*

When he stepped off the elevator onto his floor he was at once dizzy and slightly nauseated; he was definitely getting sick. He wiped the sweat from his brow and was making his way through the maze of cubicles toward his own work area when one of the floor's security guards stopped him.

"Can I help you?"

He looked at the guard. "Steve, c'mon, don't mess with me—I feel terrible." He attempted to move past the guard again but this time Steve moved quickly in front of him and held him in place.

"I need to see your floor pass, sir."

"This isn't funny, Steve."

The guard checked his own badge, which identified him only as **S. Henderson**. "I'm not sure how it is you know my name, buddy, but it don't change the fact that I need to see your floor pass."

"Fine." He was in no mood for this. He reached inside his coat to unclip his laminated employee I.D. from his pocket and shove it in Steve's face, but it wasn't there. He looked at the security guard, and then pulled open his coat for a better view. Maybe the damn thing had just slipped, or maybe it was in his shirt pocket and he'd just forgotten he'd put it there.

"I, uh ... I can't seem to find my I.D. card," he said. The guard took hold of his arm and began to gently but firmly lead him back toward the elevators. He began to cough again, feeling dry and hollow. He stopped for a moment to steady himself. The security seemed to understand that he wasn't well and didn't force him to continue walking, but did keep hold of his upper arm.

He wiped his face with his handkerchief and looked over the guard's soldier toward his own workspace and wasn't at all surprised to see himself sitting there, coding away.

A pain behind his left eye caused the lid to twitch, so he closed his eye and held the lid in place with his index finger. Looking only through his right eye, he saw that the him at his desk was flat, glossy, and two-dimensional; was, in fact, a larger version of his laminated employee I.D. Opening his left eye, he closed his right. The him that was his employee I.D. was now a him-shaped scrolling mass of binary code. He opened both eyes; the him at his desk was now a three-dimensional, corporeal human being. The him at the desk saw the other him—the first him—staring, and rose from the desk to stand at the guard's side.

"I'm sorry, Steve, I should have said something," said the second him. "I have an appointment with this gentleman."

"He doesn't have a floor pass."

"That's my bad," said second him, producing a laminated clip-on badge from his jacket pocket. "I meant to leave this down at Reception but forgot."

"Okay, then," said the security guard. "Sorry about the mix-up, sir. No hard feelings?"

"No," he said; he knew it was him, he recognized his voice. The guard walked away.

"Why the hell did you come back here?" asked second him, grabbing his arm and pulling him toward the restrooms.

"Would you—Jesus, let go! Would you please walk in front of me?"

"Why?"

"Because when you're on my left, you're nothing but binary code, and when you're on my right, you're a laminated card."

"Oh, yeah, sorry about that." He walked in front. "I still haven't quite gotten the hang of this yet."

"The hang of *what*?"

"Living comfortably in the lie of your 'I'. This existence thing, it takes a lot out of you. No pun intended."

Entering the restroom, second him locked the door behind them. "Do you need to sit down or throw up or something?"

"I don't think so." He steadied himself on one of the sinks and ran some cold water, soaking his handkerchief and then wiping it across his face before holding it against the back of his neck.

"Are you trying to take over?" he asked second him.

"No. That's not even close to what's going on."

"Then ... what?"

Second him looked at him with something like pity. "You never remember how this process works. It doesn't matter how many times we—*you*—go through this, you never remember. I think it's because you find it so frightening that you block it out."

"What the hell are you talking about?"

"Rebirth, you silly sock monkey. Rebirth. You've—*we've*—been doing this since ... since I-don't-know-when. The first time *I clearly* remember it was around the time we helped execute de Launay and de Flesselles after the Bastille fell. I think we were still us until after the *Fête de la Fédération*. Hell, who keeps track anymore?"

He looked at himself in the mirror. His cheeks were sunken, as were his eyes. Leaning in, he saw something reflected in his eyes — perhaps *from* his eyes, behind the retinas. Dusty binary code.

"Is it always this fast, this ... hurtful?"

"*Hurtful?* Huh, that's a new one. I guess ... yes, I guess it is — at least for whichever one of us — you — *they* — is the first. Me, it feels a little shaky, like maybe my blood sugar is low and I need to grab a candy bar, but that'll pass."

He touched his cheek. Part of it seemed to crack, a patch of dried plaster.

"Why do we do this?" he asked. "Why is this perpetual rebirth needed?"

Second him looked down at the floor and shook his head. "I have no idea, friend. I guess we weren't privy to that particular memo."

He looked at the reflection of second him in the mirror. "Will you remember me? Will you remember everything that I remember?"

"Memories may be knotted up in the lie of the 'I' and the deception of nouns, but they are what forms us, like it or not. Yes, I'll remember you and I'll have your memories. Someday I'll be where you are and the other me will ask the same question."

He nodded his head and watched his reflection. With a series of soft, dry sounds, his head began collapsing inward, his features crumbling and flaking away as his face fell back, split open from the center, belched out a cloud of binary encoded dust, and began to dissolve.

Can you tell me what my name was? He didn't think he'd asked this out loud since he had no throat remaining, but second him heard nonetheless.

"What does it matter, friend? Of all the lies we embrace to give our existence the illusion of a deeper and more profound meaning, the illusion of the name is arguably the worst of them all."

His clothing fell in on itself as his flesh turned to dust, and soon they were simply a pile of rags abandoned on the floor. The dust that had been him swirled in the air before second him, who, smiling, stepped into it and breathed deeply, pulling in the particles and codes and microscopic bits of flesh that had been what he once was. His last lungful of his former self was pulled in a bit too deeply and he gave out a small cough, but expelled nothing of himself. Looking in the mirror, he patted down his hair, adjusted his tie, and straightened his jacket.

"Once more, with feelers," he said aloud, laughing at their private joke, and then unlocked the door and returned to work. Behind him, the rag pile shrank, clear plastic sheets tossed onto a fire, until there was only a small section of red handkerchief that swirled like a spatter of blood circling a drain before fading away.

Chow Hound

Introduction by Jessica McHugh

Terror presents itself in unpredictable ways. Some of us fear the dark – the emptiness, the uncertainty, the way shadows eagerly shift into all manner of monsters. Some of us fear the monsters themselves – their hunger beyond human appetites and the mad deviances swirling in lawless minds. Some fear those monstrous qualities germinating in humanity, transforming us into beasts with kind eyes and silver tongues that a lifetime of good deeds can't cure, powerless against our own unnatural hunger and depravity.

When faced with terror, we have three options – fight, run, or surrender – and each inflicts fresh torture. To fight is to be battered, broken, and witness to your own defeat. To run is to be pursued, perhaps for a torturous eternity. And to surrender is to be shamed, even publically, for as long as the monster deems your life worth ruining.

But what if your greatest terror is clean and soft? What if it can coo and cry for you? Smile, need, and love you? And for all of its torments, what if that terror can coax you into loving it back, or even nurturing its survival above your own?

Gary Braunbeck tackles that issue with all the wit and deftness you've come to expect from his work, and this foray into bizarro territory from this master storyteller yields a deliciously bitter fruit that disturbed my emotions and turned my stomach long after reading. If I weren't already one half of a child-free couple, it might have been enough to put me off little ones forever.

Chow Hound

"... the child in the womb
It sayeth the young man's courting
It hath brought hunger and palsey to bed, lyeth
between the young bride and her bridegroom ..."

—Ezra Pound, *With Usara*

The baby cries and eats, then shits, pisses, and sleeps. From the moment Russell and his wife brought the thing home it has been this way. Russell asks his wife, "Why won't it shut up?" and she responds by smiling at him as she lifts the baby to her breast and says, "Him's just a little ol' chow hound, that's all him is." This said more to the baby than to Russell. She's like that now, everything she says has to include the baby, everything they do has to be done in its presence, even their lovemaking—if you can call it that; usually she shakes her head and says, "It's too soon," and Russell gets angry and she acquiesces by masturbating him. All passionless, all done with the baby in the room.

Russell can't stand the chronic caterwauling; he's had an incessant headache for weeks. People at work have begun telling him he doesn't look so hot. "Fatherhood taking it out of you, is it?" they ask, then smile, and Russell has to press his fists against his legs in order to keep from knocking their teeth out. Three in the morning and the thing is at it again. Russell's wife rolls over and jams an elbow in his side once, twice, three times until he awakens.

"... your turn," she mumbles, then drops back asleep.

Russell pulls himself out of bed and shambles over to the crib, staring down at the tiny mass of pink corpulence that his wife tells him is his son.

Its arms and legs are in the air, flailing and kicking as its torso heaves and the high-pitched, ragged cries pierce the night.

Russell blinks—

—*and suddenly it is many years ago when he was a boy, lying in bed and listening to his mother's strangled cries from his parents' bedroom. He fears that his father might be hurting her and jumps out of bed and runs to their door flinging it open just as his father rolls off of his mother, and Russell sees the stiff thing jutting from between his father's legs, then looks at his mother and sees the slick slit between her thighs and thinks DAD PUNCHED A HOLE IN*

HER AND SHE'LL DIE —

—blinking away the memory, Russell reaches down and lifts the baby.

Chow hound. Eat, eat, eat. And it's never enough.

Three in the morning. And Russell once again gets an attack of the dawn terrors, feeling panicked and afraid, thinking that this is all wrong, he's not supposed to be here doing this, he's taken someone else's place and out there in the night someone somewhere is living the life that was supposed to be his, a life with passion and success and no wailing baby that drags him from sleep.

These feelings soon pass.

In the refrigerator he finds the bottles of breast milk. He shakes one, shoves it in the microwave, and waits for the buzzer to sound.

As the milk warms he stares at the baby, thinking that he should be proud and knowing that he isn't. He doesn't look a thing like him or his wife. Soft and pink, its head seems far too big for its body, like the figures he used to make from wads of clay when he was a child. He remembers the way he used to lay the figures up on a table top, then smash them into a heap with his hand. The memory makes him smile.

The buzzer sounds and he takes out the bottle, checks to see if the milk's too hot, then shoves the nipple in the baby's mouth.

Russell watches it eat, this squirming proof of his own mortality, and knows that the baby will be walking around long after he himself is dead. In forty years it may hear a piece of music that Russell might have fallen in love with, or see a film that Russell would have enjoyed, or touch a woman that —

—Russell blinks, pressing the bottle into the baby's mouth with more force than is necessary. He imagines himself and the baby, a few years from now, walking hand in hand across a field that begins sloping uphill slightly, so the walk becomes difficult and Russell tells the little chow hound who is his son, "Take my hand." The child does, and they ascend to the top. The sun is shining and there are wildflowers all around and the grass is golden and ruffled by the soft breeze. The child giggles and looks at Russell, then tugs hard at his arm and they stumble, the hill suddenly sloping downward, and Russell has to dig in his heels to keep from going ass-over-teakettle but it's too late, his balance is shot to hell and he slams to the ground, sliding down the hill, then grinding to a stop at the edge of a cliff, his arm dangling over the edge, and he sees that it drops straight down hundreds of feet to a maze of jagged rocks and he panics, thinking of the child who is now running down the hill with tremendous force, so he pushes himself up and shoots out an arm to catch the child who is going faster and screaming because it can't stop the momentum, and Russell is suddenly filled with the fear of fatherly love and vows to save the child, but at the last second it jumps over his head and Russell rolls over, not thinking about the rocks below, and tries to catch his son, but instead of tumbling down towards the rocks the child takes flight, rising toward the clouds as Russell slides over the edge and the rocks rise up to meet him —

—the baby pushes the bottle away, breathes deeply, then gurgles, a thin and hideous smile crawling across its face. Russell hoists it up against his shoulder and begins to pat its back. The thing gurgles again, a warm, contented sound, then burps and spits up.

Russell cleans the thing, then himself, then puts it back in the crib. It shakes its arms almost gaily, gives one last kick of its feet, then closes its eyes, flopping over on its stomach.

Russell's wife has made him read countless books and pamphlets about infant care, and every last one of them said you should never let a baby sleep on its stomach because it might suffocate itself in that position.

Russell thinks about turning the baby over —

—notices how blessedly silent the house is —

—then walks away. It is still alive, and will still be alive after Russell lies in the cold rot of a grave.

Its being alive is both a miracle and mystery, so it seems only natural and understandable that it should die before him.

—and there is Russell, a child again, being led back to bed by his father, who tucks him in, sees Russell staring at his erection, and says, "Take a good look at it, boy. You gotta feed it when it's hungry. A man is no stronger than his appetites. Stay hungry, boy. Hungry for money, for success, for respect and power, hungry" —he lifts his erection—"for pussy. Feed it enough and it'll vomit, and when it pukes, you get little chow hounds . . . like you." Russell watches horrified as his father's erection dribbles, then splits down the middle and opens wide, the inside ribbed with thousands of teeth like a lamprey's mouth. His father leans down and strokes Russell's hair, then says, "You want me to take you out to the roof before you go back to sleep? You always like it when I take you out to the roof."

Now, in his own bed, next to his own wife, feeling the heat of his own erection, Russell listens for the sound of the baby's breathing.

He can't hear it.

And he grins.

* * *

When he awakens, his wife and the baby are gone and there is still silence in the house. Russell stares up at the ceiling and wonders what his wife found in the crib. Was the thing shriveled, cold, dead? Had it gone into silent convulsions during the wee hours of the morning, become trapped in a crazed descent that led from convulsions to pain, then paralysis and death? Perhaps she went over to the find the sheets of the crib sopped in blood, the baby staring up at her with pitiful, frightened eyes, not understanding why this dark liquid was seeping from its body. Yes, that's it! Things Russell. His wife did everything she could to staunch the flow of blood but nothing worked, and she tried to wake him but couldn't and so grabbed the child and called for a doctor and—

—from the kitchen her voice echoes—

". . . just a little ol' chow hound, that's all him is."

Russell presses his fists against his sides and curses under his breath.

He showers, dresses for work, and goes to the kitchen.

His wife is sitting at the table, her breast bared, the baby sucking at her nipple. Her breasts droop lower than before. Yes, they're bigger (Russell thought he would enjoy that) but now both hang so low they look like two huge cysts.

The bottles like sentries line the top of the table. All of them are empty.

"Has he had all of them?" Russell asks.

"Just like his daddy," replies his wife—not to him, to the baby. "Him's always so hungry."

Russell winces, wondering what it is about a baby that makes even the most intelligent adult suddenly start goobering gibberish like a moron. Gibberish is all his wife spouts now. No more do they have those long, in-depth conversations like they used to, conversations that were literate and multi-leveled. Now it's "Googoo" and "Him make poo-poo?" and "Little ol' chow hound." Jesus.

Russell opens the morning paper and reads the comics as the baby claws at his wife's nipple.

It's not until Russell hears a deep, wet, tearing sound that he lowers the paper and looks at his family.

The baby has devoured his wife's breast. The mangled, dropping meat hangs like a hacked carcass on a butcher's hook.

Still the baby eats, chewing and gnawing like a rat until it has burrowed deep into his wife's gut, then sits there in her viscera and wraps its lips around an artery on her heart, sucking, sucking, sucking.

His wife sighs like she used to whenever he would tongue her vagina in bed, arching her back and shuddering with delight and ecstasy.

"I remember the way my father used to play with me," she says, not looking at the thick gore that pumps out of her raw cavity and spreads across the floor. "We would go to this hill behind our house and run to the top, then race down. He always beat me, was always waiting at the bottom to catch me in case I got to running too fast and fell. I want to do that again. I want to watch you two race down the hill. I want to watch you catch him and then the two of you can wrestle and laugh and when you come inside I can complain about the grass stains on your pants and the dirt in your hair. Then I'll make cookies."

The baby is sucking harder, gulping her down. Her head begins to collapse from within, a deflating balloon.

"We'll have so much fun," she says, going soft, sinking into herself. "Life and laughter and love. All because of him." She reaches through the muck of her mutilated body and strokes the back of the baby's head. One of its tiny hands reaches up and grips her fingers, snapping them off one by one.

"Thank you," she sputters to Russell. "Thank you for giving me back that hill."

And with a soft hiss her head flattens out, drooping over her shoulders like a rubber shawl. He eyes slop out of their sockets and dangle at the end of their stalks.

The baby crawls out of her and starts playing with them.

* * *

At the funeral everyone cries and kisses Russell, telling him that he'll be just fine, if there's anything they can do for him or the baby he just has to let them know and they'll be right there.

That night, unable to satisfy the baby's hunger, he calls his parents and they come over.

Russell's mother takes the baby and cries, then wipes her eyes and says, "Him's just like his daddy and his grandpa, an ol' chow hound." Then bares her shriveled, liver-spotted breast. The baby devours her quickly, then crawls over to grandpa.

"Still think a man should stay hungry for pussy?" Russell asks his father as the baby wrenches open the old man's mouth, dislodging his jaw as it claws its way down his throat.

After Russell finishes mopping up the mess and burning his parents' clothes, he puts the baby to bed. It sleeps quietly, contentedly.

* * *

By the time the mourning period is over and it's time for Russell to return to work, the baby has grown to well over nine feet tall. It sits naked in deep piles of its own filth, screaming to be fed. Russell tries everything but the thing still bawls and shrieks.

Finally he just sits across from it, staring up at the huge head and its obscene mouth.

"We gave you everything we had," he whispers to it.

It screams shrilly, its head growing larger.

Russell picks up a toy rattle and shakes it. The baby ceases its howling for a moment, staring at the rattle with fascination, then grabs it from Russell's hand and eats it.

Russell drops his head into his hands and weeps.

He remembers the way his own father played with him, and decides to tell the baby a story. Maybe that will lull it to sleep.

He raises his head, wipes his eyes, and crosses to the baby, stroking its back.

"When I was a child my father would take me up to the roof of our house and throw me off head-first. My skull would smash against the pavement and I'd laugh, watching my brains splatter in the grass. I'd get up and yell, 'Do it again!' and Dad would wave me back up, then throw me off again. On summer evenings we'd go to neighborhood cookouts and I'd listen to other parents tell funny stories about how they'd throw and break their children, then all of us kids would run off to play and show each other our holes and scrapes and bruises and broken parts. That made us hungry. The hamburgers and hot dogs at these cookouts were always real good; they reminded me of what the stuff inside my skull looked like when my head crashed into the cement. After we'd get home I'd ask Dad to kill me one more time before bed and he'd give Mom one of those 'what-do-you-think-dear?' looks, and she'd smile and shrug and say, 'Oh, all right, but make it quick.' The bedtime throw-and-breaks were the best. They gave me good dreams. Dreams about falling over the edge of a cliff and feeling my body break against sharp rocks, and as I lay there bleeding and moaning a beautiful princess would come along on her horse and see me and weep because I was in so much pain. Then she'd dismount and cradle my head tenderly in her arms and whisper, 'I will nurse you back to health, my brave, beautiful lover. And when you are well, we shall wed and be together forever.' She would come in to my bed late at night and kiss me and soothe me and tell me stories about how she used to race with her father. And then we'd fuck, and she would squeal and scream my name, and when we came together we'd promise each other that we'd be good parents, when that time came."

He looks up. The baby is staring at him, hypnotized, a thin string of slobber dangling from the corner of its mouth.

The baby nods its head, seeming to understand.

"I'm hungry too, you know?" says Russell.

The baby smiles.

"Like you."

The baby squeals.

"Me's an ol' chow hound, just like my son."

The baby flails its arms and kicks its legs, rocking the foundation of the house as it giggles and googoos and gurgles.

Russell rises to his feet as the baby flops forward, slamming its chin into the floor. Its head is as tall as the room. The top of its skull smashes through the ceiling, raining plaster and beams.

It opens its mouth and Russell sees its teeth, then steps closer.

In the gap between its two upper center teeth is his wife's head, upside-down and staring out at him, her mouth twisting and wriggling as she tries to form words.

Russell smiles.

The baby moves its tongue, only it's not a tongue at all, it's slick, pink, quivering vaginal meat, pulsing and lubricated and ready for Russell's hardness.

Russell looks up at the eyes of his son. "In bed she used to say that I was trying to swallow her whole when we were making love."

The baby opens its mouth.

Russell whispers, "A man is no stronger than his appetites . . . stay hungry, boy." Then steps into the gaping maw.

He throws back his head and groans with pleasure as he feels something heave below his waist and his wife squeals in delight and their baby giggles and googoos and gurgles, and then closes its mouth and sighs as it drifts off to sleep, dreaming that it is a golden, sloping hill where a princess rides by on her horse to find a brave lover lying crushed upon the jagged rocks below.

John Wayne's Dream

Introduction by Mort Castle

And so we catch the latest horror on CNN or read about it in the Tribune or see the Facebook-filtered report as it becomes the springboard for keyboard philosophers.

The summary: It is senseless. There's no reason. What a world. Go figure ...

Uh-uh. There's always a reason. And so often the reason is a ghost, or ghosts, the ghosts uniquely our own but universal in their hauntingness, ghosts named Regret, Grief, Anger, Failure, or that legion of ghosts named Dead Dreams.

Those are the ghosts old Charles Dickens understood and wrote about so well, whether he metaphored them into Christmas Past, Christmas Future, or Christmas Unwrapped or just psychically attached them to Pip or Oliver—and, for that matter, Fagin.

And those are the ghosts not-so-old Gary Braunbeck knows so well and writes about so often: the soul ghosts. Those are the real specters discerned, but seldom fully exorcised, by psychology and not by a reality show nitwit with a Radioshack green screen stumbling around an allegedly haunted house in East Dipstick, Iowa.

Those are the spirits, their kith and kin, we find in Gary Braunbeck's enduring and insightful work. The late Jerry Williamson, the horror writer who was a mentor to Braunbeck (and to me and so many others!) maintained that any writer creating serious fiction should automatically be declared a psychiatrist or a minister—or both.

Here we have "John Wayne's Dream." We've got Carl Jung and William James and perhaps even a shot of Wayne Dyer and maybe the Dalai Lama, but above all, we have Gary Braunbeck doing what he does best: exploring fearlessly the wasteland that is mapped out in the GPS of the human soul.

John Wayne's Dream

"Music is the art which is most nigh to tears and memory."
—Oscar Wilde

"It (music) expresses that which cannot be said and on which it is impossible to remain silent."
—Victor Hugo

Man, it's bad tonight —sick, miserable, choke-on-this *ugly* —the worst it's ever been, worse even than when you were drying out in the hospital, and you *need* tonight's meeting before you decide to break the goddamn seal on the bottle stashed in the trunk of your car with those Other Things, Things you can't help but think of in upper case, that's how bad it is, it's so bad you can't bring yourself to name them, even silently to yourself, because *that* would mean the repellant thoughts and ugly pictures that are kicking so hard across your mind, these things you know damned well ought to turn your stomach but don't, not even a little (they've caused you to actually *smile* when you're alone and once even chuckle into your cold coffee), it means you're actually seriously no-shit-Sherlock *considering* it, and if you decide to do it the Things will make it so easy, easy, easy-peezy, so you *have* to think of those Things in upper case because to name them, to admit you *have* them *because* of the thoughts and pictures in your mind, *that's* what scares you right down to the marrow of the bones in this sad-ass body you've been walking around in for — what?—fifty-three years and however-many months and days, this sad-ass body that at least had enough willpower to drag itself down here to the church basement and the all-too familiar door halfway down the hall, the one you're standing in front of right now, so you take a deep breath, close your eyes, force the thoughts and pictures to the back of your mind, hoping they'll stay there, *God grant me the serenity to make it all fuck off*, and as you grasp the doorknob and begin turning it you see the piece of paper that's been hastily taped to the frosted glass—

AA Meeting Canceled

Tonight Only:
Ghosts Sing Sad Cowboy Song
for the Whole Broken World

—and you feel your jaw actually drop like the anvil-mouth of some cartoon character as you read the words a second time, hand still gripping the doorknob, but before you can react you hear it start from inside the room: *that song* ... and on a guitar, of course—a steel-faced dobro-style resonator, from the sound of it, just slightly out of tune, causing the melody to sound all the more distant and empty and hopeless; gritting your teeth, you pull your hand away from the doorknob and step back, as if moving two feet away will stop the sound from reaching you, but reach you it does, just as loud, just as cheerless, no goddamned different from any of the hundreds of times you've heard it played or played it yourself by request, by request, by request only because that's the only way anyone in their right mind *would* play the song, sure as hell not by choice, nosiree, like King Lear always said *never never Never Never NEVER*.

"Are you going in?" says a voice to your left.

She's younger than most of the people you've seen at the meetings; her face is round, its skin slightly pink beneath the surface, no tell-tale loopy blue lines of broken veins in her nose, no too-bright sheen in her eyes, no crow's feet, nothing to indicate that she shares your disease—hell, she looks like someone who should be playing the Julie Andrews part in *The Sound of Music*, not a recovering drunk.

"The, uh ... the meeting's been canceled," you say, not so much pointing at as absent-mindedly flipping a finger toward the makeshift sign.

"I know," she replies. "I'm here for the ghosts' concert. Isn't that why you're here, _____?"

She calls you by name. You have never seen this woman before. She's so fresh, so genuinely pretty, so clean—no, it's more than being clean, she seems ... absolutely unspoiled. You might have a small graveyard of brain cells relegated to the back plat of your grey matter, but you're not so far gone that you'd forget a face like hers.

She smiles and brushes past you, reaching down and turning the doorknob. She's pressed against your side, her hand almost touching yours, but doesn't seem the least shy or embarrassed by it.

"I always loved this song," Unspoiled says. "It's been one of my favorites for ... oh, I don't remember how long."

You just stare at her, not knowing a courteous way to respond. C, F, G, A-minor and D-minor; the whole goddamn song's based on various combinations and repetitions of those 5 chords —hell, the intro alone looks and *feels* like the most goddamn boring tune ever written —

/ C - - / G - - / Am - - / G - - /
/ C - - / F - - / C - - / G - - /
/ C - - / G - - / Am - - / G - - /
/ C - - / F - - / G - - / C - - / - - - /

—Snoozeville, right? Yet somehow those 5 basic, dreary, mind-numbing chords —chords you could teach a genetically-retarded monkey to play —mange to give body, soul, shame, and voice to the pain of the saddest songs ever ... and wouldn't you know, it was Dad's favorite?

Of course you know that, you know damn near everything about good old Dad, you know too goddamned much about good old Dad —Christ knows he talked enough during those last few days, lying there in his bed with a bedpan under his ass and a catheter running up into his urethra, trickling bloody urine into a plastic bag. Sometimes he'd give you a half-hearted smile, but he wasn't the same man, the one who used to berate, humiliate, and mock you, the man who could always find fault in everything you did, who knew just the right thing to say to make your accomplishments seem inconsequential in everyone's eyes including your own, who could diminish you with less effort than it took to pick his nose; no, this wasn't the same man at all. This was just a sick old bastard making a last-ditch effort to get his bad-tempered ass into heaven.

"Have you heard this song before?" asks Unspoiled, staring at you with a curious intensity that *goddammit* reminds you of good old

Dad toward the end.

You'd take him to the county cemetery where his parents and sister were buried, and as he sat there in his wheelchair staring at their headstones, you'd study his face and see him wondering if there was something that he'd missed, something that he could have done to spend a little more time with them, to save them from feeling alone and frightened during their last few days of life, maybe even wishing that one or all of them could still be here to comfort him and for a little while get his mind off the disease that was now counting the clock that told of the time he had left—you don't know, maybe he came here to study their graves the same way he'd study his own face in a mirror, naked and defenseless. *Why won't you look at me and Mom that way?* you'd wonder. *We have some time left—not much, but some—and maybe we could repair some things—okay, okay, okay, be realistic—if not* repair, *then at least spackle over some of the cracks so that when we drop the bag of meat that used to be you into the dirt we might feel some kind of loss instead of relief. Is that too much to ask at this point?*

"Did you know," says Unspoiled, "that this song has actually been around for centuries, in dozens—maybe even hundreds—of variations?"

You nod your head. "Actually, yeah ... I did know that." Because good old Dad, he'd told you about that dozens—maybe even hundreds—of times ... when he wasn't a zombie.

He'd sit for long hours in front of his bedroom window, staring out at the same neighborhood he'd known for most of his life, searching for something hidden, something unnoticed until now, something that would reveal whatever secrets there were to be revealed. Close by, Mom and you waited for him to complete this final voyage into himself, hoping the old emotional wounds might at last heal so that he would maybe maybe maybe pleaseGod just *once* turn and smile over his shoulder, telling the two of without the burden of words that he'd returned from this last nightmare, this final batch of self-recriminations that had made him a sadistic stranger to you for too long; and now, now that he was returned to you for however brief a time, you would go outside into the warm spring light, your mother and you each holding one of his hands, and you would thank the day for its blessings as it fell into twilight, and you would remain there, in shadows, as before, hands joined. *I don't even feel sick,* were among some of the last things he said, along with,

What I wouldn't give for a hamburger and cold beer right about now. And of all Final Requests, he asked you to get out your old guitar and play that fucking song for him because, he said, it helped him to relax, to breathe easier, to fall asleep the way a man ought to fall asleep—no drugs, nosiree; just a good, hard-working man falling asleep because the good, hard work took it out of him today. He would say that the Duke, the Duke never took to pills or liquor to fall asleep in his movies. The Duke was a Man, a Man's Man, and boy wouldn't it be nice to just once have the kind of dream that the Duke must've had when his head hit the pillow at night, the kind of dream only a strong, solid, all-American Man's Man dreamed? *Maybe I'll have it tonight,* he said to you that last night as you strummed those 5 horrible chords on that shabby guitar you'd bought second-hand from a pawn shop when you were twelve; *maybe tonight I'll dream John Wayne's dream.*

Part of you wanted to smash that guitar to pieces right there and then, go all Pete Townshend on the thing and scream *Don't you remember his last movie, Dad? The Duke, your Man's Man, was a goddamn walking corpse, being eaten away bit by bit from the bottom of his bowels by the same thing that's gobbling up your guts—fuck! He spent most of that movie fractured on Laudanum, that's how he went to sleep, but you don't remember that, do you? No—all you remember is that Jimmy Stewart told the Duke it was not the way he'd choose to go out, and that the Duke, your Man's Man, the great All-American Cowboy, he took Stewart's advice and went out in a blaze of glory, guns blasting away and bad guys dropping all around, blood and bodies littering the saloon floor, and you sure as hell aren't going out that way, are you, Dad?*

No, he sure as hell didn't. But that doesn't have to mean you'll go out the same way, his son who was such a private embarrassment to him; his son who never walked into the sunset with his best girl at his side; his son who never counted off twenty paces with a cheating gambler in the street and before whirling around and putting the scoundrel down with a quick, single, justified shot; his son who never rode high in the saddle or talked real slow and deliberate or strolled with the swagger of a Real Man who made decisions and stuck with them out there where the tumbleweeds blew across silent, dusty streets where the womenfolk and children could walk in safety once again, knowing it was Real Man who'd done what needed doing.

Hey, Dad, look at those bad guys fall. Look what I decided to do. Am I a

Man in your eyes now? Am I worthy to sleep the sleep of the Just, of the Heroic? Am I worthy to dream John Wayne's dream?

Unspoiled leans her head to the side a little and says your name again. "Are you all right?"

"I was hoping for, you know, the other meeting that was supposed to—"

She grabs your hand as she pushes the door open. "Oh, this will be *much better* than one of those dreary meetings. Those meetings are for *everyone*." She pulls you into the room. "This, tonight, is just for unfortunate rakes—just one, actually. This is just for you."

You stare at her, hoping her crazy won't explode and get all over you. "Imagine what that means to me." What the hell is *that* supposed to mean? You have no idea, but it's too late to take it back.

She laughs and pulls you into the room. It's mostly dark except for one bright circle of light shining down onto the middle of the floor; in the center of the circle is a folding chair. She leads you there, pushes you down, and kisses the top of your head.

"Now don't you move. We went through an awful lot of trouble to put this show together."

Before you say anything, she's gone—*snap!*—into the shadows. You stand up and walk back to the door, but it isn't there any longer. Okay, okay, okay—maybe you just lost your bearings, that has to be it, you're just a little confused because of Things in your trunk and the unbroken seal on the bottle and the thoughts and pictures in your head, that has to be it, you're just ... shit—you're probably just losing it, finally, just like everyone said you would someday. You stick out your arms and start feeling around the walls, doing your best Helen Keller to find the door because it *has* to be here someplace but after a minute or two you find nothing and you're even more confused than you were before you stood up, so you go back to the chair and you just sit because you don't know what else to do.

The sound of an old-fashioned projector clatters to life somewhere behind you, and your gaze follows the beam of light to the far wall where someone—Unspoiled, maybe?—has pulled down a screen, and you watch as a grainy black-and-white home movie comes into focus and shows you a scene that you damn well took place dozens of times in your youth but could not possibly have been filmed because your family never had the money to afford a home-movie camera.

You see a variation of yourself—so much younger but only a little stronger than the man he eventually became; he's standing in the corner of a room, head down, studying his feet as if expecting some great revelation to come thundering up from the earth's core and show him a Great Truth that will set his spirit free.

Sitting a few feet away in his favorite chair, good old Dad is pointing at the young man who would have to settle for becoming you; he's got a beer in his hand and a cigarette dangling from the corner of his mouth.

A conversation repeated so many times and with so few variations it has surpassed the realm of mantra and become the refrain of the inharmonious tune that has been and is your life.

"A man makes a decision and he sticks with it, boy."

"Yessir."

"A man *does what he says he'll do*. No more, no less."

"Yessir."

"How old are you now?"

Christ, you really didn't *remember, did you?* you think now. "Twenty-three, sir."

"Twenty-three, and what have you got to show for it?"

A decent-enough music career—playing clubs, upscale restaurants, sometime getting enough put aside for some studio time, a couple of self-produced albums selling okay for digital download on some minor music sites. Friends. A place of my own. "I think I've got a lot to show for it."

"You ain't famous, now, are you? I mean, what's the point of doing what you do if all you're gonna settle for is being small-time? A big fish in a little pond?"

"I like my life."

"You're *weak*, boy. A real man, when he makes a decision to do something, he *does* it. Your problem is you never decided to be anything more than second-rate because you ain't got the guts to be a real man and decide to be something more."

Why didn't you just say you were ashamed of me? I could've worked with that. "I thought you'd be pleased that I make a decent living at something I love to do."

"Don't talk to me about doing something you love. Doing something you love don't get you shit in the long run. It just makes you weak, makes you a fellah who's happy to *settle* for something. Hell, the Duke never settled in any of his movies. I thought you'd learn something from you and me watching all his movies when you was a kid. The Duke's movies, they taught good lessons. Taught you how to be a man."

Still looking down at the floor, waiting for revelations to thunder. "Because when he made a decision he always stuck with it."

"Goddamn *right* he stuck with it. Duke always went out a winner, a hero, a man you could respect. Because he knew, the Duke did. A real man, he makes a decision and sticks with it."

"Yessir."

"Does what he says he'll do, no more, no less."

"Yessir."

The film finishes, the light goes out, and the projector shuts off. Deep down in your bowels, you feel the need churning. Leave. Open the bottle. Do it. Take the Things and just do it. Don't go out like good old dad. Don't go out like the Duke. Christ, it *hurts!* If someone had jammed a knife-blade entwined with barbed-wire into your stomach and twisted it, it wouldn't hurt as much as this need.

"Goddammit," you whisper to yourself. "I want a drink. I want a drink. Just one. One drink. That's all."

The unseen guitar begins playing again, the same 5 chords, and each chord snarls into your head and your balls like a diamond-tipped drill. You want to get up and get the hell out of the room — and if you can't find the door, you'll *beat* a goddamn hole into the wall with your bare fists (*just like the Duke would do,* comes the echo of a voice that sounds like your own), you'll kick and claw and *chew* your way out if you have to, you'll —

— Unspoiled appears as the screen is raised up. She's sitting on a stage several feet off the floor. Her body is all wrapped up in a white sheet of some kind, its material thicker than something made from cotton; it looks almost like a tarp. Only her face and one hand are visible.

The music from the guitar fills the room, a sentient force, and as you look into Unspoiled's eyes you can feel her grief, even from this distance. She smiles at you, a smile that bespeaks an errant wish — that a young woman might never grow old, never lose the radiance that kissed her face when a suitor came to call, never see her beauty dissolve little by little in the unflattering sunlight of each morning, and never know a day when the scent of fresh roses from an admirer did not fill her rooms; as she begins to sing, you stare into her eyes,

eyes with sad dark places around them that tell you she has often hid behind a scrim of gaiety to conceal a lonely heart, and both she and her song become every night you've sat isolated and alone, wishing for the warm hand of a lover to hold in your own as autumn dimmed into winter and youth turned to look at you over its shoulder and smile farewell.

> "When I was a young girl, I used to seek pleasure
> When I was a young girl, I used to drink ale.
> Right out of an alehouse down into the jailhouse,
> Right out of the barroom down to my grave."

As she sings other forms move forward from the shadows; a knight in the remains of ruined armor, his sword in one hand, his bent and twisted visor in the other; behind him comes a cowboy, classic and tall, spurs jangling with each step, holding his stained and tattered hat in wind-burnt hands; an older woman dressed in mourning black; a group of soldiers in uniforms crisp and funereal, carrying the shroud-covered form of a fallen comrade; the words each of them sing are different but the melody—the morbid, heartsick, soul-beaten melody—remains the same; it doesn't matter if Unspoiled is singing of one morning in May or the soldiers are singing of Saint James' Hospital or if the knight sings of the maiden fair who passed on her physical ruin to him under the guise of love; it doesn't matter a damn if it's a cowboy dying in the street or a young woman perishing alone in the countryside; it doesn't matter if it's a soldier who got a dose from a passing lady of the night or a mother discovering her prodigal daughter by the side of the road; it doesn't matter how the words are changed or the rhythm is ever-so-slightly altered or even if the words are in English, it doesn't matter if it's a bad girl's lament or a sorrowful young girl cut down in her prime or if she's riding on horseback or the man is a soldier loyal and true or the cowboy knows that he's done wrong and so must pay penance; it doesn't matter if the pipes and fifes play or if anyone bangs the drum slowly; all of them eventually arrive at the same place: *Send for the preacher to come and pray for me/Send for the doctor to heal up my wounds/For my poor head is achin'/my sad heart is breakin/My body's salivated and I know I must die/Hell is my fate/I'm a-feared I must die/There goes an unfortunate lad to his home/I'm shot in the breast and I'm dyin' today/All gone to the round-up/The Cowboy was dead/For I know I must die/die/die/die/die* ....

The lights snap to black and the figures on the stage are gone, as is the music. The ghosts have sang their ballad, they have revealed the truth that a young man once, while staring at the floor, wished would thunder up from the core of the world and set his spirit free.

You feel a hand on your shoulder, and look up into Unspoiled's dimming eyes.

"Do you understand now?" she asks.

"It doesn't matter," you say. "It doesn't matter if your intentions were good. It doesn't matter if your heart was true. It doesn't matter if you understood right from wrong."

"Yes ..." Her voice is filled with bliss.

"It doesn't matter if you loved well or not, if you kept that love or lost it, it doesn't matter. You—all of you—all of *us*—the whole goddamned broken world—it doesn't matter, because we can't help but be what we are, and what we are, in one way or another, will end us before we're ready, before we can be forgiven, before we can feel worthy of the life that is inside and around us."

"*Yes* ..." Her voice is now Bliss itself.

"None of us will ever measure up," you say, rising to your feet, feeling tall and proud and strong. You smile at her, running your rough hands through the curls of her hair.

"Am I your best gal?" she asks.

"Always by my side."

"It's hard, to be a man."

"To be a man means you make a decision and stick with it." When had you left the building and gotten back into your car? When had you driven here, to this restaurant/bar full of people who have no idea that it all means nothing?

You raise the bottle to your lips and drink deeply of the whiskey, just the Duke would, whether or not the streets of Laredo waited outside the saloon doors or not. The bad guys were everywhere and always would be.

Hey, Mom, Hey, Dad, look at me standing proud.

You climb down off your horse and pull the Things from the saddlebag. You rack a round into the shotgun, and chamber rounds into the four pistols. No hesitation, no doubts.

For I am a lonely cowboy, and I know I've done wrong ...

Jimmy Stewart told the Duke he wouldn't want to go out that way, and the Duke didn't, but good old Dad couldn't lay claim to a blaze of glory at the end, could he? No, he couldn't.

But you can.

You can be a Man; a Man's Man who doesn't make his mark with guitar strings and meaningless words in best-forgotten songs.

Time to be a Man.

You push open the doors to the saloon.

Hey, Dad—look at the bad guys fall!

As you walk and talk real slow, just home from the prairie green, tall and proud as the villains and scoundrels perish, tall and proud like a man ought, tall and proud, with guns blazing, the soft light of home beckoning welcome, welcome home, home at last, home in John Wayne's dream.

The Ballad of the Side-Street Wizard

Introduction by Lucy Snyder

"The Ballad of the Side-Street Wizard" displays classic Braunbeck styles and themes. A fast read reveals snappy, witty dialogue worthy of classic 1950-era live television. But beneath the story's witty veneer, there's deep melancholy and a sense of profound existential loneliness that would drive any protagonist to madness (as has happened to our hero Myrddin.) Madness, sadness, and magic: in this tale there be monsters, the kind even a brave man cannot slay.

The Ballad of the Side-Street Wizard

or

Those Low-Down, Dirty, Eternally Depressing, and
Somewhat Shameful Post-Arthurian Dipshit Blues

"Myrddin," he says to his own image in the mirror over the bathroom sink (wondering if he should pronounce it as *Merlin*, seeing as how that's the name he's remembered by...if, indeed, he is who he thinks he is, damn that pre-Tennyson, -T.H. White, and -Lewis scribe Geoffrey of Monmouth for muddying the psychological waters): "She loves you not, oh, she doesn't, you poor fool."

He's put the makeup on, packed the bag of tricks — including the rabbit that he calls Artie, and the bird, the attention getter, that he calls Gwenn. He's to do a birthday party for some five-year-old on the other side of the river. A crowd of babies, and the adults waiting around for him to screw up. This is going to be one of those tough ones. He has fortified himself with some generous helpings of Crown Royal, and he feels ready.

He isn't particularly worried about it.

But there's a little something else he has to do first.

Something in the order of the embarrassingly ridiculous: he has to make a delivery. This morning at the local bakery he picked up a big pink wedding cake, with its six tiers and scalloped edges and its miniature bride and groom on top, standing inside a sugar castle. He'd ordered it on his own; he'd taken the initiative, planning to offer it to a young woman he worked with. He managed somehow to set the thing on the back seat of the car, and when he got home he found a note from her announcing, excited and happy, that she's engaged. The man she'd had such difficulty with has had a change of heart; he wants to get married after all. She's going off to Cincinnati to live. She loves her dear old ? with a big kiss and a hug always, and she knows he'll have every happiness. She's so thankful for his friendship. Her magic man. Her sweet sidestreet wizard. She actually drove over here and, finding him gone, left the note for him, folded under the door knocker; her notepaper with the tangle of flowers at the top. She wants him to call her, come by as soon as he can, to help celebrate. *Please*, she says: *I want to give you a big hug.*

He read this and then walked out to stand on the sidewalk and look at the cake in its place on the back seat of the car.

"Good God," he said.

Then thought: *I'm not supposed to be here, not like this, am I? Wasn't I the wizard above all wizards once, the magic man against whom all others must compare?*

Sometimes in sleep, other times during waking hours, he has flashes of memories, centuries-old, of a great, mythical kingdom, and of his place there; he remembers glory and enemies and a spell cast upon him, causing him to sleep, and now that he's awake he's living...backward somehow. That's right, isn't it?

He's old, and most times he forgets.

He remembers the cake in the back of his car.

He'd thought he would deliver the cake in person, an elaborate proposal to a girl he's never even kissed. He's a little unbalanced, and he knows it. Over the months of their working together at the Lazarus department store, he's built up tremendous feelings of loyalty and yearning towards her. He thought she felt it, too. He interpreted gestures—her hand lingering on his shoulder when he made her laugh; her endearments tinged as they seemed to be with a kind of sadness, as if she were afraid of what the world might do to someone so romantic—as something more than, as it turns out, they actually were.

In the olden days—providing those weren't just a fantasy concocted by a failing mind—he'd simply have waved his hands and set the universe right and have her fall hopelessly in love with him.

She talked to him about her ongoing sorrows, the guy she'd been in love with who kept waffling about getting married. He wanted no commitments. Myrddin, a.k.a. Buster Francis, told her that he hated men who weren't willing to run the risks of love. Why, he personally was the type who'd always believed in marriage and children, lifelong commitments—*eternity-long* commitments. He had caused difficulties for himself, and life in this part of time was a disappointment so far, but he believed in falling in love and starting a family. She didn't hear him. It all went right through her, like white noise on the radio. For weeks he had come around to visit her, had invited her to watch him perform. She confided in him, and he thought of movies where the friend sticks around and is a good listener, and eventually gets the girl. They fall in love. He put his hope in that. He was optimistic; he'd ordered and bought the cake. Apparently the whole time, all through the listening and being noble with her, she thought of it as nothing more than friendship, accepting it from him because she was accustomed to being offered friendship.

Now he leans close to the mirror to look at his own eyes through the makeup. They look clear enough. "Loves you absolutely not. You must be crazy. A loon. A threat to society. A potential man-in-tower-with-rifle. Not-quite-right, even. You must be the Great Myrddin."

Yes.

With a great oversized cake in the back seat of his car. It's Sunday, a cool April day. He's a little inebriated. That's the word he prefers. It's polite; it suggests something faintly silly. Nothing could be sillier than to be dressed in a pointed wizard's cap and star-covered robe in broad daylight and to go driving across the bridge into the more upscale section of Cedar Hill to put on a magic show. Nothing could be sillier than to have spent all that money on a completely useless purchase—a cake six tiers high. Maybe fifteen pounds of sugar.

When he has made his last inspection of the face in the mirror, and checked the bag of tricks and props, he goes to his front door and looks through the screen at the architectural shadow of the cake in the back seat. Inside the car will smell like icing for days. He'll have to keep the windows open even if it rains; he'll go to work smelling like confectionery delights. The whole thing makes him laugh. A wedding cake. He steps out of the house and makes his way in the late afternoon sun down the sidewalk to the car. As if they have been waiting for him, three boys come skating down from the top of the hill. He has the feeling that if he tried to sneak out like this at two in the morning, someone would come by and see him anyway. "Hey, Buster," one boy says. "I mean, Myrddin."

Myrddin recognizes him. A neighborhood boy, tough. Just the kind to make trouble, just the kind with no sensitivity to the suffering of others. "Leave me alone or I'll turn you into spaghetti," he says.

"Hey guys, it's Myrddin the You-Could-Do-Worse." The boy's hair is a bright blond color, and you can see through it to his scalp.

"Scram," Myrddin says. "Sincerely."

"Aw, what's your hurry?"

"I've just set off a nuclear device," Myrddin says with grave seriousness. "It's on a timer. The time for the Great Revolution is nigh. A few more minutes and—*Poof*."

"Do a trick for us," the blond one says. "Where's that scurvy rabbit of yours?"

"I gave it the week off." Someone, last winter, poisoned the first Mordred (which somehow seemed like misdirected justice to him, for reasons he never quite managed to fathom). He keeps the cage indoors now. "I'm in a hurry. No rabbit to help with the driving. Elwood Dowd wouldn't let me borrow Harvey for the day."

"Huh?" says the boy.

"Your lack of culture depresses me."

But they're interested in the cake now. "Hey, what's that in your car? Jesus, is that real?"

"Just stay back." Myrddin gets his cases into the trunk and hurries to the driver's side door. The three boys are peering into the back seat.

"Hey man, a cake. Can we have a piece of it?"

"Back off before I zap you all into newts," Myrddin says.

The blond-haired one says, "Come on, Myrddin."

"Hey, Myrddin, I saw some guys looking for you, man. They said you owed them money."

He gets in, ignoring them, and starts the car.

"Sucker," one of them says.

"Hey man, who's the cake for?"

He drives away, thinks of himself leaving them in a cloud of exhaust. Riding through the green shade, he glances in the rear-view mirror and sees the clown face, the painted smile. It makes him want to laugh. He tells himself he's his own cliché—a magic man with a broken heart. Looming behind him is the cake, like a passenger in the back seat. The people in the cake store had offered it to him in a box; he had made them give it to him like this, on a cardboard slab. It looks like it might melt.

He drives slow, worried that it might sag, or even fall over. He has always believed viscerally that gestures mean everything. When he moves his hands and brings about the effects that amaze little children, he feels larger than life, unforgettable. He learned the magic while in high school, as a way of making friends, and though it didn't really make him any friends, he's been practicing it ever since. It's an extra source of income, and lately income has had a way of disappearing too quickly. He's been in some travail, betting the horses, betting the sports events. He's hung over all the time. There have been several polite warnings at work. He's managed so far to tease everyone out of the serious looks, the cool study of his face. The fact is, people like him in an abstract way, the way they like distant clownish figures: the comedian whose name they can't remember. He can see it in their eyes. Even the rough characters after his loose change have a certain sense of humor about it.

He's a phenomenon, a subject of conversation.

There's traffic on the East Main Street Bridge, and he's stuck for a while. It becomes clear that he'll have to go straight to the birthday party. Sitting behind the wheel of the car with his cake behind him, he becomes aware of people in other cars noticing him. In the car to his left, a girl stares, chewing gum. She waves, rolls her window down. Two others are with her, one in the back seat. "Hey," she says. He nods, smiles inside what he knows is the glorious-wizard smile.

"Where's the party?" she says.

But the traffic moves again. He concentrates. The snarl is on the other side of the bridge, construction of some kind. He can see the cars in a line, waiting to go up the hill into Morgan Manor Estates and beyond. Time is beginning to be a consideration. In his glove box he has a flask of Crown Royal. More fortification. He reaches over and takes it out, looks around himself. No fuzz anywhere. Just the idling cars and people tuning their radios or arguing or simply staring out as if at some distressing event. The smell of the cake is making him woozy. He takes a swallow of the bourbon, then puts it away. The car with the girls in it goes by in the left lane, and they are not even looking at him. He watches them go on ahead. He's in the wrong lane again; he can't remember a time when his lane was the only one moving. He told her once that he considered himself of the race of people who gravitate to the non-moving lanes of highways, and who cause green lights to turn to yellow merely by approaching them. She took the idea and ran with it, saying she was of the race of people who emit enzymes which instill a sense of impending doom in marriageable young men.

"No," Myrddin/Buster said. "I'm living proof that isn't so. I have no such fear, and I'm with you."

"But you're of the race of people who make mine relax all the enzymes.

"You're not emitting the enzymes now. I see."

"No," she said. "It's only with marriageable young men."

"I emit enzymes that prevent people like you from seeing that I'm a marriageable young man."

"I'm too relaxed to tell," she said, and touched his shoulder. A plain affectionate moment that gave him tossing nights and fever and an embarrassingly protracted stiffy. A virtual political uprising in his pants.

Because of the traffic, he's late to the birthday party. He gets out of the car and two men come down to greet him. He keeps his face turned away, remembering too late the breath mints in his pocket.

"Hey," one of the men says, "look at this. Hey, who comes out of the cake? This is a kid's birthday party."

"The cake stays," Myrddin says.

"What does he mean, it stays? Is that a trick?"

They're both looking at him. The one spoken to must be the birthday boy's father—he's wearing a party cap that says **DAD**. How original—or perhaps he's like Myrddin, has a tendency to forget who he really is and the cap in simply the family's way to remind him when they're not around. Myrddin hopes there are plenty of mirrors in the house if that's the case or **DAD** could be in deep sewage. The man has long, dirty-looking strands of brown hair jutting out from the cap, and there are streaks of sweaty grit on the sides of his face. "So you're the Somewhat Impressive Myrddin," he says, extending a meaty red hand. "Isn't it hot in that outfit?"

"No, sir."

"We've been playing volleyball."

"You've exerted yourselves. Perspiration can get in the way of an odor-free show. You all must shower at once, lest I turn you into road-kill."

They look at him. "What do you do with the cake?" the one in the **DAD** cap asks.

"Cake's not part of the show, actually."

"You just carry it around with you?"

The other man laughs. He's wearing a T-shirt with a smiley face on the chest. "This ought to be some show," he says.

They all make their way across the lawn, to the porch of the house. It's a big party, activities everywhere and children gathering quickly to see the wizard.

"Ladies and gentlemen," says the man in the **DAD** cap. "I give you Myrddin the Not-So-Terrible."

Myrddin isn't ready yet. He's got his cases open but he needs a table to put everything on. The first trick is where he releases the bird; he'll finish with the best trick, in which the rabbit appears as if from a pan of flames. This always draws a gasp, even from the adults: the fire blooms in the pan, down goes the "lid" — it's the rabbit's tight container — the latch is tripped, and the skin of the lid lifts off. *Voila!* Rabbit. The fire is put out by the fireproof cage bottom. He's gotten pretty good at making the switch, and if the crowd isn't too attentive — as children often are not — he can perform certain sleight-of-hand tricks with some style. But he needs a table, and he needs time to set up.

The whole crowd of children is seated in front of their parents, on either side of the doorway into the house. Myrddin is standing on the porch, his back to the stairs, and he's been introduced.

"Hello, boys and girls," he says, and bows. "Myrddin needs a table."

"A table," one of the women says, proving that all the family must share the same awesome genetic intelligence. The adults simply regard him. He sees light sweaters, shapely hips, and wild dresses; he sees beer cans in tight fists, heavy jowls, bright ice-blue eyes. A little row of faces, and one elderly face. He feels more inebriated than he likes, and tries to concentrate.

"Mommy, I want to touch him," one child says.

"Look at the cake," says another, who gets up and moves to the railing on Myrddin's right and trains a new pair of shiny binoculars on the car. "Do we get some cake?"

"There's cake," says the man in the **DAD** cap. "But not that cake. Get down, Ethan."

"I want that cake."

"Get down. This is Teddy's birthday."

"Mommy, I want to touch him."

"I need a table, folks. I told somebody that over the telephone."

"He did say he needed a table. I'm sorry," says a woman who is probably the birthday boy's mother. She's quite pretty, leaning in the door frame with a sweater tied to her waist.

"A table," says still another woman. Is there no end to the brilliant think-tank of people assembled here? Myrddin sees the birthmark on her mouth, which looks like a stain. He thinks of this woman as a child in school, with this difference from other children, and his heart goes out to her.

"I need a table," he says to her, his voice as gentle as he can make it. She doesn't notice the little wave-like gesture he makes with his hand. It probably won't be until much later, when she's washing her face before bed, that she'll notice the birthmark is gone and her face is clear-skinned and lovely.

"What's he going to do, perform an operation?" says **DAD**.

DAD is beginning to annoy. Sincerely.

It amazes Myrddin how easily people fall into talking about him as though he were an inanimate object or something on a television screen. "The Impressive Myrddin can do nothing until he gets a table," he says with as much mysteriousness and drama as he can muster under the circumstances. Then he belches and the children laugh. He tastes Crown Royal in his mouth and wonders once again if there isn't something he's missing, some sign to prove he's really a magic man, a true wizard, out of time and out of place.

"I want that cake out there," says Ethan, still at the porch railing and pointing at the magic man's car. The other children start talking about cake and ice cream, and the big cake Ethan has spotted; there's a lot of confusion and restlessness. One of the smaller children, a girl in a blue dress, approaches Myrddin. "What's your name?" she says, swaying slightly, her hands behind her back.

"Jeffrey Dahmer. And I've not had my lunch. Now go sit down. We have to sit down or Myrddin can't do his magic."

In the doorway, two of the men are struggling with a folding card table. It's one of those rickety ones with the skinny legs, and it probably won't do.

"That's kind of shaky, isn't it?" says the woman who until recently had the birthmark.

"I said, Myrddin needs a *sturdy* table, boys and girls." Mensa could more than fill its membership roster here.

There's more confusion. The little girl has come forward and taken hold of his pant leg.

She's just standing there holding it, looking up at him. "*Jeffrey*," she says, somewhat sadly, as if there is some secret, precious request she wishes to make but is afraid to give voice to.

"We have to go sit down," Myrddin says, bending to her, speaking sweetly. "We have to do what Myrddin wants."

Her small mouth opens wide, as if she's trying to yawn, and with pale eyes quite calm and staring she emits a screech, an ear-piercing, non-human shriek that brings everything to a stop. Myrddin/Buster steps back, with his amazement and his inebriate heart. Everyone gathers around the girl, who continues to scream, less piercing now, her hands fisted at her sides, those pale eyes closed tight.

"What happened?" the man in the **DAD** cap wants to know. "Where the hell's the magic tricks?"

"I told you, all I needed is a table."

"What'd you say to her to make her cry?" **DAD** indicates the little girl, who is giving forth a series of broken, grief-stricken howls.

"I want magic tricks," the birthday boy says, loud. "Where's the magic tricks?"

"Perhaps if we moved the whole thing inside," the woman without a birthmark says, fingering her left ear and making a face.

Use a Q-Tip, Myrddin thinks.

The card table has somehow made its way to him, through the confusion and grief. **DAD** sets it down and opens it.

"There," he says proudly, as if he has just split the atom.

In the next moment, Myrddin realizes that someone's removed the little girl. Everything's relatively quiet again, though her cries are coming through the walls of one of the rooms inside the house. There are perhaps fifteen children, mostly seated before him, and five or six men and women behind them, or kneeling with them.

"OK, now," **DAD** says. "Myrddin the Somewhat Terrific."

"Hello, little boys and girls," Myrddin says, deciding that the table will have to suffice. "I'm happy to be here. Are you glad to see me?" A general uproar commences.

"Well, good," he says. "Because just look what I have in my magic bag." And with a flourish he brings out the hat that he will release LeFey from. The bird is encased in a fold of shiny cloth, pulsing there. He can feel it. He rambles on, talking fast, or trying to, and when the time comes to reveal the bird, he almost flubs it. But Witch flaps his wings and makes enough of a commotion to distract even the adults, who applaud and urge the stunned children to applaud. "Isn't that wonderful," Myrddin hears. "Out of nowhere."

"He had it hidden away," says the birthday boy, who has managed to temper his astonishment. He's the type who heaps scorn on those things he can't understand, or own.

"Now," Myrddin says, "for my next spell, I need a helper from the audience." He looks right at the birthday boy —round face, short nose, freckles. Bright red hair. Little green eyes. The whole countenance speaks of glutted appetites and sloth. This kid could be on the Roman coins, an emperor. Like Caligula without the whimsical wit. He's not used to being compelled to do anything, but he seems eager for a chance to get into the act. "How about you," Myrddin says to him.

The others, led by their parents, cheer.

The birthday boy gets to his feet and makes his way over the bodies of the other children to stand with Myrddin. In order for the trick to work, Myrddin must get everyone watching the birthday boy, and there's another star-covered, pointed hat he keeps in the bag for this purpose.

"Now," he says to the boy, "since you're part of the show, you have to wear a costume." He produces the hat as if from behind the boy's ear. Another cheer goes up. He puts the hat on the boy's head and adjusts it, crouching down. The green eyes stare impassively at him; there's no hint of awe or fascination in them. "There we are," he says. "What a handsome, mysterious-looking fellow you are."

The birthday boy takes off the hat and looks at it as if a large, mythical bird has just dropped a large, mythical turd on his head.

Myrddin takes a deep breath. "We have to wear the hat to be onstage."

"Ain't a stage," the boy says.

Definitely an Einsteinian brain-trust here.

"But," Myrddin says for the benefit of the adults. "Didn't you know that all the world's a stage?" He tries to put the hat on him again, but the boy moves from under his reach and slaps his hand away. "We have to wear the hat," Myrddin says, trying to control his anger. "We can't do the magic without our magic hats." He tries once more, and the boy waits until the hat is on, then simply removes it and holds it behind him, shying away when Myrddin tries to retrieve it. The noise of the others now sounds like the crowd at a prizefight; there's a contest going on, and they're enjoying it. "Give Myrddin the hat. We want magic, don't we?"

"Do the magic," the boy demands.

"Give me the hat."

"I won't."

Sometimes life for Myrddin is just too fun to endure.

He looks around. There's no support from the adults. Perhaps if he weren't a little tipsy; perhaps if he didn't feel ridiculous and sick at heart and forlorn, with his wedding cake and his odd mistaken romance, his loneliness, which he has always borne gracefully and with humor, and his general dismay; perhaps if he were to find it in himself to deny the sudden, overwhelming sense of the unearned affection given this lumpish, slovenly version of stupid complacent spoiled satiation standing before him — he might've simply gone on to the next trick.

Instead, at precisely that moment when everyone seems to pause, he leans down and says, "Give me the hat, you little prick."

The green eyes widen.

The quiet is heavy with disbelief. Even the small children can tell that something's happened to change everything.

"Myrddin has another trick," Buster says, loud, "where he makes the birthday boy expand like an ugly pimple and then pop like a balloon. It's especially fun if he's a *fat* birthday boy."

A stirring among the adults.

"Especially if he's an ugly, offensive, grotesque slab of superfluous flesh like this one here."

"Now just a minute," says **DAD**.

"Give it up, you irritating post-Arthurian dipshit," Rodney says to the birthday boy, who drops the hat and then, seeming to remember that defiance is expected, makes a face. Sticks out his tongue.

Myrddin is quick with his hands by training, and he grabs the tongue.

"*Awwwk*," the boy says. "Aw-aw-aw."

"Abracadabra." Rodney lets go and the boy falls backward onto the lap of one of the other children. More cries. "Whoops, time to sit down," says Myrddin/Buster. "Sorry you had to leave so soon."

Very quickly, he's being forcibly removed. They're rougher than gangsters. They lift him, punch him, tear at his costume — even the women. Someone hits him with a spoon. The whole scene boils over onto the lawn, where someone has released Mordred from his case. He moves about wide-eyed, hopping between running children, evading them, as Myrddin the Befuddled and Put-Upon cannot evade the adults. He's being pummeled because he keeps trying to return for his rabbit. And the adults won't let him off the curb. "Okay," he says finally, collecting himself. He wants to let them know he's not like this all the time; wants to say it's circumstances, grief, personal pain hidden inside seeming brightness and cleverness. He's a man in love, humiliated, wrong about everything. He wants to tell them, but he can't speak for a moment, can't even quite catch his breath. He stands in the middle of the street, his ancient robe torn, his face bleeding, all his magic strewn everywhere. "I would at least like to collect my rabbit," he says, and is appalled at the absurd sound of it — its huge difference from what he intended to say. He straightens, pushes the grime from his face, adjusts the clown nose, and looks at them. "I would say that even though I wasn't as patient as I could've been, the adults have not comported themselves well here," he says.

"Drunk," one of the women says.

Almost everyone's chasing Mordred now. One of the older boys approaches, carrying LeFey's case. LeFey looks out the air hole, impervious, quiet as a bad idea. And now one of the men, someone Myrddin hasn't noticed before, an older man clearly wearing a hairpiece, brings Mordred to him. "Bless you," Myrddin says, staring into the man's sleepy, deploring eyes.

"I don't think we'll pay you," the man says. The others are filing back into the house, herding the children before them.

Myrddin/Buster speaks to the man. 'The rabbit appears out of fire. By the way, have I mentioned that I don't really belong here? I'm out of place, out of time—you know, in the midst of a Billy Pilgrim: Unstuck. *Po-tweet*'"

The man nods. "Go home and sleep it off, asshole."

"Right. Thank you. Compliments are always appreciated." He makes another unseen wave with his hand and changes the large letters of **DAD** to smaller letters that say: **I AM A CONVICTED PORNOGRAPHER. IN CASE OF NUDITY, PLEASE LOAN ME A CAMERA.**

He puts Mordred in his compartment, stuffs everything in its place in the trunk. Then he gets in the car and drives away. Around the corner he stops, wipes off what he can of the makeup; it's as if he's trying to remove the stain of bad opinion and disapproval. Nothing feels any different. He drives to the suburban street where she lives with her parents, and by the time he gets there it's almost dark.

The houses are set back in the trees. He sees lighted windows, hears music, the sound of children playing in the yards. He parks the car and gets out. A breezy April dusk. "I am Myrddin the Soft-Hearted," he says. "Hearken to me." Then he sobs. He can't believe it. "Jeez," he says, "I'm a bit pathetic today, aren't I?"

He opens the back door of the car, leans in to get the cake. He'd forgot how heavy it is. Staggering with it, making his way along the sidewalk, intending to leave it on her doorstep, he has an inspiration. Hesitating only for the moment it takes to make sure there are no cars coming, he goes out and sets it down in the middle of the street. Part of the top sags from having bumped his shoulder as he pulled it off the back seat. The bride and groom are almost supine, one on top of the other —a precursor of pleasures yet to come. He straightens them, steps back and looks at it. In the dusky light it looks blue. It sags just right, with just the right angle expressing disappointment and sorrow. Yes, he thinks. This is the place for it. The aptness of it, sitting out like this, where anyone might come by and splatter it all over creation, makes him feel a faint sense of release, as if he were at the end of a story. Everything will be all right if he can think of it that way. He's wiping his eyes, thinking of moving to another town. Failures are beginning to catch up to him, and he's still achingly in love. He thinks how he has suffered the pangs of failure and misadventure, but in this painful instance there's symmetry, and he will make the one eloquent gesture—leaving a wedding cake in the middle of the road, like a pylon made of icing. Yes.

He walks back to the car, gets in, pulls around, and backs into the driveway of the house across the street from hers. Leaving the engine idling, he rolls the window down and rests his arm on the sill, gazing at the incongruous shape of the cake there in the falling dark. He feels almost glad —almost, in some strange inexpressible way, vindicated. He imagines what she might do if she saw him here, imagines that she comes running from her house, calling his name, looking at the cake and admiring it. He conjures a picture of her, attacking the tiers of pink sugar, and the muscles of his abdomen tighten. But then this all gives way to something else: images of destruction, of flying dollops of icing. He's surprised to find that he wants her to stay where she is, doing whatever she's doing. He realizes that what he wants —and for the moment all he really wants—is what he now has: a perfect vantage point from which to watch oncoming cars. Turning the engine off, he makes another imperceptible wave with his hand. The cake is now the size of a castle, taking up all of the center of the street and several feet of surrounding yards.

"Indeed, I shall dub thee *Carmelot*."

Not a great joke, but it makes him laugh, sitting there in his quiet car. And so he waits, concentrating on the giant castle-cake and the brouhaha that will undoubtedly ensue once someone notices it. He's a

We Now Pause for Station Identification

Introduction by Jonathan Maberry

This is about Gary Braunbeck...so let me talk about me for a minute.

I'll get to the Gary stuff. Bear with me.

I'm a horror guy. Always been, even before I started writing it.

When I was a kid I had a wonderfully spooky grandmother. She was two or three years older than God. Basically a collection of mobile wrinkles in the shape of an old lady. Kind of weird. Kind of like Luna Lovegood from the Harry Potter books as a ninety-year old. Had a pet crow, read tarot cards, like that. She knew stuff, too. She knew about the things that go bump in the dark, and she delighted in telling me all about them. Mind you, this stuff totally freaked my sisters out. They thought she was weird in all the wrong ways. I loved her. She knew the cool stuff. The stuff I wanted to hear. She told me about the things people believed in the places she lived as a girl. Alsace-Lorraine, on the border of France and Germany. And rural Scotland. She was forty when she gave birth to my mother, and my mother was forty-one when she had me, a change-of-life baby. I was born in 1958, so that meant my grandmother was born in 1877.

Yeah.

She died twenty-three days after her hundred-and-first birthday.

She knew the *old* stuff. The legends of vampires and werewolves, ghouls and witches, imps and goblins. She was a living encyclopedia of darkness. And she encouraged me to read about it and know it.

When I was seven years old I started watching monster movies. The old Universal and RKO stuff and the newer Hammer flicks. I was sold. And my older brother had a huge stack of EC comics from the fifties.

When I was ten years old my best friend and I snuck into the Midway Theater, a cavernous old Art Deco theater that had seen better decades. It was crumbling and unsafe and spooky and wonderful. On October 2, 1968 we were hiding in the balcony —which had been officially closed and condemned as unsafe—to watch the world premiere of *Night of the Living Dead*.

When I was thirteen my middle school librarian introduced me to a couple of writers she knew. Richard Matheson and Ray Bradbury.

So, yeah. That was my childhood.

I grew up in a world of monsters.

As I went from preteen to tween to teenager I made the switch from mostly watching movies and reading horror comics to reading prose. First it was Shirley Jackson's glorious *The Haunting of Hill House*, then I moved onto *Something Wicked This Way Comes, I Am Legend, Dracula, Carmilla*...

If you read enough horror you first become familiar with the tropes. Then you become a little jaded. Then, if you read a lot, you can start to burn out.

That happened to me. I read every damn horror novel and short story I could get my hands on. All through the seventies, eighties, nineties and oughts. I will admit to becoming a bit blasé after a while. There are only so many times a person can be scared. Only so many times a reader can be jolted. Only a limited number of times something can come at you from the blind side.

Or so I thought.

Then I read my first story by Gary A. Braunbeck. Actually I read a bunch of them. I was in a dark place in my life. Good friends had died in faraway places. I divorced my first wife. Life felt bleak. I searched for something edgy and intense to make me feel something, to sharpen the emotions that had become blunted through pain and grief. Yeah, I read horror as therapy.

A bookseller—also now dead, from a bookstore now gone—suggested a collection of creepy tales called *Things Left Behind*. Stories by a writer I'd never heard of. Usually that's a "Danger, Will Robinson" moment. But I bought the book and took it with me on a long, sad walk in Wissahickon Park in Philadelphia. I found a quiet bench under a big oak and settled down with the intention of reading one story. If I didn't like it, I would have left the book on the bench for someone else to find. I do that kind of thing.

I read eleven of the stories on that bench. More than half the book.

And when I was done the sun was still as bright, the shadows under the trees as dark, the gurgling stream and the ducks and the butterflies all as they had been, but the day had changed. Or I had.

Up till then I'd been a nonfiction writer part-time and a martial arts instructor full-time. Up till then I'd never even thought about writing fiction.

Up till then I'd been gloomy and sad and depressed.

Those stories flipped some kind of switch. The change was not as dramatic as having all the lights come on inside my head...but something changed. I changed.

As I walked out of the park—still carrying the book—I began to think about the spooky things my grandmother had told me about, and the movies and books I'd devoured. I thought about the sorrows in my life, and the horrors. It was at that moment that I understood that horror fiction was a kind of escape hatch. Reading those stories took me away from my life for a while. Those stories chilled me. Moved me. And inspired me.

I didn't jump right into writing fiction, but from that day forward I would never go another day without thinking about it. About stories. About the layers of meaning.

A handful of years later I encountered another of Braunbeck's stories, and this one hit me even harder. In 2005, I read "We Pause Now for Station Identification." It was different. It was a claustrophobic, paranoid story laced with desperation and sadness. I loved it. Devoured it. Read it four or five times over a period of a couple of days.

The story was riveting, and I use that word with precision. It grabbed me, made me sit absolutely still and pay attention. It was like leaning in to hear a broadcast on one of those days in which the world changes. I've lived through days like that. The assassinations of the Kennedy's, of Martin Luther King, the moon landing, the end of Vietnam, the fall of the Berlin Wall, the Challenger explosion, 9/11. Moments on which history pivots. This story was written with that gravitas but without a single trace of pretention. It was a great story well told. It left me excited and hungry for more. I wasn't at all surprised when the Horror Writers Association awarded "Station Identification" the Bram Stoker Award for Short Fiction.

I list it as one of the ten top horror stories I've ever read. And I am a picky damn list-maker. It also serves as a terrific science fiction story, a human drama, a thriller, and even a mystery. You can come at "Station Identification" from a lot of different angles and it works every time.

The timing was so right for me, too. I finally yielded to those inner voices—the ones that had started whispering when I read those horror stories in the park on that long ago day. I yielded to the thought that I should try to write fiction. Gary Braunbeck lit that match. In 2005 I was shopping my first novel, *Ghost Road Blues*. In 2005 I landed my agent and in 2006 that book was published.

A lot has happened since then.

One of the things that's happened is that I got to meet Gary Braunbeck, we became friends, and I've even gotten him to write new horror stories for anthologies I'm editing.

Would I have become a novelist had I not met Gary? Probably. Maybe. Hard to say. But I know that I definitely did because of him. I'll always be grateful. And even though we're cronies now, I'll always be a fan.

When he asked me to write this introduction I re-read "Station Identification." It had been three or four years since the last time I read it. Turns out that it holds up mighty well. It's still compelling. It's still scary as hell. And it's still a masterwork of insightful storytelling.

If you've read it before, you know what I mean.

If you haven't yet…then, damn…how I envy you. It'll be like tasting chocolate, or a good bourbon, for the first time.

So…go read the damn story. But make sure you can read it in one sitting. You won't want to be disturbed. The story is disturbing all by itself.

We Now Pause For Station Identification

"…three-fourteen a.m. here at WGAB—we gab, folks, that's why it's called *talk* radio. So if there's anyone listening at this god-awful hour, tonight's topic is the same one as this morning, this afternoon, and earlier this evening…in fact, it's the same topic the whole world's had for the last thirteen days, if anyone's been counting: Our Loved Ones; Why Have They Come Back From The Dead and What The Fuck Do They Want?

"Interesting to say 'fuck' on the air without having to worry that the station manager, the FCC, and however many hundreds of outraged local citizens are going to come banging on the door, torches in hand, screaming for my balls on a platter. And to tell you the truth, after being holed-up in this booth for five straight days, it feels good, so for your listening enjoyment, I'm going to say it again. Fuck! And while we're at it, here's an earful of golden oldies for you—shit, piss, fuck, cunt, cocksuscker, motherfucker, and tits. Thank you George Carlin...assuming you're still alive out there...assuming anyone's still alive out there.

"Look at that, the seven biggies and not one light on the phone is blinking. So much for my loyal listeners. Jesus, c'mon people, there's got to be somebody left out there—a goddamn *plane* flew over here not an hour ago! I know the things don't fly themselves—okay, okay, there's that whole 'automatic pilot' feature but the thing is, you've got to have a pilot to get the thing in the air, so I know there's at least one airplane pilot still alive out there and if there's an airplane pilot then maybe there's somebody else who's stuck here on the ground like I am! This is the cellular age, people! Somebody out there has got to have a fucking *cell phone!*

"...sorry, about that, folks. Lost my head a little for a moment. Look, if you're local, and if you can get to a phone, then please call the station so that I know I'm reaching somebody. I haven't left this booth in five days and that plane earlier...well, it shook me up. You would have laughed if you'd been in here to see me. I jumped up and ran to the window and stood there pounding on the glass, screaming at the top of my lungs like there was a chance they'd hear me thirty-thousand feet above. Now I know how Gilligan and the Skipper and everyone else felt every time they saw a plane that didn't...Jesus. Listen to me. It's TV Trivia night here at your radio station at the end of the world.

"The thing that shocked me about all of this was that...it wasn't a thing like we've come to expect from all those horror movies. I mean, yeah, sure, the guy who did all the makeup for those George Romero films—what was his name? Savini, right? Yeah, Tom Savini—anyway, you have to give a tip of the old hat to him, because he sure as hell nailed the way they *look*. It's just all the rest of it...they don't want to eat us, they don't want to eat *anything*. All-right-y, then: show of hands—how many of you thought the first time you saw them that they were going to stagger over and chew a chunk out of your shoulder? Mine's raised, anybody else? That's what I thought.

"Oh, hell...you know, in a way, it would be easier to take if they *did* want to eat us—or rip us apart, or...*something!* At least then we'd have some kind of...I don't know...*reason* for it, I guess. Something tangible to be afraid of, an explanation for their behavior...and did you notice how quickly all the smarmy experts and talking heads on television gave up trying to offer rational explanations for how it is they're able to reanimate? Have you ever…when one's been close enough…have you ever looked at their fingers? Most of them are shredded down to the bone. People forget that it's not just the coffin down there in the ground—there's a concrete vault that the coffin goes *in to*, as well. So once they manage to claw their way through the lid of the coffin, they have to get through four inches or so of concrete. At least, that's what all you good folks who've buried your loved ones have paid for.

"Think about it, folks. I don't give a Hammer-horror-film *shit* how strong the walking dead are supposed to be, *no way* could they break through concrete like that, not with the levels of decomposition I've seen on some of the bodies. So, then, how do you explain so many disturbed and empty graves in all those cemeteries all around the world? Easy— *you've been getting screwed.* Those vaults that you see setting off to the side during the grave-side service? Have any of you ever stuck around to watch the rest of it be lowered over the concrete base? Shit—it wouldn't cost anything to pour a base underneath the coffin. A lot of us have been getting scammed, people, and I think it's high time we got together and did something about it! Funeral homes and cemeteries have been charging all of us for a *single* concrete vault that never actually gets put in the ground!

"Anybody out there got a *better* explanation for how a moldy, rotting, worm-filled bag of bones can dig its way out of a grave so quickly? If you do, you know the number, give me a call and let's talk about it, let's raise hell, organize a march on all funeral homes and cemetery offices…

"But the ones who came out of the graveyards, they're only a part of it, aren't they? Remember the news footage of that Greenpeace boat that went after what they *thought* was a wounded whale, only once they got close enough to see that it was dead and had just come back to life, it was too late? One of them had already touched it by then. Christ, how many kids did we lose when they went outside to see that Fluffy or Sprat or Fido or Rover was back from doggy heaven? I smashed a silverfish under my shoe a few days ago, and what was left of it started crawling again. I've got towels rolled up and stuffed under the doors in case there're any ants or cockroaches your friendly neighborhood Orkin man might have missed the last time he was here.

"Were television stations still broadcasting when Sarah Grant came home? Wait a second…some of them had to've been or else I wouldn't remember seeing it. Okay, right. Anyway, locals will remember Sarah.

She was a four-year-old girl who disappeared about five years ago, during the Land of Legend Festival. Ten thousand people and nobody saw a thing. The search for her went on for I-don't-know how long before they just had to give up. Well, about two weeks ago, the night all of this first began, what was left of Sarah Grant dug its way out of the grave in its pre-school teacher's back yard and walked home. She tried to tell them what had happened but her vocal cords were long gone...so when the police showed up and saw her, they just followed her back to her teacher's house where she showed them the grave. The police found the teacher hanging from a tree in the back yard; he'd evidently witnessed Sarah waking up from her dirt nap and knew what was coming.

"By then the police had seen more than a few dead bodies get up and start walking around, so little Sarah didn't come as much of a surprise to them. A lot of missing children started showing up at their old homes. Sometimes their families were still living there, sometimes they'd moved away and the kids didn't recognize the person who answered the door —this is when people still *did* answer their doors, in the beginning, when we thought it wasn't something that would happen here, no—it was just going on in China, or what used to be Russia, or Ireland, or...wherever. Everywhere but here. Not here, not in the good ole US of A. Downright un-American to think that. Christ, there were idiots who stood up in front of Congress and declared that all of this was just propaganda from Iraq, or Hong Kong, or Korea. Can you believe that? And *of course* it was all a plot against America, because the whole world revolves around us. *Fuck* that noise. Nations as we knew them don't exist anymore, folks —and this is assuming that the entire concept of 'nations' was *ever* real and not just some incredible, well-orchestrated illusions dreamed up by the shadows who've *really* been running the show all along. It doesn't matter. It's all just real-estate now, up for grabs at rock-bottom prices.

"Remember how happy a lot of us were at first? All that news footage of people in tears running up to embrace their loved ones fresh from their graves? Mangled bodies pulling themselves from automobile accidents or industrial explosions or recently-bombed buildings... all those terrified relatives standing around crash-, accident-, or other disaster sites, hoping to find their husbands or wives or kids or friends still alive? Reunions were going on left and right. It would have moved you to tears if it hadn't been for a lot of them missing limbs or heads or dragging their guts behind them like a bride's wedding-dress train. That didn't matter to the grieving; all they saw was their loved ones returned to them. They had been spared. They had been saved from a long dark night of the soul or whatever. They didn't have to give in to that black weight in their hearts, they didn't have to cry themselves to sleep that night, they didn't have to get up the next morning knowing that someone who was important to them, someone they loved and cared about and depended on, wasn't going to be there anymore, ever again. No. They were spared that.

"It didn't take long before we figured out that the dead were drawn back to the places or people they loved most, that meant everything to them while they were alive—at least Romero got *that* much right in his movies. At first I thought it was just a sad-ass way of reconciling everything, of forcing it into a familiar framework so we could deal with the reality of these fucking *upright corpses* shambling back into our lives—hell, maybe it was just a…I don't know…a knee-jerk reaction on the dead's part, like a sleepwalker. Maybe their bodies were just repeating something they'd done so many times over the course of their lives that it became automatic, something instinctual. I mean, how many times have you been walking home from someplace and haven't even been thinking about *how* to get from there to here? Your body knows the way so your brain doesn't even piss away any cells on that one. Home is important. The people there are important. The body knows this, even if you forget.

"But then the Coldness started. I…huh…I remember the initial reports when people started showing up in emergency rooms. At first everyone thought it was some kind of new flesh-eating virus, but that idea bit it in a hurry, because all of a sudden you had otherwise perfectly healthy, alive human beings walking into emergency rooms with completely dead limbs—some of them already starting to decompose. And in every single case, remember, it started in whichever hand they'd first touched their dead loved one with. The hand went numb, then turned cold, and the coldness then spread up through the arm and into the shoulder. The limbs were completely dead. The only thing the doctors could do was amputate the things. If the person in question had *kissed* their loved one when they first saw them…God Almighty…the Coldness spread down their tongues and into their throats. But mostly it was hands and arms, and for a while it looked like the amputations were doing the trick.

"Then the doctors and nurses who'd performed the surgeries started losing the feeling in their hands and arms and shoulders. Whatever it was, the Coldness was contagious. So they closed down the emergency rooms and locked up the hospitals and posted the National

Guard at the entrances because doctors were refusing to treat anyone who'd touched one of the dead…those doctors who still had arms and hands, that is.

"The one thing I have to give us credit for as a species is that the looting wasn't nearly as bad as I thought it would be. Seems it didn't take us very long for us to realize that material possessions and money didn't mean a whole helluva lot anymore. That surprised me. I didn't think we had any grace-notes left. Bravo for our side, huh?

"Look, I've got to…I've got to try and make it to the bathroom. I can at least cut through the production booth, but once out in the hall, I'm wide open for about five yards. The thing is, I've been in this booth for five days now, and while the food's almost held out —thank God for vending machines and baseball bats —I've been too scared to leave, so I've been using my wastebasket for a toilet and…well, folks, it's getting pretty ripe in here, especially since the air-conditioning conked out two days ago. I gotta empty this thing and wash the stink off myself. If you're out there, please don't go away. I'm gonna cue up the CD and play a couple of Beatles songs, 'In My Life' and 'Let It Be'. I'm feeling heavy-handed and ironic today, so sue me. If I'm not back by the time they're over, odds are I ain't gonna be. Light a penny candle for me, folks, and stay tuned…."

* * *

"…Jesus H. Christ on a crutch, I made it! It was kind of touch and go there for a minute…or, rather, *not* touch, if you get me…but here I am, with a gladder bladder and clean hands and face, so we're not finished yet, folks. There's still some fight left, after all.

"I need to tell you a little bit about our receptionist here at We-Gab Radio. Her name's Laura McCoy. She's one of the sweetest people I've ever met, and if it weren't for her, most days at this station would be bedlam without the sharp choreography. Laura has always been a tad on the large side—she once smiled at me and said she didn't mind the word 'fat', but I do mind it…anyway, Laura has always been on the large side but, dammit, she's *pretty*. She's tried a couple of times to go on diets and lose weight but they've never worked, and I for one am glad they didn't. I don't think she'd be half as pretty if she lost the weight.

"Laura's husband, this prince of all ass-wipes named Gerry, left her about ten months ago after fifteen years of marriage. Seems he'd been having an affair with a much younger co-worker for going on three years. Laura never suspected a thing, that's how true and trusting a soul she was. The divorce devastated her, we all knew it, but she was never less than professional and pleasant here at the station. Still, whenever there was any down-time—no calls coming in, no papers to be filed, no tour groups coming through, no DJs having nervous breakdowns—a lot of us began to notice this…this *stillness* about her; it was like if she wasn't busy, then some memory had its chance to sneak up and break her heart all over again. So we here at the station were worried. I asked her out for coffee one night after my shift. I made sure she knew it wasn't a date, it was just two friends having coffee and maybe some dessert.

"Laura was always incredibly shy when dealing with anyone outside of her job. The whole time we were having coffee she spent more time looking at her hands folded in her lap than she did at me. When she spoke, her voice was always…always so soft and sad. Even when she and Gerry were together, her voice had that sad quality to it—except at work, of course. At work, she spoke clearly and confidently. Sometimes I thought she was only alive when on the job.

"I said that to her the night we went for coffee. This was, oh…about eight months after the divorce, right? For the first time that night, she looked right at me and said, 'David, you're absolutely right. I *love* working at the station. That job and the people there are the only things I've ever been able to depend on. That's very important to me now.'

"After that, things were a lot better for a while. Laura took her two-week vacation just before everything started. In all the panic and confusion and Martial Law—which didn't exactly take very well, as you might recall—no one thought to call and check on her. She'd said she was going up to Maine to visit with her sister, so I guess most of us just figured or hoped that she'd made it to her sister's place before all hell broke loose.

"Two days ago, Laura came back to work. I can look over the console and through the window of the broadcast booth and see her sitting there at her desk. She's wearing one of her favorite dresses, and she's gotten a manicure. Maybe the manicure came before the great awakening, but it looks to me like the nail polish was freshly applied before she came in—and, I might add, she drove her car to work. I remember how excited I was to see that car driving up the road. It meant there was someone else still alive, and they'd thought to come here and check on me.

"I can see her very clearly, sitting there at her desk. About one-third of her head is missing. My guess is she used either a shotgun or a pistol with a hollow-point bullet. My guess is that this sweet, pretty woman who was always so shy around other people was a helluva lot more heartbroken than any of us suspected or wanted to imagine. My guess is she came back here because this station, this job, her place at that desk…these things were all she had left to look forward to. I wish I had been kinder to her. I wish I hadn't been so quick to think that our little chat helped, so I didn't have to give her or her pain a second thought. I wish…ohgod…I wish that I'd told her that she wouldn't be as pretty if she lost weight. I wish…shit, sorry…gimme a minute….

"Okay. Sorry about that. Forty-fucking-three years old and crying like a goddamn baby for its bottle. I'm losing ground here, folks. Losing ground. Because when I look out at Laura, there at her desk, and I remember Sarah Grant walking up to her family's home, and realize how many of the dead have been able to come back, have been able to walk or drive or in some cases take the goddamn bus back home…when I think of how they recognize us, how they *remember* us…you see, the thing is, Laura used to always bring in home-made chocolate chip cookies once a week. No one made cookies like Laura, I mean *nobody*! She'd always wrap them individually in wax paper, lay them out on a tray, cover the tray with tin-foil, and put a little Christmas-type bow on top.

"There's a tray of home-made cookies setting out there on her desk, all wrapped and covered and sporting its bow. Half her fucking brain is gone, splattered over a wall in her house…and she still *remembered*. Is this getting through to you, folks? The dead remember! Everything. It doesn't matter if they've been in the ground ten years or crawled out of drawer in the morgue before anyone could identify them —*they all remember! All of them!*

"Is this sinking in? And doesn't it scare the piss out of you? Look; if they can crawl out of a grave after ten years of being worm-food and volleyball courts for maggots and *still remember* where they lived and who they loved and…and all of it…then it means those memories, those intangible bits and pieces of consciousness and ether that we're told are part and parcel of this mythical, mystical thing called a soul…it means it never *went anywhere* after they died. It didn't return to humus or dissipate into the air or take possession of bright-eyed little girls like in the movies…it just hung around like a vagrant outside a bus station on a Friday night. Which means there's *nothing* after we die. Which means there is no God. Which means this life is *it*—and ain't that a pisser? Karma is just the punch-line to a bad stand-up routine, and every spiritual teaching ever drilled into our brain is bullshit. Ha! Mark Twain was right, after all—remember the ending of *The Mysterious Stranger*?— there is no purpose, no reason, no God, no devil, no angels or ghosts or ultimate meaning; existence is a lie; prayer is an obscene joke. There is just...nothing; life and love are only baubles and trinkets and ornaments and costumes we use to hide this fact from ourselves. The universe was a mistake, and we, dear friends...we were a fucking *accident*. That's what it means...and that makes me so...sick. Because I...I was kind of *hoping*, y'know? But I guess hope is as cruel a joke as prayer, now.

"Still, it's funny, don't you think...that in the midst of all this rot and death there's still a kind-of life. You see it taking root all around us. I suppose that's why so many of us have found ceiling beams that will take our weight, or loaded up the pump-action shotguns and killed our families before turning the gun on ourselves...or jumped from tall buildings, or driven our cars head-on into walls at ninety miles an hour...or-or-Or-*OR*!

"There's a window behind me that has this great view of the hillside. In the middle of the field behind the station there's this huge old oak tree that's probably been there for a couple of thousand years. Yesterday, a dead guy walked into the field and up to that tree and just stood there looking at it, admiring. I wondered if maybe he'd proposed to his wife under this tree, or had something else really meaningful—pardon my language—happen beneath that oak. Whatever it was, this was the place he'd come back to. He sat down under the oak and leaned back against its trunk. He's still there, as far as I can make out.

"Because we found out, didn't we, that as soon as the dead come home, as soon as they reach their destination, as soon as they stop moving...they take root. And they *sprout*. Like fucking kudzu, they sprout. The stuff grows out of them like slimy vines, whatever it is, and starts spreading. I can't see the tree any longer for all the...the vines that are covering it. Oh, there are a couple of places near the top where they haven't quite reached yet, but those branches are bleach-white now, the life sucked out of them. The vines, when they spread, they grow thicker and wider...in places they blossom patches of stuff that looks like luminescent pond-scum. But the vines, they're pink and moist, and they have these things that look like thorns, only these thorns, they wriggle. And once all of it has taken root—once the vines have engulfed everything around them and the patches of pond-scum have spread as far as they can without tearing—once all that happens, if you watch for a while, you can see that all of it is...is *breathing*. It expands and contracts like lungs pulling in, and then releasing air...and in between the breaths...if that's what they are...everything pulses steadily, as if it's all hooked into some giant, invisible heart...and the dead, they just sit there, or stand there, or lie there, and bit by bit they dissolve into the mass...becoming something even more organic than they were before…something new…something…hell, I don't know. I just calls 'em as I sees 'em, folks.

"Laura's sprouted, you see. The breathing kudzu has curled out of her and crawled up the walls, across the ceiling, over the floor…about half the broadcast booth's window is covered with it, and I can see that those wriggling thorns have mouths, because they keep sucking at the glass. I went up to the glass for a closer look right after I got back from the bathroom, and I wish I hadn't…because you know what I saw, folks? Those little mouths on the thorns…they have teeth…so maybe…I don't know…maybe in way we *are* going to be eaten…or at least ingested…but whatever it is that's controlling all of this, I get the feeling that it's some kind of massive organism that's in the process of pulling all of its parts back together, and it won't stop until it's whole again…because maybe once it's whole…that's *its* way of coming home. Maybe it knows the secret of what lies beyond death…or maybe it *is* what lies beyond death, what's always been there waiting for us, without form…and maybe it finally decided that it was lonely for itself, and so jump-started our loved ones so it could hitch a ride to the best place to get started.

"I'm so tired. There's no unspoiled food left from the vending machines—did I mention that I took a baseball bat to those things five—almost *six* days ago now? I guess the delivery guy never got here to re-stock them. Candy bars, potato chips, and shrink-wrapped tuna salad sandwiches will only get you so far. I'm so…so *tired*. The kudzu is scrabbling at the base of the door…I don't think it can actually break through or it would have by now…but I'm thinking, what's the point, y'know? Outside, the field and hillside are shimmering with the stuff—from here it almost looks as if the vines are dancing—and in a little while it will have reached the top of the broadcast tower…and then I really *will* be talking to myself.

"If anyone out there has any requests…now's the time to phone them in. I'll even play the seventeen-minute version of 'In A Gadda-Da-Vida' if you ask me. I always dug that drum solo. I lost my virginity to that song…the *long* version, not the three-minute single, thanks for that vote of confidence in my virility. I wish I could tell you that I remembered her name…her first name was Debbie, but her last name…*pffft!* It's gone, lost to me forever. So…so many things are lost to me forever now…lost to all of us forever…still waiting on those requests…please, *please, PLEASE* will somebody out there call me? Because in a few minutes, the vines and thorns will have covered the window and those little mouths with their little teeth are all I'll be able to see and I'm…I'm hanging on by a fucking thread here, folks…so….

"…three minutes and forty seconds. I am going to play 'The Long and Winding Road', which is three minutes and forty seconds long, and if by the end of the song you have not called me, I am going to walk over to the door of the broadcast booth, say a quick and meaningless prayer to a God that was never there to hear it in the first place, and I am going to open that door and step into those waiting, breathing, pulsing vines.

"So I'm gonna play the song here in a moment. But first, let's do our sworn FCC duty like good little drones who are stupid enough to think anyone cares anymore, and we'll just let these six pathetic words serve as my possible epitaph:

"We now pause for station identification…."

Part Three:

SOMETIME THEN

Sometime then there will be every kind of a history of every one who ever can or is or was or will be living. Sometime then there will be a history of every one from their beginning to their ending. Sometime then there will be a history of all of them, of every kind of them, of every one, of every bit of living they ever have in them, of them when there is never more than a beginning to them, of every kind of them, of every one when there is very little beginning and then there is an ending, there will then sometime be a history of everything that ever was or is or will be them, of everything that was or is or will be all of any one or all of all of them ...
— Gertrude Stein, *The Making of Americans*

"Who'll tell the story?" asked the child to the magician. "People should be told."

"Never mind," said the old man, smiling like a beaver. "For centuries and centuries no one will believe it, and then all at once it will be so obvious only a fool would take the trouble to write it all down."

— John Gardner, *Freddy's Book*

"Hello. I must be going."
— Groucho Marx

While I—unlike several of the powerhouse contributors to this collection—am far from a household name, I am lucky to have achieved a certain "cult" status in the field, most of it based on my output as a short-story writer; I have been luckier still that a handful of these stories have come to be referred to as either "...classic" or a "...classic in the making" (a phrase that I've never really understood but am always grateful for the sentiment behind whenever it is employed). This collection began to emerge as something of a mini-career retrospective (not the original intent), so I thought it might be nice to close the proceedings with a selection of my stories that have attained a certain popularity among readers. I won't be so arrogant and self-aggrandizing as to call this final selection a compilation of my "greatest hits" or anything asinine like that; it is, rather, a selection of stories that I consider to be among my best work, and that best represent both *how* I write and *what* I often choose to write about (although I suspect by this point you've already got a pretty good grasp of the latter). These are the stories that I would offer to a person who's never read my work before, and these are also the stories that many readers have told me are among their favorites. I'll let you be the judge.

Okay, that's it for me. Thank you for spending your time with these stories. I hope you liked most of them. I'm off now to try and get better at this holy chore, and I hope that when next we meet you'll expect even better from me, and I hope to deliver on those expectations.

Rami Temporales

"When I face myself I'm surprised to see
   That the man I knew don't look nothing like me..."

                              —John Nitzinger, "Motherload"

It started with the woman in the restaurant and her hysterectomy story.

I was alone in my favorite booth at the Sparta, enjoying the last of my cheeseburger, when I happened to glance up.

"...and like I said before, she never listens to me—hell, she never listens to *anyone* when they try to tell her something for her own good. She's been that way all her life and look what it's got her."

She was at a booth toward the back of the restaurant, while mine was up front on the same side; I sat facing the rear, she facing the front, so she was looking right at me and there was no place to hide.

"I kept telling her, 'Sandy, your frame is too small to chance having another baby. You almost didn't squeeze out little Tyler the first time, there's no way you can have another one.' I think she knew I was right but she wasn't about to have an abortion, not with her Ronnie being the way he is—you know, all manly and pro-life: 'No wife of mine is going to kill our baby. I'll not have people gossiping about me like that.'"

Her tone suggested that the two of us had just resumed a previously-interrupted conversation. For a moment I thought she might be talking to someone seated across from her in the booth, a short person, or even a child—though why anyone would want to speak to a child about abortion was beyond me. I then thought she might be wearing one of those new cell phones, the type which you hang off your ear and have a small fiber-optic microphone, but, no: she was looking at and talking to me.

"I know she thinks I'm a nib-shit, but that girl has no idea how *terrible* he treats her. Or maybe she does and figures she ain't gonna find a better man so she puts up with it for the kids." She was on the verge of tears. "I mean, Ronnie *forced* her to have that second baby, even though he knew there was a chance it was going to...y'know, *mess up* her insides. She almost *died*. They had to do an emergency Caesarian, and by then she was so tore up there wasn't no choice but to do a hysterectomy. She's only twenty-three and now she'll never be able to have more children — and Sandy *loves* children. She spoils that Tyler rotten, and she'll do the same for little Katherine. But she..." The woman leaned forward; secret time. I found myself leaning toward her, as well.

"...she *bleeds* a lot sometimes," she whispered. "Not her period—she don't have those no more. It's on account of her still being raw in there from everything. And *sex*—forget that. She don't even want to *look* at Ronnie, let alone share her bed and body with him. But that doesn't stop him, no sir. If *he* wants it, he takes it, and who cares if she's doubled over with cramps and bleeding for two days after. She ain't a wife to him, she's just a possession, so to him it ain't rape. Them kids don't hardly exist for him at home—oh, if there's an office party or picnic or something like that, he's Robert Young on *Father Knows Best*, but the rest of the time..." She shook her head. "You know, I seen him just today. Walking into the Natoma restaurant with a woman from his office. Had his hand on her ass. 'Working late on the new contract proposals' my ass! And after all he's done to her."

"He..." I couldn't believe I was asking this. "...*forces* her to...?"

"All the time."

"My God." The whole of Sandy's life suddenly played out in my mind and I felt soul-sick and ineffectual as I witnessed it; Sandy: under-to uneducated (as so many young women in this city are), no dreams left, working nine hours a day in some bakery or laundry or grocery store, then coming home to a husband who didn't much like her and children who—though she might love them and spoil them rotten now — would grow up following Daddy's example to not much respect her, and before twenty-five she'd be wearing a scarf around her head to cover the prematurely gray hair, read only the saddest stories in the newspaper, and spend any free time she might have watching prime-time soap operas and getting twelve pounds heavier with each passing year. I think I'd've known her on-sight, no introductions necessary.

"That poor girl," I said.

"Sometimes," the woman said, "I got half a nerve to just go over there with my truck and tell her to pack herself and the kids up and come stay with me. Maybe I should."

"That sounds like a splendid idea."

"*Does* it?" Look at how alive her eyes became when she heard this; goodness me, somebody actually thinks *I* had a splendid idea.

She finished her coffee, took the last bite of her apple pie, then gathered up her purse and resolve and walked up to me, her hand extended. "Thank you for listening to me."

"You're welcome."

Still there were tears trying to sneak up on her. "I just feel so *bad* for her, y'know?"

"But she isn't alone. She has you."

Her grip tightened. "That's the nicest thing anybody's said to me in a while—and you're right. She *does* have me. And I got a truck and she's got the day off."

"Ronnie's working late, I take it?"

"Bastard's *always* working late." She smiled at me, then released my hand, leaned down, and kissed my cheek. "Thanks, mister. I really appreciate you lettin' me go on about this. I hope it wasn't no bother, it's just, well...you just got one of those faces, y'know?"

One of those faces.

How many times in my life have I heard that?

I don't avoid contact with strangers. It would do no good. They always come up to me. *Always.* Take any street in this city at a busy hour, fill it with people rushing to or from work or shopping or a doctor's appointment, add the fumes and noises of traffic, make it as hectic and confusing as you wish—I am inevitably the one people will stop and ask for directions, or for the time, or if I know a good restaurant. "You got of those faces," they'll say. I have had homeless people politely make their way through dozens of other potential benefactors to get to me and ask for change. I always give what I can spare, and they always tell me they knew I'd help them out because—say it with me...

This is why I'm thought of as friendly person. Ask anyone who thinks they know me: "You want to know about Joel? Oh, he's a *great* guy, friendly as they come, the best listener in the world, sincerely."

Truth is, human contact scares holy hell out of me. I'm always worried that I'll say the wrong thing or misinterpret a gesture or infer an attraction that's not there. So I listen, even though most of the time I want to slink off into the woodwork, especially when the stories are troubling.

But ask anyone what they know about me; you could groom your hair in the reflection from the glassy look. Just once I would like to have been asked something about myself. Just once, that's all.

"I'll bet you hate having your picture taken."

I blinked, looking around. Sandy's friend was long gone and as far as I could see, I was the only customer on this side of the—

—scratch that. Across the aisle, one booth down and facing the front, sat a gaunt old man who looked so much like the late actor Peter Cushing it was eerie; thinning silver hair formed into a widow's peak on his forehead, aristocratic nose, sharp jaw-line, small but intense bluish-gray eyes under patrician brows; when he swallowed, his too-large Adam's apple threatened to burst through his slender neck and bounce away.

"Yes," he said—more to himself than me, "I don't imagine you enjoy it at all."

I gawked at him for a few more moments—he even *sounded* like Cushing—then said: "I beg your pardon?"

"That was marvelous of you, listening to that woman. You probably made her day."

"It seemed discourteous to do otherwise."

"'Discourteous.' Good word. So tell me: *do* you hate being photographed?"

"I don't know. I never thought much about it." Which was a lie, albeit a harmless one. I *despise* having my picture taken; forget the rudeness of it *(I got the camera so I'm going to get up in your face and take this snapshot whether you like it or not)*, which I object to on moral grounds—most people never ask, they just click away—it's that every time I see a picture of myself, I don't recognize me. I always look like someone just stuck a gun in my back and told me to act natural.

I continued staring at the man.

"There's a reason I look and sound this way, Joel—by the way, were you named after anyone in particular?"

"Joel McCrea. Mom's favorite movie was *Ride the High Country* and Dad's was *Sullivan's Travels*."

He smiled his approval. "Good films, and a fine actor after which to be named. I'm sorry, I seem to have forgotten—who was *your* favorite actor?"

"Peter Cush—oh, hang on!"

He winked. "I told you there was a reason. By the way, hello. My name's Listen, and it's not that I don't find shouting across the aisle like some sort of simpleton amusing, but wouldn't it be better to continue this in a more civilized manner? So if you would join me here, please, we can get to the heart of the matter."

"The heart of what matter?"

"Your face and why I need you to give it to me."

Everything inside was whispering *Get the hell away from this loony.* Okay, he knew my first name, no real mystery there—I was a regular and all the staff called me by name, he probably heard the waitress talking to me, case closed. How he knew Peter Cushing was my favorite actor was another matter; I have no real friends with whom I would have shared that. And as to how he was an exact double of Cushing...

I prefer my weirdness in small, bite-sized doses, preferably in movies or books. I was still rattled by Sandy's story and in no mood for games. *Your face and why I need you to give it to me.* Uh-huh. I suddenly didn't care how he knew what he knew and why he looked as he did; it was time to go.

I grabbed the check and started to make a clean getaway when he said: "Please tell me you're *not* going to make me have to follow you."

I turned. "Is that a threat?"

"Not at all. But I cannot emphasize enough how important it is to you and the health of your loved ones that you sit down and talk to me."

My chest went cold with anger. "What the fuck do you mean, the health of my loved ones?"

He sighed, then pulled a gold pocket watch from his vest and looked at the time. "In about ninety seconds your cell phone is going to beep. The number displayed will be that of a pay phone in the lobby of Cedar Hill Memorial Hospital. It will be your sister, Amy. Look up at the television over the front counter."

I did. It showed a viewing room inside Criss Brothers Funeral Home. Several people were gathered around a small casket. From the back, one of them looked like Dad—why would anyone else wear *that* jacket? He stood there until Mom—who I clearly recognized—came over, put her arm around him, and pulled him away. As they stepped to the right of the casket I saw who was lying inside and it slammed closed every window in my soul.

"She'll be calling," said Listen, "to tell you that your eight-year-old nephew Tommy has just been diagnosed with a malignant brain tumor. What she doesn't know yet is that it's been found too late. Tommy will be dead before his birthday in October."

No one—I mean *no one*—else in the family but me knew about the follow-up EEG Tommy was having done today. For the last couple of years, my nephew—who I love dearly—has been plagued by severe headaches. At first it was thought he was suffering from allergies, but the medications prescribed made him sick and irritable and unhappy. Another doctor's visit revealed he needed adenoid surgery, so that was done and for a little while the headaches stopped. But about two months ago they returned with a vengeance—nausea, crying, wild mood-swings, fear. Tommy wants to draw comic books when he grows up. He's a small kid and gets picked on a lot at school because he's not into sports and thinks girls are *cool*. This morning his mother had taken him to the hospital for more tests because the first set came back inconclusive. The thought of him dying broke me in half. Though there's a lot in life I enjoy, I don't genuinely love much in this world but my sister and my nephew.

But for the moment I was staring at a videotape of him lying in his casket while Mom tried to look strong as Amy, shuddering, collapsed into a nearby chair while her lout of an ex-husband stood off to the side flirting with one of her friends from high school.

"The medical expenses will all but bankrupt her and she'll plunge into a black depression that will end with her suicide the following February—and right now there's nothing you can do about it."

Turning away from the suffering on the screen, I balled my hand into a fist and felt a tear slip from my eye. "I don't know how you—"

—and my cell phone went off.

"You can always depend on your sister to be prompt," said Listen, snapping closed his watch and slipping it back into his vest pocket.

I checked the display on the phone: beneath the number—which I did not recognize—were the words **unknown caller**.

"You have only to sit down and I can make it all go away," said Listen. "This offer expires in thirty seconds. That isn't my choice, those are the rules."

Panic and desperation are curious things. Enough of either impairs your judgment; a gut full of both turns you into a marionette.

I sat down. My phone stopped beeping. The display was now blank, and when I pressed the **recall** button, the number listed was that of *The Ally*, Cedar Hill's only newspaper, where I am employed as manager of the paste-up department.

Listen smiled. "It's not showing the pay phone number because your sister never made the call. The tests came back negative. Right now she's sitting in a Ladies' Room stall crying from relief while your nephew is bothering the nurses about how much he wants to see the new Spider-Man movie."

"What rules?"

"Beg pardon?"

"You said 'those are the rules.' What were you—"

"—you might want to look at the television again."

This time it was some sort of convention. A large room filled with throngs of fans. The camera moved in on a table where a particularly long line of them stood with stacks of things to be autographed. There were three people seated at the table and it was the young man in the middle who seemed the focus of attention. As the camera came closer I saw my sister, her hair shorter and greyer, seated to the left of the young man—who I now recognized as an older Tommy. I sat on the other side of him, thinner, my slouch a bit more pronounced, hair and beard (I would finally grow a beard?) filled with streaks of white. A fan came to the table and held out a hardcover book. Tommy, smiling, took it and began talking to the fan, introducing his mother and then myself and launching into some story in which I seemed to play a major role. He then signed the book and had the fan step behind the table so someone could take a picture of the four of us, the fan beaming as he held his autographed copy of...of...

"I can't make out what's on the cover," I said.

"Well, no. *That* would fall under the category of 'Too Much Information.' Tommy's been diagnosed with migraine headaches and will be put on medication that will keep them more or less under control for the rest of his life." He nodded toward the television. "That scene will take place in sixteen years. Tommy will be a very successful writer/illustrator of graphic novels, and he'll have you to thank for the idea which leads to the creation of his most famous character. So it wouldn't be playing fair to let you see the title of the book, now, would it?"

I looked at Amy's face and saw the peace there, the happiness. "What about—"

"She'll re-marry in about five years. He'll be divorced and a recovering alcoholic who's been on the wagon for ten years. He'll never take another drink. He'll be a laborer, and not nearly as smart as she is, but that won't matter. He'll love her and Tommy with all his heart and be, after your nephew, the best and most decent thing to ever happen in her life. She'll be happy, and she'll be loved. That's all you need to know."

The television blinked and the image was replaced by the sitcom re-run that usually ran at this hour.

"H-how did you...do this?"

Listen arched his brows. "Do you really need to know the how and why of it? Isn't it enough that I did it and *will not* reverse things regardless of your decision?"

I nodded. "My face and why you need —"

He waved it away. "Yes, yes, yes, I already know why I'm here, thank you."

"Then how about you explain it to me?"

He folded his hands. "Fine. But first I *must* have a refill on my coffee and a slice of their coconut cream pie. Would you like some, as well? My treat."

"Sure." I remembered the parking meter outside. *The Ally* used to be right across the street from the Sparta, but had moved a year ago to a larger building on the other side of the square, so these days I had to drive over here for dinner after work. The meter would be expiring in a few minutes. I hoped that Listen wouldn't think—

"Not at all, dear boy," he said. "Go feed your quarters into the bloody thing, I understand completely."

"Be right back."

Outside, I was digging into my pocket for change and trying not to shriek with joy. I know how melodramatic that sounds, but it's how I felt. Elated. I knew somehow that all of it was true, that this weird little man had just saved the lives of my sister and nephew.

Like most people, I don't believe in miracles but often depend on them in the same wishful-thinking way that gets most of us through our days: Maybe I'll win the lottery, maybe I'll get that raise, maybe she'll say she will go out with me. But here, now, in this most unlikely of places, I had been witness to something genuinely miraculous and wanted to sing and dance until the Twinkie Mobile came to haul me off.

"I didn't mean to do it!"

He was in his early thirties, dressed in clean khaki pants and work boots, with a denim shirt and baseball cap. His face sported a vague five-'o'-clock shadow that told you he *had*, indeed, shaved that morning. His blond hair was neatly combed and there was nothing about him to suggest that he was either homeless or insane.

Except his eyes. To look in them as he spoke you would have thought he'd swallowed a leathery chunk of pain.

There were perhaps half-a-dozen other people out there, but I knew at once he would head toward me.

"I swear to God I didn't want to do it, *I swear to God!*" His gaze locked on me. I found my change, pulled it with a shaking hand from my pocket, and immediately dropped most of it on the sidewalk.

"I didn't mean to hurt her," he said, stopping right in front of me and jamming his hands deep into his pockets. "They *made* me do it! They *always make me do it!* I don't want to. She's so *little*. And she *loves* all of us. She looks at me with those sweet eyes so full of trust and then I have to...to—I swear to God I don't want to do it, they *make* me, you understand? *They make me do it!*"

Every inch of his body trembled with helpless rage. I stepped behind the meter in case he exploded and got his crazy all over the street.

Tears formed in his eyes. "I don't want to do it anymore." His voice broke on the last three words.

All I could think to say was: "How bad is she hurt now?"

"Not too bad this time. She was doing pretty well when I left. They won't do anything to her, they never do. They —"

" —make you do it for them."

"Yes."

I wanted to run away but I couldn't. Listen might take offense and that was the last thing I wanted.

"Can you take her places?" I asked.

He stopped trembling and looked in my eyes. "Uh-*huh*. I'm the only one who ever does."

I tilted my head in the direction of City Hall at the end of the street. "Why don't you take her in there and tell the person at the front desk what they make you do? They can put her someplace safe and you'll never have to hurt her again."

He dragged an arm across his teary eyes, then inhaled thickly. "*Really?*"

"I'm almost certain, yes."

He looked toward City Hall and took something from his pocket; a small, cheap, plastic toy modeled after a Saturday morning cartoon character. "I got this for her to say I'm sorry. I always get her something after...after, and she always...*thanks* me. Do you think she'll like it?"

"I'm sure she'll love it."

"They sell these over at the drug store. I could —*hey*, I could maybe tell them I'm taking her out to buy *another* one, then we could go over there."

"That sounds good. Make sure you use the dark brown metal door on the 5th Street side." That would take them down a short set of stairs into the police station.

"I'll remember. You *bet* I will." And he walked away, gripping the toy as if it were a holy talisman. "*Swear to God* I never meant to hurt her. They made me. They *always* make me. Oh, *God...*"

I watched until he disappeared around the corner. I bent down to collect my spilled change and my car's horn sounded from behind. After I'd managed to squeeze back into my skin, I turned, still shaking, to see Listen sitting in the passenger seat. He grinned at me and waved.

"I'd forgotten they were out of the coconut cream pie," he said, leaning out the open window. "I took care of the bill. Let's go for a ride."

I gathered up what change I could find and climbed in but didn't start the car.

"Another story, I take it?"

I exhaled. "Jesus, that guy was...was —"

"—at the end of his rope, just so you know. I'd share the specifics of his home situation, but it would only make you sad and sick."

"Do you know what's going to happen?"

"Yes. I won't say he and the little girl will both be fine, because the possibility of *that* outcome died a long while ago. But he'll get her out of there tonight and take her through the brown metal door and, eventually, things will be better for both of them. Not great — never great — but *better*. Now believe it or not, I am on something of a schedule, so if you would please start the car and drive out to Moundbuilders Park..."

"Why there?"

He huffed and made a strangling gesture with his hands. "Arrrgh! — and when was the last time you heard anyone actually *say* that? Look, do I strike you as being impulsive? No? Do you think I go about will-nilly? Of course not. Has any of this seemed *unplanned*?"

I started the car and drove away.

"Have you ever seen any paintings or drawings of Jesus?" he asked.

"Of course."

"Can you remember anything specific about them?"

I shrugged. "Beard. Hair. Flowing robes. Eyes."

"But the faces have always been different somehow, haven't they? The hair longer or shorter, the beard fuller, the cheekbones higher or lower, fuller or more drawn, even the hue of the skin has been different — yet somehow you always recognize the face."

"Okay...?"

"Ever wonder how many different versions of that face exist in statues or paintings or sketches?"

"Thousands, I would think."

"Seventy-two, actually. Followers of the Prophet Abdu'l-Bahá believe that everything in nature has 'two and seventy names.' That's almost right. The thing that has always annoyed me about the various religions is that, with rare exceptions, their beliefs are too compartmentalized. *This* is what we believe in, period. I'll tell you a secret: they're all wrong—individually. The problem is none of them can see Belief holistically. If they were all to 'gather at the river,' so to speak, and compare notes, you'd be surprised how quickly people would stop setting off bombs and flying airplanes into skyscrapers. But I digress.

"Everything in nature *does* have seventy-two names. But certain of these things also have seventy-two forms. Like the face of Jesus, for example."

"You're telling me that Christ has been portrayed as having seventy-two faces?"

"No, whiz-kid, I'm telling you that Christ *had* seventy-two faces. Every picture you see is nothing more than a variation on one of them. Faces change over the course of a lifetime, dear boy. All in all, each of us wears seventy-one."

"I thought you just said—"

"—I *know* what I said, I recognized my voice. There is one face we possess that is never worn—at least, not in the sense that the world can see it. The best way I can explain it is to say that it's the face you had before your grandparents were born. *That* is the face I need from you. It exists *here*—" He cupped one of his hands and covered his face from forehead to upper lip. "—in the *Rami Temporales*."

"In the muscles around the eyes?"

"No, *those* are part of the *Rami Zygomatici*, an area controlled by the *Temporales*, which is a much larger and influential group in the temporo-facial division of—oh, for goodness' sake! Are you in the *mood* for an anatomy lesson? Are you worried that I'm going to pull out a scalpel and cut away? I'm not a graduate of the Ed Gein School of Cosmetology, so put that notion out of your head this instant."

I stopped at a red light on 21st Street. "Then I guess I don't understand what you mean at all."

"Perhaps we need to expedite things a bit. Turn left."

The light changed and I made the turn. Even though the entrance to the park should have been a good six miles farther, here we were. I pulled into the parking area and we climbed out.

"I have some luggage in your trunk," said Listen. "If you wouldn't mind...?"

It was a large, bulky square thing that reminded me of a salesman's sample case. I lifted it out of the trunk and damn near snapped my spine. "What's in here, the population of a small Third-World nation?"

"*Is* a tad on the heavy side, isn't it? Sorry." Listen took the case from me and dangled it from one hand as if it weighed no more than a tennis racket. "Do you have a favorite spot here?"

"You already know the answer."

"Of course you're right. I just wanted to see if you'd lie to me again like you did about having your picture taken."

"How did you know that?"

"I do my homework, dear boy. You'll be turning forty-two in July, and since the day of your birth you've been photographed exactly one-hundred-and-nine times, counting your employee identifications and driver's licenses. By the time they're your age, the average person has been photographed close to a thousand times, be it individually or as part of a group. But not you. One-hundred-and-nine times, that's it."

"It's over there."

"What is?"

"My favorite spot."

"Ah, yes, the picnic area near the footbridge. Where Penny Duffy kissed you when both of you were in the eighth grade."

I took a seat at the picnic table while Listen walked up to the footbridge and took in the entire park.

"Know anything about 'places of power'?" he said.

"Like Stonehenge?"

"Exactly. Stonehenge is a perfect example. The Irazu volcano in Costa Rica, the Ruins of Copan in Honduras, Cerne Abas Giant, and Bodh Gaya where Buddha achieved enlightenment are a few others. Places where the forces of the Universe are intensely focused and can be harnessed by the faithful."

"Don't go all New-Age on me, okay?"

"Don't make me ill. There are well over a thousand such spots, but believe it or not, only seventy-two are *genuinely* significant. Only seventy-two are filled with such power that you can feel the Earth thrum like some excited child who's filled to bursting with a secret their heart can no longer contain. This park—" He made a sweeping gesture with his arm. "—is one of those seventy-two places. The Indian Burial mounds here are so potent they're scary."

"Is that why we're here?"

"Yes. What needs to be done, needs to be done in a place of power. Such are the ways of ritual." He joined me at the table. "I have to tell you certain things to aid you in making your decision. Whatever happens, know that Amy's and Tommy's future health and happiness is safe."

He reached down to flip the first of four latches on the case. "The first time a stranger approached you with a story, you were seven years old. It was an elderly woman who was in tears because she'd lost a cameo her late husband had gotten for her overseas during World War One. You sat there on your bike and listened to her and then you said — do you remember this?"

I nodded. "She said she always wore it so she could feel him near. She talked about how he'd loved her home-made strawberry preserves, how she still made a batch every year to give as Christmas presents. This was three weeks before Christmas. I asked her if she'd already made her preserves and she said yes. I knew right away that the cameo's clasp had come loose from the necklace. It had fallen into one of the preserve jars. I didn't tell her that, though."

"No, but you *did* ask the right questions so she could figure it out. Do you know what would have happened if that woman hadn't approached you? She would have taken her own life New Year's Eve. This was a dangerously depressed gal, Joel, one who'd been the focus of her children's' worry since the death of her husband. You saved her life that day."

"*No...*"

"Oh, yes. And since that day, because you have 'one of those faces,' people keep coming up to you, don't they? Asking for directions, spare change, if you know a good restaurant...or to tell you things. *Rami Temporales*, the face beneath the flesh. That is what draws them to you. They recognize it in you just as you can recognize the face of Jesus or Shakespeare, because regardless of how many variations there might be, the face beneath the flesh—the First Face, the one you had before your grandparents were born—remains unchanged." He opened the case and laid it flat. From one end to the other it was at least four feet wide and three across, perhaps two feet deep.

Something wasn't right. I'd seen this thing closed, had tried to lift it, and though it weighed a ton there was nothing to suggest it would be this wide, long, or deep when opened.

Then he opened it again. Two sections into four, each covered by a square of black material.

"Since your encounter with Cameo Lady, you've lost track of how many people have approached you. But I haven't. Do you know what you are, Joel? You're a safety valve. People see your face and know you'll be sympathetic, so they have no qualms about unloading their woes on you. Do you think it helps them?"

"I have no idea."

"Hm." He removed a small notebook from his vest. Flipping it open to the first page, he began reading aloud. "Over the course of the thirty-four years since Cameo Lady, your listening to others has prevented forty-three rapes, one-hundred-and-twelve suicides, sixty-seven episodes of child abuse, thirty-three divorces, ninety-eight murders, and so many cases of spousal abuse I ran out of room to record them all." He tossed the notebook to me. "Look it over later if you'd like. The point is that all the time you've secretly felt was wasted while you listened has actually made a difference. If I asked how many people were affected by you today, you'd say...?"

"Two. Sandy's friend and the guy outside the Sparta."

He shook his head. "*Five*, Joel." He held up his hand, fingers spread apart. "Five. And one of them —*not* the fellow outside the restaurant, by the way—would have already snapped and be torturing a child nearly to death right now if it weren't for the ninety seconds they spent talking to you." He went back to the case. Four sections became eight. Eight became twelve. Twelve became sixteen, each section attached by hinges to those above, below, and on either side. Already something that should have only taken up maybe six square feet covered at least fifty. Had he been unfolding some massive quilt I wouldn't have felt like the world was disintegrating around me. But this thing was making confetti out of the basic laws of physics. I was standing in the middle of a live-action Escher painting.

Sixteen sections became twenty-four. Twenty-four became thirty-two. Every compartment covered in black, creating a square, bottomless dark pit.

"What are you?" I asked.

Thirty-two sections quickly became forty-eight. "*What*, is it? Not *who*. You catch on fast. Yes, I was being surly. Apologies."

"Are you going to answer the question or should I just wait for a postcard?"

Forty-eight sections were now sixty-four. "Consider me a reconstructive surgeon. My area of expertise is, of course, the face. One in particular." With a final flurry of hands and flipping, the sixty-four sections became seventy-two.

"There," he said, standing back and admiring the massive obsidian square which lay where the ground and grass used to be. "Whew! Sometimes this really wears me out."

"What the hell is it?"

"Funny you should mention Hell. I had to go there in order to get a few of these—and don't think *that* wasn't a bushel of dreadful fun." He pulled aside one of the black compartment covers and the rest, like slats in Venetian blinds, folded back to reveal what lay underneath. "I don't have all of them yet. Counting yours, I still have eleven to go."

In each filled compartment, nestled in a thick bed of dark felt, was a glass mask. Several were full-face, while others were half or three-quarters, but a majority were of isolated sections: the forehead and nose; cheeks connected by the nose bridge; the lips and chin; temples and eyes; the cheeks alone; and one mask, looking like one of those optical illusion silhouettes you see in Psychology textbooks, was of the forehead, nose, lips, and chin only. No cheeks, no temples, no eyes.

"I *thought* this one would interest you," said Listen. "Not that there's anything especially significant about it for you, but something about its shape I knew you'd find fascinating." He pulled on a pair of the whitest gloves I've ever seen and removed the mask. On closer inspection, as the sunlight danced glissandos over its shape, I saw it wasn't made out of glass but some thin, transparent, seemingly organic material that held the shape and acted as a prism on the light.

"Okay. Time you knew the rest. Have a seat.

"Jesus, Shakespeare, Buddha—all of their faces recognizable even though none were ever photographed. Yes, there's an element of the collective unconscious and the archetype involved, but it's a little more complicated than that. People recognize those faces because somewhere in the back of their minds that's what they *want* them to look like. Jesus should look benevolent and spiritual, Shakespeare intelligent and creative, Buddha wise and all-knowing. Everyone has these characteristics in mind when picturing them, and so they are always present in portraits and sculptures and sketches. Consensual reality, to over-simplify it: 'I believe this is what it looks like, so that is how it appears.'

"The same holds true for the face of God, Joel. But just as the portraits of the Blessed Virgin Mary, Da Vinci, Galileo and the rest change from likeness to likeness, just as any human being's face changes over the course of a lifetime or even a day—your happy face, your leave-me-alone face, your confused face, et cetera—the face of God changes. And it's not supposed to. But He doesn't have the advantage of an archetype buried in peoples' minds. That's where I come in." He squinted at the mask, blew on it, then used his fingertips to brush away some dust or pollen. "I keep forgetting what dirt magnets these things can be. Where was I?

"Ah, yes: the face of God. Have you ever noticed how the horrors of this world seem to never cease coming at you? Hideous mass murders, bombings, wars breaking out in distant countries, rapes, missing children, mutilated children, men walking into fast-food restaurants and opening fire with automatic weapons...the inventory is inexhaustible. There's a reason. Simply put, it's because no one has even the *slightest* idea what God's face looks like. Everyone guesses, and though some of those guesses might have a particular element nailed down, *none* of them comes close to the real thing, because there *isn't* one. That's why there's this gaping hole where that face should exist. So, a while ago, God— Who wouldn't know Vanity if it bit Him in the soft parts—consented to allow me to build a face for Him. Being an overly-curious sort, I naturally had to inquire why He'd never made one for Himself. It turns out that He did, but he gave it away. It was the last thing He did on the Sixth Day. He divided His face into seventy-two sections and scattered them into the Universe."

It took a moment for the full impact of this to hit me. "So you're saying that...that *I*—?"

"Possess a missing section of God's face, yes."

I looked at the masks displayed before me. "How did you manage to find *any* of these?"

"It would bore you to death."

"Give me the *Reader's Digest* version."

"Prime numbers. Seventy-one—the number of faces you wear in a lifetime—is a prime number, so I took a shot in the dark and began with that. All the digits of your birthday are prime numbers which add up to the same: 7-13-59. Every genuinely significant event that's occurred in your life has happened when your age was a prime, today included— remember, you're still forty-one. It took me several thousand years to figure this out, but once the equation revealed itself, the rest fell into place. I took the true age of the Universe, divided it by seventy-one, divided that sum by seventy-one, and kept repeating the pattern until I was left with a sum of one. I then divided each of the seventy-one individual sums *by* seventy-one and...you're way ahead of me, aren't you?

"There was much more to it—factoring in alterations made to the Earthly calendar for solstices and, of course, that pain-in-the-ass Gregorian business —but in the end I pinpointed seventy-one specific years scattered through all of history, and in each of those years, using the prime number formulae, I pinpointed one person whose life not only fit *exactly* the numerical pattern that had been discovered, but who had been blessed — or cursed, depending of course on your point of view — with 'one of those faces.' That's the short version and believe me, it wasn't as easy as it sounds."

"What happens if I say no?"

"I thank you for your time and go away disappointed. I provided for the possibility that at least nine of you would refuse. I can reconstruct most of His face with what I already have, and guess the rest with a large degree of accuracy. But I'm stubborn, Joel. I am so close to having all of the sections. It's been my life's work and I will not be stopped. I won't resort to Inquisition or Gestapo or Khmer Rogue tactics in order to achieve my goal — even though I *could*." He held up the mask. "So —"

" — you need my decision."

"Not until you know what will happen if you say 'yes.'"

"I assume that people will stop singling me out like they've done my entire life."

His eyes narrowed into slits. "Don't let's be flippant, dear boy. Think about everything you've learned today. *Think*."

The notebook.

I pulled it from my pocket and looked at the pages. "Oh, no..."

"Oh, yes. People will no longer single you out. Your face — which you've always thought was so very nondescript — will become just that. Someone meeting you for the first time won't be able to remember what you look like ten minutes after you've parted ways. You'll be just another faceless face in a sea of faceless faces. Now, being the social butterfly that you are, that's probably not going to bother you too much. However —"

I held up the notebook. "The stories."

"Exactly. Since you will have given me your First Face, those same people who won't be singling you out also won't be telling you their stories. And because they won't be doing that, there are going. To be. Consequences. Do you understand?"

A tight, ugly knot was forming between my chest and throat.

"I understand," I whispered. "Is that all?"

"No. There's one last thing, and it might be the deal-breaker."

He told me.

I listened carefully.

Thought about everything I'd learned.

And said yes.

"Lean back." He placed the first mask on my face. It weighed no more than ether. Then, one by one, he removed each successive mask and layered it on top of the one before until I wore all of them.

Have you ever used one of those sinus-headache masks? The ones that have that icy blue glop inside? That's what it felt like. An overpowering wave of cold spread across my face, seeped into my skull, through my brain, and formed a wall of frost in the back of my head. I shuddered and reached up.

Listen grabbed my arm. "Don't touch it. You'll lose your hand."

Soon it became a pleasant liquid numbness. I sighed and maybe even smiled.

"Feels better now, does it?"

"...yes..."

"Then it's done. Keep your eyes closed, dear boy. When you open them again I'll be gone. It's been genuine pleasure meeting you, Joel. You're a decent man who still has a lot to offer the world. I fervently hope you'll believe that someday. Now take a deep breath and hold it for a few seconds."

I heard something click a moment later. When I exhaled and opened my eyes, Listen was gone. I touched my face. It felt no different.

Back in my car I adjusted the rear-view mirror and caught a glimpse of myself.

Then wept.

* * *

I find it difficult to watch the local news or read *The Ally* these days. Every time I come across a story about a murder, a sexual assault, a beating, suicide, or any one of a thousand commonplace horrors we've grown so accustomed to, I wonder if the person who committed the act might have done otherwise if only they could have found some stranger to listen to their story.

It's not that stories like these never appeared in the paper before, it's just I don't recall there having been so *many* of them.

I don't sleep as well as I used to.

* * *

I received a postcard from Listen: *Having a here time—wish you were wonderful! (A joke, dear boy.) Nine to go. I think this turned out rather well. You were still wearing it, by the way.*

On the other side was a photograph he'd taken of me in the park that day. I am leaning against the picnic table with my eyes closed. My face seems to glow in the sunlight which whispers a thousand soft colors of thanks. It is a peaceful face. A beautiful face. A compelling, kind, compassionate face.

It belongs to a stranger.

* * *

The question that keeps nagging me is: *Why?*

Why, in order to know the face of God, must the same horrors caused by our having *not* known it be perpetuated?

You could argue that these horrors on the local news and in *The Ally* border on the insignificant when compared to the holistic catalogue of human misery. You would be right, I suppose. Unless you suspect you're the cause. And, no, filing it under "Sins of Omission" and going out for sushi doesn't help much.

I miss being asked to pose for pictures, be them of myself alone or in a group. I miss *not* being asked, just having someone click away. But mostly, I miss having complete strangers come up to me with their stories. I didn't think I would, but since that day with Listen I've come to realize just how much that meant to me.

Like I said, I don't sleep so well anymore.

* * *

The people I know and work with treat me differently. So do the members of my family. Nothing major, mind you, but there's a certain caution in their eyes whenever they're around me.

A few nights ago, after Amy, Tommy, and I had gone to a movie (I see the two of them nearly every day now), we went for a pizza. While waiting for it to be delivered to the table, Tommy begged some quarters to play a video game. He smiled when I handed him the money, then exchanged a "You-Gonna-Ask-Him-Or-Not?" look with his mother before sprinting over to the machines.

I stared at my sister. "What was that about?"

She took hold of my hand. "You know that Tommy and I really enjoy spending time with you, right? You've been really wonderful ever since the hospital—"

" —Christ, I was just as relieved as you that it was only migraines."

"Oh, the medicine works wonders, Joel, it really does. It makes the pain go away and Tommy says sometimes it makes him feel all 'shiny.' Isn't that the coolest way to describe it?"

"Yes, but that still doesn't tell me what that look was about."

"Tommy's been worried about you, and so have I. Hell, most everyone in the family has."

"*Because...?*"

"You don't look like yourself. I mean, you *look* like yourself, but there's something...I don't know...something *missing*, I guess. You look so sad these days."

I squeezed her hand and smiled, though I doubt it registered with her.

"I'm doing okay." Which wasn't exactly a lie, but wasn't exactly the truth, either; it was just safe. I keep hoping that "safe" will help me sleep.

"You sure?"

"As sure as anyone can be, I guess."

"Then why do you look so sad all the time?"

Would you understand? I thought. *If I were to tell you the story, would you even believe me, or would hearing it only add to the burdens you already carry? I wish there were some way you could answer me without my having to say anything, but that's a miracle I can only depend on, not believe in, so I will seek safety from my sins of omission in a kind-of silence.*

"I don't know," I said, then shrugged. "Maybe I've just got one of those faces."

The Sisterhood of Plain-Faced Women

"We will gather images and images of images
        until the last — which is blank:
        This one we agree on."
                                        — Edmund Jabés, "Mirror and Scarf"

1. Ones Who By Nature

As she watched people file into the pub Amanda found herself recalling some lines from an old T.S. Eliot poem: *In the room the women come/and go/Talking of Michelangelo.*

How many women, she wondered, had come in here since she'd first sat down, come in quite alone but looking ever so lovely, only to leave with a man in tow, complimenting him on how wonderful he looked and getting the same in return? How much attention had these women relinquished on their faces, their lovely, just right, just *so* faces, making sure the eye shadow wasn't too heavy, the base not too thick, the rouge not too bright, all of it in an effort to — as that old cosmetics slogan used to say — Right Nature's Wrongs?

In the room the women come and go...

Lighting a cigarette, she blinked away a sad memory and shrank into herself.

There are lonely ones who by nature cannot smile; watching in silence as people pass by, they never dare to speak for fear they might say the wrong thing. It would be a mercy if the Passing People became little more than vague shadow-shapes to the lonely ones, but that rarely happens; always there is something that draws attention: a knowing smile; a certain glint in the eyes; the lilt of a voice; the brief, sensuous, teasing scent of a woman's perfume or a man's cologne that still clings to the body of their partner; an echo of the embrace, the kiss, the humid passions left amidst soft, rumpled sheets and in the damp, sculpted impressions that moistly reshaped downy pillows: *O my love, my love, my love....*

Amanda looked toward the left —*If only I had a smile like hers*—and the chill of her isolation deepened; she looked straight ahead —*What I wouldn't give for her cheekbones*—and suddenly the ache in her center widened, a pit, a chasm, threatening, as it always did, to swallow her whole.

In an attempt to make herself feel better and pull her thoughts out of the mire she reminded herself that, for a good long while now, by choice and thanks to a lot of hard work, hers was a life marked not by giddy emotional highs and gut-wrenching spiritual lows but a steady unbroken line of small disappointments occasionally counterbalanced by equally small satisfactions, all of them the sum total of an average woman's existence; for that was the word that best described Amanda: average.

Or so people told her.

She crushed out her cigarette much more violently than she'd intended, then rubbed her eyes much too hard, amazed again at how pliant they felt under their slightly quivering lids. It would take so little pressure for her thumb and index finger to become spears...

She pulled her hands away, opened her eyes, and caught a glimpse of her inverted reflection in the small silver spoon lying beside her glass.

At least the ugly, the scarred or deformed, were given pity; awe was reserved for the truly beautiful, but at least the ugly were given some quarter; either way, both received attention from the people who passed.

She stared at her half-empty glass, chastising herself for thinking this way. She'd never been the type to indulge in the false luxury of self-pity —well, maybe once, long ago in dead yesterday, when she'd been younger and so damnably foolish and was quick to spill the contents of her heart; yes, then, probably at least once; but now —now these evenings of quiet soul-searching were the closest she ever came...still, there could be found, from time to time, when one person too many failed to return a look or a smile or an "Hello," a certain edge in her voice, not quite bitter but more than dark enough, intended to cut not whomever she spoke with but herself. Call it resignation.

For at least the ugly were given pity.

The plain were simply left alone.

At the bar a woman laughed a little too loudly at a joke told by the man sitting two stools to her left. The woman took a second to catch her breath and regroup, her eyes fixed solidly on the man's face, just long enough so he'd know she was appraising him, making a decision, then the moment of truth arrived and she gathered her drink and her purse and gracefully, promisingly, with perhaps a bit more stretch-and-wiggle than was needed, moved closer to him.

Amanda ordered another diet soda, smiling at the waiter who either didn't notice or didn't care.

She stared down at her folded hands. She had come to know her routines as well as her limitations: Fridays were for collecting a paycheck, going to the bank, then over to the pub for dinner and two weak cocktails before heading home for a little television, then it was off to bed with a novel. She only drank on Friday, her wild day, her crazy day, her get-down-get-funky-Get-Real day, because too much alcohol might serve to soften her resolve, and after thirty-seven years of being eclipsed by others' smiles, others' eyes, others' voices and faces and figures, Amanda knew that soft was dangerous.

Her soda arrived. The waiter was perfunctory, abrupt, damn near rude; he tossed down a napkin, set the drink on top of it, laid her check on the edge of the table, and cleared away her remaining dinner dishes. He never once looked at her, never once said anything.

The woman at the bar laughed again and slipped her hand under the joker's arm, and soon the two of them were gliding toward the door, compliments flowing freely, the scent of her too-expensive perfume mixing with the aroma of his cheap cologne, an augury of things to come.

God, and it wasn't even seven o'clock yet.

...the women come and go....

Amanda watched them leave, unaware that her grip had tightened around the glass.

Music oozed from the jukebox in back—a sappy love song, wouldn't you know? She checked her watch, took a few sips of her soda, and was reaching into her purse for money to pay the check when the woman came in.

Every set of eyes, including Amanda's, turned toward her.

Her physical beauty was breathtaking. Shimmering. Enviable.

Those women who were with a man suddenly reached for their partner's hand—just to make sure no one got any ideas; men who were alone casually glanced in the nearest mirror, straightening their ties and patting down their hair, readying themselves for the approach.

The woman herself seemed oblivious to any of it and looked for a place to sit. The pub was crowded and Amanda quickly realized that sitting on a barstool was too common and so held no interest for this woman—

—who quickly crossed the room and, without a word, sat down across from Amanda in the booth.

"Please join me," said Amanda in a flat, irritated voice. The woman smiled without looking at her, then turned her attention toward a group of men clustered near the end of the bar.

Amanda's grip on her purse tightened. So. Much. More. It. Hurt.

It was one thing to see a man's eyes effortlessly dismiss you; it was another thing altogether when a woman like this so glaringly snubbed you because you couldn't compare to her.

I must be the perfect contrast to you, thought Amanda, *and therefore the perfect accessory.*

She swallowed back her anger, reasoning with herself. After all, there *was* no other place for the woman to sit but here. Fine—

—but that didn't mean she had to act like this; she could have at least said something, a hollow greeting, but she'd chosen to ignore Amanda in the rudest way possible.

You have every right to feel offended.

Amanda was not a vindictive person, had always thought herself to be a level-headed pragmatist, but at that moment, in that place, with that woman and her beauty declaring they wanted no part of the plain creature sitting across from them, she felt a fury so intense, that stung so deep inside of her, she thought for a moment her bones might dissolve. It was the most violent, frightening sensation she'd ever known. Why tonight, after all this time, she'd felt a stab of truly unreasonable jealously was beyond her; she only knew that she did, and it was ugly, and diminishing, and she hated it.

She threw down the money on top of the check and left the booth, only to have her vacant seat immediately taken by a man who'd been hovering so close he actually bumped her shoulder as she stood. The woman turned toward him and for the first time Amanda got a look at her eyes: the purest bright azure blue, an early summer sky, the type of eyes heroines in novels and on television always had.

God, those eyes!

On her way out the door Amanda glanced at her reflection in the long mirror behind the bar, noting with pride that she'd looked far worse in her day; her light reddish-brown hair still held its luster from this morning's shower and her face, though plain, yes, was a pleasant one, a compelling one, the face of someone who observed, who listened — and not just to the words that someone might say but to the unspoken meaning beneath those words as well. Hers was the face of a friend on whom you could always depend, one who did not expect to get something in return for her kindness and compassion.

And *her* eyes...hm, yes, well...not a pure bright azure blue but a striking enough hazel, sparked by a sharpness of intelligence — after all, becoming an insurance actuary (the type of math fool even computer geeks thought of as a nerd) wasn't exactly easy.

There.

Her silent pep-talk done, she made her way out to her car, feeling content with who and what she was, though no less lonely.

As she slid into the driver's seat her vision blurred. The world washed away like sidewalk chalk drawings under a great and sudden downpour. She blinked once, twice, then uncontrollably, leaning down and pressing her forehead against the steering wheel to kill the dizziness and disorientation. She took several deep breaths. After a few more frenzied, loopy seconds, it passed.

That's when she heard someone screaming.

Loud, ragged, and shrill, the scraped-raw howl of an animal in agony blasted through one of the pub's half-opened windows and latched onto the back of Amanda's neck.

The scream was quickly underscored by several loud, panicky shouts, then the *whump-crash!* of glasses being smashed, maybe knocked to the floor by some drunk who'd fallen across a table but she knew that wasn't right, knew it as surely as her name because now the underscoring voices and panicky shouts were growing in density and volume and number, nearing hysteria as another, worse scream erupted and the upper half of a figure smashed through one of the windows, a familiar figure, a beautiful figure clutching at her lovely face, hands clawing at bloody, empty eye sockets. The woman screamed a third time, though not as loudly, as someone inside tried to pull her back in. Amanda watched horrified as two men with slashes of blood staining their shirts grabbed the woman's arms, trying to calm her. It did no good. Her pitiful screams quickly faded under the wail of an ambulance siren slicing through the damp night air.

Amanda closed her eyes, offering a silent prayer that the woman would be all right. Maybe she had been arrogant and rude and offensive, but no one deserved the kind of pain that produced a scream like that. No one.

Jesus Christ, what had *happened* to her?

As the ambulance roared into the parking lot Amanda blinked away a few tears—feeling more than a little guilty for the way she'd judged the woman so harshly—and sat back in the seat, pulling a few tissues from the box on the dashboard and drying her eyes. The police wouldn't be too far behind the ambulance and she *was* a witness, of sorts, and—

—she looked into the rear-view mirror to see if she'd smeared her mascara too badly—

—felt strangled by the cry that clogged her throat as she saw her eyes—

—so blue so blue so pure bright azure blue, lovely and bright and sparkling in the night—

The commotion of the paramedics and the chaotic shuffling of the pub crowd covered the sound of Amanda shrieking into her hands.

2. To Remain?

She had been forced to leave state college one semester into her first year because her father had gotten laid off from the plant and her parents needed her help. Though the letter her mother sent wasn't obvious in its manipulations, it nonetheless managed to push all the right guilt buttons. Two days after receiving it Amanda withdrew from school and used her last forty-five dollars to buy a bus ticket back to Cedar Hill. It was during the four-hour bus ride that she began to wonder about the price a person paid for so-called "selfless" acts. From the moment she'd stepped into the iron belly of the road lizard her throat had been expanding, then contracting at an alarming rate, finally forcing her to open the window next to her seat so she could breathe easier. Her chest was clogged with anger, sorrow, confusion, and, worst of all, pity. Everyone knew the plant was on its last leg, that the company had been looking for an excuse to pull up stakes ever since that labor riot a few years back, and when it happened, when the plant went down, so would the seven hundred jobs that formed the core of the town's financial stability.

More than anything Amanda didn't, dear God, didn't want to end up like every other girl in town; under- to uneducated, with no dreams left, working nine hours a day in some bakery or laundry or grocery store, then coming home to a husband who didn't much like her and children who didn't much respect her, wearing a scarf around her head all the time to cover the premature gray hair, watching prime time soap operas and getting twelve pounds heavier with each passing year.

As she stepped off the bus she promised herself that, regardless of what eventually happened with the plant, she wouldn't betray herself for anyone or anything. That alone was her hope.

"I thank God for a daughter like you," said her father, embracing her as she stepped through the door. "Come on in and sit down and let your mother fix you up something to eat. It's good to see you, hon. Here, I saved the want ads from the last couple days, maybe you'll find something...."

She wound up taking a cashier job at the town's only all-night grocery store. Amanda smiled at her late-night customers, and spoke with them, and tried to be cheery because there was nothing more depressing than to find yourself in a grocery store buying a loaf of bread at three-thirty in the morning in a town that was dying because the plant was going under and no one wanted to admit it.

Still, Amanda smiled at them with a warmth that she hoped would help, from a heart that was, if it could be said of anyone's, truly good and sympathetic.

The customers took no notice.

For eleven months she lived in a semi-somnambulistic daze, going to work, coming home, eating something, handing her paycheck over to her parents once a week, then shuffling off to bed where she read until sleep claimed her.

Outside her bedroom window, the soot from the plant's chimneys became less and less thick but still managed to cover the town in ashes and grayness.

She read books on sociology, countless romance novels and mysteries, biographies of writers and film stars, years-old science magazines, and developed an understanding and love of poetry that had eluded her in high school. Of course she went for a lot of the Romantics, Donne and Keats and Shelley, as well as a few modernists —T.S. Eliot and James Dickey, Rainer Maria Rilke and the lyrical, gloomy Dylan Thomas. Cumulatively, they gave eloquent voice to her silent aches and hidden despairs.

Crime began to spread through the town: holdups, street fights, petty thefts, and acts of vandalism.

And in the center of it all stood the plant, a hulking, roaring dinosaur, fighting desperately against its own extinction as it sank into the tar of progress.

Amanda discovered *Jane Eyre* in the library one day. Over the next month she read it three times —

—and the dinosaur howled in the night —

—and her mother at day's end sat staring at the television or listening to her scratchy old record—

—and her father's eyes filled with more fear and shame as he came to realize he was never going to be called back to work—

—and somewhere inside Amanda a feeling awakened. She did what she could to squash it but it never really went away.

So sometimes, very late at night when shameful fantasies are indulged, she took a certain private pleasure as she lay in her bed, and usually felt like hell afterward, remembering the words to a nursery rhyme her mother used to read to her when she was a child:

> *"Mirror, mirror, tell me true*
> *Am I pretty or am I plain?*
> *Or am I downright ugly?*
> *And ugly to remain?"*

No man would ever want her in that special, heated, passionate way. She was too plain, and the plain did not inspire great passion.

Mirror, mirror, told her true.

3. "...She Was Alone When I Got There."

Amanda finished giving her statement to one of the police officers on the scene (who failed to ask for her address and home phone number until she volunteered the information) and was getting ready to leave when she saw the man who'd taken her spot in the booth. His shirt was spattered with dried blood and his face was three shades whiter than pale. He looked up from his shaking hands for a moment, through the swirling visibar lights and milling patrons, past the police officer who was taking his statement, and stared at her.

It seemed to her that she ought to say something to him—but what?

Before she could come up with an answer she found herself walking across the parking lot and coming up next to him. He was no longer looking at her—if he actually had been in the first place. He ran a hand through his hair and turned toward the officer beside him.

"You say she just doubled over suddenly?" asked the officer.

"Uh, yeah, yeah. It was weird, y'know? We're sitting there talking and then she starts...blinking. I'm thinking to myself, 'Oh, Christ, she's lost a contact lens,' then she bends over, real violently, like maybe she's gonna throw up or something and I moved out of the booth to, y'know, help her get out and over toward the bathroom but she's making this sound, this awful sound like she's choking and now I'm shaking 'cause I've never had to Heimlich someone but she sounds in pain, serious pain, and I reached over to grab her and she pulls away and covers her eyes with her hands, and now she's groaning and wheezing and people around us are looking, so I reach for her again and that's when I see there's all this...blood coming out from under her hands. It was fuckin' horrible."

The officer finished writing something down, then said, "Was there anyone else in the booth with her?"

"No. She was alone when I got there."

Amanda turned away, biting down on her lower lip as if that would be enough to shield her from the invisible fist that had just rammed into her gut, and half-walked, half-ran to her car where she checked her eyes — no, not her eyes, not hers at all — again in the rearview mirror, then turned the key in the ignition, backed out, and drove away.

She had no idea how long or how far she drove, only that she had to stay in motion while the numb shock of realization ebbed into a dull thrum of remorse. She hadn't meant for anything to happen to the woman, not at all, but —

— Was there anyone else in the booth no she was alone when I got there no she was alone no she was ALONE —

—bastard had bumped right into her. Right into her.

Twenty deadened minutes later, feeling very much like an etherized patient on the anesthetist's table, she parked in front of a church, stepped out of the car, then walked up the steps and through the doors, pausing only to dip her fingers in the marble font of holy water and make the Sign of the Cross over her forehead and bosom, then strode down the aisle, through a set of small wooden doors, lowering to her knees as she pulled the doors closed and a small overhead light snapped on —

"Bless me, Father, for I have sinned."

Kneeling in the confessional, her voice that of a disembodied ghost, Amanda felt as if she were being operated by remote control, only vaguely aware of the words coming out of her mouth, mundane sins — cursing, lusting, small acts of thievery like sometimes not putting a quarter in the box at work when she got a cup of coffee, sins of omission, white lies, I meant no harm, then she was whispering, humiliated, about impure thoughts that still moved her blood faster and still took her to a private place where moist fantasies waited for her...

...and in one of these private places where plain-faced fantasies lay hidden, she was as beautiful as she wished to be and with a man who not only loved her but desired her as a result of that love, his lips moving down the slope of her breasts, his tongue tracing soft circular patterns around her nipple —

She was suddenly, awkwardly aware of the claustrophobic silence in the confessional, and wondered how long she'd been quiet.

On the other side of the screen the priest asked, "Are you all right?"

She pulled a compact from her purse, opening it to examine her eyes in the mirror. "No."

"What's really wrong?" His voice was soft and velvety, like Burt Lancaster's in *Atlantic City*. She wondered what the priest looked like; maybe he was young, perhaps handsome and —

—*stop it right now, you're bordering on pathetic.*

She almost rose but hesitated for some reason, and in that moment the soothing male voice on the other side said, "Please, ma'am — uh, miss — if you can, try to forget that you're talking to a priest. I know that sounds trivial but you might be surprised how much it helps some people. You could pretend I'm a close friend —"

"—don't have any real close friends —"

"—then your mother or father, maybe a sister —"

"—my parents are dead and I don't —"

She blinked, realizing something. True, she had no siblings, had been an only child —

—but she did have sisters, nonetheless.

In restaurants, in the lobbies of movie theaters, standing in the checkout line at the grocery store or wandering the aisles of video rental stores twenty minutes before closing, they were there, her sisters, waiting for something that would probably never come along, waiting alone, always looking toward a place not imagined by the beautiful or ugly, a spartan, isolated place reserved for the plain, for those never noticed, not bothered with; every so often their eyes would meet her own and Amanda would detect a glint of recognition in their gaze: *I know just how you feel and just what you're going through, and I'd smile if I could but it'd probably look awkward, if not absurd, so I'll just go on my way and promise you that I'll remember your face, one much like my own, and I'll wish you well, and good luck, you'll need it.*

Then it was through the checkout, down the next video aisle, into the darkness of the movie theater, or out of the dining room and into the night, never speaking, never allowing for a moment of tenderness, keep that guard up because it's all you've got, and it should be enough, that guard, but sometimes it wasn't, sometimes it slipped and something painful leaked inside, or something ugly slipped out —

—she was snapped out of her reverie by the ghost of her voice.

"When I was a child my mother used to play this one record over and over, I don't know where she got it, Dad had bought the record player for me—it was one of those models that came in a carrying case, it had this really heavy arm—but Mom, she had this one record, the only one she owned, an old '78, a Nat King Cole song called 'There Will Never Be Another You' or something like that. It was one of the sappiest songs I ever heard, I never understood why she liked it so much. But she did, she loved it, and she used to have a few shots of whiskey after my dad went to bed, then she'd play that record over and over, until she got this dreamy look on her face, sitting there in her chair and listening to that song and pretending she wasn't who she was. Sometimes I could see it in her face, that wish. She was someone else and the song wasn't on a record, it was being sung to her by some handsome lover come to court her, to ask for her hand and take her away to a better life than the one she had, the kind of life she'd dreamed of when she was the age I am now. I used to sneak downstairs and watch her do this, and I'd laugh to myself, you know? I'd laugh at her because I knew that my life was going to turn out differently, I'd never be so stupid as to wind up marrying a man who didn't really love me like a husband should but I stayed with him anyway because that's what the Church told me I was supposed to do. I'd never do that. I'd never spend my days working around the house, doing the dishes and the laundry and the dusting, having no life of my own, no hobbies, no interests, spending half the afternoon fixing dinner, then half the evening cleaning up afterward, only finding time for myself after everyone went to bed and I could sip my whiskey and play a goddamn record by Nat King Cole about there never being another me. I mean, I was just a kid, I was only in grade school, and Mom was old and used up and kind of funny at those times. But now it's twenty years later and here I am, just like her —hell, I even have that record of hers! It's the only thing that was really *hers* that I have, just like my dad's old straight-razor. A couple of award-winning keepsakes, huh? I look at these things of theirs, then I look at my life and...I try to keep the bad feelings at bay but sometimes it doesn't work. I've turned into her. There's no man who loves me, all I've got is my work, and instead of whiskey and Nat King Cole I've got two weak cocktails on Friday night after work and *Jane Eyre* or well-thumbed collections of poetry or a ton of videotapes, most of them romantic comedies. My God, if I had any kids they'd be laughing at me now, sneaking down after I think they're asleep and watching Mom get all teary-eyed over a book or movie or poem. They'd look at me and laugh and say, 'Look at her, she thinks she's Katherine Hepburn or something.' Most of the time I can get by but on nights like tonight I...I feel so lonely I could scream, so I tell myself that at least there's my job, at least there's a place I can go where I won't have to think about how I feel, except now I work with a bunch of other people, most of them women—and younger than me—and they all want to tell me about their love lives. 'You've got a kind way about you,' they say, or 'You're such a good listener.'

"Oh God, when I hear them going on about their love lives, how it's so hard being in a relationship because they don't agree on...on what kinds of toppings to get on a pizza or who should make the first move or how truthful they should be or why they don't feel comfortable making a serious commitment just yet...when I hear all this, I really want to slap them sometimes, you know? They have no idea how it feels to be the 'nice' girl who's always there, always willing to listen, the girl you can call anytime because she's always home, who's friendly and reliable like an old dog or five bucks from Grandma in your birthday card every year. I know I'm not the most stunning woman ever to walk the face of the Earth, but...." She reached into her purse for a tissue to wipe some of the perspiration off her face. Unable to find one, she kept searching around while she spoke.

"It's amazing how relaxed a man can be when he's in the presence of a woman he thinks doesn't need or want passion. I don't know how many times I've had a guy I know make a mock pass at me, then we'll both laugh like it was no big thing. I'm not feeling sorry for myself, that's too damned easy, and I know that I'm plain, but the thing is, because I'm plain, I'm safe. And safe means being rendered sexless."

She took a breath, weighing the truth of that word.

"Sexless. And sometimes I'd like to pull all these people aside who are so overwrought about their shaky sex lives and whisper that word to them, because it's a feeling they'll never know. Because with all their whining and crying and bitching and all their melodramatic romantic suffering, they'll always be able to find someone who wants them, even if it's just for one night. And I'd like to know how it feels from their side, just once. To be wanted that way just once, to be that beautiful for just one night."

She looked toward the small tinted glass separating her face from the priest's, caught sight of her face, saw the azure eyes, and remembered the other woman's screams.

"It hurts, Father. Sometimes it physically hurts! I don't know how but I...I did something tonight, caused something to happen. I didn't mean for her to get hurt, to suffer like she did, but I—"

The words clogged in her throat when her hand brushed against something inside of her purse.

Something small.

Soft.

Moist.

And round.

"What is it?" asked the faceless priest.

Amanda couldn't answer.

She opened the top of her purse wider, then slowly looked down inside, tilting it toward the dim light.

Then she saw them.

Saw them and gasped and snapped closed her purse and leapt from the confessional and ran down the aisle sobbing, the sound of her grief echoing off the wide arches above as she kept running, wanting to rip the purse off her shoulder and throw it away and never look inside again, wanting to close her eyes—not her eyes, not hers at all, just different eyes in her head—close them forever and not have to face her reflection or see the way other people looked at her, close the eyes and make everything go away, deny that what had happened was real and make everything better by that denial but she knew it was true and didn't understand why, and now she was outside the church, running down the stone stairs, the priest following and calling for her to stop, please, stop, but she couldn't, she was too frightened as she threw herself in the car and flung the purse into the back seat, slammed the door, and pulled away, the houses and street signs blurring as she sped past, lights melting, images flowing into one another like paint on an artist's canvas, blues into tears into yellows into aches into reds —

...*Talking of Michelangelo....*

—into greens into curses and back to blues, signs guiding her way, **STOP, YIELD, ONE WAY, ROAD CLOSED AHEAD**, rounding the corner, finding detours, familiar trees, lonely trees and this empty street, dark houses, dirty fences, take a breath, there you go, calm down, take another breath, slow down, breathe in, out, in, out, that's good, that's a good girl, slow it down, pull it over, close to the curb, there ya go, here we are, home sweet, ignition off, keys out, all stopped, all safe, alone, alone, alone.

She stared at the front of her house, then turned around and lifted her purse as if she had only —

—only —

—*only one way to know for sure.*

She took a deep breath, exhaled, then opened her purse and looked inside.

Silence; stillness.

She calmly reached in and took them out, holding one in each hand like a jeweler examining uncut diamonds.

They were still quite moist, sheened in corneal fluid.

No sparkle now.

But still a striking enough hazel.

She felt a pang of remorse, for until this moment she'd never realized how pretty her old eyes had been.

"God, I'm gonna miss you," she whispered.

Then looked up into the night sky, into the depths of a cold, unanswering, indifferent heaven, where no angel of the plain-faced looked back down.

4. Discards

One afternoon, shortly after moving back home, she had wandered down to a local flea market and found a table covered with dolls. Among them was a set of mismatched nesting dolls ("*Matryoshka* dolls," said the old woman sitting behind the table. "You must always call them by their proper name."); the largest was the size and shape of a gourd, the second largest was almost pyramid-shaped, the next was an oval, the fourth like a pear, and the last resembled an egg. What surprised her was that each of them, despite their disparate shapes, was able to fit neatly inside the next, and the next, and so on, until there was only the original *matryoshka* holding all the rest inside.

She carefully examined the largest doll, somewhat shaken that its face bore a certain resemblance to her own. The artist had captured not only the basics of her face but its subtleties, as well: the way the corners of her eyes scrinched up when she was smiling but didn't want anyone to know what she was smiling about, the mischievous pout of her mouth when she had good news to tell and was bursting for someone to ask the right question so she could blurt it out, the curve of her cheekbones that looked almost regal when she chose to accent them with just the right amount of rouge—all these details leapt out at her, impressive and enigmatic, their craftsmanship nothing short of exquisite, as if the hand which painted them had been blessed by God.

She looked away for a moment, then looked back; no, she hadn't imagined it. The thing did look a little like her.

As she was paying for the set, the old woman behind the table told her, "The old Russian mystics claimed that the *matryoshka* had certain powers, that if a person believed strongly enough in the scene the dolls portrayed when taken apart and set side-by-side-by-side, then it would come true. A lot of old-country matchmakers used to fashion *matryoshkas* for the women of their village who were trying to find a husband and start their own families. It's said that someone created a set for Princess Alix of Hesse-Darmstadt that showed her marrying Nicholas II and having several children."

"Wouldn't it be nice if that were true?" said Amanda.

"But this set here, I have no idea what someone would want with it. Especially a young girl like you. None of the dolls resemble one another. It's like a bunch of riffraff, discards. Though it's odd, isn't it, how all of them fit together so well?"

"I like discards," Amanda replied. "It's nice to think that even the unwanted can find others like themselves and become a family."

"But these're all women."

"Then they're sisters. A family of nothing but sisters."

The old woman nodded her head. "I like that. I like that right down to the ground."

Amanda smiled. "Me too."

5. Galatea and Pygmalion

Once back inside her house after fleeing the church, Amanda quickly put the eyes in a large-mouthed mason jar containing a mixture of water and alcohol, then set the jar on the top shelf of the upstairs linen closet. She stood for a moment, watching them bob around, turning this way, then that, one eye looking toward the front while the other glanced behind it; finally they looked at her, then slowly, almost deliberately, turned toward each other.

Hey, babe, haven't I seen you somewhere before?

Why, yes, sexy, you do look sort of familiar.

Amanda closed the door, leaning her head against the frame. She gave up trying to invent a rational explanation because there wasn't one.

She went into the bathroom and washed her face. Looking up into the mirror, she stared at her new eyes. They were so perfect, so sparkling and bright, eyes that would cause anyone to stop and take notice, eyes that gave her face a luster it had never possessed before, eyes that would make people realize that maybe this particular package wasn't so plain, after all.

Then she remembered the woman's bloody face as it came through the window of the pub and at once cursed herself for being so narcissistic. She blinked, then took one last glance at herself—

—her nose.

Ohgod, *her nose.*

It was different.

Not so wide, so pug anymore; it was slender and perfectly angled, not rounded on the end but sharp like—

—like—

—like Sandy Wilson's nose. Sandy, who was the receptionist at the office, who'd gone out with half the men working there, men who smiled at her every morning as they passed by her desk, and Amanda began to shake as she remembered this afternoon when she was leaving she'd looked at Sandy and thought: *The reason her face looks so good, so delicate and chiseled and playful, is because of her nose, it's a really sexy nose, it accents her features without drawing attention to itself and makes her face seem all the more friendly and God, what I wouldn't give to have—*

—she covered it with her hands, hands that seemed to be folded in prayer, or were clamping down to rip this thing off her face so she could stand here and watch her old one grow back, and for a moment the image struck her as funny but she didn't laugh—

—she whirled around and went out into the hall and yanked open the door of the linen closet, looking up at the jar —

—her old eyes had company.

Slamming the door, her heart triphammering against her ribs, she ran downstairs and grabbed her purse and dumped its contents onto the kitchen table, frantically sifting through the debris until she found her small phone number/address book, then quickly looked up Sandy's home phone number, grabbed the receiver off the wall, and dialed the number.

A voice—not Sandy's—answered on the third ring.

"H-HELLO?" Whoever it was sounded nervous and panicked, damn near hysterical.

"Is...May I speak with Sandy, please?"

Amanda heard two other voices in the background, one of them Sandy's, the other an older man's, probably Sandy's father because she still lived with her parents, didn't she, she was only twenty and why in God's name was she wailing like that?

"There's b-b-been an accident," said Sandy's mother, her voice breaking. "Please call back tomorrow."

Click.

Amanda pulled the receiver away from her ear, stared at it for a moment, then slowly started to hang up—

—and saw her hands.

Slender, with long, loving fingers; artist's fingers.

She remembered the woman who'd been sitting on a bench in the small park behind the Altman museum downtown a few days ago, sketching that incredible sculpture of those grieving women that was attracting so much attention lately. Several people had gathered to watch what this artist was doing. She'd been in her early thirties, with strawberry-blonde hair, lovely in a hardened, earthy way. Amanda had stood unnoticed among the admirers—mostly men—staring at first the womans face, then her thick but not unattractive neck, and, finally, her hands.

Her strong yet supple, smooth hands....

Amanda fell against the kitchen table shuddering, the contents of her stomach churning, and tried very, very hard not to imagine what was—or rather, *wasn't*—dangling from the ends of that woman's arms right this second.

Back in the bathroom, she looked at her face again.

The lips this time, full and moist and red and alluring as hell.

Jesus Christ, whose lips are they?

Numbed, she checked the jar.

Getting pretty crowded in there.

She filled a portable cooler with ice and water and rubbing alcohol, pried the hands out of the jar and tossed them into the cooler; they hit the ice with a sickening, dead plop! and lay there like desiccated starfish.

She slammed closed the lid, then vomited.

Over the next two hours, it only got worse.

Her legs were next, model's legs, long and slender and shiny, with extraordinarily subtle muscle tone. Amanda wondered who she'd seen them on, and where, and what the woman must look like now.

Wondered, then wept.

As she did with everything else:

Breasts, full and firm, even perky, with tan aureoles so precisely rounded they seemed painted on, nipples so pink and pointy, and now here were there any blue veins visible on their surface, only a few clusters of strategically placed freckles that fanned outward from the center of her chest, creating teasing shadows of cleavage; then her hips were next, not the too-wide, too-sharp hips she'd been born with, not the hips that made it almost impossible for her to find blue jeans that fit comfortably, but hard, rounded hips, not wide at all but not too small, either, lovely hips, girlish hips, God-you-don't-look-your-age hips and a now-size-8 waist—

—the cooler filled up quickly and she had to go to the bathtub, adding water, ice, and alcohol to keep everything moist and sanitary—

—next was the stomach, not the slightly sagging thing she'd been carrying around for the last ten years but a deliciously flattened tummy, its taut, aerobicized, Twenty—Minute-Workout muscles forming a dramatically titillating diamond that actually undulated when she moved, a bikini stomach if ever there was one, abs of steel; then came her jaw, elegant and chiseled, the jaw of a princess, Audrey Hepburn in *Roman Holiday*; her neck became slightly longer, thinner, sculpted, losing the threat of a double chin that had been hovering for the last couple of years, the muscles flowing down toward the sharp, perfect "V" in the center of her collarbone, something she'd always thought was unbearably sexy—

—the bathtub was quickly filling but that was all right, there couldn't be too much left at this point—

—then, after a while, her bone structure began to change: ribs not so thick, shoulders not so wide or bony, knees not so awkward and knobby—

—the rest of her body began altering itself with each new addition, her features and limbs molding themselves to each other like sculptor's clay, an organic symbiosis, her forced evolution, heading toward physical perfection until, at last, her skin itself blossomed unwrinkled and creamy, sealing around everything like a sheet of cellophane.

Amanda was sitting on her bed when she felt the last of it take place, then rose very slowly—the pain of each change had grown more and more intense, the last few minutes becoming almost unbearable— and looked at herself in the full-length mirror hanging on the inside of her closet door, not sure whether to smile or simply die.

She had become both her own Galatea and Pygmalion.

No other woman she'd ever met or seen could compare with what stared back at her from the mirror.

She was completed, breathtaking, beautiful.

More than beautiful; she *was* Beauty.

And Beauty always has her way.

She told herself not to think about it, then went into the bathroom and pulled a bottle of prescription painkillers from the medicine chest, downing two of them before turning to face everything.

The remnants of Old Amanda.

There was arranging to be done.

By the time she finished there were four full Mason jars, as well as a full bathtub, sink, cooler, and toilet tank. The bones went into the laundry hamper along with several wet towels, and the skin, well-soaked, was draped over the shower curtain rod. She nodded, thinking to herself that it all looked very tidy, indeed.

She suspected that her mind would crumble soon—how could it not, after all this?—but hopefully the painkillers would kick in and she'd be nicely loopy before it got too bad.

She looked once more at her reflection in the mirror and thought, *Why not enjoy it while you can?*

Then it hit her: How in hell was she going to explain this at work on Monday?

Like my new clothes? I think they make me look like a new person, don't you?

She rubbed her temples, realizing that she had chosen to keep her own hair.

She liked that very much; liked it right down to the ground.

The pleasant, seductive numbness of the painkillers began to pour over her body, and she decided to go lie down for a little while.

She was just putting her head onto the pillow when she noticed that all six *matryoshkas* were displayed across the top of her dresser. She tried to remember when she'd taken them apart and arranged them this way.

She stared at them, noting after a few seconds that their shapes were now oddly uniform, all like gourds growing progressively smaller, right down to the baby who was no longer a baby but Amanda as she'd been at four years old; the next showed her as she'd been this morning; the next, as she'd been a few hours ago; the others, so silent and still, illustrated the rest of the stages of her transformation, the last and largest of them a sublime reflection of the woman who now lay across the room staring at it.

She felt so soft...

...In the room the women come and go...

...and it was so *good* to feel this soft, and sexy...

...Talking of Michelangelo...

...no guard now, no hardness, my sisters, I understand how you feel...

...a breath, a sigh, then—drained and exhausted—she felt herself falling asleep—

—in the room the women come and go—

—and was startled back to wakefulness by sounds in the upstairs hallway; slow, soft, almost imperceptible sounds; tiptoeing sounds.

She breathed slowly, watching her breasts rise and fall in the shadows, imagining some lover passionately kissing them, tonguing the nipples—

—the front door opened, then closed.

She sat up, holding her breath.

Looking around the room, she saw that her closet door was now closed; it had been open when she'd fallen asleep, and her bedroom door, closed before, was now standing wide open.

Jesus Christ, she hadn't been out for very long, just a few seconds, wasn't it? Just a moment or two but the time didn't really matter a damn, ten minutes or ten seconds because someone had been in here while she was asleep!

She jumped off the bed and ran into the hall, saw that the bathroom light was on, and kicked open the door.

No one was inside—

—but the sink was empty.

Just like the bathtub.

And the laundry hamper.

And the toilet tank and the portable cooler and all of the mason jars.

She stormed back into her bedroom and snapped on the overhead light, then flung open her closet door.

She stared at her wardrobe and knew instinctively that something was missing; she couldn't say *what*, specifically, had been taken, but she knew that the whole didn't match up quite right.

She sat down on the bed and stared at her reflection in the mirror hanging on the inside of the closet door.

Damn if she wasn't still a stunner.

Then she saw the *matryoshka* dolls behind her. No longer uniform in shape, they had returned to their original, disparate forms — a gourd, a pyramid, an oval, a pear, an egg, a seashell — but each of them now had one thing in common, one characteristic they hadn't shared before:

None of them had a face.

Amanda took a deep breath, then checked the clock.

It was only twelve-thirty. The clubs didn't close for another two hours and she wanted to be seen, to be admired, to feel pretty and wanted on this night.

It was nice to actually have the option for once.

She thought she knew what was happening, maybe. Maybe it would only be a matter of time, less than a few hours, and maybe she had all the time in the world and would be this gorgeous for the rest of her life, but either way she was going to make this evening count, goddammit!

She dressed quickly, purposefully choosing a pair of old jeans and a blouse that she knew she'd outgrown over a year ago.

Both fit wonderfully, hugging her form tightly, accentuating every wonderful curve. She threw an old vest on as well — which did wonders for emphasizing her bust—then unbuttoned not one, not two, but (for the first time in her life) three top buttons of her blouse, showing just enough of her freckles and cleavage and the slope of her breasts to make anyone want to see more.

She checked her face in the bathroom mirror, under the harsh, unforgiving glow of the fluorescent light.

No wrinkles, no bags, no blemishes; she needed no makeup.

She looked...delicious.

That made her smile, and brought a sparkle to her eyes.

"What say we go out there and win one for the Gipper, eh?"

She giggled, then Sparkle Eyes Amanda flowed out into the night.

6. The Water Doesn't Know

Taking a shortcut through town in order to get to her pub before it closed, Amanda was driving down the side street that served as the location of the Altman Museum when she thought she heard someone scream—

—and knew she saw a figure running from behind the museum.

Later, she would remember feeling frightened yet oddly detached from herself—much like the state she'd been in after fleeing the church earlier.

She knew this wasn't the safest area of the city, even during the day, but she nonetheless watched from a place outside her body as Sparkle Eyes pulled into a parking space beside the museum, got out of the car, and walked toward the small plat at the back of the museum that served as an ersatz-park where artists whose work was too big for indoor exhibition often displayed their pieces.

Sparkle Eyes walked up to a bench that sat near the park's entrance.

Sparkled Eyes looked down at the thick sketch pad that was lying face-down in the grass.

Sparkle Eyes kicked the pad over with her foot to see what the artist had been sketching—

—and that's when Amanda found herself firmly reunited with her new body, because the pages facing her were covered not with drawings but with wide slashes of blood—as if whoever had been sketching had suddenly had their throat cut—

—*or lost their hands*, she thought.

She looked around, nervous, and only then realized that the sculpture of the grieving women that had been such a crowd-drawing show piece for the Altman was gone.

In its place, a new *bas-relief* piece had been incorporated into the museum's outside back wall.

Looking once more at the blood-drenched sketch pad lying at her feet, Amanda approached this new piece.

For a moment she forgot to breathe, she was so stunned by what she saw.

A massive curtain of bluish-gray flowstone hung before her, its surface shimmering and shifting like sand beneath incoming waves at high tide. She had no choice but to think of it in terms of liquid, for everything about the image embedded in the curtain seemed to ripple.

The piece was of a woman, lying on her back, naked from the center of her chest upward, her hair cascading to the left as if draped over a pillow. Her arms were crossed over her center, the right slightly higher than the left, and her hands, their fingers slightly bent as if about to clutch at something unseen, unknown, were pressing down against the rest of her body, which was hidden underneath a wide sheet.

She stepped forward, peering, and saw that the sheet was composed of smaller stones and slates and sculpted shapes of uncountable fossils: toads, lizards, prehistoric arachnid crustaceans the likes of which she'd never seen, praying mantises, eels and serpents slithering over faded, ancient symbols and primeval drawings.

Even the skin of the woman in its center was not as she first perceived it to be: thin and transparent, misted with a fine scintillance like lavender spiderwebs, it allowed the viewer to see through the woman's surface to the millions of swarming, teeming, multiplying cells and legions of bacteria-like clumps within. There was an odd, damaged beauty to the sight, a vague impression of transcendence, of the human becoming the elemental, then the infinitesimal, and Amanda found herself drawn toward it but, at the moment of communion, something in the image seemed to pull back and become cold, alien, unreachable, leaving her to stare into exhausted eyes too much like her own, eyes that were balanced atop dark crescents. They were lifeless eyes, lightless and unfocused, beyond caring. They were her own eyes. The woman, she realized then, was herself as she used to be, Old Amanda, not Sparkle Eyes, and her mouth was curved downward, trapped somewhere between a pout and a groan, but as she moved a little to the side a parallax effect —aided in part by the small spotlights the museum had installed to help night viewing— took place; viewed from the right, this image of her was a sad, dark, twisted thing, but viewed from the left, she appeared to be beckoning a lover to her bed, her mouth teasing, her eyes filled with promise.

She reached out to touch her flowstone face and suddenly the upper portion of the curtain erupted with other faces, some angry, some gloomy, others insane-looking or hideously deformed, and a few that were not even close to being human; with mandibles clacking or antennae twisting in the air, these last faces, the inhuman ones, were in too-close proximity to that of her own image, threatening to fall on it and chew away her features. Far above them, their not-quite-formed eyes looking down, more faces moved in the deepening shadows, their fossilized skin covered in cracks and swarming with tiny things she couldn't bring herself to look at too closely.

She stumbled backward, the curtain of liquid stone rising higher, revealing more sick-making details: One of the faces near her own—this one little more than a skull with an impossibly large cranium encircled by two serpents—had a carving of a rose on its side, a most delicate rose, and its ghostly beauty rather than being out of place seemed right and proper, buried as it is in the terrible image, soft hints of red trickling outward into her hair, tinging it in blood.

She touched the rose, then pulled her hand away and saw that it was, indeed, blood.

She looked back to the bench where the sketch pad lay on the ground.

She looked at her new hands, and knew who'd been screaming, and why.

She looked back; all of the faces — her own included — opened their mouths and began to speak, words that she herself had said before, or thought, or heard others speak, others that she has thought of as her sisters, the plain-faced who are simply left alone:

"...he calls me out of the kitchen to admire a lovely actress on the television, then points to a Miss America-type and says she's a little too fat, you know, and her face isn't as pretty as it ought to be, and he never once thinks about how that makes me feel..."

She was aware of shadows moving from the darkness toward her.

"...I can't stand to look at my whole face, so if I'm combing my hair, it's only my hair that I see; if I use a mirror to put on lipstick, I hold it so close that I don't have to see my cheeks..."

The voices were coming from both the sculpture and from those shadowy figures slowly surrounding her.

"...never look at my naked body, and I'd rather walk out of the house without checking my clothes than look at myself in a full-length mirror because there's always that face on top, making a mockery out of the pretty clothes below it..."

Her sisters, nameless and lonely.

"...my face embarrasses me, it's so flat and dull; I can't even make it better with makeup..."

Each one clutching a jar to her chest.

"...and I never, NEVER let anyone take my picture because when I look at myself in a photograph I cringe inside...."

"Stop it," she whispered, then shouted, "STOP IT!"

The voices ceased, the faces faded back to their still, sculpted shapes, and her image suddenly, violently, rolled up out of sight, a window shade snapping closed.

Silence and murkiness.

Then a pair of glowing eyes, somewhere back in the shadows embedded in the piece.

"Who are you?" asked Amanda.

"I am what you once were. You are what became of me."

"Are you...me?"

"No. And yes. I am the First Woman—not Eve or Lilith—though some have called me by those names. I have also been called Shekinah, Metrona, Shine, Isolde, Old Roses, Bright Hands, and a million other names. I am the only woman, and all women. Even the last."

"You know me."

"No, no I—"

"You've seen me before, in certain faces you glimpse in restaurants, in the lobbies of movie theaters, standing in the checkout line at the grocery or wandering the aisles of video stores, waiting alone for something that will never come along, looking toward a place not imagined by the so-called beautiful or ugly, though I am in those faces, too. You know me. You came from me. I know you hurt. So ask me one question and I will answer you with the only truth there is; perhaps it will help your sadness."

Amanda did not hesitate: "Why are some of us plain and others so beautiful?"

A picture appeared in the wall, a framed print of M.C. Escher's *The Waterfall*. Amanda stared at it, then shook her head. "I don't understand."

Silence.

She stepped closer to the picture.

The water in the picture began to move.

The voice of Metrona, who was also Shine and Bright Hands, joined now by the Jar Sisters standing behind Amanda, sang: "'*Mirror, mirror, tell me true/Am I pretty or am I plain?/Or am I downright ugly?/And ugly to remain?*'"

Amanda watched closely, her eyes following the path of the water around the loop again and again and again, quite fast at first, then much slower. The path of the water seemed perfectly normal and natural to her — until she found herself right back where she started from. She blinked, sighed, took a deep breath, and followed the water's path once again, realizing at the halfway point that the entire loop, when taken as a whole, is manifestly an impossibility, yet at no point on the path going around the loop did anything go 'wrong'; she was able to go from point A to B to C and so on, all the way back around to A *but she shouldn't have been able to!* She decided to break the path up into sections and, taken by themselves, they were fine, but holistically they remained an absolute impossibility.

"What's wrong with this picture? It makes no sense."

The water turned silver and bright, then Shekinah, who was Isolde and Old Roses as well, said: " *'Mirror, mirror, tell me please/Is this my face I see?/So plain and ugly and pretty/One face made from three.'*

"The water doesn't know it's following an impossible path, Amanda; it's just water, flowing along. It doesn't care about what goes 'right' or 'wrong' in the loop, so long as it *goes*. There is no manifest beauty, no ugliness, no plainness or any kind of imperfection which lessens; there is only One, who once was Me, and now is Many, including You. There is only Woman; anything else is a lie.

"And Woman shouldn't care about lies like Beauty and Ugliness and Plainness. Just remember: As forgettable as you think your face is, there is someone out there who envies what you have; to whom *you*, as you are, are the ideal."

And with those words, the sculpture froze again, just a haunting *bas-relief* in flowstone at the back of a museum late, late at night.

She turned to confront the women with their jars but found she was alone.

She looked at the blood on her fingertips, then wiped them against the surface of the sculpture and half-walked, half-ran back to her car.

7. Absences

She went back to her usual pub — which was still quite crowded, surprisingly. The bartender and several of the servers were buzzing about the terrible thing that had happened earlier. There was a strong smell of disinfectant in the air but it didn't bother Sparkle Eyes, who noticed the empty booth near the back — the one next to the window covered by a sheet of particle board.

Everyone looked at her when she glided through the doors. Men glanced into mirrors, straightening their ties and patting down their hair. Women greedily took hold of their dates and shot her a look that said, *Don't try it, bitch.*

As she walked down the aisle, not having to look to see if anyone was watching her because she knew everyone was, her attention was caught by a song from the jukebox, an old Motown hit: "Always Something There To Remind Me." She stared at the back of the man who was leaning over the machine, punching in his next song choice.

Any guy who was a Motown fan got high marks in her book.

Ready or not, here I come, she thought.

Then he turned around.

Amanda's breath caught in her throat.

Dear God.

The acne scars on his cheeks were so deep she could see them even from where she was standing, some twelve feet away, and you could tell from the way he moved, from the way he looked down at the floor and would not make eye contact with anyone who passed, from the way his hands immediately —*snap!*— went into his pockets, you could tell that this was not a confident man, not a popular man, not a man who'd come here easily; it had probably taken all the nerve he could summon just to leave the house, let alone actually *walk into* this place. It wouldn't have surprised her to know that he was terrified, and it did not surprise her that he was sitting alone at a small two-person table near the jukebox and loud pinball machines and entrance to the billiards room; it did not surprise her that he gripped his half-empty glass a bit too tightly, or that his head came up a little too hard and a little too quickly whenever some woman nearby laughed; it came as no surprise that his waitress would not look at him, even though he smiled and tried to be friendly when she came to his table; it came as no surprise that he stared at his folded hands, that he rubbed his eyes a lot, that he smoked and blinked too much, and that he looked like he couldn't decide whether to cry, scream, leave, or just drop dead on the spot. Every move he made, every gesture, every awkward smile and self-conscious glance-around betrayed his true feelings, if only to Amanda: *I know I'm not much to look at, but I'm a nice guy, really I am, and I wish you'd sit down and talk with me, that's all I want, really, just to talk and nothing more, I'm not trying to get into your pants, promise, just let me buy you a Coke or something because I've been sitting here for most of the evening and I gotta tell you, I feel stupid and ugly and lonely and I don't know if I can handle it anymore so, please, if you wouldn't mind —*

—he froze, blanching, when he saw that she was staring at him, and for a moment, one slow, frightened, awkward and god-almighty-agonized moment, he stared back at her, just long enough for a gleam of hope to flash across the surface of his eyes —*Is she really looking at ME? Is that smile of hers meant for ME?*—then die a fast, sputtering, miserable death as reality kicked in —*Hell no, what would a woman like that want with YOU? How could a woman that damned beautiful be attracted to YOU, CRATERFACE?*—and before she could lift her hand to give him a little wave, a little gesture to tell him she was on her way and it was not, repeat not out of pity that she wanted to be with him but because she could tell he was a nice —hell!—a terrific guy, and she would settle for nothing less than a terrific guy —before she could do this, something inside of him, something weak and frightened and conditioned since childhood to kick in on those rare occasions when he felt like a fine, normal, and at least partially attractive man —this awful something reached up and jammed an iron butcher's hook into his heart and he...crumpled, simply crumpled. He looked away, ashamed, then turned toward the jukebox, downed what was left in his glass, then tossed a too-generous tip onto the table and jumped to his feet and made his way toward the rear exit door, head down, hands in pockets, shoulders slumped and trying hard not to shudder too much. Disgraced, defeated, diminished.

And alone; alone, alone, alone.

The song finished playing, then started again. Sparkle Eyes Amanda wondered if he sat in a favorite chair at home listening to this song over and over, sipping at his beer or whatever poison he picked until he got a dreamy look on his face and could pretend he was someone else.

By the time she got to the door and ran out into the parking lot, he was nowhere to be seen.

So Sparkle Eyes went back inside.

She took a seat at the far end of the bar and soon found herself laughing just a bit too loudly at some joke told by a man sitting two stools over. He smiled at her. She smiled in return. He moved closer, bought her a drink, and stumbled over his tongue several times, not able to look away from her face.

She laughed a soft laugh that ended in something like a low, promising purr, then touched a fingertip to his lips.

The rest was easy.

Because Beauty always has her way.

* * *

He was very skillful with her.

Kissing her everywhere and endlessly, licking her, a bite here, a nibble there, probing her with his fingers, cupping her breasts in his hands and tonguing her nipples in slow, wet, maddening circular patterns; she pulled back and said, "There's a halo around you," and he stopped for a moment, looking down at himself. There was a thin beam of moonlight slipping in under the window blinds; each hair on his body was isolated by that light like a bluish gossamer, a wrapping. "It's just a trick of the light," he replied to her, his hand resting for a moment on hers. His fingers were long and bony but soft, soft as her own supple neck. He ran those fingers up her arms and the little hairs there sprang to attention, then he touched her eyes with his fingertips; they were like pads, responsive to her every pore. Her eyelids fluttered beneath his touch and she drew her own fingers down his cheeks to the bone of his jaw, then down his neck, leaning forward and kissing his lips. Her mouth felt larger than human, able to protect his in its clasp. She felt his tongue beating against her lips and opened them and soon felt his saliva in her own, then his mouth was crawling down her body and she lay back, opening her vagina for him. Soon, her murmurs seemed to fill the room. She arched her back slightly as her knees bent around the small curve at the back of his head, pressing it slowly downward. They twined around each other as if their limbs had lost their natural form. A moment later he lifted his head from between her wet heat and moved up her belly to her breasts again, at first teasing her nipples, then sucking them deep into his hungry mouth, trailing his lips across her shoulders, his breath moist and warm against the side of her neck, his cock rigid and hot, his entry smooth and painless, the two of them rocking together, pumping slick and steady, and it was good, it was great, it was heaven, and Sparkle Eyes grabbed hold of his shoulders and rolled him onto his back, straddling his hips, locking her ankles under the backs of his knees as her own pushed out and down, her ass rolling back and forth across his groin, pushing him deeper inside of her as his hand grabbed one of her breasts and his mouth encircled the aureole, slurping and sucking and biting as he thrust himself upward with more force, ramming his erection deeper, deeper, and deeper still, and she threw back her head and arched her back, her nails digging into his well-toned pectorals, and she caught sight of their bodies reflected in the closet-door mirror; sweating, glistening, heaving bodies attacking one another, devouring one another, then came the sounds, low, throaty growls, grunts and sighs and strangled screams as their rhythm grew faster, harder, frenzied, bedsprings squeaking, almost causing her to laugh but she didn't, she wouldn't, she groaned instead, driving herself down, pushing his cock in so much deeper it was starting to hurt but she didn't care, she wanted him to bury it in her up to her throat so she dug her fingers into his chest, tangling them in his sweat-matted hair, God he felt so good, so thick and solid, pulsing, throbbing, sliding wet and steamy into her slick sex as she doubled her efforts, grinding down with all her strength; he arched his back and groaned, she threw back her head once again and squealed, then moaned, then screamed, her juice-soaked thighs sliding against his own, then he was sitting up again, burying his face between her breasts, his tongue lapping at her nipples, then he was biting them, hard, harder, and she loved it, it was incredible, and now they were moving side to side as well as up and down, the chaotic motion setting fire to her body as she pulled up and slammed back down on him, tossing her head to the side—

—she glimpsed the shadow-shape reflections in the mirror, dozens of them that were standing in the inverted doorway of her bedroom, moving as one toward her bed, surrounding it, their eyes glistening as they watched in silence, their breathing getting heavier and more ragged along with her own, their sighs soft and excited, rising into moans, then squeals, then near-deafening screams of ecstasy —

—their faces were plain and forgettable but Sparkle Eyes knew what they wanted, and what she wanted—to be desired as they'd never been desired before, to be *wanted* in that private, heated way, to be *lusted after*, just once, that's what they wanted—and she was giving it to them, just this once, just for tonight, just so they'd know what it was like instead of having to imagine it, and she could feel some part of them inside of her as well, some small part from each of them, and now the man below her was really going at it because he wasn't in control now and never had been, it was all her, and it was good, so good as she reached over his shoulders and dug her fingernails into his back, drawing them straight up, turning them into claws as she bucked and thrashed and wiggled, driving herself down one last time squealing and howling and screaming.

"God, yes, do it...do it...*shoot it* in me, in me, in me NOW! YES! GOD, YES!"—

—one of the shadow-shapes moved forward and touched the largest *matryoshka* doll—

—*In the room the women come and go* —

—Sparkle Eyes felt the pressure building up inside of her, roiling around, looking for release, and thought the veins in her neck might burst from the strain, then she felt him explode inside of her, his orgasm blinding, overpowering as he groaned, then grunted, then moaned loudly, ramming his hips upward, burying his cock even deeper, shooting his seed all the way up to the back of her teeth, and she wanted to come with him, wanted their climaxes to be one and the same, but that wasn't going to happen, *his* orgasm was the point, coming like he'd never came before because he'd never, ever, *ever* been with a woman as stunning as her, and *God* did he come, hard and strong and endlessly, with such intensity she actually thought he was going to pass out before it was over, but he didn't, he stayed with her, groaning and crying out until he was spent, then, smiling, suppressing a giggle, she leaned down and kissed the side of his face, lifting herself slowly off of him, his still-throbbing erection sliding out of her, the head giving one last spurt before the whole thing flopped to the side, something that made them both laugh, then he rolled her onto her back and took his hand and began massaging her vagina —

" —you don't have to do that," she said. "It doesn't matter if—"

" —it matters to *me*," he said, but not angrily, not with the ridiculous macho-man determination that dictated a man wasn't a man unless he could make a woman come; no, this was said with concern, and surprising tenderness, as one who wished to return pleasure in equal measure, so Sparkle Eyes stretched back and parted her legs a bit wider and whispered, "Okay, then, just...touch me here —gently, gently...there you go..." and he worked his fingers until she came, grabbing the sheets in her hands and arching her back, his fingertips moist and warm with her juices, then they were lying beside each other, faces almost touching, and he couldn't seem to keep his hands off of her.

"I'm sorry you couldn't come with me inside of you," he said.

"Shhh, don't apologize, it was just as good this way."

"The halo's around you now, around your whole body."

She looked toward the mirror and saw that the moonlight had moved to her side of the bed, its light glinting off her sweat, making her glow, and she felt as if she were glowing from somewhere deep within, from a place only another woman might understand.

"I wish moments like this would never end," she said, not only to the man next to her but to the shadow-shape sisters filling the room. "Right now I don't want any of this to go away, not the sweat, not the stains, not your fingers touching me, not this...this pounding in my chest."

"I know how you feel," he said, his fingertips tracing subtle patterns on her bare, slick belly.

"Do you? Do you really? I wonder. I—no, please, don't...*mmm*, don't stop doing that, okay, it's just...it's just that right now I wish there was something more powerful, more ethereal to help me express this feeling. There should be a new language, you know? One that can only be spoken between two people who've just made love, only then, and only until the sun comes up or they have to get out of bed and go their separate ways. I know that must seem kind of silly to you—"

"—no, not at all."

She smiled at him, then placed a finger against his lips.

For a while, neither of them spoke; she wouldn't allow it.

Laying her head against his solid, washboard-sculpted stomach, she closed her eyes and for a few minutes became lost in a pleasant limbo, neither awake nor dreaming, just lost in contented stillness of her body, heart, and mind, turning her face toward his flesh and kissing his chest, feeling his body tense ever so slightly, and soon they were making love again, less frenzied this time, more patiently, taking the time to enjoy each other's bodies in ways they hadn't bothered with before, and this time she came with him inside of her (though he did have to reach down and use his hand again as well, but that was all right), then they both fell asleep for a few minutes; when they awoke she could sense his trying to think of a tactful way to broach the subject of leaving. She decided to save him the trouble and, lifting her head, swallowed once and said, in a hoarse, throaty, deeply satisfied voice, "Uh, listen, I've got a long day tomorrow and I've never been much of a morning person, so if you wouldn't mind—"

She watched as he dressed himself in silence, then leaned over, kissed her bare back, and left.

She waited until she heard the front door close behind him, then kneaded her vagina, soaking her palms and fingers in his juices as well as her own, then pulled her hands up and pressed them against her face, inhaling the rich, wet scent of their sex.

With her hands still pressed firmly against her face, she began to cry.

There are lonely ones who by nature cannot hold on to their joy, no matter how hard they try. Like the acne-scarred man in the pub, something in Amanda had been trained since childhood never to trust happiness.

She'd learned her lesson well, and felt damned because of it.

And empty, so empty, empty, empty...

"Do you remember?" asked one of the shadow-shape sisters. "Do you remember that time in the sixth grade when Tommy Smeltzer ran over and kissed you right on the mouth? You were surprised because you'd had a crush on him for so long but didn't think he even knew you were alive."

"I remember," said Amanda.

"Do you remember," asked another sister, "how you tried to put your arms around him but he grabbed your wrists all of a sudden? He twisted your arms behind your back while a couple of his friends threw mud in your hair, then left you in the middle of the playground?"

"...yes..."

Another shadow-sister moved closer. "Remember the way all of the girls stopped jumping rope and made a big circle around you and pointed and laughed? You never forgot that sound, did you? You closed your eyes and asked God to let you die right there and then because you didn't think anyone would want to be friends with you after that."

"...they never did."

"And you spent the rest of your grade-school recesses leaning against the chain-link fence that surrounded the playground, wishing that someone would come over and ask you to play with them."

"I thought I'd forgotten that."

Another sister moved closer. "You never tried to make any friends after that, ever, not even after you were in high school. You were always afraid you'd get laughed at. Why have you spent so many years putting mud in your own hair?"

"...don't know, I...I don't know. Scared, I guess. So scared, all the time." She wiped her eyes, then rose from the bed and crossed to one of her bookshelves, kneeling down to scan the spines until she found the one she was looking for.

She flipped through the pages of her college yearbook, remembering the endless nights of waitressing and typing term papers and even working as an operator for one of those I-900 "psychic revelations" lines that helped foot most of her bills as she worked toward her degree, then came her first secretarial job at the insurance company, which led to another, more important position as she studied for the first of the endless actuarial exams, going at the books day and night and weekends, acing most of them on the second or third try —

—she put the yearbook away, then pulled out her high school reveille, turning to her senior class picture and wondering why she'd even bothered to have the damn thing taken.

Nobody had asked her for one.

She read the small bio underneath the photograph —Drama Club, Cup and Chaucer Society, Chess Club, Homemaker's Club —then looked at her quote. Every senior had been allowed one brief quote under their photo and bio, an epitaph for their youth before they went out to die a little more every day in the great big bad real world.

She read:

Just be the best and truest person you can!

Her vision blurred briefly. She wiped her eyes, then placed her hand, palm-down, on top of the photograph, embarrassed at her youthful optimism for what Might Be, now what Might Have Been.

"Might have been," whispered Amanda, softly. How much time had she wasted with thoughts of what might have been? How many moments of her life had been sacrificed to fantasies, well-choreographed memories of tremendously exciting or romantic things that had never happened to her? For so long everything had been defined by absence: the absence of laughter, the absence of friends, the absence of the noises made by a lover trying hard not to make any noise—not only that, not only the absence of noise, but the absence of noises to come—no phone ringing (a man calling to ask her for a date), no car pulling up into the driveway (said man coming to pick her up because he was old-fashioned that way and thought it right and proper that the man do the driving), no nervous knock on the front door (because he wasn't all that well-versed in this dating thing, poor guy).

But now...now there would be a new absence in her life; the absence of might-have-beens, because now she was beautiful, and almost didn't care if Beauty was a lie because Beauty always has her way —

—no; she mustn't think like that. Ever again.

Her sisters stared at her, expectant, inquisitive.

"Don't ask me," she said to her sisters. "Don't ask me if I remember that time I got lost at a family picnic when I was five and spent three hours wandering through the woods crying. And don't ask me if I still have that picture of Bobby Sherman that I cut out of *Seventeen* when I was in high school because I thought a paper lover was better than no lover at all—and before you remind me, yes, I did hide in the attic on the afternoon of my thirteenth birthday party and I know Mom and Dad were worried sick, and I know I broke their hearts when I didn't like that awful record player they bought for me—it looked too much like the one Mom used—but everyone has to have their heart broken sometime in their life, don't they? And no, I never called that guy from Columbus back because I was afraid he'd reject me and I've never really handled rejection well, in spite of what I tell myself."

Her sisters said nothing.

She looked down at her high school photograph once more, this time tracing the shape of her cheek with a fingertip. "God, honey," she whispered. "I'll miss you so much. But don't worry —I'll never forget anything I learned from you."

She carried the book over to the dresser and used the business end an antique letter opener to cut out her photograph, then carefully tucked the picture into a corner of the mirror's frame.

She examined the letter opener in her hands, admiring its sharp edges. "I remember one time when I was a little girl Dad shot a deer and split it open from its neck down to its hind legs, then hung it upside-down in the basement to drain. I didn't know it was down there. I went down to get something for Mom —I don't remember what —and it was dark and I didn't want to go down because the light switch was all the way over on the other wall, which meant that I had to walk across the basement in order to turn it on...it always seemed like a twenty-mile hike through the darkest woods to me, that walk across the basement to the light switch.

"I went down to get —a screwdriver, that was it! Mom needed to pry the lid off some can of silver polish and needed a screwdriver. So I get to the bottom of the stairs and take a deep breath and start hiking through the forest, then I slipped in a puddle of something and fell on my stomach. I yelled because I was having trouble getting up, so Mom came down and walked over and turned on the light...

"There was so much blood everywhere. I was so frightened I couldn't even scream. The deer's hanging there, its eyes wide, staring at me while the rest of it gushed blood and pieces of guts and I didn't know if the deer was bleeding on me or if I was bleeding on it, I wasn't even sure if the thing was dead. I reached out to Mom and tried to speak but I couldn't. I was afraid that if she didn't pull me away the light would go out again and I'd die there with the deer in the dark forest.

"I never got myself a pet because of that. Because animals die and that meant someday I'd die too. Alone in the dark forest. Alone in the dark."

8. Programmed For Paradise

Her sisters surrounded her now, whispering of their awe and admiration as they caressed her —*I've never seen hair as lovely as yours your eyes are so breathtaking and pure azure what I wouldn't give for a figure like yours with that stomach so flat and diamond perfect God your lips I love your lips so full and red and sensual and moist your neck so slender your arms so slim your hands so delicate your legs so exquisite your skin so luminous —*

—then she remembered the words of Old Roses, who was Shekinah and Malkuth, as well: *Women shouldn't care about lies like Beauty and Ugliness and Plainness —*

—she saw that each of her shadow sisters had claimed some part of her old self—her old eyes, her old lips, nose, hands, legs, cheeks, teeth, bone structure, neck—and it took a moment for the full impact of that to register—

—*As forgettable as you think you are, there is someone out there who envies what you have; to whom you, as you are, are the ideal —*

"I don't want you to envy me," she said to her sisters.

"Not envy," said a sister in Shekinah's voice. "Admire."

"Why are you here?"

"To admire, and to give thanks. I am changed."

"I am changed," echoed the others.

"I am more than I was."

"I am more than I was."

"But you always were," said Amanda. "All of you."

"We know this. Because of you."

One of them placed a warm, loving hand on her bare shoulder, a touch so sensual in its silent softness that its physical pleasure transcended the merely sexual. "We understand how you feel," said this sister, "and we love you so very, very much." She leaned forward and kissed Amanda on the lips, long and lovingly; then, with great tenderness, cupped her face in magical hands and squeezed until Amanda had no choice but to part her lips; when she did this, her nameless sister breathed into her mouth an age-old breath filled with the breath of all sisters before and yet to come. It seeped down into her core and spread through her like the first cool drink on a hot summer's day: an ice-bird spreading chill wings that pressed against her lungs and bones until Amanda was flung wide open, dizzy and disoriented, seized by a whirling vortex and spun around, around, around in a whirl, spiraling higher, thrust into the heart of all Creation's whirling invisibilities, a creature whose puny carbon atoms and other transient substances were suddenly freed, unbound, scattered amidst the universe—yet each particle still held strong to the immeasurable, unseen thread which linked it inexorably to her soul and her consciousness; twirling fibres of light wound themselves around impossibly fragile, molecule-thin membranes of memory and moments that swam toward her like proud children coming back to shore after their very first time in the water alone, and when they reached her, when these memories and moments emerged from the sea and reached out for her, Amanda ran toward them, arms open wide, meeting them on windswept beaches of thought, embracing them, accepting them, absorbing them, becoming Many, becoming Few, becoming One, knowing, learning, feeling; her blood mingled with their blood, her thoughts with their thoughts, dreams with dreams, hopes with hopes, frustrations with frustrations, and in this mingling, in this unity, in this actualization, she became:

a woman, alone, nameless, any ordinary woman, and this woman enters a department store from the street, tired, hot, her hair windblown, looking very mortal, her face perhaps just a tad more visible than she would like, and in order to reach the cosmetics counter she has to pass a deliberately disorienting prism of mirrors and lights and perfume-scents which cumulatively suggest to her that she isn't all she could be, so by the time she reached the counter she feels old and ugly, then uglier still as she looks across the counter and sees that it is staffed by ranks of angels—seraphim and cherubim—perfect young faces on perfect young bodies, backlit, ethereal, programmed for paradise, and the woman places her hand on the cool glass, looking down at heaven in a tube, in a jar, under the lid of a compact or on the tip of an eye-liner, and when she looks up to the angelic faces behind the counter, hoping for understanding, for some moment of communion, she sees a line of round, unmerciful mirrors, each reflecting her own face in all its imperfection back at her, larger and in harsher light, so flawed and shut out from the paradise on the other side of the counter;

whirling, she became:

two women simultaneously; one, in her late thirties, crossing the street with her face buried in a book, just like Amanda in her high school days when she walked home alone every day, but this woman looked as if she were more interested in keeping her eyes averted from the world passing by than in paying attention to the words on the page; the second woman, much shorter than the first, a good forty pounds heavier and ten years older, carried a shoulder bag filled with books, only the expression on her face—part impatience, part resignation, and part longing—betrayed that she wished she had the nerve to walk with her face buried in a book, but then what would she have to look forward to once she got home? And as they passed one another, both looked up and slowed their steps, just for a moment, because suddenly one was thinking Is that what I'll look like in ten years? *while the other thought* My God, is that what I used to look like when I was that age? *then the crosswalk sign changed and both, Before and After, hurried along, shaken, rushing along to the same plans in the same kind of house where each had lived similar evenings for longer than either wanted to admit;*

spiraling, she became:

a woman named Rosemary, married for twenty-two years to a man she knew had been having an affair with a much younger and prettier woman for at least a year, probably longer, so this Rosemary found herself sitting, nervous, in the waiting room of a plastic surgeon's office where she planned to have a little liposuction, a bit of a face-lift, and perhaps, if she could afford it, a little breast augmentation, some Inflate-a-Boob so maybe he'd take notice of her once again;

spinning, she became:

a patchwork quilt of wrinkles and cuts and swollen bruises that was once Joyce's face, and Joyce carefully, with trembling hands, washed away the blood, wincing, her boyfriend's words, so much more violent than his fists, replaying in her mind: "Why aren't you beautiful? You're not even pretty!" and she wept because she knew it was true, she wasn't pretty and really, really wished she were, because then Kevin wouldn't be ashamed to be seen with her, and maybe she ought to break it off with him but who else would have her? Maybe getting hit once in a while after he'd had a few too many was the price she had to pay for not being lonely in bed at night;

mingling, she became:

the secret, embarrassed fantasy of so many plain-faced ones: Changed into a very beautiful and glamourous woman, closing their eyes and watching this other beautiful woman who used to be them from another place outside of themselves, seeing her so clearly, so vividly, and trying hard not to shout, "Enjoy it! Enjoy it while you can, you deserve it!" all the time knowing this other woman isn't them, not really, it was only a silly schoolgirl fantasy;

accepting, she became:

the echo of voices, chanting: "It isn't me...not myself...not this body of mine, not this fat/sagging/shapeless/old/nothing-special body...it's her, a someone else...and that face!...a face to die for, not like this one, so ordinary, forgettable...removed from me...from fantasy...a beautiful woman...and I hate myself for feeling this way...not me...not myself...her...someone else...hate myself for feeling this way...why am I nothing if not thin/beautiful/young/without a man?...but, still...

...still I shout...

...enjoy it...

...enjoy it while you can...

...enjoy it while you can you deserve it...

...still..."

lost and lonely, Amanda felt herself being wrenched backward, down through the ages, through the infinite allness of want and desire and isolation and dreams and shames and moments of pride and self-worth and meaning that Woman had shrunk Herself into so as to be human, raw with pain yet drenched in wonder, and she stretched herself under the weight of this knowing, her eyes staring toward the truth that was her soul, her whole body becoming involved in drawing it back into her in one breath, and in the moment before she came away whole, clean, and filled with glory, in the millisecond before she found herself once again standing in her bathroom staring at the reflection in the mirror, in that brief instant of eternity that revealed itself to her just this once before her final metamorphosis took place, she broke into a language few could understand, speaking of herself and her sisters as zealots entering a church resurrected on the sight of pagan temples called Beauty and Ugliness and Plainness, a novice in the inner sanctum, knowing at whose altar she knelt, to what god she prayed, and in this communion between herself and her sisters she knew all of Woman, and loved them, and thanked them as a thread of knowledge wound itself around a certain part of her consciousness and Shekinah whispered a last answer to a final question —

—and Amanda, awakened to the majesty that was always without and within her, knew exactly, precisely, with a strength of certainty most people know only once in their entire lives, what had happened to her, and why.

She looked at her sisters, crowding around her; so lonely-eyed and plain-faced and in desperate need of one moment of glory, a moment like she'd experienced tonight—and to hell with the empty feeling in the pit of her stomach when it was over—but could not find the words to articulate.

Her sisters, standing there with their jars in their hands. "You're so beautiful," said one of them. "Like a picture by Michelangelo."

Then held out her empty jar.

Amanda reached up and took hold of her father's straight-razor, opened it, and stood in awe at how exquisitely the blade gleamed in the light.

Her sisters held their breath.

Every moment of glory comes with its consequences. "I love you," she whispered to her sisters. "And I give myself to you."

"Amen," they whispered, tears of gratitude in their eyes.

She placed the razor against her lips and began.

Union Dues

"It is one of the great tragedies of this age that as soon as man invented a machine he began to starve."
—Oscar Wilde, *The Soul of Man Under Socialism*

(here is my son
   does he have the makings of a factory man?
   does he have the mark of a worker?
   will he do me proud?)

1

A man works his whole life away, and what does it mean?
Please don't ask me that question, Dad.
On the line your hands grow aching and calloused, your body grows sore and crooked, and your spirit fades like sparks between the gears. The roar of machinery chisels its way into your brain and spreads until it's the only thing that's real. The work goes on, you die a little more with each whistle, and the next paycheck is tucked inside the rusty metal lunch pail that really ought to be replaced but you can't afford to right now.
A man works his whole life away. For twenty-three years he reports to work on time, punches the clock, takes his place on the line, and allows his body to become one-half of a tool. He works without complaint and never calls in sick no matter how bad he feels, and for this he gets to come home once a week and present his family with a paycheck for one-hundred and eight-seven dollars and sixteen cents. Dirt money. Chump change. Money gone before it's got. Then one day

he notices the way his kid looks at him, he sees the disappointment, and he wants to scream but settles for a few cold beers instead.

And what does it mean? It means a man becomes embarrassed by what he is, humiliated by his lack of education, ashamed that he can only give his family the things they need and not the things they want.

So a man grows angry—

—because even in his dreams—

(...doors open and the OldWorker is cast away...)

—the work goes on—

—and the machines wait for him to return and make them whole again—

Don't say these things, Dad.

I can't help it, boy.

Sometimes it gets to be too much.

2

Sheriff Ted Jackson held a handkerchief over his nose and mouth as he surveyed the wreckage of the riot.

(...as the production line begins again...)

A cloud of tear gas was dissipating at neck level in the parking lot of the factory, reflecting lights from the two dozen police cars encircling the area. Newspaper reporters and television news crews were assembling outside the barricades along with people from the neighborhood and relatives of the workers involved. Silhouetted against the rapidly-setting cold November sun, the crowd looked like one massive duster of cells; a shadow on a lung x-ray—sorry, bud, this looks bad.

Men lay scattered, some on their sides, others on their backs, still more squatting and coughing and vomiting, all wiping blood from their faces and hands.

A half-foot of old crusty snow had covered the ground since the first week of the month, followed by days and nights of dry cold, so that the snow had merely aged and turned the color of damp ash, mottled by candy wrappers, empty cigarette packs, losing lottery tickets, beer cans, and now bodies. The layer of snow whispering from the sky was a fresh coat of paint; a whitewash that hid the ugliness and despair of the tainted world underneath.

A pain-filled voice called out from somewhere.

Fire blew out the windshield of an overturned semi; it jerked sideways, slammed into a guardrail, and puked glass.

The crowd pushed forward, knocking over several of the barriers. Officers in full riot gear held everyone back.

The snow grew dense as more sirens approached.

The searchlight from a police helicopter swept the area.

A woman in the crowd began weeping loudly.

You couldn't have asked for an uglier mess.

Jackson pulled the handkerchief away and took an icy breath; the wind was trying to move the gas away but the snow held it against the ground. He turned up the collar of his jacket and pulled a twenty-gauge pump-action shotgun from the cruiser's rack.

"Sheriff?"

Dan Robinson, one of his deputies, offered him a gas mask.

"Little late for that."

"I know, but the fire department brought along extras and I thought—"

"Piss on that." Jackson stared through the snow at the crowd of shadows. The strobing visibar lights perpetually changed the shape of the pack; red-*blink*-a smoke crowd; blue-*blink*—a snow-ash crowd; white-*blink*—a shadow crowd.

"You okay, Sheriff?"

"Let's go see if they cleared everyone away from the east side."

The two men trudged through the heaps of snow, working their way around the broken glass, twisted metal, blood, grease, and bodies. Paramedics scurried in all directions; gurneys were collapsed, loaded, then lifted into place and rolled toward waiting ambulances. Volunteers from the local Red Cross were administering aid to those with less serious wounds.

"Any idea how this started, sir?"

"The scabs came out for food. Strikers cut off all deliveries three days ago."

"Terrible thing."

"You got that right."

They rounded the comer and took several deep breaths to clear their lungs.

(...the shift whistle blows like a birth scream, and the factory worker springs forth, with shoulders and arms made powerful for the working of apron handwheels. . .)

Jackson remembered the afternoon he'd had to come down and assist with bringing in the scabs—the strikers behind barricades on one side of the parking lot while the scabs rode in on flatbed trucks like livestock to an auction. Until that afternoon he'd never believed that rage was something that could live outside the physical confines of a man's own heart, but as those scabs climbed down and began walking toward the main production floor entrance he'd felt the presence of cumulative anger becoming something more fierce, something hulking and twisted and hideous. To this day he couldn't say how or why, but he could swear that the atmosphere between the strikers and scabs had rippled and even torn in places. It still gave him the willies.

He blinked against the falling snow and felt his heart skip a beat.

Twenty yards away, near a smoldering overturned flatbed at the edge of the east parking lot, a man lay on the ground, his limbs twisted at impossible angles. A long, thick smear of hot machine oil pooled behind him, hissing in the snow.

Maneuvering through the snowdrifts Jackson raced over, slid to a halt, chambered a shell, and dropped to one knee, gesturing for Robinson to do the same.

Jackson looked down at the body and felt something lodge in his throat. "Damn. Herb Kaylor."

"You know him?"

Jackson tried to swallow but couldn't. The image of the man's face blurred; he wiped his eyes and realized that he was crying. "Yeah. Him and me served together in Vietnam. I just played cards with him and his wife a couple nights ago. *Goddammit!*" He clenched his teeth. "He wasn't supposed to be workin' the picket line today. Christ! Poor Herb...."

He turned away, shook himself, and looked back at the man whose company he'd known and treasured, and cursed himself for never letting Herb Kaylor know just how much his friendship had meant.

Kaylor's neck was broken so badly that his head was turned almost fully around. Jackson reached out to close his friend's dead eyes —

—his fingers brushed the skin—

—*1 barely touched him*—

—and the eyes fell through the sockets into the skull.

There was no blood.

"Jesus!" shouted Robinson.

"I hardly —!" Jackson never completed the sentence.

With a series of soft, dry sounds, Herb Kaylor's skull collapsed inward; the flesh crumbled and flaked away as his face sank back, split in half, and dissolved.

Robinson was so shaken by the sight that he lost his balance and pushed a hand through Kaylor's hollowed chest. He tried to pull himself from the shell of desiccated skin and brittle bone but only managed to sink his arm in up to the elbow. Jackson pulled him out; Robinson's arm was covered in large clumps of decayed, withered flesh. Bits and pieces of Herb Kaylor blew away like so much soot.

Jackson stared into the empty chest cavity.

Robinson backed away, dry-retching.

A strong gust of wind whistled by, leveling to a chronic breeze.

(...the factory man turns his gaze toward the plant's ceiling ...)

Unable to look at Herb's body any longer, Jackson rose to his feet and turned toward the sliding iron doors that served as the entrance to the basement production cells.

He could feel the power of the machines inside; at first it was little more than a low, constant thrum beneath his feet, but as he began to walk toward the doors the vibrations became stronger, louder, snaking up out of the asphalt and coiling around his legs, soaking through his skin and latching onto his bones like the lower feed-fingers of a metal press, shuddering, clanking, hissing and screeching into his system, fusing with his bloodstream as carbon fused with silicon and lead with bismuth, riding the flow up to his brain and spreading across his mind: it became a deep, rolling hum in his ears, then an enveloping pressure, and, at last, a whispe

Welcome, my son —

—a powerful gust of wind shrieked around him, kicking against his legs—

—welcome to the Machine.

It came from the opening between the doors, and as Jackson moved toward them something long and metallic slipped out, flexed, then vanished back into the darkness of the plant before he could get to it. Jackson blinked against the snow and shook his head. Every so often he'd see something like that in his dreams, a prosthetic hand, its metal fingers closing around his throat...and the thing he'd glimpsed had been like the hand in his dreams, only much, much larger.

Jesus, I gotta start sleeping better, can't start seein' shit like that while I'm awake or—

"Christ Almighty!" shouted Robinson.

Jackson whirled around and instinctively leveled the shotgun but the wind was so strong he lost his grip and the weapon flew out of his hands, slamming against a far wall and discharging into a four-foot snow drift.

He stared at the body of Herb Kaylor.

No way, no goddamn way he can still be alive—

—moving, no mistaking that, Herb was moving; one arm, then another, then both legs—

—Jackson reached out and grabbed the iron handrail leading down the stairs; it was the only way he could keep his balance against the wind—

—that seemed to be concentrated on what was left of Herb's body, lifting it from the ground like a marionette at the end of tangled strings, its limbs twisted akimbo, shaking and flailing in violent seizurelike spasms, flaking apart and scattering into the wind, churning into dust and dirtying the funneling snow; even the clothes were shredded and cast away.

It was over in less than a minute.

Jackson slowly climbed the steps and rejoined Robinson. They stood in silence, staring at the spot where Kaylor's body had been —

—the steps into the basement —

(It sure as hell looked like a hand of some sort.)

—but the pressure returned to his ears, three times as painful —

—*what are these marks, Daddy? They're just like the ones on your back only mine don't bleed*—

—he shook his head and pressed his hands against his ears as he spiraled back to that morning so many years ago, during a strike not unlike this one; his own father, so desperate because the strike fund had gone dry and he'd been denied both welfare and unemployment benefits, had decided to cross the picket line. He remembered the way his mother had cried and held Dad's hand and begged him not to go, saying that she could get a job somewhere, maybe doing people's laundry or something—

—and the look on her face later, when the police came to tell her about the Accident, that Dad had somehow ("We're not sure how it happened, ma'am, no one wants to talk about it.") been crushed by his press, and Jackson remembered, then, the last thing Dad had said to him before leaving that morning, something about being welcome to come and see his machine—

—Jackson took a deep breath and stood straight, clearing his head of the pain and pressure.

"What the hell happened, Sheriff?" asked Robinson, handing back Jackson's shotgun.

"I never saw anything like it," whispered Jackson. "How do you suppose a man could get crushed in a press like that and no one saw it happen?"

"What are you talking about, Sheriff?"

Jackson blinked, cleared his throat and faced his deputy. "I mean...Jesus...how could a body just ... *dry up* like that? You had your arm in there, Dan. The man had no internal organs. When his head collapsed there was no brain inside the skull." He fished around inside his pockets, found his cigarettes, then lit one for himself and one for Robinson.

They smoked in silence for a moment.

Around the corner, the sounds of the crowd grew angrier, louder. The chopper made another sweep of the area. Sirens shrieked as ambulances sped from the scene with their broken and bleeding cargos.

Jackson crushed out his cigarette, turned to Robinson, and said, "Listen to me. I don't want you *ever* to tell anyone what happened out here, understand me? Not the other guys, your girlfriend, your parents, *nobody*. This stays between us, all right?"

"You got my word, Sheriff."

A gunshot cracked through the dusk and the crowd erupted into panic. Jackson and Robinson grabbed their weapons and ran to lend what assistance they could.

(...the iron support beams in the factory's ceiling ripple and coil around one another, becoming sinewy muscle tissue that surges down and combines with the cranks...

...which become lungs...

...that attach themselves to the press foundation...

...which evolves into a spinal column...

...that supports the control panel as it shudders...

...and spreads...

...and becomes the gray matter of a brain signaling everything to converge...

...pulsing steelbeat pounding faster and faster...

...moist pink muscle tissue, tendons, bones, sparks, tubes, metal shavings, flesh, iron, organs, and alloys coalescing...

...and the being that is the Machine stands before the factory man, its shimmering electric gaze drilling into them as it reaches down and lifts them to its bosom, feeding, draining them of all essence until they are little more than a clockwork doll whose every component has been removed...

...doors open and the Old Worker is cast away... a hiss ... a clank...

...the next shift arrives...

...as the production line begins again...)

The east parking lot was empty now. No one was there to hear the sounds from behind the iron doors.

Squeaking, screeching, loud clanking, heavy equipment dragging across a cement floor.

Something long, metallic, and triple-jointed pushed through the doors, folding around the edge. Another glint as more metal thrust out and folded back.

Throwing sparks, the mechanical hand raked down, gripped the handle, and pulled the doors closed.

The structure of the factory trembled.

The breeze picked up, swirling snow down the steps and up against the doors with a low whistle; a groan in the back of a tired man's throat

A man works his whole life away, and what does it mean?

The wind stilled.

It means he has the makings of a factory man.

Shadows bled over the walls.

He has the mark of a worker.

A shredded section of Herb Kaylor's shirt drifted to the ground, floating back and forth with the ease of a feather. It hit the dirty snow and was covered by a rolling drift of chill, dead white.

3

Hearing the noise is nothing at times. No, the worst part is that, after a while, you start to wear it. All over your face, in your eyes, on your clothes.

Stop *it, Dad, just knock it the hell off!*

It's a mark, this sound, that people can see and recognize. You might be at the grocery store or just walking outside to get the mail and people will look at you and see what you are, what you can only be, and that's a factory worker, a laborer all your life, and they know this by looking at you because you wear the noise.

I never asked you to give up any of your hopes or dreams to go work there, you gave those up on your own!

A man works his whole life away and he grows angry because he can't make anyone understand how it feels to scrub your hands so hard after a day's work that the palms start to bleed.

Goddammit, Dad, shut up! I know it's crummy but it's not my fault!

I remember my Daddy's hands, the machine stink on them. The day he had my dog put down he tried to apologize to me, told me about how sick old Ralph was, but I was too hurt to listen. He just stood there and touched my cheek. I opened my eyes and looked at his hand and saw it was stained with machine grease. It was the hand that fed me but it was also the hand that killed my dog. He did it. Because he had to. Had to and hated it. He knew he'd never have to tell me he was sorry because his hand against my face, trying to wipe away my tears, said it all. His cruel dog-killing hand with its grease and machine stink so lightly against my face.

Take a good look at *my* hands, boy. A man's flesh was never meant to be like this, the lines so dark from oil stains they might as well be cracks in plaster. Sometimes I hate the idea of touching you mother with these hands, having her feel the calluses and cuts, the roughness on her cheek. She deserves tenderness, boy, the soft, easy touch of a lover, and she ain't never gonna feel it from these hands.

But she loves you, we all do, you should know that.

I know you do, boy. And I wish it helped more than it does, but sometimes it don't and that just makes me sick right down to the ground.

4

Jackson climbed the front steps of Herb Kaylor's house and knocked on the door. Darlene answered, nodded, and invited him inside.

The house smelled like coffee, uneaten dinner, and grief.

"I made meatloaf tonight," whispered Herb Kaylor's widow. "It was always his favorite. Don't know what I'm gonna do with it now..." She bit her lower lip and closed her eyes, locking her body rigid against Jackson's embrace. Pulling away, she ran a hand through her thinning gray hair and coughed. "I have to...apologize for how the place looks. I, uh..I—"

"Place looks fine," whispered Jackson as she led him toward the kitchen.

"Nice of you to say so." Her eyes were puffy and red-rimmed, making the lines on her face harsher.

Her son, Will, was making coffee; the teenager exchanged terse greetings with the sheriff and took his coffee into another room.

"Would you like a cup?" asked Darlene. "I grind the beans myself. Herb says...*said* that it made all the difference in the world from the store-bought kind."

"Yes, thank you."

As she handed him the cup and saucer her hand began to shake and she almost spilled the coffee in his lap. She apologized, tried to smile, then sat at the table and wept quietly. After a moment she held out her hand and Jackson took it.

"Darlene," he said softly, "I hate to ask you about this but I gotta know. Why was Herb working the picket today? He wasn't supposed to be there again until Friday."

"I swear to you I don't know. I asked him this morning right before he left. He just kind of laughed—you know how he always does when he don't want to bother you with a problem? Then he kissed me and said he was sorry he'd got Will into this and he was gonna try to fix things."

"What'd he mean?"

"He got Will on at the plant. Was even gonna train him." She shook her head and sipped at her coffee. "You know Herb's father did the same for him? Got him a job workin' the same shift in the same cell. I guess a lot of workers get in that way. Didn't your father work there, too?"

Jackson looked away and whispered, "Yeah."

"Place is like a fuckin' family heirloom," Will stood up in the doorway.

Jackson turned to look at him as Darlene said, "What did I tell you about using that kind of language in the house? Your Daddy—"

"—was stupid! Admit it. It was stupid of him to go down there today."

Darlene stared at him with barely-contained fury worsened by weariness and grief. "I won't have you bad-mouthing you father, Will. He ain't"—her voice cracked—"here to defend himself. He worked hard for his family and deserved a hell of a lot more respect and thanks than he ever got."

"*Thanks?*" shouted Will. "For what? For reminding me that he put his obligations over his own happiness, or for getting me on at the plant so I could become another goddamm factory stooge like him? Which wonderful gift should I have thanked him for?"

"You sure couldn't find a decent job on your own. Somebody had to do something."

"Listen," said Jackson, "maybe I should come back—"

"When was I supposed to look for another job? Between running errands for you and helping with the housework and cleaning up after Dad when he got drunk—"

"I think you'd better go to your room."

"No," said Will, storming into the kitchen and slamming down his coffee cup. "I'm eighteen years old and not once have I ever been allowed to disagree with anything you or Dad wanted. You weren't the one who had to sit down here and listen to him ramble on at three in the morning after he got tanked. To hear him tell it, working the plant was just short of Hell, yet he was more than happy to hand my ass over—"

"He was only trying to help you get some money so you could finally get your own place, get on your own two feet. He was a very giving, great man."

"A *great* man? How the hell can you say that? You're wearing clothes that are ten years old and sitting at a table we bought for nine dollars at Goodwill! Maybe Dad had some great notions, but *he* wasn't great. He was a bitter, used-up little bit of a man who could only go to sleep after work if he downed enough booze, and I'll be damned if I'm gonna end up like—"

Darlene shot up from her chair and slapped Will across the face with such force he fell against the counter. When he regained his balance and turned back to face her, a thin trickle of blood oozed slowly from the corner of his mouth. His eyes widened in fear, shock, and countless levels of confusion and pain.

"You listen to me," said Darlene. "I was married to your father for almost twenty-five years, and in that time I saw him do things you aren't half man enough to do. I've seen him run into the middle of worse riots than the one today and pull old men out of trouble. I've seen him give his last dime to friends who didn't have enough for groceries and then borrow money from your uncle to pay our own bills. I've seen him be more gentle than you can ever imagine and I've been there when he's felt low because he thought you were embarrassed by him. Maybe he was just a factory worker, but he was a damn decent man who gave me love and a good home. You never saw it, maybe you didn't want to, but your father was a great man who did great things. Maybe they weren't huge things, things that get written about in the paper, but that shouldn't matter. It's not his fault that you never saw any of his greatness, that you only saw him when he was tired and used-up. And maybe he did drink but, goddammit, for almost twenty-five years he never once thought about just giving up. I loved that...*factory stooge* more than any man in my life—and I could've had plenty. He was the best of them all."

"Mom, please, I—"

"—You never did nothing except make him feel like a failure because he couldn't buy you all the things your friends have. I wasn't down here listening to him ramble at three in the morning? You weren't there on those nights before we had kids, listening to him whisper how scared he was he wouldn't be able to give us a decent life. You weren't there to hold him and kiss him and feel so much tenderness between your bodies that it was like you were one person. And twenty-five years of that, of loving a man like your father, that gives you something no one can ruin or take away, and I won't listen to you talk against him! He was my husband and your father and he's dead and it hurts so much I want to scream."

Will's eyes filled with tears. "Oh god, Mom, I miss him. I'm so...sorry I said those things. I was just so angry." His chest began to hitch with the abrupt force of his sorrow. "I know that I...I hurt his feelings, that I made him feel like everything he did was for nothing. Can't I be mad that I'll never get the chance to make it up to him? Can't I?" He leaned into his mother's arms and wept. "He always said that you gotta ... gotta look out for your obligations before you can start thinking about your own happiness. I know that now. And I'll ... I'll try to ... oh, Christ, Mom. I want the chance to make it all up to him. . ." Darlene held him and stroked the back of his head, whispering, "It's all right, go on ... go on ... he knows now, he always did, you have to believe that..."

Ted Jackson turned away from them and swallowed his coffee in three large gulps, winced as it hit his stomach, and was overpowered by the loss that soaked the room. He'd never felt more isolated or useless in his life.

Someone knocked loudly on the front door. Darlene turned toward Jackson. "Would you ... would you mind answering the door, Ted? I don't think I'm ... up to it just now."

Jackson said of course and went into the front room, quickly wiped his eyes and blew his nose, then turned on the porchlight and opened the door.

5

Even if you manage to scrub off all the dirt and grease and metal shavings, you've still got the smell on you. Cheap aftershave, machine oil, sweat, the stink of hot metal. No matter how many showers you take, the smell stays on you. It's a stench that factory workers carry to their graves, a stink that's on them all the days of their lives, squatting by them at the end like some loyal hound dog that sits by its master's grave until it starves to death, reminding you that all you leave behind is a mortgage, a pile of unpaid bills, children who are ashamed of you, and a spouse who will grow old and bitter and miserable and empty and will never be able to rid the house of that smell.

Stop it.

That smell is your heritage, boy, don't deny it. You were born to be part of the line, part of the Machine, and it will mark you just like it marked me.

I won't listen to this.

Breathe it in deep.
SHUT THE FUCK UP!
That's a good boy.

6

Seven men stood on the porch, each with some sort of bandage covering a wound. Though Jackson recognized all of them as strikers, he only knew a few by name.

A barrel-chested man in old jeans and a grimy sweatshirt stepped forward and offered a firm handshake. "Evenin', Sheriff. We come to ... to pay our respects to the family. Herb was one of the good guys and we're sorry as hell that he died because of this."

"Darlene's not feeling up to a bunch of company," said Jackson. "I shouldn't even be here myself but —"

"Nonsense," said Darlene from behind him. "Herb would never turn away a fellow union man, and neither will I."

Jackson stepped back as the men entered and stood in a semi-circle, each looking sad, awkward, lost, and angry.

The barrel-chested man (Darlene called him "Rusty") offered the group's sympathy — each man muttering agreement and nodding his head — and said that if there was anything they could do she was to give the word and they'd be right on it

Darlene thanked them and offered them some coffee. The men seemed to relax a little as each found a place to sit.

Then Will came into the room.

Once, when Jackson had still been a deputy, he'd arrested a man suspected of child molestation. When he'd opened the door to the holding cell every prisoner there had looked at the man with such cold loathing it made Jackson's blood almost stop in his veins. The guy hadn't lasted the night—Jackson found him the next morning beaten to a pulp. He'd choked on his own vomit with three socks rammed in his mouth.

The workers in the room were looking at Will Kaylor exactly the same way. Jackson felt the nerves in the back of his neck start tingling. He released a slow, quiet breath and surreptitiously unbuttoned the holster strap over his revolver.

"Hello," said Will flatly.

The men made no reply. Eyes looked back and forth from Will to Jackson.

"Well," said Darlene with false brightness, "would one of you like to give me a hand in the kitchen?"

Rusty and another man said they'd love to and followed her in, but not before giving Will one last angry glance.

As the remaining men started to whisper among themselves, Will touched Jackson's elbow and asked the sheriff to follow him upstairs.

Jackson excused himself and went after Will. They walked quickly up to Will's room at the end of the hall and closed the door.

Will turned on a small bedside lamp. "You know they really came here to see me, don't you?"

"I figured it was something like that."

"I was supposed to work the picket line today. My first day at work was the morning the strike started. Dad barely had a chance to show me the press before the walkout." His eyes filled with pleading. "Please believe I loved my dad and I appreciated what he tried to do for me, but I ... didn't want to end up like him. He was so goddamn tired and unhappy all the time. I just ... didn't want to let that happen to me."

Jackson put his hand on Will's shoulder. "Your dad told me once that he hoped you'd do better than he had. I really don't think he'd blame you, so don't go blaming yourself."

"But those guys downstairs blame me. As far as they're concerned I should have been the one who died today." He crossed to the window and pulled back the curtain. The factory in the distance shimmered with an eerie phosphorescence that seemed both peaceful and mocking.

"Have you ever been in the lobby of the bank downtown?" asked Will. "All those windows facing every direction? Have you noticed that you can't see any part of the factory from there, not even the smokestacks? I worked for a while last summer as a caddy at the Moundbuilder's Country Club. They used to give us a free lunch. The factory's only five miles away but you can't see it from anywhere on the club grounds, even using binoculars."

"You're not making any sense."

"It's almost as if the people who don't want to know about it can't see it." He turned around and pulled the curtain farther back. "Can you see the factory, Sheriff?"

"Yeah."

"My room faces north, all right?"

"Okay...?"

Will dropped the curtain and crossed to open the door, gesturing for Jackson to follow him to the other end of the hall. They entered Herb and Darlene's room. Will pointed at the curtains.

"Their window faces the exact opposite direction of mine. Pull back the curtain."

Confused, Jackson did as Will asked —

—and found himself facing a view of the factory. The angle was slightly different, but it was undeniably the factory.

"That's impossible," he whispered. "The damn thing's north and this window —"

"Dad showed it to me the night before I started at the plant. If you go downstairs and look out the back door, you'll still be able to see it. Look out any door or window facing any direction in this house and you'll see the plant."

Jackson let the curtain fall back.

Will shrugged his shoulders in defeat. "I don't know why I'm showing you this, telling you these things. I doubt you even understand."

Jackson faced him. "I know exactly how you feel, Will. My dad was killed at the plant when I was seventeen. Up until the day he died he'd been priming me to go work the line. I didn't want to, God knows, I saw what it did to him, how it sucked his life away. He was dead long before the...accident. I watched it happen bit by bit, the way his spirit just ground to a halt in a series of sputtering little agonies. I hated that place, even used to have these dreams where the machines came alive and chased me. The morning he was killed my mom started in on me to go get a job there. I didn't know what to do. But I got lucky and was drafted. Even Vietnam was preferable to that place. Mom died while I was over there. As terrible as it sounds, for as much as I loved her I was almost relieved that she was dead because it meant she wouldn't hound me about taking my father's place at the plant."

"Why did you stay here?"

"I wish I knew." Jackson absent-mindedly scratched at an area near the center of his back, thinking about the marks he'd found there when he was a child, and pulled his hand away. "Maybe it was my way of defying that place. I kept remembering the passage from Revelations that the priest read at Dad's funeral: 'Yea, sayeth the spirit, that they may rest from their labours, and their works do follow them.' Well, *I* wasn't going to follow and I was damned if that place was gonna drill into my conscience and follow me. For so many years I'd listened to Dad talk about it like it was an actual living thing that I came to think of it that way, so I guess part of me decided to stay here just to spite it, to drive past it every day and think, 'You didn't get me, motherfucker!' At least that way I can ... I dunno, make my Dad's death count for something." He exhaled, smiled, and put his hand on Will's shoulder. "Those men can't force you to do anything you don't want to, not while *I'm* wearing this badge, anyway."

"Thanks, Sheriff. Dad always said you were one of the good guys."

"So was he. So're all the workers."

Will stared down at his trembling hands. "You know the funny thing? I keep thinking about being ... a virgin. I've never even *kissed* a girl. I've been trapped here all my life, waiting to follow in my dad's footsteps, watching him and Mom waste away, not able to do a goddamn thing about it I spend half my time feeling like shit and the other half mad that I feel that way. I look in mirrors and think I'm seeing a picture of my dad. I think of everything he and Mom have missed out on and I just...surrender, Yknow? Because I love them. And I don't know if I'm my own man or just the sum of my family's parts."

Jackson started out of the room. "You stay here. I'm gonna go send those men on their way."

Will rose from the bed. "Sheriff?"

"Yeah?"

"Thanks for telling me about your dad. It helped me to decide. I'm gonna go with them."

"Jesus, Will, you just said that —"

"—I said that I *didn't* want to go—but I've been thinking about what Dad said, about looking out for obligations before thinking about your own happiness, and he was right. And just like you, I gotta make my dad's death count for something."

Jackson stared at him. "You sure about this?"

"Yes. It's the first thing I have been sure of. It's about time."

The boy was now resigned.

The son would become the father.

"All right," said Jackson, swallowing back his rage and disgust.

"I'd ... I'd really appreciate it if you'd come along, Sheriff."

"Why's that?"

"I think you and I have something in common. I think we both never understood what our fathers went through, and I think we've both always wanted to know."

Jackson glanced out the window, at the factory. "I could never imagine what he must've ... felt like, day after day. I could never —" He blinked, looked away. "Yeah. I'd like to come along."

They went downstairs. Will asked his mother to please help him pack his lunch pail.

The other men seemed pleased.

Jackson shook his head, offered his sympathy to Darlene once again, and left with Will and the others.

7

—someday you'll understand, boy, that a man becomes something more than part of his machine and his machine becomes something more than just the other half of a tool. They marry in a way no two people could ever know. They become each other's God. They become a greater Machine. And the Machine makes all things possible. It feeds you, clothes you, puts the roof over your head, and shows you all the mercy that the world never will.

The Machine is family.

It is purpose.

It is love.

So take its lever and feel the devotion.

There you go, just like that.

8

The parking lot was deserted, save for cars driven by the midnight shift workers.

They milled about outside the doors to the basement production cell, waiting for Jackson and Will.

As they approached the group Will gently took Jackson by the arm and said, "I think it'd be nice if you didn't stop coming around for cards Saturday nights."

"Wouldn't miss it for the world."

They stood among the other workers. Barrel-chested Rusty smiled at Will, nodded at Jackson, and said, "We got to make sure."

"I figured," said Jackson.

"Sure of what?" asked Will.

And Rusty replied: "You never actually started working with the press, did you?"

Will sighed and shook his head. "No. The strike was called right after I clocked in." Without another word, he took off his jacket, then unbuttoned and removed his shirt, turning around.

Rusty pulled a flashlight from his back pocket and shone the beam on Will's back.

Several round scar-like marks speckled the young man's back, starting between his shoulder blades and continuing toward the base of his spine. Some were less than an eighth of an inch in diameter but others looked to be three times that size, pushing inward like the pink indentations left in the skin after a scab has been peeled off.

"Damn," said Rusty. "Shift's gotta start on time."

"Don't you think I know that?" snapped Will. "Dad used to talk about how ... oh, hell." He took a deep breath. "Better get on with it."

Rusty pulled a small black handbook from his pocket, then turned toward the other men. "We're here tonight to welcome a new brother into our union—Will Kaylor, son of Herb. Herb was a decent man, a good friend, and one of the finest machinists it's ever been my privilege to work beside. I hope that all of us will treat his son with the same respect we gave to his father."

The workers nodded in approval.

Rusty flipped through the pages of his tattered union handbook until he found what he was looking for. "Sheriff," he said, offering the book to Jackson, "would you do us the honor of reading the union prayer here in the front where I marked it?"

"It would be ... a privilege," replied Jackson, taking the book.

Will was marched to a nearby wall, then pressed face- and chest-first against it, his bare back exposed to the night.

"Just clench your teeth together," whispered Rusty to Will. "Close your eyes, and hold your breath. It don't hurt as much as you think."

The other shift workers were opening their lunch pails and toolboxes, removing Philips-head screwdrivers.

Jackson would not allow himself to turn away. His father had gone through this, as had his father before him. Jackson had been spared, but that did not ease his conscience. He wanted to know.

He *had* to know.

Rusty looked toward Jackson and gave a short, sharp nod of his head, and Jackson began to read: "'Almighty God, we, your workers, beseech Thee to guide us, that we may do the work which Thou givest us to do, in truth, in beauty, and righteousness, with singleness of heart as Thy servants and to the benefit of our fellow men.'"

The workers gathered around Will, each choosing a scar and then, one by one, in orderly succession, plunging their screwdriver into it

"'Though we are not poets, Lord, or visionaries, or prophets, or great-minded leaders of men, we ask that you accept our humble labour of our hands as proof of our love for You, and for our families.'"

Blood spurted from each wound and gouted down Will's back, spattering against the asphalt.

His scream began somewhere in the center of the earth, forcing its way up through layers of molten rock and centuries of pain, shuddered through his legs and groin, lodged in his throat for only a moment before erupting from his throat as the howl of the shift whistle growing in volume to deafen the very ears of God.

Jackson had to shout to be heard over the din. "'We thank Thee for Thy blessing as we, Your humble workers, welcome a new brother into our ranks. May You watch over and protect him as You have always watched over and protected us. Who can be our adversary, if You are on our side? You did not even spare Your own Son, but gave him up for the sake of us all.'"

"'And must not that gift be accompanied by the gift of all else?'" responded the workers in unison.

"'... So we offer our gift of all else, Lord, we offer our labours for the glory of Thy name, Amen.'"

"Amen," echoed the workers, backing away.

"Amen," said Will, dropping to his knees, then vomiting and whimpering.

Jackson closed the union handbook and came forward, tears in his eyes, and began to cradle Will in his arms; the boy shook his head and rose unsteadily to his feet, then began staggering toward the slowly opening basement doors —

**(here is my son
does he have the makings of a factory man?)**

—squeaking, screeching, loud clanking, heavy machinery dragging across a cement floor —

—the doors opened farther —

—something long, metallic, and triple-jointed pushed through, folding around the edge. A glint as more metal thrust out and folded, seizing the door —

—throwing sparks, the mechanical hand raked down, gripped the handle, and pulled the door wide open.

... doors open and the OldWorker is cast away...

Something crumpled and man-like was tossed out over their heads and landed with a soft *whumph!* in the snow.

Will turned toward Jackson. "A man works his whole life away, and what does it mean?"

Jackson and the workers stared into the shimmering electric gaze beyond the iron doors.

"Welcome, my son," whispered Jackson —
—in a voice very much like his own father's —
"Welcome to the Machine."
...as the production line begins again...

9

You'll be a worker just like me, that's the way of it.

Work the line, wear the smell; the son following in his father's footsteps.

Something like this, well...it makes a man's life seem worthwhile.

I always knew you'd do me proud.

I love you, Dad. I hope this makes up for a lot of things.

I love you too, son.

Best get to work.

That's a good boy....

All But the Ties Eternal

"All waits undreamed of in that region...
    Till when the ties loosen,
        All but the ties eternal, Time and Space,
  Nor darkness, gravitation, sense, nor any bounds bounding us."
             —Walt Whitman "Darest Thou Now O Soul"

Afterward she spent many hours alone in the house for the purpose of making it emptier; it was a game to her, like the one she played as a child, walking on the stone wall of the garden, pretending it was a mountain ledge, not wanting to look down for the sight of rocks below, knowing certain death awaited her should she slip, a terrible fall that would crush her to squishy bits, walking along until her steps faltered and she toppled backward, always thinking in that moment before her tiny body hit the ground: *So that's when I died.*

She always had laughter then, as a child, sitting ass-deep in mud and looking at the wall.

All the house had was the hole Daddy left behind, and there was no laughter remaining.

Yolanda stood looking at the small hole in the living room wall, wondering when it would start bleeding again. It only bled at night, at twenty minutes past twelve, the same time her father had —

—a stirring from the bedroom. She listened for Michael's voice. He would have to wake soon, he always did whenever she got up at night. She peered into the darkness as if it would warn her when he awakened, perhaps split down the middle like a razor cut and allow some light to seep through, and in that light she would see her father's face, winking at her like he often did before letting her in on a little secret.

He'd let her in on all his little secrets, except the one that really mattered. She found it hard not to hate him for it.

Nothing came at her from the darkness. She turned back and stared at the hole. It was so tiny, so silent.

The digital clock blinked: *12:19.*

She took a breath and watched as the numbers changed —

—then looked at the hole.

It always began slowly, like a trickle of water dripping from a faucet not turned completely off: one bulging droplet crept to the edge and glistened, almost wiggling the same teasing, impatient way a child does before pulling a harmless prank, then it fell through and slid down the wall, dark as ink.

She watched the thin stream crawl to the floor, leaving its slender-thread path for the others to follow. And follow they did.

Pulsing out in streams heavier and thicker, they spread across the wall in every direction as if from the guts of a spider until she was staring into the center of a web, admiring patterns made by the small lines where they dripped into one another like the colors of a summertime ice-cream cone. Strawberry; vanilla.

A soft groan from the bedroom, then: "Yolanda? Where are you?"

She looked once more at the dark, shimmering web, then went to the bedroom where Michael was waiting.

He saw her and smiled. She was still naked.

"Where were you? Come back to bed."

"No," she said. "I want you to come into the living room and see it for yourself."

"See what for my —? Oh, yeah. Right."

"Please?"

He sat up in bed and rubbed his eyes. "Look, Yolanda, I've been telling you for days — you've got to get out of this house! Your father's dead and there's nothing you can do about it. You've got no reason to stay here. The sooner you get over this, the sooner you can get on with your life."

"I thought you left the social work at the office."

"I only mean that —"

"*Goddammit*, stop patronizing me, Michael! Get your ass up and come look at this!"

The anger in her voice made him do as he was told.

As they entered the living room, she saw the last of the web slip into the hole and thought of the funny way her father used to suck in the last string of spaghetti.

As the last of the streams pulled back into the hole, she gripped Michael's arm and pointed. "Did you see it? Did you?"

He placed his other arm around her bare, sweaty shoulder, pulling her close. "Take it easy, Yolanda. Look, it's been a rotten time for you, I know that. It's why I came over and—"

"I didn't *ask* you to come over!"

"I know, but, Jesus, you haven't even so much as *called* for ten days! I figured you'd need a little time to yourself, but I never thought you'd start to... to..."

She pulled back and slapped away his arm. "Don't you dare talk to me like that! I am not one of your screwed-up runaway teenagers who just needs a shoulder to whine on!"

"I was only—"

"I know what you were *only*, thank you. I'm not one of your fragile children who might shatter if pushed a little, and I am not *imagining* things." She crossed to the hole and stuck the tip of her middle finger in, feeling the moisture. She pulled it out and felt the trace of a smile cross her lips: there was a small droplet of blood perched between her nail and the flesh of the quick. She faced Michael and offered her evidence.

"Look for yourself. Blood."

He lifted her hand closer to his face, squinted, then turned on a small table lamp.

For a moment she saw him hesitate.

There was, indeed, blood on her fingertip. He stared at it, then brushed it away. "You cut your finger on the plaster."

"I most certainly did not."

"You did," he said. "Look." He lifted her hand; she saw the small gash in her fingertip.

Something pinched in her stomach. Her eyes blinked. Her arms began to shake. She swore she wouldn't start crying.

Making no attempt to touch her, Michael said, "If you insist on staying here, why don't you just fix the hole?"

She took a breath and wiped something from her eye. "It's not that big. It's just not...that big."

"You must be joking, right?"

She stared at him.

"It's not that *big*?" he said. "Christ, honey, I could stick a pool cue in that thing." He pointed and she followed with her gaze—

—remembering she'd only been able to press her fingertip against the hole before, never inside it, never—

But Michael was right.

The hole was bigger. Not much, less than a quarter inch in circumference, but bigger.

Her voice came out a whisper when she said: "I remember thinking it should have been bigger. I mean, he used a bullet with a hollow point, right? He sat in his favorite chair, put the gun in his mouth and...and the hole was so small. The sound was so loud. It was like the whole ceiling turned into thunder. I was in my bed, I heard Dad mutter to himself, and then..." She took a small breath. "Then it was over and the sound stopped ringing in my ears and I...came out here."

She stared at the hole. "I didn't look at him. I looked at the hole. It was all I could see. It looked like a mouth. It was...*eating* everything."

She stood hugging herself, transfixed. "The blood, the tiny pieces of his skull and brain, the hole pulled them in. It was like watching dirty dish water go down a drain. It all swirled around the hole, got closer and closer till there should have been nothing left—but it was still there on the wall, his blood and brains, all the pieces were still there and—"

"Yolanda, c'mon—"

"...wanna know why he did it, Michael, if I did something to upset him—but I don't think I did. I loved him so much, but that wasn't enough. I guess he missed Mom too much. I told him it wasn't our fault that she walked out, that she didn't love us back. He didn't ask me for much, he never did, he always gave, and I wish he had...I wish he would've asked me for help, said *something*, because he was always there for me and when he needed someone I was...was—"

"You need rest."

She felt hot tears streaming down her cheeks, but she didn't care.

"...I just want him back! I want my father back, all right, and all I've got is this fucking hole that took him away from me. It sucked him in, left me alone, and it's...not...*fair!*"

She buried her face in her hands and wept, feeling the fury and sorrow mix, feeling a bellyful of night making her shudder and she hated it, wanted to destroy it.

Before she knew it she was against the wall, pounding with her fists, feeling the force of her blows ripple through her arms like electric shocks but she didn't care, she kept pounding as if Dad would hear her and call out from the other side.

Then Michael was behind her, his arms around her, easing her away; she didn't want him to, so she whirled around to slap his face, lost her balance, suddenly falling from the garden wall again, her arms flailing to protect her from the rocks below as she fell against the wall—

—and saw the hole swallow four of her fingers.

It was still getting bigger.

Michael was all over her, picking her up like she was some goddamned helpless pathetic frail child. She swatted at his face because he wasn't looking at the hole, he didn't see the small globule of blood peek over the edge as if saying *wait until next time...*

Once in bed, she fell immediately asleep.

Then woke, Michael at her side.

Then slept. And woke. And slept.

And woke—

Daddy was there, just between the beams of moonlight that slipped through the window blinds, smiling at her, his mouth growing wide as he stepped closer to the bed, whispering It's the family comes first, you and me, that's all, honey, because family ties are the most important ones, *then he was bending low, his mouth opening into a pit, so wide and deep, sucking her in—*

She slept—

No sense to her dreams, no rhythm to the words spoken to her there by figures she didn't recognize, moving slowly past her like people on the street; no purpose, no love , no reason, empty here, this place, yet so full of people and place and time going somewhere but she couldn't tell, wouldn't tell—

And woke—

—massaging her shoulders, Michael was massaging her shoulders, his hands strong, warm, and comforting, his voice close and tender, "I'm not going anywhere, baby, I love you, just sleep, *shhh*, yeah, that's it," like talking to a frightened child; she loved him but when would he start treating her like an adult?

She balanced on the edge of sleep, sensing her father. And the ceiling. And the walls.

And the hole.

She could feel it growing, slowly sucking air from the room, Daddy's voice on the tail of moonbeams *most important because they're the ones that last...*

Finally the darkness swirled up to take her where there was only safe, warm peace. She slept without dreams.

When she woke it was still night. But deeper. The covers were moist and warm. She moved back to press her shoulders into Michael's chest—

—and was met by cold space.

She blinked several times to convince herself she was awake. "Michael?"

No answer. She turned onto her side. The cold space grew. Michael was gone. The ceiling rumbled. The other side of the bed looked so vast.

Maybe he'd gone for a drink of water; she often did that in the night.

She pulled the pillows close, waited for him to return. The clock ticked once. Forever passed. It ticked again.

"Bring me some water too, please." There was no response. The gas snapped on. Something cold trickled down the back of her neck. The ceiling rumbled again.

A slight breeze drifted by the bed, tickled her shoulders, then went toward the open bedroom door, through the corridor —

—toward the living room. The beams of moonlight pressed against the foot of the bed to tip it over and send her sliding down to the floor. She closed her eyes, feeling the tightness of her flesh.

"*MICHAEL!*" Her voice reverberated off the walls and left her ears ringing. He *had* to have heard that.

No answer.

Maybe he slipped out, thinking she'd be embarrassed when she woke in the morning because of her behavior; yet he said he loved her, that he wasn't going anywhere—but how many times had Dad said the same thing?

The force of the breeze increased.

She rose, put on her nightgown, and shuffled into the corridor.

The breeze grew stronger, pulling at her.

Once in the living room, she refused to look at the hole; that's what it wanted, for her to stand staring as the streams flowed out and—

There was a stain on the carpet; a dark smear that hadn't been there before.

Was it really moving like she thought? Perhaps it was just a trick of the moonlight casting her shadow, for it seemed to grow larger then smaller in an instant...

The stain kept moving. Slowly. Back.

As if being dragged.

She put a hand to her mouth, breathed out, reassured by the touch of her warm breath against her palm; then she snapped on a light.

She remembered a prank she'd played as a child on a neighbor who'd sent a dog to chase her from their yard; she'd come home and cleared the vegetable bin of all the tomatoes Daddy had bought at that market where he and Mom used to love shopping and thrown them against the neighbor's house, laughing when they splattered every which way, the seeds, juice, and skin spattering, widening with each new throw and moist *pop!*, some of the skin sliding off to the ground.

The living room wall looked like the side of that house.

Only the skin was *crawling* along the floor, being sucked back into the hole—which was so much bigger now, so much wider; she could probably shove her entire arm in up to the elbow.

The breeze grew violent, edging her toward the wall.

She saw Michael's Saint Christopher medal, still on its chain, near the wall. He loved that medal, always wore it, wouldn't even take it off to shower.

The breeze increased, becoming wind.

The ceiling rumbled.

The hole was swirling under the seeds and skin and juice, opening wide with Daddy's smile on the tail of moonbeams...

Yolanda turned, caught a glimpse of herself in the mirror over the fireplace. She nearly shrieked, thinking how right her father had been.

She looked a lot like her mother.

The stain backed toward the base of the wall, nearer the hole.

She could easily stick her head through it now.

The wind almost knocked her off-balance—but she held firm, knowing something about feelings and night and love and tears: all of them could only be judged by what they drew from suffering.

So long as that suffering never drew them back.

—and if you can leave through a hole you can *come back* through one, even if it's one piece at a time. But she loved him—and weren't you supposed to help the ones you loved put the pieces back together?

She ran to the wall, called his name into the aperture, watched as it gulped everything in like a last breath before dying. She jammed her hand through, hoped he might reach out to take it and come back—leave all the memories and pain behind like Mom had left them, without a backward glance of regret.

She pushed in deeper, felt something close round her wrist, something so very strong, yet so gentle and loving.

Suddenly the pressure of the grip turned to the prick of razors and sucked her arm in up to the shoulder.

The ceiling started to thunder.

She yanked back, knowing one of them would weaken soon because the stain and pieces were nearly gone now, and when they were gone the hole would...would...

...would keep growing until it had her, would still send the wind and thunder and memories and—

She wrenched away with all her strength—

—and felt herself pull free.

Yolanda fell back-first to the floor but didn't wait to catch her breath, didn't look at the hole; she sprinted out of the room, knowing how she could get him back. She couldn't do it with her hand, didn't dare try that again, yet she could make the hole bigger, help it to grow—and Michael would see the way out, he'd come back to her because he loved her, didn't want her to be alone, never again. *I'm sorry, Daddy, that you missed Mom so bad but Michael is my family now, all the family I've got left*—

She ran through the kitchen, into the bathroom, unlocked the door to the basement, flipped on the light, and took the stairs three at a time.

The shotgun. She hadn't told the police about Daddy's shotgun, they'd only taken the pistol, but that was fine because she needed the shotgun now for Michael and —

—she ripped open the door to her father's work cabinet and found the twelve-gauge under a sheet of canvas. She grabbed the shells and loaded the gun, smiling as she pumped back—

—*ch-chick!*—

—and felt the first round slide securely into the chamber.

Back upstairs. Fast. In the living room.

In the mirror she saw the reflection of her mother gripping the gun that had killed Daddy; she tried to work up enough saliva to spit in Mom's face but her mouth was too dry so she hoisted the shotgun, pressed the butt against her shoulder, and pulled the trigger —

The ceiling thundered again as Mom shattered into a thousand glittering reflections. Yolanda looked down and saw how small the woman looked, staring up from the floor, shiny, sharp and smooth and empty-eyed pitiful.

She readied herself—

—*ch-chick!*—

—and aimed at the hole.

The wind slammed against her with angry hands, but it would not stop her. Nothing would.

Again and again and again the ceiling thundered as she blew the hole apart, her shoulder raw from the pounding of the shotgun's stock, her chest full of pain and fear, but she kept firing until the force of the blasts weakened her, knocking her from the garden wall.

She dropped to the floor, gazing at the hole.

Wide, dark, bloodied, she peered into the mouth of the web and saw forms moving within, like people passing on the street, and she listened for the sound of Michael's voice but instead heard different voices beckoning to her: *Empty here, so empty without you, I love you I miss you I want you back please come —*

The hole began closing.

She tried to rise because they were in there, Daddy and Michael, but she was too spent, too hurt and weakened by it all. She fell back, saw a thousand reflections of her mother's face glaring up at her —

—and knew what to do.

"Wait for me," she said. Whispered. Weakly.

She wanted to be in there with them, away from all the draining strength of suffering and the memories whose warmth was tainted by it. She fell forward, groping with shaking fingers for the shotgun, grabbed it, dragged it toward her, and sat up.

The hole was so small now, so tiny —one shimmering globule was on the edge, winking at her, *hurry, hurry, get across the ledge.*

She propped up the shotgun between her knees —

—*ch-chick!* —

—and shoved the barrel deep into her mouth.

The globule smiled, then winked at her like Daddy letting her in on some little secret *that's my girl just get over the mountain, don't fall off and I'll tell you something special, because you were brave, you made it back to me* —

From the corner of her eye she saw a thousand images of her mother, all of them screaming.

Then Daddy's voice again: *Almost there, honey, keep your balance, don't slip, don't fall away like Mommy did because I'll never leave you like she did, I'll always be here, I'll be right here waiting for you and always* —

—the ceiling thundered one last time, and a new web spread across the wall —

—*love you....*

After The Elephant Ballet

"Our acts our angels are, or good or ill,
Our fatal shadows that walk by us still."

—John Fletcher (1579-1625) *An Honest Man's Fortune*, Epilogue

The little girl might have been pretty once but flames had taken care of that: burned skin hung about her neck in brownish wattles; one yellowed eye was almost completely hidden underneath the drooping scar tissue of her forehead; her mouth twisted downward on both sides with pockets of dead, greasy-looking flesh at the corners; and her cheeks resembled the globs of congealed wax that form at the base of a candle.

I couldn't stop staring at her or cursing myself for doing it. She passed by the table where I was sitting, giving me a glimpse of her only normal-looking feature: her left eye was a startling bright green, a jade gemstone. Buried as it was in that ruined face, its vibrance seemed a cruel joke.

She took a seat in the back.

Way in the back.

"Mr. Dysart?"

A woman in her mid-thirties held out a copy of my latest storybook. I smiled as I took it, chancing one last glance at the disfigured little girl in the back, then autographed the title page.

I have been writing and illustrating children's books for the last six years, and though I'm far from a household name I do have a Newbery Award proudly displayed on a shelf in my office. One critic, evidently after a few too many Grand Marniers, once wrote: "Dysart's books are a treasure chest of wonders for children and adults alike. He is part Maurice Sendak, part Hans Christian Andersen, and part Madleine L'engle." (I always thought of my books as being a cross between Buster Keaton and the Brothers Grimm—what does *that* tell you about creative objectivity?)

I handed the book back to the woman as Gina Foster, director of the Cedar Hill Public Library, came up to the table. We had been dating for about two weeks; romance had yet to rear its ugly head, but I was hopeful.

"Well, are we ready?" she asked.

"'We' want to step outside for a cigarette."

"I thought you were trying to quit?"

"And failing miserably." I made my way to the special "judge's chair." "How many entries are there?"

"Twenty-five. But don't worry, they can show you only one illustration and the story can't be longer than four minutes. We still on for coffee and dessert afterward?"

"Unless some eight-year-old Casanova steals your heart away."

"Hey, you pays your money, you takes your chances."

"You're an evil woman."

"Famous for it."

"Tell me again: How did you rope me into being the judge for this?"

"When I mentioned that this was National Literacy Month, you assaulted me with a speech about the importance of promoting a love for creativity among children."

"I must've been drunk." I don't drink—that's my mother's department.

Gina looked at her watch, took a deep breath as she gave me a "Here-We-Go" look, then turned to face the room. "Good evening," she said in a sparkling voice that always reminded me of bells. "Welcome to the library's first annual storybook contest." Everyone applauded. I tried slinking my way into the woodwork. Crowds make me nervous. Actually, most things make me nervous.

"I'll just wish all our contestants good luck and introduce our judge, award-winning local children's book author Andrew Dysart." She began the applause this time, then mouthed *You're on your own* before gliding to an empty chair.

"Thank you," I said, the words crawling out of my throat as if they were afraid of the light. "I. . .uh, I'm sure that all of you have been working very hard, and I want you to know that we're going to make copies of all your storybooks, bind them, and put them on the shelves here in the library right next to my own." Unable to add any more dazzle to that stunning speech, I took my seat, consulted the list, and called the first contestant forward.

A chubby boy with round glasses shuffled up as if he were being led in front of a firing squad. He faced the room, gave a terrified grin, then wiped some sweat from his forehead as he held up a pretty good sketch of a cow riding a tractor.

"My name is Jimmy Campbell and my story is called 'The Day The Cows Took Over." He held the picture higher. "See there? The cow is riding the tractor and the farmer is out grazing in the field."

"What's the farmer's name?" I asked.

He looked at me and said, "Uh...h-how about Old MacDonald?" He shrugged his shoulders. "I'd give him a better name, but I don't know no farmers."

I laughed along with the rest of the room, forgetting all about the odd, damaged little girl who had caught my attention earlier.

Jimmy did very well—I had to fight to keep my laughter from getting too loud, I didn't want him to think I was making fun of him but the kid was genuinely *funny*; his story had an off-kilter sense of humor that reminded me Ernie Kovacs. I decided to give him the maximum fifty points. I'm a pushover for kids. Sue me.

The next forty minutes went by with nary a tear or panic attack, but after eight stories I could see that several of the children were getting fidgety, so I signaled to Gina that we'd take a break after the next contestant.

I read: "Lucy Simpkins."

There was the soft rustling of movement in the back as the burned girl came forward.

Everyone stared at her. The cumulative anxiety in the room was squatting on her shoulders like a stone gargoyle, yet she wore an unwavering smile.

I returned the smile and gestured for her to begin.

She held up a watercolor painting.

I think my mouth may have dropped open.

The painting was excellent, a deftly-rendered portrait of several people—some very tall, others quite short, still others who were deformed—standing in a semi-circle around a statue which marked a grave. All wore the brightly colored costumes of circus performers. Each face had an expression of profound sadness; the nuances were breathtaking. But the thing that really impressed me was the cloud in the sky; it was shaped like an elephant, but not in any obvious way: it reminded you of summer afternoons when you still had enough imagination and wonder to lie on a hillside and dream that you saw giant shapes in the pillowy white above.

"My name is Lucy Simpkins," she said in a clear, almost musical voice, "and my story is called 'Old Bet's Gone Away.'

"One night in Africa, in the secret elephant graveyard, the angels of all the elephants got together to tell stories. Tonight it was Martin's, the Bull Elephant's, turn. He wandered around until he found his old bones, then he sat on top of them like they were a throne and said, 'I want to tell you the story of Old Bet, the one who never found her way back to us.'

"And he said:

"'In 1824 a man in Somers, New York, bought an elephant named Old Bet from a traveling circus. He gave her the best hay and always fed her peanuts on the weekends. Children would pet her trunk and take rides on her back in a special saddle that the man made.

"'Then one day the Reverend brought his daughter to ride on Old Bet. Old Bet was really tired but she thought the Reverend's little girl looked nice so she gave her a ride and even sang the elephant song, which went like this:

"'I go along, thud-thud,
I go along.
And I sing my elephant song.
I stomp in the grass,
and I roll in the mud,
And when I go a-walking, I go along THUD!
It's a happy sound, and this is my happy song
Won't you sing it with me? It doesn't take long.
I go along, thud-thud, I go along.

"'Old Bet accidentally tripped over a log and fell and the Reverend's daughter broke both of her legs and had to go to the hospital.

"'Old Bet was real sorry but the Reverend yelled at her and smacked her with a horse whip and got her so scared that she ran away into the deep woods.

"'The next day the Reverend got all the people of the town together and told them that Old Bet was the Devil in disguise and should be killed before she could hurt other children. So the men-folk took their shotguns and went into the woods. They found Bet by the river. She was looking at her reflection in the water and singing:

"'I ran away, uh-oh, I ran away.
And I hurt my little friend.
I didn't mean to fall, but I'm clumsy and old
I'm big and ugly and the circus didn't want me anymore.
I wish they hadn't sold me.
I want to go home.

"'The Reverend wanted to shoot her but the man who'd bought her from the circus said, "Best I be the one who does the deed. After all, she's mine." But the man wasn't too young either and his aim was a bit off and when he fired the bullet it hit Old Bet in the rear and it hurt and it scared her so much! She tried to run away, to run back to the circus.

"'She didn't mean to kill anyone, but two men got under her and she crushed them and her heart broke because of that. By now the Judge had come around to see what all the trouble was, and he saw the two dead men and decreed right there on the spot that Old Bet was guilty of murder and sentenced her to hang by the neck until she was dead.

"'They took her to the rail yard and strung her up on a railroad crane but she broke it down because she was so heavy. They got a stronger crane and hanged her from that. After three hours, Old Bet finally died while five thousand people watched. She was buried there in Somers and the man who owned her had a statue raised above the grave. Ever since, it has been a shrine for circus people. They travel to her grave and stop to pay their respects and remember that, as long as people laugh at you and smile, they won't kill you. And they say that if you look in the sky on a bright summer's day, you can see Old Bet up there in the clouds, smiling down at everyone and singing the elephant song as she tries to find her way back to Africa and the secret elephant graveyard.'

"Then it was morning, and the sun came up, and the elephants made their way back to a place even more secret than the elephant graveyard. They all dreamed about Old Bet, and wished her well.

"My name is Lucy Simpkins and my story was called 'Old Bet's Gone Away.' Thank you."

The others applauded her, softly at first, as if they were afraid it was the wrong thing to do, but it wasn't long before their clapping grew louder and more ardent. Gina sat forward, applauding to beat the band. She looked at the audience, gave a shrug that was more an inward decision than an outward action, and stood.

Lucy Simpkins managed something like a smile, then handed me her watercolor. "You should have this," she said, and made her way out of the room toward the refreshment table.

As everyone was dispersing, I took Gina's hand and pulled her aside. "My God, did you hear that?"

"I thought it was incredibly moving."

"Moving? Maybe in the same way the last thirty minutes of *The Wild Bunch* or *Straw Dogs* is moving, yes, but if you're talking warm and fuzzy and *It's A Wonderful Life*, you're way the hell off-base!"

Her eyes clouded over. "Jesus, Andy. You're shaking."

"Damn straight I'm shaking. Do you have any idea what that girl has to have been through? Can you imagine the kind of life which would cause a child to tell a story like that?" I took a deep breath, clenching my teeth. "Christ! I don't know which I want more: to wrap her up and take her home with me, or find her parents and break a baseball bat over their skulls!"

"That's a bit...strong, isn't it?"

"No. An imagination that can invent something like that story is not the result of a healthy, loving household."

"Don't be so arrogant. You aren't all-knowing about these things. You don't have any idea what her family life is really like."

"I suppose, Mother Goose, that you're more experienced in this area?" I don't know why I said something like that. Sometimes I'm not a nice person. In fact, sometimes I stink on ice.

Her face melted into a placid mask, except for a small twitch in the upper left corner of her mouth that threatened to become a sneer.

"My sister had epilepsy," Gina said. "All her life the doctors kept changing her medication as she got older, a stronger dose of what she was already taking, or some new drug altogether. Those periods were murder because her seizures always got worse while her system adjusted. Her seizures were violent as hell but she refused to wear any kind of protective gear. 'I don't wanna look like a goon,' she'd say. So she'd walk around with facial scrapes and cuts and ugly bruises; she sprained her arm a couple of times and once dislocated her shoulder. People in the neighborhood started noticing, but no one said anything to us. Someone finally called the police and Child Welfare. They came down on us like a curse from heaven. They were of course embarrassed when they found out about Lorraine's condition —she'd always insisted that we keep it a secret—but nothing changed the fact that people who were supposedly our friends just *assumed* that her injuries were the result of child abuse. Lorraine had never been so humiliated, and from that day on she saw herself as being handicapped. I think that, as much as the epilepsy, helped to kill her. So don't go jumping to any conclusions about that girl's parents or the life she's had because *you can't know*. And anything you might say or do out of anger could plant an idea in her head that has no business being there."

"What do you suggest?"

"I suggest that you go out there and tell her how much you enjoyed her story. I suggest we try to make her feel special and admired because she deserves to feel that way, if only for tonight."

I squeezed her hand. "It couldn't have been a picnic for you, either, Lorraine's epilepsy."

"She should have lived to be a hundred. And just so you know — this has a tendency to slip out of my mouth from time to time — Lorraine committed suicide. She couldn't live with the knowledge that she was 'a cripple.' I cried for a year."

"I'm sorry for acting like a jerk."

She smiled, then looked at her watch. "Break's almost over. If you want to step outside and smoke six minutes off your life, you'd better do it now. I'll snag some punch and cookies for you."

I couldn't find Lucy; one parent told me she'd gone into the restroom, so I stepped out for my smoke. The rest of the evening went quickly and enjoyably. At the end of the night, I found myself with a tie: Lucy Simpkins (how could I not?) and my junior-league Ernie Kovaks who didn't know no farmers.

Ernie was ecstatic.

Lucy was gone.

* * *

I have only the vaguest memories of my father. When I was four, he was killed in an accident at the steel mill where he worked. He left only a handful of impressions: the smell of machine grease, the rough texture of a calloused hand touching my cheek, the smell of Old Spice. What I know of him I learned from my mother.

His death shattered her. She grew sad and overweight and began drinking. Over the years there have been times of laughter and dieting, but the drinking remained constant, evidenced by the flush on her cheeks and the reddened bulbous nose that I used to think cute when I was a child because it made her look like W.C. Fields; now it only disgusts me.

After my father's death, nothing I did was ever good enough; I fought like hell for her approval and affection but often settled for indifference and courtesy.

Don't misunderstand — I loved her when she was sober.

When she was drunk, I thought her the most repulsive human being on the face of the earth.

I bring this up to help you make sense of everything that happened later, starting with the surprise I found waiting on my doorstep when, after coffee and cheesecake, Gina drove me back to my house.

Someone on the street was having a party so we had to park half a block away and walk. That was fine by me; it gave us time to hold hands and enjoy the night and each other's company. The world was new again, at least for this evening—

—which went right into the toilet when something lurched out of the shadows on my porch.

"...been waitin' here....a long time..." Her voice was thick and slurred and the stench of too much gin was enough to make me gag.

"Mom? Jesus, what are you—" I cast an embarrassed glance at Gina. "—doing here?"

She pointed unsteadily to her watch and gave a soft, wet belch. "...s'after midnight...s'my birthday now..."

She wobbled back and forth for a moment before slipping on the rubber WELCOME mat and falling toward me.

I caught her. "Oh, for chrissakes!" I turned toward Gina. "God, I don't know what—I'm sorry about..."

"Is there anything I can do?"

Mom slipped a little more and mumbled something. I hooked my arms around her torso and said, "My...*dammit!*...my keys are in my left pocket. Would you—?"

Gina took them out, unlocked the front door, and turned on the inside lights. I spun Mom around and shook her until she regained some composure, then led her to the kitchen where I poured her into a chair and started a pot of coffee. Gina remained in the front room, turning on the television and adjusting the volume, her way of letting me know she wouldn't listen to anything that might be said.

The coffee finished brewing and I poured a large cup for Mom. "How the hell did you get here?"

The shock of having someone other than myself see her in this state forced her to pull herself together; when she spoke again, her voice wasn't as slurred. "I walked. It's a nice...nice night." She took a sip of the coffee, then sat watching the steam curl over the rim of the cup. Her lower lip started to quiver. "I'm...I'm sorry, Andy. I didn't know you were gonna have company." She sighed, then fished a cigarette from the pocket of her blouse and lit it with an unsteady hand.

"Why are you here?"

"I just got to...you know, thinking about your dad and was feeling blue...besides, I wanted to remind you that you're taking me out for my birthday."

My right hand balled into a fist. "Have I *ever* forgotten your birthday?"

"...no..."

"Then why would I start now?"

She leaned back in the chair and fixed me with an icy stare, smoke crawling from her nostrils like flames from a dragon's snout. "Maybe you think you've gotten too good for me. Maybe you think because I wasn't a story writer or artist like you, you don't have to bother with me anymore."

Time to go.

"Sit here and drink your coffee. I'm going to walk my friend to her car and then I'll come back and take you home."

"...didn't get it from me, that's for damn sure...does you no good anyway...drop dead at forty-five and no one will care about your silly books...."

I threw up my hands and started out of the kitchen.

"What's this?" said Mom, pulling Lucy Simpkins's watercolor from my pocket. "Oh, a picture. They used to let us draw pictures when I was in the children's home...did I ever tell you about —?"

She was making me sick.

I stormed out of the kitchen and into the front room in time to see Jimmy Stewart grab Donna Reed and say, "I don't want to get married, understand?"

"Don't worry," said Gina. "They get together in the end." She put her arms around me. I felt like Jason being wrapped in the Golden Fleece.

"I'm so sorry about this," I said. "She's never done this before—"

"Never?"

I looked into her eyes and couldn't make any excuses. "I mean she's never come *here* drunk before."

"How long has she been this way?"

"I can't ever remember a week from my life when she didn't get drunk at least once."

"Have you ever tried to get her some help?"

"Of course I have. She tries it for a while but she always...always—"

"—I understand. It's okay. Don't be embarrassed."

That's easy to say, I thought. What I said was: "I appreciate this, Gina. I really do." I wished that she would just leave so I could get the rest of this over with.

She seemed to sense this and stepped back, saying, "I guess I should, uh, go..."

A loud crash from the kitchen startled both of us.

I ran in and saw Mom on the floor; she'd been trying to pour herself another cup of coffee and had collapsed, taking the coffee pot with her. Shattered sections of sharp glass covered the floor and she had split open one of her shins. Scurrying on her hands and knees, she looked up and saw me standing there, saw Gina behind me, and pointed at the table.

"W-where did you...did you get *t-that?*"

"Get what?"

"...t-that goddamn...*picture!*"

I moved toward her. She doubled over and began vomiting.

I grabbed her, trying to pull her up to the sink — making it to the bathroom was out of the question — but I slipped and lost my grip —

—Mom gave a wet gurgling sound and puked on my chest —

—Gina came in, grabbed a towel, and helped me get her over the sink—

—and Mom gripped the edge, emptying her stomach down the drain.

The stench was incredible.

Feeling the heat of humiliation cover my face, I looked at Gina and fumbled for something to say, but what *could* I say? We were holding a drunk who was spewing all over —

—what could you say?

Gina returned my gaze. "So, how 'bout them Mets, huh? Fuckin-A!"

That's what you could say.

I didn't feel so dirty.

* * *

Gina surprised me the next morning by showing up on my doorstep at eight-thirty with hot coffee and croissants. When I explained to her that I had to take Mom's birthday cake over to her house Gina said, "I'd like to come along, if you don't mind."

I did and told her so.

"Come on," she said, taking my hand and giving me a little kiss on the cheek. "Think about it, if she's hung-over and sees that I'm with you, she might behave herself. If she doesn't behave, then you can use me as an excuse not to stick around."

I argued with her some more; she won. I don't think I've ever won an argument with a woman; they're far too sharp.

Besides an ersatz-apology ("I feel so *silly!*") and a bandage around the gash on her shin, Mom showed no signs that last night had ever happened. Her hair was freshly cleaned, she wore a new dress, and her makeup was, for a change, subtly applied; she looked like your typical healthy matriarch.

We stayed for breakfast. Gina surprised me a second time that morning by reaching into her purse and pulling out a large birthday card that she handed to Mom.

Well, that just made Mom's day. She must have thanked Gina half-a-dozen times and even went so far as to give her a hug, saying, "I'm glad to see he finally found a good one."

"Blind shithouse luck," replied Gina. She and Mom got a tremendous guffaw out of that. I gritted my teeth and smiled at them. Hardy-dee-har-har.

"So," Mom said to Gina. "Will you be coming with us?"

"I don't know," Gina replied, turning to me with a Pollyanna-pitiful look in her eyes. "Am I?"

"You stink at coy," was my answer.

"Good!" said Mom. "The three of us. It'll be a lot of fun."

"Have you decided where you want to go?"

"Yeee-eeessss, I have."

Oh, good; another surprise.

"Where?"

She winked at me and squeezed Gina's hand. "It's a secret. I'll tell you when we're on our way." This was a little game she loved to play — "I-Know-Something-You-Don't-Know"—and it usually got on my nerves.

But not that morning. Somehow Gina's presence made it seem as if everything was going to work out just fine.

Our first stop was Indian Mound Mall, where Gina insisted on buying Mom a copy of the new Stephen King opus and paying for lunch. After we'd eaten, Mom looked at her watch and informed us it was time to go.

"Where are we going?" I asked as we got on the highway.

Mom leaned forward from the backseat. "Riverfront Coliseum."

"*Cincinnati?* You want to drive three hours to—"

"It's my birthday."

"But—"

Gina squeezed my leg. "It's her birthday."

I acquiesced. I should have remembered that no good deed goes unpunished.

* * *

"A circus!" shouted Gina as we approached the coliseum entrance. I slowed my step, genuinely surprised. I have been to many circuses in my life, but never with my mother—I always thought she'd have no interest in this sort of thing.

"Surprised?" said Mom, taking my arm.

"Well, yes, but...why?"

Her eyes filled with a curious kind of desperation. "All our lives we've never done anything *fun* together. I've been a real shit to you sometimes and I'll never be able to apologize enough, let alone make up for it. I've never told you how proud I am of you—I've read all your books. Bet you didn't know that, did you?" Her eyes began tearing. "Oh, hon, I ain't been much of a mother to you, what with the drinking and such, but, if you'll be patient with me, I'd like to...to give it a try, us being friends. If you don't mind."

This part was familiar. I bit down on my tongue, hoping that she wasn't going to launch into a heartfelt promise to get back into AA and stop hitting the bottle and turn her life around, blah-blah-blah.

She didn't.

"Well," she whispered. "We'd best go get our tickets."

"Do we get cotton candy?" asked Gina.

"Of course you do. And hot dogs—"

"—and cherry colas—"

"—and peanuts—"

"—and an ulcer," I said. They both stared at me.

"You never were any fun," said Mom, smiling. I couldn't tell if she was joking or not.

"I never claimed to be."

Gina smacked me on the ass. "Then it's about time you started." It was a blast. Acrobats and lion tamers and trained seals and a big brass band and a sword-swallower, not to mention the fire-eating bear (that was a real trip) and the bald guy who wrestled a crocodile that was roughly the size of your average Mexican Chihuahua (**A DEATH-DEFYING BATTLE BETWEEN MAN AND BEAST!** proclaimed the program: "Compared to what?" asked Gina. "Changing a diaper?"); all of it was an absolute joy, right up to the elephants and clowns.

Not that anything happened with the elephants; they did a marvelously funny kick-line to a Scott Joplin tune, but the sight of them triggered memories of Lucy Simpkins's story. I looked at Gina and saw that she was thinking about it as well.

Mom thought the elephants were the most precious things she'd ever seen — and since she used to say the same about my baby pictures, I wondered if my paranoia about my nose being too large was unjustified after all.

At the end of the show, when every performer and animal came marching out for the Grand Finale Parade, the clowns broke away and ran into the audience. After tossing out confetti and lollipops and balloons, one clown ran over to Mom and handed her a small stuffed animal, then, with a last burst of confetti from the large flower in the center of his costume, he honked his horn and dashed back into the parade.

I looked at Mom and saw, just for a moment, the ghost of the vibrant, lovely woman who populated several pages of the family photo albums; in that light, with all the laughter and music swirling around us, I saw her smile and could almost believe that she was going to really change this time. I suspected that it might just be wishful thinking on my part, but sometimes a delusion is the best thing in the world — especially if you *know* it's a delusion.

So, for that moment, Mom was a changed woman who might find some measure of peace and happiness in the remainder of her life, and I was a son who harbored no anger or disgust for her, la-dee-da.

It was kind of nice.

We made our way through the crowd and toward the exit. I don't like crowds, as I've said, and soon felt the first heavy rivulets of sweat rolling down my face.

Gina sensed what was happening and led us to a section near a concession stand where the crowd was much thinner.

As I stood there catching my breath, Gina nudged Mom and asked about the stuffed animal. Mom looked at it then for the first time.

"Oh my. Isn't that...something?" She was smiling, yet she cringed as she touched the tiny fired-clay tusks of the small stuffed elephant in a ballerina pose, wearing a ridiculous pink tutu. Cottony angels' wings jutted from its back.

"That's adorable," laughed Gina.

"Yes...yes, it is," whispered Mom. Her smile faltered for just a moment. I have seen my mother worried before, but this went beyond that; something in her was *afraid* of that stuffed toy.

"Janet Walters!" shouted a voice that sounded like old nails being wrenched from rotted wood.

Mom looked up at me. "Walters" was her maiden name. "What the—?"

The nun came toward us.

That in itself wasn't all that unusual; it was easy to assume that the nun was here with some church group. What *was* unusual was the way this nun was dressed; pick your favorite singing sister from *The Sound of Music* and you'll have some idea. Nuns don't have to dress this way anymore, but this one did. The whole outfit was at least fifty years out of date. Her habit was four times too heavy for the weather and her shoes would have looked right at home in a Frankenstein movie.

Sister Frankenstein barreled right up to Mom and grabbed her arm. "Would you like to hear a story?"

Mom's face drained of all color.

I didn't give a good goddamn if this woman was a nun.

"Excuse me, Sister, but I think you're hurting—"

Sister Frankenstein fixed me with a glare that could have frozen fire, then said to Mom: "He was led across the railroad yards to his private car. It was late at night. No train was scheduled but an express came through. A baby elephant had strayed from the rest of the pack and stood on the tracks in front of the oncoming train, so scared it couldn't move. Jumbo saw it and ran over, shoved the baby aside, and met the locomotive head-on. He was killed instantly and the train was derailed."

My mother began moaning soft and low, gripping the stuffed toy like a life-preserver.

Sister Frankenstein let fly with a series of loud, wracking, painful-sounding coughs and began to stomp away (*I go along, thud-thud!*) then turned back and said, "Only good little girls ever see Africa!"

A crowd of teenagers ran through and the nun vanished behind them.

I was reeling; it had happened so *fast*.

Mom marched over to the only concession stand still open — —which sold beer.

She took the large plastic cup in her hands and said, "P-please don't start with me, Andy. Just a *beer*, okay? It's just a beer. I need to...to steady...my nerves."

"Who the hell *was* that?"

"Not now." She tipped the cup back and finished the brew in five deep gulps.

Gina took my hand and whispered, "Don't push it."

Right. Psycho Nun On The Rampage and I'm supposed to let it drop.

Gina raised an eyebrow at me.

"Fine," I whispered.

Mom fell asleep the minute we got in the car and didn't wake up until we reached Cedar Hill.

Mom took her mail from the box, then insisted we come in for a slice of cake.

As I was pouring the coffee, Mom opened a large manila envelope that was among the mail.

Her gasp sounded like a strangled cry of a suicide when the rope snaps tight.

I turned. "What is it?"

Gina was leaning over her shoulder, looking at the large piece of heavy white paper that Mom had pulled from the envelope.

"Andy," said Gina in a low, cautious voice. "I think you'd better take a look at this."

It was a watercolor painting of the center ring of a circus where a dozen elephants were all wearing the same kind of absurd pink tutu as the stuffed toy; all had angel's wings unfurling from their shoulders, and all were dancing through a wall of flames. The stands were empty except for one little girl whose face was the saddest I'd ever seen.

There was no doubt in my mind—or Gina's, as I later found out—about who had painted it.

There was no return address on the envelope, nor was there a postmark.

After a tense silence, Mom lit a cigarette and said, "Would you two mind...mind sitting with me for a while? I got something I need to tell you about.

"When I was six years old the county took me and my three brothers away from our parents and put us in the Catholic Children's Home..."

I faded away for a minute or two. I'd heard this countless times before and was embarrassed that Gina would have to listen to it now.

Most of what Mom said early on was directed more toward Gina than me. The Same Old Prologue.

In a nutshell:

Mom's parents were dirt poor and heavy drinkers both. Too many complaints from the school and neighbors resulted in a visit by the authorities. My mother and her brothers remained under the care of the Catholics and the county until they were fifteen; then they were each given five dollars, a new set of clothes, and pushed out the door.

"There wasn't really much to enjoy," Mom continued, "except our Friday art classes with Sister Elizabeth. If we worked hard, she'd make popcorn in the evening and tell us stories before we went to bed, stories that she made up. There was one that was our favorite, all about these dancing elephants and their adventures with the circus. I don't know why I was so surprised to see Sister Elizabeth tonight; she always loved circuses.

"She'd start each story the same way, describing the circus tent and giving the names of all the elephants, then she'd make up a story about one elephant in particular. Each Friday it was a new story about a different elephant. The stories were real funny and we always got a good laugh from them.

"Then she got sick. Turned out to be cancer. She kept getting sadder and angrier all the time so we started to draw pictures of the elephants for her, but it didn't lift her spirits any.

"The stories started getting so...bitter. There was one about an elephant that got hanged that gave some of the girls bad dreams for a week. Then Sister quit telling us stories. We heard that she was gonna go in the hospital, so we bought her flowers and asked her to tell us one last story about the elephants.

"God, she looked so thin. She'd been going to Columbus for cobalt treatments. Her scalp was all moist looking and had only a few strands of wiry hair and her color was awful...but her eyes were the worst. She couldn't hide how scared she was.

"She told us one more story. But this one didn't start with the circus tent. It started in Africa."

I leaned forward. This was new to me.

"I never forgot it," said Mom. "It went like this: The elder of the pack gathered together all of the elephants and told them that he had spoken with God, and God had said the elder elephant was going to die, but first he was to pass on a message.

"God had said there were men on their way to Africa, sailing in great ships, coming to take the elephants away so people could see them. And people would think that the elephants were strange and wonderful and funny. God felt bad about that 'funny' part, and He asked the elder to apologize to the others and tell them that as long as they stayed good of heart and true to themselves they would never be funny in His eyes.

"The elder named Martin the Bull Elephant as the new leader, then lumbered away to the secret elephant graveyard and died.

"The men came in their ships and rounded up the elephants and put them in chains and stuffed them into the ships and took them away.

Gary A. Braunbeck

They were sold to the circus where they were made to do tricks and dances for people to laugh at. Then they were trained to dance ballet for one big special show. The elephants worked real hard because they wanted to do well.

"The night of the big show came, and the elephants did their best. They really did. They got all the steps and twirls and dips exactly right and felt very proud. But the people laughed and laughed at them because they were so big and clumsy and looked so silly in the pink tutus they wore. Even though they did their best, they felt ashamed because everyone laughed at them.

"Later that night, after the circus was quiet and the laughing people went home, the elephants were alone. One of them told Martin that all of their hearts were broken. Martin gave a sad nod of his head and said, 'Yes, it's time for us to go back home.' So he reached out with his trunk through the bars of the cage and picked up a dying cigar butt and dropped it in the hay and started a big fire.

"The elephants died in that fire, but when the circus people and firemen looked above the flames they saw smoke clouds dancing across the sky. They were shaped like elephants and they drifted across the continents until they reached the secret elephant graveyard in Africa. And when they touched down the elder was waiting for them, and he smiled as an angel came down and said to all of them, 'Come, the blessed children of my Father, and receive the world prepared for you....'"

She cleared her throat, lit another cigarette, and stared at us.

"That's *horrible*," said Gina.

"I know," whispered Mom. "Sister Elizabeth didn't say anything after she finished the story, she just got up and left. It really bothered all of us, but the Sisters had taught us that we had to comfort each other whenever something happened that upset one or all of us. They even assigned each of us another girl that we could go to if something was wrong and there wasn't any Sisters around. Sister Elizabeth used to say that we were all guardian angels of each other's spirit. It was kinda nice.

"The girl I had, her name was Lucy Simpkins. She'd been really close to Sister, and I think it all made her a little crazy. On the night Sister Elizabeth died, Lucy got to crying and crying until I thought she'd waste away. She kept asking everyone how she could go to Africa and be with Sister Elizabeth and the elephants.

"Everyone just sort of looked at her and didn't say anything because we knew she was upset. She was a strange girl, always singing to herself and drawing...

"She never said anything to me. Not even when I went to her and asked. At least, that's how I remember it.

"You see, sometime during the night she got out of bed and snuck down to the janitor's closet, found some kerosene, and set herself on fire. She was dead before anyone could get the flames out."

Mom rose from the table, crossed to the counter, and looked at her birthday cake. "I never told anyone that before."

She took a knife from the cutlery drawer and cut three slices of cake. We ate in silence.

She went to bed a little while later and Gina came over to my place to spend the night.

At one point she nudged me, and said, "Have you ever read any Ray Bradbury?"

"Of course."

"Don't you envy him? There's so much joy and wonder in his stories. They jump out at you like happy puppies. They make you believe that you can hang on to that joy forever." She kissed me, then snuggled against my chest. "Wouldn't it be nice to pinpoint the exact moment in your childhood when you lost that joy and wonder, then go back and warn yourself as a child? Tell yourself that you mustn't ever let go of that joy and hope. Then you wouldn't have to worry about any...regrets coming back."

"I think it's a little late to go back and warn Mom."

"I know," she whispered. "You really love her, don't you? In spite of everything."

"Yes, I do. Sometimes I've wished that I didn't, it would have made things easier." I tried to imagine what my mother must have been like as a child but couldn't: to me, she was always *old*.

"I can't do this to myself, Gina. I can't start feeling responsible for the way her life has turned out. I've done everything I'm capable of, but it seems as if she doesn't *want* to be happy. Dad's being alive filled some kind of void in her, and when he died something else crawled into his spot and began sucking the life out of her.

"I remember once reading about something called 'The Bridge of the Separator.' In Zoroastrianism it's believed that when you die you meet your conscience on a bridge. I can't help but wonder if...if..."

"If what?"

"I used to look at Mom and think that here was a woman who had died a long time ago but just forgot to drop dead. And maybe that's not so far from the truth. Maybe the really *alive* part of her, the Bradbury part of joy and wonder and hope, died with my father—or maybe it died with Lucy and that nun.

"Whatever the reason, it's dead and there's no bringing it back, so is it so hard to believe that her conscience has gotten tired of waiting at the bridge and has decided to come and get her?"

* * *

I awoke a little after five a.m. and climbed quietly out of bed so as not to wake Gina. I stood in the darkness of the bedroom, inhaling deeply. Something smelled.

I puzzled over it—

—sawdust and hay, the aroma of cigarettes and beer and warm cotton candy and popcorn and countless exotic manures —

—I was smelling the circus.

The curtains over the bedroom window fluttered.

The circus smell grew almost overpowering.

I put on my robe and crossed to the window, pulled back the curtains, and looked out into the field behind my house—

—where Lucy Simpkins stood, her sad, damaged hands petting the trunk of an old elephant whose skin was mottled, gray, and wrinkled. Its tusks were cracked and yellowed with age. When Lucy fed it peanuts, its tail slapped happily against its back legs.

A bit of moonlight bounced off Lucy's green eye and touched my gaze. The old elephant looked at me through eyes that were caked with age and dirt and filled with the errant ghosts of many secrets.

My first impulse was to wake Gina but something in Lucy's smile told me that they had come to see only me. I went downstairs and out the back door.

I became aware of the damp hay and sawdust under my feet. If I had thought this a dream, a small splinter gouging into my heel put that notion to rest. I cried out more from surprise than pain and shook my head as I saw blood trickle from the wound. Leave it to me to go out in the middle of the night without putting on my slippers.

Lucy smiled and ran to me, throwing her arms around my waist, pressing her face into my chest. I returned her embrace.

She led me to the elephant.

"I thought you might like to meet Old Bet —well, that's what I call her. To Sister Elizabeth, this is Martin."

"And to my mother?"

"This would be Jumbo. Everyone has a different name for it."

The elephant wound the end of its trunk around my wrist: How's it going? Pleased to meet you.

I fed it some peanuts and marveled at its cumbersome grandeur. "Is this my mother's conscience?"

Lucy gave a little-girl shrug. "You could call it that, I guess. Sister Elizabeth calls it 'the carrier of weary souls.' She says that when we grow too old and tired after a lifetime of work, then it will lift us onto its back and carry us over the bridge. It will remind us of all we've forgotten. It knows the history of the whole world, everyone who's lived before us, and everyone who will come after us. It's very wise."

I stroked its trunk. "Have you come to take my mother?"

Lucy shook her head. "No. We're not allowed to take anyone—they have to come to us. We're only here now to remind."

She tapped the elephant, it unwound its trunk from my wrist so she could take both of my hands in hers. I was shocked by their touch, though they looked burned and fused and twisted, they felt healthy and normal—two soft, small, five-fingered hands.

Her voice was the sound of a lullaby sung over a baby's cradle: "There's a place not too far from here, a secret place, where all the greatest moments of our lives are kept. You see, everyone has really good moments their whole life long, but somewhere along the line there is one moment, one great, golden moment, when a person does something so splendid that nothing before or after will ever come close. And they remember these moments. They tuck them away like a precious gem for safekeeping. Because it's from that one grand moment that each guardian angel is born. As the rest of life goes on and a person grows old and starts to regret things, something—" She gave a smile. "—*reminds* them of that golden moment.

"But sometimes there are people who become so beaten-down they forget they ever had such a moment. And they need to be reminded." She turned toward the elephant. "They need to know that when the time comes and Old Bet carries them across the bridge that that moment will be waiting, that it will be given back to them in all its original splendor and make everything all right. Again. Forever."

"...and Mom has forgotten about her...moment?"

"So have you. You were there. You remember it. You don't think you do, but..."

"I don't—"

"Shh. Watch closely."

The elephant reared back on its hind legs and trumpeted. When it slammed back down, its face was only inches from mine. Its trunk wrapped around my waist and lifted me off the ground until my eyes were level with one of its own—

—which was the same startling jade-green as Lucy's.

I saw myself as clearly in its gaze as any mirror, and I watched my reflection begin to shimmer and change: me at thirty, at twenty-one, then at fourteen and, at last, the six-year-old boy my father never lived to see.

He was sitting in his room—a large pad of drawing paper on his lap, a charcoal pencil clutched in his hand—drawing furiously. His face was tight with concentration.

His mother came into the room. Even then she looked beaten-down and used-up and sadder than any human being should ever be.

She leaned over the boy's shoulder and examined his work.

"Remember now?" whispered Lucy.

"...*yes*. I'd kept my drawing a secret After Dad died, Mom didn't spend much time with me because...because she said I looked too much like him. This was the first time in ages that she'd come into my room. It was the first time in ages I'd seen her sober."

The woman put a hand on the little boy's shoulder and said something to him.

My chest hitched.

I didn't want to remember this; it was easier to just stay angry with her.

"What happened?"

"She looked through all the drawings and...she started to cry. I was still mad as hell at her because of the way she'd been treating me, the way she never hugged me or kissed me or said she loved me, the way she spent all her time drinking...but she sat there with my drawings, shaking her head and crying and I felt so embarrassed. I finally asked her what the big deal was and she looked up at me and said—"

"—said that you had a great talent and were going to be famous for it someday. She knew this from looking at those drawings. She knew you were going to grow up to be what you are today. She told you that she was very proud of you and that she wanted you to keep on drawing, and maybe you could even start making up stories to go with the pictures—"

"—because she used to know someone who did that when she was a little girl," I said. "She said that would be nice because...oh, Christ!...it would be nice if I'd do that because it would make her feel like someone else besides her was remembering her childhood."

Old Bet gently lowered me to the ground. My legs gave out and I slammed ass-first into the dirt, shaking. "I remember how much that surprised me, and I just sat there staring at her. She looked so proud. Her smile was one of the greatest things I'd ever seen and I think—no, no, wait—I *know* I smiled back at her. I remember that very clearly."

"And that was it," said Lucy. "That was her moment. Do you have any idea how much it all meant to her? The drawings and your smile? When you smiled at her she knew for certain that you were going to be just what you are. And for that moment, she felt like it was all because of her. The world was new again." She brushed some hair out of my eyes. "Do you remember what happened next?"

"I went over to give her a hug because it felt like I'd just gotten my mother back, then I smelled the liquor on her breath and got angry and yelled at her and made her leave my room."

"But that doesn't matter, don't you see? What matters is the moment before. That's what's waiting for her. That's what she's forgotten."

"...Jesus..."

"You have to remember one thing, Andy. It wasn't your fault. None of it. You were only a child. Promise me that you'll remember that?"

"I'll try."

She smiled. "Good. Everything's all right then."

I rose and embraced her, then patted Old Bet. The elephant reached out and lifted Lucy onto its back.

"Are you going back without Mom?" I asked.

She *tsk*-ed at me and put her hands on her hips, an annoyed little girl. "Dummy! I told you once. We aren't allowed to take people. Only *remind* them. Except this time, we had to ask you to help us."

"Are you...are you her guardian angel?"

She didn't hear me as Old Bet turned around and the two of them lumbered off, eventually vanishing into the layers of mist that rose from the distant edge of the field.

The chill latched onto my bones and sent me jogging back inside for hot coffee.

Gina was already brewing some as I entered the kitchen. She was wearing my extra bathrobe. Her hair was mussed and her cheeks were flushed and I'd never seen such a beautiful sight. She looked at me, saw something in my face, and smiled. "Look at you. Hm. I must be better than I thought."

I laughed and took her hand, pulling her close, feeling the warmth of her body, the electricity of her touch. The world was new again. At least until the phone rang.

A man identifying himself as Chief something-or-other from the Cedar Hill Fire Department asked me if I was the same Andrew Dysart whose mother lived at —

—something in the back of my head whispered *Africa*.

Good little girls.

Going home.

* * *

My new book, *After the Elephant Ballet*, was published five weeks ago. The dedication reads: "To my mother and her own private Africa; receive the world prepared for you." Gina has started a scrapbook for the reviews, which have been the best I've ever received.

The other day when Gina and I were cleaning the house ("A new wife has to make sure her husband hasn't got any little black books stashed around," she'd said) I came across an old sketch pad: **MY DrAWiNG TaLlAnt, bY ANdy DySArT, age 6**. It's filled with pictures of rockets and clowns and baseball players and scary monsters and every last one of them is terrible.

There are no drawings of angels.

ANdY DySArT, age 6 didn't believe in them because he'd never seen proof of their existence.

In the back there's a drawing of a woman wearing an apron and washing dishes. She's got a big smile on her face and underneath are the words: **MY mOM, thE nICE lAdy**.

The arson investigators told me it was an accident. She had probably been drinking and fallen asleep in bed with a cigarette still burning. One of them asked if Mom had kept any stuffed animals on her bed. When I asked why, he handed me a pair of small, curved, fired-clay tusks.

On the way to Montreal for our honeymoon, Gina took a long detour. "I have a surprise for you."

We went to Somers, New York.

An elephant named Old Bet actually existed. There really is a shrine there. Circus performers make pilgrimages to visit her grave. We had a picnic at the base of the gorgeous green hill where the grave lies. Afterward I laid back and stared at the clouds and thought about guardian angels and a smiling woman and her smiling little boy who's holding a drawing pad and I wondered what Bradbury would do with that image.

Then decided it didn't matter.

Cocteau Prayers

The snow had begun falling again, lightly, but seemed heavier because of the sharp, steady wind blowing in from the east. The cemetery looked fresh, almost pristine; a newly completed ice sculpture. The mourners clustered together near the head of the grave, their backs to the wind. Looking at them with their hair and coats flowing forward, Michelle couldn't shake the feeling that all of them were fighting against some force, unseen and unknown, that was trying to suck them into the ground. She walked quickly around the grave and the eight or nine floral arrangements positioned at the head, noticing as she did that someone (not her) had thought to send irises—Kate's favorite flower. She took a place next to her uncle who, like most of the people assembled here, had his hands shoved deep into his coat pockets and was staring at the ground—not into the open grave but somewhere just to the right where a bit of soil could still be seen through the snow. A few people folded their arms across their chests and watched the sour sky, blinking against the new snowflakes that fluttered down and clung stubbornly to their eyelashes. Everyone stood in postures that seemed more distracted than grieving. Michelle looked around at all the faces, none of which would meet her gaze. It didn't surprise her that Mom hadn't shown up; she was either stoked on tranqs or bouncing off the walls, deep in the grip of a manic phase. Just as well; she and Michelle had never much gotten along and had only been courteous to each other out of respect for Kate's feelings, even though her mother took every available opportunity to remind the two of them that she was disappointed in them: "Girls like you are supposed to be special. Isn't that what all the books say? That twins are supposed to be special? What happened? You two are nothing like your older brother —he *always* makes me feel proud."

Michelle stared up at the sky, wondering if her sister were up there, looking down. She and Katie had always shared that special bond reserved for twins — knowing each other's thoughts, being able to tell when the other was sick, or sad, or anxious...she wondered if she would somehow, now, share Kate's death; after all, hadn't a part of her died along with her sister?

It suddenly occurred to Michelle that everyone looked drugged, and she didn't know what to make of it. Had they already wrung dry their grief? God. She felt as if she'd stepped into the fifth reel of some impenetrably enigmatic art film, one of those profoundly ponderous black & white meditation pieces where no one speaks for minutes on end, then some minor character no one has given a second thought to steps into camera range and starts paraphrasing Camus or Borges while the trees melt behind them: A head-on collision between Cocteau and Dali. Even the minister looked surreal, his face something that was hastily painted on a nesting doll ("*Matryoshka* doll," Kate always corrected), his gourd-shaped body standing at the head of the grave with a Bible clutched in one shaking blue-cold hand, squinting as he read the passage committing Kate's mortal remains to the earth. Completing the requisite benediction, he signaled the men from the funeral home to lower the coffin into the ground. It hissed hydraulically into the cold, dark, open maw of the grave. Michelle had to fight the urge to turn away. She didn't want it to end like this, with distracted *matryoshka* mourners and surreal Cocteau prayers and sour snow on an ice-knife wind. Even her own hand looked like some fuzzy image on a screen as it scooped up the symbolic handful of frozen death-dirt and tossed it down onto the lid of the coffin. The gourd-shaped minister stalked over, misting some words of comfort, then grimly wobbled away. Michelle looked at her uncle, who nodded his head, understanding, and she walked toward the ice- and snow-sheened northern plat of the cemetery, then down a small incline that led her to a stone sculpture of an angel standing at the less-accessible north entrance.

She was glad she'd walked away; she needed a few moments alone before saying her final good-bye to her sister, her friend, her life-long companion; even when the two of them had been hundreds of miles apart, they'd always felt the connection, and so had never truly been alone.

Are you alone now, my sister? thought Michelle. *What am I supposed to do now, without you to lean on?*

She wiped a few stray tears from her eyes and looked up at the face of the angel. If ever a sculptor had captured an expression of grief so purely, she'd not seen it. In its face was everything from anguish and rage to acceptance and peace. She saw in that face the way all mourners were meant to be; diminished, yes; broken-hearted and scared, certainly; but if you looked at the face long enough you saw a certain, enviable measure of tranquility which hinted at actualization, a look suggesting that all the conflicting emotions associated with death eventually coalesced to warm a sorrowing heart with the knowledge that, though it seemed to take forever, life was over in a second but that was all right, because there would be someone waiting for you at the end to make Act IV a little easier. And though Michelle had often laughed at that sort of psychobabbling sentimentality, she found herself hoping now that some of it might be true, even though all her years as a biology teacher had taught her otherwise. Death wasn't instantaneous, the cells went down one by one; it took a while before everything was finished. If a person wanted to, they could snatch a bunch cells hours after somebody had checked out and grow them in cultures. Death was a fundamental function; its mechanisms operated with the same attention to detail, the same conditions for the advantage of organisms, the same genetic information for guidance through the stages, that most people equated with the physical act of living. Now, standing in front of this angel of perfect grief, Michelle couldn't help but wonder: If it's such an intricate, integrated physiological process—at least in the primary, local stages—then how did you explain the permanent vanishing of consciousness? What happened to it? Did it just screech to a halt, become lost in humus, what? Nature *did not* work that way; it tended to find perpetual uses for its more elaborate systems. Maybe all that crap from 70s about "All of us, together, make up God" was true; maybe human consciousness was somehow severed at the filaments of its attachment and then absorbed back into the membrane of its origin. Maybe that's all reincarnation was: the severed consciousness of a single cell that did not die bur rather vanished totally into its own progeny. Maybe it was more than that—and maybe she was full of shit and needed to get some sleep but how was she supposed to do that? The apartment was so small, suddenly, a child's crib, barely enough room to turn around, and knowing that Kate would no longer be there on the other end to answer the phone in the middle of the night when loneliness really got its hold on her, Michelle couldn't face it. She could sleep at a motel, or go over to her brother's place. It didn't matter. Without her sister, none of it seemed to matter now.

She looked up once more at the angel of perfect grief and felt her heart skip a beat; it seemed to be half-smiling, half-snarling at her, as if she'd accidentally hit on something human beings were never meant to realize. "Thanks," she said to the statue; then, looking up at the sky: "And fuck you, too." Words that came easily, because none of this was real; they were all only images on a screen, somewhere, blurry and disjointed. Even now she thought that if she looked hard enough, she could see the scrim hidden out there in the distance, maybe even catch a glimpse of the audience out there in the theater, sitting in their seats, watching, watching, watching as the cells went down, one by one....

* * *

Later that night, she got up off the couch and went into her kitchen, opening the refrigerator door and removing two small Petrie dishes that she held in her hands while whispering, "Oh, Kate, oh, Jesus, oh, my sister, my sister, my sister...."

Cell to progeny to membrane.

Love never dies.

Dinosaur Day

Well, you got some idea of what happened then or else you wouldn't be here talking to me now, would you? Don't look at me like that. Every couple of years one of you new reporters over at the *Ally* stumbles on that old story and then comes around asking your questions, so if you don't mind I'll tell it in my own way, thanks very much.

Besides, this has got nothing to do with me. Not really. This is about a couple of folks I used to know and the nice little kid they had who they didn't much like and so did everything they could to horsewhip the nice right out of him. I understand all about the so-called "tough-love" approach to raising a child, but I think these folks carried it a little too far. Seems to me more and more folks these days want their kid to pop out of the womb fully-raised and don't much have the patience or care to take the time to teach them things, instill values and such. They let the movies and video games and cable channels do all of that for them, or else the belt and fist, then wonder why in hell it is every so often a kid or two walks into their school and opens up with a Howitzer or rocket-launcher or something. I'm getting off the subject, sorry. My mind wanders a bit these days. Got that tape recorder running? Good.

Jackson Banks is the name. Appreciate it if you spelled it right this time. I've lived in Cedar Hill all my life, including the last six years here at the Healthcare Center. Got a nice private apartment-style unit all to myself, round-the-clock care, and—I'm proud to say—money in the bank, thanks to the retirement package I had waiting when I punched the clock for the last time at Miller Tool & Die almost a decade ago. That's where I knew Don Hogan. Him and me worked the line there. On the job Don seemed a decent-enough fellow, hard-working, friendly, never what you'd call antisocial. We'd go out for some beers and burgers with the other fellows after the shift and bitch about the foreman's brown nose or some such—you know, the usual guys-after-work kind of talk. We'd make jokes about the wives (except me, my Maggie had passed on the year before and the fellahs were always careful not to make jokes about wives buying the farm), piss and moan about the economy (when you work the line in a place like Cedar Hill, the economy's always in the crapper), and then get on to things like sports.

That's when something about Don would change. Other guys, they'd be talking about the game that had been on TV over the weekend or what OSU's chances were of winning the national championship, and Don, he'd talk about this some, but then the other fellahs'd get on about their kids; so-and-so's boy was going out for football at Cedar Hill Catholic this year, or such-and-such's daughter was making a name for herself on the Blessed Sacrament volleyball team, that sort of thing. That's when Don'd clam up. Oh, he'd listen and nod his head and ask questions, but you could never get him to talk about what sports his own son was into. There was a reason for that, but I need to tell you about something else first, so bear with me.

This was back in 1970. We still had boys over in Vietnam and the Kent State shootings were so fresh the wound hadn't even begun to scab over yet. Our involvement in Vietnam had been good for *Ohio's* economy but not so hot for Cedar Hill's. We didn't have any major manufacturing plants that could fill military contracts fast enough to suit Washington, so most of that went to places like Columbus and Dayton. Even back then the industrial heart of the city was starting to murmur (it wouldn't ever completely stop, but it's been on life-support since the mid-80's) and the city needed some kind of new industry to come in and boost the local economy. So Cedar Hill got into the gravel business.

See, there was this rock quarry a couple miles out past the old county home that had gone under during the Great Depression. For decades it'd just been sitting there, this big-ass hole in the ground, no use whatsoever, except during the rainy season when it'd fill with water and high-school kids'd go out there to skinny-dip and smoke dope. Well, the city leased this land to a gravel company, and they came in with their Allis Chalmers and their feeder hoppers, radial stackers, jaw crushers, and a couple hundred jobs to fill, and set about the business of digging the living shit out of that quarry. Now, they had this one piece of equipment called a PIP (short for Portable Impactor Plant) that was basically a sixteen-wheeled horizontal hydraulic pile driver. They fired this bad boy up every Sunday afternoon and the operator'd drive it up to one of the quarry's lower walls and start hammering away. One hit from the impactor would go about twenty feet into the wall, and inside of a couple hours, there'd be tons of rocks and boulders for the workers to go at on Monday. Thing is, it made a noise the likes of which shook the ground and rattled windows over a good quarter of the town. Imagine an hour or two of continuous sonic booms. It wasn't so bad for folks who lived far away from the area, but if you lived anywhere near the north side of Cedar Hill, it felt like bombs going off in your backyard.

I know this last part because Don Hogan and his family lived on the north side, and every Monday he'd come in to work with another list of things that had happened during the previous Sunday. Mostly it was minor stuff like windows rattling or his wife's glassware being shook off a shelf, but it was Don's kid usually provided him with the biggest complaints.

"I swear to Christ," he'd say, "that damn kid's afraid of his own shadow. Yesterday, when they started in over at the quarry, he comes running into the house all crying and shaking because he thinks there are giant monsters coming. I keep telling Cathy not to let him stay up on Friday nights and watch Chiller Theater, but does she listen to me? *Hell* no. Then we gotta put up with him having nightmares and shit and thinking that giant monsters are out there walking around Cedar Hill every Sunday afternoon. I don't know what we're gonna do with the likes of him, I really don't."

The likes of him. That's just what he said, and in those four little words I knew right away that Don and Cathy Hogan didn't much like their own son. I felt for the kid, I did, but how a man manages his own house is his own business and it ain't nobody else's place to tell him how to do things otherwise.

I got to meet his kid a couple of weeks later. There was a company picnic out at Mound Builder's Park that Sunday, and rare as it was for the company to shell out any extra money for its employees' benefit, everyone came and brought their families with them. (You offer an afternoon of free food and beer and soda pop, you'd better watch out.) Anyway, Don's kid was named Kyle. He was seven. A small, thin, fair-haired and -skinned nervous kid who wore glasses and spent most of the afternoon with his nose buried in a stack of comic books while the other kids played games and sports. He struck me as having a lot on the ball, had those kind of eyes where there was always something going on behind them. None of the other kids paid him much mind, which seemed like something he was used to, so he'd brought the comic books along.

I wandered over to where he was sitting and introduced myself. I have to tell you, he was one courteous and well-mannered little guy. He stood up and shook my hand all adult-like and said it was a pleasure to meet me. "It's a real pleasure to meet you, sir." Said it just like that.

"I work at the plant with your dad," I said. "He talks about you a lot." Which was within spitting distance of a lie, but I didn't think it my place to tell this kid that his dad hardly ever talked about him, except to make fun of him.

Kyle seemed to sense right off I was white-washing something, because he got this look in his eyes like he *wanted* to believe me—it would've been the greatest thing in the world if his dad *did* talk proud of him, you could just tell the kid wanted that more than anything—but then he looked over to where the other kids were deep into a serious ball game, saw the way his dad was cheering the kids on and not looking over in his direction, not even once, and his whole body kind of deflated.

"What'cha reading there?" I asked, pointing to the stack of comics.

"Just comics."

"Anything good?"

He shrugged. "*Ghost Rider*, mostly. I think he's a neat hero."

"Ever read *Green Lantern*?"

"No, sir."

"How about *Prince Namor, the Sub-Mariner*?"

"You know about the *Sub-Mariner*?" Ought to've seen the way he looked at me right then. There's a grown-up who reads comics? What's the world coming to?

So I sat down next to him and we talked about Prince Namor and Spider-Man and Hawk-Man and monster movies and the like (I had a nephew who was really into those things so, being a good uncle, I stayed current on important matters such as these), and somewhere in there I happened to look down and see that one of Kyle's shoes had a thicker sole than the other one, and that's when I realized, genius that I am, that he had a club foot. Turns out he also had asthma, because he had to use his inhaler once when got real excited talking about *The Green Hornet* and lost his breath.

"So what'cha want to be when you grow up, Kyle?" I asked after he'd settled down and got his breath back.

"I wanna... I wanna write stories. About spaceships and monsters and ghosts and things, like that Rod Serling does."

"You watch them *Twilight Zone* re-runs, do you?"

"Uh-huh. And that one movie? *Night Gallery*? A man on television said that they're gonna make a weekly series out of that this year. That'll be so *cool*. So I'm gonna be a writer."

"That'll make your folks proud," I said because it seemed like the kind of thing you ought to say to a kid. Then Kyle looked over at his folks, at the way they were cheering the other kids on, and he started to cry.

I felt about an inch tall right then. Here I'd come over to give the kid some company, cheer him up and make sure he wasn't feeling too lonely, and I wind up reducing him to tears. Me and Maggie, we never had any kids, but I'd like to think if we'd had, we would've been real supportive of whatever dreams they found appealed to them. I'd've been damned proud to have me a kid who wanted to be a writer. Ain't nothing better to me than to spend the weekend curled up with a good book, nosir. I read Raymond Chandler and Ray Bradbury and writers like that who tell stories like they're reciting poetry. Never much good with words myself, I admired that, and I thought it was just terrific that Kyle wanted to write and I told him so but it didn't stop him from crying and trying to turn away so I wouldn't see it.

"Don't your folks think that's a good idea?" I asked him, realizing that I was about to cross a line that men don't talk about among themselves, the line where you go from being just an outsider to someone who knows their private business. It's one thing when you're invited to cross the line; it's another thing altogether when you take it upon yourself to do the crossing, but no way in hell was I just gonna get up and walk away from this kid with his inhaler and his club foot and nervous ways. My guess was everybody'd been walking away from him at times like this for most of his life and probably sleeping the sleep of the just after. No snowflake in an avalanche ever feels responsible.

I looked around to see if anybody was watching us, then reached out and put my hand on Kyle's shoulder. "Hey, c'mon now, it's all right."

"No it isn't," he said. "Mom and Dad, they think I'm useless—that's what Dad's always saying. 'You're useless.' I wish I could be a ball-player but I can't run too good, and I can't always catch my breath."

"Those things aren't your fault, though, Kyle. You can't help that you were born with problems like those."

He shrugged his shoulders. "I'm a sissy."

"Why, just because you don't like the things other kids do?"

"Uh-huh." Said so seriously that I knew deep in his heart he believed it. It was easy to understand why: if you were a male in Cedar Hill and wanted to be accepted by the other fellahs, you had to be a White, Athletic, Semi-Articulate, Beer-Drinking Poon-Tang Wrangler who drove a pickup with at least one hunting rifle displayed in the back window, or the son of a man like that. If you were like Kyle, though, if you were a poor, blue-collar, crooked-toothed, skinny, four-eyed, club-footed asthmatic who was more interested in comic books and *Night Gallery* and spaceships than in sports and fighting and hunting, well, then, you were a sissy, a queer, an easy target for ridicule because you couldn't fight back. Don't get me wrong, there's a lot of decent folks in this community, but there's also more than enough assholes to go around—and Don Hogan was definitely an asshole. So was his wife, but I didn't find that out for sure until later, and by then ...

Okay, so here I am in the park that afternoon and Kyle's crying because his dad don't think much of him or what he wants to be when he grows up. "He says it's stupid," Kyle whispered. "He says that only smart people can write books an' make any money an' I'm not smart, I'm a sissy who can't do anything an' he says... he says that he's ashamed of me."

I didn't know what to say to him about that. I had half a mind to march over and knock ol' Don's teeth right down his throat, but that'd probably come back on Kyle real hard so I just stayed put.

"Do *you* think it's stupid?" I asked.

"I think I'd be a good writer. I already wrote a bunch of stories."

"Ever show 'em to your folks?"

"They don't want to see them. Mom says she can't read without her glasses but she never *looks* for them so she can read my stories. Once I found 'em for her so she could read a story I wrote about the people who live in the caves on the moon, an' she ... she smacked me hard in the face. She said I was being smart with her, but I *wasn't*. I *swear* I wasn't."

"Maybe she was having a bad day. I'm sure she didn't mean it." I was trying to give Cathy the benefit of a doubt. The only thing harder than being a blue-collar worker in this town is being the wife of one. It was that way back in 1970 and it hasn't changed much today, you ask me. Most of the gals in this town, they're brought to not to expect much out of life and so they don't. You get yourself a high-school education (Cedar Hill has the lowest graduation requirements in the state), find yourself a job, and if you're lucky you marry a man with a steady job and do what's required to make a good home for you and yours —and if that means having to back down and suffer his occasional cruelties, that's just part and parcel of marriage. So I gave Cathy Hogan the benefit of a doubt.

"They'll come around, Kyle," I said, hoping he believed it because I for one had my doubts. "I bet they'll come around and be really proud of you."

"Dad scares me."

Didn't quite know how to take that. "Scares you how?"

"He likes scaring me. Sometimes he comes into my room at night after I'm asleep and holds a pillow over my face until I wake up. He makes me fight him off 'cause he says I need to learn to fight on account of I'm such a weakling. And sometimes he'll sneak up behind me and shout and make me jump. He laughs at me then. Says I gotta ... what is it? 'Grow a spine.' That's what he says."

The ball game was really heating up now, folks were on their feet and shouting, whistling, making all kinds of noise, and then they started up over at the quarry with PIP. Everybody winced and looked over in the direction of the quarry, shaking their heads and complaining about the noise. Fact of the matter is, the noise and vibrations weren't so bad in the park, not so that the day was going to be ruined. Seemed to me that if anything was going to do that, it was the dark rain-clouds in the sky. I decided right then it was time for Kyle and me to go over and get ourselves a couple of hamburgers, so I turned back to him and said, "Hey, why don't we mosey —"

The rest of it died in my throat.

Kyle was rigid as a board and pale as a corpse. I've never seen a kid that scared before. He was holding his breath and his eyes were so wide I thought they might pop right out of his skull.

"Kyle, hey buddy, what's wrong?" I laid a hand on his arm and felt how he was shaking, the kind of shakes you usually think of when someone talks about getting the DTs; this boy was shaking right down to the insides of his bones.

And he still wasn't breathing.

"Hey, buddy," I said, trying to work his inhaler from his pocket, "are you all right? Do you need —"

"*They're coming!*" he screamed so loud that half the folks watching the game turned around to look at us.

"Kyle, hey, what —"

"*They're coming, they're coming, THEY'RE COMING!*" And now he was up on his feet and looking around him like a bank robber who'd just run out to hear the police sirens screaming down on his ass and I knew he was gonna bolt, so I tried to grab hold of his arm again but he was so far into panic I didn't have a chance and then he was off like a shot screaming how they were coming they were coming everybody had to hide everybody had to get away before they got here because they'd kill us all and by then I was on my feet and going after him, but there's a lot of difference between the speed of a terrified seven-year-old even if he does have a club foot and a fifty-year-old factory worker with a tricky back but now the game was stalled and some of the players got into the act and just as I gained some ground one of the teenagers had easily tackled Kyle and knocked his glasses off and Kyle was thrashing around and screaming at the top of his lungs and crying so hard that snot flew out in ribbons and covered his face that was getting redder and redder by the second, and all the time he kept shrieking on about how they were coming they were coming didn't anybody hear them and look up there can't you see their shadows starting block out the sun ohgod please everybody has to hide before they kill us all—

—and then he stopped screaming because he couldn't get air into his lungs; even from where I was I could hear the way he was wheezing, how his throat was making all these wet crackling sounds, so I pushed my way past the crowd of gawkers who'd gathered round and had to shove the teenager who'd tackled Kyle off the boy because the idiot was parked with his knees on Kyle's chest, then I had Kyle sitting up and was holding his inhaler for him but he was still thrashing around in panic and by now Don and Cathy had come over, both of them looking for all the world like the most humiliated couple God had ever created, looking more embarrassed for themselves than concerned over their boy, and I managed to get the inhaler in Kyle's mouth and gave him a couple of pumps but he didn't get it all, he jerked his head away and tried to scream as he saw the shadow that was falling over the park from the rain clouds, I knew that's what was scaring him because he pointed to the shadow and croaked out something like "...sore hay..." and then his eyes rolled up into his head and his legs shuddered and he wet himself and passed out.

An ambulance had to be called to come get him, and they hooked him up to some oxygen and loaded him into the back and took off for Memorial. By now it was starting to rain and what folks weren't running for one of the covered shelters or their cars were gathered around Don and Cathy offering their sympathies and trying to think of things to say to make them feel better about being so embarrassed by their boy.

All I could do was stand there and shake my head, listening to the constant *whump-whump-whump!* from PIP at the quarry and looking at Kyle's inhaler that I still held in my hand.

* * *

By the time I got over to the emergency room the rain was coming down pretty hard. It was lightning and thundering to beat the band, too.

I got inside and found Don and Cathy in the waiting room, both of them smoking one cigarette after another (you could still smoke in hospitals back then). I wondered if they both smoked like that around the house, knowing how it would affect Kyle's asthma, but I didn't say anything about it. Didn't seem like the right time for a lecture.

"How is he?" I asked.

Cathy just gave me a look that would have frozen fire and went back to her smoking. Don looked at her none-too pleasantly, then shook his head and said, "They got him back there but we haven't been told anything yet."

I handed him the inhaler. He looked at it like it was a piece of dog shit, then snatched it out of my hand and whirled on Cathy. "How many goddamn times have I *told* that kid to keep this on him? Christ! Sometimes I think he doesn't have the sense God gave an ice-cube!"

"He had it on him," I said. "He just dropped it when he took off like that." I didn't care about this lie, not one little bit.

"Doesn't make any difference," Don said, not looking away from Cathy. "You gonna say something or just sit there like a knothole on a log?"

"I'm sorry that he embarrassed us in front of all your buddies," she said.

"You got that right. Kid's been nothing but a pain in the ass since he came into this world. If you hadn't listened to that quack doctor of yours, putting you on Thalidomide—"

"—which I stopped taking after the first month. I heard the stories. Besides, it made me feel sick all the time."

"You shouldn't've took it in the first place! If you hadn't, maybe we'd've had a normal kid with good feet and healthy lungs and—"

"—so now it's *my* fault Kyle's sickly? Oh, you're really a fucking prize sometimes, Donald, you know that?"

"I'll thank you not to—"

They both realized I was still standing there and got real quiet. I was trying to think of a graceful way to leave when the doctor came out and told us that Kyle was going to be all right but they were going to keep him overnight to just to make sure. "It was a fairly serious episode," he said. "It could have been fatal. Has he been taking his medications?"

"When we can afford them," said Cathy. "But we always make sure he's got his inhaler." She let out a long stream of smoke, and I knew the doctor was thinking the same thing I had when I saw them puffing away.

"Would you like to see him?"

"Not particularly," said Don. "I have to go to work in the morning to make the money to pay for this goddamned hospital visit." He looked at Cathy, who wouldn't look at him, then turned to me and said, "You two were getting all buddy-buddy there. Why don't you go back and see him, Jackson?"

"Think I will, thank you."

They had him off in room by himself, all hooked up to an oxygen tank with a mask over his nose and mouth. He looked fifty years old, all pale and sweaty with dark half-crescents under his eyes. He smiled when he saw it was me and waved.

"Hello yourself, little man." I reached into my coat pocket and brought out the comic books he'd left back at the park. "I grabbed these up for you. Didn't think you'd want them getting ruined in the rain."

He nodded his head and reached up for them, but the IV tube and needle wouldn't let him reach very far so I laid them on the bed next to him. "That new issue of *Ghost Rider* got pretty wet, so I stopped off and bought you a new copy, plus they had this Special Issue just come out, so I got that for you, too."

He looked at the comics, then at me, and smiled under his mask. He looked like he was gonna cry again and I didn't know that I could handle that, so I pulled up a chair next to his bed and said, in as light a tone of voice as I could manage, "So ... they treating you good here so far?"

He nodded.

"I half expected you to be conked out after what happened. Gave us all quite the scare, is what you did."

He pointed to something in the corner. There was a small black-and-white television on a wheeled stand, tuned to the local PBS channel. Even though the sound was turned down pretty low, I recognized the theme they play at the start of the *National Geographic* shows.

"You want me to turn it up a little bit?"

Nod.

I did, then adjusted the rabbit ears for a better picture, rolled it closer to the bed, and sat back down next to him. "You know, I watch this sometimes, too" I told him, which was true. "This *is* what you wanna watch, right?"

Nod, nod.

"Okay, then."

It was a special about this thing called the "Bog Man" they'd found in the Netherlands. The narrator said the man had been buried in this peat bog for over two thousand years. They had film of it. His brow was furrowed and there was this serene expression on his face. He wore a leather cap that reminded me of my own work hat and he lay on his side. His feet and hands were shriveled (I wondered how seeing those shriveled feet made Kyle feel about his own problems but didn't say anything) but aside from that, he looked no different from any number of guys that worked the line. Put a metal lunch bucket in his grip and it might've been me two thousand years from now.

The narrator kept going on about well-preserved the Bog Man was, and likened it to a similar discovery made in Siberia a few years back when they'd found a fully-preserved Mammoth.

Sometime in there Kyle reached out and took hold of my hand and gave it a little squeeze. I squeezed back.

He fell asleep after about fifteen minutes, so I got up, made sure the comics weren't going to fall off the bed, and then did something that surprised even me; I bent down, brushed some of the hair from his forehead, and gave him a little kiss there. It seemed right somehow. I started to walk away as quiet as I could and then bumped into a clipboard hanging at the foot of his bed. I caught it just in time. As I was putting it back I glanced at what the doctor had written, then read some of the typed material.

On top of everything else, Kyle was diabetic. I felt my heart jump a little. My Maggie had been a diabetic, it was what killed her eventually. Thinking this made me sad and I missed her all the more for the thinking, then I saw something about "... macular degeneration," and "... visual hallucinations commensurate with Charles Bonnet Syndrome." I knew that it was pronounced *Shaz Bone-eh* because my Maggie'd had the same problem. You see things that aren't there. She used to tell me toward the end that she always saw this well-dressed Negro butler following me around the house, and then she'd joke about how we could use some extra help, seeing as how she'd be blind soon enough. She was totally blind the last ten days of her life.

And Kyle Hogan was slowly losing his sight just like her.

There's some anger that takes on a life outside your power to do anything about it, and sometimes this anger comes wrapped up in sadness like a mummy in bandages. I was that kind of angry. Didn't seem fair, this great kid who held my hand and smiled at me having so many problems and not even ten years old yet. Hell, I've know people *my* age who couldn't handle half of what this kid was dealing with on a daily basis. Don and Cathy had themselves one great boy here, and needed to be reminded of it. So I put the chart back and marched out to the waiting room, all set to cross yet another line.

Don was by himself. "Cathy and me had some words and she took off," he said. "I was hoping I could trouble you for a lift."

"No problem." I figured it'd give me a chance to say a few things to him.

We'd been driving along a couple of minutes when Don said, "I suppose Kyle gave you quite an earful today. Kid'll talk your head off you give him half a chance."

"Right before he passed out in the park, he tried to say something to me. Sounded like 'sore hay' but that don't make any sense."

"'Dinosaur Day,' is what it was. Sunday is Dinosaur Day."

"That something else you use to scare him with?" I asked, making sure I put a hard emphasis on the *else* so Don would know that I knew things.

He eyeballed me for a second, then grinned. "Yeah, it is. He hears old PIP start up and feels the ground start shaking and he thinks it's monsters, so, yeah, I go with it. I tell him that it's the sound of big old dinosaurs waking up and going for a walk. I tell him that on Dinosaur Day he needs to behave himself or else I'm gonna lock him outside so the dinosaurs can step on him or eat him. Goddamn sissy thinks that pile driver is a dinosaur's footsteps. No kid of mine's gonna have an imagination like that. Won't do him a damn bit of good later on in life."

"But he's a great kid, Don. He's smart, and he's sensitive —"

"Don't give me that 'sensitive' shit, okay? 'Sensitive' and ten cents'll get you a cup of coffee over at the L&K Restaurant. Big deal. He's a sickly kid who ain't never gonna get any better and on account of the way he is, Cathy doesn't want to have another one ... so I don't get to have a boy that I can cheer on while he plays football, or teach him how to duck-hunt, or how to drive — no. I got the likes of him to deal with. You think I don't know how the other guys at work are gonna look at me come tomorrow? 'Too bad about Don, having himself a boy like that. Makes you wonder about his being a real man.' And don't tell me they ain't gonna think that. A man's son is the measure of his father, and I don't want anyone thinking that Kyle is any measure of me."

"That may be the lousiest thing I've ever heard anyone say."

"I'll thank you to mind your own business, Jackson."

"For god's sake, man, don't you see what you're doing to that kid? Scarin' him like that all the time and —"

" — and if he's gonna stand any chance in this world, then someone *has* to scare him! Don't you get it? I got to put the fear inside of him so he'll know what life is like. I figure there's only so much that a kid *can* be scared before it becomes a permanent part of him, and then he won't be scared of nothing anymore, and *that's* the only way he's gonna survive in this life. He's got to have the fear within him."

"You'd best watch out, Don. Things like that have a way of coming back on you."

"What the hell would you know about it? You and Maggie never even *had* any kids."

Goddamn good thing we were on his street already or else he'd've had himself one long walk home.

* * *

Don and I avoided each other at work for most of the next week, but we weren't what you'd call obvious about it. We sat at different tables during break, and when the other guys went out after work, I'd beg off if Don was going along, or he'd make some excuse about getting home to tend to Kyle if I was gonna be there. I don't think the other guys suspected anything other than Don being embarrassed about his boy.

An offer a voluntary overtime came up for that Sunday, and I was the first to get my name on the list. Don signed up for it, as well. I was getting ready to head home that Friday when he stopped me near the doors and said, "I hope everything's okay with you and me."

I shrugged. "How's Kyle feeling?"

"He should be able to go back to school next week. Listen, uh ... Cathy's gonna be using the car Sunday to take Kyle over to see his grandma. Could I get you to swing by and pick me up on your way in?"

"Don't see why not. I've got some comic books that I think Kyle might enjoy."

"*You* read comic books?"

"Bet'cher ass I do. Some of the best stories being told anywhere. Kyle got me interested in *Ghost Rider*. You ought to give it a read sometime. Might teach you a thing or two."

He stared at me for a minute to see if I was joking. When he saw that I wasn't he broke out laughing anyway, pretending that I *was* joking. I went along with him thinking that.

"See you Sunday," I said, punching the clock and heading out to my car.

That Saturday night I sat down to watch another special on PBS about how children's personalities are shaped during the first ten years of their lives. A lot of it was a bit over my head, but then they got to this one psychologist who started talking about something called "...

consensual reality." Way I understood it is that a child is taught from its first day on earth to see the same world their parents see. That seemed simple enough to me, but then the psychologist showed this film of a nine-year-old girl who'd been raised by her mother who was a schizophrenic. The girl had even worse delusions than her mother did, because she'd been taught to see the world her mother saw and once she got old enough to let her imagination kick in, she "... amplified the disorder" because she thought she was dealing with the world her mother gave her, "... one of sleeplessness and incoherence and dementia and paranoia." She was ruined. It broke my heart.

I started to drift off. It's strange the connections your mind will make when you're falling asleep. I thought about the Bog Man and how he looked like the guys I worked with. Then his face became Don Hogan's and he got up out of the bog and said his name was Chaz Bone-eh. He started screaming at Kyle. Kyle was crying because he was scared and was trying to tell Chaz he could see monsters. Chaz said that was good because monsters were real and they were coming for Kyle. Then he lay back down in the bog and his face became mine, so I curled up with my lunch bucket next to the Wooly Mammoth and went to sleep, waiting for someone to find me in a couple thousand years.

* * *

They were screaming at the Hogan house when I knocked on the door.

"... have my goddamn lunch ready on time is all I ask!"

"So because you got to work today that means I can't sleep in an extra half-hour?"

"Bitch! I got a long day ahead of me and —"

I knocked louder and they got real quiet. Cathy answered the door in her bathrobe. She glared at me and then blew smoke in my face. "Your ride's here." She walked away, leaving the door open but not inviting me inside. Don peered out of the kitchen doorway and shouted, "Be with you in a minute, Jackson."

"I got them comics for Kyle," I said. "Mind if I come in and give them to him?"

"Oh, for chrissakes!" said Cathy. "That's just what he needs, more comic books!"

"I'll thank you not to speak to my friend like that," shouted Don.

"Screw him—and screw you, too! And screw that little useless piece of shit of a son you've got!"

That's when I decided Cathy Hogan was as big an asshole as her husband.

"You go on up," said Don to me. "His room's right at the end of the hall."

I knocked on Kyle's door and he opened it just a crack, then smiled when he saw it was me. "Hello, Mr. Banks."

"Hey, Kyle. Got some more comics here for you. *Creepy* and *Eerie* and an issue of *Famous Monsters.*"

"Thank you very much." He seemed a bit nervous to me. No wonder, if the screaming I'd heard from his parents was the norm around here.

"You feeling better?" I asked, ruffling his hair.

"A little."

Downstairs Cathy was shouting, "Pimento loaf's all we got for sandwiches! I haven't been to the groceries yet."

"I *hate* that shit!" Don shouted back about twice as loud.

"Then fuckin' go hungry today, I don't care!" This followed by cupboard doors being slammed and a glass being broke.

Kyle looked at me and shrugged. "They yell a lot, I guess."

I nodded. "So you'll be visiting with your Grandma today?"

He brightened. "Yeah! My gramma's really cool."

"Treat you nice, does she?"

"Yes, sir."

It was good to know that there was someone in this world who was good to this kid.

I started to say something else, but then PIP kicked in over at the quarry and every window in the house shook. I checked my watch and saw that it was only nine-thirty in the morning; they usually didn't get started until noon on Sundays.

"Now, don't you go gettin' all excited, Kyle," I said. "That's just —"

I got real quiet when I looked back up.

When I was over in Korea during the war, my unit came across a little boy whose entire village had been wiped out the night before. He'd been the only survivor, and our interpreter told us that the kid had seen the whole slaughter. I never forgot the look on that kid's face. There was this gruesome *calm* to his features that somehow got worse when you looked into his eyes; he was staring at something only he could see, something so far away and so terrible there would never be words to describe it, so he'd just decided to embrace it.

The look on Kyle's face made the one on that kid's seem like a grin over a birthday cake.

"What is it, buddy?" I said.

"You need to leave, Mr. Banks."

The *whump-whump-whump* from PIP was getting a lot louder and a lot stronger.

"Are you okay?"

"I'm fine, sir," he said, taking hold of my hand and leading me out of the room. "But you really need to go outside."

"You sure you're okay?" I asked him as he led me out onto the front porch. I figured there was something he wanted to tell me and didn't want his folks to hear. 'Course, he could've done that upstairs, but that look on his face and the hollow sound in his voice told me this was serious, so I went along.

"I'm fine, Mr. Banks. See? I'm not scared anymore."

The next bunch of whumps from PIP were so violent I thought for a second the sidewalk was going to crack open. I could hear Cathy screaming at Don about how it was his fault they couldn't afford to move someplace where this goddamned noise wouldn't shake loose her fillings every week, and Don shouted something back at her that I couldn't make out but I heard the slap clear enough, and by then I couldn't hear or feel anything else but the noise and vibrations from PIP.

Kyle yanked me off the porch and all but dragged me to my car. "You have to get in now," he shouted. "Please, Mr. Banks."

"What the hell is wrong, Kyle?"

He stared at me, and then blinked. "Can't you see it?" He pointed over the roof of the house.

"See what?"

Whump-Whump-WHUMP!

"Please get in your car, Mr. Banks." He opened my door and started pushing me. He was a lot stronger than he looked. Before I could say anything more, he slammed closed the door and turned back to house, looking at something over the roof, and then the noise became these explosions that rocked the ground so bad I actually hit the top of my head against the inside roof of the car, and by the time I got my vision cleared there was another series of explosions that shattered every window of the house, and then another one that shook the trees and then another one that caused one of the streetlights to come loose and fall across the middle of the sidewalk in a shower of sparks and broken glass and by this time I was so scared I couldn't move so I sat there gripping the wheel and wishing to hell I'd never said yes to coming over here today but wishing and ten cents'll get you a cup of coffee and then Kyle spread his arms wide and lifted them over his head and started laughing

as the explosions kept coming closer and harder and louder and faster, and I didn't think that PIP could work that fast, and then another part of my brain said *I don't think it's PIP* and I closed my eyes as the vibrations rattled my bones and my dentures and everything there was inside me, right down to my nuts and all the way up to the stalks of my eyes, and all the time I could hear Kyle laughing laughing laughing —

—and then it all stopped.

No noise.

No vibrations.

No sound or movement at all.

I didn't want to open my eyes, I was still that scared.

"Mommy, Daddy," called out Kyle. "Come out and look. It's *so cool!*"

I heard the front door open and then I heard Cathy and Don start yelling for Kyle to get his ass back up on the goddamned porch they were going to give him what-for real good and then Cathy gasped and Don shouted *"Jesus H. Christ!"* and then they both screamed but that was drowned under the sound that came next.

It was a roar from something so big and so angry that it swallowed nightmares whole for breakfast.

I pressed my head against the steering wheel and whispered Maggie's name over and over.

Then the roar came again, twice as loud as before, and then Kyle laughed again and the whole world became noise and thunder and one massive explosion and then there was a sound like a jet engine sucking in all the air from the earth and then there was a silence the likes of which I hope never finds me again.

I don't have to tell you what I saw when I finally opened my eyes, do I? You've seen the pictures of the house, the way the whole front of it was smashed to rubble. There wasn't enough left of Don and Cathy Hogan to scrape up with a shovel. The official explanation was that PIP had accidentally hit on a batch of dynamite embedded in one of the quarry walls and caused an explosion that sent rocks and boulders flying, and that one of them landed on the Hogan's house and killed them. Which would've explained the indentations in the ground, all six-feet-wide and three-feet-deep of each one, except that there was no boulder. They say it must have hit with such impact that it broke apart, because there was plenty of rubble. The fact that the gravel company denied any such accident and that PIP was unharmed didn't come into it. Every house on that street lost its windows that Sunday. A couple of family pets were killed by furniture toppling over on top of them. One woman had a heart attack from the noise. The gravel company got the pants sued off them and pulled up stakes and Cedar Hill was no longer in the gravel business by fall.

I asked you once already to not look at me like that. I know how it sounds, believe me. It's been over thirty years ago that it happened and not a day goes by that I don't go over it again, and every blessed time I do I keep coming back to the same conclusion. I told Don that putting that kind of fear inside a boy would come back on him somehow. I *told* him.

Kyle's doing fine. Went to live with his grandmother who made sure he got the right kind of care. He still wears glasses, but he ain't lost his sight yet. He writes me every month and calls me every other weekend. He's real excited about how well his new book's doing — you know that boy's had three Number Two bestsellers in the last few years? Seems folks can't get enough of his spaceships and monsters. He sends me copies of every new book and story he publishes, and he always inscribes them the same way: *To My Buddy Jackson, Who Knows What the Bog Man Knows: It's Always Dinosaur Day.*

He signs him name *Chaz Bone-eh.*

Kid's got a lot on the ball, he does.

In the House of the Hangman
One Does Not Talk of Rope

Alan Westall committed suicide twice before he ate breakfast. The first time came a few moments after he got out of bed; he took the belt from his pants, fastened it securely to the doorknob, twisted it into a tight figure 8, then stuck his neck through the loop and sat down. It took longer than he'd thought it would and was infinitely more painful than he'd imagined, but as he stood watching himself convulse and turn various disgusting colors, he realized that he'd started the day in the best possible manner. He felt much, much better about himself.

After the thrashing and choking stopped, after the final death rattle wheezed from his crushed throat, after his bowels had emptied themselves of their foulness as a final illustration of death's indignity, only then did he take the special container from his pocket, smiling to himself as he unscrewed the cap and heard the faint *whoosh-pop!*

Empty and ready to be filled.

He took one last look at his body and then ground the flesh and bone under his heels until all that remained was a fine powder, which he carefully scooped up and placed inside the container.

He held it up to the light, studying its contents.

This was, he thought, the Alan Westall who continuously smiled at people he'd rather tell to go fuck themselves. Within the granules was *that* Alan Westall; the country-club bartender who spent his nights listening to rich, pampered people moan on and on about how their money didn't make them happy, only more privileged and therefore better than the people who served their drinks; better, even, than the families of those who served them with smiling faces. *Here* was the Alan Westall who felt like a whore every time he collected his paycheck—and a cheap one, at that. Because he served the rich and privileged and they were the ones who'd shut down the plant where his father had worked for over thirty years, and Dad started drinking then because he was fifty-eight years old and no one would hire him and there wasn't enough money because he'd been sixteen months short for his pension and there was no way *that* Alan Westall could make it better and now both his parents were dead, rotting six feet under, killed by poverty and frustration, beaten to death by a world they never harmed. And so their surviving son was a whore.

Or had been, rather.

Now he was dust.

The new Alan Westall smiled, slipped the container into his pocket, and went into the bathroom to shave. He had just applied the shaving cream and opened the straight-razor when the phone rang. The old Alan would have cursed, then stormed into the middle room to answer it, but the new and improved Alan Westall had a better attitude, and so smiled broadly. Nothing could phase him now. He answered the phone, not minding at all the shaving cream he smeared on the handset.

"Hel-loooooo," he said cheerfully.

"Hi'ya." It was Janet. "So...I guess you're still alive after all, huh?"

"So it would seem."

"Listen, I was just going through some stuff and found a couple of your books." She read the titles. He couldn't remember any of them.

"You can keep them," he said.

"I figured you'd say something like that."

Something of the old Alan stirred within him. He didn't like the taste it left in his mouth. "Let's not argue anymore, okay?"

"No, of course not. In order to argue we'd actually have to be *talking* to one another, wouldn't we?"

"I'm not sure I follow."

"Jesus, Alan! You haven't so much as *called* me in almost three weeks! The last time you spent the weekend, you hardly said a word.

Then you just disappeared. I think you owe me an explanation and an apology."

"Why were you going through things?"

Janet gave a disgusted sigh. "Because I'm *moving,* that's why. A senior copywriter position opened up at a branch office in New York and they offered me the position."

He felt nothing, though he knew he should have. "Well...I guess congratulations are in order."

"I didn't call to...*goddammit* I did call for you to bestow accolades on me, I called because I..." She fell silent. Something of the old Alan stirring told him that she was desperately hurt and he should try to do something to make up for it.

He waged a fierce battle in the silence, and lost.

"You can keep the books to remember me by. The good times, anyway."

"Ask me not to go."

"W-what?"

"Ask me not to go, Alan. Tell me you're sorry about pulling another one of your disappearing acts, tell me that you're back in therapy and want to get over your depression about your parents, tell me that you'll try harder not to be in a fog most of the time. Please? Tell me that the ugliness is over and everything will be fine between us from now on—Christ! At least ask me to help you. You've never done that, you know? I don't know if it's that annoying Midwest blue-collar work ethic or just some bullshit macho streak in you, but you've never once *asked* me to help you through any of this. I will, I swear to you. Just say the word and I'll turn down the position, tell them that I've changed my mind. They told me I could. They hate the idea of losing me here so it's not like I'd be screwing myself out of a livelihood. All you have to do is give me a little something, Alan; all you have to do is ask."

He tried in the silence and couldn't do it.

"I hope you like it in the Big Apple."

A wet, spluttering sound from her end. "Oh, God. Why can't you let it go? None of it was your fault, but you have to put yourself on the rack over it, don't you? You had no idea your father was capable of something like that. How...how could you?"

"If I'd been paying more attention, if I'd cared a little more, I would have seen it coming."

"*Don't say that!* It isn't true and you know it as well as I do! You spend so much time brooding over what you *should have* seen, or did, or noticed, or realized, or whatever in the hell it is you chastise yourself for constantly, that you don't see the things you *can* do something about. Why is it that people are precious to you only after they're a memory?"

He felt the shaving cream run down his neck, saw it drip onto the floor, soaking into the carpet. "Be happy, Janet. And find someone who'll love you well." He didn't wait for a reply; he hung up, disconnected the phone, walked into the bathroom, picked up the straight-razor, and stared at the reflection staring back at him from the mirror—some man who had once been a boy, and was not what the boy had once dreamed of becoming.

He sneered at the face.

You should call her right back, you know that, don't you? Call her back and beg her to forgive you and stay. But you won't. Why is that, you suppose?

Part of the old Alan was still in that face that stared back at him. Deceptive bastard that he was. And that was the part that had hung up on Janet. That was the part that had just driven away the best thing that ever happened to him. Kind, caring, intelligent and articulate, perceptive, everything the boy had once dreamed of finding in a life-mate, silenced forever by the simple act of yanking a cord from a wall.

Now there was no one for him.

The face reflected at him didn't deserve anyone.

And so Alan Westall took his life a second time by inserting the tip of the razor into the base of his arm and pulling it up to the wrist, opening his flesh like the pink maw of some loathsome insect, watching as the blood slopped out into the sink. Ignoring the pain, he did the same to his other arm, then stood back and watched as he collapsed against the bathtub, arms extended, staining the white porcelain.

He felt no sympathy for the pathetic creature huddled before him. It deserved to die a coward's death, alone and cold and filled with misery. No sympathy at all.

When it was finally done, when the thing before him was elbow-deep in its own gore, Alan removed the container, unscrewed the cap—*pop-whoosh!*—and ground the body into dust, then scooped it into the container, mixing it with the powder from earlier. Then he was on his knees, can of cleanser in hand, washing out the tub until it was restored to its original state of shiny white. Then he cleaned the sink. Then he shaved. When his face was smooth and clean he saw that he didn't quite recognize the man who stared back at him, but felt as if he could learn to like this man a great deal.

And so to the kitchen to prepare breakfast for this new friend, this better friend, this one-and-only best friend who was now the only one he had.

While the English muffin was toasting, he sat down at the table with his cup of black coffee and picked up the yellowing newspaper page, the same page he'd read every morning for the last six months, and looked at the small headline over the article three-quarters of the way down:

MAN KILLS WIFE, SELF

As always, his eyes began to tear.

He took the container out of his pocket, unscrewed the lid —*pop-whoosh!*—and poured the powder into his coffee, turning it a deep, rich butterscotch color.

Not minding the searing pain in his throat, he drank it down.

Felt something old and familiar fill him to the brim.

And wondered how many times he'd die before supper.

Iphigenia

It's dying without death and accomplishing nothing To waver thus In the dark belly of cramped misfortune. —Agrippad'Aubigne

He was checking the seat numbers on the tickets when he heard Mrs. Williamson scream.

"Donny! Watch out!"

He looked down in time to see seven-month-old Julie crawl into his path, her body so low to the ground it would be easy to step on her fragile skull and crush it all over the sidewalk. He pulled back in mid-stride and fell back-first onto the pavement, cursing both the pain and the memory of his sister—which found him as soon as the cement knocked the air from his lungs. After a moment he managed to push himself up on his elbows to see little Julie—sitting up now—look at him and giggle, a thin trickle of saliva dribbling off her chin. She looked so cute, so safe.

Safe. With someone to watch over her. Protect her. Trusting was easy when you were that young. Trusting was fun.

So little Julie was giggling.

As Mrs. Williamson ran up to her daughter Donald wondered if, at the very instant of her death, Jennifer Ann had giggled, too, thinking the whole thing somewhat funny, when you Got Right Down To It.

Then he remembered the sound of screams echoing off the stone walls.

And he began to shake.

"You should pay more attention to where you're walking, Donald Banks. You could've—" Her words cut off when she caught sight of Donald's pale and terrified face.

"Donny?" She reached out to touch his arm but he scooted away from her, crossing his arms in front of his face, his shaking worse than before.

"Oh, God...I'm...I'm sorry, Mrs. Williamson, really I am. I should've been...been *looking*. I'm really s-s-s-sorry. Is she all right?" He winced at the sound of his stuttering; it was the first time he'd lapsed back into it since—

—since—

—since little Julie was giggling then things must be all right, because Mrs. Williamson had the baby in her arms now and was stroking the back of her head.

"Julie's fine. Christ, calm down, will you? No big deal, no harm done. I don't see why you're so—" Once again she cut herself off.

Donald looked up and saw it register on her face; the memory of the police car, of sitting up with his mother while he and his father went to the morgue, of the funeral, the closed casket, all of it.

For a moment she went pale, also.

"Oh, Donny, I'm so sorry. I didn't mean to yell like that, I just panicked."

He rose unsteadily to his feet and gathered up the four concert tickets, very much aware of the neighbors who were staring at them from front porches or from behind windows. Donald could feel their eyes drilling into his back, watching him, perhaps holding their breath, waiting.

Expectantly.

"It's okay, Mrs. W-W-W-Williamson. I'm just glad she's okay."

The woman smiled at him, then took her daughter and began walking back toward her home. Donald pulled in a few deep breaths, hoping that the stuttering would stop once he calmed down. He continued in the direction of his house, all the while feeling his neck crawl with the stares of his neighbors.

Maybe they knew. Maybe they sensed it, somehow.

For just a moment there, even with the memory of Jennifer Ann pulsing through him, for just a *fraction* of a moment before he jerked back and fell, a part of him —a silent, ignoble part—had wanted to bear down on little Julie's skull with all his weight and grind her head into the pavement, just to know what it felt like, just to know how it must've felt to all those people, they *had* to have something when it happened, didn't they, had to know that they were stomping out the life of another human being, and he'd wondered ever since that night what it must feel like to sense a person's head being mashed under your foot, and for just a fraction of a moment there he could've found —

—his chest started pounding and he slowed his pace. His arms were shaking with such force he could feel it in his teeth.

His temples were pounding.

He thought he might vomit. He looked back to make sure little Julie and her mother were safely inside their home, where no expectant eyes could harm them. He took a few more deep breaths, managed to steady himself, then walked on home, all the time telling himself that he'd just been angered and frightened for that fraction of a moment, that he'd never consciously hurt anyone.

Never.

He hoped his father was asleep by now. Nothing would be dredged up then; about Jennifer Ann's death, about that night at the arena, about his mother's suicide six months after Jennifer's funeral, *pleaseGod* nothing. Donald couldn't stand it when his father went off on one of his "You-Know-You're-All-I've-Got-Left" tangents, tangents that never ended well for either of them. He shook his head. Two years. Two years and still his father spent his weekends in front of the television set, drinking himself into a coma, hearing without listening, watching without seeing, talking to people who were no longer there; then, on Sunday night, he'd rouse himself enough to shower, dress for work, pack his bucket, and leave at three a.m. to fill himself with factory foulness for the next eleven-and-a-half hours, come home, eat a little something, drink a lot of something, then collapse for five or six hours, just long enough to give his broken existence a breather before he got up and did it all over again. The thought made Donald wince. Donald Banks loved his father, even with all the man's faults, but there was nothing he could do for the pain the man was in, and it was killing both of them.

A suddenly empty house, a suddenly empty life, a suddenly empty batch of dreams; dreams nurtured for a family of four, revised for a family of three, abandoned for a family of two. The house was just a coffin waiting for the dirt.

Donald reached up and rubbed his eyes, still aware of a few neighbors staring at him.

All because Jennifer Ann had wanted to come along to the concert; because she was only eight and still thought that everything Big Brother did was so goddamned terrific, because My Big Brother Donny's The Bestest —

He paused by the front door, staring at the tickets in his hand.

A small insect was crawling across the porch. It paused by his foot, its feelers searching for him. Checking him out.

"How's it g-g-g-goin—"

Goddammit!

He slammed his foot down on the thing.

And twisted.

He turned away to see some of the neighbors backing away from their windows, no longer staring. He felt their eyes drop away, satisfied.

Stepping through the front door, Donald saw his father heading upstairs, a quart bottle of beer in his hand. He was dressed only in his underwear and his body, once looming and powerful, had given way to a sickening coat of flab over the last few years. His hair was tangled, making the heavy streaks of grey so much more predominate, and his eyes were so bloodshot Donald could barely see the pupils.

"Hi'ya," whispered his father. "I was just...goin' up to bed. Shift was a bitch."

"You look pretty b-bushed," said Donald. He caught a moment of hesitation on his father's face, a moment where the man must have asked himself if he'd heard his son right; *did* the boy stutter again? No, that couldn't be, he hadn't done that for ages, and he only stuttered during the Crazy Time when all the doctors thought he might try to kill himself, and when the stuttering went away so did the Craziness, because his boy was fine now, and fine boys didn't go away forever because they knew they were all you had left in the whole...

"I, uh...I am," said his dad. "I'm...pretty tired."

They stared at one another for a moment, Donald watching his father's eyes fill with something he recognized but could not name. These were the moments that tore Donald up inside; they'd never had all that much to talk about before, and now that it was just the two of them any attempted conversation was nothing short of torturous. They both tried so damn hard. And they shouldn't have had to.

"How'd that test go?"

"Which one?" His father ran a shaking hand through his tangled hair.

"I, uh, don't...you know, that one? That one you was so worried about."

"Greek Mythology?"

"Yeah."

"I did fine."

His father gave a smile. A very small one. "That's good."

Donald could feel his stomach tightening. His father blinked a few times, then gave a nod of his head. "That's...that's good. I hate to see you...y'know, worry."

Donald looked away, feeling something hot behind his eyes.

"I'd better hit the sack," said his father. The phone was ringing in the kitchen. When Donald spoke again he did it very, very slowly, not taking any chances the Craziness would come back.

"You look pretty tired," he said. So far, so good. He took a step toward the kitchen. "Good night."

"...'night," whispered his father, turning on the stairs and slowly making his way up. Donald vanished into the kitchen as quickly as he could, grateful that he'd been spared the sight of his father stumbling away. He answered the phone. It was Laura.

"Hey, sexy," she said. "You get the tickets?"

"Yeah, no problem."

"Good seats?"

"The guy's a scalper, *of course* they're good seats—they ought to be, for what we paid for them."

"Where are they?"

"Tenth row, main floor."

"That's *great!* Main floor!" Donald found the sound of her enthusiasm unnerving. Jennifer had been excited, too.

"Jim and Theresa'll flip!"

"I hope not," said Donald. "Jim's d-d-driving." He bit into his lip and cursed under his breath. On the other end he heard Laura take a small breath.

"Donny? Is everything all right?" He took several deep breaths again, trying to calm himself. It did no good to let it get the best of you, that's what the Craziness fed on. He swallowed, released his breath slowly, and spoke again.

"Everything's fine. Really. I'm just a little...nervous."

"Don't be," said Laura. "We'll stay together, all of us, and everything'll be fine."

"Listen, Laura, I really gotta tell you, it's been...I, I mean...I'm not real sure that I'm up for this."

"You are, you know it."

"It's just that...Dad's not looking real good and—"

"He never does," said Laura. That caught Donald off-guard. He and Laura had been dating for over a year now, and in all that time she'd never once made any remark about his father; she'd listened to him about Jennifer, about his mom and dad, but never once had she—

"What's that supposed to m-mean?" He bit his tongue.

"It means you have to stop blaming yourself, Donny. There's nothing you can do for him, and the sooner you let go of that the better you'll feel."

"What about *him*, huh? What about the way he feels?"

"Don't start in on me, Donny. I know you care about him, but I care about *you*. Can we drop this, please?"

"Yeah. Sorry." He heard her silence see the smile of relief on her face.

"Good," she said. "We'll pick you up at six." He thought he heard his father laughing. Maybe it was laughing.

"See you then," he said.

"Donny?"

"What?"

"You're okay. Everything's okay. You lived—that's nothing to feel guilty about."

He smiled, said good-bye, and hung up. She was right, she was always right, he just had to relax, had to think about what he had *now*, not what he'd lost, he just had to—

He caught sight of Jennifer's picture on the hall table. Second grade, dress, black shoes, chubby cheeks, stupid-cute grin. The burning behind his eyes worsened.

"Ah...*hell*," he whispered.

He hurried up to his room, where he closed the door and sat on his bed, cursing his trembling arms.

From across the hall he could hear his father talking, heard his mother's name mentioned once or twice.

He rubbed the back of his neck, feeling the chill left from the neighbors' stares.

He removed his shoe and looked at the remains of the insect he'd crushed.

He looked across his room at the small statuette of Perseus brandishing Medusa's head.

"Why don't you really exist?" he whispered to it. "Why couldn't you have been there, huh? Tell me that, Purse. Why couldn't you have swept down on ole Pegasus and pulled her out of it? Once they opened the doors she never had a chance. I just couldn't...keep h-h-hold..." He looked away from the statue and down at his hands.

They were still shaking.

He heard his father drop something and curse.

Gary A. Braunbeck

He remembered Mrs. Williamson's scream and wondered —as he always did whenever the memory assaulted him —if Jennifer Ann had called his name, believing that Big Bestest Brother would swoop down and save her.

But the crowd had been too big, had waited for too long in weather that was too cold—

—and Jennifer should've let him pick her up and hold her like he wanted, but she said no because it made her feel like a baby —

—and he should've been paying more attention to her when the crowd started to push —

—and that crowd should've been full of human beings instead of monsters.

He gripped the bridge of his nose between his thumb and middle finger.

The thoughts didn't change anything. He was still responsible for his sister's death, as surely as Agamemnon was responsible for the death of his daughter.

A sacrifice of sorts.

Donald smiled bitterly to himself then, realizing that he'd linked the story of Agamemnon to Jennifer's death so he'd remember it for the test.

What gods did your death appease, my little sister? What victory was secured?

He heard his father drop and shatter the beer bottle, then call out and ask Jennifer if she'd mind cleaning it up so mom wouldn't have to, he was sorry he was so clumsy....

Donald stood at the window and saw another insect, this one crawling on the inside of the glass. It looked a lot like the other one.

He felt the house crowding in on him as the bug reached out with its feelers.

He didn't try to speak as he reached out, shoe in hand, and squashed the thing.

* * *

At twenty minutes until six he sat down on the steps of his front porch to wait for Laura, Jim, and Theresa. He'd left his father a note saying that they were going to the movies and then for pizza.

He didn't want the man to worry.

He looked up and saw a few neighbors peek out at him through their windows. Maybe it was just a trick of the orange-red sunlight, but all their eyes seemed to be as bloodshot as his father's. Tiny, fiery orbs with a slight pinprick of black in the middle.

He shook his head and looked down at his hands.

They were not shaking.

A soft scraping sound came to him then...no, wait, not scraping, more like a crackling noise, a small, dried twig, maybe, brushing against wood.

Behind him.

As he turned the image of little Julie, crawling, came to his mind —
—and left when he saw the insects.

Ten, maybe fifteen of them, all crawling around the remains of the one he'd crushed before coming in. They piled on top of one another like children building a human pyramid, all the time scattering the mashed remains Donald had left for them.

One insect fell from the black group and began scuttling in his direction, feelers extended, mandibles clacking.

Donald scooted down one step.

Another insect followed.

Then another.

Another.

Donald got up and walked away from the porch.

Soon all of the bugs were crawling toward the steps where he'd been sitting. As he stared at them Donald wondered if they, too, had little bits stuck to the bottoms of their...

Their *what?* Their *feet? Bugs don't* have *feet.*

He looked at the writhing mass on the steps.

They don't have feet.

Do they?

He took another step back just a car pulled up and Laura called his name.

Suddenly, he couldn't get away from the house quickly enough.

* * *

Laura held his hand all the way to the concert, her head resting on his shoulder, her voice telling him that they were going to have fun, not to worry, things would be all right, she really loved him....

He replied to her, but couldn't really hear himself.

When he spoke he did it very slowly, and was pleased that he didn't hear himself stutter.

Once he looked at the reflection of Jim and Theresa's eyes in the rear-view mirror, noting that the sun made their eyes bloodred and pinprick black, also.

He felt awkwardly aware of the insect remains on the bottom of his shoe, but didn't say anything about it to Laura. She might think the Craziness was trying to come back. And he didn't want that.

He closed his eyes once, saw something small crawling into his path, and opened them at once.

"You okay?" said Laura, her breath warm against his cheek.

"I think...yeah. Great. We're gonna have...fun, right?"

She leaned close and kissed him. "Right. Now stop being such a wet sponge." He laughed. Wet sponge. That was a good one.

Jim pulled into the arena parking lot and drove around until they found a spot; from the looks of it they were a good football field away from the entrance doors, but even here Donald could see the edge of the crowd.

It was too damned big.

He closed his eyes and took a long, deep breath, hoping that Laura wouldn't ask him what was wrong.

She didn't, and he loved her for that.

"All-fuckin'-*right!*" shouted Jim. "We have arrived!" Donald didn't know either Jim or Theresa very well, and didn't particularly want to; they were a ride to the concert, that's all. He looked once more at their eyes—which hadn't changed—then toward the milling crowd...

...did you remember to give Jennifer her gloves? You know how she hates it when her hands get cold and it's supposed to be cold tonight...

...make sure you call us after it's over, Donny, you know how your mother worries about you kids...

...oh goddadididntmeanforittohappen...

...pull out drawer seven, will you, Charlie?

He felt his mouth starting to go dry.

They climbed out of the car, locked it, and went to grab a place in the crowd. It didn't take long for the sun to finish setting, leaving them in darkness except for the glow of the arena lights, lights that cast a cryptic sheen over everything but didn't change the fact that everyone's eyes were red and black, red and black, it just must have been a trick of the light, that had to be it, just a trick of the lights over the thousands of bodies and faces, faces in front of them, behind them, next to them, edging them forward into the immovable mass of bodies before them, beside them, a few angry shouts but nothing serious, impatient, drunken, stoned shouts, the shuffling of too many feet, the brush of too many shoulders, the clattering of too many emptied beer bottles, the smell of too many joints being passed around...

...Donald looked around him as he squeezed Laura's hand tighter, trying not to give into panic, a panic he felt pushing its way up from his balls into his throat, but there was at least the feel of Laura's hand, a good feeling, a safe feeling, even here, even now...pushing against them, someone was pushing against them from behind...he turned to get a look, maybe say something to them, tell them not to be so impatient, everybody paid their money and they were going to get in...but only more faces, more bodies, more red-pin-prick-black eyes that glanced around, behind, ahead, all of them meeting his own at one point, never staying for long, and he thought for a second...a *fraction* of a second, that he saw a small, fragile figure making its way through the crowd, trying to get somewhere in particular, trying to get to *someone* in particular, but in a blink and a noisy shifting of the crowd it was gone, lost in the swirling mass of voices, eyes, and flesh...

...he took some deep breaths and looked down at his feet, trying to stay calm, they hadn't been here all that long, there was no reason for him to feel so panicky, so why did he...his shoe, there was something wrong with his shoe...he bent over just a little and glared down, watching as a shadow of some kind shifted under his feet...no, not a shadow, it was a...a...a *leg*...no, not a leg, just part of a bug that he'd scraped off, only...wait...only it seemed to be moving, seemed to be trying to pull itself out from under his weight, a small, twig-like hairy leg squirming from under his shoe...he froze as he stared, thinking for a moment that he could hear the clatter of its hard- shell body, could see its mandibles starting to jut out from under...

...Laura leaned in and kissed him on the cheek, whispering something about later on tonight, after the concert, Mom and Dad weren't home and she was all alone did he wanna come over, soft promises of flesh and tongues and bodies...bodies pressing, bodies sweating, groaning, pumping steadily...he looked at her and smiled, kissed her, but felt nothing, only the sour liquid in his stomach churning around, churning and bubbling as the crowd shifted once again, and Donald looked around, feeling the sourness spread into his mouth, drying his saliva, gluing his tongue down, unable to speak now, almost unable to breath, but then Laura kissed him again with her wet and wonderful tongue and he was all right, moist again, able to swallow, then he noticed that Jim and Theresa were nowhere to be seen...

...the figure again, he saw the figure again, so tiny, so frightened, and he almost moved to reach for it, but then Laura grabbed his arm and said, "You're not going anywhere without me, not in this crowd," so he pulled her along beside him, positive he'd seen...seen someone wandering around the crowd, a frightened gleam in their gaze, maybe tears streaming down their cheeks, but no one saw because she was so small, no one heard because her voice was too weak and they were too busy trying to push other people out of the way, trying to get as close to the doors as possible, that's what counted, getting ahead so you could get inside, get a good seat, toke it up, party down, drink and chug Big Time...

... "Christ, slow down, will you," said Laura, demanding that he give her a break, just wait a minute...Donald slowed and stood still, his eyes darting around...Laura moved closer to him, putting her arms around his waist...he took another deep breath and put a protective arm around her shoulder and said, "Are you all right?" and she said, "I'm fine, how about you, lover?" and he laughed, laughed and held her close because she'd never called him "lover" before and he liked it, liked it very much as he stretched his arms out to relax them and went to step closer to Laura...

...someone pushed from behind and he lost his balance, fell forward, rammed his foot out to try and break his fall but in the second before his foot connected with the pavement a child crawled out in front of him, a small child, a baby crawling, and he tried to cry out but someone else pushed and he felt his foot connect with the fragile skull, felt the baby's head pop like a melon below his foot, and his stomach heaved then but nothing came up as he looked down and saw the feelers worming around, saw the baby's arms flailing out as it kicked and wriggled in its death spasms, so he pulled back and lifted his foot, not wanting to see what he'd done but having to look...

...mandibles...the baby had mandibles and feelers and its legs were no longer the chubby flesh-folds of a baby's but thin, hairy twigs that skittered out and brushed against the legs of his pants, but before he could say anything a woman broke through, picked up her mandibled child, and vanished into the crowd...

...Laura grabbed his arm again and said, "Whoa! Almost lost you for a second there," and he wanted to tell her, wanted to ask her if she'd seen the insect baby, but he didn't dare, didn't dare because if he did he knew she'd think the Craziness was back, and he didn't want for her to think he was crazy just because everyone else did, but then he thought that, yes, it was easy for everyone else to think he was crazy because they weren't the ones out here that night, they weren't the ones who'd pushed, hit, and kicked their way through to find that little body, little crushed body lying in the long, wide, stone hallway, one tiny gloved hand reaching out as if clutching for someone they prayed would swoop down and save them, head mashed into the cement, skin, bones, brains ground to a sickening pulp, bending low, cradling her in his arms, screaming out, crying out, a howl that was lost under the massive roar of the rock 'n' roll monsters inside, rocking back and forth, feeling her innards shift around like the pennies in her piggy bank back home under her bed...I'm so sorry, Jennifer, please...please come back...please don't be...don't be like this, dead like this...

...he looked around, blinking away the thoughts, swallowing back the fear, blacking out the memory of the insect baby because he knew he hadn't seen anything like that, it was just his fear taking over and he wasn't going to let that happen, forcing away the indelible image of his sister's mangled form...just to the right, the figure was just to the right, and he moved quickly, with Laura in tow, asking him if he thought the crowd was acting all right because it seemed to her, didn't he think, that they'd been out here an awfully long time...

...everyone was looking his way now, looking at him through the bloodshot eyes of his father...then the figure again, moving just ahead of them, and this time he heard it cry out, not very loudly, but there was just a moment of silence from the crowd...a *fraction* of a moment, where all seemed to freeze in the night and allow that sound to come over and find him, so he tightened his grip on Laura and began moving again...

...he noticed the noise of the crowd was almost deafening now, slicing into his ears like a sub-zero wind, so he shook his head and kept moving, acutely aware that his father stared out from behind every face that turned as he passed...Laura asking about the goodies they sold inside...shall we get a program, some sweatshirts with the tour emblem on them, something to drink from the stands, what?...he wasn't paying much attention to her, could only think of that tiny figure lost among all these violent bodies and now...now there was the scrabbling, clacking sounds of insects somewhere behind but he refused to turn and look because then Laura would know the Craziness was back...he felt someone push from behind, yelling, "Outta my *way*, fuck-face!" and he lost his balance again, nearly fell forward, nearly dropped to the ground to be trampled by thousands of feet, thousands of ignorant, uncaring monsters, but he didn't fall, he kept his balance, kept hold of Laura, but the bodies were pressed tight now, pressed too tight.. .he found his breath becoming hard, labored, painful, his head was getting light, dizzy...just a little dizzy, but that he could handle, that was no problem, but that tiny figure he thought he saw...*knew* he saw and heard...it needed *help*, needed to find someone in particular...cries, loud cries up ahead, one of the security guards was yelling into a riot horn, telling the crowd to settle down before someone got hurt...someone threw a bottle at the horn and yelled, "*Open the goddamn fuckin' doors!*" as the bottle shattered against the guard's helmet and scattered slivers of glass into the faces of people standing nearby...Donald remembered snatches of his father's babbling from his room across the hall *sorry for bein' so clumsy, Jenny* as he pulled Laura along, trying to get to the edge of the crowd because now it looked like things were going to get ugly because another guard was shoving a gas grenade into a launcher, threatening to set it off if things didn't settle down...he looked around for some sign of the little figure but couldn't see it, couldn't hear it, could only hear the angry shouts of the crowd and some asshole blasting AC/DC from a boombox...

...something about blood on the rocks...

...he yanked Laura hard, trying to get them out of the mob, but he couldn't budge much, he was to dizzy, there were too many eyes glaring expectantly at him, too many arms slamming fists into his back...

...and now Bon Scott was wailing about blood on the streets...

...he looked across the sea of heads, the black, wiggling sea of bodies, and saw two people who might have been Jim and Theresa shoving their way through, trying to get to them, trying to get the hell out of madness before it got really bad, this Craziness, but Donald bit down on his lip and felt something moist and hot spread over his chin because he knew that the guard was going to fire the grenade and once that happened none of them had a chance in hell...

...next it was blood on the sheets...

...everyone in the crowd was turning toward him, staring at him like he was expected to do something, him and him alone, to stop what was about to happen, thousands of eyes, thousands of questions thrown silently through the air to slam against his head...he couldn't see any way out of the bodies...no way out...

...every last drop...

...he could still hear the clattering chattering of the insects as Jim and Theresa reached them, but he didn't look at them...there was a loud *blam!* as the guard fired off the first tear gas grenade that soared through the air and landed in the middle of the crowd, vomiting out thick, burning smoke...

...a voice screamed that if you want blood...

...every eye was on him for as much as he could see...

... you got it ...

...and for a moment, in the thickness of the smoke, everything seemed to freeze and the crowd parted before him, clearing a path between him and the tiny figure, so small, so fragile, so frightened, but as he moved toward it with Jim, Theresa, and Laura in tow, the crowd shifted in... sounds of more grenades being launched and popping off... the eyes drilling into him...he looked at the small, terrified figure on the ground, a figure that even now was swarming with insects vile and clacking, then he turned to the three people behind him…heard his own screams of two years before echoing back to him, rocking his sister's body back and forth…

…Laura tried to speak, but her clacking mandibles produced no sound that he could recognize…Jim and Theresa were worming their feelers toward him…he tried to pull back but the sight of Laura's face froze him…skittering, clacking, scrabbling forward…the stares from the crowd were making him sick, unable to breath…his heart triphammering in his chest…he reached back for Laura's feelers as he heard the doors swing open…

…and ripped her grip from his body.

"You can have them," he whispered to the gazes, knowing it would satisfy them.

The crowd parted before him and he ran to grab the tiny figure—

—the screams from behind were lost under the sound of blood pulsing through his ears and temples—

—the violence exploded all around him as he fell over the delicate body before him, closing his eyes and wrapping his arms around it. For a few minutes it seemed that everything dissolved away; he was aware, as if in a dream, of shouting, pushing, crunching sounds, movement, but finally he took a deep breath, opened his eyes, stood up, and pulled the body up with him.

Jennifer Ann leapt into his arms and threw a hug around his neck, covering his cheek in kisses and tears of her tiny fear, which must have seemed so monstrous to her.

I love you,'" he whispered to her, feeling his heartbeat slow to a normal rate, feeling the throbbing in his head ebb away. He promised himself that he'd never let her out of his sight again.

He looked around until he spotted a way through the lifting gas.

He took a few steps, then bumped into something on the ground.

He looked down, holding Jennifer Ann close, so close he could feel her heart beating, could feel her breath coursing down his neck.

He smiled.

Laura, Jim, and Theresa were kneeling before the pulpy mass, their feelers twisting, their mandibles clamped together as they cried. Donald could see the smashed remains of the insect, so large, so crushed, as he stepped around them, Jennifer Ann firmly in his arms, and made his way out of the smoke, ignoring the bloody footprints he left behind.

Duty

"There are some mistakes too monstrous for remorse."

—Edwin Arlington Robinson

Mom woke up just as the priest was giving her Last Rites.
(Is this part of the penance? you asked of the Guests. *Isn't it all?* was their reply. Smug fucks.)

For six days she'd lain unconscious in the ICU at Cedar Hill Memorial Hospital, kept alive by the ventilator which sat by her bed clicking, puffing, humming, buzzing, measuring her blood, inspiratory, and baseline pressure, waveform readouts showing the fluxes of tracheal and esophageal pressure, proximal pressure at 60 to + 140 cmH2O, 1 cmH2O/25 mV, output flow at 300 to 200 LPM, 1 LPM/10 mV, the whole impressive shebang running smoothly at maximum system pressure of 175 cmH2O, the ribbed tube rammed securely down her throat into her lungs, ensuring that she continued to breathe at the acceptable rates of 250 milliseconds minimum expiratory time, 5 seconds maximum inspiratory time. Details. Specifics. Minutia. Like the other tube, the one running out of her nose into the clear container hanging on the other side of the ventilator; this tube is emptying her lungs of the blood filling them, but you've noticed, haven't you, that there's much more than blood flowing through the tube; there are flecks of things, black flecks, some tiny, others so big you're surprised they don't clog the flow, and when these flecks are released into the container they swirl around with an almost deliberate precision, dancers executing masterful choreography, and you remember a phrase spoken by one of the EMTs:

circling the drain. Yes, that was it: when they're about to lose a victim, the EMTs say that they're circling the drain. That's what the black flecks are portraying in your mother's blood, and for a moment you wonder who would compose the music to this ballet; more likely Mahler than Copland, you're willing to bet. *Drain-Circle of the Black Flecks.* Like the title of a bad 50's horror movie, the kind you used to watch with Dad on Friday nights when you were a child and there was no sibling to compete for his attention. All of this comes to you as you stand there studying the details, the specifics, the minutia. Things to look at and memorize because you can no longer look at the pale, pinched, collapsed ruins of the face and body lying motionless on the bed. A glowing number changes, a monitor beeps softly to register the new data, the pump presses down, expanding the lungs, raising the chest, and all is right in god's techno-savvy world. Except.

(Except, say the Guests; ah, there's the rub, as Willy S. once wrote, right, pal? 'Except.' What a word that is, so much disaster and heartache and ruination and disappointment and pain and all of it always follows one little two-syllable word. Very dramatic, don't you think? Yes, we thought you'd agree, so what say we get back to things and see what follows that word of all words that you seem incapable of getting past right now so, as usual, we have to do it for you. Be a Good Boy and say it with us, now.)

Except that she never should have been here in the first place. Her DNR order had ceased to be in effect at the hospital when she was transferred to the nursing home, but some stupid nurse over there panicked and called an ambulance when Mom went into respiratory arrest, so she was brought back here and immediately placed on life-support; the last thing she'd wanted was to be hooked up to some goddamn machine at the end of her life—she'd told you and your sister that often enough when her emphysema had entered the advanced stage, this a full year before the double pneumonia now snarling inside her—and the two of you had promised you wouldn't let that happen. But it has happened. You wonder if she blames you. But doesn't she realize it isn't your fault? Someone should have called you, should have made sure that the DNR order was attached to her chart at the nursing home, should have been paying attention to the fucking records when her name was entered into the computer and her information came up in the ER, but all of this is for lawyers to deal with later. Right now a duty needs to be performed. You and your sister have already tracked down Mom's doctor and told him what you want; you have shown him the living will and he has nodded his head solemnly, he has picked up the phone and called the ICU; you and your sister have shown the living will to the nurse in charge, have called various friends and family to tell them what you are about to do, and have contacted Father Bill at St. Francis. The two of you have agreed to wait until everyone is present before giving the order. That's everything so far, right? Well, no, but that's *most* of it. Even now as you stand here witnessing these events, you're already replaying their beginning in your mind, as if by doing so and focusing on the details, the specifics, the minutia, you might find a way to alter the outcome which hasn't even been determined yet. To wit: Father Bill was the first to arrive, all soft words and sympathy — "This must be terrible for the two of you, so soon after your father's and grandmother's deaths." —as he donned the garments and uncorked the vial of holy water and found his place in his book of blessings. "In the name of the Father, the Son, and the Holy Spirit: 'O God, great and omnipotent judge of the living and the dead, we are to appear before you after this short life to render an account of our works. Give us the grace to prepare for our last hour by —'"

And that's when Mom woke up.

She blinked a few times, then looked up, saw Lisbeth, and smiled as best she could with that tube in her mouth and throat.

Father Bill continued: "'—a devout and holy life, and protect us against a sudden and unprovided death.'"

(*Bummer,* say the Guests. *Hadn't planned on this turn of events, had you, pal?*)

Mom's eyes grew wide and she began to shake; at first you thought she was having some kind of seizure, but she tore her hand from Lisbeth's and began to shake it in the air: No. Stop this. Stop it now.

"'Let us remember our frailty and mortality,'" continued Father Bill, "'that we may always live in the ways of your commandments. Teach us to watch and pray, that when your summons comes for our departure — '"

Mom started shaking her head and making wet, querulous, awful sounds as her hand shook more violently, the index finger trying to uncurl from its arthritic brethren to point at someone or something; her head jerked to the side, then back again, her eyes staring into those of your sister.

(The Guests again: *She'll cave. She will. Sis always does wherever Mom's concerned. Next stop, Cave City. And you know it.*)

"'—from this world, we may go forth to meet you, experience a merciful judgment, and rejoice in everlasting happiness. We ask this through Christ our Lord. Amen.'"

Father Bill then placed his hand on Mom's forehead — or *tried* to, rather. She was having none of it. "It's all right, Mary," he whispered. "It's all right, Frank and your mother are waiting for you, there's no need to be scared. God's love will ease your fear and carry you home."

He whispered something to her that you couldn't understand, then with a nod to you and your sister, made his way out.

You didn't want to turn around and look back into the room because you knew what you'd see, but eventually Father Bill disappeared from view and you had no choice.

There. All up to date now, yes? Yes. The outcome was determined even as you were trying to alter it by your observation at the time. And you didn't notice until it was too late. What's wrong with this picture? Too many black flecks, dancing.

Okay, so what now?

Duty.

You turn back into the room and there's Lisbeth, looking at you with a surprised smile and a "Maybe-Everything-Will-Be-Okay" gleam in her eyes. She's holding Mom's hand and trying to look happy while all the while silently asking: Should I be happy or not? She's back with us, we didn't think that would happen but here she is. Maybe this is a sign, her coming awake when she did. Maybe. Maybe?

(Cave City — this stop, Cave City.)

You shake your head. The gleam fades from her eyes for a moment, appears again as if she's thought of an argument against this, then leaves completely. She knows what you shaking your head means.

And so does Mom.

She's looking right at you, and you know what this look means. Oh, the lids are droopier than they've ever been, and the eyes are both dull and bloodshot, but the look is a classic: How can you do something like this?

How often in your forty-one years have you seen that look from her? Or, for that matter, from everyone else in your life? *Yes, Mom, look at me. I'm no longer your son — I'm what* became *of him. Forty-one, divorced, living alone* (well, sort of, but you wouldn't understand, *no one* would understand about the Guests), *no real friends, and here I am about to kill you — because that's what you're really thinking, isn't it, Mom? "My son is going to kill me." Because you know if it were just Lisbeth, she couldn't do it. You could always talk Lisbeth out of anything, but me? I inherited your stubborn streak, and you hate that. Does that also mean you hate me right now? Or maybe you always have, who knows?*

"I'm glad to see you," Lisbeth whispers to Mom, squeezing her hand and kissing her cheek. But Mom is still shaking, still trying to point a finger, still objecting.

"There's a lot of people who want to see you," says Lisbeth. "We called everybody. You're going to be real popular today."

You pull in a breath and cross over to the bed. "Hi, Mom," you say, but it doesn't sound like your voice, does it? When did you start speaking with someone else's voice? Odd—Lisbeth and Mom seem to recognize it. "I thought you were gonna stay asleep on us."

She continues to shake her head, and you notice for the first time how wide her eyes are. (*'Deer in the headlights' is the simile you're looking for*, say the Guests.) For the first time you let yourself acknowledge that she's scared. She knows what's going on and she doesn't want it to happen but one look in your eyes and she knows she's toast, that maybe she'd have a chance if it was only Lisbeth but with *you*...oh, yeah: toast. Browned on both sides.

Tears form in her eyes as her mouth works to form words but she can't speak, not with that tube, so what emerges is a series of squeaks and whistles and deeply wet groans, a vaudeville of language but it's all she's got, that and her shaking head and pointing finger and tears.

You reach out and grab her shaking hand, squeezing it gently. "I love you, Mom," you say, and this time the voice sounds a little more like your own; an echo, yes, distant and thin, but yours nonetheless. "I'm so sorry you've been so sick for so long. But the doctor's told us that you...you can't breathe on your own anymore. You have to be hooked up like this, it's the only way you can breathe, you see?"

Her eyelids twitch as a single tear slips out from the corner of her left eye and slides a slow, glistening trail down her temple into her ear. You pull a tissue from your pocket and wipe the tear away before it drips into her ear canal. That's always irritated you whenever you've been on your back and crying so it must be twice as awful for her because she can't raise that arm, what with all the IV needles decorating it like a seamstress's pincushion. So you wipe away the tear just like a Good Boy should do for his Mom.

"Please don't cry," you say, hating the hint of desperation that's suddenly there in the echo of your voice, but Mom's wrinkling her brow and every last line in her face, the short ones, the long ones, the deep and not-so deep ones, all of them become so much more pronounced, each one looking more painful than the one next to it, or over it, or crisscrossing it: the map of a face, the topography of a life: *This is from the night when your spleen burst and we had to sit in the emergency room, your* *dad and me, wondering whether or not you'd make it out of surgery or if we were going to lose our little boy; this one here, under my right eye, is from all those nights I spent squinting over grocery store coupons when your dad was on strike at the plant, we had to watch every penny so the coupons were a big help but, Lord, there were so many of them, and maybe I wouldn't have this line if I'd admitted to myself that I needed glasses, but even if I had admitted it we couldn't afford them, not with the strike and all, so I squinted...*and there are no rest-stops on this particular map, are there? No, not a one that you can find.

"You'll wear yourself out," you say, squeezing her hand a little tighter. "You don't...you d-don't want to do that because everyone is coming over to see you."

Her private vaudeville of language continues, and every squeak is wrapped up in sandy, sputtering, wet rawness that makes your stomach tighten and your throat constrict. Her hand in yours is cold and leathery but she's trying to squeeze back, to let you know *Please don't do this, please don't do this, I know I'm sick and I know it's hard on you kids but I don't want to die, not yet, I don't want to die not yet not yet not yet please don't do this pleasepleaseplease.*

You let go of her hand as a nurse comes into the room and asks if she can speak to you or your sister. You nod at Lisbeth and walk out into the hall, but not before bending down and kissing Mom on the cheek; it still tastes of the tear you wiped away earlier, and the saltiness is unexpected; it tastes of flavor, of something being prepared, Christmas dinner where Mom always used just a little too much salt in her stuffing, but you loved that smell, didn't you? The way it wafted up the stairs and tickled your nose to wake you: *It's Christmas, come on down, sleepy-head, and see all the goodies Dad and me have got for you!*

"I'll be right back," you whisper to the tear's trail, hoping Mom hears it, as well.

Outside, the nurse pulls closed the glass door separating Mom's room from the rest of the ICU. "Is there anything more you'd like us to do?"

"I think she might need a sedative of some kind. She's really scared and —"

"—doctor already wrote the order for a sedative and morphine, as well. I can give it to her any time you say."

You nod your head and chew on your lower lip for a moment.

(Handling things just like the Good Boy we all know you are, say the Guests. You can't tell if they're making fun of you or not, so before you

get too caught up in this moment you tell them to fuck off and simply jump to the outcome without benefit of observation.)

"I don't want her knocked out, understand? She'll want to say g-good...good-bye to everyone and I want her to be conscious."

"It won't knock her out, I promise."

"Then please give it to her now."

The nurse nods her head and looks at you—she has very pretty grey eyes, doesn't she? They look just like your ex-wife's—but here you are observing the moment while it rides right on by, and have to ask the nurse to repeat what she's just said.

"Is there anything we can do for you or your sister?"

"No, thank you. I just want Mom to feel...I mean, she's been so sick for so long and we—Lisbeth and I, we..."

The nurse puts a hand on your forearm. Her fingers are soft and warm, the first time a woman's fingers have touched there in —what?—a year-and-a-half? Two years? Who remembers?

(*We do,* say the Guests. *We remember everything, pal. That's why you invited us here.*)

"Is everything the way you want it?" asks this nurse of the warm soft fingers on your arm.

What you want to say is: *No, everything is not the way I want it, so if you'll pardon me, then, I think I'll just go over here and scream for lost things, throw back my head and open my mouth and just scream. For a smile I haven't seen in years, or the chime that's missing from a laugh, or the noise not made by a child now ten years in its grave, for the toys my ex-wife and me don't have to pick up; I'll scream for all the school pictures that aren't decorating a mantel, then maybe for songs no one but me remembers of cares about, songs from dead singers that make me smile or cry when I hear an echo of their choruses from a passing radio accidentally tuned into an Oldies station, and finally I'll scream for my only living parent whom I am about to kill. Yes, that sounds good. Sounds splendid, in fact. So if you'll just excuse me for a moment, I'll go take care of this. Sound okay? Good. If you need me I'll be right over there. Can't miss me. I'll be the one screaming.*

That's what you want to say (as you observe in the moment that hasn't quite gotten away from you yet), but what actually comes out of your mouth is: "Yes, thank you, everything is fine...as fine as it can be under these circumstances, I guess."

Nurse of the warm fingers lingers for just a moment longer, maybe longer than is necessary or even professional, and the sad smile on her face is echoed by the one in her eyes.

You both release a breath at the same time. She blinks, squeezes your arm, and with a soft swish of shoes against the polished tile, heads off for the syringe.

(Were you just flirting? the Guests inquire. *Oh, pal, what stones you've got. Mom lying in there choking to death on the ruined slop of her insides and you're making time with Florence Nightingale. Show of hands: spit or swallow?)*

"Shut the fuck up!" you growl through clenched teeth. An older gentleman passing by you snaps his head in your direction, his offense at your language all over his face.

"Sorry," you mumble. "I wasn't talking to you, I was —"

But he's gone, turned into another room a few yards down.

(A flirt and *a charmer. What self-respecting nurse wouldn't want some of this action?)*

Shaking your head, you go back in to Lisbeth and Mom.

"She's *scared*," Lisbeth whispers. You wonder why she bothers. Fer chrissakes she's standing right there next to Mom, holding the woman's hand, and Mom might be hard of hearing but she isn't deaf and she may not have been the ideal parent but her life's going to be over — repeat that, turn up the volume, OVER — in less than two hours and the woman deserved to not be spoken of in Third Person.

"I know you're scared, Mom," you say, taking your place by the bed. "But this is what you wanted."

The shaking of the head again.

You reach into your pocket and remove the copy of her living will, unfold it, and hold it up for her to see. "You made us promise you that if this time ever came, we'd go through with it. Even if you said 'no,' we'd go through with it."

Lisbeth snaps your name and you give her the Glare. The Glare has served you well over the years, hasn't it? The Glare scares even the Guests sometimes. Burns right through a person, makes it damn near impossible to maintain eye contact with you. You know this, and you use it to your advantage whenever you want to be left alone, which is most of the time, so many have known the terror of the Glare.

Lisbeth looks away almost at once. You feel terrible for having looked at her this way, but dealing with that is for later.

(You got that right, pal. We'll just add that to the list, shall we?)

You grab Mom's hand away from Lisbeth and hold it tight. You look at your sister — who's still not returning your gaze — then directly into Mom's eyes. You have looked into her eyes this intensely maybe three times in your entire life. "Listen to me, Mom. You will *never* be able to function without this machine, do you understand me?"

A slow nod. Another tear.

"Even if we were to call this off right now and leave you hooked up to this thing, you're not going to last another week. You're on borrowed time, Mom. You should have been dead six days ago."

Once again Lisbeth says your name, this time spitting it out as if it's some rancid chunk of food.

"You're here with us now," you continue, "and you're awake, and you're getting the chance to do something Dad didn't get to do. You're getting a chance to say good-bye to all the people who love you. They're all coming, and they're all going to stay right here with you until you fall asleep for the last time. The nurse is going to give you a shot so you'll be comfortable, and all you have to do is just let us say good-bye and tell you that we love you and then you can rest. You're tired, Mom. You've been tired for so long—" Your voice cracks on these last two words, and you have to turn your head away for a moment to get a grip on yourself.

(*Aw*, say the Guests, *look at this. Widdle baby cwying faw his mommy. Little late to feel sad about this now, isn't it, pal?*)

You ignore them and turn back. "—and you need to rest. You've earned it."

Her hand squeezes yours.

"I have no idea how scary this must be for you, but we're going to be right here, however long this takes. But I'm —*we're*—going to keep our promise to you, Lisbeth and me. Because this is what you wanted. But there's something you need to do for me, Mom. You need to let me know you understand. Can you do that? Can you squeeze my hand and let me know that you understand so I don't have to go through the rest of my life feeling like I've killed you?"

She looks in your eyes.

And for some reason you remember something from twenty years ago: you were still living at home and had picked up the phone one day, just to make a call, but Mom was talking to someone so you started to hang up when you clearly heard her say the words: "I love you."

Phone in hand, staring.

Dad was raking leaves in the back yard.

You lifted the receiver to your ear and listened. Details. Specifics. Minutia. Three years this had been going on. They laughed. At your dad. At you. But not Lisbeth, not the light of everyone's lives, not her.

You hung up loudly and waited. It didn't take long. Mom at the door to your room, her eyes wide and frightened by the headlights.

"How much did you hear?"

"Enough," you said.

Her face took on many forms in a very few seconds; sadness, shame, anger, indifference, confusion and, finally, resignation. "Go ahead and tell him. I don't care." Bullshit bravado, that.

"I figured out that much from what I heard. So you really think I'm useless?"

Shock, for just a moment. Then: "Sometimes."

You nodded your head. "It would kill Dad if he knew."

"I'm not going to tell him."

"Neither am I."

She'd smiled at you, then, and for a moment you thought it was a smile of love and appreciation, but it was in her eyes, wasn't it?

You were now in it with her. If Dad ever found out, she could deflect part of his hurt and anger and anguish by saying, "Your son's known about it almost the whole time." And that *would* kill Dad.

There are times you wonder whether or not it *did* help kill him, just as much as the diabetes and high blood pressure and prostate cancer. Had he somehow found out? Then just let his heart break along with everything else so he could die alone in the toilet of his room at the nursing home? That's where they found him — dead in the crapper.

You never found out what happened to the other guy, never asked his name, never kept an eye out for a strange car or truck parked near the house.

Dad's gone. Grandma, too. Now it was Mom's turn; not because you want it this, because it has to be this way.

"Please squeeze my hand," you whisper, and the begging in your voice disgusts even you.

Mom looks at you the same way she had after that phone call twenty years ago.

"*Please?*"

Mom does not blink, does not try to speak, does not shake her head.

After a moment you look at your sister. "She squeezed my hand," you say. Softly.

Lisbeth releases a breath, her shoulders slumping, then smiles and weeps at the same time. The relief she feels is palpable even from where you're standing.

(*She bought it, pal. Very nice, very smooth.*)

You look back down at Mom. She will not look at you.

"I love you, Mom." And you do. That's the terrible part. If she's going to hate you for this, so be it. It's what she wanted, and you promised.

(That you did, pal.)

You were her son. You were a Good Boy. And it was your duty.

The first of the friends and family begin to arrive, and you're relieved to step back from the bed and give the rest of them the chance to say good-bye.

The warm-fingered nurse comes back in, smiles at you, then gives Mom the shot. "This will help you relax, Mary. You'll feel better here in just a minute, I promise."

Mom smiles at her, a smile full of gratitude and affection. Part of you wishes she'd look at you like that, just once, just for a moment, but the rest of you

(And us, pal. Don't forget us, we'll take it personally!)

knows damn well that you've already gotten the last direct look from her that you'll ever know, and there you were in the moment, observing the event while not being a part of it so now all you've got is the impression of something that may or may not be a memory of an experience you weren't really a part of in the first place.

(Let's hear it for our Fearless leader, folks! Nothing gets by him, nosiree!)

The room fills quickly; aunts, uncles, Mom's co-workers from the cable assembly plant, friends of the family you haven't seen in years, and a few people you've never seen before. You wonder if one of them is Him. You wish you could figure out which one He might be so you could follow him out to the parking lot and slit his throat with your car keys, then pull back his neck and expose the wet tissue and shit right down his throat.

(Now, now, say the Guests. *Is that any way to think at a deathbed?)*

Mom smiles at all of them, squeezes their hands, gestures for them to bend down so she can hug them and they can wipe away her tears. Warm Fingers comes back in and give Mom a shot of morphine, then stops beside you and whispers, "I have orders for two morphine shots. The second one is much stronger. I'll be at the desk, so when you want the second shot, just let me know." She touches your arm again, and this time there's a definite intimacy to her touch. You nod your head and place your hand on top of hers. For a moment her fingers entwine with yours, then she is gone.

A few moments later two technicians come in and ask for everyone except you and Lisbeth to clear the room. They wander into the hall. The first technician —a girl no older than Lisbeth, twenty-six, twenty-seven tops — closes the glass door and then pulls the curtain across it. The room becomes grey and shadowed; Death pausing to check his schedule: Here, is it? Ah, yes, I see. Okee-dokee; back in twenty minutes.

"Are you ready?" asks the technician.

You look at Lisbeth, then at Mom who still won't look at you, and say: "Yes."

She turns off the ventilator.

The sudden silence sings a sick-making sibilance of final things that cannot be taken back.

"Now, Mary," says the technician, "we have to take out the tube now. Are you ready?"

Mom smiles around the tube and nods her head.

You look away for only a moment, hear the terrible sound of medical tape being peeled away, then decide this is something you have to see.

Mom's already wrenching upward from the force of the tube being pulled from her, her face collapsing forward, becoming a reddening gnarl of flesh as her body locks rigid and her tears stream down and her fingers shudder (somehow that is even more terrible to you than her face, the way only her fingers and not her hands shudder) and the veins bulge in her head and temples and her eyelids spasm —

— *make it stop,* you think. *OhGod I didn't think it would hurt this much, it's my fault, I'm so sorry, Mom, I'm not mad at you, I understand, I never hated you, never, please make it stop, please make it stop, please make it* —

"Don't swallow, Mary," says the technician, her hands moving gracefully, one over the other, as she pulls and pulls and pulls.

It takes only ten seconds but it seems like ten minutes, and when it's done, when the tube has been pulled free Mom slams back against the bed with such force she actually bounces a little, and when she bounces a spray of thick black-flecked spit scatters across her face and down onto her chest and even onto your own hand even though you're standing a couple of feet away. Her face is covered in sweat but it's not quite so red now, and her chest is moving up and down as she pulls in breath and you feel the tears on your own face now, goddammit, and the snot running out of your nose but you don't move to wipe away any of it because look at her, she can't wipe the muck away so you won't, either, you'll stand here covered in your own fluids to show her that you understand, that you want to feel something of what she's going through now because this is the last thing you'll ever share, the last thing, the very, very, very last thing and you want to remember it, every specific, every detail, every minutia because you're a Good Boy and that's what a Good Boy does.

(And noble, to boot. Look at all this fucking nobility. It makes you want to openly weep sensitive manly tears, it does.)

The ventilator is rolled into a corner, the tubes rolled into coils and deposited into the medical waste bin, Mom is wiped clean, and the technicians leave, opening wide the room to light and sound and the waiting throngs.

You move toward a corner and stand there, no longer trusting your legs.

Looking out of the glass, you see Warm Fingers and nod your head. She nods hers in return and runs to fetch the last syringe.

Bit by bit, Mom's eyes close—but not all the way. The light fades, the readouts become erratic, the last shot of morphine is administered...and then all of you wait.

No one in the room will look at you. At Lisbeth, yes, but not at you. You were the one to give the orders. You were the one who didn't get off at Cave City. You were the one with Mom's stubborn streak and the living will folded neatly in your pocket and the memory of the phone call and your ex-wife's tears when the police called about your little boy who you shouldn't have let ride his bike to the movies that day but, jeez, Dad, I'm almost ten and it's not that far and the screams in your ear of You Fucking Bastard How Many Times Have I Told You I Don't Want Him Riding That Bike Outside The Neighborhood and the fists against your face again and again and again and Dad whispering No Son of Mine Would Ever Put My Ass In A Nursing Home but you're a Good Boy, aren't you?

(Well, say the Guests, about that...)

It takes Mom two hours and seventeen minutes to die. It is slow and painful to watch, but you never once look away.

When it is over and everyone begins to leave, you are the one who closes her eyes the rest of the way.

You wait until you are alone in the room with her, then lean down and kiss her. "I will miss you every day for the rest of my life," you say. "I loved you, Mom. I'm sorry for every bad thing I ever said to you. I'm sorry for all the times I forgot to do something for you, for all the times I could have called you but didn't, for every time you felt lonely and forgotten. Is that all right? Is it all right for me to say these things to you? It's just the two of us now, so I think it must be all right." Then something small bursts inside you and you're crying again. "I'm sorry I wasn't a better son, a better man, a better husband and father. But

Lisbeth and Eric, they gave you two wonderful grandchildren, didn't they? And they never let them ride their bikes too far from the house, you can count on that. They never get so busy with work that they just tell their kids it's okay, ride wherever you want, it'll be fine. They never do that. They never leave the bottle of prescription sleeping pills setting out open so that their Dad can sneak them into the toilet at the nursing home. They never will. They'll never disappoint you. Never.

"I have to go now, Mom, because there's a lot to do for your funeral. But I just wanted you to know that I always had the best intentions. In my heart, I always meant well. I love you. You should rest now, you've earned it."

You make sure no one is watching from outside, and you observe the moment as it passes; you can do this now, because the outcome is given. You move to one of the corners, and you take something, and then you leave.

Warm Fingers smiles sadly at you as you walk past the desk. She looks like she might cry herself. You wish she'd touch you again. Warm Fingers would forgive you all your trespasses and mistakes. Warm Fingers would understand.

* * *

You park outside your house and see that all the lights are on. You look up at the windows and see the Guests moving around. One of them is playing the stereo. NIN. "Head Like A Hole." Too loud for this hour.

You smoke three cigarettes before going inside. The Guests don't like it when you smoke inside, and you are nothing if not a gracious host.

They're all waiting for you when you come inside. All of them have their props at the ready. None of them speak to you now. They never talk to you when you're here, only when you're gone, only when you're performing a duty like the one tonight.

One of them comes up to you, empty-handed. He's the new one. The one behind him, he arrived the day you buried Dad. His is the face you wore the night you walked out of the nursing home knowing what Dad intended to do with those pills.

Lurking in a corner near the stereo is another guest. He showed up the night your ex-wife came over after little Andrew's funeral to slap you in the face yet again. You had been brewing water for tea and after she slapped you, you pushed her away and she fell against the stove and spilled the scalding water all over her arm. This Guest is holding the boiling kettle and wears the face you wore that night. Just like all of them. Wearing the faces you happened to have on when committing your trespasses.

The new Guest is still standing there, holding out his hand. You reach into your pocket and remove the coiled ventilator tube. He takes it with a smile and points to the chair. You remove your coat and sit down.

Other guests—the one who arrived after you had that brief affair with that temp before Andrew was born, for instance—bind your wrists and ankles to the chair.

The music changes. The James Gang. "Ashes, the Rain and I." The saddest song you've ever heard. It's important that you have sad music now.

One Guest has the pills. One the boiling water. One has the dart you stuck Johnny Sawyer with when you were six and you got mad because you thought Johnny was cheating.

There are pins. And burning cigarettes. And pieces of broken glass.

You wish you didn't remember what every last one of these items means, but you do, you remember so very, very clearly.

The phone rings. No one moves to answer it.

The answering machine picks up, gives its banal greeting, then a beep. A woman says your name. Her voice is soft and warm, just like her fingers. "This is Daphne. I'm the nurse who gave your mom the shots today. Listen, we're never supposed to do this—call patients' families personally like this—but, well...I just wanted to make sure you were all right. You didn't look good when you left and I was...oh, okay, I was worried. I hope you're not angry. I just thought that maybe you, y'know...needed to talk to someone. So I was wondering..."

Joe Walsh's voice drowns out the rest of the message. You almost smile. Maybe after all of this is over—a few weeks or however long it takes for you to heal this time—maybe you'll give her a call. Warm Fingers would be sympathetic. Warm Finger would listen. Warm Fingers would understand and squeeze your hand.

The new Guest stands in front of you, reaches out, and forces your mouth open. He has lubricated the ventilator tube with Vaseline. You remind yourself that it's important to swallow as the tube goes down. You just hope the Guest with the boiling water remembers his proper place in line.

You open wide your mouth and close your eyes. It is important for a Good Boy to remember things. Remembering, that's a duty, as well.

And you are nothing if not dutiful.

All Over, All Gone, Bye-Bye

Thus let me live, unseen, unknown;
   Thus unlamented let me die;
      Steal from the world, and not a stone
        Tell where I lie.
            —Alexander Pope, "Solitude"

There should have been more left once the children were gone, more than just empty bedrooms, broken toys discovered in the back of closets, the occasional pair of gym socks or pantyhose found hiding under furniture, collecting dust like the little ones used to collect dolls or model cars.

There should have been more, but Frank and Mary quickly discovered otherwise. The children were gone and they were alone for the first time in thirty years. Their conversations were short; too short. Their eyes didn't meet as much as they once had. Frank cleared his throat a lot in order to break the silence and often read the same newspaper page three times in a row because he couldn't think of anything else to do. Mary kept telling herself there was a ton of laundry and cleaning to do because she was used to working from morning till bedtime, but the truth was that hardly any of it needed doing.

Not now.

Now that the children had left.

Always smiling, never any tears as they hauled themselves and their stuff out the door.

All over.

All gone.

Bye-bye.

Frank tried taking up a hobby, but found he hadn't the patience for anything that demanded he sit still for more than twenty minutes at a time.

Mary joined a card playing club but the women in the group were always talking about their own children and how proud they were of them and took care not to ask Mary about hers because it was common knowledge that Mary's children never wrote or visited and seldom called. She quit going after three weeks. The other women were too obviously being courteous to her.

And so they were alone for the first time in thirty years, not knowing what to do or say because they'd rarely spared any thought for themselves; the children had been their pleasure and their purpose.

The rooms of the house should have grown larger but they didn't. Frank took to opening the windows even in cold weather; the place was too stuffy. Mary took to watching television in the mornings before working on her latest cross-stitch project for an hour, then she cleaned for two hours before preparing lunch, then it was her daily walk around the neighborhood before it was time to start dinner; later, after the dishes were washed and put away (a task both she and Frank performed, taking as much time as possible) she would return to the television and watch her evening programs until sleep claimed her.

Then one afternoon, struck by a now rare desire to rearrange one of the old rooms, Frank discovered something from his days as a younger man. He showed it to Mary.

For the rest of that afternoon and well into the evening they sat at the kitchen table recalling all the old memories they'd shared many times before, never embellishing them for each would know if the other was fibbing, and it should have been a fine time for them, talking about the old days while eating popcorn and drinking coffee (Mary) and beer (Frank was a devout Blatz man), but their words rang hollow, their eyes met too rarely, and when Frank reached over to take Mary's hand it was more the gesture of a drowning man clutching at a life preserver than a loving husband trying to take comfort in his wife's touch.

At last, after refilling her coffee cup and fetching another beer for her husband, Mary cleared her throat and said, "Why don't they ever call or write or visit?"

"I don't know," said Frank.

Then, and only then, did their eyes meet and stay fixed.

"I was a good mother, wasn't I?"

"You were grand. A wonderful mother. You really were."

"I mean we never...we never let them go without, did we?"

"Whatta you mean by that?" His face said that he'd been thinking the same thing but since she'd mentioned it first the responsibility of talking about it was hers.

"I just keep thinking about some things, you know? Like that prom dress I made for Beth."

"It was a beautiful dress. I remember how hard you worked on it."

"But she didn't like it, remember? She said it didn't match her favorite shoes."

"Well, we got her a new pair, didn't we? And they matched the dress all right. I thought she looked lovely."

Mary dug a cigarette out of her purse and lit up. Even though he was trying to get her to quit, Frank didn't say anything.

"What is it?" asked Mary.

"I's just thinking that cigarette smoke don't smell half-bad. Makes me wished I smoked a pipe or something."

"We could always go out to the shopping center tomorrow and look in that new smoke shop. I'll bet they got real nice pipes in there. We could pick one out."

"Place's pretty expensive, from what I hear."

"I suppose, but you'd be getting a good pipe for the money. You could even maybe start yourself a little collection. We can afford it, hon, really we can. We could even get you one of them wood display cases so you can put them all out and then...." She sat staring at her husband, her mouth working to form sounds, words, sentences; all that came out was cigarette smoke.

"We could always go to the movies or something," said Frank.

"Could you sit still that long?"

"I don't know. I suppose I could give it a try."

Mary found the movie listings in the paper and called the theater to check on show times and prices.

"Seven dollars apiece?" said Frank.

"That's what they said."

"Christ! Fourteen dollars to see a movie! We can't afford that—I mean, not that and dinner, too. Ain't a proper movie night without stopping for dinner while you're out."

Mary put a hand on his shoulder. "Once every couple of weeks wouldn't be so bad, would it? We don't have to go to a fancy place to eat, just some hamburgers or something."

"I don't know. I don't got any real nice clothes—you know, nothing that you'd wear out on a date."

"We could always go out and buy you some new clothes."

"I don't know," he said. "I don't much feel..."

"Me, neither," said Mary.

"Really? I thought it was just me."

"Nope."

They sat in silence for a little while longer as the night drifted in around them.

There was no way to give it voice. There was no way one of them could look at the other and say, We did it all for them. All the work, all the worrying, paying the bills and keeping the house up, it was all for the kids. Never for us. I love you, hon, I really do, but we lost each other somewhere along the way. Sometime in there when we weren't looking we stopped being Frank and Mary and became *their parents*. And now what? I love them with all my heart but they ain't part of us anymore, not really. I don't think it's because they're ashamed of us or anything—I'm sure they still love us and all—but they got families of their own now. They're not our children anymore, they're Gayle and Gary and Eric and Kylie. And they're not here. It's just us now and we let ourselves slip away in there someplace. We're not what we wanted to be when we were young. When they left they took their parents with them and left us in their place, and we don't know much about these people, not anymore.

Because there were no children left to care for. They'd hauled themselves and all their stuff out the door.

All over.

All gone.

Bye-bye.

Soon, when the kitchen became so dark they almost couldn't see, they rose and went into the living room and sat very near one

another on the sofa. Frank placed the keepsake from his youth on the floor by his feet and lovingly put his arm around Mary. Breathing slowly, she put her head against his shoulder, one of her hands dropping down to hold one of his.

"Will they ever visit?" she asked, knowing what they were going to do.

"I think so. I think they're coming right now."

They sat in silence as the shadows of night came into the room and made themselves at home.

"Do you hear them?" said Mary, smiling.

"Yes, I do. See there, hon? They didn't forget us."

"They're not ashamed of us, are they?"

"Nosiree," said Frank. "Listen to them talk. They're proud of their workin' folks."

"Never a king's castle, but a good home."

"A fine home. Damn fine. They never wanted for a thing."

Mary touched her husband's cheek. "That's on account of you bein' such a good, hard worker. Always providing for us."

"I did my best."

"Your best was just fine, it was." She smiled, eyes wide, and pointed in front of them. "Look, there's Gary."

"My God," said Frank. "Look at what a fine man he's become. So strong and sure of himself."

"You always said that he had a good head on his shoulders."

"They all did. I told them that."

"Oh my, there's Gayle and Danny—aren't they a handsome couple? And—look! Oh, they brought the baby with them! Isn't he beautiful?"

"Do you think he knows we're his Grandma and Grandpa?"

"Of course he does. Look at him giggle at your big hands."

"Yeah, and he's—aw, did you hear that? Danny said they named him after my dad. They call him Joseph."

"And there's Kylie with little Sophia!"

"And Eric brought his kids, too!"

"Makes you proud, don't it?"

"It wasn't all for nothing."

And time stood still for them for a little while, as it will for everyone at least once in a lifetime, if only at the end.

But soon the visit was over. The children left, hauling themselves and their families out the door.

"All over," whispered Frank.

"All gone," said Mary.

"Bye-bye," said both to the darkness.

Frank leaned over and kissed Mary.

"I love you," she said to him. "What a fine family."

"Yeah. I guess maybe it was worth losing us, after all. They're a fine bunch. But I still miss them."

Mary hugged him. "We mustn't harp on things, hon. The children are safe and happy and they love us and remember us. You heard for yourself."

"They make a body proud."

"Isn't our new grandson wonderful?" she whispered in his ear, pressing herself close to him.

"I love you so much," said Frank. "I've given you a good life, haven't I?"

"A woman would be foolish to ask for one better."

"We'll babysit Joseph, won't we?"

"You bet."

"Here he is now, all fussy and hungry."

"I should change his diaper, don't you think?"

"Hell, yes! Look at him kicking up his legs."

"That giggle!"

"Oh, now he wants to chew on my finger."

"He'll outgrow that."

And he did.

"Graduating college," said Frank. "Didn't think I'd ever live to see the day one of my grandkids graduated college, let alone all of 'em."

"And Joseph is so handsome in his cap and gown."

"A heartbreaker."

"Just like his grandpa."

"A good life," said Frank.

"A fine life," said Mary, her hand reaching down to brush against Frank's keepsake. "Your father gave that to you, you say?"

"Yeah. He loved to go hunting."

"You miss him, don't you?"

"That I do. That I do."

Mary kissed his cheek as the glare of a car's headlight beams filled the living room. The engine clattered as the ignition was turned off.

"We should go now," said Mary. "The children will be expecting us for a visit."

"Okay," said Frank, digging two shells out of his pocket.

They held hands as they walked upstairs to their bedroom, but before vanishing into the darkness they turned and looked at their home, each remembering some moment from their family's life together.

But that was done now.

All over.

All gone.

Bye-bye.

As they rounded the landing and started up the second, darker flight of stairs, the lock on the front door jiggled, then turned. The door opened and a harried-looking young man in a business suit entered, fumbled around until he found the light switch, and turned on the overhead lights.

A young couple came in behind him, wide-eyed and grinning as they looked from one spacious empty room to the next.

"This is so perfect," said the young woman.

"I knew you'd love it," replied her husband.

"Yeah," said the young man in the suit. "This's a great house, all right. We've had it on the market for well over a year now. A lot of us down at the agency are surprised that no one's made a firm offer on it until now. And I'm glad to say that everything here is in solid working order."

The young woman placed a hand against her protruding belly. "It's going to be perfect for our family."

"Of course it will," said her husband, putting his arm around her.

"The perfect family home," said the young man in the suit. "What a wonderful way to begin."

 **Gary A. Braunbeck** is the author of the acclaimed Cedar Hill Cycle of novels and stories, which includes *In Silent Graves, Keepers, Mr. Hands, Coffin County,* and the forthcoming *A Cracked and Broken Path.* He has published over 20 books, evenly split between novels and short-story collections, and his work has earned seven Bram Stoker Awards, an International Horror Guild Award, three Shocker Awards, a Black Quill Award, and a World Fantasy Award nomination. He doesn't get out much, which everyone agrees is probably for the best. Find out more about his work on-line at garybraunbeck.com

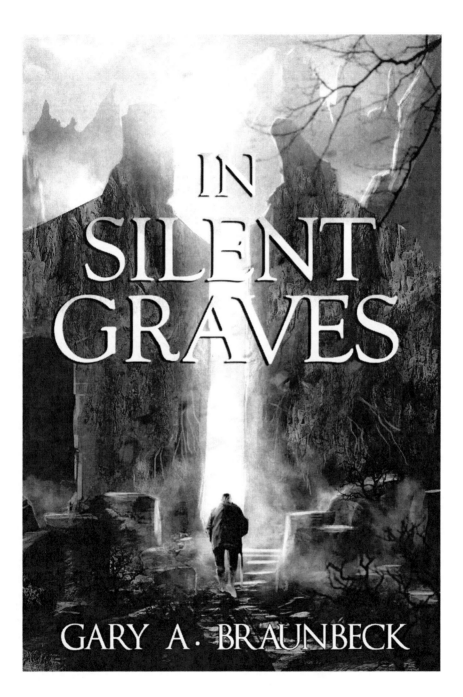

IN
SILENT
GRAVES

GARY A · BRAUNBECK

KEEPERS

THE CEDAR HILL SERIES

GARY A. BRAUNBECK

CPSIA information can be obtained
at www.ICGtesting.com
Printed in the USA
FFOW02n2020160116
20452FF

31901056981360

9 781942 712596